TREASURE CAVE

GREGG BOGOSIAN

Illustrated by Mary Anne Quill

ISBN: 978-0-9987130-1-4 (sc)
ISBN: 978-0-9987130-0-7 (hc)
ISBN: 978-0-9987130-2-1 (e)

Because of the dynamic nature of the Internet, any web
addresses or links contained in this book may have changed
since publication and may no longer be valid.

Published by Gregg Bogosian
Saint Louis, Missouri

Rev. date: 07/10/2017

Dedicated to Nelle Harper Lee
(28 April 1926 – 19 February 2016), whose novel *To Kill A Mockingbird* provided much inspiration for this story.

Contents

PREFACE

This novel is based on the "Seckatary Hawkins" stories written by Robert F. Schulkers from 1918 until 1942. These stories related the adventures of a boy called Seckatary Hawkins and his band of chums who had formed a club, complete with clubhouse, along the banks of a river in Kentucky. There they encountered many mysteries they worked to solve, while they struggled with gangs of troublemakers who descended upon the river landscape around the clubhouse. The stories were published as weekly episodes serialized in ever-increasing numbers of newspapers as the series became wildly popular in the 1920's and 1930's. Seckatary Hawkins clubs formed all across the United States, with some chapters boasting hundreds of thousands of members.[1]

Starting in 1921, Schulkers began publishing some of the early stories in book form. The books were compilations of about 30-40 of the weekly newspaper episodes that went together as one storyline. Schulkers had published eleven such novels by 1932. There was also a daily comic strip that ran from 1928 to 1934, and live radio broadcasts of some of the stories. Starting in 2007, the modern-day Seckatary Hawkins Club embarked on a project to publish the entire set of newspaper episodes. This project was completed in 2017 after the publication of 30 novels, and a two-volume set of all the comic strips. A complete bibliography of these books is listed at the end of this book.

Robert F. Schulkers was born in 1890 in the Eastside neighborhood of Covington, Kentucky, just two blocks from the Licking River. In about 1900 he and his comrades formed a club, including a clubhouse in an old shack on the bank of the Licking

River, about a mile upstream from Covington in an area of woods and fields where they had fun and adventures away from the everyday concerns of school and adults. It was a glorious setting in which to grow up, as Schulkers attested in an unpublished autobiographical manuscript:

> I was born near a river and played, during most of my early days, on the river bank. One summer when I was about nine years old a group of us boys started a little club down in an old shack on the river bank. Since a boy always wants to do everything like his daddy, I insisted that I be allowed to write down the minutes of the meeting. I was pretty young and didn't know much about spelling, so I wrote "seckatary" instead of "secretary". This first book was a half-full copy-book left over from school.
>
> We boys played around the bank, swam in the river, and had a regular time – mostly by fighting with the boys from across the river. These boys are the "Pelhams" of the Hawkins stories. It seems that there is always a feud between boys separated by water – or any boundary line for that matter. One crowd thinks that it is better because it is on one side of the line, while the ones on the other side think their side is better – and they fight about it. I think that I had the most glorious boyhood of any lad in America![2]

Concerning the odd moniker "Seckatary", Schulkers went on to point out "It does not seem strange, however, to say 'seckatary'. Not only boys pronounce it that way – many grown-ups, careless of proper pronunciation, use it in the very same-sounding manner."[2]

In addition to recording the minutes of his Club, Schulkers began to write other material:

I have always wanted to write. I started writing in school, and at the age of twelve or thirteen I began fiction. I used to go down to the Covington office of the *Cincinnati Commercial Tribune* and watch the branch editor write. It seemed wonderful to me to think that I was actually seeing something before it came out in print. I think that I would have done anything to have been allowed to write something that I knew was going to be printed.[2]

In early 1911, at the age of 20, Schulkers joined the staff of the *Cincinnati Enquirer* newspaper as the personal secretary and stenographer for the editor. In addition to his regular duties, later that same year Schulkers began writing short stories for young readers, published at irregular intervals in the Sunday supplement of the *Enquirer.* These proved immensely popular, and his editor challenged him to write a regular series of stories to be published on a weekly basis. Casting about for ideas, Schulkers came across, in his desk at home, the old copy-book with the minutes of the club of his childhood. Each page was signed "R. Schulkers, Seckatary". The word Seckatary "seemed to leap off the page" at him, and the Seckatary Hawkins series of stories was born.[1,2]

Just as he had experienced in his own childhood, Schulkers placed Seckatary Hawkins and his comrades into a club with their own clubhouse on the bank of a river in Kentucky. In the Seckatary Hawkins stories, the river meanders through a landscape of forests, cliffs, caves, creeks, and an island verdant with a dense tanglewood. As described in a recent biograpy of Schulkers, Hawkins and the other boys enjoyed a life that would be the envy of anyone, youngster or adult:

> While the Hawkins stories all revolve around plots filled with mystery and danger, the boys also enjoyed the many pleasures of this landscape, gathering and eating blackberries, pawpaws, beechnuts, walnuts, hickory nuts, and chestnuts,

hunting and trapping in the woods, and fishing along the river. They often built campfires on the riverbank, and would cook the fish they caught. They had their favorite swimming holes, and would spend a few weeks nearly every summer camping down on Seven Willows Island or in other similarly remote locations. Most winters were cold and snowy, and the boys enjoyed skating on the frozen river and bobsledding on nearby hills. They sometimes rode through the woods on horses borrowed from the farms on which some of the boys lived. All in all it was a tapestry of an enviable life, appreciated not only by Schulkers' young audience but also by older readers who led much more complicated lives.[1]

A passage from the Schulkers novel *The Gray Ghost* illustrates the "mystery and danger" that permeated the Seckatary Hawkins stories. Hawkins and his self-appointed guardian Perry Stokes, who always carried his "trusty rifle," were high on a cliff looming over the river. They saw their fellow clubmembers Link Lambert and Will Standish coming up the river in a launch. Hawkins and Perry knew their arch-enemy, named Stoner's Boy, was in the vicinity with his vicious and ugly dog Big Boy, and Hawkins was worried Stoner's Boy was planning to ambush Link and Will. Hawkins had Perry fire a warning shot into the air:

> It was the wrong thing to do, but I didn't realize it till too late. As the gun went off we heard the angry barking of the ugly dog, and it was close to us. I turned my head and saw the brute galloping up the rocks toward us. I saw Perry working out the empty cartridge and going through his pockets again –
>
> "Aha," came a voice; oh, how well I knew that voice. "So, my fine Seckatary, you are here. Get him, Big Boy."

I caught first a sight of the gray hat, then the kerchief that hid the lower half of his face. Before I could see more of him, the big dog was upon me. I struck him as he bounded against my chest, and I felt his hot breath on my face, but down I went, and as I fell I managed to drop away from the dog, for there was a step-off to a ledge that hung out over the side of the cliff. I was more afraid at that minute of falling off that ledge than I was of the dog, but before I had time to realize my greatest danger, I heard Perry's gun bark again – and the howl of a dog and the angry shout of Stoner's Boy –

I pulled myself back upon the top of the cliff again as quickly as I could. As I did so I saw the dead body of the ugly dog flash past me, and I watched it, fascinated as I lay there upon my stomach on the cliff top. With a splash it hit the river fifty feet below, and sank out of sight. There was a red tinge in the circling waves where it had hit the water. That was all.

But I had to leap to my feet quickly, for even as I turned my head I saw the gray ghost spring upon Perry and wrench the rifle from his hands. The next second the gray figure had flung his bulky form upon the slight, freckle-faced boy, and although Perry resisted stoutly, Stoner was slowly but surely bending him back over the edge of the cliff.

I sprang for the fallen rifle and raised it to my shoulder. The gray ghost never missed a thing. He saw me. He must have thought it was loaded, for he suddenly let go of Perry and flew down the rocky path.

This dramatic passage, involving a dog shot and killed, blood in the water, and a desperate struggle at the edge of a cliff, is typical of the level of grittiness Schulkers wove into the Seckatary

Hawkins stories. No mere pablum for children, Robert F. Schulkers was writing stories at a level of maturity similar to Robert Louis Stevenson's books such as *Treasure Island*, appealing to an audience of both older children and adults.[1]

For this novel, I have drawn most heavily on the first nine Seckatary Hawkins books published from 1921 to 1926, namely *Stoner's Boy* through *The Yellow Y*. In fact, the start of this story picks up a few months after the end of the events in *The Yellow Y*. However, I have turned back the clock, placing this story in the summer of 1914.

I have woven in many elements from stories written by Samuel Clemens, Robert Louis Stevenson, and Harper Lee. Copious use was made of old maps and atlases, and reference books on Northern Kentucky (with a focus on Covington and surrounding areas), steamboats, railroads, Kentucky flora and fauna, the Licking, Kentucky, and Ohio rivers, and many others. The endnotes and bibliography at the end of this book list these reference materials.

The grandson of Robert F. Schulkers, my good friend Charles R. Schulkers (Randy Schulkers), has provided me copies of many letters, untitled typescript documents, and other papers he has been curating since his grandfather passed away in 1972. These materials are referred to as "the Schulkers papers" in the endnotes and the bibliography. The generosity and patience of Randy Schulkers has greatly enriched this book with interesting details that otherwise would not have been known to me.

Special mention needs to be made of the book *Woodford County, Kentucky 1910 Census* compiled by Dona Adams Wilson, and published in 2003 by the Woodford County Historical Society in Versailles, Kentucky. The village of Clifton along the Kentucky River is in Woodford County, an area that Schulkers often visited as it was the home of his wife's family. Most of the names of the young characters that appear in this novel are the actual names (or composites of first and last names) of teenaged white and black boys and girls listed in this 1910 census book.

Schulkers never named the town Seckatary Hawkins and his comrades lived in, nor the name of the river where their clubhouse stood in the woods lining the bank. I have taken the liberty of naming their town Austinberg, a neighborhood of Covington near where Schulkers grew up. I have named the river the Looking Glass; the name is taken from the Lewis Carroll 1871 novel *Through the Looking Glass, and What Alice Found There*. To me, there is a special element in the first nine books Schulkers wrote, one where every day after school and on Saturday mornings Hawkins and his chums hurried down the path from town to their clubhouse on the riverbank and pushed through the evergreens lining the path, as if "through the looking glass" into a wonderland of adventure and excitement seldom interrupted by adults.

But my book starts in another real Kentucky town, Morning View, located along the Looking Glass about 20 miles downstream from where Seckatary Hawkins and his comrades live. There we meet the Morgan children, whose lives are jolted by a series of events that send them on a journey into Seckatary Hawkins territory.

PART I

MORNING VIEW, KENTUCKY.
MID–JUNE TO EARLY JULY 1914

CHAPTER I

THE SECRET ROOM

Ah, summertime! No more school until September! Not that I minded school that much this past year, since I went into the ninth grade – it's combined with grade ten, and I liked being with the older kids. Plus, our teacher Miss Geldreich is a good teacher. She had given me a bunch of projects to work on over the summer. I was sitting cross-legged on the dining room floor, surrounded by papers and measuring tape.

"What are you working on, Scout?" Mom was standing in the doorway between the kitchen and the dining room.

"I'm making a diagram of our house. It's part of a math and geometry assignment Miss Geldreich gave me. I'm striving to improve my grasp of geometric principles."

Mom began to bite one of her fingers. It was something she did when she was trying not to laugh. "And working on your vocabulary, too, I see."

"Yes'm."

Mom went back into the kitchen. Tom-Tom, our cat, was sleeping on the floor next to me. Suddenly he woke with a wild look in his eyes. He leaned over and furiously chewed at the fur on his hind leg, then sagged back down. He yawned a big toothy yawn, licked around his mouth, and then closed his eyes and sank back into sleep. Cats are so weird.

"Whatcha doin', Scout?" My little sister Jessamine came into the room and sat down next to me, her dress making a big circle on the floor.[1] She always wore dresses. Frilly girl things like that make my stomach hurt.

"Making a map of our house."

"What for?"

"To put my math and geometry skills to practical use."

"What does that mean?"

Tom-Tom opened his eyes a bit. I guess he was wondering the same thing.

"Here, Jessamine. See, I measured all the rooms, and up and down the halls, and around the outside of the house. Then I put all that onto these papers, like a map. See, there's your room."

Jessamine leaned over the paper. "Oh! And there's Stone and Cliff's room!" Our brothers Stonewall and Clifton are identical twins, and share a bedroom. They were only a year older than me, and we did a lot together.

"Yes. And there's Clay's room." Clayton was our oldest brother, 17 years old, and worked at the J.W. Brookie Distillery.[2] Prohibition fever was rampant in the nation, but had not yet taken hold here in Kentucky.[3]

Tom-Tom lifted his head and cocked an ear toward the front door. A few seconds later, Stone and Cliff came charging in from the steamboat landing, with our cousin Mickey Maus carrying a suitcase. "Whatcha doin', Scout?" shouted Cliff. I had to explain everything over again.

Mickey traced around the map with his finger. "What are these gaps here?"

I sighed. "I don't know yet. I can't get everything to line up."

Mickey stared at me. "It's because you don't know what you're doing."

That's Michael Ethelbert Maus for you. What a ridiculous name! You can see why everyone just calls him Mickey. I must admit, Mickey and I do not like each other. He lives up in Cincinnati with Uncle Adolphus and Mom's sister Aunt Sarah. He has a younger sister, Narcissa, who is an invalid and needs a lot of care. She has consumption.[4] After school is out for the year, they send Mickey down by steamboat to spend the summer with us in Morning View.[5] Here he was, just arrived, and already insulting me.

Mom came into the room. "Here you are, Mickey! Did you have a good trip coming down the river?"

"Yes'm."

"Do you want to wash up before dinner?"

"No'm." Mickey Maus had an aversion to soap and water, and was usually adorned with the consequent distinctive odor!

Mom paused for a second. The corner of her mouth was twitching, meaning that she was about to say something serious. "Let me rephrase that. Stone, you will take Mickey's bag up to his room. And Cliff, you will take Mickey to the washroom."

"Yes'm" they sang in unison, and away they went.

That's one thing I didn't like -- I normally do a lot with Stone and Cliff, who are only a year older than me, but when Mickey is here, they don't do much with me.

After dinner, I showed Dad my map, and asked him if he could tell why there were gaps all over the place. He studied the map carefully.

"It seems to me that you have neglected to take account of the thicknesses of all the walls. You have them here as simple lines, with no thickness."

"Oh, brother! How dumb is that?"

"It's an understandable omission. This is just your first draft. The challenge now is to accurately determine the thicknesses of all the different walls, the inside and outside walls."

Clay came into the room and overheard that last remark. "Sam, it should be a simple matter of subtraction from the inside and outside measurements. That's sort of what we do when rolling barrels into position in the barrelhouse, to make sure the bunghole in each barrel is facing up."

I like Clay a lot. Even though he was three years older than me, he never talked down to me.

I got back to my task the next morning. It was a lot of work, and I made a lot of mistakes, and covered page after page with lists of measurements, and erased sections until I wore holes in the papers, but finally I had it done -- at least I thought it was done, but there was still a problem with my diagram of the second floor.

I couldn't wait for Dad to come home, so I decided to walk into town to see him at his office. Jessamine insisted on coming with me. She always wanted to hang around me for some reason.

The sign over the door read "Septimus Morgan, Attorney-at-Law". We walked in. Dad was poring over some papers at his desk.

"Hiya Dad!" shouted Jessamine. "I brought Scout to see you."

"Hello, Jessamine and Sammy! Just what I needed! A break from all these papers."

Dad always made us feel welcome, no matter how busy he was. "What's up, Sam?"

"I think I have this thing done, but look here -- look at the second floor. All the interior walls still do not line up here in the center. They make a box instead of intersecting."

Dad went over the map with a pencil, checking and re-checking my math. "Are you positive that these measurements are accurate?"

"Yes." My response was probably too curt.

He glanced up at me. I must have had quite a look on my face, because he smiled. "I don't doubt it."

He looked at the map again, took off his glasses, and rubbed his eyes. "Sam, do you remember the famous quote by Sherlock Holmes?"

"When you have eliminated all which is impossible, then whatever remains, however improbable, must be the truth. That quote?"

"Yes. Very good."

Jessamine gasped. "How did you know that, Scout?"

Dad smiled again. "Sammy reads a lot, honey. Just like you do. Keep it up, and you'll be as wise as Sam."

It was true. In my room I had a big shelf of boys' adventure novels, *Tom Sawyer*, *Huckleberry Finn*, *Treasure Island*, *Kidnapped*, and many others.

But I was still confused. "I don't feel wise. I don't understand how the Sherlock Holmes quote applies."

Dad stood up and poked his finger at the box in center of the map. "All of your measurements are correct. You have eliminated any error. Therefore, your map is accurate."

I stared at the map. "You mean that there really is . . ." and there I paused, hardly able to believe what he was saying.

"Yes. There really is a square chamber, right there. A secret room."

Jessamine's eyes grew wide. "How do we find it?"

"Sam's already found it. What we need now is to find a way in. Let's go."

This I could hardly believe. "You mean you're going home?"

"You don't think I can stay here and concentrate on these boring papers, do you? Let's go see what's in this room."

Mom was the only one home when we got there. Clay was working down at the distillery, and Stone, Cliff and Mickey were off fishing or something. She was certainly surprised to see us with Dad, but I showed her my map and explained it.

Mom had a serious look on her face. "You know, I have always wondered about that closet in our bedroom. It's in an odd location, crammed in that corner. I think that is where we should start."

We went upstairs, and Mom swiftly pulled all the clothing and boxes out of the closet. Dad got an oil lamp off the wall, lighted it and turned up the wick, and he and I began examining the closet walls. They were all paneled with wood, not plastered like the other walls in our house. Tom-Tom padded into the room and sat down to watch us.

"See here, Sam. There's a fine gap in the wood, starting there, up and over, see?"

"A door!"

"Now where is the latch?" Dad ran his hands along the edges of the door. "The hinges must be on this side. And here, see, on the other side the wood is worn a bit. Like someone has pressed there many times." He pushed hard on the spot. There was a click, and the door began to swing open.

Tom-Tom stood up, eyes huge and black. As the door opened more, he suddenly darted in.

"That cat is fearless," laughed Dad. "Let's see what he's found."

Mom shook her head. "Probably a mouse town!"

We pulled the door all the way open, hinges protesting with loud cries. The secret room! It was square, just like on my map, about four feet on a side. The air smelled old, and the room was very dusty. The only object in the room was a small wooden chest, on the floor and shoved up against the rear wall. Tom-Tom jumped up on top of it.

Dad shooed him off, and grasped the handles of the chest. "Ooh, kinda heavy. Give me a hand, Sam."

We carried the chest out into the bedroom. On top, a hot iron had been used to burn the initials "B.G." into the wood.

"Benjamin Gunn!" breathed Mom.[6] "My father. He was a river merchant. This looks like a seaman's chest."

"Then you open it, Emma."

She unlatched it, and pulled up the top, struggling a bit against the stiff hinges. A strong smell of tobacco and tar rose from the chest.

She nodded. "To help preserve clothing." Indeed, there was a suit of very fine cloth on top, with several sticks of tobacco intermingled within. She carefully lifted them out and laid them aside. Under that were the instruments of a river merchant – a sextant, a compass, a brass spyglass, and two very handsome pistols. Beneath this was a heavy cloth coat, which she pulled aside to reveal the last two objects in the chest: a bundle tied up in oilcloth, and looking like papers, and a canvas bag, that gave forth, at a touch, the jingle of coins.

We carried the oilcloth bundle and the canvas bag down to the dining room table.

"What do you want to open first, Scout?"

"The bag."

Mom unfastened the cord on the bag, and dumped it out onto the table. Coins, lots of them! Silver and gold coins. The silver coins were Seated Liberty quarters, half dollars, and dollars. The gold coins were Liberty Head and Indian Princess Head dollars, Liberty Head quarter eagles, Indian Princess Head three dollar coins, and Liberty Head half eagles, eagles, and double eagles. All of the dates on the coins were before 1873.[7] We organized the coins into stacks, and added them up. It came to eight hundred fifty-three dollars! I never thought I would see so much money in one place.

"Well," observed Mom, "I think I know what this money is. My mother told us many times that shortly before he disappeared, my father took all his money out of the old Pioneer Bank that was here in town.[8] This money was his savings from his river merchant business. She explained that at the time he withdrew all his money, there was about eight or nine hundred dollars in the account. We never did find out what happened to this money, and all the time, it was right here in this house! This money belongs to you, Scout! It was your hard work that led us to it."

I was surprised. "Doesn't it belong to Gamma?" That's what we called our grandmother, our mother's mother.

Dad stroked his chin. "No. She sold us this house and everything in it when we got married. We paid her a handsome sum for this property, and that plus the big pension check she gets from her husband's company, means she certainly is in no need of money. I'm sure she would want you to have it."

Mom nodded. "I agree. Scout, if it wasn't for your hard work on that map, we never would have found this money. Who knows when, and into whose hands, this money would have been discovered. Maybe not until this house eventually gets torn down, long after we are all gone from this earth. This is your money to do with as you please. If you want, we could meet with Mr. Drysdale, the president of Morning View Bank, to decide what to do with it."[9]

I think I was getting too excited to notice what they were saying. "Now let's open the packet."

The bundle was sewed together, and Mom had to get out her fine-bladed sewing scissors and cut the stitches to open the package. It contained two things – a book and a sealed paper.

"We'll try the book first," observed Dad.

Mom and Jessamine and I were peering over his shoulder as he opened it. On the first page was written "Benjamin Gunn, his book."

Jessamine pointed at the name. "Grandpa."

The next twelve pages were filled with a curious series of entries. There was a date at one end of the line, and at the other a sum of money, as in common account books, but instead of explanatory writing, only a varying number of crosses and other symbols between the two, looking all the world like hieroglyphics. The record lasted over twenty years, from 1850 to 1872.

Dad ran his finger down the pages. "This is as clear as noonday. This is Gunn's account book, but danged if I can tell where the money was coming from. It's all encoded in these symbols."

Mom nodded. "Just looking at those sums, they total a lot more than eight hundred fifty dollars. There are the old family rumors that he was in a gang of river pirates."

My grandfather Benjamin Gunn, a river merchant, married my grandmother Artemesa Darnell. They had three daughters, my mom Emma being the oldest, and her two sisters Hannah and Sarah. Aunt Sarah lives up in Cincinnati with her husband Adolphus Maus, the parents of my cousins Mickey and Narcissa. Aunt Hannah lives out in the country near Morning View with her husband Clifford Berryman and my four girl cousins Becca, Matilda, Kacy, and Lilly.[10] "Gamma", as we call grandmother Artemesa, lives in a log cabin up the hill from the Berryman house. This cabin had been her childhood home, and the Berryman's bought the property from her when they got married and built a fine home down the hill from her log cabin. Our house in Morning View was where Mom and her

8

sisters were born. Grandpa Gunn disappeared in 1872, shortly after Sarah was born, and Gamma had to raise the three girls by herself. After Mom and Dad married, Gamma sold them the house and she moved back into the log cabin of her childhood, up the hill behind the Berryman house.

There are old family stories that Grandpa Gunn was in a gang of river pirates. For a long time there has been a booming steamboat trade up and down the Looking Glass River that flows south past Morning View, and several gangs of river pirates have operated along this stretch of the river.[11]

"Clearly," observed Mom, "my father built this house to include the secret room. The items we found today are probably legitimate property from his river merchant business, and he hid them here before disappearing."

Dad stroked his chin. "Agreed. Let's open this last piece."

The oilcloth bundle had been sealed with wax in several places with a thimble by way of a seal. Mom opened the seals with great care, and there fell out a map. The map was quite detailed, showing a river, cliffs and other landmarks, and then an inset map of a complex cave system that was labeled "Treasure Cave", with the cryptic notation "To the edge of the pit and thence down to the chamber where the treasure is hidden". The map had red crosses indicating two entrances to the cave along the cliffs, and then the location in the cave of the pit and a drawing of something called "the treasure chamber".

"This cave," exclaimed Mom, "is where the bulk of the money listed in the account book could be hidden!"

"Perhaps," replied Dad, "but who can make sense of this map? Where are these places? Are they near here? Are they on the Looking Glass? I don't recognize this area."

Tom-Tom cocked his ear toward the door, and seconds later Stone, Cliff, and Mickey came crashing into the house. They saw all the coins on the table.

Stone pointed to the stacks of coins. "Where did that come from?"

We told them the whole story. I was surprised to see that Mickey

Maus was the most interested. I thought, maybe there's hope for him yet. But then he did something that showed me how dumb I was to think such a thing. It happened after dinner.

Mom had asked me to clear the table and set it for dinner, so I put all the coins back into the bag and took it and the book and the map up to my room.

Before dinner was over, Mickey excused himself and went upstairs. I went up several minutes later and found him in my room, sitting at my desk and intently studying something.

"Mickey Maus! What are you doing in here?"

"None of your business."

"It is my business! This is my room!"

"Too bad! Get out of my way!" as he pushed me aside and stormed out.

I went over to my desk. The map was lying there. I had put it away in the top drawer. He must have gone through my desk, found it, gotten it out, and been studying it.

Tom-Tom came padding into my room. He sniffed the air, and looked at me with squinted eyes.

Yes, even I could smell Mickey Maus had been there. "That's right, Tom-Tom. He is one stinky creep."

CHAPTER 2

PLESSY FERGUSON[1]

The next day found me stuck alone with Jessamine, who was pestering me to play games with her. Stone, Cliff and Mickey were off on some adventure, and had not invited me along. I was feeling sore, and maybe was being a little mean to Jessamine.

Mom and Dad and I were supposed to meet with the banker Mr. Drysdale, to decide what to do with my eight hundred fifty-three dollars, but he was out of town until tomorrow on business up at Lake Tapaho.[2] I kept the bag of money in my room.

Mom had a group of lady friends over for lunch, members of the Kentucky Equal Rights Association.[3] They were advocating for the right of women to vote in elections. Mom and Dad often talked to us kids about the importance of this effort. I knew it was important, because the lunch guests included Harriet Railey, wife of the mayor, Mattie Drysdale, wife of the banker, and Evaline Pepper, wife of the town doctor.

Jessamine and I helped serve the lunch. While the ladies were enjoying lunch and talking, there came a strong boom, which rattled the windows and the glasses in the china cabinet.

"Goodness!" exclaimed Mrs. Railey. "What could that have been?"

"I don't know," replied Mrs. Pepper, "but it didn't sound good."

A few minutes later I saw Tom-Tom cock his ear toward the

front door. "I think Stone, Cliff, and Mickey are coming," I told Mom. "Maybe they have some news."

Sure enough, Mickey Maus came barging through the front door. Mom and I went into the entrance foyer. Mickey was out of breath. He must have run ahead of Stone and Cliff.

"What was that loud boom?" asked Mom.

Mickey leaned over, hands on his knees, breathing hard. Between breaths he blurted out, "A boiler – a boiler exploded – on the steamboat *Hudson Lee*".

The other women came rushing to the entrance foyer. "Oh, dear goodness!" gasped Mrs. Railey. "Was anyone hurt?"

"No'm. Killed a nigger."

That set Mrs. Railey back. There was a stunned silence. I saw Mom's mouth twitching, and knew she was about to say something serious, but I couldn't control myself and I sailed in ahead of her.

"Who was it?"

Mickey stared at me and shrugged. "I don't know. I don't know the names of your niggers."

I could feel my face getting hot. I knew I was flushing red with anger. "Stop saying that word!"

Mickey gave me an ugly look. Just then, Stone and Cliff stumbled in through the door.

"Who was it?" I shouted. "Who was killed?"

Stone opened his mouth, and shut it. Cliff swallowed hard, and looked at me. "What do you mean?"

I was frustrated to the point of fury. "The name of the person who was killed, you moron! Who was it?"

Cliff hesitated, studying my face, and finally spoke. "It was ol' Plessy."

I stared at him. "Mr. Ferguson? That's all? That's all you're going to say? His wife died last year! Those kids have no parents anymore!" I could feel hot tears welling up in my eyes. I didn't know what to say, except to burst out: "He taught us kids how to tie fishing lures!" I was choking up, unable to control my voice.

There was dead silence, finally broken by Mom. She spoke in a low, controlled tone. "You three boys will go up to your rooms and wait there until Mr. Morgan comes home. When he hears about this, he will want to speak with you."

Mickey glared at her. "You're not my mother. I don't have to do what you tell me."

Mom didn't hesitate this time. Her voice was a thunderclap. "Young man, as long as you are staying in this house, you are my responsibility and you will do as I say. If my sister Sarah were to hear about this, I would not want to be in your skin. Now march!"

Mickey opened his mouth, but then an intelligent thought must have come into his measly brain, because he clapped his trap shut and sullenly marched up the stairs. As he went up, he turned and caught my eye. The look of hatred on his face was at a pitch so pure that it practically sang.

Stone and Cliff followed. As they started up the steps, I heard Stone say to Cliff, "Scout called you a moron. What does that mean?"

"I don't know. Let's look it up in the dictionary."

Tom-Tom glanced at me, and then went padding up the stairs after them. I guess he wanted to see their faces when they looked up the word moron. I'd like to have been there for that. I've never seen a cat laugh.

Mom and the other ladies talked briefly about what had happened, and how they didn't know what to do about the four orphaned Ferguson children. The women left after a short time.

After Dad came home and had a talk with Stone, Cliff, and Mickey, they were unusually quiet. At dinner, Dad explained what he had learned about the terrible accident. The steamboat *Hudson Lee*, a regular at our landing, was having trouble with one of its boilers. Plessy Ferguson, an ironworker by trade, was working on it when it exploded. He was killed instantly. The steamboat was being towed up to Cincinnati to be repaired.

The atmosphere around the dinner table that night was gloomy. Abruptly, Mickey Maus announced that he wanted to return home.

He wanted to go as quickly as possible, meaning not on a steamboat. Mom and Dad glanced at one another. I, for one, was glad to hear it.

Cliff blurted out, "But you just got here!"

Mickey was adamant. "I don't like it here. I want to get out of here."

The next morning, my parents put him on the Kentucky Central Railroad bound for Covington, from where he could take the Green Line streetcar across the Suspension Bridge to his home in Cincinnati.[4, 5]

Well, maybe Mom and the other leading ladies of the town didn't know what to do about the four orphaned Ferguson kids. I wasn't sure myself. But I knew one thing for sure.

I set off for the Ferguson house. It was in Trenchtown, the colored section of Morning View, across the train tracks from the white section of town, and down low close to the river.[6]

My route took me past the J.W. Brookie distillery, where Clay worked. As I walked past the distillery and began to cross the tracks, I saw Clay and some of his co-workers sitting on the loading dock, taking a break.

"Hey, Scout, where you goin'?" called out Clay.

"To Trenchtown" I replied.

Clay just watched me go.

I came up to the Ferguson house, and tapped on the door.

The door opened, and Jemima Banks stood there. She was the aunt of the Ferguson kids.

"Hello, Mrs. Banks. I am a friend of the Ferguson family."

She nodded to me, pushed the door wide open, and motioned for me to come in.

There were a lot of folks there, all colored. I scanned the room, and saw the Ferguson kids over at one side, sitting around a table. The oldest boy was Mercury, who was Clay's age. Then there were the identical twins, Romulus and Remus, who were the same age as Stone and Cliff. Finally, there was the one girl, Venus, who was the same age as Jessamine.

I nodded to them and walked over. "Mercury, Romulus and Remus, Venus, I'm very sorry about what happened to your daddy."

Mercury Ferguson nodded. "Thank you for coming, Sam. We appreciate it."

There was a moment of silence. I sensed everyone was wondering why I was there.

"I've come to bring you something." With that, I heaved the canvas bag onto the table and dumped the coins out. "There's eight hundred fifty-three dollars there. That's for you. I remember how kind your momma always was to us, and your daddy teaching us all kinds of things, and I'll never forget it."

Mercury Ferguson stood up. His eyes were wide, his mouth open. "We can't . . ." was all he could muster. Romulus and Remus looked shocked, and Venus was looking around, wondering what was going on.

I shook my head. "It's mine to do with as I please. I choose to give it to you."

The preacher from the Colored Baptist Church, Reverend Reuben Mulcahy, came over to me.[7, 8] "Do your parents know what you are doing?"

"They did say this was my money to do with as I please. I please to give it to the Ferguson family."

The preacher shook his head. "I will need to speak with your father."

"Yes, sir. But this money is staying here."

There was another uncomfortable silence.

Mrs. Banks came over to me. "We have some cold lemonade over there, honey. Would you like some?"

"Yes'm."

She bowed slightly to me, took my hand, and led me over to the sideboard and poured a glass of lemonade. I sipped it, and nodded to the Ferguson kids.

Mercury Ferguson looked dazed. "Is this really happening?"

"Yes," I replied.

I got home just before lunchtime. Tom-Tom and I were in the dining room, as I was setting the table for lunch. He cocked his ear toward the front door. I looked out, and saw a formidable group of men approaching the house. There was Dad, the mayor Mr. Railey, the town doctor Dr. Pepper, the banker Mr. Drysdale, and a hero of the old Confederacy, General Lyon.[9, 10, 11]

"Mom! Some men coming to visit."

They came in, and greeted her.

The mayor bowed. "Good afternoon, Emma," to which she replied, "Good afternoon, Logan."

The doctor bowed. "Good afternoon, Emma," to which she replied, "Good afternoon, Oscar."

The banker bowed. "Good afternoon, Emma," to which she replied, "Good afternoon, Leonidas."

The general bowed. "Good afternoon, Emma," to which she replied, "Good afternoon, Hylan."

After all that nonsense, she asked "What is this all about?"

Dad responded, "Naturally, this is all about our Sam."

"What?"

Dad turned to me with a stern voice, but a twinkle in his eyes. "Sam, did you think a white child, carrying a big bag of money, and going into Trenchtown all alone, would not be noticed? We heard about it right away."

I figured that was Clay's doing. That was alright. He was always looking out for me.

Mr. Drysdale turned to Mom and held up his hands. "Emma, little Sammy here has given the Ferguson children eight hundred fifty-three dollars in silver and gold coins."

Mom glanced at me, but with more of a smile on her face than a look of surprise.

Mr. Drysdale turned to me. "Sammy, many of those coins are worth more than their face value. Many of them are quite old, or rare, or both. Some of them are worth even more than two times their face value. Being a banker, I am something of a coin collector, and offered to buy the whole bag of coins from the Ferguson children. Dr. Pepper knows a lot more about coins than I do, and he made

16

an independent appraisal of the coins. I have opened an account at my bank for the Ferguson children in the amount of two thousand dollars. That is somewhat more than the coins are worth, but I am following your lead and I made a donation above and beyond the value of the coins, in the name of the Ferguson Family Trust, which I have opened in my bank."

I looked down at my hands. "Thank you, Mr. Drysdale."

Mayor Railey responded, "Sammy, don't thank us. We thank you. You have pulled our town together. Many citizens are coming forward, and contributing, including me."

"And me," chimed in both Dr. Pepper and General Lyon.

"Indeed", added Mr. Drysdale, "the Ferguson Family Trust is already approaching twenty-five hundred dollars."

The funeral for Plessy Ferguson was held two days later, in the Colored Baptist Church down in Trenchtown, near the distillery. The weather was blazing hot and humid.

It seemed like the whole town was there, and people came in from the countryside. There were lots of horses, carriages, and wagons in the streets around the church.

We went in, and some very serious looking men from the colored funeral home, in black suits, escorted us to the second pew, right behind the Ferguson kids. Mercury, Romulus and Remus all turned and nodded at me.

Speaking of black suits, Mom had insisted I put on black dress clothes and a white starched shirt.

Venus leaned over the back of the pew. "Hey, Jessamine! Mrs. Railey gave me a brand-new doll! Do you want to play with it?"

Jessamine glanced at Mom, who nodded. "Sure, Venus. You can come to my house, and I'll show you my dolls, too."

That kind of frilly girl talk made my stomach hurt.

The church was dark and unpainted. Kerosene lamps hung on the walls, and the pews were rough pine. There was no piano, no organ, not even any hymn books.

The church was getting crowded. They opened all the windows, but it was still getting real warm inside. They had placed cheap cardboard fans at each seat, courtesy of Berryman's General Store, with a picture of Jesus on one side, and bright lettering on the other side shouting, "Buy Hogsden Mill flour!"[12] Even though I fanned my face furiously, I could feel rivulets of sweat trickling down my chest and from my underarms. My starched shirt was beginning to melt.

As more and more people entered the church, some of the colored folks began to get up from the pews, to let the white folks have a seat, but there was a lot of hand waving and quiet words, and everyone just began to squeeze together. I saw the old Confederate general, Hylan Lyon, seated between two colored Union veterans, Charles Clay Buntain and William Rice.[13] And they were talking to each other!

The mayor, Mr. Railey, and the colored preacher, Reverend Mulcahy, stood up in the front of the church. The casket behind them was closed. I shuddered when I realized what that meant. The church got very quiet.

Mr. Railey spoke first. "I just want to say one thing, before turning this over to Reverend Mulcahy. I am very proud of how our town of Morning View has come together at this time of great tragedy." Murmurs of approval rippled through the congregation. "This news has spread across our region. We even have a newspaperman here today from the *Cincinnati Enquirer*, a Mr. Schulkers, and he has brought his camera. We all know why he is here, and that is to join us in recognizing young Sam Morgan there, for putting into motion the amazing response our town has made to the Ferguson family in their time of sorrow and great need." More murmurs, and someone behind me patted my head. "But today is mostly about honoring Mr. Plessy Ferguson, and his life with us here in Morning View."

With that, Mr. Railey sat down with the Ferguson kids, and Reverend Mulcahy stood before the casket. "Will the music superintendent lead us in the first hymn. We'll sing number three sixty-two, *Nothing but the Blood of Jesus*.[14] This is a wonderful song. You don't hear it sung much anymore. Someone, I believe it was brother Roberts, said Sunday night that they're trying to take the blood out of the songbooks. They'd like to take it out of the Bible. But we can stand for the word of God, and certainly the blood of Jesus cleanses us of all sin."

A murmur of "Amen" rippled across the pews.

Old Cyprian Clamorgan got up from his pew, stiffly walked down the center aisle, turned to face the congregation, and called out *"Nothing but the Blood of Jesus."*[15]

I turned to Mom and whispered, "How we gonna sing it if there ain't no hymn books?" Mom put her finger to her lips.

Mr. Clamorgan called out the first line. "What can wash away my sin?"

Miraculously on pitch, a hundred colored voices sang the line, followed by Mr. Clamorgan calling out the next line "Nothing but the blood of Jesus." And on it went for each line.

The first verse and the refrain were:

What can wash away my sin?
Nothing but the blood of Jesus;
What can make me whole again?
Nothing but the blood of Jesus.

Oh! Precious is the flow,
That makes me white as snow;
No other fount I know,
Nothing but the blood of Jesus.

I looked at Mom, who smiled at me. I could hardly believe it, but I had heard it. He was lining out the song for the congregation!

His performance continued for four more verses.

This was followed by a tedious prayer, and another hymn called *Meet Me There*, lined out again by Mr. Clamorgan. It was about meeting all your dead relatives after you die.

It was getting uncomfortably hot inside the church.

Reverend Mulcahy began to speak. He sketched out the life of Plessy Ferguson, and his wife, Percella, who died last year, and the four Ferguson children. He was doing a good job. But when he got to the point in the story where I found the money, he dropped this howler: "It was the hand of God Himself laid upon young Sam Morgan, guiding this child to a hidden bag of money."

I leaned over to Mom and whispered, "That's a bunch of hooey. It was my map that led me to the money." Mom closed her eyes, shook her head, and bit her finger.

The preacher continued, "Who can explain what has happened to the Ferguson family? What have these innocent young folk, Mercury, and Romulus and Remus, and little Venus, done to deserve these two heavy blows of tragedy? Why must they suffer so, we must ask ourselves?"

Here I thought the preacher was getting dangerously close to making a point, but then he veered off into safer waters.

"This is one of the great mysteries of life. God works in mysterious ways, and while we know He has a purpose for everything He does, we cannot always understand what that purpose may be."

When he had finally finished, there was one more hymn, *Precious Memories* about more dead relatives. Then we were finally released to get out into the fresh air.

The pallbearers were the three Ferguson boys, plus Mayor Railey, Dr. Pepper, and Dad. Reverend Mulcahy led them out of the church and into the graveyard on the side, to the freshly dug grave next to the grave of Mrs. Ferguson. They laid the casket next to the gravesite, and we all gathered around. Mom and Jessamine were on either side of Venus Ferguson, holding on to her.

Reverend Mulcahy opened a large book and spoke in a strong voice. "Solomon teaches that the just, though they die early, shall be at rest. For the age that is honorable comes not with the passing of time, nor can it be measured in terms of years. Rather, understanding is the hoary crown, and an unsullied life, the attainment of old age. Those who pleased God were loved; they who lived among sinners were transported, snatched away, lest wickedness pervert their mind or deceit beguile their soul, for the witchery of paltry things obscures what is right and the whirl of desire transforms the innocent mind. Having become perfect in a short while, they reached the fullness of a long career, for their souls were pleasing to the Lord, therefore he sped them out of the midst of wickedness. But the people saw and did not understand, nor did they take this into account."[16]

The preacher closed the book, and there was a long moment of silence. The casket had been covered with a white cloth as it was carried out of the church, and the preacher laid his hand on the cloth.

The preacher spoke in a strong voice. "For all of you who were baptized into Christ have clothed yourselves with Christ, in his baptism Plessy Ferguson put on Christ. In the day of Christ's coming, he shall be clothed with glory." Then he nodded to the pallbearers.

With ropes strung under the casket, they moved it over the open grave and began to slowly lower it into the ground. I could hear soft sobbing from many in the gathered crowd. Warm tears were welling up in my eyes.

When the casket was lowered, they pulled up the ropes. The Ferguson children dropped some lumps of earth into the grave, and then many others did the same. Mom ushered me over, and we picked up pieces of soil and gently tossed them in. I felt my face streaking with tears.

It was over. The preacher led us away from the graveyard, over to the other side of the church.

Everyone gathered in the shade of the chestnut trees next to the church, and a group of white and colored men and women began serving cold drinks. They were shaving ice off big blocks. I never thought a glass of ice cold lemonade could ever taste so good.

I was standing with Mom. "Mom, how did Mr. Clamorgan do that? He knew the lines for all three of those hymns."

"You saw that church. They can't afford much, including hymn books. Mr. Clamorgan has memorized all the hymns from the Colored Baptist hymnal."

I thought that was just plain incredible.

Lots of folks came over to talk to me. My teacher Miss Geldreich was one of them. "Sam, I always knew you were special, and destined for great things. But my goodness, you've already exceeded my expectations!"

I could feel my face blushing. "Thank you, Miss Geldreich. You are my favorite teacher ever! I'll never forget you."

Mercury Ferguson was standing nearby, and heard that last remark I made. He shook my hand. "You saved my family, Sam. I'll never forget that. I just don't know how I can ever repay you."

I shook my head. "I wouldn't worry about it. We never know what the future holds."

I saw a man, someone I did not recognize, talking to Mayor Railey. The mayor was pointing to me. The man came over to Mom and me.

"Hello, Mrs. Morgan, and this must be the famous young Sam Morgan. My name is Robert Schulkers. I'm a newspaperman, work for the *Cincinnati Enquirer.* I'm a Kentuckian, too, born and raised in Kentucky. I have been interested in the habits and adventures of boys, and am considering writing some stories about a group of boys who have adventures like young Sam here has had. These sorts of experiences would make for some good reading."

He shook our hands, and Mom patted my head. "We're pleased to meet you, Mr. Schulkers, but . ."

Mr. Schulkers talked real fast. He seemed to have more to say, and as soon as Mom started to say something, he just talked even faster. He did this in a friendly way, and it made him seem funny at the same time. I had to keep from laughing.

"I'm just going to take a minute of your time, ask a few questions, and get a photograph of the famous Sam Morgan." He pulled out a stenography pad and a pencil.

I opened my mouth to speak, but he pointed the pencil at me and rushed forward. "One thing I've learned is that a story like this gets all mixed up as it gets told up and down the river. The treasure you found, for instance, I've heard it was buried, or hidden in a cave, or a barn, or under the floor in your house? And it was either gold coins or gold bars, I've heard both. And it was guarded by the skeleton of a pirate, that's just incredible. I'm sure the real facts are mixed in there somewhere, and I'm here to listen to the story straight from you and then I can be sure to get it straight for the newspaper. That's my job."

He opened his notebook, poised his pencil over the page, and looked expectantly into my face. He was ready to listen. I took a deep breath, glanced at Mom who smiled and nodded, and then I began to straighten out the facts for him.

He was very appreciative of the time I took to explain everything, and he took a whole lot of notes. After I was done talking, he commented "This is wonderful. The real story is even better than all the mixed-up information I have been hearing. I'm glad to get this on the record." After that, he had me pose for a photograph, and then he worked his way through the crowd, interviewing the mayor and the banker, and lots of other people.

The colored Union veteran, William Rice, was making mint juleps at a table off to one side, away from most of the crowd. A group of other colored men were standing around him, sipping on the drinks.[17] The Confederate veteran, General Lyon, hobbled over to them. I edged closer to hear what would happen.

General Lyon spoke first. "Mr. Rice, are those bourbon mint juleps?"

"Yes, General," replied Mr. Rice. "You are welcome to one.'

"I would be honored and delighted."

At the sight of that, a whole bunch of other white men moved over to the table, and Mr. Rice started making mint juleps as fast as he could. Mr. "J.W." Brookie, owner of the distillery, walked over, and I heard him say "Mr. Rice, you are going to run out of bourbon right quick." He turned and motioned for two boys who worked at the distillery, Russel Railey, son of the mayor, and a colored boy, Elijah Craig.[18]

"Here is the key to the cabinet in my office. You boys each get two bottles of our Hand Made Sour Mash."

Elijah Craig looked startled. "But Mr. Brookie, that's your special reserve."

"Never you mind. Just scoot over there and get it." Russel and Elijah dashed off.

General Lyon was talking to the colored Union veterans, Charles

Clay Buntain and William Rice. Mr. Buntain was saying, "Yes, we were in the Fifth United States Colored Cavalry. You and your boys whooped us good at the battle of Hopkinsville."[19]

General Lyon smiled. "Your unit fought well, and honorably, for the whole war. Even after the Saltville Massacre. That scoundrel Champ Ferguson was a coward and a disgrace to the Confederacy."

I knew this story from my history lessons. The Saltville Massacre was the murder of captured and wounded white and colored Union soldiers, including about 50 members of the Fifth US Colored Cavalry, by Confederate soldiers and irregular guerilla forces under the command of the notorious Champ Ferguson. Champ Ferguson was one of only two Confederates hanged for war crimes after the war.[20] Quite a contrast to the Mr. Ferguson we were honoring today.

Mr. Brookie was talking to the Ferguson children. He looked at the three boys. "You three look mighty strong. What do you do for a living?"

Mercury Ferguson responded. "We are woodhawks.[21] We collect driftwood, big tree trunks, from the Looking Glass, and split them into kindling wood, to sell to the steamboats."

Mr. Brookie nodded. "Hard, honest work. A steamboat burns two hundred cubic feet of firewood every hour."[22] He looked at Romulus and Remus. "Are you two still in school?"

Remus looked at Romulus, who spoke. "No, sir. Our school goes through eighth grade. We've been out of school for two years now."

Mr. Brookie paused. He looked real serious. "I would like to offer all three of you jobs at my distillery. If you do that, who would take care of your little sister Venus?"

Mrs. Banks stepped forward. "I'm their aunt, live just a couple doors away. Venus can stay at my house while they're at work. We're most appreciative to you, Mr. Brookie."

"I can always use strong, hard-working men. The work is hard, but the pay will reflect that. When can you start?"

Mercury glanced at Romulus and Remus, who nodded to him. "We can start tomorrow."

Mr. Brookie shook hands with all three of them. "You young men are made of some stern stuff."

All in all, even though it was a funeral day, I would say the whole day was plain amazing.

CHAPTER 3

A VISIT WITH GAMMA

The next several days were a whirlwind of activities, including special dinners at the mayor's house, and at our house, with all the important people in town. The article by Mr. Schulkers in the *Cincinnati Enquirer*, including a photograph of me, was pasted up all over the place.

People were always sending me gifts, too, mainly dress clothes. I would probably never wear them, but Mom made me wear them for the dinners and other events. I would just as soon stay in my jeans and plain shirts. One time Cliff and Stone and I made some dye out of butternut hickory nuts.[1] I had read about this in an old botany book in Dad's study. We used the dye on some of our white cotton shirts, and they turned a beautiful yellowish olive green. Mom nearly fainted when she saw them hanging on the line to dry, but it's my favorite shirt.

Venus Ferguson began coming to our house, to play with Jessamine. Dolls and dresses and hair bows and all that frilly girl stuff. It just made my stomach hurt.

One day the steamboat *Hudson Lee* returned from repairs in Cincinnati, and stopped at Morning View. Cliff was our steamboat expert, and kept a logbook of the steamboats that worked the Looking Glass. The *Hudson Lee*, a sternwheeler, mainly carried passengers. It was an incredibly ornate boat, of the type often referred to as a "bride of Babylon", or a "floating wedding cake". It was on its way south to Memphis and points further downstream.[2]

Captain Lee and his son Hudson Lee and daughter Rosalind Lee came up to our house. Rosalind had a rag doll, and she and Venus and Jessamine ran upstairs to play with their dolls.

Captain Lee came over to me. "Sam, I am hearing your name up and down the river. I always figured you were destined for great things, but my goodness, what you have done is making the news in a big way."

"Thank you, sir."

Hudson Lee, who was about my age, shook my hand. "I am glad I know you, Scout."

I waved my hand by my head, like I was batting away a cloud of gnats. "Thank you, Hudson. I'm glad to know you, too. Can I ask you a question, Captain Lee? Are there any cliffs and caves anywhere close to the banks of the Looking Glass?"

Captain Lee furrowed his brow. "Well, south of here, the river valley keeps getting wider, and the hills and bluffs along the floodplain are set far back from the river. Upstream, however, about halfway between here and Cincinnati, there is an extensive section known as The Palisades, where the Looking Glass cuts a deep and narrow valley, with cliffs right on the riverbank.[3] There are lots of caves in that area. Why do you ask?"

I hesitated. "I was just wondering. I saw a map that showed some cliffs close to a river, and wondered if there were any areas like that along the Looking Glass."

Later that afternoon, after the mail was delivered, Mom handed me a letter she had received. "You need to read this."

I read the letter, and sucked in my breath. "Wow."

"Wow is right," replied Mom.

The next day was a Saturday. All seven of us were at breakfast.

I turned to Mom. "Mom, I've been studying Grandpa Gunn's account book, and that map, again. Those figures add up to a little over one hundred thousand dollars. The map says the money was hidden in a cave. Do you think there could be that much money, that he hid in a cave around here?"

Mom thought for a minute. "I think that is a question for your Grandma Gunn. Why don't you visit her?"

Cliff and Stone were all for that. "Let's ride horses up there!"

Clay nodded, and then surprised me. "I'm coming, too."

That was all set. Mom turned to me. "Take your little sister."

"Yay!" shouted Jessamine.

I searched my brain for an excuse. "We only have four horses."

"She can ride with you."

"Mom . . ."

"Hush, Scout."

"Yes'm."

After breakfast we saddled up the horses. I had the white horse, Joe Cotton.

Jessamine was watching me strap on the gear. "Can Tom-Tom come with us?"

"No. Cats don't like to ride horses."

We set off on four horses, Clay, Cliff, and Stone had their own horse, and I had Jessamine sitting in front of me. She was wearing a dress. A dress! On a horse!

Clay was riding on a gray horse, Aristides, Cliff was on the black Wintergreen, and Stone had his chestnut horse, Stone Street.[4]

We turned into the lane that ran by our barn, and rode over to the Independence Turnpike.[5] Up the hill we rode, out of the river valley. At the top of the hill was a toll booth.

Old Mr. Venable hobbled out into the turnpike. "Four horses. That'll be one dollar."

Mom had given me the money. "Here you go, Mr. Venable."

He seemed startled as he looked up at me. "Oh, it's you, Sam!

I didn't recknize you behind that lil' girl. You fellers can go by for free. Matter of fact, jus' a second here . . ." and he fumbled in his pocket. "Here's two quarters. Put that in the Ferguson bank account for me, would ye?"

Clay nodded. "Awful good of you, Mr. Venable."

"Thank you!" we all called out, and then proceeded on our way.

It was beautiful countryside, with stone walls lining the pike, and horse farms on either side. Kentucky coffeetrees were growing alongside the pike next to the walls, and black cherry trees were growing between the walls and the fences around the pastures.[6]

Jessamine leaned back against me. "I love you, Scout."

"I love you too, Jessamine."

"I'm going to marry you."

That brought the parade to a standstill. Clay, Stone, and Cliff were bent over in their saddles laughing. Joe Cotton turned his big horsey face at us and looked pathetically at Jessamine.

Stone was gasping for breath. "You can't do that, Jessamine, not even in Kentucky!"

"Why not?"

"Because you have to marry a feller who ain't one of you own kin."

"Plus," added Cliff, "you're too young to get married."

Jessamine sat up. "But I saw Scout kissing Becky Thatcher!"[7]

Oh, man. I could feel my face turning red.

Clay was looking up at the sky, like he was studying the clouds. "Do Mom and Dad know anything about this?"

"No. But I don't think they'd mind."

Clay turned and looked at my face. "You just be careful, Sam."

We turned into the lane that led up to the Berryman house, home of Uncle Clifford, husband of Mom's sister, Aunt Hannah, and our four girl cousins: Becca, Matilda, Kacy and Lilly.

Kacy was on the front porch. She saw us and jumped up. "Mom! Guess who's coming!"

Uncle Clifford and Aunt Hannah and all four of the girls were there. They came out, and we all got smothered with hugs and kisses. We see them about every month, but they acted like we hadn't for years.

We tied up the horses, and went inside for some cold drinks and snacks. I told Aunt Hannah we had come to talk to Gamma. "Well, you know where she is. She hardly ever comes down from that cabin."

Uncle Clifford laughed. "Sam, you tell her she needs to come down here more often and get a decent meal!"

Gamma had been born in a one-room log cabin up the hill behind the house. She grew up there, and only moved away when she married Grandpa Gunn. He built the house we live in down in Morning View. When Aunt Hannah married Uncle Clifford, they bought this property and built their house. Gamma stayed in the big house in town until 1895, when Mom and Dad got married and they bought that house. After that, Gamma moved back into the log cabin of her childhood.

We started up the path, through the cedar trees. It was steep going, and the cabin was high up on the hillside. The smell of woodsmoke gave away the cabin before we saw it.

The cabin was small, with tiny windows and a cedar shake roof. Smoke was coming out of the limestone chimney. Gamma kept a fire going, no matter how hot the weather was.

We knocked on the door, but it swung open on its own. Gamma was sitting on her bed, and smiled a big smile when she saw us. "There you are, you Morgan kids! Come in here and give me a kiss!"

It wasn't easy to bring myself to kiss that wrinkly face, but I did it anyway. It was like kissing melted butter.

Gamma was very happy to see us. "Jessamine, sweetie! And Clayton, how big you are getting! Clifton and Stonewall, I can hardly tell you apart! And Sammy, you rascal, come over here and sit next to me. I want you to tell me all about what's happened."

One thing I will remember about Gamma's cabin, for as long as I live, was the strong smell of woodsmoke. There could be other aromas, such as fried bacon or baked apples or cornbread, but always over the top of everything else was the powerful woodsmoke odor. It permeated everything and everyone in that cabin. After every visit, all my clothes and all of me smelled of woodsmoke until a good bath and laundry.

I sat on the bed next to Gamma and told her all about how I found the secret room, and the chest and the bag of money that was in it. I mentioned that Mom thought it was from his river merchant bank account.

Gamma nodded. "I think that's exactly what it was. Your grandpa Gunn pulled that money out shortly before he disappeared. It was in the old Pioneer Bank of Morning View, and it was a good thing he took it all out in '72, because in the Panic of '73, that bank failed, and everyone lost all of their money.[8] He told me at the time it was about eight hundred fifty dollars, and that he was going to hide it somewhere safe. Then he disappeared, and I had no idea where the money was. You are very clever, Scout, the way you found that money sitting right under our noses all these years."

"Are you mad at me for giving it away, Gamma?"

"Oh, no, dear goodness no. I have plenty of my own. And what you did with it, that was such a noble deed, and I am very proud of you. Tell me the whole story!"

I told her what had happened to poor Mr. Ferguson, and the funeral. When I mentioned about General Lyon being seated at the funeral between Mr. Buntain and Mr. Rice, she laughed so hard I was worried she was going to bust a rib.

"Oh, dear me!" she managed to say. "That old Confederate, seated between two colored Union veterans! I guess the Civil War really is over!"

When I told her about the mint juleps episode with General Lyon and Mr. Rice, she clapped her hands together. "I'd've given good money to see that! Oh! By the way . . . Stone, would you hand me my purse there?"

It was just a plain black coin purse. She opened it and fished out two silver dollars. "That's for the Ferguson account."

I shook my head. "Gamma, you don't have to do that. You don't have much money."

Gamma waved her bony hand. "Sammy, I've got more money than I could possibly ever use. Your grandfather Gunn set me up as a partner in his river merchant business, and I get a big check every month from the company. You don't need to worry about me. My money is with Mr. Drysdale at the Morning View Bank, and there is more in my account than I could ever spend. Your mother had called Hannah on the telephone, to tell her about all the stuff that was in the chest, and asked her to check with me to see if I wanted any of it, but I did not."

I opened my knapsack. "There were a couple of other things in the chest I want you to see, Gamma." I brought out the account book, and the map.

She studied the account book first. "That's his handwriting, sure thing."

Jessamine was sitting on the bed on the other side of Gamma. "His name is in the front, too."

"You're right, sweetie. I see it."

I pointed to the symbol writing. "Can you understand these strange symbols?"

"No, honey. I guess he had made up some code, but I don't know anything about it."

"Was he a river pirate?"

Gamma sighed a weary sigh. "He was a river merchant, with several partners, and a fleet of steamboats, running freight between New Orleans and St. Louis.[9] His company did real well, and we had no lack of money. But I found out later he had somehow gotten mixed up with some river pirates. That led to a lot of trouble."

"What happened to him in '72?"

Gamma shut the book. "I didn't know this at the time, but the police were closing in on the river pirates. Most of them were caught and sent to prison. Grandpa Gunn was getting ready, taking care of his affairs, taking his legitimate money out of the bank and hiding it, along with his pistols and the other things you found in the chest. Then he disappeared."

"Have you ever heard from him?"

The question surprised Gamma. She considered her answer. "No, he has not contacted me."

I persisted. "Do you think he could still be alive, somewhere?"

Gamma laughed lightly, and patted my hand. "You're just like your father! I guess you'll grow up to be an attorney, too!"

I took that as Gamma's gentle way of asking me to change the subject.

"The numbers in that account book total more than one hundred thousand dollars. Did he really have that much money?"

"Well, not that I ever knew, but you see, Sammy, since we can't read the entries in that account book, we don't know if it was all money coming in, or if it was money coming in and going out."

I opened the map. "But here is some evidence there was a lot of money. It says on this map, there is in a treasure chamber in a cave."

Gamma pored over the map for a minute. "This was done in his hand. It is his map, for sure."

I asked her "Do you recognize this area? Is it along the Looking Glass?"

Gamma shook her head. "I can't say for sure."

"Captain Lee told me about a stretch of the Looking Glass, between here and Cincinnati, where there are cliffs all along close to the river, just like this map, and there are caves in the cliffs.'

Gamma nodded. "Your grandfather and I did travel up to Cincinnati several times, and I remember that area. It is beautiful. I just don't remember enough to be able to say if any part of it matches this map."

"Do you believe this map? Would Grandpa Gunn have hidden treasure in a cave somewhere?"

"He had his secrets, yes he did. If the river pirates had amassed a lot of money, he very well may have hidden it away somewhere, as the police were getting close to catching them." Gamma paused, and looked intently at me. "You want to try to find the treasure mentioned on this map, don't you?"

"Yes'm."

She was still looking closely at my face. "Well, you've always been a keen observer. That's why we call you Scout. I think you just need to go up there and see what you see. See if you can find the cliffs that match this map, and then find the cave and the treasure chamber. If there is a treasure there, I want to know it."

I knew Gamma would have the right answer.

CHAPTER 4

WE GO UP THE RIVER

Mom was real doubtful about a trip up the Looking Glass, and didn't want me to go, even though Stone and Cliff explained they would go with me. We spent all day Sunday arguing about it. Part of the problem was that Dad, who I thought would be on my side, was distracted by the news from Europe. Sent by the trans-Atlantic telegraphic cable, word spread across our nation that Serb nationalists had assassinated Archduke Franz Ferdinand of Austria and his wife Sophie while they were visiting the Bosnian capital of Sarajevo.[1] This had set off an anti-Serb pogrom in Bosnia and elsewhere, and Dad and lots of other people in town were worried that war was brewing.[2]

On Monday, when Clay came home from working at the distillery, he had some news. He had asked for a few days off, and Mr. Brookie had replied yes. Therefore, Clay stated he would be able to go with us. That turned the discussion to the right decision, and Mom and Dad agreed we could go.

We spent the next day, Tuesday, getting our tent and other gear ready. Mom was preparing enough food for us to last a month, I think.

Finally, the day came when we were all set. It was Wednesday, the first of July. We were getting ready for Dad to take us and the two canoes and all our gear down to the wharf in the wagon, and were saying our goodbyes to Mom and Jessamine.

Jessamine was hugging me. "Is Tom-Tom going with you?"

"No. Cats don't like to ride in canoes. You take good care of him, hear?"

"Yes." I could tell she was about to cry.

"Don't worry. We'll be home soon, and with bags of gold coins!"

Clay rolled his eyes. "I think half of that statement is true."

The Morning View wharf was a bustling place. There were three steamboats tied up, taking on freight: the side-wheel packet *Kentucky Belle,* and two sternwheel packets, the *Crescent City* and the *Cynthianne.*[8] There were smaller boats, flatboats and lighters, selling firewood and moving some freight. The most activity was around the *Kentucky Belle,* which seemed to be about ready to get underway. Dark gray smoke was pouring out of its twin stacks. The whole wharf was alive with noise, laughing and singing, and activity. It was a fun place to visit and take in the show.

We went to the upper part of the wharf, which was much quieter. We got the canoes in the water, and loaded up all our gear. Stone and Cliff had one canoe, and Clay and I were going to be in the other.

Dad pulled Clay aside, and spoke to him in a low voice. I couldn't hear what he was saying, but his tone was scary dead serious. I knew he was telling Clay that he held him responsible for us. Clay had a stony face when he climbed into the canoe and gave me a significant glance.

Away we went, waving goodbye to Dad. I turned around a few times, and he was still standing there as we went around the first bend, and I lost sight of him.

We knew this stretch of the Looking Glass well, and Clay was an especially skilled boatman.

"Keep close to the right bank here," he called out to Cliff and Stone, who were ahead of us. "That's where the slack water is, easier to go upstream out of the main current."

It felt great to be out on the water with my brothers, and being able to spend a lot of time with them. Mom and Dad and Jessamine are great, but I thought the four of us needed to do things together.

A great blue heron took off in front of us, crossing the river with powerful wing strokes and landing on a log sticking out of the far bank.

Around mid-day, we stopped in the shade of some towering sycamore trees and had lunch – cornbread, dried fruit, and spring water.

There was a pile of mussel shells on the bank next to where we stopped. Stone explained it was a midden, and that the footprints in the mud around it were those of a raccoon. He was an expert on freshwater mussels, and had a collection at home. He pointed out the various species in the midden. "Threehorn wartyback. Yellow mucket. Hickorynut. Butterfly. And there's a Northern elktoe! That's a rare one!" He slipped off his boots and socks, rolled up his jeans, and stepped out of the canoe. He picked up "the specimen", as he called it, and carefully put it in his knapsack. "A great addition to my collection!"[4]

"See!" I exclaimed. "We're already finding treasures on this adventure!"

Clay nodded. "The Looking Glass is full of treasures."

Back underway again, and our canoe was in front this time. I spotted four turtles on a log ahead, red-eared sliders, and silently pointed to them. Clay held up his hand, our signal for silence, and we stopped paddling and drifted. We got real close to the turtles before plop, plop, plop, plop! They all slid into the river and disappeared.

"Steamboat a-comin'!" called out Cliff behind us. I turned around and saw the steamboat approaching from downstream.

"We need to cross here," responded Clay, "to get into better slack water on the other shore. Let's snap to it, and we can cross in front of that boat."

We swiftly crossed the river, and then slowed as we turned into the slack water. The steamboat was slow in coming, thrashing against the current. As it grew near, we could read the name: *Kentucky Belle*, the steamboat we had seen this morning down at the Morning View wharf. The distinctive whistle blew out a warning at us. It was a big side-wheel packet.

Cliff called out "One of the biggest on the Looking Glass. The engines are thirty-fours, ten feet." I knew that was "river shorthand", and meant the engine cylinders were 34 inches in diameter, with the pistons having a 10 foot stroke.[5]

The *Kentucky Belle* mainly hauled freight, and as it passed, we could see bales of cotton, sacks of flour, barrels and cases of bourbon, bundles of tobacco, and livestock. All of Kentucky's finest, headed for Cincinnati. We waved to the crew who were out on deck, and they waved back.

"Now!" called out Clay. "Turn into the wake!"

We turned perpendicular to the bank, and paddled hard into the approaching wake. It was fun, bouncing up and over the waves.

The river valley had stayed wide since we left Morning View, with forests and tobacco and horse farms lining the banks. Now, for the first time, we started seeing some low hills closer to the river. The forests became denser, with towering trees and dark, swampy areas. We spotted an ivory-billed woodpecker, a female with a black crest, on a huge bald cypress tree with an opening in the trunk – probably a nesting site.

We floated silently close to the bald cypress. The ivory-billed looked down at us. "Wow," I whispered. "We are really lucky. Those birds are getting extremely rare."[6] We watched her for a few minutes then quietly resumed paddling.

This was the furthest upstream from home I had ever been, but Clay had gone up further and knew a good spot to stop for the night.

When we reached our stopping point, I saw why he had picked it out. It was on the right bank, next to a hill with a low rock face along the river. There was a cove there and a low rise to a flat wooded area. There were huge sycamore, cottonwood, and silver maple trees, and an understory of pawpaw trees. This is where we made camp. Cliff and Stone got busy setting up our tent, and Clay and I gathered a pile of firewood and started a campfire. I noticed lots of zebra swallowtail butterflies flitting around among the pawpaw trees, the host plant for their caterpillars.[7]

Then we set up our fishing poles. Clay knew how to find the best fish. He put Stone and me up the bank a bit, where there was a deep hole. We used chicken liver as bait, with split-shot sinkers, and dropped them in. It wasn't too long before we hauled in a couple of fine flathead catfish.

Meantime, Clay got out our net, and cast it over a shallow gravel bar down from camp. The net came back up with a bunch of minnows. Cliff and Clay used these as bait, and cast into quiet water. This yielded them some fine crappie.

"What kind of crappie are those?" I yelled down to them.

"Hard to tell the white and black crappie apart," called back Clay. "Probably white crappie, more common in rivers than black crappie."

Another side-wheel steamboat went past, the *Bonanza*.[8] It was another freight hauler, this time headed down the river with goods from merchants in Cincinnati. Textiles, grains for the bourbon distilleries, Rookwood pottery, paper, and cured meats.

"Twenty-twos, seven and a half feet!" called out Cliff.

"Look at that, Clay!" I called, and pointed into the river near where we were sitting. An immense turtle had come up for air.

"An alligator snapping turtle!" exclaimed Clay. "The biggest turtle in Kentucky! You hardly ever see 'em!"

For dinner, we grilled the fish, and we made a rock oven by the fire where we baked potatoes. We had apples from last year, and passed around a jug of homemade root beer. Man, oh man, the fresh fish tasted good! Also, Mom had packed us cookies for dessert. We sat there, full and sleepy, and watched the fire dying down. Stone was telling stories about the creatures that come out at night, wood nymphs and the half goat–half man, Pan – but he couldn't scare me.

"Look!" whispered Stone, and he pointed up the river bank.

A deer had appeared there, and was drinking from the river. I had never seen a deer before![9] We watched it until it turned and melted back into the forest.

I turned to Clay. "Clay, why do you think Gamma lives in that old log cabin?"

Clay was quiet for a moment. "She was born there. It must have good memories for her."

"But our houses are a lot better."

"Well . . . maybe she does worry that Grandpa was a river pirate, and most of her money came from him stealing from other folks. Maybe she wants to live a simple life, instead of a showy life with other folks' money."

That was something to think about.

"But we can't read the account book," I reminded him. "Even Gamma thought it could be money coming in and going out. And we don't know if those entries were for regular business, or pirate business."

Clay thought for a bit. "Look, Scout, if we do find a hundred thousand dollars in gold coins," and here he leaned over at me, "and I'm not thinkin' we will, but if we do, you don't think Grandpa earned that much from regular business, and chose to hide it in a cave, do you?"

I had to agree with Clay, that didn't make much sense. "Well, what are we going to do with the money? – if we find it."

"Talk it over with Dad, and Mr. Drysdale. They'll figure it out."

We went around and around on it for a bit, but it was a puzzle to figure out the right way to handle it.

Finally, Clay decided it was time to turn in. It had been a long day of paddling upstream, and I was ready. We all went into the tent and laid on our bedrolls.

"Goodnight, Stone."

"Goodnight, Scout."

"Goodnight, Cliff."

"Goodnight, Scout."

"Goodnight, Clay."

"Goodnight, Scout."

"Clay?"

"Yes, Scout?"

"I gotta pee."

There was a pause. "Well, Scout, I guess you know what to do about that."

I opened the flap and went out. The fire was out. I saw that some of the pieces of firewood in our pile were glowing – the greenish blue of foxfire. Miss Geldreich had told us it was caused by a fungus in the wood.[10]

As I was returning to the tent, I heard some thrashing in the underbrush and then a loud splash in the river, right near our camp. I shivered and hurried back, glad that Clay and Stone and Cliff were there.

Just as I was about to drift off to sleep, a barred owl started calling. The call sounds like *Who cooks for you, who cooks for you, all?* This went on for a minute, then a second barred owl joined in, and they got into a "shouting match". It is one of the most wonderful sounds to hear at night, out in the forest, safely inside a tent!

The next morning, I was looking forward to a hot breakfast of eggs, bacon, and coffee.

Clay was standing on the river bank, staring at the sky to the southwest. It was dark and bruised, and below the black sky some small low white clouds were scudding fast in our direction. He turned when he heard me approaching. His face was as gloomy as the sky. "Storm coming. We need to break camp and secure all our gear."

"No breakfast?"

"Don't have time. Maybe grab a piece of cornbread."

"Wouldn't it be best to stay here?"

"No. We got to get our tent and other gear secured, and keep 'em dry."

All four of us quickly got to work, bundling up all our gear and putting it on tree branches laid in the middle of the canoes, to keep them out of any water that got in the canoes, then covering it with sheets of canvas. Then we shoved off. We were all barefoot, as we had stowed our socks and boots away.

It was strangely calm, but the sky was getting ugly. The muttering of far-off thunder began. Then we heard a rushing sound.

Suddenly the trees along the river began to pitch and sway violently. The silver maples flashed the bright undersides of their leaves.

Downstream behind us, it looked like a gray wall was approaching. Seconds later, the rain started, and man did it pour down hard. We got totally soaked. The storm passed quickly, and things calmed down again. There was only about an inch of water in the canoes, but all our gear was high and dry on the branches. The air was cooler after the rain.

Cliff and Stone came up next to us. Cliff grinned at me. "That wasn't too bad."

Stone twisted around and looked a Cliff. "What do you mean? I don't have a dry spot on me!"

I laughed. "There's a dry spot!" and I smacked my paddle in the river and splashed him good.

"Hey!" he yelled. "You're getting me – " Then he stopped, realizing the absurdity of what he was about to say.

Instead, he splashed me back, and then we all started doing it. The river water was much warmer than the rain water, and it felt good. We were laughing so hard our canoes got turned all cattywampas in the river.

"Steamboat a comin'!" called out Clay. We got the canoes back in formation. The steamboat was the *Crescent City*, a sternwheeler we had seen yesterday down at the Morning View wharf.

"Twenties, six and a half feet!"

The clouds were breaking up, and the sun came out. Up around the next bend we went and came in sight of an island. On this south end of the island was a big sandy beach.

"We'll land there," called Clay, "and get into some dry clothes."

"And have our breakfast," added Cliff.

We nosed our canoes into the beach. I jumped out and pulled our canoe up onto the sand. Stone did the same with their canoe.

We got out dry clothes. Clay, Stone and Cliff started stripping off their wet clothes. I went behind a big sycamore tree.

"Where you goin', Scout?"

"Never you mind!"

We spread our wet clothes on the canoes to start drying in

the sun. Clay and I built a fire, and got breakfast underway. Hot scrambled eggs and bacon, washed down with hot coffee. It was just what the doctor ordered.

When we got underway again, the sun was shining strong, and we left our wet clothes draped around on the canoes.

I had to laugh at the sight. "We look like the George Caleb Bingham painting, *The Jolly Flatboatmen*." Mom was a member of the American Art-Union, and had purchased a print of this painting, which was hanging in our dining room.[11] The flatboatmen were floating along, with their laundry draped all over the boat.

"We certainly are jolly," observed Clay.

The steamboat *Hudson Lee* passed us, going downstream, but we didn't see our friend Hudson Lee on board. Maybe he was below deck.

As we reached the upper end of the island, we saw huge colonies of water willows growing along the bank and on shallow sandbars. Some of the willows were draped with the bright yellow dendrils of dodder. Miss Geldreich had told us that dodder was a parasitic plant, with no chlorophyll and thus no ability to carry out photosynthesis. It fed on the sap of other plants. Mother Nature is fascinating!

A couple of miles above the north end of the island, we passed the mouth of a large creek on the left. Shortly after that, we came upon a small hamlet on the right, with a ferryboat tied up at the dock. We passed close by the ferryboat. A man was standing on the deck.

He scowled at us. "Where do you fellers think yer goin'?"

Clay answered. "We're going to do some exploring a little further upstream."

The man glared at Clay. "Upstream? Wouldn't go up there if I was you. Nothin' but trouble up there. Some bad trouble right now, even got my boy mixed up in it. He be gone up there for days."

Clay nodded. "We'll keep our eyes peeled, sir."

The man continued to scowl at us as we paddled on.

A sternwheel steamboat passed us, going downstream. It was a small boat, the *City of Clifton*, and was all decked out in red, white and blue bunting and flags.[12] The Fourth of July was coming soon. It must have been out on some sort of excursion because there were a lot of passengers on the decks. We all waved at each other.

Cliff called out "Sixteens, seven feet." It almost made me laugh, how much he knew about these steamboats.

There were hills and low cliffs on both sides of the river. I knew we were getting close to the area we wanted to examine. I had made a copy of Grandpa's map, and got it out now.

We paddled past an ancient steamboat wreck on the left bank. Not much left of the moldering old hulk, a huge side-wheel packet. The name was mostly rotted away, something "City".

Cliff was staring hard at the wreck. "That's the *Smokey City*, wrecked by ice.[13] Twenty-eights, eight feet."

We reached a bend where tall cliffs came into view. Suddenly it became hard to paddle, maybe because the cliffs dropped straight into the river here, and the stream was squeezed into a narrower channel. It was taking us longer to paddle past here.[14]

I had plenty of time to study the rock features of the cliffs, and compare them to the sketches of the cliffs on my copy of the map. I could hardly believe my eyes. The cliffs looked just like the sketches on the map! I shouted, "I think this is the place!" I was so excited that I nearly tipped over our canoe.

"Really?" asked Clay.

"Are you sure?" asked Stone.

I nodded. "We need to find a place to land at the upper end of these cliffs. The map says there is a path up there, leading up to the main entrance to the cave."

Passing through a spot where we were close to the cliffs, we scared up a great number of turkey buzzards from their roost on a rocky ledge. They shot into the air with a great whirring of wings, sounding for all the world like the whirring of an airplane.[15]

We swung around a bend and saw where the cliffs suddenly decreased in height and at their end was a wooded area along the riverbank.

I pointed to a flat area on the bank. "Let's land there."

As we headed for shore, we saw three boys coming down from the cliffs, along a path. They spotted us and stopped on the bank.

Our canoes nosed into the soft mud. Clay stood up in the back of our canoe. "Hello. We're the Morgans, from down at Morning View. My name is Clayton, but everybody calls me Clay."

He motioned over to the other canoe. "These are our twin brothers, Stonewall and Clifton, but everybody calls them Stone and Cliff."

Then he pointed to me. "And this is our sister Samantha, but mos' everybody just calls her Scout."

One of the boys on the bank smiled at me. "Scout, eh? I like that nickname. I have a nickname, too. Around here, everybody calls me Seckatary Hawkins."

PART II

AUSTINBERG, KENTUCKY.
LATE JUNE TO EARLY JULY 1914

CHAPTER 5

STORM CLOUDS

Ah, summertime! No more school until September! Not that I minded school that much this past year, since I went into the ninth grade – it's combined with grade ten, and I liked being with the older kids. Plus, our teacher Brother Francis is a good teacher.[1] He had reviewed some of my writing books, where I record the minutes of our meetings, and gave me a bunch of assignments to work on over the summer, to improve my writing. Right now, I was spread out on the long pine table in our clubhouse, getting all the papers from Brother Francis organized.

"What are you working on, Seck?" Shadow Loomis was standing the doorway.

"I'm organizing all these worksheets. They're part of some writing assignments Brother Francis gave me. I'm striving to improve my grammatical, compositional, and writing effectiveness skills, as well as my lexicon."

Shadow laughed lightly. "And working on your vocabulary, too, I see."

"Yep."

It was time for the meeting to start, and the fellas were coming in from the ballfield in the hollow. Perry helped me gather up the papers and folders, and we put them away in my little writing room at the back of the clubhouse.

All thirteen of the boys were present. Shadow Loomis and

49

Robby Hood, who lived up in Cincinnati, had come down in Robby's motorboat to our town of Austinberg.[(2)] Dick Ferris, who had been our captain for several years now, was getting ready to start the meeting. Lew Hunter, the boy who could play almost any kind of musical instrument, was there, too. Lew was the one who always made us practice songs, and he had us all singing in the church choir on Sundays. He had a battered old melodeon in the clubhouse.[(3)] Jerry Moore was the biggest and roughest fellow in our club; Shadow called him "old hippopotamus", but he was someone you were glad was on your side in a fight. Roy Dobel was the fellow whose parents had a farm nearby, and Roy would sometimes let us sneak into the barn and take the horses out. Bill Darby, the captain of our baseball team, and Johnny McLarren, our first captain, were my two oldest friends – we played together long before we started our club. Perry Stokes, whose father was the butler up in Judge Granbery's house, had joined the club while I was away in Cuba. They let him join provided he would be the caretaker of the clubhouse. He had appointed himself to be my personal guardian. The Court twins had arrived for the summer several days ago, having come down from their fancy school in Boston. Harold was the rowdy twin, but a good fighter. His identical twin brother Oliver was the quiet one, but seemed smarter and more logical than Harold. Finally, one of my best friends ever, Link Lambert had come up from Lexington a few days after the Court twins had arrived, to spend the summer with us.[(4)] He was staying at my house.

There were thirteen of us in all. And that's where the trouble started.

Bam! Dick Ferris hit the table with his wooden hammer. "Meeting will come to order."

All the boys took their seats and quit talking. "Any new business?" asked Dick.

Jerry Moore stood up. "Yes, there is. I count thirteen boys around this table."

I knew where this was going. Dick looked at him. "So what? Our best friends, all old-timers, and we all been through a lot together over the years."

Jerry remained standing. "It's just not right. It's bad luck, you know. We keep it at thirteen, and somethin' turrible bad is gonna happen to us. You know it's true."

Shadow Loomis smiled. "I don't believe in that kind of superstitious stuff, but anyway, what do you suggest? Dick is right. Everyone here belongs. Who do you suggest we get rid of?"

Jerry scowled at him, and sat down. "Nobody. We need a new member."

That startled everyone. Johnny McLarren responded first. "Okay, you got anyone in mind?

Just at that moment there was a knock at the door. Before I could say anything, Perry Stokes sprang over and yanked open the door. "Ah! Come in."

In walked one of the most striking figures I had ever seen. It was a tall colored boy. He stopped just inside the door and surveyed the room. He was very handsome, dressed neatly in khaki pants that were tucked into polished boots and a long-sleeved khaki shirt. But most striking was the flaming orange turban he had wrapped around his head, like a volcanic plume.

There was a stunned silence in the clubhouse. The colored boy finally broke it: "May I inquire as to which one of you is Seckatary Hawkins?" His English was impeccable, and I thought I detected the hint of a British accent.

I stood up. "That's me. I am Seckatary Hawkins."

He smiled and walked around the table to where I stood and extended his hand. I shook his hand and noticed what a firm grip he had. "I am honored to meet you. My name is William."

"William, good to meet you. What brings you to our clubhouse?"

He smiled a big pearly smile. "I have heard a lot of very fine things about you, Seckatary Hawkins, and all the boys in this club," sweeping around the table with his arm, "and I would like to join this club."

That set me back. I dropped my eyes from his face and stared at my hands. Odd, there was a dirty brown smudge on the fingertips of my right hand. This William fellow seemed too clean and tidy to have dirty hands.

Shadow Loomis had a coughing fit, and turned away from the table. I glanced over at him, but he had his back to me.

I looked helplessly at Dick and the other boys, but most of them avoided my look. Those who did look at me seemed very uncomfortable.

I turned back to William. "Well, um . . . see, we only take in new boys if one of our members knows them, and can vouch for them." I looked back at the boys. "Does anyone here know William?"

Shadow made another strange noise in his throat, like he was having some problem, and remained turned away from the table.

Nobody responded.

"No," growled Jerry. "Nobody knows him. We don't even know his full name. What is your last name?"

William looked over at Shadow. Shadow seemed to gather himself, but without looking at William, he chuckled lightly. "He's got you. You have to answer the question."

William smiled again and looked at me. "Standish. My last name is Standish."

That sucked the breath out of me. I stared hard into his face. "Will Standish!" I yelled. "Boys, it's Will Standish!"

At that, Shadow bent over with peals of laughter. Tears were rolling down his face as he fumbled in his black bag and pulled out some cloths. "Oh, man! I could hardly breathe! Will, you had them going! Wow, that was a fantastic performance!" He poured a bit of fluid from a small bottle onto the cloths, and handed one to Will and one to me.

Will pulled off the turban, and his light locks spilled out. He began wiping off his face and hands, and I saw the cloth staining brown. I wiped off the fingertips on my right hand, and began to laugh, too. All the boys were laughing, slapping Shadow on the back and coming over to greet Will.

Link Lambert and I had first met Will Standish when we were in Cuba. He helped us out of some mighty tight fixes and is one of our best friends. He visits us occasionally, and is one of our club members kept on the membership roll even though he isn't around all the time.

We were all delighted to have Will join us. He still lived in Cuba, but since he turned sixteen, he had been going to a college in Pennsylvania.[5] He told us he had arranged with his parents that he could spend a few weeks with us before returning to Cuba. I invited him to stay at my house, sharing the guest bedroom with Link as it had two beds.

Bam! Dick hit the table with his wooden hammer again. "Meeting come back to order! Problem solved, Jerry, we are fourteen now."

Shadow looked at Dick. "Dick, what do you think about this? Would we have let a colored boy join the club?"

Dick grimaced a bit, like he had a twinge of pain. "I don't know. Hawkins is right, our rule is he would have to be someone that a member knows, and can vouch for. That's all I know."

After the meeting, most of the boys went back to baseball practice. I stayed at the table, along with Link Lambert, Shadow Loomis, Robby Hood, Harold Court, and Will Standish. What a great group! All my best scouts, my confidants. The six of us had only been together one other time. You see, back in that one summer during our troubles with Harkinson, Shadow and Robby were not yet members of our club. Will and Link and Harold were around all that summer, but they had to leave when school started. We needed some new members, and got Shadow and Robby to join us. The next summer, during our troubles with the Gray Ghost, Will came to visit again, and Link and Harold were here, too, making that the only other time all six of us were together.

But what need now for this elite group of scouts and confidants? It had been quiet on the old riverbank. I guess I should have appreciated the opportunity to luxuriate in the presence of such special friends and comrades.

Harold Court stood up, shoved his hands in his pockets, and stared gloomily out one of the windows at the Looking Glass. "Nothing happening, Will. We're in the doldrums here. Been here over a week, and no excitement at all."

Will laughed, a cheerful pleasant laugh. "I'm thinking I've burned up all my excitement tickets from my last two visits. First, there was that frightening Harkinson bully."

Robby turned to him. "You do know how that ended, right?"

"Yes. Hawkins wrote me about what happened after I returned to Cuba, about the coming of the Red Runners, and how they split up between Harkinson and Long Tom and then how Harkinson died. Terrible, terrible."

I nodded. "But then you came back."

"Yes, and we had all that excitement with the Gray Ghost, and Androfski the Silent, and that Simon Bleaker fellow – quite a chap he was. And the unicorn on Burney's Field that Androfski shot and killed, and regained his voice.[6] Yes indeed, Harold, maybe it's time for a more relaxing visit. Fishing, swimming, maybe we could go camping on Seven Willows Island."

"Fishing, swimming, camping," grumbled Harold, an edge of sarcasm in his voice. "I can hardly wait."

Link Lambert laughed. "Come on, Harold. I've got my launch *Cazanova* tied up at the landing. How about we go out for a spin on the river?"

That seemed to brighten Harold up a bit. "Sure! Let's go down and look at the old boat."

We stepped out onto our porch, and two five-lined skinks who were sunning themselves there skittered away under the boards.

We walked down to our little landing, where the launch *Cazanova* was rocking gently in the river, and walked up the gangplank onto the deck. Harold may have called it "the old boat", but it was only a couple of years old, and in beautiful condition.

We walked around to the rear deck, took a seat, and looked out at the river.

I smiled at Harold. "We've had some excitement on this boat, haven't we? You remember that night in this very spot . . ."

Harold finished my sentence. "At the going away party for Link, Will, Oliver and me! When the ugly hand came over the gunwale, right there, and I smacked it twice with a heavy wooden pin."

"How did I miss that?" asked Shadow.

"I looked for you when Harold and I decided to come out on deck," I chuckled, "but you were more interested in the ice cream and Bill Darby's sister Lillian."

"Ah, yes, Lillian Darby," sighed Shadow. "I remember her."

Harold wanted to get back to the story. "We thought it was Harkinson, didn't we?"

I nodded. "Yes, but we found out a short time later that it was Briggen."[7]

"Briggen!" laughed Harold. "Maybe we can stir up some excitement with him and the rest of the Pelhams."

I waved my hand. "No need to go looking for trouble, Harold. Trouble will find us, sure as shootin'."

Just then there came a call from the river. We turned and saw coming downstream a group of ten long dark canoes. Each one carried two boys, and between them the canoes were laden with a lot of gear. Some of the canoes had big dogs in them, and I even thought I could pick out a few rifles sticking up. Then I noticed the canoe at the rear had three boys. The boy in the middle did not have a paddle. All of the boys were staring at us, and they even stopped paddling for a moment. The boy in the middle of the rear canoe stood up and shook his fist at us. He shouted something in an angry voice, but it was inaudible. They resumed paddling, glaring at us, and swiftly passed our landing and disappeared around the lower bend at the cliffs.

Will laughed a nervous laugh. "Such pleasant chaps!"

Harold smacked his knees. "Storm clouds! That's what those canoes looked like. Storm clouds of trouble descending on us!"

I sighed. "I'm afraid you're right, Harold. Looks like we are going to have a storm of trouble."

Which we did.

CHAPTER 6

THE MUDMUCKS

The next day, at our regular meeting, we informed everyone about what we had seen the day before – the dark canoe gang of twenty-one boys who seemed so unfriendly.

Johnny McLarren looked worried. "It looks like we're in for some big trouble. You say they had dogs and rifles?"

Jerry Moore waved his hand by his head, like he was batting away a cloud of gnats. "Who knows? Maybe they didn't stop around here, maybe they kept on going downstream. Let 'em go, down to Rabbit Hash or to Paducah, or heck, for all I care, they can go down all the way to New Orleans or the Gulf of Mexico."[1]

Indeed, the next couple of days remained quiet. We saw no sign of the twenty-one boys in the dark canoes.

However, a bit of a mystery developed. On my desk are an oil lamp, a little brass clock, an inkwell, a pen, my current writing book, and a telephone. I generally keep these items in the same location when I am done writing for the day, but one day I noticed that they had been moved around a bit. I thought nothing of it, straightened up my desk, and then the next day saw again that they had been moved.

At our next meeting, I mentioned this and asked if anyone had been at my desk. All the boys stared at me.

"Good night, Hawkins," gasped Dick Ferris. "Why would any of us disturb your desk? Are you sure about this?"

"Maybe I'm imagining things," I replied. Shadow Loomis was studying my face intently.

That evening, before I left for the night, I put a tiny slip of paper in the back door that leads from my writing room to the outside, between the door and the doorframe.

The next day, I was sure. Under my desk are my twelve writing books from the past several years, all neatly stacked and in chronological order.[2] Today, I noticed that the stack of writing books was disheveled, and out of order. I turned to look at the back door. The slip of paper was on the floor near the door.

I summoned my top lieutenants into my writing room: Link Lambert, Shadow Loomis, Robby Hood, Harold Court, and Will Standish. I explained to them what I had been seeing for the past three mornings and told them about the slip of paper on the floor.

Shadow Loomis nodded. "This is as clear as noonday. Somebody has been coming in here each night, picking the lock to that door after we leave and going through your writing books."

"What do we do?" I asked.

"Set a watch," replied Harold. "Find out who is doing this."

We set the first watch for that very night. Link Lambert and Will Standish, who were staying at my house, remained with me after all the other boys had left. I had told Mom we had other plans for dinner, which was true since we'd be sitting in the clubhouse instead, and that we would be home late. Moms are real astute, and she lightly mentioned that she might have an apple pie waiting for us, for dessert.

We sat quietly in the meeting room. All the oil lamps were out. The clubhouse was pitch dark.

We didn't have long to wait. We heard a scratching noise from the back of my writing room, and then the lock turning, and the door creaking open. We heard a match struck, and then the glow of the oil lamp on my desk could be seen under the curtains between the meeting room and my writing room. The next sound we heard was the stack of my writing books falling over, some fumbling noises and then the sound of someone turning the pages of one of the books.

Link leaned close to my ear, and in a barely audible whisper asked, "Why don't you go take a look? We'll be right behind you."

I got up as quietly as I could, and slowly and carefully stepped over to the curtains. I pulled back one edge a tiny bit, and peeked in with one eye. There was a strange boy sitting at my desk, leafing through one of my writing books. I watched him for a long time. Every now and then he would stop turning pages, read intently, and make some brief notes on a piece of paper he had. Abruptly, he put the book away, blew out the lamp, and went out the back door with a slam.

"Why did you let him get away?" asked Link, as I lit the lamp again.

"He wasn't doing any damage. I was afraid if we confronted him, he might break the door, or knock over the oil lamp, or run off with one of my books."

Will smiled. "Probably a good idea. I wonder what he was up to?"

"I'm not sure yet. It is a mystery. But I bet we find out soon. In the meantime, tomorrow let's get better locks put on the doors – including a deadbolt on that door in my writing room."

"Another good idea," replied Will. "Now let's go and get some of your mom's apple pie!"

"Yet another good idea," I responded, as we locked the doors and headed up the river path for home.

At our regular meeting the next day, I did not mention what we had seen the night before. After the meeting, most of the boys headed out for the old swimming hole. I had motioned for Link Lambert, Shadow Loomis, Robby Hood, Harold Court, and Will Standish to stay behind. We sat around the long pine table. Link,

Will and I described what we had seen in my writing room last night.

Harold let out a low whistle. "A spy! Maybe from the dark canoe gang!"

At that, the door burst open. A fearsome figure entered, a muscular boy with an ugly face. His nose had clearly been badly broken at some point, and he had some jagged red scars on his face. When he spoke, we could see that he was missing several front teeth.

"Yes, it was a spy from the dark canoe gang. We are the Mudmucks from Cincinnati, and you will be sorry if you cross us. My name is Rafael Peralta, and I have come here on orders from our leader, to warn you."

I was startled by the name. "You are not Rafael Peralta!" Uncle Rafael, as Link and I knew him, was the evil uncle in Cuba who nearly did away with us.

The ugly boy laughed a nasty, sarcastic laugh. "That is the name you will know me by. We know the names of all your old enemies, and those are the names you will know us by."

"Ah!" I exclaimed. "So, that is what your spy has been doing! Reading my writing books, and making a list of the names of our old enemies that you will take as pseudonyms."

Peralta sneered at me. "I don't know what that fancy word means, but you will only know us by the names of your old enemies. Cross us, and you will be sorry!"

I stood up and spread my arms open wide, palms facing outwards. "We don't want any trouble. What do you want?"

He glared at me. "Our leader says if you clear out of this clubhouse, and stay away from this riverbank for two weeks, you won't get any trouble from us."

I thought for a moment. "Who is your leader?"

"What does that matter?"

"We need to know who we are dealing with."

Peralta paused. "His name is the Cincinnati Kid. You know him?"

"No. But that is not the name of one of our old enemies."

"No. That is his real name. He is known from Cincinnati up and down the Looking Glass."

"Sorry. Never heard of him."

Peralta shook his fist at me, and stormed out.

"Pleasant chap," commented Will.

I turned to the group. "Any of you ever heard of the Cincinnati Kid? Shadow, Robby, you live up in Cincinnati."

They all shook their heads. "Never heard that name."

At our next regular meeting, I described the visit yesterday from the ugly boy calling himself Rafael Peralta.

"He told us he is a member of the gang we saw in the dark canoes a few days ago. They're a Cincinnati gang. They call themselves the Mudmucks. Their leader, who is called the Cincinnati Kid, sent Rafael Peralta here to warn us."

Dick Ferris stood up. "Not so fast, Hawkins. Why does he call himself Rafael Peralta? We all know who that was."

Link Lambert smiled. "You don't miss much, do you Dick?"

Then I had to explain how I had figured out that someone was picking the lock and coming into my writing room each night, and how Link, Will and I had waited in the clubhouse two nights ago and had seen the spy making notes from my writing books.

Dick's voice had an edge to it. "Why, Hawkins, did you not inform us of all this?"

"I wasn't sure the spy was from the gang we had seen in the dark canoes. I was trying to figure out who he was, and what he wanted to learn from my writing books, before I worried any of you about this."

Dick shook his head. He clearly was not happy with me. "If ever any one of us learns that someone has broken into this clubhouse, we should all be informed immediately."

A murmur of approval ran around the table.

I nodded my head. "You're right, Dick. I'm sorry I didn't tell you. I just wanted some time to think, but I should have told you right away."

Dick sat down. "Alright. You told us this Peralta fella was sent here to warn us. What was the warning?"

I hesitated. "He told us he had a message from the Cincinnati Kid. The message was that if we were to clear out of this clubhouse and stay away from the riverbank for two weeks, then we wouldn't have any trouble from the Mudmucks."

"Two weeks!?" shouted several of the boys.

Dick thought for a moment. "What do you think we should do?"

I looked at him. "Are you asking me? We should all make this decision. There are two options in front of us."

Oliver Court stood up. "We could go camping on Seven Willows Island."

I smiled. "I hadn't thought of that. There are at least three options in front of us."

Lew Hunter nodded at Oliver. "That is a non-confrontational solution, Oliver. I like it for that reason. At the same time, I do not like a gang of strangers from Cincinnati coming down here and ordering us to go away. I assume one your two options, Hawkins, is for us to abandon the clubhouse and stay in town away from the riverbank for two weeks."

"Yes," I nodded. "And the second option is . . ."

Roy Dobel cut me off. "Is to stand up to them."

Oliver Court sat down, but Bill Darby stood up. "Not 'zactly, Roy. We're not in a fight with the Mudmucks."

Harold Court stood up, too. "That's right, Bill. We need to find out more about them. Where are they? What do they want?"

Dick Ferris hit the table with his wooden hammer. "Everybody sit down!"

But the meeting had destabilized into a babble of voices, everyone talking excitedly and arguing about what we should do.

Bam! Bam! Dick pounded the table with his wooden hammer. He was putting dents into the pine tabletop. "Order! This meeting will come to order!"

There was silence. Dick put his wooden hammer down. "That's better. Now, Hawkins, how do you think we should proceed?"

I thought for a minute. "We have three options on the table.

One, go camping on Seven Willows Island for two weeks. Two, go home for two weeks. Three, stay here and find out what is going on. We should discuss these options and then take a vote."

Dick stood up. "Okay. But everyone will raise their hand and be recognized before speaking."

Perry Stokes raised his hand, and Dick nodded at him. "Beggin' your pardon, sir." Perry Stokes always called me 'sir'. "Beggin' your pardon, but without more information, we can't just go away home or to the island for two weeks. Just on the threat from one boy. Other fellas get wind of that, and we'll always be getting pushed around."

I stroked my chin. "Are you saying we only have one option?"

"Yes, sir. That's what I'm saying."

Dick was still standing at the head of the table. "Let's make this official. Anyone opposed to us staying here, and finding out what the Mudmucks are up to? If you are opposed, raise your hand."

Not one hand went up.

Bam! Dick hit the table with his wooden hammer. "That settles it. We will see this through no matter what. Now, how do we proceed?"

Robby Hood was recognized next. "There are twenty-one boys in the Mudmucks, and several dogs. We need to be careful."

"Yes," agreed Lew Hunter. "We have done this sort of thing before, when faced with this kind of trouble. We always go out in groups, say three boys in each group."

"Scouting parties!" exclaimed Roy Dobel. "Sure! We can get out and find their camp, or whatever. That will tell us a lot about what they might be up to."

The meeting was getting rambunctious again, but Dick let the discussion flow for a minute. Finally, he hit the table with his wooden hammer again. "Hawkins! When Judge Granbery deputized us as his Junior Police, he made you the chief. I'm turning this over to you, to form the groups of three, and give them assignments."

"Okay, Dick. There are fourteen of us. I suggest we form four scouting parties of three boys each and have two boys stay here and keep the clubhouse secure."

With that, the meeting was adjourned, and we got busy getting the scouting parties organized. We decided we would go out at first unarmed, no rifles or clubs or anything, because we didn't want to provoke any Mudmucks we might encounter. However, I did tell Perry to get my best rifle, the fine rifle Larry King had given me several years ago, and give it to Roy Dobel.[3] Roy and Dick Ferris were going to take the first watch at the clubhouse.

The scouting party I was part of included Johnny McLarren and Bill Darby, my two oldest friends. We were to scout around in the woods and ravines behind the hill with the cave complex.

"We've been exploring these woods since we were five years old!" exclaimed Bill.[4]

We stopped by a patch of sassafras trees. Johnny crushed a leaf, and passed it around, and we all took in the lemony aroma. "Just like old times," he commented. "We would make sassafras tea from the bark of the roots."[5]

I laughed. "Those were the good old days!" But then I got serious. "Fellas, we got work to do, and we need to be careful. Let's go into the ravine behind the caves."

We headed east toward the cave complex. There was a ravine on the backside of the hill, opposite from the cliffs along the river, and there were more cliffs lining that ravine with cave openings in them.

"Here," I pointed up to the top of the cliffs. "See that big old cedar tree? The opening to the Cave of Wonders used to be in the cliff below that tree."[6]

"Look!" exclaimed Bill. Three figures had appeared on the top of the cliff and were looking down at us.

"Is that one of our scouting parties?" asked Johnny.

I whipped out Dad's fine binoculars. I don't think he would be too pleased to know I had taken them from his study. I turned them on the three figures on the cliffhead. "No, I don't recognize them. Not any of us and not Pelhams, either."

"Mudmucks?" asked Bill.

"Uh oh," I replied.

"What's wrong?" asked Johnny and Bill together.

"They're using hand signals. Someone else is down here, near us."

I had a very uneasy feeling about this, and a tingle started on the back of my head and down my back. The woods around us suddenly had a dark and sinister look. "This doesn't feel right. We may be about to be ambushed."

"Let's stay calm," muttered Bill, "and stay together and start heading back."

"Follow me," commanded Johnny in a low voice. "Let's swing out of here and take a more roundabout route back."

Quickly we moved off the path through the woods. We knew this area, rich with beech and walnut trees, where many times we had gathered nuts. [7] But this time we hustled along quickly, trying to be as quiet as possible.

There was a rushing sound behind us. I started to turn, but was too late. Bam! Something hard and wicked smashed into the side of my head. Down I went. I was seeing a million stars, and the world seemed to be spinning. I heard Bill and Johnny yelling, and other strange voices, angry voices, and knew a fight was going on. I tried to stand up, but toppled over again. Then I heard more voices, some of our boys, including Jerry Moore and Harold Court, and knew the cavalry had arrived.

A moment later, strong arms lifted me from each side. "Come on, Hawkins, let's get you back to the clubhouse." It was Harold Court talking.

Jerry Moore was on my other side. Slowly we walked, and my head began to clear. I turned and saw others, Oliver Court, Link Lambert, Will Standish, and Lew Hunter. They were helping Bill and Johnny, who were both injured. Bill was bleeding from his nose, and Johnny had an eyebrow split open and blood was streaming down that side of his face.

"What happened?" I gasped.

Jerry Moore growled, "We saw those fellas on the cliff signaling down to where we knew you would be. We got here as fast as we could, but four Mudmucks had bushwhacked you. One of them hit you in the head with a club, and that put you down leaving two Mudmucks each attacking Bill and Johnny."

"Did you get 'em?" I asked.

"We got some good licks in, and sent 'em running, but I'd say we got the worst of it."

As we approached the clubhouse, Dick Ferris and Roy Dobel, who had been on sentry duty there, saw us coming and rushed over to help us. "Good night!" gasped Dick. "What happened?" Jerry quickly related the events to him.

Roy shook his head. "What kind of gang are we dealing with?"

I shook off Jerry and Harold, wobbled into the clubhouse and sat down in a chair. I was beginning to return to normal. Oliver Court examined my head. "You've got quite a lump developing there, but the skin is not broken."

Lew Hunter came over to me. "Do you think we need to take Johnny up to see Doc Waters?"

"No!" exclaimed Johnny. "We can't let Doc know about the trouble we're in. He would tell Judge Granbery, and then we'd be in worse trouble."

"Alright," replied Lew. "Let's get some sticking plaster from the medical kit and get that bleeding stopped." Lew and Link Lambert got to work on Johnny.

I looked over at Bill. Oliver Court and Will Standish had him in a chair with his head tilted back and cotton stuffed into his nose. Oliver looked at me. "We've just about got the bleeding stopped, Hawkins."

I turned to Dick and Roy. "We still have one scouting party out. Shadow Loomis, Robby Hood, and Perry Stokes. Where did they go? I can't remember."

Roy looked closely at me. "You alright, Hawkins? You gave each scouting party their assignments."

I shrugged. "I guess that blow to my head just knocked it out of me."

Roy and Dick exchanged worried glances. Roy sat down next to me. "They were supposed to go out in Robby Hood's motorboat and scout along the river bank, looking for the canoes of the Mudmucks."

Jerry Moore was out on the porch, with the rifle. "Here they come now!" he called.

Shadow, Robby and Perry came in. They were startled to see the scene in the clubhouse. Jerry explained what had happened.

Robby shook his head. "Glad we didn't run into any of them. But we did find their canoes. They're all beached on the rocks along Cave River."

Cave River was a branch of the Looking Glass, that flowed into an opening where the cliffs dropped straight into the river. The water had cut a tunnel that wound around under the cliffs for a couple miles before coming back out into the Looking Glass further downstream.[8]

"Cave River!" exclaimed Lew. "You went into Cave River?"

"Yes," replied Robby. "I cut the motor, and we drifted in. The ten canoes are all lined up on the shore near Table Rock."[9]

Lew looked worried. "Did they have a sentry? Did anyone see you?"

"No. Just the canoes there. We turned around and went back out into the Looking Glass and scouted downstream further along the cliffs. We went as far as the wreck of the steamboat *Smokey City*, but we didn't see any other sign of the Mudmucks. We came straight back here after that."

Lew whistled. "Sounds like they've squirreled themselves away inside Cliff Cave."

I nodded. "That's right, Lew. That would explain their scouts up on the cliffhead, too. We've got to go up to Cliff Cave and find out what's going on. But we'll need some reinforcements. There's twenty-one of them, and only fourteen of us."

I turned to Robby. "Robby, take your motorboat down to Hobbs Ferry. Shadow and Perry, go with him. We need to keep the scouting parties of three intact. See if you can get Lige Hobbs to come up here. Then go down to Banklick Creek and see if Rube Muller can get away from the farm and come up here." Elijah "Lige" Hobbs and Reuben "Rube" Muller were both members of our club, but since they had to work most days, they were not around a lot.[10]

Robby, Shadow and Perry shot out the door.

I motioned to Dick Ferris. "Dick, you are closest of any of us to the Pelham fellas. Do you think we can enlist their help?" The tumbledown village of Pelham was across the Looking Glass from our little wharf. The Pelham boys generally didn't get along with us, but I was hoping they would let bygones be bygones and help us out now. We had certainly gotten them out of some tight spots over the years.

Dick frowned. "I'll do the best I can. Lew and Roy, why don't you come with me?" Dick, Lew and Roy left to go across the river and visit the Pelhams.

I turned to the rest of the boys. "We're going to find out what the Mudmucks are up to in Cliff Cave. We will probably have a hot time of it."

Which we did.

CHAPTER 7

FIASCO

It took us a couple of days to get organized. Lige Hobbs helps his dad run the ferryboat down at Hobbs Ferry, and he had a hard time getting away. Rube Muller helps his dad on their farm down along Banklick Creek, and he too had a hard time convincing his parents to let him take some time off from the chores. But they finally made it up here. They were going to sleep in the clubhouse, and we had set up cots for them in the meeting room.

The Pelhams, on the other hand, refused to help us. Briggen came over to see me. He walked into my writing room and sat down. "Lookee here, Hawkins. We ain't got a dog in this fight. Them mudhens hain't bothered us none. We stay on our side of the river, and y'all stay on your side of the river. They's fightin' you, not us."

"But Briggen," I protested, "We have helped you Pelhams out of many fixes. You remember Harkinson, when he took over your gang? You remember the time there were all those strange things happening on Burney's Field, and the unicorn that was terrorizing your neighborhood? We came over and helped you out. You remember all that?"

"Sure I do. But they was enemies of both of us. Them mudballs hain't come over to our side of the river."

"Mudmucks."

"Whatever. But if they try'n spread to our side of the river, we'll all take care of 'em."

I waved my hands. "You're no match for them. We have to band together."

"We'll see." With that, Briggen stalked out.

At our first meeting with Lige Hobbs and Rube Muller present, Dick Ferris welcomed them. "Now we're at sixteen. Better odds than before."

Lige responded first. "I am glad to be here to help our club. You don't call on me very often, and I know this time you really need my help."

"Same for me," chimed in Rube. "We can't have some mudheads from Cincinnati come down here and push us around."

There was a murmur of approval around the table and nodding of heads.

Perry Stokes was standing over by one of the front windows. "Somebody approaching! Looks like the Mudmucks. A bunch of 'em – with dogs. But they're carrying a white flag."

All the boys jumped up and rushed to the front of the clubhouse. Jerry Moore yanked open the door, and we crowded out onto the porch. The Mudmucks were standing off a short distance. I counted sixteen of them, and they had seven dogs with them, on long leashes. I recognized among them the boy who called himself Rafael Peralta.

One boy with a dog stepped forward. "This is a flag of truce! We come only to talk. Agreed?"

I had a flash of recognition. This was the boy I had seen in my writing room, reading my minute books and making notes! The dog he had was bigger than any dog I had ever seen, bigger even than a Great Dane.

Dick Ferris went down the steps. "Agreed. I am the captain of this bunch. What is your business here?"

"I want to speak to Seckatary Hawkins!"

Dick motioned to me, and I went down and stood by him. "I am Seckatary Hawkins. Who are you?"

"I am the Cincinnati Kid." He was a bit smaller than the

other Mudmucks but was sturdy and stout. He seemed to bear a perpetual sneer that had warped his face into something unpleasant, something rat-like.

I gave him a close look. "You like to go into other people's rooms, and read their personal papers?"

He was surprised by my question. He didn't know I had seen him that night in my writing room.

There was an uncomfortable silence. I decided to break it. "What kind of dog is that?"

"Irish wolfhound."

"What's his name?"

"Lion."[1]

"Hello, Lion." I took a step toward the dog and extended my hand, but the Cincinnati Kid yanked the dog back. "Don't do that. He could crush your hand with one bite. He's my personal guard dog."

I straightened up. "Your boys have attacked us. It was unprovoked. Three of us were injured."

The Cincinnati Kid squinted at me. "Unprovoked? You don't listen very well. I sent Rafael Peralta to warn you. You ignored the warning. We were defending our territory – our response was not unprovoked."

I started to object, but he held up his hand. "However, we did see that your patrols were unarmed in any way. I ordered that my boys respond in kind. But I have learned that one of my boys, Cheeky, clobbered you in the head with a club. Cheeky, come here!"

Cheeky had been the name of another of our old enemies, a particularly bad one.[2]

The boy who stepped forward was tall and lean, but seemed fit and strong. His face was pinched and drawn, leathery, like he was dried out. He reeked of tobacco smoke. In his hands was a stout club.

The Cincinnati Kid snatched the club from Cheeky, and handed it to me. "You kin hit him back. Hit him in the head!"

I shook my head, and handed the club back to Cheeky. "No. That is not our way. We do not hit defenseless boys." I turned back to the Cincinnati Kid. "However, I appreciate your gesture. I'm sure we can work this out, but you see, we can't have just anybody from another town come here and push us around. What is your business here? If you have legitimate business, we are willing to help you. If you don't, then you should go back to Cincinnati."

The Cincinnati Kid studied my face. "Our business is our business, and not yours. We have warned you. Go away for two weeks, or else suffer the consequences."

"Why are you here? Are you up to something in Cliff Cave?"

"Never heard of it. I hear you like to use fancy words. Well, put these in your pipe and smoke 'em. We are geologists, from the University of Cincinnati. We are studying the geological succession in the caves and cliffs in this area. We need to work undisturbed. Two weeks, and we will be gone. Keep meddling with us, and you will understand one thing – I am the Cincinnati Kid, and we are the Mudmucks, and nobody, not even you, can resist us. Resistance is futile! Try it, and you will be sorry!"

With that, he turned and waved his hand angrily, motioning for them to leave. The Mudmucks followed him, across the hollow toward the path that went up the cliffs to the main entrance to Cliff Cave.

We resumed our meeting but were frankly puzzled by the visit of the Mudmucks and their leader, the Cincinnati Kid.

"We have had gangs come down here on legitimate business," commented Robby. "Pooley, for example, was seeking the hidden money that was rightfully his. We just didn't know at first why he and his gang were here."

"The same thing applies to Ching Toy," added Lew. "He was helping his daddy recover the Magic Triangle medal the Chinese government had awarded him, that the Chinese mafia in Cincinnati had stolen."

Oliver nodded. "That's right. But Pooley and Ching Toy wouldn't tell us what they were up to. Neither will the Cincinnati Kid, it seems. We always have to figure these things out ourselves."

"What makes you think," I asked, "that the Cincinnati Kid and his Mudmucks could have a valid reason to be here? They ambushed us and brutally attacked us. To me, that makes their being here suspicious."

"That's true," agreed Oliver. He thought for a moment. "Their behavior is certainly hard to fathom. The Cincinnati Kid seemed almost reasonable in some ways, coming here under a flag of truce, and saying he ordered his boys not to be armed when he saw we weren't, and pulling Cheeky out to face the consequences of hitting Hawkins in the head with a club. But then the next moment the Kid is nasty and threatening. He's kind of spastic."

That caused some of the boys to laugh. We all liked Oliver because he had a good head when it came to reasoning and logic.

Jerry snorted. "I know one thing, they're no geologists from the University of Cincinnati. Too young, only about our age, fourteen, fifteen, maybe sixteen."

Rube shrugged. "They could be high school interns, working for a professor at the university. Maybe the professor hired them to come down here and do just what the Kid claimed they were doing."

Lige Hobbs shook his head. "Consider the facts we have. They are in Cliff Cave. They don't want us around here for two weeks. They have sent warnings and violently attacked our patrol that came near the cliffs. We don't know what they want, but we sure know what they don't want. They don't want us in Cliff Cave or anywhere around the cave."

I looked at Lige. "That's very linear, Lige. Now, we have already made the decision that we won't let them drive us away. We have to consider our next steps carefully."

Dick Ferris hit the table with his wooden hammer. "Okay. Hawkins, you work out a plan, and let's discuss it at our meeting tomorrow. The rest of us, let's help get Lige and Rube set up in here."

Meeting adjourned.

Most of the other boys got to work helping Lige and Rube get settled in. I called Shadow, Robby, Link, Harold and Will into my writing room.

I was thinking about the comments Lige had made, about how serious the Cincinnati Kid and the Mudmucks were about us staying away. It seemed obviously true but left one big question. Why? "What do you think they are up to in Cliff Cave?"

Harold drummed my desk with his fingers. "We need to get in there and see what they're up to."

"Yes," I replied. "I agree with Jerry. I don't think they are geologists."

Link shook his head. "But I don't think they'll invite us in for a look-see."

"I know!" exclaimed Robby. "You remember when I told how we had gone into Cave River and found the Mudmuck canoes? Lew asked if there was a sentry, if we had been seen. But there was nobody there. We can sneak in that way!"

I nodded my head. "That's good, that's very good. Let me think for a minute." They watched my face as I stared up at the ceiling for a moment, turning things over in my head. "Here's what we do. There are three entrances to the Cliff Cave system. There's the main entrance, up the cliff path. There's the entrance to Cave River. And there's the back entrance, that little hole in the hillside under a tree where we chased Lasky out that one time."[8]

"What about the entrance to the Cave of Wonders you told me about, the one Spider used to go in with his rope web?" asked Will.

"Mr. Dobel closed that one, to keep people out of the Cave of Wonders. He was running the Cave of Wonders as a show cave, and people had to pay to get in. There was another entrance down on his farm that he was using as the way into the show cave, but it collapsed in a rock fall last year. We only know of these three ways into the Cliff Cave system."

Shadow leaned forward. "The Mudmucks must know about the route from Table Rock along Cave River, up the slab-stone stairs to the upper chambers of Cliff Cave. And they must know about the main entrance up on the cliff path, since that is the way they went back today. But they aren't watching the Cave River entrance, and

I'll bet they don't know about the back entrance – that's hard to find from inside Cliff Cave."

Robby's face brightened. "That's right! We can sneak in both entrances and spy on them."

I held up my hands. "Hold it. We need to be careful. We need to distract them. Assuming they are only using the main entrance, I suggest we send a big group up there to confront them, and . ."

Link jumped in and finished my sentence. "And send smaller spy teams in through the other two entrances!"

It seemed like a brilliant plan.

The meeting the next day was spent planning the spy missions into Cliff Cave. We got everything organized and ready to go by mid-afternoon. The team going in through Cave River was Harold, Will and Link. The team going in through the back entrance was Shadow, Robby and Roy. Roy knew the most about that part of the cave since the back entrance was close to his farm. The rest of us were to go up to the main entrance and create as much distraction as we could. However, I told Perry to stay behind and watch the clubhouse.

I handed him the rifle Larry King had given me. "Just in case you need to scare anybody away." He nodded gravely, and took the gun.

Dick turned to me. "What about the rest of us? Going up there unarmed?"

"Yes," I replied. "We don't need any escalation. The Mudmucks haven't shown their rifles yet."

Our two scouting parties took off first. We needed to give them a head start, so we waited in front of the clubhouse for about ten minutes.

There were nine of us in the group as we headed up the cliff path. Jerry Moore was leading the way, followed by me, Dick Ferris, Johnny McLarren, Bill Darby, Lew Hunter, Oliver Court, Lige Hobbs, and Rube Muller.

"Look!" called out Johnny in a low voice. He was pointing up to the cliffhead. There were two figures standing there.

I whipped out my binoculars and watched them for a second. "They see us, and they're making hand signals to someone I can't see, down below, near the cave entrance."

We continued up the hill. The path grew steeper, and we began to dislodge some of the loose rocks.

"They don't need lookouts," grumbled Bill. "Anybody could hear us coming from a mile away."

Jerry held up his hand in our signal to stop. The sound of the tumbling rocks did not stop, however. It seemed to be coming from up ahead.

Oliver Court came up to me. "Somebody is throwing rocks down this way, Hawkins."

"I think you're right, Oliver. At least we know we have their attention." I turned to the rest of the group. "They're trying to scare us away. Keep an eye out for incoming rocks!"

As we reached the final approach to Cliff Cave, quite a shower of rocks came down at us from the cliffs above. But we stayed close to the cliff face, and most of the rocks missed us. A few found a target, however, and several of our boys were struck. I turned and saw Bill Darby bleeding from a laceration on his forehead, and Lew Hunter had a gash on his forearm.

Around the last corner, finally we stood in front of the main entrance to Cliff Cave. A group of eight Mudmucks were standing there, including the ones named Peralta and Cheeky. Four of them had dogs on leashes. Mudmucks indeed! These boys were filthy, simply coated with mud. I noticed a pick leaning against the cave wall just inside the entrance, and a coil of muddy rope. Cliff Cave had many muddy areas. I began to wonder about the comment the Cincinnati Kid had made, about them being on a geological expedition of some sort.

"What's the meaning of this?" one of them snarled. He even had mud in his hair.

"Who are you?" demanded Dick.

"My name is Sawyer," replied the Mudmuck. "You have no business here. Go back the way you came before you get hurt."

I stepped forward. "We want to talk to the Cincinnati Kid. Tell him we are here."

Sawyer turned and spoke to one of the others. "Quayle, tell the Kid we have company."

The Mudmuck named Quayle disappeared into the cave. As with the names Rafael Peralta and Cheeky, Sawyer and Quayle were the names of some of our old enemies.[4]

I pulled Dick aside, and spoke in a low voice. "So far, so good. We've seen ten Mudmucks, these eight here and the two lookouts up on top, and there must be more up along the cliffs, the ones who were throwing rocks down at us."

Dick nodded. "Yep, and none of them seem to be worried about anything except us. They don't act like they know we have spies inside the cave."

A minute later, Quayle reappeared along with another Mudmuck, and they both had a dog. The nine Mudmucks crowded out in front of the cave and spread out. The Cincinnati Kid came next with his dog Lion on a leash.

He glared at us. "Oh, ho! If it isn't Seckatary Hawkins and his band of clowns! You morons just can't seem to get it through your thick skulls that you are not wanted around here. I'll show you just how serious we are."

He turned to his band of muddy cronies. "Cry havoc! And let slip the dogs of war!"[5]

With that, the Mudmucks unleased all seven dogs, and the brutes came at us, barking and growling.

"Call off your dogs!" I yelled.

The Cincinnati Kid laughed and folded his arms across his chest. "Now let's see how well you can dance!"

Dick Ferris was pulling at my sleeve. "We need to retreat, Hawkins." I nodded, and he turned to the other fellows. "Fall back! Back to the clubhouse!"

We began backing down the cliff path. More stones rained down on us, and one struck me in the cheek. I could feel blood streaming down my face.

The dogs went wild and began to close in on us. They were howling with fury and began to lunge at us. Lion went for my arm, and as I pulled away his teeth closed on my shirt and tore the sleeve. He backed off for a second, and began to charge me again.

Crack! – came the sound of a rifle shot! Lion was hit, and he flinched violently. He broke off his attack.

I turned around, and saw Perry Stokes with the rifle down the path a bit. The cliff path made a big sweeping turn here, and from where he was, Perry had a clear shot up towards where we were. He was down on one knee, preparing to shoot again.

"No, Perry!" I shouted, but too late! I heard Perry's gun bark again, and the howl of the dog and the angry shout of the Cincinnati kid.

I saw the dead body of the dog Lion tumble off the cliff It splashed into the Looking Glass fifty feet below and sank out of sight. There was the red tinge of blood in the circling waves where it had hit the water. That was all.[6]

The remaining dogs fell back, but an enraged Cincinnati Kid screamed angry orders and led his ten thugs in a charge at us. I thought the Kid was going for me, but he rushed right past me. I turned back just in time to see Peralta throwing a punch at me. I bobbed down, and his blow missed. Then, remembering some boxing moves that Harold Court and Will Standish had taught me, I led with my right, began to swing with my left, and then threw everything I had into my right. Perlata had bobbed to avoid my left, and my right caught him fair and square. He went down and out.

There was a huge uproar on the cliff path behind me. I turned and saw the Cincinnati Kid spring upon Perry and wrench the rifle from his hands. He turned the rifle around and used the butt end like a sledge to smash Perry in the head. Perry fell onto the path. The Kid began beating on him with the rifle. Jerry Moore grabbed hold of the rifle and they struggled furiously.

I shouted and ran over to them. I slugged the Kid as hard as I could on the side of his head, and he let go of the rifle and staggered back against the cliff face. He seemed shocked by the force of my punch and began yelling "Get the dogs! Let's get these guys!"

Our two groups separated, the Mudmucks pulling back up toward Cliff Cave and calling for their dogs. We regrouped, and Jerry Moore and Rube Muller picked up Perry Stokes, who was unconscious, and we began retreating down the cliff path as fast as we could.

The Mudmucks had regrouped, too, and seemed ready to attack us again, when there came urgent shouts from the area up by the entrance to Cliff Cave. They turned and rushed back up the cliff path to the cave.

We hustled along as fast as we could to, and reached the clubhouse without incident. We went in to assess the damage. Almost every one of us was injured in some way – lacerations, bruises, dog bites. Perry had gotten the worst of it – what with that rifle blow to his head and the beating upon his body with the rifle.

We laid him on one of the cots in the meeting room, and Lew Hunter and Oliver Court got the spirit of hartshorn out of our medicine chest.[7] That brought him around, but we made him stay on the cot. We began to tend to the others who had lacerations and bites.

I went over and sat down next to the cot Perry was on. I tried to be gentle. "Perry, what were you doing? You were supposed to stay here and guard the clubhouse."

He studied my face for a moment. "I heard lots of shouting, and dogs barking. I knew you were in trouble. I ran up the cliff path, and saw that dog Lion attacking you. I had to stop him."

"All he did was tear my shirt. I think they were just trying to scare us. We had been successful in creating a distraction at the entrance to Cliff Cave, and it was time for us to retreat. You shouldn't have shot that dog. The Cincinnati Kid is in a rage. This whole situation has just gotten a lot worse."

"I'm sorry, Hawkins. I saw him tearing at your arm. I thought I had to stop him."

I smiled. "I know, I know. You are always watching out for me. What's done is done."

About thirty minutes later, Shadow Loomis, Robby Hood and Roy Dobel came in, completely smeared with mud. They were stunned by the scene in the meeting room.

Shadow came over to me. "Looks like your attempt to distract the Mudmucks worked, but at what a cost!"

"Did you learn anything?"

"Yes, a little. Let's get things under control here, then we can report to you."

"I wonder why they didn't attack us again, as we retreated down the cliff path? We were going slow, having to carry poor Perry Stokes. There was a lot of yelling up there about something, and they hustled back to the cave entrance."

"I think I know what it was," came a voice from the door. It was Harold Court, and he looked like he had been through a ferocious struggle, bruised and bleeding and clothing torn. "They had found out we had infiltrated the cave."

"What happened?" I gasped.

He slumped down in a chair. "We went in and then up the slab stone steps from Cave River. We got into the first level of upper passages. Then we got ambushed, Mudmucks and dogs. They got Link and Will."

Dick Ferris came over. "What do you mean?"

Harold looked at him. "They are captives of the Mudmucks. I barely got away myself. We were overwhelmed, must've been six of 'em at least. We fought 'em, but Link and Will got knocked down, knocked out, I think. I couldn't help them. The dogs were tearing me up something awful. I broke away, but they were between me and the slab stone steps back down to Cave River. Good thing we know that cave so well, I had to run deeper into the cave – managed to lose 'em. I waited a long time till it seemed safe, and then I was able to get out. I'm sorry I couldn't help Link and Will. This is terrible!"

I sat down next to him. "It's worse than you think. Perry shot and killed that dog Lion. The Cincinnati Kid is in an awful bad state. I don't know what he's going to do to Link and Will."

Harold stared at me. "Good night, Hawkins! They are in real danger!"

Dick Ferris came over. He looked grim. "There is only one thing for us to do. We are going to have to figure out a way to go into the cave, and rescue Link and Will."

Johnny McLarren heard that. "We need time to get ready. Nobody's eaten anything since breakfast. Lots of the guys have injuries. It's getting late, will be getting dark in less than two hours."

I groaned. "Johnny's right. We can't do anything today. We need to get some rest, and we have to have clear heads to plan how we're going to do this."

Dick stared at me. "You want to leave Link and Will in the hands of those devils all night?"

Jerry Moore was outraged. "Are you out of your mind?"

I held up my hands helplessly. "We are nowhere near ready to launch a rescue attempt. I think we must wait until tomorrow. Anybody else got a better idea?"

There was an uncomfortable silence in the meeting room.

Jerry Moore went over to Harold Court, and they were whispering.

Jerry straightened up, took a deep breath, and came back over to me. "Okay. But this is your fault. You sent that spy team into the Cave River entrance, when you knew the Mudmucks knew about it."

Dick and Johnny started to object, but Jerry cut them off. "I know, I know, we all have to stand together. I want Hawkins to figure this out, how we rescue Link and Will early tomorrow. That's all."

I looked at Dick, and then held my head in my hands. "This whole day has been a fiasco."

Dick had a scary dead serious look on his face. "Okay. I'm ordering everyone home. Get something to eat, get some rest, take care of your injuries. Tomorrow we are going to try to figure out how to rescue Link and Will. It's going to be very dangerous, going into Cliff Cave. We are probably going to pay for this now."

Which we did.

CHAPTER 8

INTO THE HORNET'S NEST

That night I came back down to the clubhouse. It was pitch dark and raining hard. I slipped going up the steps, then had to fumble around to get the key in the lock.

I stepped inside. The meeting room was dark, but I could see a light coming around the curtain from my writing room. I heard low voices. Someone was in there! It sounded like two people.

I tried to walk over to the curtain, but my legs felt heavy. I had the sensation of walking through molasses.

I could clearly hear two people in my writing room talking about something, but I could not make out what they were saying. I reached my hand out and grasped the curtain. My heart was pounding. I yanked back the curtain, and I gasped! There stood two familiar figures!

Stoner's Boy and Long Tom! I never thought I would see either of them again. But here they were, in their long gray coats, floppy broad-brimmed gray hats, and Stoner with the gray handkerchief tied over his lower face.

They turned and stared at me. Long Tom had the mocking sneer he always wore, and he laughed at me, a laugh of complete disdain. "Seckatary Hawkins! You are such a fool! You don't understand what you're up against this time."

Stoner's Boy nodded his head. "You thought my old gang was tough. You have no idea how tough these Mudmucks are."

Long Tom laughed again. "And my Red Runners. You think they were bad? They were nothing, nothing, compared to these Mudmucks."

"Are you part of them?" I asked.

Stoner's Boy shook his head. "No. We have just come to warn you. You are way out of your league."

"But . . ." I protested, but they just began laughing at me. That made me angry, and I started shouting at them, "Get out! Get out!"

Suddenly I felt my whole body shaking violently. My legs felt restrained by something. Someone was yelling at me. "Hawkins, wake up! You're having a nightmare!"

I awakened with a violent start. I was in the clubhouse, in the meeting room. One of the oil lamps had been turned up, and Rube Muller and Lige Hobbs were bent over me.

"Easy, Hawkins," Lige was saying. "You're okay."

Then it all came back to me. Dick Ferris had ordered everyone home yesterday evening. That had created a problem for me that I had not considered. Link Lambert and Will Standish had been staying at my house. With Link and Will in the hands of the Mudmucks, I had to come up with some explanation of why they weren't at the house tonight. I told my parents we were all staying down by the river, which was true enough since Link and Will were being held captive in Cliff Cave. Johnny McLarren had brought a bedroll down to the clubhouse for me, and I was going to spend the night there with Lige and Rube.

"Oh, man." I sat up. I was drenched with sweat. "I dreamed that Stoner's Boy and Long Tom were here. They were here to warn me, to warn us, about the Mudmucks."

Rube smiled. "Those two old birds would give anyone a nightmare. But their warning was true enough."

I got up and went into my writing room, lit the oil lamp on my desk, and sat there. I was still shaky, and trying to calm myself. But what was troubling me was Rube's comment about the warning from Stoner's Boy and Long Tom in my dream. What had we gotten ourselves into? Would it have been better if we had just stayed away from the riverbank and the cliffs? I glanced out the window, imaging all sorts of danger lurking out there. And I thought of my old friends, Link and Will, in the hands of those devils, and felt sick.

Daylight put a new prospective on things, and I began to feel a little better.

I stepped outside. Lige was standing on the river bank, staring at the sky to the southwest. It was dark and bruised, and below the black sky some small low white clouds were scudding fast in our direction. He turned when he heard me approaching. His face was as gloomy as the sky. "Storm coming. Can't build a fire."

"So much for a hot breakfast," I grumbled. We went back into the clubhouse.

Just in time! – there was a lightning strike nearby and a huge crack of thunder, and it began to rain, and man did it come down hard! But it passed quickly, and the clouds started shredding apart.

We had some dry wood behind the stove in the clubhouse, and Lige and Rube used that to build a campfire out front at the base of the steps, while I got the fixin's organized for breakfast. The sun came out, and my mood brightened along with it. We got busy and prepared the meal. Hot scrambled eggs and bacon, washed down with hot coffee. It was just what the doctor ordered.

The other boys began arriving, and soon almost everyone was present. Perry Stokes was absent, which was understandable given that blow to the head he had received. Dick Ferris ordered us into an emergency meeting, to plan a rescue mission for Link and Will.

It was a sorry sight around the long pine table. Practically every boy had a bruise or laceration of some kind.

Jerry Moore looked around the table. "We're down to thirteen again. Bad luck, mark my words."

Roy Dobel glared at him. "That's baloney, Jerry, and you know it. We are sixteen, not thirteen. It's just that three of our members are not able to attend this meeting."

Robby Hood stood up. "That's right, Roy. What we need to figure out is how to rescue Link and Will, and right now."

Lew Hunter was stroking his chin. "Given what happened yesterday, it doesn't seem like we are going to be able to go into Cliff Cave and get them."

"Why not?" asked Shadow Loomis. "We got in and out safely, without being seen, through the back entrance."

Dick Ferris hit the table with his wooden hammer. "That's right! We haven't heard your report yet. What did you learn?"

"Well." Shadow paused and glanced at Robby Hood and Roy Dobel, who had been with him.

Robby motioned with his hand. "Go ahead, Shad."

"Well, Roy knows that section of Cliff Cave better than anybody else, I think. As soon as we went in the back entrance, he showed us a cheese hole in the top of the passage that I had never noticed before. But it wasn't a cheese hole, it was an opening to a small passage, of crawling height. We climbed up into it, and Roy led the way. It was a long crawl, with many twists and turns and other passages branching off, but Roy knew exactly where he wanted to go. We finally reached a ledge, from where we could look down on the Mudmuck camp."

"Camp?" asked Rube Muller.

"Yes. It's in the main passage, where it gets wide and tall, and the cave floor is dry rock and flat. They have set up tents there, seven I think, right?"

"Eight," responded Roy.

"Eight. That's right. But nobody was around. I guess you had them all engaged at the main entrance."

Harold Court corrected him. "Not all of 'em. There were at least six who bushwhacked us."

"Right. Sorry, Harold. Anyway, from where we were, there was no way to climb down, the cave wall was too sheer, nothing to climb down on. But there were lanterns lit in the camp, and we could see lots of rope, and some shovels and picks. It did sort of look like a camp of geologists."

Jerry Moore snorted. "Those mudballs are no more geologists than I am a ballerina!"

That got a light laugh from the boys.

I held up my hand. "Hold on. Hold on a minute. Let me think." All the boys were looking at me. "We can approach this camp without being seen, right? – in this little passage that only Roy knows about. But you can't climb down into the camp, the cave wall is too steep, right? Could we get down on ropes?"

Roy stared at me. "Yes, but why in thunder would we want to do that?"

"Because," Bill Darby smiled, "Hawkins thinks Link and Will would be held in the camp, or near it."

"That's right," I nodded my head. "That's right, Bill, that's exactly what I'm thinking."

Lew Hunter looked startled. "Are you suggesting we create another diversion at the main entrance, and send in a rescue team by the back entrance?"

"Yes, that's how we rescue Link and Will."

There was an uncomfortable stir around the table. I knew many of the boys were not happy at the prospect of being sent up the cliff path again. They began talking all at once.

Bam! Dick hit the table with his wooden hammer. "Order!" He turned to me. "What if they're not being held in that part of the cave? There are all sorts of little rooms, chambers, all over in Cliff Cave, that could be used as a prison cell."

"That's true," I agreed. "But in that part of the main passage, right near where the Mudmuck encampment is, there is that prison chamber where Stoner's Boy held Briggen captive. There is even a wooden door to that prison room. I'll bet that's where they are holding Link and Will."

An approving murmur ran around the room, as some of the old-timers recalled that incident.[1]

Oliver Court stood up and shocked me. "We at least have to try. With the shooting of that dog Lion, who knows what the Cincinnati Kid will do to Link and Will. We should get going right now!"

That settled it for the rest of the boys. If timid Oliver Court was willing to go into battle, so were they.

Lige Hobbs held up his hand. "I went up the cliff path yesterday, and it was an ugly mess. But seems to me the most dangerous part of this mission is on the rescue team. They're gonna climb down on ropes, right into that hornet's nest. They could get captured, too."

Dick held his head in his hands. "You are right about that, Lige." He looked up at the ceiling. "How am I supposed to choose who to send, when they will be at such great risk of being captured by those devils?"

My stomach was in a knot. I knew I couldn't let this go on. This whole situation was my fault. I stood up. "This situation is due to the fiasco I created yesterday, this dangerous mission is my idea too, and it is my responsibility to choose. I choose Roy, who is the only one who knows the way for sure. And I choose Shadow and Robby, who have been there already. And I'm going, too."

Dick gasped, "Why you?"

"Because what happened yesterday was my fault, and now I've come up with another idea that may just be another fiasco."

Dick opened his mouth, but I waved my hands. "Let's go! Our friends are in danger!"

There was a step on the porch, and in came Perry Stokes. "Reporting for duty, sir."

I was glad to see him, and to show him how much I trusted him, I gave him the job again of guarding the clubhouse with Larry King's rifle. I didn't say anything about not coming up the cliff path and shooting another dog. I knew he wouldn't leave his post this time.

We got organized, my team with a heavy knotted rope and flashlights. I slipped a small folding saw and some other tools into my pockets.

The other boys gathered around us, putting on brave faces and wishing us good luck. I began to get nervous, and just wanted to get going. I did not have a good feeling about this at all.

Dick ordered Harold Court and Jerry Moore, our best brawlers, to lead the rest of the boys up the cliff path after giving us a thirty minute head start.

With that, Roy, Shadow, Robby and I started off at a hustle. We went up the river path a good bit, then veered off left and crossed the upper end of the hollow. We wanted to go on a route that would prevent us from being seen by any Mudmuck lookouts up on the cliffhead. We cut through the woods south of the hollow, and picked up the lane that leads down to Dobels farm along the river. We crossed the pasture, then up the steep hillside to where, next to a big cucumber magnolia tree, was a little hole – the back entrance to Cliff Cave.[2]

We paused to gird ourselves for what was to come. From this vantage point we had a good view of the river. A steamboat was thrashing upstream, the *Crescent City*. I felt very strange, looking at that symbol of normalcy here on the Looking Glass, and thinking of the dark dangers we were about to expose ourselves to.

But our friends were in need. I took a deep breath. "Let's go."

Roy led the way. We stooped down low and ducked into the cave. Boy! – that cave floor was muddy! A few steps in, and Roy pointed with his flashlight. "There is the entrance to the passage." It was a small hole in the passage roof. I didn't see how I was going to make it. Roy and Robby climbed up, then turned around and with Shadow pushing me from behind, I managed to get up the wall and they pulled me in.

I looked around. "This is a tight squeeze."

"Shhh!" Robby put his finger to his lips, and I shut up.

It was a crawl the whole way, in single file. Roy leading, then Robby, then me, and Shadow bringing up the rear. On and on we went. It was very muddy, and cold mud at that! My hands began to feel numb.

After what seemed like hours, we reached the ledge. There was room enough for all four of us to creep to the lip and peep over, down into the camp of the Mudmucks. It was just as Shadow had described, eight tents in two rows in the big wide cave passage. Hung all around the tents were oil lanterns. There were three

Mudmucks standing among the tents, talking in low voices. One of them I recognized as the one called Cheeky, who had clobbered me in the head with a club. Though I could not understand what they were saying, their voices echoed all around the cave.

Roy leaned up next to my ear, and mouthed in a breathy whisper, "What'll we do?"

"We wait here, either until our boys reach the main entrance, or we see some other opportunity."

Abruptly, the three Mudmucks picked up some tools and ropes and lanterns and began to walk away, but deeper into the cave rather than toward the main entrance. They went around a corner and disappeared. They must have stopped a short distance down the passage, as we could still hear them talking and then the sounds of shovels and picks being worked.

I turned to the others. "Now's our chance." I looked over the ledge. It was about fifteen feet to the cave floor. We fastened our rope to a boulder and gently lowered it down.

Robby went first, and he went down that rope like a spider. Roy followed, then it was my turn. It was much harder than I imagined, with the rope so tight at spots against the rock wall, but I made it. A moment later Shadow stood with us.

"This way," I mouthed softly, and we headed up the passage in the direction of the main entrance. As we passed the last tent, I heard rustling inside. Mudmucks! My heart began pounding, and I started trembling.

We kept going, but suddenly a great cry came from up ahead. "Alert! Alert! Enemies at the gate!"

I thought we were going to get caught, but Robby knew this section of Cliff Cave. He pulled us into a small chamber, almost like a closet, and we switched off our lights. Not a second later, two Mudmucks came out of the tent and rushed past us, toward the main entrance.

"Don't move," whispered Robby.

Sure enough, a few seconds later the three Mudmucks we had seen earlier charged past. We waited, but no more sounds came from the camp. There were low muffled sounds coming from up the passage, probably from outside the cave.

Flipping our lights back on, I quickly led the way to the prison chamber. It was down a side passage, which was like a long hall with other passages and rooms off to each side, but I knew the way. We reached the spot, and there was a small hole like a tiny window in the rocky wall. I looked in. "Link, Will," I called softly. "You in there?"

"Hawkins!" It was Link.

"We're going to get you out of there!"

We rushed around the corner of the wall, to where Stoner had built a door. Sure enough, it had been repaired, with heavy oak boards, the hinges fastened to the rock with big iron spikes, and a brass padlock on the hasp.

I got out my folding saw, and began to hack furiously at the wood around the lock. It was making a lot of noise. My hands began to rub raw.

"Here, let me." Shadow took over, and he made that saw fly. When his hands gave out, Robby took the saw and with a few last slashing cuts broke the door open.

Link and Will were inside, bound hand and foot. Roy got out his knife, and freed them.

Link came over to me. "Hawkins, the Mudmucks haven't even given us any water!"

I shook my head. "Let's get out of here."

We raced back to the rope, and one by one began climbing up. We sent Roy first, to lead the way out, and then Link and Will. Shadow was next, and I heard him gasp as he climbed up. My turn, and I immediately knew why Shadow had gasped. My raw and bleeding hands could hardly hold the rope, and the pain was awful, but the excitement somehow got me up to the ledge. Robby came last, and we pulled up the rope and were on our way out. We crawled fast, but it was still a long time before we saw a patch of daylight ahead, and a few minutes later we clambered out and were standing under the cucumber magnolia.

"Thank you!" exclaimed Will, and he wanted to shake our

hands, but when I showed him my palm, he pulled back. "I can't imagine what you went through to do this."

We slipped and stumbled down the steep hillside. At the base of the hill was a small gully, with some mud puddles in it. Will and Link ran over and cupped their hands and began drinking the water.

I turned to Shadow, Robby, and Roy. "Those Mudmucks are the worst we have ever dealt with. They didn't even give them water to drink."

We hurried back the way we had come, to avoid being seen. As we approached the clubhouse, I saw Perry on the porch with the rifle. My heart leaped into my mouth. Were our other boys still up on the cliff path?

"Hey everybody!" shouted Perry. "Here they come now! And they got Link and Will!"

Johnny McLarren, Oliver Court, Lew Hunter, and Lige Hobbs came out onto the porch and gave us a cheer.

"Where is everyone else?" I asked.

Lew jerked his thumb toward the door. "Inside. We got hit bad."

I pushed past them and went into the meeting room. It looked like a Civil War field hospital. Jerry Moore and Harold Court, our chief brawlers, had gotten it the worst. Jerry had two black eyes, the first time I had seen that on him.

Harold was seated, having gashes on his forehead being tended to by Dick Ferris. He heard me come in. "I hear you got Link and Will. That's great, Hawkins."

"Yes. We were in the Mudmuck camp when they sounded the alarm for trouble at the main entrance. What happened up there?"

Dick shot me a look. "Let me tend to Harold. Johnny can tell you all about it."

Johnny was standing in the doorway. "Kinda the same drill, Hawkins. Rocks dumped on us, and then they came out of the cave and attacked us. We stood our ground for as long as we could, to cover for you guys inside the cave and give you as much time as we could, but then they sicked the dogs on us again. We were overwhelmed and started retreating down the cliff path, but when we reached the flat area on the riverbank, the dogs surrounded us. The Mudmucks charged us, and a wild fist fight that was, with the nasty dogs in the thick of it, too. Then Perry began firing the rifle from the clubhouse, and the dogs ran off."

I turned to Perry. "You didn't kill any more dogs, did you?'

"No, sir. I was just firing warning shots into the ground near the clubhouse. Worked, though, huh?"

"What happened then, Johnny?"

"Well, the Mudmucks went wild after Perry fired the rifle. Jerry and Harold managed to knock a couple of 'em down, but that even made them angrier. There were nine of us, and about thirteen of them, so they had us outnumbered. They were beating up Jerry and Harold something terrible, and the rest of us were having a tough time, when a steamboat whistle began screaming at us. It was the *Hudson Lee*, headed downstream, but the steamboat turned right at us and I thought Captain Lee was going to ram our wharf. He spun the boat sideways, up close to the wharf, and they began to lower the gangplank. The Mudmucks saw that, and sounded the retreat, back up the cliff path. Haven't seen a Mudmuck show his face since then."

I thought for a moment. "We saw five Mudmucks in the cave, near their camp. They all went up to the main entrance. You say you fought about thirteen of 'em?"

Johnny turned to the others. "Yes, there was the Cincinnati Kid, and I'd say maybe twelve others, you think?"

There was general agreement on that.

Lige came over to me. "That makes sense. We saw two up on the cliffhead head as lookouts, and to throw rocks down. That makes about fifteen in total around the main entrance."

Link nodded. "Yes. When we went in through Cave River yesterday, we were captured by a group of about six. If they had six there again today, that would account for all the Mudmucks.'

Harold pulled away from Dick for a moment. "Again today, they had six guarding the Cave River entrance. They don't know about the back entrance. That gives us an advantage."

I sat down and tried to think. "They do know, or will in a

minute, that we got Link and Will out. Their guards at Cave River will report they didn't see us come in, and they will figure out there must be another entrance."

"So what?" asked Rube. "They don't know where it is. And Shadow explained it's hard to find from inside Cliff Cave."

"Well," I replied, "that's true, but they will be looking for it. We might not have that advantage for long."

"We have one other advantage," growled Jerry Moore. "We have seventeen members now."

"What do you mean?"

Jerry jerked his head over to the back of the meeting room. "Hudson Lee got off the steamboat, and we elected him into our club."

Indeed, there was Hudson Lee, helping to put a bandage on Rube Muller. I went over. "Hey, Hudson. Glad to have you join us, but I wish it was under better circumstances."

"That's alright, Hawkins. After we saw the brawl on the riverbank, I told my dad that I needed to stay here and help you."

I wanted to shake his hand, but my palms were too raw.

I went over to Dick, and talked quietly with him. "Dick, this situation is getting out of hand. We can't risk having any more of our boys captured by the Mudmucks. Will and Link were in a dreadful position."

We argued quietly for a couple minutes. He finally agreed to my proposal, and turned to the other boys. "Hawkins and Johnny and I are going back up, under a flag of truce, and try to cool things off with the Mudmucks."

Some of the boys thought we were crazy, but Dick reminded them that the Cincinnati Kid himself had come to the clubhouse under a flag of truce.

We rigged up a white flag, and began slowly walking up the cliff path. When we got high enough up the path, we had a good view of the river. A sternwheel steamboat passed us, going downstream. It was a small boat, the *City of Clifton*, and was all decked out in red, white and blue bunting and flags. The Fourth of July was coming soon. It must have been out on some sort of excursion because there were a lot of passengers on the decks.

There were two Mudmuck lookouts on the cliff head, and they were signaling down toward the cave entrance. However, when we reached the area where the rock attacks had started, there were none. I began to think our flag of truce was working. Indeed, when we reached the entrance to Cliff Cave, the Cincinnati Kid was standing out in front, by himself. We could see a crowd of Mudmucks milling about just inside the entrance.

The Cincinnati Kid had his face screwed up into a ferocious expression. I could tell he was not pleased with the way things were going. "What do you want, Hawkins?"

I walked up to him and stuck my face in his. "Just this. We got our boys back, see?" I could tell by his eyes that he knew Link and Will had been rescued. "We can do things like that, see? You thought we were no match for you. Well, we are, even though we are fewer in number."

"Is there some point to this idiotic babbling?"

"Yes. We offer you five days of peace. We stay out of the cave, and you stay away from our clubhouse. Five days, then whatever you are doing in the cave must be finished, and you and your gang go back to Cincinnati and never come back down here."

He studied my face for a minute, glanced at Dick and Johnny and then walked over to the Mudmucks standing in the cave. I could see him talking to the ones named Peralta and Sawyer, who I was beginning to think were his top lieutenants.

The Kid walked back over to us. "It's a deal. If we can work undisturbed in the cave for five days, then we will leave. Just be sure to keep your boneheads away, I mean truly away, from the cave and this hilltop. You've been meddling in our business ever since we got here, and we can't hardly get any work done. You follow?"

"I follow. But I don't want to see any of your gang come down around our clubhouse. You follow?"

He sneered at me, and walked back into Cliff Cave, waving his arms over his head.

I turned to Dick and Johnny. "Let's go. We will hold up our end of the deal."

We walked back down the cliff path. As we neared the bottom, we spotted two canoes approaching our bank, each with two boys in them. The canoes were loaded with camping gear, fishing poles, and other supplies.

"Now what?" asked Johnny.

"They're definitely not Mudmucks," replied Dick.

We stopped on the bank. The two canoes nosed into the soft mud.

One of the boys stood up in the back of his canoe. "Hello. We're the Morgans, from down at Morning View. My name is Clayton, but everybody calls me Clay."

He motioned over to the other canoe. "These are our twin brothers, Stonewall and Clifton, but everybody calls them Stone and Cliff."

Then he pointed to the boy in the front of his canoe. "And this is our sister Samantha, but mos' everybody just calls her Scout."

Sister? I looked closer. She was barefoot, dressed in jeans and a simple shirt, and had a boy haircut, but now I saw her facial features were indeed that of a girl, a very pretty girl.

I smiled at her. "Scout, eh? I like that nickname. I have a nickname, too. Around here, everybody calls me Seckatary Hawkins."[3]

PART III

AUSTINBERG, KENTUCKY.
EARLY JULY 1914

CHAPTER 9

A BRIEF INTERLUDE

"Seckatary Hawkins?" Scout looked intently at me. "Why, you are famous up and down the Looking Glass!"

Maybe that blow to my head had scrambled my noggin, but I finally put two and two together, and realized just who I was talking to!

"Samantha Morgan from Morning View?" I replied with a laugh. "You are more famous up and down this river. Captain Lee and Hudson Lee have told us all about you, and we read about you in the *Cincinnati Enquirer*."

We had them move their canoes over to our little landing, and helped them get their gear and the canoes up on the log wharf. Dick and Johnny shook hands with them. My right hand was in no condition for shaking. We started walking toward clubhouse.

"What brings you to our riverbank?" I asked them.

The Morgans glanced at each other, then Scout spoke. "We will fill you in on the details, but we are looking for something and probably will be here for a few days. We'll need a place to put our tent."

"You can put it right next to our clubhouse."

We went up the steps and into the meeting room, and I addressed all our boys. "Fellas, these are the Morgans from down at Morning View. Clay, there, the twins Cliff and Stone, and Samantha. That's the Samantha Morgan we have been hearing so much about."

"Just call me Scout."

All the boys greeted her and her brothers warmly.

"What's going on here?" asked Clay, as he looked around the meeting room with all the injured boys.

"We have had a lot of trouble with a gang of boys from Cincinnati calling themselves the Mudmucks," I replied. "We've been trying to drive them away."

"We could use some reinforcements," growled Jerry.

Clay nodded. "We'll be here for a few days, at least. We'd be glad to help you."

I held up my hands. "Hold on, Jerry. We have just reached an agreement with the Mudmucks, if they stay in Cliff Cave and away from everywhere else, they can have five days undisturbed by us, and then they must go back to Cincinnati and never come back."

A lot of the boys vocalized strong doubts about that, including Jerry. "And you believe 'em? This, the worst gang ever, won't even give water to their captives, hit us with rocks and clubs, and sick dogs on us?"

"Yeah!" "Right!" came from many voices.

Jerry continued. "I don't trust 'em. I think we are in for worse to come. We need all the members we can get. Now, this Morgan clan here are upstanding folk. I know we only let in new members if we know 'em. But we all know Scout, from the newspaper and Hudson Lee and others, and that means we know all the Morgan bunch. Sign 'em up."

Hudson Lee came over. "That's right. I can vouch for all of them. Fine folk."

I looked at Jerry in amazement. "Sign up a girl?"

"Yes!" he snapped. "Sign 'em all up!"

Dick called for a vote, and it was unanimous. We added to the membership rolls the names of Clayton, Clifton, Stonewall, and Samantha Morgan.

Jerry folded his arms. "That's better. Now we have twenty-one members, same as the Mudmucks. They won't be able to put two or three on one, like they have been doing."

I saw Will go over to Jerry, who had two black eyes, and Harold, who had a bandage over his eyebrow that had been split open – both injured in the wild brawl with the Mudmucks. "Jerry, Harold, I want to thank you for what you did – it was the key to giving enough time to Hawkins, Roy, Shadow and Robby – the time they needed to get us safely out of the cave."

Harold smiled. "Always glad to help someone like you, Will."

Will shook his head. "A few days ago, when I first got here, you said you were bored – you were wishing for some excitement. Now what do you think?"

Harold laughed. "Probably more than I bargained for, but we didn't start this."

"That's right," agreed Jerry. "And it ain't over yet. This peace treaty Hawkins mentioned won't last more'n a day. We're going to be back in battle with the Mudmucks by tomorrow, take my word for it."

Scout came over to me. She was very pretty, I thought. "Seckatary Hawkins, I want to hear about this Cliff Cave you mentioned. But first, where is the nearest telephone? I need to call home and tell our mom what we are doing."

I led her into my writing room and pointed to the telephone on my desk. "There. You can use that one."

"You have an office, with a telephone? That's fantastic!"

The call from the clubhouse had to be routed through the operator in Austinberg, and then the operator in Morning View, before it was connected to the Morgan house.[1]

Scout spoke briefly with her mother. She told her where they had landed. "And you won't believe this. We are with Seckatary Hawkins! Yes, it's him, and the clubhouse, and all the boys. We have been elected into the club!" There was a pause, then she continued. "Yes, we think the cave is near here. I'm sure Seckatary Hawkins and the other boys can help us. OK. I love you too, Mom. Bye. Sure, put her on."

There was a pause.

"What cave?" I asked.

Scout glanced at me and smiled. Then she spoke back into the mouthpiece. "Hi, Jessamine! Yes, it's me! We're all doing great.

How's Tom-Tom? That's good. I miss you too. Jessamine! Stop that, good grief, we've only been gone one night. Give Mom and Dad a kiss for me, OK? Yes, I'll tell Clay and Cliff and Stone. I love you too, Jessamine. Bye."

"What cave?" I repeated.

Scout called her brothers into my writing room. Shadow, Robby, Link, Harold, and Will crowded in, too.

Scout explained that in the secret room where she found the money that she gave to the Ferguson children, she had also found a map to a cave called Treasure Cave. She got out of her knapsack a copy of the map she had made and showed it to us.

We spread it out on my desk and pored over it. It showed a long cave passage leading to a deep pit, and indicated there was an opening into a side passage down in the wall of the pit, leading to a chamber where it was written that a treasure of gold coins was hidden.

"Sure looks like Cliff Cave, and the route to the deep pit over Cave River," observed Robby.

"But Robby," I protested, "we have gone down the pit before, to the side cave where the brown man and the pearls were hidden. There were no gold coins in there."

Shadow looked at the map. "No, there wasn't. But maybe that's the wrong side cave. There may be other side openings in the walls of the deep pit."

Scout was excited. "You think so?"

I put my hand on her shoulder. "Maybe. All of Cliff Cave is a crazy maze of passages, rooms, and pits. But we have another problem. The Mudmucks have taken over Cliff Cave. For over a week we have been fighting them, trying to get them out of there. We don't like to be pushed around by gangs from Cincinnati or anywhere else. But we have been unable to dislodge them. You see out in the meeting room, how hard we have tried."

"Yes," Scout nodded. "You have fought hard. What do they want in the cave?"

"They say they are geologists. We have been in the cave twice, through a secret back entrance, and spied on them, and it sure looks like they have set up the camp of a geological expedition."

"But you don't believe it?"

"Most likely I don't."

Scout frowned. "What'll we do?"

"Well, today we made a peace treaty with them. We promised them five days of undisturbed work in the cave, after which they must go back to Cincinnati. They have to stay up on the cliffs, and leave us alone down here around the clubhouse."

Cliff Morgan came over to me. "And then we can go in the cave?"

"Yes."

"We'll have to stay here for five days and wait?"

"That's the deal we made with the Cincinnati Kid."

"Who the dickens is that?"

"The leader of the Mudmucks. Ever hear of him?"

"Never."

"Well, hopefully you'll never have to deal with him, or any of them. They are plain nasty thugs."

We helped the Morgans set up their tent next to the clubhouse, and get settled in. Link and Will were going to join me in spending nights in the clubhouse with Rube and Lige and Hudson Lee.

It was looking like it was going to be a peaceful five days around the clubhouse.

Mom had invited us up for dinner, so the four Morgans, Link, Will, Rube, Lige, Hudson and I walked up to my house.

Mom looked at me. Moms don't miss much. "Greg, what happened to your right hand?"

"I was doing a lot of sawing." That was the truth.

Then Mom looked at Link, Will, Rube, and Lige, with their bruises and bandages. She gave me a significant glance, but said nothing more. She didn't need to. Her glance spoke volumes. She was reminding me that I was held responsible for the safety of all guests. Now added to my burden of worries was this Morgan clan, and their pretty sister Scout.

We sat outside on the patio behind the house and had some cold lemonade. Our next door neighbors, the Bechtolds, came home in their carriage. Their carriage house had a turntable, and we watched them pull in, and use the turntable to turn the carriage around, leaving the front facing out. [2]

Scout turned to Clay. "That's slick. We should build one of those."

Dad seemed a little distracted. He had the *Cincinnati Enquirer* with him, and the front page had more bad news from Europe, following the assassination four days ago of Archduke Franz Ferdinand of Austria and his wife Sophie.

Scout looked at the front page. "Our dad is worried, too. He thinks war is brewing."

Dad glanced at her, folded the newspaper shut and put it down, and smiled. "Well, that's not a subject we should discuss here and now. I am very glad to meet you in person, and tonight we are going to celebrate new friends and Club members for Greg and the other boys. You are just the kind of person to be in his Club, generous and caring for the less fortunate."

Mom nodded her head. "And her brothers, too. And Will and Lige and Rube and Hudson, we hardly ever see you boys. I hope your visit here is fun and relaxing."

Link was sitting next to me, and he nudged my arm and whispered, "Fun and relaxing?"

Will looked sideways at Lige and Rube before he spoke. "I have always liked coming here, and it is good to be here with my old friends, and my new friends the Morgans."

Mom had made burgoo, and we stayed on the patio and ate the stew along with cornbread. [3]

Mom and Dad asked Scout a lot of questions about the secret room and the bag of money and Plessy Ferguson and all that. It was like we had a celebrity at our house.

When Scout was done telling the whole story, Mom asked her, "What brought you up here today?"

Scout paused for a moment. "I've never seen the Palisades area. Our grandmother told us it is beautiful, and it certainly is. We had no idea when we stopped to camp for the night that we would find Hawkins and the clubhouse."

I noticed Scout was careful not to mention anything about the map of Treasure Cave.

After dinner we went back down to the riverbank. The days are long now, and it was getting near the Fourth of July. Some of the other boys went to the hollow to practice baseball. The Morgan boys wanted Link to show them his launch *Cazanova*.

"I want to see the entrance to Cliff Cave," announced Scout.

I shook my head. "A deal's a deal. We promised we would stay off the cliffs and hill where the cave is."

"Can we see it from the river?"

I thought for a moment. "I guess there's no harm in that. Being out on the Looking Glass in a canoe should be okay."

We got out my faded old red canoe. My birthday was coming up in a few weeks, and I had asked for a new canoe, a gray one.

Scout and I pushed off, and began paddling downstream. My right hand was raw and sore, and I was having some trouble handling the paddle, but Scout was a strong paddler and ended up doing most of the work.

I pointed out Pelham to her on the left, and then the entrance to Cave River on the right. I swung us out across the current, over to the wooded bank down from Pelham. From here we had a better view of the tall cliff. The sun was getting low behind the cliffhead, but I could still point out the features.

"There, coming up from the right, is the cliff path, winding along the side of the cliffs. And you see that big cedar tree, right above those boulders?"

"Yes."

"From there follow along the cliff path a bit more to the left, and you see where the rocky face of the cliff looks like a stone mason laid it?"

"Yes! I see it! There's a dark opening there!"

"I see why they call you Scout! That's the main entrance to Cliff Cave."

I handed her Dad's binoculars, and she studied the cave

entrance. She let out a long breath. "I can hardly wait to get in there. It's deserted right now. Nobody up there."

"No. They just want to be left alone in the cave, for some reason."

The sun had dropped behind the cliffhead, and long shadows from the cliff were thrown across the Looking Glass. It did look like a looking glass this evening, the surface completely smooth, and in this type of light you could see your reflection perfectly in the water.

We began to slowly paddle back toward our little landing. Swallows were dipping and swooping over the river all around us.

Daylight was fading fast. I never thought I would be out on the river on an evening like this, in my canoe with a girl!

I guess I overslept because by the time I got out of the clubhouse, the Morgans had already caught some fish and started a campfire. All the other boys were up and about, too – Link, Will, Lige, Rube, and Hudson.

"Good morning, Sunshine!" teased Scout when she saw me.

I shook my head. "I was bushed. Yesterday was a long day, crawling around in Cliff Cave and all that."

They had caught some black bass and sauger. Sauger was one of my favorite eating fish. We had the fish along with coffee and leftover cornbread from dinner last night.

Our other boys began trickling in, and we got to work decorating the clubhouse for the Fourth of July, which is tomorrow. We hung red, white, and blue bunting all around the porch, and had little flags lining the walk from the river path to the steps. Scout even put some bunting on their tent.

I went into my writing room, and got to work catching up on my writing. I was way far behind! I was scribbling away when Scout came in.

"Whatcha doing, Hawkins?"

I showed her my writing book and explained how I kept a record of all the goings on around here, and the big stack of writing books under my desk. She was very interested.

"But, hey, Hawkins, some of the boys are going with Roy Dobel to go horseback riding. Can we go with them?"

I threw down my pen. "Let's go!"

The Morgan boys were going to walk into town with some of our boys, to look around and get some supplies. The other boys stayed at the clubhouse, doing some painting and cleaning and touch-up repairs. We usually do that at the beginning of summer vacation, but the arrival of the Mudmucks had set us back.

It was thus just a group of six of us set who off with Roy Dobel. Our party included Lew Hunter, Oliver Court, Will Standish, Scout Morgan, and me.

We walked directly across the hollow, no longer afraid of being seen by Mudmuck lookouts on the cliffhead. Still, we looked up there, but saw nothing except a kettle of turkey buzzards floating in circles high above the hill.

Oliver commented dryly, "The buzzards are circling over the Mudmucks. Their days are numbered."

We all laughed heartily. Oliver is a very clever and funny guy.

"But I don't believe that," added Oliver.

That surprised me. "You don't?"

"Not at all. I think Jerry is right. I think the Mudmucks will go back on the deal. You probably shouldn't have given them the five days."

"But I didn't think we could take more beatings and dog attacks. And I didn't want any more of our fellow members captured by the Mudmucks."

Oliver shrugged. That surprised me, and worried me, too.

We went through the woods on the south side of the hollow, then onto the dirt road leading down to Dobel's farm. We passed the low buildings and the pen in which Roy kept his flock of turkeys [4]

The horses were out in a pasture. Roy zipped into the house, and then came out with six apples. "Here, you're gonna need these to get your horse."

There were eleven horses in the pasture, and we had our pick. I selected a chestnut beauty named Lookout, and Scout picked a white horse named Apollo[5].

We led our horses over to the livery stable, and Roy began showing us how to saddle them up. To my surprise, Scout knew how to do it without any help. She was some girl.

Just as we were getting ready to set out, Mrs. Dobel came out with a bulging knapsack and handed it to Roy. "A little something for your outing."

"Thank you, Mrs. Dobel!" we all sang out in unison.

I was standing next to Apollo with Scout. Mrs. Dobel looked over at us. "Greg, is that a girl you have there? Well, I'm damn pleased!"

Scout laughed gaily, and bowed. "Pleased to meet you, Mrs. Dobel. Samantha Morgan, from down at Morning View."

Mrs. Dobel came over and clasped Scout's hands in her own. "My dear, I am very happy to meet you! We have heard all about you. What brings you to Austinberg?"

"Hawkins is going to show me around Cliff Cave."

"Oh, is that right? There are some beautiful chambers in that cave. A lot of it is under our property, and we used to have it as a show cave. But Greg and my boy Roy can show you the whole place. OK, you kids, have a good time!"

We mounted up, waved goodbye to Mrs. Dobel, and headed back up the lane toward Banklick Pike. There we turn left and headed south away from town. It was a sunny day, and we were all in a good mood after our many days of trouble. Scout and I rode side by side, and she told me about Morning View, and her parents and sister Jessamine, and her grandmother, and her cat Tom-Tom. I told her about some of our adventures on the old riverbank, including how I had found the secret room in the Lonely House by pacing across the rooms on the first floor and comparing them to the rooms on the second floor. It was a very similar approach to how she found the secret room in their house, and we had fun comparing stories. Will Standish came up on the other side of Scout, on his horse Vagrant, and we talked about his life in Cuba and our adventures together there.[6]

We entered some beautiful country. Banklick Pike ran right next to Banklick Creek here, with the creek to our right, and to our left the beginnings of the forested Parks Hills. On the other side of the creek ran the Kentucky Central Railroad, with a trestle crossing the creek as the tracks headed into Austinberg.

We came to the turn-off to Hobbs Ferry, turned left into that lane, and rode down toward the river through the valley of Banklick Creek. To our right, we could see the tower of Lonely House above the trees, and then we caught a glimpse of the barns of Rube Muller's farm across the creek. Near here, in a bend of the creek, was where we had our summer camp during our adventures with Pooley and his Knights of the Square Table. I told Scout about that, and the many bags of gold coins that had been hidden in the old mill.

"Gold coins have been found around here before!" exclaimed Scout.

"Don't start counting your gold coins just yet!" called Oliver from his horse Meridian[7].

Now we could see the old mill itself, across the creek, moldering away. Steentzen's Mill, it was called.[8]

Just a little further down the lane, in the hills to our left, was the gorge with the cave of Simon Bleaker. I told Scout about those adventures, with the unicorn on Burney's Field. I explained that what everyone thought was a unicorn turned out to be a gnu that had escaped from the Cincinnati Zoo, and had broken off one of its horns.[9]

We passed the tobacco farm of Stringbean Wilson, and soon came in sight of the Looking Glass, and the sleepy hamlet of Hobbs Ferry across the river.[10]

We stopped at the landing, and waited while old Mr. Hobbs brought the ferry over. Hobbs Ferry was the only crossing on the Looking Glass for miles around, although there was one spot further downstream that could be forded in low water.[11]

The ferryboat was a single stack steamer. Mr. Hobbs cut the engine, coasted in close to the landing, then came out of the pilothouse and lowered the ramp onto the landing just right to stop the boat.

"Slick," commented Scout.

"He's been doing it for decades," replied Lew.

We led our horses onto the ferry. Mr. Hobbs came up to us. "Six horses. That'll be a dollar twenty."

I held out the money for him. He seemed startled as he looked up at me. "Oh, it's you, Hawkins! I didn't recknize you behind that big horse. You fellers can cross for free. You takin' care of my boy?"

"Yes, sir, Lige is fine," I answered. "He's staying with us through the Fourth, should be coming home shortly after that."

Mr. Hobbs squinted and looked closely at Scout. "Didn't you pass by here yistidday, with some other fellas, in a couple canoes?"

"Yes, sir."

I spoke up. "Mr. Hobbs, this is Samantha Morgan, from Morning View."

"Please to meet ya," as he started to extend his hand, then stopped cold and his eyes widened. "Morning View? Is this *the* Samantha Morgan?"

"Yes, sir," she answered with a laugh.

"Well, well, young lady. I am honored to meet ya. Matter of fact, jus' a second here . . ." and he fumbled in his pocket. "Here's a silver dollar. Put that in the Ferguson bank account for me, would ya, when ya get back home?"

"Yes, I will, thank you very much, Mr. Hobbs."

I had to shake my head in wonderment, at the effect Scout had on complete strangers.

We crossed the river, led our horses onto the landing, and then mounted up and headed out. We passed by the handful of houses that made up the hamlet of Hobbs Ferry, and then we were back in the woods again. The hills around here were also called Parks Hills, as they made a long ridge that started on the western side of the Looking Glass up near the Cliff Cave complex, ran southeast to this area, where the Looking Glass had cut a water gap through the ridge, and then the ridge continued south on the eastern side of the river.[12]

After a couple miles, we turned right onto a trail that took us down to the river. We stopped on the bank.

"This is the back channel of the Looking Glass that runs behind

Seven Willows Island," I explained to Scout. "The main channel is on the west side of the island. We can cross here, it's real shallow."

"I think this is the island we had breakfast on yesterday," replied Scout. "We stopped on a sandy beach on the downstream end of an island."

"Yep, that's on this island. We have had our summer camp right there on that sandy beach, three times now."[18]

We urged our horses forward, into the river. Lew Hunter had to press his horse, Chant, and Roy Dobel had a lot of trouble with his horse Donerail[14]. "He don't like water. I didn't know we were going to the island, or I would've picked a different mount."

"Sorry, Roy," I called. "I didn't have a plan."

Scout laughed. "That's the way to do this sort of thing!"

The horses splashed through the water, and up onto the island. We rode along the bank for a short distance, under the overhanging willows, until we were forced to stop by the dense underbrush. Most of Seven Willows Island is covered by a thicket of trees, shrubs, and vines.

We sat on the bank, and opened the knapsack. Mrs. Dobel had prepared sandwiches for us, along with the apple dumplings she was known for. There was a big jug of the delicious spring water from their farm.[15] We talked about how Mrs. Dobel often prepared a picnic lunch for us, one time at Oscar Koven's camp in Cliff Cave, and another time here on the island, when we met the Yella Kid Stevens at our hidden houseboat.[16]

Scout wanted to see that, so after our lunch we started the trek to the backwater pool. Roy stayed behind to watch the horses.

"Wow, this is quite a jungle," exclaimed Scout, as we threshed our way through the bushes and curtains of vines. "Ouch!" A lot of the bushes had thorns.

The backwater pool is a little cove off the back channel of the Looking Glass, and there, a couple of years ago, we had found the hidden houseboat of Link Lambert and his daddy. They had lived in it before Link came into his inheritance, the Cazanova sugar cane plantation in Cuba, and found his long-lost mother. His Uncle Lucio ran the plantation now, and the Lamberts lived in a fine home in

Lexington. Every time I see this old houseboat, I can hardly believe Link and his daddy lived in it for so long.

Scout looked all around the backwater pool. "This is a gorgeous spot. How long have you had the houseboat hidden here?"

Oliver, Will, Lew and I had a good laugh at that one. "Well, we call it our hidden houseboat, but it has been found quite a few times. One time, a boy named Ching Toy and his gang even moved it, across the back channel and smack up against a cliff at the base of the Parks Hills ridge over there."

We went up the old plank that led from the shore to the houseboat. Inside the place was in a shambles, but there was still the little table in the center of the room with shreds and bits of the tablecloth that I had seen many times when Link lived in the houseboat. Scattered around were the little tin dishes, cups and saucers and plates that Link and his daddy had used.

I showed Scout the little ladder in the corner, leading up to the room under the roof where there were two cots. "This was their second houseboat. The first one sank near our clubhouse, and we had it hauled up on the bank and used it for our first clubhouse. Then old Judge Granbery ordered it hauled away after Stoner's Boy had his accident in Cliff Cave. We later convinced Doc Waters to get the judge to let us use the shack in the hollow for a new clubhouse. It had been built by some college runaways, Rufe Rogers and his two pals Homer and Phil."

"What happened to Stoner's Boy in Cliff Cave?"

"He fell." I paused for a second. "He fell into the deep pit."

Scout stared at me.

"I wasn't sure if I should tell you, but I guess you need to know. Cliff Cave is a place where many bad things have happened. We are going to have to be on guard, very careful."

"What happened to Stoner's Boy?"

"He was real lucky. He landed in a deep spot in Cave River, and survived. He returned two years later, during the adventures with Simon Bleaker we were telling you about."

I was quiet for a moment, thinking about Rolling Stone John Loomis, the older brother of Shadow Loomis, who also fell into the deep pit but landed on the rocky shore of Cave River and was killed. I didn't want to say anything about that to Scout, at least not yet. "We should head back. Roy is going to wonder what happened to us."

On the way back, we swung past the stockade and log house that Harkinson and the Pelhams had built a couple of years ago, just before the coming of the Red Runners. We had many adventures around this structure, and told Scout about some of them.

"Wow!" exclaimed Scout. "The Looking Glass indeed! I feel like Alice, like I've gone through the looking glass and into this wonderland you inhabit here! The river, the island, the forests and hills, the cliffs, the caves!"

I pointed to the log house. "There's an entrance to a system of tunnels inside that log house, under a trap door."

Scout clapped her hands. "Tunnels!"

"Yes. We've been told they were originally started by river pirates. Stoner's Boy and his gang expanded the tunnels. We know of four entrances to the tunnels, including the one in this log house."[17]

"River pirate tunnels? I wonder if it was my grandfather. Maybe the treasure is hidden in a pit in these tunnels."

"Maybe. But the map you found sure looks like the main passage of Cliff Cave up near our clubhouse. However, there are many pits in this cave complex. We might have a hard time finding the right place."

We rode the horses across the back channel to the eastern shore, then up to Hobbs Ferry, and crossed the river on the ferryboat. Then we rode back to the Dobel farm, and returned the horses.

Scout went over to Roy. "That was fun! Thank you, Roy!"

Roy smiled. "You're welcome. I'm glad my mom got to meet you."

As we were crossing the hollow, we looked up on the cliffhead again. We were startled to see several figures up there, undoubtedly Mudmucks, looking down at us. One of them was looking through binoculars.

Oliver shook his head. "Just as I feared. The Mudmucks are back."

This was confirmed when we reached the clubhouse. Dick Ferris came up to me. "We had a visitor. That Mudmuck named Peralta. He delivered this for you."

It was an envelope with my name on it. I tore it open, and pulled out a note.

The boys all crowded around me. Hudson Lee leaned in to look at the note. "Read it out loud, Hawkins."

"Okay. Here's what it says. *You and your clowns have broken the treaty. You weren't allowed to get more members. Either send those five new boys away, or we will stay in the cave for as long as we please, and declare war on you. You and your clubhouse are in danger.* And it's signed *The Cincinnati Kid*. That's all."

Clay Morgan came up to me. "That right? Did the treaty say no new members?"

"No, no. I don't know what he's talking about."

"Who are the five new members? We Morgans are only four."

"He means the four of you, and Hudson Lee, who same as you just joined our Club yesterday."

Jerry took the note and read it. "Just as I said yesterday, this peace treaty wouldn't last even one day."

Stone Morgan took the note from Jerry and looked at it. "No. Let's not jump to that conclusion. Let's find out what he means, before we assume hostilities are about to resume."

Dick Ferris nodded his head. "I agree. Let's send a group up to Cliff Cave and get an explanation. We don't want any more trouble. But we need to go now – it's going to be getting dark soon, and I don't want anyone up on the cliffs at night, with those Mudmuck devils in control of the area."

Everybody wanted to go, but I insisted we keep a good contingent at the clubhouse. In the end, ten of us went up the cliff path, the four Morgans, Hudson Lee, Dick Ferris, Jerry Moore, Harold Court, Will Standish, and me. We went under a flag of truce.

When we reached the entrance to Cliff Cave, four Mudmucks were there, with three dogs. They included Peralta and Sawyer, and two other whose names I did not know, but the Cincinnati Kid was not there. Peralta had a rifle slung over his arm. I saw several more Mudmucks up on the cliffhead, looking down at us.

"We want to speak to the Cincinnati Kid!" declared Dick.

Peralta stepped forward. "He's busy. Get lost!"

I waved the note at him. "We need to speak to him. He sent me this note. It doesn't make any sense."

"We need to speak to him. He sent me this note. It doesn't make any sense."

Peralta glared at me. "Are you some kind of moron? Can't read?"

"It says we have broken the treaty because we have these five new members here", and I indicated the Morgans and Hudson Lee, "but that was not part of the treaty. We have kept our end of the deal."

"The Kid says get rid of those five new boys, or we will stay in the cave and attack you and destroy your clubhouse and drive you out of here for good!"

Scout stepped forward. "I'm a girl! Or are you and the Kid some kind of morons?"

"Makes no difference! Having a girl in your gang won't stop us!"

Hudson Lee went chest to chest with him. "Seems to me the only ones who have broken the treaty are you Mudmucks. You must have been spying around the clubhouse to know we had joined the club."

I hadn't thought of that! Hudson was right.

Hudson continued, "Seems to me you Mudmucks have four days left under the treaty. You'd be lucky that we allow the treaty to stand. Take that message back to the Cincinnati Kid, and stay in your hole and don't come out anymore!"

I thought Peralta was going to bite Hudson right in the face, he got so close, with his teeth bared. But Hudson didn't budge, he just stared him down. Finally, Peralta stepped back and hissed, "You been warned! Nobody can save you now!" With that, he rejoined his comrades, and they stood blocking the cave entrance, faces firm and hard with hatred and anger.

Dick turned to us. "Let's go." He turned back to face the Mudmucks. "You tell the Cincinnati Kid that we will abide by the treaty for four more days."

As we cautiously made our way back down the cliff path, I walked with Jerry. "Jerry, you were right, and I was wrong. These Mudmucks are completely untrustworthy, completely unpredictable. Our peace treaty had no chance of holding."

Jerry put his arm on my shoulder. "No, Hawkins. About the peace treaty, I hoped you were right, and I hoped I was wrong. But I disagree with what you just said – the Mudmucks are not unpredictable. They are very predictable – you can count on them cheating, lying, deceiving. They are the worst we have ever dealt with. We are in for it now."

Harold came up beside us. "I heard that, and I can't say I disagree. We have a chance for a fair and square fight now, twenty-one to twenty-one, but the Mudmucks will find some way to unfairly gain the advantage again."

My gut told me that Jerry and Harold were right.

When we reached the clubhouse, it was getting dark outside. Dick ordered everyone who was not staying on the riverbank to get ready to walk home together. The boys wanted to know what was going on, but Dick said he wanted them to get on their way home as quickly as possible, and that we would discuss the situation at a meeting in the morning.

We walked Shadow Loomis and Robby Hood down to our little wharf, and saw them safely off in Robby's motorboat, back to their homes in Cincinnati.

Spending the night at the clubhouse were Rube Muller, Lige Hobbs, Link Lambert, Will Standish, Hudson Lee, and me. The four Morgans were staying just outside in their tent. That meant ten of us would be here, keeping the clubhouse safe.

The other nine boys, Perry Stokes, Jerry Moore, Roy Dobel, Bill Darby, Lew Hunter, Johnny McLarren, Harold and Oliver Court, and Dick Ferris, got ready to head up the river path to home.

Dick came over to me and grasped my arm. "Hawkins, I am very worried. The Mudmucks seem intent on resuming hostilities. We need to prepare. Tomorrow morning we need to have a meeting and decide how to proceed. I am afraid we are going to have a hot time of it."

Which we did.

CHAPTER 10

FOURTH OF JULY FIREWORKS

The next day was the Fourth of July, which fell on a Saturday this year. There was a package on the clubhouse porch when we woke up this morning. It was from good old Doc Waters, and inside was the newest United States flag, this one with 48 stars. Our old flag had 46 stars. There have now been three different flags during my lifetime. The flag with 45 stars came into existence in 1896 after the admission of Utah, four years before I was born. In 1908, with the admission of the Indian Territory as the new state of Oklahoma, the flag had a 46th star added. With the admission of New Mexico and Arizona two years ago in 1912, the flag now has 48 stars. I waited until all of the other boys had arrived, to admire the new flag, and then we ran it up the flag pole.[1]

Normally we wouldn't have a meeting on a holiday, but Dick wanted to discuss our unpleasant encounter with Peralta the day before, up at the cave entrance.

Dick called the meeting to order, and briefly related the tense exchange with Peralta.

"Those were his exact words?" asked Link. "He told you 'Get rid of those five new boys, or we will attack you and destroy your clubhouse' ?"

"Close to exact," replied Dick. "And he also said 'You been warned. Nobody can save you now.'"

"Those are vile threats," observed Oliver. "We've been warned indeed. It's up to us be prepared, to be ready to protect ourselves."

Harold smiled at the bravery of his brother.

Dick nodded. "There's more. I've been informed of reports of trouble in the area."

Bill Darby had the first report. "Last night, someone broke into Spennenberg's grocery and feedstore, at the corner of Bush and Twelfth streets, just a couple blocks from my house.[2] They took a bunch of groceries, and smashed the place up real bad. Sounds like the Mudmucks to me, just a bunch of thieves and vandals."

"Do we have any reason to think the Mudmucks are involved?" asked Stone Morgan.

"Yes," replied Roy Dobel. "Last night, someone broke into our turkey pen and stole a couple of turkeys. I think the Mudmucks are getting low on supplies."

"And," added Jerry Moore, "last night someone broke into our barn and stole some of our ropes and pulleys and stuff."

Dick looked grim. "The Mudmucks seem to be getting bolder. We need to keep a close eye on the clubhouse."

I held out my hands. "What else can we do? We've got six of us sleeping in the clubhouse every night, Link Lambert, Will Standish, Rube Muller, Lige Hobbs, Hudson Lee, and me, and we've got the four Morgans in their tent right outside."

"You got any dogs?" asked Clay Morgan.

Everybody thought that was a good idea, and after the meeting some of the boys who had dogs went home to get them. Roy Dobel brought two of his farm collies, Copper and Chief. Jerry Moore brought his water spaniel Buck, and Dick Ferris brought his big German shepherd Pepper.

Dick told us to try to forget about the Mudmucks and enjoy the holiday. We had planned a day of playing baseball, or horseshoes, or going out on the river in our canoes or in the launch *Cazanova*, followed by a picnic-style supper, after which we had some fire crackers to set off. We all agreed we would remain watchful, but that we weren't going to let the Mudmucks ruin our Fourth of July.

Shadow Loomis, Robby Hood, Harold Court, Will Standish, Clay and Scout Morgan, and I went out in the *Cazanova* with Link. Clay was interested in the pilot house, and Link had him in there, showing him how things worked. First we went upstream, going slowly as Link was letting Clay take the controls.

The other boys were sitting on the back deck. I wanted to talk to Scout, so she and I sat up on the front of the boat, with our legs dangling over the prow.

"How far is it to Morning View? I've never been down that far."

"It took us most of two days, hard paddling, to get up here." Scout was watching my face intently. "You want to visit, don't you?"

I felt myself blushing. "I know you'll have to go home sometime. I just can't think that we'll never see each other again. I thought I could come down in my canoe."

"We figure that if we get a real early start, we could paddle downstream to Morning View in one long day. I don't think you could do that by yourself, just one paddler. Maybe coming by steamboat, or on the Kentucky Central railroad, would be better."

"I wouldn't want everyone to know where I'm going. Maybe I would just say I need to get away, go off camping for a few days."

"And we could come back up here sometimes. We are club members."

"Would you bring your brothers?"

Scout looked serious and arched her eyebrows. "Seckatary Hawkins, are you thinkin' what I think you're thinkin'?"

I took a deep breath, and blurted something reckless. "That I want to spend some more time alone with you, like that first night on the river in my canoe, without a bunch of other guys and your brothers around."

I felt stupid, but then she leaned over, put her hand on the back of my neck, and kissed me on the cheek. "That's sweet. You come down anytime you want, and we can do some things with just the two of us, fishing or horseback riding."

"Hey, you lovebirds!" That startled me. It was Shadow Loomis. "Link says he's going to turn downstream and get the launch flying. He wants you two to get off the prow and come around to the back deck."

As we got up, I looked at Shadow, but he seemed nonchalant about the whole thing. The three of us joined Will, Robby and Harold in chairs on the rear deck. Clay was in the pilot house with Link.

Link turned the *Cazanova* downstream, and away we went. I think the *Cazanova* could beat just about any boat on the Looking Glass. Within minutes we were passing our little wharf. Some of the boys were fishing under the willows near there, and we all waved We swung around the cliffs past the entrance to Cave River, and passed under the entrance to Cliff Cave. We looked up, but could not see the entrance, since we were close to the cliffs. We continued south, past the wreck of the *Smokey City*, Hobbs Ferry, the mouth of Banklick Creek, and then down the western main channel past Seven Willows Island. Link slowed the launch down and turned left around the lower end of the island and then up into the eastern back channel behind the island.

The channel was narrow, with lots of trees hanging over the water, or fallen in. We saw a cottonmouth snake in one of the trees, and it dropped into the water as we got near.

The channel was shallow here, and Link had to pick his way carefully around all the snags in the water. I knew where he was headed. Yep! To the backwater pool, to see his old houseboat. It was a short distance up the back channel, and then Link expertly turned left into the backwater pool and pulled up to the houseboat. Will and Robby took ropes in their hands, jumped over to the houseboat, and tied us on.

Link hesitated before stepping over. "Been a long time."

Scout and I went right behind him, and we went inside. He looked around wistfully.

"What are you thinking?" asked Scout.

Link shrugged. "Pop and I had some good times, living on the river. Simple. But that was another life, seems like ages ago.

Everything is different now, more complicated. I know it's better, got my mom back and all, but I still think about the old times." His eyes were misting up.

I patted him on the back. "You still got all us old friends, and new friends, like the Morgans."

"I know. You and me been best friends for a long time, Hawkins. It means a lot."

Scout put one hand on Link's right shoulder, and another one on my left shoulder. "I admire you two, sticking together through thick and thin, no matter what. Good friends are one of the most important things in a good life."

We each put an arm on Scout's shoulders, and just stood there for a moment. Link straightened up. "Okay. Let's go. Think I can get all the way up the back channel?"

"Nope. We were down here yesterday on horseback. Near the upper end, it was so shallow we didn't even have to hold our feet up when we crossed over to the island. River's pretty low."

"Alright. We'll go back the way we come down."

"And Link, on the way back, when we pass Cliff Cave, go way over against the Pelham shore on the east. I want to get a look at the cave entrance."

"Aye, aye, captain!"

At that we all laughed, and trooped back over to the *Cazanova*. Link eased the boat out of the backwater pool into the back channel, and we went downstream and around the south end of the island, then out into the main channel and headed upstream back north.

As we came around the last bend before the cliffs, Link slowed the launch down and steered over toward the eastern shore. We glided up to a point just opposite Cliff Cave, and Link brought the *Cazanova* to a stop.

There was quite a group of Mudmucks standing on the ledge in front of the entrance to Cliff Cave. They had their hands on their hips, or arms folded, and were looking down at us. A couple of them were looking at us with binoculars.

I pulled out dad's binoculars. "There are about ten of 'em there. I see Peralta, Cheeky, and Sawyer. No Cincinnati Kid, though."

Scout tugged playfully at the binoculars. "Let me see!" I let go, and she put them up to her eyes. The strap was still around my neck, and she pulled my head over against hers. The other fellas laughed at us.

Link got us underway again, and we crossed over to our wharf and tied up.

It was time to get ready for our Fourth of July picnic dinner. Jerry Moore had a good campfire going, and the boys were getting ready for a fish fry. They had caught a mess of good eating fish, flathead catfish, black crappie, black bass, and sauger. We had brought down all sorts of other food, pickles, strawberries, coleslaw, German potato salad, cheese and crackers, cornbread, root beer and lemonade, and baskets of cookies and pastries.

After we had finished eating, we got our box of firecrackers out and began setting them off. The dogs didn't care for that, so Roy and Dick took the four dogs over into the hollow and got them busy chasing after sticks.

Suddenly we heard two loud cracks, like big firecrackers, coming from the direction of the hollow.

"Why would they do that to those dogs?" I asked.

Perry Stokes looked puzzled. "We don't have any firecrackers that big."

"Help!!" came screaming from the hollow. It was Roy Dobel!

We all ran over into the hollow, and came upon a shocking scene. Two of the dogs lay dead. It was one of Roy's collies, Chief, and Jerry's water spaniel Buck.

"What happened?" I yelled.

Roy turned Chief over. "Look, he's been shot, right in the head." Roy was choking back sobs.

"The same with Buck," called Dick. "We heard two shots, thought you guys had tossed some big firecrackers at us. This had to be the Mudmucks."

Jerry Moore cradled Buck in his arms. He glanced at me, and the smoldering look in his eyes would have even set Peralta back.

Stone Morgan looked grim. "This is terrible. Does this sort of thing happen a lot around here?"

"No, of course not," I responded. "We did have a gang here once, stealing dogs. Their leader was named Stormie Petry. They did kill two dogs.[3] That gang had some bad actors, but Stormie and some of the others reformed and we ended up on peaceful terms. But these Mudmucks, I don't think there's a single one of 'em with a shred of decency."

Clay Morgan came over. "Let's get these other dogs into the clubhouse."

I motioned for some of the boys to do that. "And you other guys, let's get these two dogs buried."

Most of the boys headed back to the clubhouse, while the rest of us considered where to bury the two dogs.

"Fire! Help!" came shouting from over at the clubhouse.

We tore over there. I was shocked to see smoke churning up from one side of the clubhouse. Most of the other boys were there, struggling with something. Then I saw that the Morgan tent had collapsed, too. Some of the boys ran over there.

I dashed up to the clubhouse, and saw that the fire was confined to a large pile of dead grass that had been piled near the side of the shack. The boys were using sticks to drag the burning grass away from the clubhouse, and they were stamping on it to put the fire out. Mostly there was just a lot of smoke.

I turned to the collapsed tent. "What happened?"

Stone Morgan shook his head. "Don't know. It was folding in on itself as we came up here with the dogs, and then we saw the fire."

Johnny McLarren was walking around the tent. "Some of the stakes have been pulled up, and the interior poles kicked down."

We got busy getting the tent set back up and secured. There was no serious damage inside the tent.

"Sir!" called Perry Stokes from the porch. "There's an envelope tacked to the door!"

"Good night!" exclaimed Will. He turned to Harold. "Exciting enough for you?"

Harold nodded as he yanked the envelope off the door. "I think this is addressed to Scout."

"What do you mean?" I asked as he handed the envelope to me. It was addressed to *That moron girl*. That made me mad.

Scout and her brothers came over. "Is it addressed to me?" she asked.

I hesitated, and then handed her the envelope. She looked at it and snorted indignantly. "We're gonna get these creeps." She tore the envelope open and read the note. She looked defiant.

I admired her determination. "Read it out loud, Scout."

"Okay. Here's what it says. *Hey moron girl. You have joined the biggest bunch of clowns from St. Louis to New Orleans. I wrote this ahead of time, knowing you morons would all run off from your clubhouse when we shot the dogs. Then we set the little fire and knocked your tent down. That was just to show you what we could do, how much worse this could have been. This is our last warning. You and the other four new boys must go away from here, and Hawkins and his band of clowns must go home and stay away. If not, we will return in the dead of night sometime and burn down your clubhouse and tent. I am dead serious. This is your last warning.* It's signed *The Cincinnati Kid*."

Dick Ferris shook his head. "What is going on? Why have the Mudmucks broken the treaty, and attacked us again, down here, nowhere near the cave? And threatening to attack again and try to burn us out. What has gone so terribly wrong?

I thought for a long time. "That's a good question. No point in us going up there to ask them – they won't say anything. I know it's a bit risky, but we need to send a patrol into Cliff Cave, to try to get an idea of what in tarnation is going on in there. In through the back entrance, just to the ledge, and spy on their camp – see what is going on."

Roy Dobel raised his hand. "I'll go. I have to lead the way."

Scout jumped at the chance. "Me, too!"

I made a cutting motion with my hand. "No!"

"Why not? Because I'm a girl?"

"No. You haven't been in the cave yet. I told you it's a dangerous place. It's not time yet for you to go in."

She put her hands on her hips, pursed her lips, but didn't say anything more.

I turned to the other boys. "Who wants to go with Roy?" The fellows looked uneasy. "Listen, you're just going in the back entrance, to the ledge that overlooks the Mudmuck camp. No further than that. Nobody will even see you."

Scout was stubborn. "Then why can't I go?"

"No! I'm in charge of this sort of thing. My answer is no, and that's final!"

She threw up her hands, spun around, and stalked off. Cliff and Stone went after her.

Lew Hunter and Lige Hobbs volunteered, giving us the three we needed for the scouting party. They set off immediately, the long way around the hollow so as not to be seen from the cliffs.

Cliff and Stone were talking to Scout. I walked over to them. "Scout, I'm sorry I was sharp with you. I just don't want you in the cave yet, until we clear out the Mudmucks."

"It's okay, Hawkins. I'm just always an impatient person."

Stone laughed. "That's an understatement!"

I shook my head. "This is no laughing matter. Listen, I told you lots of bad things have happened in Cliff Cave. You remember when I told you about Stoner's Boy, who fell into the deep pit? He landed in Cave River, which is real deep there, and he survived. But Shadow Loomis had an older brother, John Loomis, who wasn't so lucky. When Pooley got hold of the bags of gold coins that belonged to him, he hid them in Cliff Cave, on the other side of the deep pit. John Loomis was guarding them, but he slipped and fell into the deep pit. He landed on the rocks along Cave River and was killed. We saw the whole thing."[4]

Scout sucked in her breath. "That's horrible! Poor Shadow!"

"That's the kind of thing I've been warning you about, and why I don't want you to go into Cliff Cave until the Mudmucks clear out of there."

Dick called everyone into the clubhouse. Perry Stokes stood by the door with Larry King's rifle. We talked about what else we could do, but agreed that we needed to wait and see what Roy, Lew and Lige saw in the cave.

It was taking a long time. The sun set, and it was getting dark. I began to get nervous.

"Here comes somebody!" called Perry from the door. We crowded over to the door and the front windows. It was Peralta, carrying a white flag.

"We should just take him," muttered Jerry.

Dick shook his head. "We can't. We need to maintain some line of communication with these goons. Hawkins, you talk to him."

I stepped onto the porch. Peralta was at the bottom of the steps. "Why did you kill two of our dogs?"

Peralta had a bad look. "You killed the Kid's dog. You had it comin'. Plus, we warned you, things would get ugly around here if you didn't get rid of those new guys. Here!"

He thrust out his hand, with an envelope. I grasped the porch post and leaned out to take it, like I was reaching gingerly into a steel trap. Peralta laughed, a rough crow laugh, and walked away.

I opened the envelope, and pulled out a note. I read it, and gasped. I staggered a bit, and felt faint.

"What is it?" Dick Ferris pulled me back into the clubhouse. "Read it out loud, Hawkins."

"I can't. Here, you . . ."

Dick took the note, and read it. He swallowed hard. "This is unbelievable. Here's what's written here. *You guys are the biggest bunch of clowns we have ever dealt with. You think we didn't find your secret way into the cave? You couldn't have left a more obvious trail. We have a bloodhound, and you left your bloody pawprints all the way from the jail door, up to the ledge, and out of the cave. We have been waiting for you. We caught your three spies, and have them in a new place you'll never find. There is worse yet to come if you don't get rid of those new guys, and the rest of you stay away from this riverbank.* It's signed by you know who. Fellas, Roy Dobel, Lew Hunter, and Lige Hobbs have been captured by the Mudmucks."

"Oh, man." Jerry Moore was holding his head. "We're down to eighteen now."

Everyone was talking. "What are we going to do?" asked a bunch of the boys.

Most of the boys were looking at Dick, who looked at me. "What's the answer to that question, Hawkins? You sent Roy and Lew and Lige on this mission, and it was a disaster."

I took a deep breath. "The truth is, we are in big trouble. They outnumber us twenty-one to eighteen. They have all three entrances guarded. We need some serious reinforcements, and I don't see where they're coming from. Unless someone has a better idea, I think tomorrow morning we go up there and make a deal to get our boys released. It will probably mean we'll have to clear out of here for as long as they want. I think we're whipped. Down to eighteen, we can't beat them."

"What?" blurted out Jerry Moore. "We're just going to go home? And leave our friends captives?"

Dick frowned at him. "I am not putting anyone in danger. Going up the cliff path is dangerous at night, and we might walk into a trap, or get captured. Imagine if someone fell off the cliff. It's fifty feet to the river, and they could land on rocks. No, I'm not allowing any risks like that."

There was a lot of grumbling and angry muttering, but nobody had any other suggestions.

"Look, fellas," I sighed. "Let's sleep on it. Maybe somebody will think of something."

Dick looked out the window again. "Everyone who isn't staying here needs to get going. It won't be safe after dark. Plus, we've lost Lige Hobbs who was staying here in the clubhouse every night. Johnny, I have a special mission for you. Jerry, you go with him in case there's any trouble."

Jerry objected. "I want to stay here and stand by you guys in the fight that's sure to come tonight."

Dick shook his head. "I need you to go with Johnny – it's getting dark, and you might encounter a Mudmuck scouting party. I need you two to deliver some messages. First, stop by my house and tell my folks I'm spending the night here. And then go by the preacher's house, and tell him Lew is staying down by the river for the night.

Then I want you to go to Dobel's and tell them the same thing about Roy."

Johnny and Jerry nodded. Bill Darby and Perry Stokes volunteered to go with them, safety in numbers. What a great bunch of guys. They began to file out, to head up the river path to the pike.

Harold Court turned to his twin brother Oliver. "Tell mom and dad that I'm staying here tonight." Oliver nodded, grasped his brother's hand, then sped out to catch up with the other guys.

Shadow and Robby were talking in low voices, then Shadow came over to me. "We're going to use your telephone to call our homes, and let our folks know we're spending the night here." They both lived up in Cincinnati.

There we were, Dick Ferris, Shadow Loomis, Robby Hood, Link Lambert, Harold Court, Will Standish, Rube Muller, Hudson Lee, Clay Morgan, Stone Morgan, Cliff Morgan, Scout Morgan, and me, along with two dogs. Even so, I began to get real jittery. Then my stomach jumped into my throat, as I realized there were thirteen of us spending the night here. What would Jerry Moore think?

"Okay," sang out Dick, trying to sound cheery. "Let's get organized. We're probably going to have a long night."

Which we did.

CHAPTER II

ESCALATION

Everyone else had gone home. Left in the clubhouse were a lucky thirteen of us – Dick Ferris, Shadow Loomis, Robby Hood, Link Lambert, Harold Court, Will Standish, Rube Muller, Hudson Lee, Clay Morgan, Stone Morgan, Cliff Morgan, Scout Morgan, and me, along with two dogs, the collie Copper belonging to Roy Dobel, and the big German shepherd Pepper belonging to Dick Ferris.

We gathered around the long pine table. Pepper and Copper sat on the floor next to Dick.

I spoke first. "I am sure we are going to be attacked tonight. Just a feeling I have."

Clay Morgan looked thoughtful. "These Mudmucks seem to have no bounds. Plus, we will probably be seriously outnumbered, even if they keep some back in the cave as guards."

Dick Ferris sighed. "We need to stand our ground here, and defend the clubhouse. Otherwise, we may as well go home. Hawkins, you have a plan?"

"Yes. We need to hang some lanterns outside, around the clubhouse and the tent. Lights on, dogs outside. We need to show them that we are on alert. Sunrise is in about eight hours. We'll post watches, three of us on two hour shifts. Sleep with your boots on. No way I can get to sleep right now, so I'll take the first shift. Scout and Shadow, want to join me? Yes? Okay, the rest of you try to get some sleep."

I assigned the next three shifts, and those guys turned in. We took oil lamps outside, turned up high, and hung them in the trees around the clubhouse and the tent. Then Scout, Shadow and I sat on the clubhouse steps. I was holding Larry King's rifle. We had Pepper and Copper on the porch behind us.

"What's a-matter, Seck?" asked Scout. My legs were shaking, almost drumming on the steps.

"I just can't calm down."

Just then the bells up at St. Joseph's chimed out ten o'clock.[1] "We'll stay on until midnight."

A twig snapped, and all three of us nearly jumped out of our skins. It was Stone Morgan, coming out of their tent. "I can't sleep at all. May as well sit with you guys for a bit."

We were talking in low voices, when both dogs stood up and growled. The hair on the back of my neck was standing up.

The dogs were looking across the river path, toward the shrubs that lined the path.

"Something there," muttered Shadow.

"Where?" Then I saw. Our lanterns threw a pretty feeble light that far away, but I could make out several black shapes standing among the shrubs. They raised up long objects. Rifles! Then, crack, crack, crack! – came shot after shot. The lanterns exploded and the flaming oil spilled onto the ground. Our dogs were barking furiously, but the black shapes were gone.

Everyone else came spilling out of the clubhouse and tent. "What's happening?" "Are we under attack?"

"Let the oil burn out," I directed. "We need another source of bright light."

"A bonfire!" declared Clay Morgan.

"Everyone gather firewood!" ordered Dick Ferris.

Soon we had a blazing bonfire, with a big pile of firewood nearby. The others went back inside, and we resumed our watch. The bells chimed eleven.

The dogs started growling again. Stone, Shadow, Scout and I stood up. Something whizzed past us and crashed against the front of the clubhouse. I turned and saw a green walnut rolling across the porch. Then came another, and another, coming so hard I figured they were being fired by slingshots.

Scout was standing on the porch. Most of the walnuts seemed to be aimed at her. A walnut smashed one of the front windows. That brought everybody outside again. Then a walnut hit Scout in the stomach, and she went down on her knees in agony.

That made me mad as a hornet. "Let's get those guys!"

"There they are, behind those trees!" yelled Stone. "Let's get 'em!"

We rushed forward toward the trees. The dogs ran with us, barking and snapping. A few more walnuts were fired, then the attackers disappeared.

Hudson Lee was shaking his head. "We'll never get any sleep tonight."

I went over to Scout. "Are you okay?"

"Yeah. Gonna have a beaut of a bruise, I think." She pulled her shirt up, revealing a nasty red welt on her stomach.

Boy, that made me angry! "Those cowards! Why don't they come out of the shadows, and fight fair and square?"

Robby Hood came over. "I don't think that's going to happen. But we haven't seen the last of them tonight, either. Their pattern, these brief attacks, probably by just a few Mudmucks, seems designed to wear us down."

I took a deep breath. "Like they're planning something major later tonight."

"Maybe. Let's change shifts, you guys need a break."

Shadow and I went inside the clubhouse, and Scout went into their tent.

I laid awake. I heard the bells chime midnight, then one AM, then two AM. I heard the shifts changing. I thought I was still awake when the boys were shouting an alarm again.

Groggily, I stumbled across the meeting room. There was a bright light outside and a lot of yelling. I looked out a side window. The Morgan tent was on fire!

Outside a great struggle was underway. There must have been at least twelve Mudmucks, and several of their dogs. They were all grappling with our boys, and the dogs were barking and lunging. Our two dogs were in the thick of it, too. It was a surreal scene, in the bright glow of the flaming tent. I stood for a moment, trying to take it in. The Mudmuck calling himself Sawyer seemed to be in charge. One thing I noticed was that the Cincinnati Kid and Peralta were not present. I was alarmed, however, when I didn't see Scout, either.

I hustled down the steps and headed toward the tent, to see if Scout and her brothers were safe, but a Mudmuck came up behind me and clobbered me on the side of the head. I staggered, then turned and put all the steam I could muster into a right punch on the side of his jaw. He fell, and I turned back toward the tent. It was in full flame, and beginning to collapse.

Then I saw down closer to the river that Scout had pinned a Mudmuck on the ground, and she was holding him there. Our other boys were standing their ground, too, and we seemed to be battling the Mudmucks to a standoff.

I paused. The thought occurred to me that if we could capture a few of these hooligans, we could negotiate an exchange for Roy Dobel, Lew Hunter, and Lige Hobbs.

Wishful thinking! For just then, the tide turned against us in a very bad way.

"Oh, no!" "Look out!" yelled several of our boys. They had turned and were pointing back toward our clubhouse. I turned and gasped! There was a group of about six or seven Mudmucks there, furiously piling burning brush against the clubhouse. The flames were shooting high!

"Let's get em'!" I yelled, and charged over into this new group of Mudmucks. One of 'em kicked me in the leg, and I stumbled. As I fell, the brute kicked me again, this time in my ribs. That knocked the breath out of me, and for a moment I could only get up on my hands and knees.

I saw Shadow, Robby, Harold, Hudson, and Clay break off from the main fight and rush over, wrestling with the Mudmucks. I staggered to my feet, and kicked the burning branches off the side of the clubhouse.

"Alright!" I yelled. "The fire is off the clubhouse!"

The six of us regrouped and stood between the clubhouse and the Mudmucks facing us. The pile of burning brush was behind us. We had to keep the Mudmucks from pushing that fire back against the shack. There were eight of them, including Cheeky. We were outnumbered. They were poised and tense, and slowly began to advance on us.

"Look!" I hissed, and pointed. The other fight on the riverbank was not going well for us. Our guys down there, Dick, Link, Will, Rube, Stone, and Cliff were badly outnumbered, being swarmed upon by at least ten Mudmucks. I didn't see Scout at all!

It was a terrible moment for me. I hesitated – my choice was between protecting the clubhouse, and protecting Scout. Then I remembered the glance Mom had given me the other day.

"Where's Scout?" I yelled. I began to run down toward where I had last seen her, but that thug Cheeky had his club and swung it at my head as I passed him. I ducked and dodged, but still the club caught me on the shoulder and spun me around. I fell backwards, but jumped back up and began running toward the riverbank.

I got to the spot where I had seen Scout holding down one of the Mudmucks. There was nobody there. I looked around desperately, but saw nothing.

"Hawkins!" It was Dick Ferris. "Help us!"

The ten Mudmucks there had Dick, Link, Will, Rube, Stone, and Cliff down on the ground, and were giving them a bad thrashing.

I felt like I was being torn in two. I wanted to look for Scout, but didn't even know where to start, and my other friends were in need. I choked back a mixture of panic and rage. What could I do against so many? I picked up a stout branch. I hated to use such a weapon, but we were getting a real drubbing.

"Let's get 'em!" came a great shout from up the river path. It was Jerry Moore! And he was leading Johnny McLarren, Bill Darby, and Oliver Court.

They charged into the group holding Dick and our other boys. I threw aside the branch, ran over and joined in the melee. The Mudmuck dogs began tearing at us.

Crack! – came a rifle shot from the clubhouse porch. It was Perry Stokes, with Larry King's rifle. He began firing round after round into the ground at the base of the steps. The Mudmuck dogs howled in fear and ran off.

The Mudmucks pulled back. I saw Sawyer cup his hands to his lips. "Cheeky! Pull back!"

Up at the other fight on the side of the clubhouse, Cheeky pulled his boys back. He shouted at Sawyer, "Are we finished?"

"Yes!" came a shout from the riverbank. It was Peralta! "Back to the cave!"

The Mudmucks ran toward the cliff path. Jerry Moore led a bunch of our guys on a hot pursuit, and they got in a few good licks, then broke off and came back to the clubhouse.

Jerry came up to me. "Clubhouse safe?"

"Yes. Some of the wood scorched on that one side, but that's all. What are you doing here?"

"I couldn't sleep at all. I finally gave up and went around to the other guy's houses. They were ready to go, too, and they slipped out and we came down here."

"What time is it?"

"About four thirty. It'll be getting light soon."

I went over to Dick Ferris. "Did you see what happened to Scout?"

He hesitated. "Yes. Peralta and another big Mudmuck came out of nowhere, and grabbed her. The big Mudmuck ape threw her over his shoulder and ran up the cliff path with her. I'm sorry, Hawkins, but we were outnumbered. We couldn't help her."

Shadow joined us. "I heard that. I think that was their plan all along, to get Scout. They created a diversion with the attempt to set fire to the clubhouse. That forced us to divide our forces, and that gave them the upper hand down by the river. That's how they got Scout."

"This is terrible." I wobbled over to the steps and sat down. Shadow came over and sat down next to me.

"Take it easy, Seck."

"I can't. We need to do something. We can't just sit around. We need to go in Cliff Cave and get Scout back. We have to!"

Shadow looked worried. "You're not talking sense, Seck. You know we can't do that."

I put my head in my hands, and spoke quietly. "Shadow, I have to try. I think I'm in . . . I think I'm in love with Samantha Morgan."

He put his arms around me. "That's obvious to everyone. What you must do now, to help her, is get past your feelings, and think. Think, man! You are the smartest guy around here!"

"I'll try. I need a moment to pull myself together."

Cliff Morgan was standing behind us. "Shadow, I need to talk to you." Shadow got up, and they moved off a distance. I couldn't hear what they were talking about.

I looked up and saw Link walking around the smoldering ruins of the Morgan tent. Clay Morgan joined him, and they were talking in low voices. Clay had a very worried look on his face, but one set with grim determination.

"Alright!" called Dick Ferris. "Everyone inside for an emergency meeting!"

I got up from the steps, to let the fellas standing there get by, and I went into the clubhouse with them. Some of the other boys were still outside, talking about the events of this terrible night.

"Come on," I heard Hudson Lee call. "Captain wants a meeting."

The other boys trickled in slowly, and we gathered around the long pine table. It was a somber group for sure.

Dick rapped the table with his wooden hammer. "It appears that Scout has been taken captive by the Mudmucks. Add her to our three members taken yesterday, Roy, Lew and Lige, and we're down to seventeen."

I was casting about the room with my eyes. "Where are Link and Clay?"

Nobody knew. We went back outside, but they were nowhere to be found.

Johnny McLarren shook his head. "Who was the last person to see them?"

The question shocked me. "I was! It was right before Dick called us into the meeting. They were down there, by the ashes of the Morgan tent. As we started inside, they were still standing there, talking. Good night, Dick! – what if they . . ." I couldn't finish my question.

Dick finished it. "What if some Mudmucks had snuck back and when we all went inside, they grabbed them?"

Harold Court looked defeated. "I don't mind fighting them, but now we're down to fifteen. We don't stand a chance."

Dick put his hand on my shoulder. "Hawkins?"

I thought for a long time. "We have to get our six friends, Roy, Lew, Lige, Scout, Link and Clay, out of the hands of the Mudmucks. We saw the terrible way they treated Link and Will. With just fifteen of us, and the Mudmucks in control of all three entrances into the cave, and we don't even know where they might be holding the captives, there is no way we can mount a rescue mission. I'm sorry, fellas, but I think as soon as the sun comes up, we go up the cliff path and negotiate a new peace treaty. We can offer them more time in the cave, in exchange for them releasing our six friends."

There was some half-hearted arguing, but everyone knew we had no other choice.

Shortly after sunrise, we sent a group up the cliff path under a flag of truce, comprised of Dick Ferris, Shadow Loomis, Robby Hood, Hudson Lee, Stone Morgan, Cliff Morgan, and me. When we reached the entrance to Cliff Cave, Peralta was standing there with a rifle in his hands.

He pointed the rifle at us. "Stay back, or I'll shoot. I swear I will."

Dick Ferris held out his hands. "We want to talk to the Cincinnati Kid, to negotiate a new peace treaty."

Peralta gave a short, nasty laugh. "We'll send orders down soon. Now git!"

We tried to reason with him, but he just kept threatening us, and steadfastly refused to bring the Cincinnati Kid out to talk to us. We finally gave up and went back down the cliff path.

As we neared the bottom of the cliff path, Perry Stokes came running up to us. "The *Cazanova* is gone! Maybe that's where Link and Clay are!" That got everyone excited.

I waved my hands. "But what if the Mudmucks stole it?" That made everyone gloomy again.

Dick Ferris looked hard at me. "Hawkins, I've known you a long time, and I've never seen you so pessimistic."

"I know, Dick, I know. I just can't think straight. Let's get back to the clubhouse." We resumed walking over that way.

Shadow walked with Dick and me. "He's worried about Scout, Dick."

Dick turned to me and raised his eyebrows. "Ah, I see. Well, Hawkins, everyone is worried about Scout. And don't forget our other guys the Mudmucks have captured – we need to help all of them. You got to start thinking with your brain, or I'm gonna relieve you of your position as chief of our town's Junior Police."

We walked into the clubhouse. I tried to think. "Give everyone something to do. The Morgans need help. Get our summer camp tent, and other supplies. Send some of the boys into town to buy whatever other things the Morgans need. Get other boys up to the hardware store to get a new window pane and get that window fixed. And have 'em buy some more oil lamps to replace ours that got shot up, and some more flashlights."

Dick nodded. "Alright. Give me a hand here."

Dick and I pried up the loose floorboard, and we got out the old tin box where we kept our dues. We counted out what we thought would cover the purchases we needed.

Dick got the boys hopping, and by late morning we had the Morgans all set up in our tent, our broken window repaired, all new oil lamps, and several more flashlights.

Perry Stokes remained vigilant, watching the area around the clubhouse, clutching Larry King's rifle in his arms. "A Mudmuck approaching! Peralta again! Under a white flag!"

Jerry grabbed my arm. "Can I knock him down now?"

"No! We must maintain some form of communication."

Peralta approached me with an envelope. I nodded to him and took it. He turned and sped away.

There were two objects inside the envelope, a note and something else. I read the note and felt like I was going to get sick. I handed it to Dick Ferris.

He read it, and turned to the boys. "I'll read it. *We got the girl. Here is a lock of her hair. If you clowns don't do as we say by noon, and get rid of those new guys and get off the riverbank, we will shave her head. If you don't do as we say by sundown, we will cut off her ears. We will not release the captives until our work in the cave is done.* It's signed by you know who." Dick held up the other object in the envelope, a lock of hair tied up with a string. He turned to Cliff and Stone. "Is this Scout's hair?"

Stone took the clump of hair. "What difference does it make? We know they got her. Yeah, this looks like her hair, but what are we going to do? He's threatening to cut her ears off!"

We convened a meeting in the clubhouse. Cliff and Stone Morgan excused themselves, and stepped back into my writing room. I knew they were worried about their sister Samantha and their brother Clayton.

We had a vigorous discussion about if we should surrender to the Mudmucks, get Scout, Roy, Lew, Lige, Link and Clay released in exchange for the Morgans and Hudson Lee leaving the area, and the rest of us pulling back from the clubhouse and riverbank. A lot of the boys, including me, hated the very thought.

"But what else can we do?" asked Oliver Court.

Everyone turned to me. "Don't look at me. With six held captive, there are only fifteen of us here now. We can't go up against the Mudmucks without some serious reinforcements."

Just at that moment there was a knock at the door. Before I could say anything, Perry Stokes sprang over and yanked open the door. "Ah! Come in."

In walked one of the most striking figures I had ever seen. It was a tall colored boy. He stopped just inside the door and surveyed the room. Although dressed in the plain clothes of a working man, he was very handsome. But what was most striking about him were his arms, bulging with muscles that made his arms bigger around than my legs.

There was a stunned silence in the clubhouse. The colored boy finally broke it: "Which one of you is Seckatary Hawkins?"

I stood up. "That's me. I am Seckatary Hawkins."

He smiled and walked around the table to where I stood and extended his hand. I shook his hand, and noticed what a firm grip he had. "I am honored to meet you, Seckatary Hawkins. My name is . . ."

At that moment, Cliff Morgan stepped out of my writing room, and gasped. "Mercury Ferguson!" He rushed over and grasped his hand. "You are most welcome!"

Stone Morgan came into the room, and he grabbed the colored boy and hugged him.

My head was swimming a bit. "What is going on?"

Cliff turned to me. "This is fantastic. This is Mercury, one of the Fergusons you have heard about." He turned back to Mercury. "What are you doing here?"

"Well, real early this morning, your brother Clay and somebody named Lincoln Lambert arrived at the Morning View wharf with a powerful launch. Clay came up to the distillery and explained that Scout was in bad trouble."

"Hold on." I held up my hands. "We can't get you involved in this. This is our problem."

Mercury smiled at me. "Seckatary Hawkins, Scout Morgan saved my family. We are indebted to her forever. We are here to make a little payment on that debt. We will do whatever it takes to get her out of trouble."

I stepped back.

Cliff grasped the hand of Mercury Ferguson. "You mean you're not alone?"

Mercury closed his eyes, took a deep breath, shook his head and smiled. "When we told Mr. Brookie what had happened to Scout, he closed the whole barrelhouse operation and said anyone who wanted could come up here, and for us to get Scout. Every single boy in the barrelhouse volunteered for that. We came up here at full speed in that launch of Lincoln Lambert."

Cliff looked worried. "Do my folks know?"

"No, of course not. Mr. Brookie promised he would keep it quiet, but he ordered us to get Scout out today. That's what we're here to do. The others are outside."

We stepped out onto the porch. There was a huge group of boys out there, some of them even bigger and more muscled than Mercury. I saw standing off behind them Clay and Link, who smiled and nodded to me.

Jerry Moore was standing next to me. "We need to sign 'em up as club members."

I turned to Jerry in amazement. "About half of them are colored."

Jerry grabbed my arm and squeezed it until it hurt. "Shut your mouth! Makes no difference. They are here to help Scout, and Roy, and Lew, and Lige. Cliff and Stone and Clay know 'em, and have vouched for 'em. Sign 'em up!"

Dick Ferris came out. "We need to vote on that."

The vote was unanimous in favor, and we added to the club membership rolls the following names:

Fourteen white boys, Russel Railey, Jesse Venable, Hurst Early, Lankford Burns, Cotton Darnell, Buford Broadhead, Thornton "Bull" Frazier, Rowland Bismarck, Nimrod Ledridge, Isaac Nuckols, Jinks Gore, Woodford Parrish, Noah Gastineau, and Stewart Kidd.

And ten colored boys, Mercury Ferguson, the identical twins Romulus Ferguson and Remus Ferguson, Elijah Craig, Trot Rice, Luther Deadmon, Alford Lumpkins, Anderson Taylor, Sanford Washington, and Volentine Umphansaw.[2]

I pulled Lankford Burns aside. "We know a boy across the river, in a little village called Pelham, named Dave Burns."

"Yep, he's my cousin."

"Dave Burns is your cousin?" I motioned for Dick Ferris. "This is Lankford Burns, a cousin of Dave Burns."

Dick caught my meaning immediately. "We will go over to

Pelham and reason with them. They have a dog in this fight now." Dick and Lankford took off, down to our landing and into a canoe to cross the river.

Shadow Loomis smacked me on the back. "Atta boy, Seck! That's using your noggin!"

I told all our fellas to pick out two or three of the distillery boys, and explain the lay of the land around here, particularly pointing out the cliff and cave complex, and tell them all about what had been going on for the past week with the Mudmucks.

I chose Mercury Ferguson and Cotton Darnell. From the porch of the clubhouse, I pointed out the cliffhead. "Up there is the main entrance to Cliff Cave. That's where they're holding Scout, and three other of our members who the Mudmucks captured yesterday."

Mercury nodded. "We heard that they had other prisoners, besides Scout. We'll get them all out of there!"

"Yep," agreed Cotton. "We're gonna rescue everyone, and right this morning! What'll you want to do with the Mudmucks?"

"Well, they've committed a lot of crimes," I explained, as we went back into the clubhouse and sat down. I filled them in on the events that had transpired since the arrival of the Mudmucks on our riverbank. "We need to flush them out of the cave, that's for sure."

Mercury smiled. "I'm looking forward to that!"

"Not so fast, Mercury. They are violent and nasty and don't fight fair."

"They'll be sorry when we're done with them!"

"Well, I'm trying to figure out, with all these guys we have now, how we can pull this off without another bloody fight. If we are successful, I just want the Mudmucks to go back to Cincinnati and never come back."

Suddenly, Perry Stokes called out from the porch. "Pelham flatboats coming across the river!"

We went out to meet the Pelhams. Dick and Lankford led Briggen and the Pelhams up to the clubhouse.

There were eleven Pelhams present: Briggen Crockett, Hamill "Ham" Gardner, Dave Burns, Timothy "Little Tim" Mundy, Jake

Grubbs, Newton "Booby" Warren, Steve Lanigan, Jouet Curd, Bell McConnell, Miller Miguer, and Patrick Flinn.[3]

I counted our forces. We had been up to twenty-one Club members, but with Scout, Roy, Lew and Lige captives of the Mudmucks, we were down to seventeen. Add to that the twenty-four new boys from the distillery, and we had forty-one Club members. Then add to that the eleven Pelhams, and we had fifty-two boys on hand.

Briggen came up to me. "Understand those mudcreeps have kidnapped a girl. We ain't gonna stand for that sort of thing. We are here to help you finally drive them away."

"It's Samantha Morgan from Morning View they've kidnapped."

"I know, Dick Ferris told us. Lankford Burns is her friend, and he's a cousin of Dave Burns, so we got that connection. We're all friends of Samantha Morgan."

I shook Briggen's hand. "We'll never forget this. I have to tell you, it's gonna be dangerous and lots of us could get hurt."

Briggen grinned. "Not as bad as we're gonna hurt the mud boys."

Dick Ferris frowned. "I don't want any more violent battles, if we can help it. We have might, and right, on our side. There must be a way to end this today, right now, with all the guys we have."

I knew Dick was right. We had sent our boys up against the Mudmucks too many times, and suffered the consequences. I didn't want to send all these new boys, especially the distillery boys we had just met, to the same fate. I was racking my brain for a solution. The large group of boys gathered around me was dead quiet, except for the nervous shifting of feet.

Shadow Loomis broke the silence. "What's the plan, Seck?"

Everybody was looking at me.

"Hold on a minute." An idea had been forming in my head, a possible trick we could employ to surprise the Mudmucks and get into the main entrance to Cliff Cave without a bloody brawl. It would take a carefully choreographed dance of deception, leading to a split second of shock when the Mudmucks just might drop their guard.

I called into my writing room the three sets of identical twins, Harold and Oliver Court, Stone and Cliff Morgan, and Romulus and Remus Ferguson. I spoke quietly to them, and then scribbled out a note and walked back outside and handed it to Bill Darby. He looked at the note in surprise.

"Buying more flashlights I understand. But what do you need all this other stuff for?"

"Just run uptown and get it. Take someone with you, to help carry everything."

Bill grabbed Johnny McLarren, and they took off at a run. I turned to the others.

"Alright. We're going to split up into four groups. The biggest group is going to go in the main entrance to Cliff Cave. I want each of the other three groups to have ten boys, ready to deal with up to five Mudmucks. First, we need to capture the high ground. There will probably be about four or five Mudmucks on the cliffhead, watching for us and ready to rain rocks down on us. Robby, I want you to pick out nine more guys, and go up there the back way, you know, up the Steps to Heaven, through the Big Arch, and onto the cliffhead.[4] Take some rope. Capture those Mudmucks, and tie 'em up good. Take Stoner's old brass horn, and signal us when you have secured the high ground."

Shadow was smiling at me.

"Next, Johnny, you pick out nine more guys, and wait outside the back entrance to Cliff Cave. When you hear the horn, go in. There will probably be about four or five Mudmucks waiting in there to ambush you. You have to capture them, and tie them up."

"Aye, aye, Seck."

"And Dick, same thing, pick nine more guys and wait in canoes by the entrance to Cave River. When the horn is sounded, go in to Table Rock and up the slab stone steps. You will probably be ambushed by four or five Mudmucks. Capture 'em and tie 'em up."

"With pleasure."

I looked around at everyone. "Get this straight. I want all three entrances to Cliff Cave seized and guarded. I don't want any

Mudmucks to escape. That's why I'm sending such large teams in each entrance. I want those exits closed and watched."

Everyone nodded.

I swallowed hard. "That leaves nineteen of us for the most dangerous part. We are going directly into the main entrance to Cliff Cave, and resistance there will be stiff. Peralta will be there with his rifle. We cannot take a chance with that. We will need to distract him and grab that rifle, before he has a chance to even think of firing the dern thing."

Mercury Ferguson laid his hand on my shoulder and locked intently at me. "I don't care who else goes where, Seckatary Hawkins, but I'm going with you into the main entrance."

Several others volunteered to join Mercury and me, thus I had Shadow Loomis, Will Standish, Link Lambert, Jerry Moore, Perry Stokes, Rube Muller, Hudson Lee, Clay Morgan, Russel Railey, Bull Frazier (the biggest of the distillery boys), Mercury Ferguson, Elijah Craig, and Luther Deadmon (another fearsome-looking distillery boy), and two Pelhams, their leader Briggen Crockett, and Steve Lanigan, in my group.

Robby Hood looked puzzled. "We have fifty-two boys, but your four groups only add up to forty-nine. And you only got sixteen in your group, not nineteen. You're missing six boys."

I nodded. "That's right. I need three of the remaining boys to go on a special mission that could very well be the key to this whole thing ending quickly and without a big brawl where a bunch of us get hurt. And the last three remaining boys will be in my group. Just wait and see."

Shadow Loomis came over to me. "This is the old Seck I know. Good job."

Bill and Johnny returned with their packages. We had enough flashlights now for everyone. I pulled all the twins back into my writing room, and explained what they were going to do. After they were ready, Oliver Court, Cliff Morgan, and Remus Ferguson set off alone, up the cliff path.

"Why are they going up there?" asked Dick Ferris. "They'll be captured!" Then he saw Harold Court, Stone Morgan, and Romulus

Ferguson come out of my writing room. "Hawkins, what in dickens are you up to this time?"

I quickly explained my plan. There were approving nods, and some of the boys even smiled a little.

I turned to the other three twins. "Harold, Stone, and Romulus, you are in my group. With any luck, this might work."

The four groups were organized, and standing in front of the clubhouse. Robby was ready to lead his group up onto the high ground. I stood on the porch, and leaned forward on the railing. "This is serious. If things get out of control, many of us could get hurt. The Mudmucks don't fight fair and square. They have our friends captive. They are threatening to hurt them. I am going to try to distract Peralta at the main entrance. If we are successful there, this could be a quick operation. Let's go!"

With a great hurrah, we set off. Robby Hood and his group went running across the hollow toward the back path up onto the cliffhead. Johnny McLarren and his group headed out for the back entrance to Cliff Cave. They went directly across the hollow, too. We were not trying to conceal our assault.

The rest of us went down to our little wharf, and put five canoes into the river for Dick Ferris and his group, who were going into the Cave River entrance to Cliff Cave.

My group of nineteen stopped at the bottom of the cliff path to wait for the signal. We could see Dick and his team in their canoes, just below us on the Looking Glass, holding their position. I got my group organized. I needed them to go up the cliff path in a carefully orchestrated formation.

More quickly than I expected, the brassy notes of Stoner's horn were sounded from high above us.

"That's it!" I shouted. "The high ground is taken! Let's go!" I turned toward Dick, but already his canoes were in motion, the boys digging into the river with their paddles and driving into Cave River.

We rushed up the cliff path as fast as we could go. I looked up on the cliffhead, but saw nobody. I began to get worried. What if our plans had been compromised? Were we running into a trap? But no rocks were being thrown down at us.

Around the last corner we went, and arrived at the entrance to Cliff Cave. Peralta was standing in front of the cave, and threatening us with his rifle. "Go away!" he screamed. I could see a bunch of Mudmucks milling around just inside the cave.

I looked up at the cliffhead, and saw Robby. He signaled to me that they had been successful, and then signaled they had captured four Mudmucks.

My group moved forward slowly, maintaining our formation. As we approached Peralta, Mercury Ferguson moved slightly off to one side, and I saw him tense his body and get ready to spring.

I stepped forward. "Peralta, this is over. I want to speak to the Cincinnati Kid, to discuss your unconditional surrender."

Peralta looked uneasy. "What do you mean, this is over?"

"We have taken the cave, and rescued everyone you captured. Here, see?"

Harold Court, Stone Morgan, and Romulus Ferguson stepped out of our formation, from behind where they had been shielded by the bigger boys Russel Railey, Bull Frazier and Luther Deadmon, and stood in front of Peralta. Each was dressed identically to his twin brother, with the three sets of clothing I had sent Bill and Johnny to purchase.

Peralta was stunned. His eyes bulged wide, and his mouth fell open. He began to turn toward the cave, and at that moment Mercury Ferguson sprang forward like a mountain lion and grabbed the rifle. They struggled furiously, grunting and kicking up dust. I was terrified the gun would go off, but Mercury was way too much for Peralta. With a ferocious twist, he yanked the gun away and threw it over toward us. Perry Stokes darted forward and grabbed it. Peralta tried to run into the cave, but Briggen Crockett and Rube Muller tackled him, and my group had captured our first Mudmuck.

Robby Hood and several others from his group clambered down from the cliffhead and joined us. I had four boys, two of the distillery boys Elijah Craig and Luther Deadmon from my group, and two of the Pelhams Booby Warren and Patrick Flinn from Robby's group, stay at the main entrance to make sure no Mudmucks escaped from the cave that way. The rest of us charged into Cliff Cave with war whoops.

We saw Sawyer and Cheeky and about seven other Mudmucks just inside the entrance, but they turned and ran down the main passage toward their camp. We chased them, and when we arrived at the camp, it was in complete disarray. Our boys were coming from all directions, and I knew that Johnny and his group and Dick and his group had broken through the Mudmuck defenses and that we had all the exits from Cliff Cave under our control.

It was a quick roundup, and we started lining up the Mudmucks, hands tied behind their backs, and secured their dogs. The other Mudmucks that had been captured on the cliffhead, at the back entrance, and down by Cave River were brought into the camp. There were twenty of them. The Cincinnati Kid was missing.

I waved my hands and shouted "Fellas! You boys who know your way around in this cave, pick out a couple other of our boys, and form teams! Fan out! Search the cave! We must quickly rescue our friends!"

They obeyed immediately, and began to head down the various passages. The others stayed behind to keep an eye on our Mudmuck captives.

I went over to Peralta. I wasn't thinking I would get any cooperation from him, but I at least had to try. "Where is the Cincinnati Kid? And where are our friends?"

He sneered at me. "Think you brought enough guys, Hawkins?"

Dick Ferris came over. "When you do something as stupid as you did, this is what you get."

Peralta glared at him. "What do you mean, we did something stupid?"

Mercury Ferguson slammed Peralta against the cave wall and pinned him there. He hissed, "Do you know who you had kidnapped?"

Peralta winced, and his breath was short. "No, the Kid just told us to get the girl."

I laughed. "The Cincinnati Kid had you kidnap Samantha Morgan." I could tell from his reaction that he knew who she was. "That brought twenty-four boys from her town up here in a hurry, ready to do whatever was necessary to rescue her. And our old rivals across the river heard about it, and joined us. Everybody wanted to help Samantha Morgan."

Peralta shook his head. "I thought something was up. When the Kid wanted us to capture the girl, I asked him why. I could tell he knew something about her, but he wouldn't say. If I had known who she was, I would have stopped him. I swear I would have. He's an idiot!"

I pulled Dick Ferris aside, and we spoke in low voices for a minute. He agreed to what I was thinking.

I went back over to Peralta. "Look, Peralta, here's the best deal you're going to get. Take us to our friends that you have captive, and then take us to the Cincinnati Kid, and we will let all of you go back to Cincinnati. But if you don't, I'm going have the sheriff come down here and take you all away. For the crimes you have committed, kidnapping, assault, arson, burglary and theft and vandalism, Judge Granbery will put you all away in the School for Bad Boys. Believe me, you don't want to be standing in front of old Throckmorton Granbery, answering for the crimes you have committed."[5]

Peralta looked surprised. "You mean it? You'd let us go?"

"Yes. We keep our word. You know that. You know we didn't break the terms of our peace treaty. The only thing we want is for you to go back to Cincinnati and never come down here again."

Peralta thought for a moment. "Then follow me."

I held up my hand. "Hold on." I went over to some of our other fellas. "Go find our search teams, and bring them back up here." They nodded, and scattered out through the cave. I turned back to Peralta. "Let's go."

He led us into a section of Cliff Cave that was a maze of passages and side rooms. He pointed to one, and we went in. Our seven friends were there, tied hand and foot, blindfolded and gagged. We quickly freed them.

Roy Dobel, Lew Hunter and Lige Hobbs were in the worst shape, having been held captive the longest. We brought in canteens of water for them.

I helped Scout stand up. She was wobbly, and steadied herself by placing one hand on my shoulder. "I knew you'd come for me, Seckatary Hawkins." I put my arm around her and held her up.

She looked over, and saw some of our boys helping the other captives. "Remus Ferguson! I didn't know you were in here with us! How did you get here?"

Remus smiled. "Hey, Scout. Good to see you safe and sound!"

Mercury and Romulus came over. Mercury explained how Clay had come down to Morning View. "When we found out what had happened to you, we all came straight up here to get you out of trouble. All the boys in the barrelhouse came with us."

Scout gave them all big hugs. "I will never forget this. And it looks like you managed to do it without anyone getting hurt."

"I guess your plan worked, eh, Hawkins?" laughed Oliver.

"Yes," replied Will Standish. "It was brilliant. After we got Peralta, it was all over for the Mudmucks at the main entrance. They just cut and ran. It was a real display of brains over brawn. We have to hand it to Hawkins."

Dick Ferris came over to Oliver, Cliff and Remus. "What happened to you three twins who came up the cliff path?"

"They were just watching us from up on the cliffhead," explained Oliver. "They didn't throw any rocks down at us."

"No," agreed Cliff. "But they were signaling down to the area around the cave entrance. They probably thought we were a scouting party"

Remus chuckled lightly. "They must've thought we were a scouting party of dumbheads. When we got to the cave entrance, there was nobody there. We were trying to get captured, but there was nobody there! We didn't know what else to do, so we walked in! And boom! They grabbed us. That Peralta fella there led the ambush. He was laughing at us. I don't blame him!"

Shadow Loomis shook hands with Oliver, Cliff, and Remus.

"That was very courageous of the three of you, to allow yourselves to be taken captive by these devils."

I stepped up to Peralta. "Speaking of devils, what is wrong with you? Don't you know you must at least give water to your captives? They could die quickly without water."

Peralta shook his head. "It wasn't any of us. The Kid ordered us not to give them water, threatened to whip anyone who did."

"And where is the Cincinnati Kid?" I asked. "He's in here somewhere. We have all three entrances to this cave being watched." I turned to our club members who had been captured by the Mudmucks. "Did you see the Cincinnati Kid?" But none of them had seen him.

Peralta shrugged. "I guess it's over. He's hiding, afraid of something, I don't know what. I'll take you to him."

"Peralta, what is your real name?"

"Valentine Ostendorff. Mostly I just go by Val."

"Val, you seem to have some shreds of decency in you. I think you should get away from the Cincinnati Kid and get your life on a straight path."

"There are lots of good guys in this gang, we've just had a tough life in some mean sections of Cincinnati, where we live is just slums. We never seemed to catch a break from trouble."

"Well, you are all getting a big break this time. You would have been in deep trouble if we had turned you over to our sheriff. You should remember that, before you try anything like this again, joining a bad gang like the Mudmucks and that Cincinnati Kid demon."

Val nodded. "I'll talk to the other guys."

"Good. Let's go. It's time to get the Cincinnati Kid."

"And say, Hawkins?"

"What?"

"I see now how you did it. You had three sets of twins, each pair dressed the same. I heard your guys congratulating you. I just want to say it was slick. That's all."

"Val, you have some good stuff in you. I think you know what

149

to do with your life from this point forward. Let's get started – take us to the Cincinnati Kid."

Val led us back to the main passage, through their camp toward the deep pit, and pointed to a low hole in the cave wall. I knew this place, it led to a large room where Stoner's Boy used to hide his loot. "He's in there."

I went in first, followed by a bunch of our members. Everyone wanted to be in on the taking of the Cincinnati Kid.

I crawled through into the chamber. It was pitch dark. I stood up, swept around the room with my flashlight, but saw nothing. I knew there was no way out of this room except the way we were coming in. There was a cheese hole in the ceiling of this room, where Stoner's Boy had stashed the ivory quiver arrow box that he had stolen from Robby Hood, along with a bunch of other loot, but that hole was too small for a person to get in.[6]

The room was strewn with boulders, and I assumed the Cincinnati Kid was hiding behind one of those. "Come out, Kid," I called in a loud voice. "The game's up. Come out into the open."

I kept sweeping the room with my flashlight. Our other boys were crowding into the room, and playing their flashlights around. We spotted a movement over to the right, among a large cluster of boulders, and all the lights were turned on that spot. We had him. Slowly the miserable wretch stood up. He was sniveling and had a look of terror on his face.

Scout Morgan pushed her way to the front. "Let me see this creep!"

She gasped when she saw the Cincinnati Kid. "Mickey Maus!"

CHAPTER 12

TREASURE CAVE

Scout strode rapidly over to Mickey Maus and slugged him hard in the face. Blood came spurting out of his nose.

"Ow! Ow! Why'd ya do that, Scout?"

"That was nothing, compared to what Aunt Sarah is going to do once she finds out what you've been doing down here! You've assaulted these boys, held them captive without water, killed their dogs, committed burglary, vandalism, even arson. You had me kidnapped, and you had them chop a hunk out of my hair. You even threatened to shave my head and cut off my ears! When Aunt Sarah gets ahold of you, I would not want to be in your skin!"

"You're not going to tell her, are you?"

Scout laughed. "She already knows. She wrote us a letter, saying you had run away from home and formed a gang. She told us you and your gang went on quite a crime spree, stealing guns and tents and canoes and stuff, and that the Cincinnati police are looking for you. They think you went upstream toward St. Louis. You may have fooled 'em then, but you can't get away anymore."

"Alright!" yelled Dick Ferris. "Let's clear the cave. Get everybody down to the clubhouse!"

We untied the Mudmucks, and had them help us carry their tents and other supplies down to the clubhouse. Mickey Maus was escorted by Romulus and Remus Ferguson, and "Peralta" Val Ostendorff was escorted by Mercury Ferguson and me. Some of our boys got the ten Mudmuck canoes out of Cave River, and put them on the bank next to our little wharf.

I sat down in the meeting room with Dick Ferris, Shadow Loomis, Robby Hood, Link Lambert, Harold Court, Will Standish, the four Morgans, and the three Fergusons, and we questioned Mickey Maus.

"I know what they were doing in Cliff Cave," explained Scout Morgan. "Mickey had gone into my room and studied my grandpa's map of Treasure Cave. He had been up and down the Looking Glass every summer on a steamboat, each year when he came to stay with us. He got to know that stretch of the river, and he recognized the area that the map showed. He went back to Cincinnati, organized his gang, and came down here to try to find the treasure before we got here."

"Ah!" I exclaimed. "Then, when you and your brothers and Hudson Lee arrived, Mickey got rattled. He knew you had the treasure map. They had only four days left to find the treasure, under the terms of the peace treaty. He had his gang break the peace treaty, and escalate the violence. They demanded that the four of you and Hudson Lee go away because you would have recognized Mickey. And that's why Mickey never showed his face again until we caught him."

I turned to Mickey. "This is all true, isn't it? Did you find the treasure?"

He scowled at me. "Yes, it's true, but there is no treasure, that map is worthless. We went down into the deep pit and found the side chamber, but there's nothing in there but a mummy."[1]

"I see."

Mickey shrugged. "We went all over that cave, down every pit in it, and found nothing."

I stood up. "Alright. You got any money?"

Mickey looked confused. "No. Why?"

"I'm putting you and your gang on the Kentucky Central, back to Covington, and then you can get yourselves home to Cincinnati and take your lumps with the law there. There's a train in about one hour."

Mercury Ferguson pulled out a wallet. "Mr. Brookie gave me some money, for anything we needed while up here. Should be plenty enough to cover their train tickets."

We marched Mickey Maus and the Mudmucks up to the train station and bought them the tickets. We waited until the train pulled in, they boarded, and left Austinberg. They left with just the clothes on their backs and their dogs.

Back at the clubhouse, we carefully went through all their tents and other belongings, and found not one gold coin.

"Do you think they found the treasure and hid it somewhere else in the cave?" asked Dick.

"No," I replied. "If they had found the treasure, they would have left in their canoes right away. Mickey Maus was very worried when he saw that the Morgans and Hudson Lee had joined us. And while Mickey did say they went down into the deep pit, I'm guessing they missed the side entrance to Treasure Cave."

"What side chamber did they get into down in the deep pit?" asked Scout. "And what did Mickey mean about a mummy they found in there?"

"Ha!" I laughed. "It was hard for me not to give it away. We know all about that side chamber they went into. We've been in it. It was the hiding place of a treasure, but it was a string of pearls, not gold coins."

Scout looked puzzled. "I don't understand."

I nodded my head, and told the story. "There was a gang around here recently, led by a boy who called himself the Yellow Y. His grandfather had been a river pirate. The leader of the river pirates was named Burney, and he lived across the river near Pelham. He had a man living in a cabin behind his house, who had been his slave before the Civil War, but this slave was not from Africa. His name was Zakir Mokka, and he was a Tamil from Ceylon.[2] Mokka had stolen a valuable string of pearls from a Hindu temple in Ceylon, and was trying to get to America, but the ship he was on sank in a storm. He and a few others made it into a lifeboat, and they were rescued by a slave ship. When the captain of the slave ship saw his brown skin, he forced Mokka into slavery. Mokka ended up here in Kentucky along the Looking Glass, a slave of Burney. When slavery ended, Mokka remained with Burney for some reason. The story goes that a little over forty years ago, when the police were closing in on Burney, he had Mokka help him carry the river pirate treasure up into Cliff Cave and down into the deep pit. Burney entombed Mokka in that side chamber, without knowing he had a valuable string of pearls hidden in his clothing. Mokka died in that cave chamber, holding the string of pearls in his hands. His body was mummified by the minerals in the cave water that had dripped on him for over forty years. The great-grandson of Zakir Mokka, a Tamil boy named Ali Mokka, found out what had happened, and came here to search for the pearls. Ali Mokka was part of the Yellow Y gang, and he and the Yellow Y boy got away with the pearls, intending to return them to the rightful owners back in Ceylon."

Stone Morgan looked skeptical. "How in thunder did this Ali Mokka boy in Ceylon know to come to this place, to this stretch of the Looking Glass in Kentucky? How did he know his great-grandfather had been living here?"

I shrugged. "That's a good question. It's a real mystery. All I know is, he did."

Scout was excited. "What about the river pirate treasure?"

"It was never found." Suddenly I understood what Scout was driving at. "Maybe it's the same treasure that your grandfather's map shows the way to!"

"Enough of that for now!" exclaimed Clay Morgan. "We got rid of the Mudmucks! We need to have a celebration!"

Everyone agreed with that. We sent a bunch of boys up into town, with some of the money from Mr. Brookie, to buy supplies for a party. We used the telephone in my writing room to call Mr. Brookie at his office in the distillery. Clay gave him the good news, and asked if everyone could stay overnight and return tomorrow morning. Mr. Brookie agreed without hesitation.

We set up the eight tents of the Mudmucks, next to the clubhouse, for all the distillery boys to spend the night in. It was looking like a little village down on the riverbank.

We borrowed a huge cast iron pot from Mrs. Moore, and made burgoo. Roy Dobel was our head chef. His burgoo recipe included chicken and beef, beef stew bones, onions, parsley, carrots, tomatoes, turnips, green peppers, butter beans, salt, black pepper, sugar and red pepper. It had to cook the whole afternoon. Roy also made cornbread in big cast iron skillets. While Roy and his assistants were getting the burgoo underway, we sent other boys up to Droscher's Deli to get sandwiches and cold drinks for everyone for lunch. The Pelhams brought over a bunch of jars of pickled vegetables.

Bill Darby organized a baseball tournament. We played horseshoes, went out in the canoes and on the *Cazanova*, and set off the firecrackers that we had left over from our interrupted Fourth of July picnic.

I went up to the colored boy Trot Rice. "We used to have a member, years ago, named Hal Rice."

Trot broke a little smile, and nodded his head. "I know about him. We have the same great-grandfather. Before the Civil War, in slave times, these things happened."[3]

"Well, there were many families in Kentucky who had slaves. However, Hal Rice's grandfather fought for the Union in the Civil War."

"That's interesting. My grandfather, William Rice, was a slave, and he served in the Fifth United States Colored Cavalry."

"That's a famous unit. Is your grandfather still alive?"

"Yes. Matter of fact, he was at the funeral for Mr. Ferguson."

Scout came over and joined us. "I heard that! Whatcha guys talking about?"

I smiled at her. "The Civil War veterans in our families. My grandfather on my mother's side, Logan Darnell, was in the Turnverein Regiment, the Ninth Ohio Volunteer Infantry. They were a mostly German-speaking unit."

"Darnell?" It was Cotton Darnell, and he joined us, too. "From where?"

"Down the river, in the Bluegrass, in the area known as Little Germany in Woodford County."

Cotton was astonished. "That's where my family is from! I bet we're related!"

"I'm sure we are!" I shook his hand. "Cousin Cotton!"

Scout laughed. "My grandfather Benjamin Gunn was in the First Regiment, Kentucky Infantry. And my other grandfather Atticus Morgan was in the First Kentucky Cavalry. Those were both Union units."

Cotton nodded. "The First Kentucky Cavalry was also known as Wolford's Cavalry."

I knew about that unit. They were famous for the scouting missions they carried out, including in this area. "Around here, there were defensive batteries put up to protect Cincinnati. Most people don't know it, but the sixth largest city in the Union was defended from the hills of northern Kentucky.[4] That included the first Union colored unit, the Cincinnati Black Brigade. My other grandfather, Uriah Hawkins, was in the 104th Ohio Infantry. When the rebels attacked this area, he was killed in combat. September 10th, 1862. Right near here, around Fort Mitchell."

Cotton, Trot, and Scout stared at me. Trot took a deep breath. "That was a great sacrifice."

"Yes. But as Abraham Lincoln once said, sometimes sacrifices must be laid on the altar of freedom. My great-grandfather Eli Hawkins was an abolitionist."

Trot looked startled. "Here in Kentucky?"

"Yes. Right around here. He helped slaves get to freedom with the Underground Railroad. There were several routes that went through this area, for slaves trying to make it into Ohio."

"That was dangerous work in a slave state!"

I nodded. "Lots of people around here were opposed to slavery." I pointed to Link Lambert. "That boy over there? His great-grandparents were very active abolitionists. His parents even named him after Abraham Lincoln. Lincoln Lambert is his name, though we just call him Link."

Trot extended his hand, and we shook warmly. "I am very

pleased to meet you and all the boys in your club, Seckatary Hawkins."

"Your club, our club," I replied with a smile. "Thank you for coming up to help us and to help Scout."

Just before our dinner was ready, Dick Ferris got up and made a little speech. "We are here to celebrate the end of the Mudmucks!" This was greeted with loud cheering and clapping. "We couldn't have done it alone. Our new friends and club members from Morning View, the Morgans, the Fergusons, and all you other boys, came to help us." More cheers and clapping. "And we were helped by the Pelham boys, from across the river. We will never forget their help, too." Another roar and applause. "Finally, we mustn't forget this. These Mudmucks were the most vicious and violent gang we have ever encountered. The final assault on Cliff Cave, to rescue Scout and our six boys, could have been terribly bloody. I'll tell you, I was worried sick about it. But Hawkins, here, saved the day. His plan with the three sets of twins, how brilliant was that, and just enough to throw the Mudmucks off guard and give us the break we needed." Lots of cheering and clapping. "Finally, the key moment was when Mercury Ferguson got that rifle away from Peralta, then the Mudmucks fell like a line of dominoes! Three cheers for Mercury!" We made the riverbank echo with our cheers for the hero of the day.

Mercury waved his hands for attention. "Thank you, everyone. I just want to say that because of what Scout did for me and my family, I would have done anything to help her. I felt it was my duty to go for that gun and get us into the cave."

Scout came over and gave Mercury a big hug. "Thank you." She turned to the boys crowded around. "Thank you all. I will never forget this day for as long as I live."

"A song, Lew! Let's have a song!" called out Dick Ferris.

We helped Lew carry his battered old melodeon onto the clubhouse porch. He turned to the boys gathered around the steps. "What should we sing?"

"How about *My Old Kentucky Home*?" suggested Johnny.

"Perfect!" agreed Lew, and he struck up the familiar opening notes.

We all joined in:

The sun shines bright in the old Kentucky home.
'Tis summer, the darkies are gay . . .

"Whoa, whoa, whoa!" I called out, and held up my hands. The voices died out, and Lew wobbled the melodeon to a flat stop. "Sorry about that, fellas. Poor choice."

Most of the colored boys began cracking up with laughter.

I was puzzled. "What's so funny?"

"We learned all about that song in school," explained Volentine Umphansaw. "It's a fine song!"

"It is?"

"Yes!" agreed Alford Lumpkins. "It was written before the Civil War by Stephen Foster. It's actually an anti-slavery ballad."

Luther Deadmon nodded. "It tells a story, about a Kentucky farm with slaves that fell on hard times. They had to sell the slaves. The song is the lament of a slave who is being sold to a cane plantation way down in the Deep South."

"Worse'n a Kentucky farm," added Anderson Taylor. "Much harsher working conditions, lots of slaves worked to death."

Mercury Ferguson smiled at me. "A bit of a history lesson for you, eh Hawkins? Not many white people understand this song.[5] C'mon, Lew, let's take it from the top and sing the whole song!"

Lew pumped up the bellows and got the melodeon cranking out the notes again.

The sun shines bright in the old Kentucky home.
'Tis summer, the darkies are gay,
The corn top's ripe and the meadow's in the bloom
While the birds make music all the day.
The young folks roll on the little cabin floor,
All merry, all happy and bright.
By 'n by hard times comes a-knocking at the door,
Then my old Kentucky home, good night.

Weep no more my lady, oh! weep no more today!
We will sing one song for the old Kentucky home,
For the old Kentucky home far away.

We white fellas only knew this first verse, but the colored boys knew the whole song, and kept singing. Lew stayed right in there with them:

They hunt no more for the 'possum and the coon,
On the meadow, the hill and the shore,
They sing no more by the glimmer of the moon,
On the bench by that old cabin door.
The day goes by like a shadow o'er the heart,
With sorrow where all was delight.
The time has come when the darkies have to part,
Then my old Kentucky home, good night.

Weep no more my lady, oh! weep no more today!
We will sing one song for the old Kentucky home,
For the old Kentucky home far away.

The head must bow and the back will have to bend,
Wherever the darkey may go.
A few more days and the trouble all will end,
In the field where the sugar-canes may grow.
A few more days for to tote the weary load,
No matter 'twill never be light.
A few more days till we totter on the road,
Then my old Kentucky home, good night.

Weep no more my lady, oh! weep no more today!
We will sing one song for the old Kentucky home,
For the old Kentucky home far away.

Everybody clapped with enthusiasm, and then we gathered together to share our meal.

It was a good celebration all around. We had to call an early night, as the distillery boys needed to get back to Morning View early the next morning.

After an early breakfast of coffee and leftover cornbread, we bade our goodbyes to the Fergusons and the other distillery boys, and thanked them again for helping us get rid of the Mudmucks.

Jerry Moore went up to Mercury Ferguson and shook his hand. "That was a courageous thing you did, wrestling for that rifle with Peralta. That just broke the backs of the Mudmucks. I'll never forget it. You know, all you guys are members of our club now. You can come up here anytime you want, and maybe we'll have some more adventures together."

Mercury smiled. "Thanks, Jerry. I just hope the adventures don't include needing to take rifles away from big guys like Peralta!"

With that, they boarded the *Cazanova*, and Link took them back down to Morning View.

While Link was gone, I used my telephone to call Mr. Jeckerson, the Cincinnati detective who was our good friend. I explained that we had recovered rifles, tents, canoes, and other supplies that we understood had been stolen from Cincinnati merchants. He told me to have it all brought up to the riverfront landing at Cincinnati, and he would have some officers there to meet us.

So, when Link got back, we loaded all that stolen gear onto the *Cazanova*, and Link and a few other boys went up to Cincinnati. When they returned, Link was waving an envelope at me. "There was a reward, Hawkins! Fifty dollars!"

I turned to Clay Morgan. "That's for you, to replace all the stuff you lost in the fire, the tent, fishing gear, everything."

Clay scuffed the ground with his boot. "Well, you should at least take what it cost you to repair the window and replace your oil lamps, and buy us some basic supplies after the fire."

That was a satisfactory compromise.

The next day, we got ready to go into Cliff Cave and look for the treasure chamber. All twenty-one of us were going on the adventure.[6] We took some tools, including a long pole with a hook on one end, flashlights and lanterns, and big coils of rope, and headed up the cliff path.

It was a peaceful morning, with a great view of the Looking Glass valley. All was quiet again, so different from the recent treks we made up here while the Mudmucks were in control of the cliffhead!

Robby Hood was walking with Scout and me. "My grandfather, Hank Hood, was a member of the river pirates. There is another club we chum with, called Sadler's Seventeen, and one of their former members, a boy named Sargent, has a grandfather named Silas Sargent who was one of the river pirates.[7] Both Hank Hood and Silas Sargent were caught and sent to prison, and were just released earlier this year. And the Yellow Y boy that Hawkins mentioned? His proper name was Siegfried Wye, and his grandfather, also named Siegfried Wye, was one of the river pirates."

"We don't know what happened to my grandfather, Benjamin Gunn. He disappeared in 1872."

"That would have been right around the time all this happened. Hawkins was correct, it was a little over forty years ago. We should ask my grandfather and Silas Sargent."

"What happened to the leader Burney, and old Siegfried Wye?"

"Siegfried Wye was caught too, and he died in prison. Burney was not caught, but died under mysterious circumstances in Cincinnati, a short time after the other river pirates were caught."

We were approaching the entrance to Cliff Cave. I motioned for Roy Dobel to walk with me. "Roy, I have promised Scout a tour of the cave. Before we go to the deep pit, I want to show her the Cave of Wonders and the Wonder of Wonders. You know the route from this entrance better than anyone else. I want you to lead us there."

We made our way to the entrance to Cliff Cave. Roy Dobel

sprang in first, drawing out his flashlight as he went and lighting up the dark hole. I expected him to take us far into the cave, far under the hills, to a secret opening. But he turned sharply to the left as he entered, and then, to my surprise, climbed up a series of steps that I never knew existed.

And there in the rock his flashlight showed a rugged hole about three feet high by two feet wide. "Here is the opening, but only one can enter at a time. Take it slow." I saw Roy get down on his hands and knees and crawl in. We all followed. The ground beneath our hands and knees was wet. The wind whistled past us through the narrow place. The air grew colder as we pushed on. After a long crawl, we came to a larger place, a ledge in the cave wall where we could stand up. We all gathered there, and pointed our flashlights down the rocks, into the high and wide Cave of Wonders. We were looking down into one of the loveliest caves in the whole world. Its ceiling was one great mass of glistening white stalactites, breaking up our lights into all the colors of the rainbow; its walls were covered in white flowstones, radiating a kaleidoscope of colors; its floor was covered with a million sparkling stones and long stalagmites that glittered like rock candy.

Scout was standing next to me, and gripped my arm. "This is unbelievable. There is more treasure under these cliffs than just gold coins!"

I turned to Roy. "Let's show her the next chamber!"

Roy led the way, down the rocky slope to the floor of the Cave of Wonders, then we wended our way through the beautiful stalagmites to the far side of the room. Here there was an opening, about the size of a doorway, and we crossed through into the next chamber, the Wonder of Wonders cavern. Myriads of brilliant crystals formed the walls, all the colors of the rainbow, and incredible, great stalactites hung to meet stalagmites of equal size, forming huge pillars that continued to run upward along an incline and around the whole cavern, as much like a gallery as if it had been carved by the hand of man.

"It's like being in a great cathedral," breathed Scout.

Stone Morgan was examining the colorful crystals. "The cave

minerals in here are unbelievable. Red rhodochrosite! That's a rare one! Orange quartz and yellow metavoltine. Over there, green aragonite. And this is blue hydrozincite, and there's some purple azurite. Look here! Pink cerussite."

I looked quizzically at Scout, who laughed. "Stone knows a lot about geology and minerals."

Stone came over to me. "What's the story behind these caverns?"

Everyone gathered around, and I told of the adventures we had in these caves. "There used to be a clever stone door here, between the Cave of Wonders over there and this room, the Wonder of Wonders. A special Chinese coin was needed to put into motion the gears and things that opened this door. The Chinese coin that operated the door was a small coin, about the size of a nickel, round with a square hole in the center, and on one side of the square hole was a nick – it was this nick that was the key to making this coin be able to open the door."

"Wow," breathed Scout. "Who came up with that, and why?"

I continued to tell the story. "The Chinese Mafia in Cincinnati, called the Tong, had built the door. They had hidden in this room a casket of gold coins they had stolen from merchants in Cincinnati, worth nearly a hundred thousand dollars. They accidentally lost the Chinese coin, and we had some scary times with them as they tried to get the coin back, and we tried to figure out why there was such intense interest in that coin. The members of the Chinese Mafia were finally arrested, and a Javanese boy, named the Spider, showed us how to use the Chinese coin. We recovered the money, and it was returned to the rightful owners in Cincinnati. We received a large reward."

Stone patted me on the back. "You and the boys have certainly had some interesting adventures around here."

"And," added Scout, "there has been a second treasure of gold coins hidden in this cave!"

"Just wait!" I held up my hand. "There is one more, remember, I told you about it. Roy, lead us back to the main passage, and then to the deep pit."

We returned the way we had come in, and when we reached the

main passage, Roy turned left, away from the main entrance, and we went to the edge of the deep pit. Far below we could hear the rumbling waters of Cave River.

I turned to Scout. "You remember what I told you about a boy named Pooley and his gang the Knights of the Square Table?"

"Yes. You said Pooley was seeking bags of gold coins hidden in the old mill along Banklick Creek. The coins rightfully belonged to him. But you told me someone was trying to steal them, so Pooley hid them in this cave."

"Right. Pooley put them right over there, on that ledge on the other side of this deep pit. Eighty-seven bags of gold coins, with a face value of about a hundred thousand dollars."

Scout glanced over at Shadow Loomis. "And your brother died, guarding those gold coins for Pooley."

Shadow nodded. We were all silent for a moment, recalling his older brother "Rolling Stone" John Loomis, who fell into the deep pit and was killed when he landed on the rocky shore of Cave River.

I broke the silence. "We who know this cave well think the side cave on your grandfather's map is down in this pit."

"How do we go down?"

"With a rope slung over that." I pointed my flashlight to the ornate iron hook mounted in the cave ceiling right over the deep pit.[8]

Clay Morgan turned his flashlight on the iron hook. "Scout, look at that hook!"

"We know where that came from!" exclaimed Scout.

"How do you know that?" I asked.

"We have a big barn on our property. Up in the loft there are openings on both ends, to hoist hay bales up. There were four big iron hooks, two on each end, to use for hoisting up the hay. But one has been missing since before my mom can remember. That hook there is identical to the three remaining hooks in our barn!"

I slapped my leg. "That practically proves it! This must be the place where your grandfather hid his treasure!"

We got busy, preparing a big rope. We put loops in one end of it, and then used our long pole to drape it over the hook. We pulled the looped end over to our side of the pit, and I stepped into the lower loop and held on to an upper loop. A bunch of the boys were holding tight onto the other end of the rope.

"Here I go." I swung out over the pit, and waited until my swinging had settled down. "Lower me down slowly!"

Down, down I went, twisting around a bit, and swaying a little. I played my flashlight over the walls of the pit. Soon I passed the opening on our side of the deep pit, leading to the chamber where the mummified body of Zakir Mokka was located. I knew the treasure was not in there, and that the Mudmucks had confirmed that.

"More!" I shouted. "Lower me more!"

Deeper I want. The roaring of Cave River grew louder, echoing off the walls of the cave. I was so deep now I could even see the water with my flashlight, and it was clear why Stoner's Boy and John Loomis, who both fell into this pit, had such different fates. Stoner's Boy fell straight down the center of the pit, where I was at that moment, and I could see directly below me the deep waters of Cave River. He landed in the water and escaped alive. But John Loomis had fallen down the far side of the pit, and now I could see there was only the rocky shore of Cave River below that part of the pit. He fell onto those rocks and was killed.

Then I saw it. Another opening, this one on the far side of the pit! "Stop!" I shouted. My downward motion halted. I had to pump back and forth, like I was on a rope swing, to get over to the opening. The opening was wide and tall, with a broad ledge, and I could easily step off the rope and onto the ledge.

"Alright!" I yelled. "I'm in! Send down the next person!"

I could hear whoops of excitement from far above, and the rope went flying back up to the top.

Next to come down was Scout. She swung her way over, and I grabbed the rope and pulled her to where she could safely step onto the ledge.

"All clear!" I yelled. "Send down the next person!" The rope was yanked back up into the darkness.

"Is this the place?" asked Scout. "Is this Treasure Cave?"

"I think so. I couldn't have gone much lower without being clear into the passage that Cave River has cut through this cave system. This has to be the place."

Scout turned her flashlight into the cave passage. "I don't see anything."

"Let's wait until the others have come down here."

We had arranged the members of the team that was to join us, and in short order the others arrived. Clay, Stone, and Cliff Morgan, Roy Dobel, and Shadow Loomis.

The seven of us began to venture carefully forward.

Roy Dobel led the way. "My dad warned me to look for sandstone or other weak rock. We must be wary of a possible cave-in. But this rock looks good, solid Kentucky limestone."

The passage wound this way and that, but remained high and wide, of easy walking height. We came to the end, and there sat a chest.

Scout sprang forward. "This is identical to the chest I found in the secret room in our house! The chest my grandfather hid there! They're the same!"

The chest was coated with a glistening sheen of calcite, from over forty years of sitting in this wet, dripping cave passage.

Scout stepped forward and attempted to open the chest, but it was frozen shut by the cave minerals.

"Nobody has touched that in decades," commented Roy.

Cliff Morgan had a hammer, and he stepped up and beat lightly on the chest. Sheets of calcite, looking like pieces of glass, shattered and fell onto the ground around the chest.

Scout grasped the latch again and lifted. With a groaning of long frozen hinges, the lid lifted an inch or so. She grabbed under the rim of the lid and wrenched it back with gusto. We aimed our lights into the chest. Gold coins! Lots of them!

Clay Morgan looked stunned. "Scout, I thought we were on a fool's errand! I can hardly believe my eyes!"

Scout was quiet. She scooped up a handful of the coins and examined them. "These are old, all dated before the early '70's.

They will be worth more than their face value. Plus, if this is river pirate treasure, and it probably is, then we have to find a way to return it to the people it was stolen from."

I put my hand on her shoulder. "That's right. I know just the person who can help us."

Scout nodded. "Let's get these coins to the clubhouse, and then decide how to proceed."

Which we did.

CHAPTER 13

THE BEST TREASURE OF ALL

It took a long time, but slowly we had the gold coins hauled up, in small batches in burlap bags, to the top of the deep pit. Scout wanted the chest, too. We had a shovel and a crowbar lowered down, and Cliff and Stone carefully freed the chest from where it had become cemented to the passage floor by the cave minerals.

"This whole cave system is very alive and active," commented Stone.

We returned to the clubhouse and counted the money. The face value was a little over ninety-five thousand dollars. Not the one hundred thousand plus that Scout was expecting, but close enough!

"What should we do with this money?" asked Dick Ferris.

I thought for a moment. "There is still a mystery here. The story we heard, from Hank Hood and Silas Sargent, was that old man Burney had his ex-slave carry the treasure up into Cliff Cave, and entombed it and his ex-slave in the upper chamber where the mummy is. The gold coins were said to have been in carpet bags, which I saw when I first entered that tomb earlier this year, but those bags were empty.[1] The mystery is, how did the treasure get moved to where we found it, and why did the Morgan's grandfather's map accurately show where it was? Why was the money in his chest? And why was an iron hook from his barn mounted in the cave, above the deep pit? It seems there is more to this story than we have been told."

Shadow Loomis smiled at me. "What do you suggest we do, Hawkins?"

Robby Hood answered for me. "I think we go up to Cincinnati, turn this money over to Detective Jeckerson, and then go talk to my grandfather Hank Hood and his friend Silas Sargent."

That was exactly what I was thinking!

Dick Ferris appointed a group to do just that. Link Lambert was to take us on his launch the *Cazanova*, and the rest of the party was Harold Court, Robby Hood, Shadow Loomis, Will Standish, the four Morgans, and me.

I used the telephone in my office to call Jeckerson, and arranged for him to be waiting for us in his office. I did not tell him why we were coming.

Before we departed, Robby Hood used my telephone to call his parents, and ask that his grandfather Hank Hood and Silas Sargent be summoned to meet us. The meeting was to be held in the Hood home.

When we had tied up at the riverfront landing in Cincinnati, we hired a livery driver to take us and all the bags of gold coins into central downtown, to Jeckerson's big office on Main Street. When we walked in, he was standing by his open window puffing on a cheroot, one of the long thin black cigars that seemed to be perpetually in his mouth. We plopped the bags down on the floor in front of his desk.

Jeckerson looked amused. "What's in the bags?"

"A little over ninety-five thousand in gold coins," I replied.

He was astonished. He came around the desk and opened one of the bags. "I see." He looked up at me. "And?"

"And, we're going up to Mount Adams to get some answers. Then we'll come back here."

Jeckerson shook his head in amazement. "I'll keep an eye on these bags until you get back. Both eyes! This is going to be a good story, I can tell already! And is this the famous Samantha Morgan?"

I had forgotten my manners. I introduced the four Morgans to Jeckerson.

Jeckerson shook their hands warmly. "Hawkins is always in the middle of something complicated and exciting!"

Scout laughed. "This has been quite the adventure, and it isn't over yet!"

She had no idea how true that was going be.

From Jeckerson's office, we took the streetcar up the Mount Adams incline. That dropped us off on Ida Street at the top of Mount Adams. From there it was a short walk to the Hood home on Paradrome Street.

Robby Hood led us inside, and we were greeted by Mrs. Hood. We went into the parlor, where three elderly people were seated, two men and a woman.

Robby introduced us. "This is my grandfather, Hank Hood, and his good friend Silas Sargent. They were members of Burney's river pirates and just got out of prison a few months ago, after serving 42 years. And this is my great aunt Samantha Hood, sister of my grandfather."

Samantha Hood got up and came over to Scout. "Samantha Morgan, I am pleased to meet you. We have heard many good things about you!"

"Thank you very much, Miss Hood."

"I imagine you have some questions for my brother and Mr. Sargent."

"Yes'm."

"Such as, was your grandfather Benjamin Gunn a member of Burney's river pirates."

"Yes'm."

"And you want to know what happened to your grandfather."

"Yes'm." Scout looked quizzical. "Miss Hood, you seem to know a lot about all of this."

"Yes, I do." Samantha Hood looked over at the two old men. "Gentlemen, I think it's time Samantha Morgan and her brothers heard the truth."

We all gathered in more closely. Hank Hood spoke first.

"My sister Samantha never married. She devoted her life to helping the less fortunate in life, including us poor fools sitting in prison. She visited us often, including Siegfried Wye, until the very day he died."

Silas Sargent nodded, then cleared his throat. He straightened up. It was clear he was about to make some sort of announcement. The parlor was completely silent. "Samantha relayed messages between us and your grandfather, Ben Gunn."

The Morgans gasped. Scout went closer and grasped his hands. "Is my grandfather still alive?"

"Indeed, he is. But he's in trouble. At this very moment he's sitting in a cell in the Cincinnati jail."

Scout nearly fell over.

A babble of conversation followed, which got very confused with everyone talking over everyone else. One thing was clear, Scout wanted to see her grandpa as soon as possible. Samantha Hood suggested the best course of action, which was for me to telephone Detective Jeckerson and ask his advice.

When I got Jeckerson on the telephone, I told him everything I knew. I told him about the treasure map Scout had found in her Grandfather Benjamin Gunn's chest and how it led us to the river pirate's treasure, and all about the coded account book found in the chest, and that book was in the Morgan house down in Morning View. I told him we had met with the old river pirates Hank Hood and Silas Sargent, and that they had told us Benjamin Gunn was in the Cincinnati jail.

Jeckerson called back several minutes later and informed me he had arranged a meeting with the judge who was handling the case. We were to be at the courthouse in two hours.

Robby's mother had prepared a delicious lunch for us. We were all very hungry, as we hadn't eaten anything since before we went into Cliff Cave this morning.

Samantha Hood pulled Scout aside. "Samantha, everything I have heard about you says you are destined for greatness. Maybe you'll be a famous attorney, fighting for the poor and the weak. Let's go into the study and talk for a bit."

As they moved away, I heard Scout say, "One thing you should know about me, Miss Hood, is that I'm not a normal type of girl."

"I see. Neither am I. But let's find another way to put that, instead of saying you are not normal. But that does create additional obstacles you will face, beyond the obstacle of being a woman."

Shadow Loomis was standing next to me. I turned to him. "What did all of that mean?"

Shadow put his hand on my shoulder. "Let's go outside."

When we left to go to the courthouse, Hank Hood, Silas Sargent, and Samantha Hood accompanied us. We rode the streetcar back down the incline and through downtown to the courthouse.

Jeckerson was waiting in the lobby, and he had Doc Waters and Judge Granbery with him. This time I remembered my manners and introduced the four Morgans, as well as Samantha Hood. Hank Hood and Silas Sargent were already acquainted with Doc, Jeckerson, and the judge.

Doc Waters gave Scout a warm embrace. "I am very glad to meet you!" he exclaimed. "We have heard many good things about you, but it seems like your story is still underway!"

"Yes, indeed," nodded Judge Granbery. "Remarkable developments. Jeckerson has shown us the gold coins, and told us about your grandfather. It seems that you are a lot like Seckatary Hawkins. Wherever he goes, whatever he does, surprise and amazement seem to accompany him – like it does for you, too!"

"Thank you, Judge Granbery and Doctor Waters. Hawkins has told me all about you, and everything I've heard speaks very highly of you."

Scout turned to Jeckerson. "Where are the gold coins?"

"Still in my office. My two best officers, Danny Columbo and Matt Phillips, are guarding them.[2] Don't worry."

Jeckerson came over to Hank Hood, Silas Sargent, and Samantha Hood. "You will be of great assistance here. Okay, everyone, follow me into the judge's chambers. His name is Montmorency Evan Keys.[3] Please refer to him as your honor. He is very old fashioned, very formal. Let's go."

Judge Keys had a large office with dark paneled walls and a huge dark desk. Jeckerson introduced everyone. The judge nodded and had just a hint of a smile when Scout was introduced, but he didn't say anything.

He shook hands with Judge Granbery. "Good to see you, Throcksey."

Judge Granbery nodded. "Wouldn't want to miss this. There are some loose ends from that Yellow Y business, and I hope we get some answers today."

"I hope so, too," replied Judge Keys. He then shook hands with Doc Waters and Mr. Jeckerson. "Always a pleasure, Doctor Waters, and same to you, Alvin."[4]

The men exchanged a few pleasantries, and then began to look around for a place to sit. Judge Keys had his assistants bring in some more chairs, and we all sat down.

The judge turned to a clerk. "Have the prisoner brought in."

Scout was seated next to me. I could tell she was nervous and expectant, as her legs were bouncing and drumming her feet on the floor.

A side door opened, and two police officers came in, escorting an old man in handcuffs. Another man, in a suit, was behind them.

The judge motioned to the officers. "Take those off." They uncuffed the old man. "That will be all. You can go." The officers left.

Hank Hood and Silas Sargent stood up and went over to the old man. Silas Sargent spoke. "Ben Gunn! Do you remember us?"

The old man looked closely at their faces. "Yes, indeed. Silas Sargent and Hank Hood. And that looks like your sister over there, Samantha Hood. Right?"

"Yes," responded Hank Hood. He pointed to Scout. "Do you know who that is?"

"Well, I've never met her, but I'm guessing that's my granddaughter Samantha Morgan."

Scout was trembling. She stood up and went over. "Are you really my grandfather Gunn?"

"Yes, my dear. I came back because of you."

They hugged for a long time. They both had tears streaking down their faces. As did I. I think everyone did. The Morgan boys went over and embraced their grandfather.

"Alright!" The judge rapped on his desk. "This is a hearing on an important and serious legal matter. Everyone sit down." He pointed to the other man, in the suit, who had come in with Ben Gunn. "This is the Hamilton County Assistant Prosecuting Attorney, Roger Montilla.[5] He has filed some serious charges against the prisoner, Benjamin Gunn, charges of river piracy."

Mr. Montilla nodded. "These charges carry a prison sentence of fifty years. Now, I understand the prisoner, Benjamin Gunn, is eighty-four years old. I have no desire to put a man who is eighty-four into prison, to die there. It is my understanding there are some extenuating circumstances that we should consider. Let's have them."

Jeckerson stood up. "Indeed, there are. Before he went into hiding, Mr. Gunn prepared a map, indicating where the money the river pirates had stolen was hidden. His granddaughter, Samantha Morgan, found the map, and then the money. It is in my office, a total of ninety-five thousand six hundred eighty dollars."

Judge Keys looked at Scout. "Is this true?"

"Yes, your honor."

"You turned over all of the money to Detective Jeckerson?"

"Yes, your honor."

"You didn't keep any of it?"

"No, your honor."

"Not even one coin?"

"No, your honor."

"Come on, young lady. You must have kept one little coin as a keepsake."

"No, your honor."

The judge seemed satisfied. "Alright. The word of Samantha Morgan is good enough for this court. Agreed, Mr. Montilla?"

"Well, your honor, she is the granddaughter of the defendant, and she would naturally have some personal bias that could taint her credibility. However, she is Samantha Morgan, and that carries some weight with my office."

Judge Granbery thumped his cane on the floor. "It should be more than some weight. There should be no doubt in your mind."

Mr. Montilla smiled. "I am sorry, Judge Granbery, but I do think a bit of skepticism is not out of order."

I saw Judge Granbery begin to react, but Doc Waters laid his hand on his arm and the judge restrained himself.

Jeckerson stood up. "If there is any doubt here, I would add that, in addition to her three brothers, seventeen members of the Fair and Square Club, including Seckatary Hawkins himself," pointing to me, "were all present in the cave where the hidden money was found, and they would all attest to the fact that every single coin they found has been turned over to me."

Mr. Montilla waved his hands. "Alright, yes, yes, Seckatary Hawkins and his chums are all admired by my office and this court for the many good deeds they have done. We are satisfied, detective. Let's move on. What other extenuating circumstances do you want to bring up?"

Jeckerson turned to Hank Hood and Silas Sargent. "The two of you were arrested, convicted, and sentenced to fifty years in prison. You served forty-two years of that prison sentence, and were just released a few months ago. Your fellow river pirate here, Ben Gunn, escaped and never saw the walls of a prison. What do you think about that?"

Silas Sargent stood up. "Hank and me been talking about this ever since we got out of prison. It's true, Ben Gunn never was in a prison with stone walls, but all this time, all these forty-two years, he was in a different kind of prison. He was in exile. And we know how he suffered there, knowing that while we would eventually be released and able to rejoin our loved ones, he could never return. Every day, he thought about the fact that if he ever returned, he would immediately be sent to prison, and would die there. It was when he heard what Samantha Morgan had done, he knew he had to come back. He had to see her before he died. We both would like to see Ben Gunn spend the rest of his days with his family, and not in prison."

It was silent for a moment in the judge's chambers. The judge was scribbling some notes. "Interesting. No ill will toward Benjamin Gunn from his comrades who spent most of their lives in prison."

Mr. Montilla turned to Ben Gunn. "Alright. I think it's time we heard from the prisoner, Benjamin Gunn. Tell us everything that happened to you from when you joined Burney's river pirates, and what you did during the days the police were closing in forty-two years ago, and everything else you did until you returned to Cincinnati a few days ago."

Ben Gunn shifted around in his chair, then he began to speak. A most amazing story rolled out in his words.

"I was a young man, back before the Civil War, and was learning the steamboat business. We formed a company, Incandescent Freight, and my partners and I were modestly successful. Then I met old Legran Burney, who lived in a grand stone house along the river a few miles downstream from Cincinnati. He told me there was better money to be made on the side by river pirating, and that he had three other young men who would join us. Nobody would suspect us, he insisted, since we were all engaged in other legitimate businesses. In hindsight, we were all fools, but old man Burney had a convincing way about him."

"Who were the other three men?" asked Mr. Montilla.

"Hank Hood and Silas Sargent, sitting there, and one other, Siegfried Wye, who died in prison."

"Go on."

"Ben Gunn had a slave named Zakir Mokka. He was one of the smartest men I ever met, and he and I became friends. Mokka told me he was not like the other slaves, the slaves who came from

Africa. He told me he was from Ceylon, a Hindu Tamil from Ceylon. I asked him how he came to be a slave in Kentucky. It is a sad tale."

I saw Samantha Hood nod her head, and I wondered what she knew about all of this.

Ben Gunn described how Zakir Mokka had ended up a Kentucky slave, but one in possession of a valuable strand of pearls.

"Why didn't the slave takers get the pearls from him?" persisted the judge.

Ben Gunn took a deep breath. "Mokka was very clever, as I told you, and he managed to keep them hidden, sewn into the lining of his pants. He then concealed them in his log cabin for many years. He showed them to me one night, in his log cabin, and was very ashamed by what he had done. He felt the sinking of the ship he was on, and his enslavement, were punishment for his crime."

"What year was this when he showed you the pearls?" asked the judge.

"Let me think. Burney formed his river pirate gang with us in 1850. That's when I met Zakir Mokka. Our friendship grew over the years, until he felt he could confide in me about the pearls. I guess that would have been in the late 1850's."

"What about after the Civil War started?" persisted the judge. "Why didn't Zakir Mokka return to Ceylon?"

"He was still a slave then."

"Kentucky was a border state. It stayed in the Union."

Ben Gunn nodded. "That's true. But Kentucky didn't abolish slavery until the Thirteenth Amendment went into effect in December 1865, well after the war had ended."

"Why didn't he return to Ceylon then?"

Ben Gunn shifted in his seat. "After the war started, I volunteered for the First Regiment, Kentucky Infantry, in April 1861. We saw action against Morgan's invasion of Kentucky, among other battles."

Judge Keys glanced at Mr. Montilla. "A Union combat veteran, defended his home state. Noted for the record." He paused and made a few notes, and then turned back to Ben Gunn. "But you haven't answered my question."

Ben Gunn nodded and continued. "When I returned in early 1865, I talked to Mokka about going back to Ceylon. There were several reasons he chose to remain with Burney. First, as a former slave, Zakir Mokka had little or no money, and was in no financial position to travel halfway around the world to Ceylon. Second, to restore the honor of his family, another family member would need to come here from Ceylon and take the pearls from him. Finally, Zakir explained that he himself was permanently dishonored, and could never return to Ceylon."

He paused for a moment. "I felt sorry for Mokka, and made him a promise that I would help him restore the honor of his family. I didn't know how I could do that, but I made him that promise."

The judge was scribbling notes. "Go on."

"We resumed our pirating. We only seized gold coins, nothing else. Easier to hide. But the gold coins were beginning to accumulate in Burney's house. We knew we needed a better place to hide them. Burney knew his way all around in a cave across the Looking Glass from his house. We went in the cave, and he showed me the deep pit. He explained that an old timer, long dead, had once told him there was a cave passage down in that pit that nobody but him knew about. We built a wooden scaffold across the pit, and went down on a rope ladder. Sure enough, we found the passage. I got a big iron hook from my hay barn, and Burney and I mounted it in the cave ceiling above our scaffold. From then on, we used that hook to climb down on rope ladders and to lower carpet bags of gold coins and hid them there."

I saw Doc Waters and Judge Granbery put their heads together, whispering. They had long been curious about the iron hook in Cliff Cave, and I knew this news was very interesting to them.

Judge Keys continued his questioning of Ben Gunn. "How much money did you hide in there?"

"Just before our gang got busted in '72, there was about one hundred five thousand dollars there."

"But Detective Jeckerson has just told us that Seckatary Hawkins and Samantha Morgan and friends only brought about ninety-five thousand dollars in gold coins to his office."

Ben Gunn nodded. "Yes, I took ten thousand for myself."

I couldn't contain myself any longer. "But the coins were not in the chamber Burney knew about. They were in another chamber, further down, and they were in your chest, not in carpet bags. Those carpet bags were in the upper chamber, and they were empty. And your map described that lower hiding place." Doc Waters and Judge Granbery looked alarmed.

Judge Keys looked at me and raised his eyebrows, and I thought I was going to get yelled at. But he turned back to Ben Gunn. "Explain all this."

Ben Gunn coughed. "One day, I was taking a bag of coins down to the hiding place, by myself. The rope ladder was swinging a lot, and the bag hit the edge of the ledge and got a small tear. A few gold coins fell out. I lowered the rope further and went down to try to recover the coins, but could see that there was a river at the bottom of the pit, and those gold coins were lost. However, that was when I found the second cave passage in the side wall of the pit, and decided to keep that my secret. Something told me that it was going to become useful."

"How did it become useful?"

"In 1872, we made a big haul from a steamboat. Biggest haul we ever hit. It was big news, and the police stepped up their efforts to find us. They were getting closer all the time. Burney had Mokka help him carry the big haul up into the cave, and into the hiding place. A short time later, Burney was arrested. He made a deal with the law. In exchange for his freedom, he gave up Hank Hood, Silas Sargent, and Siegfried Wye, who were hiding in a tunnel running from Burney's house to Mokka's log cabin.[6] He told them about me, too, and he claimed I was the leader of the gang."

"How do you know this?"

Ben Gunn looked at Samantha Hood.

"The police came to see me," she explained. "They told me what Burney had done, and they wanted my help in catching Ben."

"Did you tell Ben Gunn this?"

"Yes, he came to see me in Cincinnati, before leaving the country."

The judge turned back to Ben Gunn. "You need to fill in the gaps here."

"Yes, okay. Everyone else was caught. I had to lay low. I hid in some tunnels we had dug on Seven Willows Island. After several days, I came back up the river. I searched for Mokka, but couldn't find him. I decided to move the gold coins, just to be safe. I found the chamber down in the pit had been sealed with rocks and clay. I broke in and found Mokka there, tied up and dead. Burney had left him there, tied up, and he died from lack of water. Burney had murdered him, and left him in that indecent position. I untied him and braced him up in a sitting position, and found the pearls in the lining of his pants, just as Mokka had shown me. I placed them in his hands, and vowed to make good on my promise to him."

"Then what?"

"I returned to Morning View, got my affairs in order, had my wife move our legitimate money from the bank and I hid it in a chest in the secret room in my house, and I put in that chest a map showing where the gold coins were hidden. I took another one of my seaman's chests into the cave, and put it in my secret side passage further down in the deep pit, and moved all the gold coins down into there. I resealed the tomb of Zakir Mokka. Then I went up to Cincinnati, to see Samantha Hood. She told me that Burney had ratted on us, and was out on bail. She told me where he was staying, at a hotel, and I found him there. I confronted him, told him I knew he had murdered Zakir Mokka, and that I knew he was planning to take all the gold coins for himself once the rest of us were safely behind bars. I told him I was going to the law and tell them what he had done. Burney pulled a pistol on me. We struggled, and the gun went off and Burney was shot and killed."

The judge turned to Mr. Montilla. "Do you want to add any charges here, murder or manslaughter?"

Mr. Montilla shook his head. "Sounds like self-defense to me, and Legran Burney got what he deserved."

Judge Granbery was nodding his head. Judge Keys glanced at him.

"Alright." Judge Keys made some more notes. "Go on, Mr. Gunn."

"Well, I knew I was in big trouble then. I went back to the cave, and took ten thousand dollars in gold coins out of my chest, and travelled to Cuba. That's where I've been for the past forty-two years."

Mr. Montilla went over to him. "You expect us to believe you've lived in Cuba for all this time?"

"It's true."

Mr. Montilla looked skeptical. "Hablas muy bien el español?"

Ben Gunn smiled. "Sí, estoy con fluidez en español."

"Qué hiciste cuando estabas viviendo en Cuba?"

"Formé un consorcio de inversión con varios socios, con intereses en la caña de azúcar, tabaco y ron."[7]

Doc Waters was chuckling at this exchange. I knew from the time we spent together in Cuba that Doc could speak pretty good Spanish.

Mr. Montilla turned to Judge Keys. "I'm satisfied. He's fluent in Spanish, almost better than me. He tells me he and some Cuban partners formed an investment consortium, with interests in sugar cane, tobacco, and rum."

The judge pursed his lips. "With the money you stole? Pirate loot?"

Ben Gunn nodded. "I lived modestly. My partners in Cuba will prepare affidavits on that. I donated some money to an orphanage, and to a girls' school. I have arranged with my partners to liquidate my holdings, and have the money sent by wire transfer to the control of this court. That should be a little over forty thousand dollars."

"Are you telling me your investments of the original ten thousand dollars have grown to over forty thousand dollars?"

"Yes, your honor."

"That is still not rightly your money."

"Yes, your honor. I agree. I will turn it all over to this court. That money will help in reimbursing the people we stole from, plus some interest on top of that."

"Who knew you were in Cuba?"

"I corresponded by letter with Samantha Hood. I wanted to protect my family, but wanted to let my wife know I was alive. Samantha secretly visited her on occasion, and we relayed messages back and forth. My wife and I knew I couldn't return to America, and she didn't want to leave Kentucky and all her family here."

"What about your promise to Zakir Mokka?"

"I spent many years researching that. I wrote countless letters to government officials in Ceylon. They took many months to go back and forth, sometimes over a year before I got a response, but finally I found officials who could help me. They located the Mokka family I was looking for. It was a couple of years ago, that I left Cuba and travelled to Ceylon. The ocean liner went through the Suez Canal, but it was still a long journey.[8] I found the Mokka clan, and more intelligent people I have seldom met. As part of the British Empire, they all spoke excellent English, and they welcomed me as if I was their long lost relative. I told them what had happened to Zakir Mokka. One of his grandsons, Ali Mokka, was given the task to return with me and attempt to recover the pearls."

"This court knows of Ali Mokka, and the Yellow Y gang he was in. You brought him here?"

"No, your honor. I brought him to Cuba. I sent a letter to Samantha Hood, asking for her help, asking her to help Ali Mokka. She wrote back that young Siegfried Wye, grandson of my fellow river pirate of the same name, had recently been orphaned, and that she had taken him in to live with her. She wrote that he was a good boy, and she thought that Siegfried would be the one to help Ali Mokka. It was arranged that I would send Ali to Cincinnati. He travelled from Havana to New Orleans on the ocean liner *Lusitania*, and then from New Orleans to Cincinnati on the steamboat *Louisiana Lou*. Samantha Hood and Siegfried Wye met him at the steamboat landing."

"That was the nucleus of the Yellow Y gang?"

"Yes, your honor. Siegfried Wye knew they were headed into the territory of Seckatary Hawkins and his club. He was worried that Seckatary Hawkins could interfere with their mission into Cliff Cave. He formed a gang of his own. Matters might have gone smoothly, except that Lembacher Burney, grandson of old Legran Burney, found out what was going on. I heard that the boys called him the Rat-Faced Man. That would describe the Burney clan alright. Lembacher convinced Siegfried that he was his uncle, and became 'Uncle Lem' to him.[9] He was after the river pirate treasure, of course, but he nearly ruined the whole mission."

This was astounding testimony. We who had dealt with the mysterious Yellow Y gang were on the edge of our seats, including Judge Granbery, Doc Waters and Jeckerson.

Judge Keys nodded. "We know what happened, that the Rat-Faced Man was about to use a pick-axe to murder Seckatary Hawkins in Cliff Cave, and how Ali Mokka shot and killed Rat Face with an arrow. Ali and Siegfried were ultimately successful, and fled with the pearls. Do you know what happened to them?"

"Yes, your honor. Samantha Hood and I had it all planned. She sent them back to Cuba. Once there, I booked them in first class on an ocean liner bound for Ceylon. Ali Mokka will return the pearls, and restore the honor of his family."

"Why did you come back to Cincinnati a few days ago?"

"Samantha Hood sent me a copy of the article in the *Cincinnati Enquirer*, about my granddaughter Samantha, and the finding of the secret room, and the story of the Ferguson family. I knew that meant she had found my map showing where I had hidden the gold coins. I knew right then that I had to return here immediately, to be sure she didn't get herself and her family into trouble. I wanted to meet her before I died, even if it was through the bars of a prison cell."

Judge Keys was silent for what seemed like a long time. He turned to Mr. Montilla. "Roger, I think we have a pretty good picture of what we have here. Any objection to an SIS?"

"Seems like the right thing to do, judge. Plus, a remand to you know who."

The judge's face broke into a smile. "Yes! Perfect." He turned to Ben Gunn. "How do you plead to the charge of river piracy?"

"Guilty, your honor."

The judge made some notes. "Your guilty plea has been accepted.

I sentence you to fifty years in prison. Now I am going to suspend that sentence, what we call an SIS or a suspended imposition of sentence, in exchange for the following. First, all the gold coins will be turned over to this court. Second, your money in Cuba will be wired to this court. Third, you will decode the entries in your pirate's account book, to help this court identify all the parties who have legitimate claim to this money plus interest. You will pay all legal fees and accounting fees required to find these merchants or their living descendants. When all is settled, Mr. Gunn, there may be no money left at all. Is this acceptable to you?"

"Yes, your honor. I wouldn't want any of it for myself, under any condition."

"Very good. Perhaps if there is any left, you could create a college fund for your granddaughter. You wouldn't be looked on favorably by this court if it wasn't for her. Now, Mr. Gunn." And here Judge Keys paused, and glanced at Scout. He had a twinkle in his eye! "The suspended sentence means you are on monitored probation for the rest of your life. One misstep on your part, and I will cancel the suspension and into the clinker you will go. Furthermore, I want you to report back to me on a regular basis, once a month. I will appoint someone to be your legal custodian, to make sure you follow these instructions. Is this all understood?"

"Yes, your honor. Perfectly. Thank you for being merciful to me."

The judge turned and pointed to Scout. "Mr. Gunn, I remand you to the custody of Samantha Morgan! This hearing is adjourned!"

Everyone jumped up, cheering and clapping. Hank Hook and Silas Sargent shook hands with Ben Gunn, and we all gathered around to welcome him back to freedom and his family and friends.

Judge Granbery grasped the hand of Ben Gunn. "Mr. Gunn, you have cleared up the mystery of the Yellow Y. I was never satisfied that we had the whole story. Now we do."

Jeckerson smiled. "Simply amazing, the lengths you went to – to keep your promise to Zakir Mokka, and to help Ali Mokka get here and get the help he needed to recover the pearls."

Doc Waters nodded. "I was worried about those boys, Ali and

Siegfried, after they up and disappeared with the pearls. I am relieved they are safely on their way to Ceylon. Little Siegfried will have an interesting life in that part of the world!"

Jeckerson came over to where I was standing with Scout. "I know Judge Keys can be gruff and blunt. But I'll wager that as all this gets straightened out, deciding who the rightful parties are to receive their share of this money, that he will let them know who is responsible for it happening at all. Scout, if you hadn't found that map, and if your grandfather had died in Cuba, that gold would have lain hidden deep in Cliff Cave for who knows how long, maybe long centuries. All trace of who it belonged to would be gone. And maybe there would have been an earthquake or something, and the cave collapsed and buried it forever. I'll wager that there will some rewards coming to you."

Scout smiled a bit, but shrugged. "I got my grandpa back. That's more'n enough for me."

We talked for a good long while about everything, and then bade our goodbyes to Doc Waters, Jeckerson, and Judge Granbery.

The four Morgans, along with Ben Gunn, Hank Hood, Silas Sargent, Samantha Hood, Link, Harold, Robby, Shadow, Will, and I, walked out of the courthouse. My head was simply spinning with the amazing developments in this story.

Our next stop, at Scout's insistence, was back up on Mount Adams, to the Maus home on Monastery Street near the famous Rookwood Pottery.

Samantha Hood stopped us as we approached the house. "You young folk go up first, and get your hellos and introductions taken care of. We'll be up there in a minute or two."

We walked up the hill to the Maus home. There was a woman sitting on the front porch, and when she saw us approaching, she jumped up and exclaimed "Scout! And Stone and Cliff and Clay! Come up here and give me a kiss!"

Scout turned to me. "It's our Aunt Sarah, Mickey's mother."

The Morgans went up and hugged and kissed their aunt.

Suddenly, a girl came out of the house. She was pale and thin, but Scout exclaimed "Narcissa! You look good! Are you getting better?"

"Yes," replied Mrs. Maus. "The doctors tried a plombage technique. They collapsed the lobe of her lung with the consumption in it."

"I've been getting better every day!" beamed Narcissa. "They say I can even go to school this fall!"

Scout hugged her. "That's wonderful!"

Scout introduced Link, Harold, Robby, Shadow, Will, and me to Mrs. Maus and Narcissa, and explained how we had helped her. Then Scout turned to her aunt. "Where's Mickey?"

The question surprised me. I had put him completely out of my mind.

Mrs. Maus sighed. "He's in the custody of the police. Your Uncle Adolphus is there now, seeing what's to be done."

Narcissa put her hands on Scout's shoulders. "We are all very sorry about what he did to you, and your brothers, and Seckatary Hawkins and all the other boys."

Scout arched her eyebrows. "How do you know about that?"

Narcissa was still holding onto Scout's shoulders. "When they got back to Cincinnati yesterday, the whole gang forced Mickey to the police station and turned him in. They all turned themselves in."

Scout persisted. "But how did you know what he had done to us?"

Mrs. Maus came over. "The police released the other boys to the custody of their parents. One of the boys, Valentine Ostendorff, came here earlier today and told us all about what had happened. He said he knew we were going to hear about it sooner or later, and that he and the other boys wanted us to hear it from them first. He apologized for the gang having kidnapped Scout, and all the other bad things they had done."

Will turned to me. "Who the dickens is Valentine Ostendorff?"

"That's the real name of Peralta. He told me."

Samantha Hood, Hank Hood, Silas Sargent, and Ben Gunn

came up the sidewalk and stopped in front of the house. Mrs. Maus looked quizzically at Scout.

Scout smiled and walked over and pulled on the hand of Ben Gunn, leading him up to Mrs. Maus. "Aunt Sarah, I want you to meet someone. This is your father."

Mrs. Maus looked intently at the old man. "My father? My father disappeared when I was just a baby."

Samantha Hood stepped forward. "It is your father. I knew him before he fled America, as did my brother Hank, and his friend Silas Sargent. We can all attest that this is your father, Benjamin Gunn."

It was another emotional moment, and there was a lot of explaining to do. Mrs. Maus told everyone come into the house and we sat down around the dining table to talk.

The sun was beginning to set on this long day, and we had to make some plans. The Morgans were going to spend the night with the Maus family, and the rest of us were going to split up and spend the night either at the Hood home, or at the home of Shadow Loomis around the corner on Celestial Street.

Scout's Uncle Adolphus got home from the police station and found out what was going on. He and Mrs. Maus decided that they and Narcissa would travel with us the next day on the launch *Cazanova*, down to Morning View for what was going to be an amazing family reunion.

Then Scout surprised everyone. "Mickey is welcome to come, too."

The room was silent. Mr. Maus cleared his throat. "No. He's in Juvenile Detention right now, and he's going to stay there. I have enrolled him in Laird's Military Academy here in Cincinnati.[10] He starts there next week."

Ben Gunn nodded. "From what I've heard, the young man needs some straightening out. I will work on that with him, too."

The next day we all boarded the launch *Cazanova* and got underway.

I was sitting by myself on the front deck. Scout came around and sat down next to me. There was a real uncomfortable silence.

"Seck, there's something I have to tell you."

"I know what it is. Shadow Loomis told me."

"How did he know?"

"Your brother Cliff told him."

"I see."

I took a deep breath. "Look, Scout, it's okay. You and I have become friends, and that's the most important thing. You and your brothers are members of our club, and I want you to come back up to the clubhouse as often as you can."

Scout looked relieved, and happy. "Sure! And you come down to visit us, too!"

"Well, maybe we will find some treasure we can keep."

Scout smiled. "Seck, we found my grandpa, and that's the treasure I'm taking home. That's the best treasure of all!"

"I heard that!" It was Clay Morgan. We turned to look at him.

He smiled and shook his head in amazement. "Scout, when you said you wanted to come up here and look for a treasure of gold coins, I thought the whole expedition was crazy. I was wrong. But being wrong about the gold coins was nothing compared to what has happened. We are taking our grandpa home! And it is all due to you and what you did. Mom and Gamma and Aunt Hannah and everyone else will be in shock and disbelief! It will be something to see, and be part of!"

Scout clapped her hands. "We should include everyone who was involved!"

She turned to me. "Why don't you and all the boys, including the Pelham boys, come down to Morning View for the day? We'll invite the Ferguson boys and all the other boys from the distillery, too! We'll have a great time!"

I was very happy. "I think we'll have lots of adventures together!"

Which we did.

ENDNOTES

Endnotes for the Preface.

1. For more details on the life of Robert F. Schulkers, and the origin of the "Seckatary Hawkins" stories and books, see O'Dell, Gary A., and Gregg Bogosian. "Fair and Square. Robert F. Schulkers, Seckatary Hawkins and the Literature of an Ohio Valley Childhood." *Ohio Valley History* 15 (Fall 2015), 43-67.
2. The unpublished autobiographical manuscript, circa 1926, is part of the Schulkers papers, a loosely organized collection of documents and papers curated by the author's grandson, Charles R. Schulkers, in Powhatan, VA.
3. This passage was taken from pages 205-207 of the Robert F. Schulkers novel *The Gray Ghost*. Robert F. Schulkers, Cincinnati, OH, 1926.

Endnotes for Chapter 1.

1. Jessamine Morgan. Her first name is taken from Jessamine County, located just south of Lexington. The county has as part of its border the Kentucky River, and is the site of Camp Nelson and Daniel Boone Cave. West of Jessamine County is Woodford County, site of the village of Clifton and Clifton Cave, and childhood home of Julia Darnell, wife of Robert F. Schulkers.
2. J.W. Brookie Distillery. The 1877 *Atlas of Bourbon, Clark, Fayette, Jessamine and Woodford Counties, Kentucky* has a

detailed map of the village of Clifton. Even though Clifton was a very small river town, it boasted two distilleries, the Miller and Brothers distillery at the north edge of town, and the J.W. Brookie Distillery at the south edge of town along the creek called Rowe's Run. Further upstream along Rowe's Run was the entrance to Clifton Cave.

3. Prohibition in Kentucky. Kentucky went dry by act of the state legislature in November 1919. The entire nation followed suit two months later when the Eighteenth Amendment to the United States Constitution was ratified on 16 January 1920. Prohibition ended with the ratification of the Twenty First Amendment on 5 December 1933, repealing the Eighteenth Amendment (the only US Constitutional Amendment ever rescinded).

4. Consumption. An older, and now outdated, name for the wasting disease pulmonary tuberculosis.

5. Morning View. A small town on the west bank of the Licking River, about 17 miles upstream from southern Covington. It is located near the southern border of Boone County. The 1883 *Atlas of Boone, Kenton and Campbell Counties, Kentucky* shows it to have been a small village sitting astride the Kentucky Central Railroad which ran north as far as Covington.

6. Benjamin Gunn. The name is taken from Robert Louis Stevenson's *Treasure Island*, being the pirate who had been marooned on the island by Captain Flint.

7. The coins listed were all general circulation coinage issued in the years before 1873.

8. Pioneer Bank was one of the older banks of Kentucky.

9. Mr. Drysdale, the president of Morning View Bank. The name is taken from the banker character in the television series *The Beverly Hillbillies*.

10. Clifford Berryman. The name is taken from the real-life Clifford Berryman, born in 1869 in Clifton, Kentucky. The Berryman name was a prominent one in the area. Clifford Berryman went on to become a well-known editorial cartoonist in Washington, DC, first for *The Washington Post* from 1891 to 1907, and then

for *The Washington Star* from 1907 until his death in 1949. He won a Pulitzer Prize in 1944 for Editorial Cartooning for one of his compositions. He was even better known for a 1902 cartoon showing Teddy Roosevelt cuddling a bear cub. This image was the basis for the "teddy bear".

11. The Looking Glass River. The name is taken from the Lewis Carroll (a pen name taken by Charles Lutwidge Dodgson) 1871 novel *Through the looking glass, and what Alice found there*, the sequel to his 1865 novel *Alice's adventures in Wonderland*. While the river in the Seckatary Hawkins stories is never named, there was a "through the looking glass" aspect to how Hawkins and his chums would leave the real world of family and school, and go down the river path into a world of rugged natural beauty and exciting adventure.

Endnotes for Chapter 2.

1. Plessy Ferguson. The name is taken from the landmark 1896 United States Supreme Court decision *Plessy vs. Ferguson*, upholding the constitutionality of state laws requiring racial segregation in public facilities under the doctrine of "separate but equal". In 1890 Louisiana passed the Separate Car Act, requiring passenger trains to have separate cars for whites and blacks. This was challenged in 1892 by Homer Plessy (an "octoroon", meaning he was 1/8th black and 7/8th white), who was arrested for attempting to sit in a car for whites. First heard at the state level, Judge John Ferguson ruled against Plessy, and his decision was appealed up to the US Supreme Court. Their near-unanimous decision against Plessy led to the institution of segregation-based laws that became known as the Jim Crow system. This decision and these laws held until they were all repudiated by the 1954 *Brown vs. the Board of Education* decision. The idea to combine the two names into one was inspired by the Plessy and Ferguson Foundation, created in 2009 by descendants of Homer Plessy and John Ferguson and dedicated to teaching the history of civil rights in the US. The

recent events in Ferguson, Missouri, also played a role in the different uses of the name Ferguson in this chapter.

2. Lake Tapaho. The locale for the Seckatary Hawkins story *The Ghost of Lake Tapaho*. Lake Tapaho is a fictional lake, but was closely based on Indian Lake in mid-north Ohio. Indian Lake was a popular summer vacation spot for wealthy whites during this era.

3. Kentucky Equal Rights Association. Founded in 1888, this was the first statewide women's rights organization in Kentucky. It later became the state chapter of the League of Women Voters, formed in 1920 after the ratification on 26 August 1920 of the Nineteenth Amendment giving women the right to vote. The wording of the Amendment is simply, "The right of citizens of the United States to vote shall not be denied or abridged by the United States or by any State on account of sex."

4. Kentucky Central Railroad. This railroad was established in 1854, linking Lexington to Covington. It was an important means of travel between those two cities. In addition, it transported hogs and other livestock to the meatpacking operations in Covington and Cincinnati. The railroad did not have a bridge from Covington over the Ohio River, and passengers and freight had to cross the river by other means to reach Cincinnati.

5. Green Line streetcar. The Green Line Company, officially the Cincinnati, Newport and Covington Railway Company (CN&C), linked Covington and other northern Kentucky cities along the Ohio River to Cincinnati, crossing on the Suspension Bridge. This bridge, opened to pedestrians and horsedrawn vehicles in 1867, added the CN&C electric streetcar line in 1891. Their cars were painted green to distinguish them from the orange streetcars that plied the streets of downtown Cincinnati.

6. Trenchtown. A neighborhood in Kingston, the capital city of Jamaica. Trenchtown was the birthplace of the ska, rocksteady and reggae genres of popular music. It was the home of international reggae star Bob Marley, along with many other musicians and reform-minded political leaders of Jamaica,

who together successfully raised world consciousness of the impoverishment and political corruption rampant in the island nation during the 1960's.

7. Colored Baptist Church. The 1877 *Atlas of Bourbon, Clark, Fayette, Jessamine and Woodford Counties, Kentucky* has a detailed map of the village of Clifton. This map shows the Colored Baptist Church on the south edge of town, near the J.W. Brookie distillery.

8. Reverend Reuben Mulcahy. The name is partially taken from the character Father John Mulcahy on the television series *MASH*. The first name was changed from John to Reuben to reflect both that he was Baptist, not Catholic, and that Reuben was a relatively common first name for northern Kentucky black men of his age in this story.

9. Mayor Railey. The Railey family was a prominent one in Woodford County and the area around Clifton. The family tree of Julia Darnell, who married Robert F. Schulkers, has direct connections to the Raileys.

10. Doctor Pepper. The name is based on the popular soda of the same name. However, with his first name being Oscar, it is also based on the Oscar Pepper Distillery (today called the Woodford Reserve Distillery, and located close to Clifton). The Oscar Pepper Distillery gained fame due to the research there by Dr. James Crow, who developed and perfected the sour mash fermentation, pot still distillation, and barrel maturation steps that led to the distinctive taste, aroma and appearance of modern bourbon.

11. General Lyon. Based on Hyman Lyon, a United States Army career officer, who joined the Confederate forces upon the outbreak of the Civil War. Serving as a brigadier general, he was a brilliant combat leader whose forces defeated or stymied Union forces in many skirmishes and battles.

12. Berryman's General Store. The Berryman family was prominent in Clifton. They operated several businesses in the town. The family tree of Julia Darnell, who married Robert F. Schulkers, has direct connections to the Berrymans.

13. Charles Clay Buntain and William Rice. Based on real veterans of the Fifth United States Colored Cavalry. There was a boy named Hal Rice, a member of the Fair and Square Club in the early Seck Hawkins stories (present in the books *The Rejiment Stories Volume I*, *The Rejiment Stories Volume II*, and *Stoner's Boy*), and a Rice family lives to this day in Clifton.

14. The hymn *Nothing but the blood of Jesus*. Composed by Robert Lowry in 1876, this striking hymn is a Baptist standard to this day, especially in sects that hold true to older Baptist traditions. The commentary by Reverend Mulcahy reflects a general lament that "they're trying to take the blood out" of the more modern hymnals.

15. Cyprian Clamorgan. Based on the name of the author of *The colored aristocracy of St. Louis*, an intelligent and well-educated man of mixed race (American white and West Indian black). The Mr. Clamorgan of this story is likewise highly intelligent, having memorized all the songs in the Baptist hymnal.

16. This reading was taken from the Wisdom of Solomon, Chapter 4. A common reading at Baptist funerals. Protestant churches generally consider it to be non-canonical (apocryphal), and thus not Biblical "scripture". Catholics usually change the name to the Book of Wisdom. It is one of the seven Sapiential or wisdom books included within the Septuagint, along with Psalms, Proverbs, Ecclesiastes, Song of Songs (Song of Solomon), Job, and Sirach.

17. Men sipping on bourbon mint juleps. While the use of tobacco products was a common occurrence in the Seckatary Hawkins books, the consumption of alcohol was not. There was one mention in *Trilogy II: The Dog Snatchers* pages 114-115. Doc Waters was talking to Hawkins about how Judge Granbery was grieving the loss of his dog:

> "Strange! How a person can get to love a dog. Yesterday I went over to call on the judge. Stokes, his butler, warned me that the judge was in no mood to receive me. But I went on in. He was slowly pacing

up and down in his library, his eyes on the floor, his hands locked behind his back. Stokes told me he had been doing that almost constantly since Saturday night. Once he had ordered Stokes to bring him a drink. And while he was drinking it, he said to Stokes: 'You remember The Champ, Stokes! Don't forget him! He was a great hound. We'll never see his like again.' And then he set to pacing the floor again."

18. Elijah Craig. The name is based on a Baptist preacher from Virginia who is credited with inventing bourbon, in that he is believed by some as having discovered the virtues of aging new whiskey in charred oak barrels. The facts are that this is, at best, simply a charming legend, since this "invention" was made simultaneously by many shippers of whiskey. The legend lives on in the form of Elijah Craig bourbon made by the Heaven Hill Distillery.

19. The Fifth United States Colored Cavalry and the Battle of Hopkinsville. General Hyman Lyon and his Confederate forces engaged the Union forces, including the Fifth US Colored Cavalry, at Hopkinsville, Kentucky, in December 1864. The Confederate forces prevailed, but faced a gallant defense by the Fifth.

20. Champ Ferguson. The Saltville Massacre recalled here by General Lyon and Scout is true, and stands as one of the most despicable war crimes of the Civil War. The other Confederate officer who was hanged for war crimes was Captain Henry Wirz, commandant of the infamous Andersonville, Georgia prison for Union soldiers.

21. Woodhawks. An early American slang term, long out of use, referring to men who sold wood to passing steamboats for fuel. Two paintings by George Caleb Bingham, *Boatmen on the Missouri*, and *The Wood-Boat*, depict woodhawks at work. These are shown and described in the catalog *Navigating the West. George Caleb Bingham and the river* (Nenette Luarca-Shoaf et

al., Amon Carter Museum of American Art, the Saint Louis Art Museum, and Yale University Press) that accompanied the 2015 Bingham exhibition (pages 44-46).

22. Steamboat consumption of firewood. The typical steamboat consumption of 200 cubic feet of firewood per hour is accurate, a figure taken from informational placards accompanying the 2015 Bingham exhibition (see the previous endnote). In the catalog for this exhibit, the term "wooding up" is used to describe the "frantic labor" required to rapidly load a steamboat with the tons of firewood it required at frequent intervals.

Endnotes for Chapter 3.

1. Butternut hickory nuts. Obtained from the butternut hickory tree, also known as the white walnut (*Juglans cinerea*). This tree is actually a species of walnut, so the name "butternut hickory" is misleading. The nuts can indeed be used to prepare an olive yellow dye. Unfortunately, today the butternut hickory tree is on the edge of extinction due to the butternut canker, an accidentally introduced fungal disease.

2. Memphis mentioned as being on the Looking Glass River. Schulkers wrote that the river in the Seck Hawkins stories was a composite of the Ohio, Licking, and Kentucky rivers (the Schulkers papers). There are passages in the stories that suggest the river runs south from St. Louis, past Cincinnati, past their town, and on downstream past Paducah and on to New Orleans and the Gulf of Mexico. Obviously for this fanciful river to have such a course would put Memphis on the banks of the Looking Glass.

3. The Palisades along the Looking Glass River. In the Bluegrass region of Kentucky, the Kentucky River cuts a gorge several hundred feet deep lined with picturesque cliffs known as The Palisades which extend for more than a hundred miles from Frankfort to Boonesborough. This same geologic feature is used in this story.

4. The horse names are taken from the names of horses who won the Kentucky Derby, all before 1914 (the year this story is set). Joe Cotton won the Derby in 1885, Aristides in 1875, Wintergreen in 1909, and Stone Street in 1908.

5. Independence Turnpike. The 1883 *Atlas of Boone, Kenton and Campbell Counties, Kentucky* shows the Independence Turnpike running from the vicinity of Morning View north to Independence. There the road becomes the Banklick Turnpike, and continues north to Covington.

6. Bluegrass countryside. The landscape as described is common along rural roads in the central Bluegrass near Clifton. The roads are lined with stone walls, with Kentucky coffeetrees (*Gymnocladus dioica*) growing between the walls and the roads. Beyond the walls wooden fences surround the horse pastures, with black cherry trees (*Prunus serotina*) growing between the walls and the fences.

    In recent years, some horse farms have been removing the black cherry trees around their pastures. An outbreak in 2001 of "mare reproductive loss syndrome", with up to 30% of foals being aborted dead, was eventually linked to the hairs of Eastern tent caterpillars being ingested by pregnant mares. These caterpillars favor black cherry trees as their host plant, and their hairs can be consumed after they fall onto the grass in the pastures. Another solution to this problem is to keep pregnant mares out of the pastures during severe outbreaks of the Eastern tent caterpillar.

7. Becky Thatcher. The name is taken from that of Tom Sawyer's secret girlfriend.

8. Panic of '73. The Panic of 1873 plunged the United States and Europe into economic depression until 1879. The crisis was set off by several factors, including over-investment in railroads in the US. In September of 1873, when the investment bank Jay Cooke and Co. was about to secure a loan for the Northern Pacific Railway, the bank's credit was called into question. The bonds behind the loan failed, and the bank declared bankruptcy. This set off a chain reaction of bank failures across the US.

9. Running freight on the Looking Glass River between New Orleans and St. Louis. Near the end of the Seckatary Hawkins book *Stormie the Dog Stealer*, it is mentioned that Stormie Petry has become captain of the steamboat *Louisiana Lou* and, with Big Ike handling the boilers, will be running a route from St. Louis to New Orleans (*Stormie the Dog Stealer* page 291; unabridged *Stormie the Dog Stealer* page 336). This is recalled twice in the unabridged edition of *Knights of the Square Table* pages 129 and 151. These two passages were omitted from the original edition of *Knights of the Square Table*.

Endnotes for Chapter 4.

1. Trans-Atlantic cable. The Trans-Atlantic telegraph cable between Europe and North America commenced operation in 1858.

2. Start of World War I. The assassination by Serb nationalists of Archduke Franz Ferdinand of Austria and his wife Sophie in the Bosnian capital of Sarajevo on 28 June 1914 set off a firestorm of protests and angry exchanges between the governments of Serbia and the allied nations of Austria-Hungary and Germany. Diplomatic breakdowns over the next few weeks led to the outbreak of war by late July.

3. The steamboats *Kentucky Belle*, *Crescent City*, and *Cynthianne*. The *Kentucky Belle* was not ever the name of an actual steamboat. It appeared in many Seckatary Hawkins books, namely *The Rejiment Stories Volume II*, *Stoner's Boy*, *The Red Runners*, *Ching Toy*, *The Chinese Coin*, *Gideon*, *Trilogy II: Jericho*, and *Hackbury*. In these books, it is stated that the *Kentucky Belle* ran from the clubhouse vicinity downstream to Paducah and New Orleans. It was wrecked by river ice in *Hackbury* pages 120 and 126.

The *Crescent City* was an actual steamboat, built in Cincinnati in 1880. It was named after the Crescent City nickname for New Orleans, so-called because the Mississippi River makes a crescent curve around that city. It appears in two Seckatary Hawkins books. In the unabridged *Knights of the Square Table*, Chapter 10 *The Mysterious Stranger* and Chapter 11 *The Mystery Solved* both feature the *Crescent City* extensively. These two chapters were omitted from the original edition of this book. In *Ching Toy*, the steamboat is seen at the Watertown wharf (page 26 of the original edition, page 25 of the unabridged edition). There were two earlier steamboats of the same name, one built in Cincinnati in 1854 (lost in 1861) and the other built in Evansville, Indiana in 1867 (lost in 1873). The *Crescent City* built in Cincinnati in 1854 ran St. Louis to New Orleans, and was the steamboat young Samuel Clemens (1835-1910) stood his first pilot watches on.

The *Cynthianne* was not ever the name of an actual steamboat. It appeared extensively in *Trilogy II: Jericho*, and briefly in *Hackbury* (pages 29, 54, and 98).

Information on steamboats for this story came from two books, *Way's Packet Directory, 1848-1994*, and *Way's Steam Towboat Directory*. Both books were compiled by Frederick Way, Jr., and published by Ohio University Press in 1994 and 1990, respectively.

4. Freshwater mussels. The rivers of the central United States, especially the Ohio and the upper Mississippi and their tributaries, contain the richest diversity of freshwater mussels in the world. The state of Kentucky is home to over 100 species of mussels. The fact that these little-known invertebrates have been given trivial names, such as those called out by Stone Morgan, is due to their importance in the late 1800's to early 1900's as raw material to manufacture "pearl buttons" for clothing. Stone mentions the threehorn wartyback (*Obliquaria reflexa*), yellow mucket (*Lampsilis radiata luteola*), hickory nut (*Obovaria olivaria*), butterfly (*Ellipsaria lineolata*) and the Northern elktoe (*Alasmidonta marginata*). Stone is correct when he mentions that the Northern elktoe is a rare one. Uncommon at best in the northern portions of its range in the upper Midwest, it is indeed rare south of the Ohio River.

5. Steamboat engine dimensions. In general, the larger the steamboat, the larger the engine dimensions. One of the largest steamboat engines was on the famous *Robert E. Lee*, which had 40 inch cylinders and a piston stroke of ten feet. The immense *Delta Queen* had tandem compound cylinders of 26 inches and 52 and a half inches, respectively, and a piston stroke of ten feet.

6. Ivory-billed woodpecker. Believed to be extinct today, this magnificent bird (*Campephilus principalis*) was the largest woodpecker in the United States (and second in the world only to the imperial woodpecker of Mexico) with a length of 19 to 21 inches, a wingspan of 30 to 33 inches, and a bill 2.5 inches long. The plumage was glossy blue-black, glossed with green below; head crested, red in the male, black in the female; and a white stripe extended down each side of the neck onto the fore back. The most distinctive feature, distinguishing it from similar birds such as the pileated woodpecker, was that the wings had large white patches. The habitat of the ivory-billed woodpecker was old growth bottomland forests and swamps; habitat destruction in the 1800's was the main cause of the demise of this bird. By the 1880's, the bird had become quite rare throughout its range. The range of the bird was the South Atlantic and Gulf States from eastern Texas to North Carolina, and north in the Mississippi and Ohio Valleys to Missouri, Kentucky, southern Illinois and southern Indiana. The ivory-billed woodpecker also ranged into eastern Cuba, where the last confirmed sighting was in 1987. There has not been a confirmed sighting of the bird in the US since 1944. Reported sightings in Arkansas in 2004 and in Florida in 2005 have not been confirmed, and are rejected by nearly all experts.

7. Pawpaw trees. The pawpaw tree (*Asimina triloba*) produces a large fleshy fruit with a custard-like consistency and a flavor reminiscent of mango. In the Seckatary Hawkins books, there are a couple of passages where Hawkins and the boys are seeking out this fruit, either in Parks Hills (*The Gray Ghost* pages 209 and 219; unabridged *The Gray Ghost* pages 249 and 251) or

across the river in the woods near Burney's field (unabridged *Ching Toy*, in the short story *Two boys and a dog* page 280).

8. The steamboat *Bonanza*. The *Bonanza* was an actual steamboat, built in Cincinnati in 1885. The engine dimensions called out by Cliff Morgan, 22's – 7 and a half feet, are correct. It was the boat that put Lew Hunter off at the clubhouse (*The Rejiment Stories Volume II* page 413), while he was travelling upstream from Paducah to Cincinnati (*The Rejiment Stories Volume II* page 439). There were several other mentions of the *Bonanza* in this book, but it did not appear in any other Seckatary Hawkins books.

9. The sighting of a deer. Prior to European settlement, eastern North America had a white-tailed deer (*Odocoileus virginianus*) population estimated at 30 million. Over-hunting had reduced that number to about 300,000 by 1900. Most of these deer were in remote forested areas without extensive farmland or other development. In northern Kentucky and the Bluegrass, sightings of deer were extremely rare from the late 1800's to the 1930's.

In the Seckatary Hawkins books, deer are seldom mentioned. In *The Rejiment Stories Volume I* pages 388-402 describe an incident in which a pair of deer antlers are stolen from Judge Granbery's house and then returned. When and where the antlers were obtained from a deer is not mentioned.

In *The Red Castle*, Chapter 11 is entitled *The deer hunt*. Lige Hobbs comes to the clubhouse to report that he has seen a deer that morning, stating "I'm meanin' big game, like you hear the old folks tell about when their great granddaddies used to live in log houses around here, and when the redskins was a-pesterin' the life out o' 'em day in and day out". Hawkins replies "You mean to stand there and tell me you can scare up deer meat around this old river bank, when we know the last of the deers around here was shot more'n a hundred year ago?" Lige dismissively refers to ". . . that old belief – that no more deers are on these shores . . .". But Jerry Moore is determined to hunt the deer. Hawkins says to Jerry of the deer that:

". . . they've been exterminated for years – you ask your daddy."

"I did ask him," cut in Jerry, softly, laying his hand on my arm. "I asked him last night, and he said there wasn't. He said, 'No, there ain't been deer around here since the year Great-Granddaddy Moore shot the last one'."

"Well," I said, "wouldn't you believe your own father?"

"I would," answered Jerry, "only that I happened to see a deer myself – last night – before I asked him."

The illustration on page 107 shows Jerry taking aim on the animal with the rifle that Hawkins "got from Larry King some years ago". He shot and killed the animal, which turned out be an American elk that had escaped from the Watertown Zoo five days earlier.

In *Gideon* page 156, Hawkins states "Lige Hobbs says that there's been a deer seen in the Pelham timber during the winter . . ."

Other than this latter passage, which was not followed up on in the storyline, there was never a confirmed deer sighting in any of the Seckatary Hawkins books.

10. Foxfire. There are several species of bioluminescent fungi that grow in decaying wood, exhibiting a surprisingly bright bluish or greenish glow. The biochemistry of this light production is closely related to the mechanism by which fireflies glow. A pile of firewood, gathered in the summer from the floor of a damp bottomland forest, will often contain luminescent pieces of branches. Foxfire was mentioned in the Seckatary Hawkins stories one time, where it was referred to as "witch-fire". In the short story *A Wager in the Mill* (this was published in the newspaper on 19 July 1925, one of three single chapter short stories inserted between the end of *The Chinese Coin* story and the beginning of *The Yellow Y* story), when Rube Muller saw a

mysterious light in the old mill on Banklick Creek, his father told him "That was witch-fire!" Rube told Hawkins, who responded ". . . if it was witch-fire, why of course it's because there is some rotting, wet stuff under the floor or something like that to make a little light like a fire-fly . . ." (in the short stories at the end of the unabridged *The Chinese Coin* book, pages 470-471. This incident and the word "witch-fire" also appeared in the comics (*The Chinese Coin* comics, *Comic Book 2* page 57).

11. George Caleb Bingham and the American Art-Union. The American Art-Union (AA-U), formed in 1840, promoted the fine arts in the United States. As described in the catalog *Navigating the West. George Caleb Bingham and the river* (Nenette Luarca-Shoaf et al., Amon Carter Museum of American Art, the Saint Louis Art Museum, and Yale University Press) that accompanied the 2015 Bingham exhibition, it was his involvement with the AA-U that brought Bingham to national attention when in December 1846 the Bingham painting *The Jolly Flatboatmen* was chosen as the engraving to be distributed to all AA-U subscribers the following year. It proved immensely popular, and was displayed in many homes in Cincinnati, Louisville, St. Louis, New Orleans, Pittsburgh and elsewhere across the region.

12. The steamboat *City of Clifton*. This was an actual steamboat, built in Jeffersonville, Indiana, in 1900. The engine dimensions called out by Cliff Morgan, 16's – 7 feet, are correct, and reflect a relatively small steamboat, as stated in this story. The *City of Clifton* did not appear in any Seckatary Hawkins book, but it was included in this story because of the link to Clifton, Kentucky.

13. The steamboat *Smokey City*. This was not ever the name of an actual steamboat, but it was the name of a steam towboat. The name is based on one of the nicknames of Pittsburgh, Pennsylvania, due to the many steelmills in the city around 1900. The steamboat *Smokey City* was featured extensively in *The Rejiment Stories Volume II*. It was wrecked in ice, *The Gray Ghost* page 66 (unabridged *The Gray Ghost* page 75) and the

wreck was featured that book and in *Stormie the Dog Stealer*, *Ching Toy*, *The Chinese Coin*, the unabridged edition of *Herman the Fiddler*, and *The Red Castle*.

14. "We reached a bend where tall cliffs came into view. Suddenly it became hard to paddle, maybe because the cliffs dropped straight into the river here, and the stream was squeezed into a narrower channel. It was taking us longer to paddle past here."

This passage is drawn from a description of the river just downstream from the clubhouse in *The Gray Ghost* pages 43-44 (unabridged *The Gray Ghost* pages 52-53). Seckatary Hawkins and all the other boys were paddling their canoes upstream on their way back to the clubhouse, and were approaching the cliffs that lined the river just down from the clubhouse:

> ". . . until we reached the bend where the cliffs came into view . . . It always seemed like this was the hardest place in the world to paddle. . . . Maybe because the cliffs go steep into the river here, and the water is squeezed into a narrower bed . . . It takes you longer to paddle past here . . . We swung around the bend by the cliffs with a splash and a go, and we started on the last stretch for home shore . . ."

15. ". . . we scared up a great number of turkey buzzards from their roost on a rocky ledge. They shot into the air with a great whirring of wings, sounding for all the world like the whirring of an airplane." This passage is taken from a real-life experience of Robert F. Schulkers, as well as two passages in Seckatary Hawkins books.

In his journal of a trip on 6 September 1915 to the cliffs along the Kentucky River near Clifton (the Schulkers papers), guided by his father-in-law Charlie Darnell, Schulkers wrote:

> "As we neared the cliff a whirring noise greeted our ears . . . I saw a great number of turkey buzzards

rise into the air . . . sounding for all the world like the whirring of an aeroplane."

This experience must have made an impression on Schulkers, for he wove it into two Seckatary Hawkins books.

In *Gideon* page 267, Hawkins was going up the cliff path when ". . . once I scared a flock of turkey-buzzards, and they all scared off at once, making a sound like an airplane taking off."

In *Trilogy IV, The Gang of Usher* page 194, Shadow and Hawkins were headed to Cliff Cave. "And so we hurried down the path that leads from the Main Road to the river, and so on to the Cliff Path that winds up toward the caves. At one spot on the cliff-side we startled a bunch of turkey buzzards, and they flew away with a whirring of wings that sounded like an airplane taking off."

Endnotes for Chapter 5.

1. Brother Francis. In the Seckatary Hawkins books, at first their teacher was Miss Sally and then later it was Brother Jim. There were two mentions of Brother Francis as their teacher, first as Brother Frank (*Little Gil* page 47) and then as Brother Francis (*Trilogy III: The Backwater Pool* page 223).

    There was a real Brother Francis (Francis Laehr), who was the principal at St. Joseph's High School during the years when Robert F. Schulkers attended (he graduated in 1906). The school was just two blocks north of his boyhood home.

    Francis Laehr was born on 17 October 1857 in Cincinnati, and died on 5 August 1939 in Beacon, New York.

    The date of his death may be significant. The chapter in *Trilogy III: The Backwater Pool*, where Brother Francis was mentioned, was originally published in the newspaper on 9 April 1939. Perhaps Brother Francis, then 82 years old, was critically ill and RFS wanted to honor him before he died.

    The information on Brother Francis was provided by Father Paul Vieson at the Marianist Archives in Dayton, Ohio.

2. Austinberg. While "our town" was never named in the Seckatary Hawkins books, Austinberg was chosen as the name for this story. It is a neighborhood of Covington near the Eastside neighborhood where the Schulkers home was located.

3. Melodeon. There are several passages in the Seckatary Hawkins books that refer to Lew Hunter's organ as a melodeon (*Knights of the Square Table* pages 6 and 112, unabridged *Knights of the Square Table* pages 3 and 225, *Herman the Fiddler* page 174, unabridged *Herman the Fiddler* page 299, *The Lavender Light Mystery* page 13, and *Trilogy III: The Backwater Pool* page 260). A melodeon is a small organ, popular in the 1800's. In the melodeon and the closely related harmonium, notes are produced by air driven through metal reeds by foot-operated bellows.

4. Lexington, home of the Lamberts. At the end of their adventures in Cuba, it is announced that the reunited Lambert family will purchase a home in Lexington (*Seckatary Hawkins in Cuba* page 403, unabridged *Seckatary Hawkins in Cuba* page 329).

5. Will Standish at a college in Pennsylvania. Following the events in *The Gray Ghost*, Hawkins wrote at the beginning of the next book, *Stormie the Dog Stealer*, of the departure of several Club members, including Link Lambert, Harold and Oliver Court, "Rolling Stone" John Loomis, and that "Will Standish had to go Pennsylvania, where his father was waiting to enter him in a college there." (*Stormie the Dog Stealer* page 2, unabridged *Stormie the Dog Stealer* page 3). College in this case would refer to a residential preparatory high school.

6. The unicorn on Burney's Field. The "unicorn" was shot and killed by Androfski (*The Gray Ghost* page 275, unabridged *The Gray Ghost* page 317). Doc Waters identified the animal as one that had escaped from the Watertown Zoo during a fire (*The Gray Ghost* page 276, unabridged *The Gray Ghost* page 320). Hawkins later wrote that the animal was a gnu, or horned horse, that had broken off one horn when it fell off the cliff (*The Gray Ghost* page 279, unabridged *The Gray Ghost* page 322). Gnu is another name for wildebeest; the description of the animal

in this story suggests it was a black wildebeest (*Connochaetes gnou*).

7. Briggen confused for Harkinson. This incident occurred at night on the launch *Cazanova*, at the end of the summer going away party for Link Lambert, Will Standish, and Harold and Oliver Court. Hawkins and Harold were sitting on the rear deck, when an "ugly big hand" grasped the gunwale. Hawkins was convinced it was Harkinson. Harold grabbed a wooden pin and smashed the hand (this scene illustrated in *The Red Runners* page 115, unabridged *The Red Runners* page 137). Two chapters later, Briggen (with a bandaged hand) admitted it was him (*The Red Runners* page 136, unabridged *The Red Runners* page 157).

Endnotes for Chapter 6.

1. The Looking Glass River flows to New Orleans and the Gulf of Mexico. Robert F. Schulkers wrote that the river in the Seckatary Hawkins stories was a fanciful river, a composite of the Licking, Kentucky, and Ohio rivers (the Schulkers papers). There are several passages in the Seckatary Hawkins books that suggest the river runs south from St. Louis, past Cincinnati, past their town, and on downstream past Rabbit Hash and Paducah and on to New Orleans and the Gulf of Mexico. The town of Rabbit Hash, Kentucky is on the Ohio River a short distance downstream from Cincinnati. It was mentioned twice in *Gideon* (pages 105 and 120), referring to Rabbit Hash as being "down the river far past Seven Willows Island". Paducah, Kentucky is on the Ohio River far downstream from Cincinnati, near the confluence of the Ohio and Mississippi rivers. It was mentioned in several Seckatary Hawkins books. The steamboat *Smokey City* first appeared coming upstream from Paducah (*The Regiment Stories Volume II* page 144), the steamboat *Hudson Lee* was seen travelling from Paducah to Cincinnati (*The Regiment Stories Volume II* page 235), and Lew Hunter was a stowaway attempting to travel from Paducah to Cincinnati when he was kicked off the steamboat *Bonanza* at the little landing near the

clubhouse (*The Rejiment Stories Volume II* pages 413 and 439). In *Gideon* (page 45) it states of the steamboat *Kentucky Belle* that it "travels sometimes to Paducah and sometimes as far as New Orleans."

2. Twelve writing books of Seckatary Hawkins stacked under his desk. The number of writing books Hawkins accumulated grew as the years passed, and the few times the number of books was mentioned in the Seckatary Hawkins books indicated that there was one writing book per book-length set of episodes.

The first mention of the number of writing books was in *Stormie the Dog Stealer* page 4 (unabridged *Stormie the Dog Stealer* pages 3-4):

> Every day after school we have our meeting, and I write the minutes of the meeting. I got to like this writing so much that I didn't stop at the minutes, but wrote down in this "seckatary" book everything that happened to us boys. I have been doing this work ever since we started our meetings, and believe me, I have written many books full. They are big books, too, but this is the eighth one I am writing now. The other seven, full to the last page with my scribbling, are stacked under my desk.

Stormie the Dog Stealer was the fifth book in the original ten hardback books published from 1921 to 1930. That Hawkins refers to the corresponding writing book as being his eighth reflects the fact that Schulkers had intended to publish three volumes of the Rejiment-era stories that predated *Stoner's Boy* and the other nine original books.

There were 103 Rejiment-era stories. These have been published by the modern Seckatary Hawkins Club as *The Rejiment Stories Volume I* (episodes 1-47; 47 chapters), *The Rejiment Stories Volume II* (episodes 48-99; 52 chapters), and *The Rejiment Stories Volume III* (episodes 100-103; 4 chapters, published at the beginning of the unabridged edition of *The Red Runners*).

Schulkers intended to publish the Rejiment-era stories in three books with the titles *Seckatary Hawkins and the Rejiment*, *Seckatary Hawkins and the Skinny Guy*, and *Seckatary Hawkins and the Stranded Houseboat*. From short descriptions of these books listed on the rear dustjacket of the 1921 first edition of *Seckatary Hawkins in Cuba*, as well as more detailed notes found among the Schulkers papers, these three books were intended to be comprised of the following Rejiment-era episodes:

Seckatary Hawkins and the Rejiment   1- 38 (38 chapters)

Seckatary Hawkins and the Skinny Guy   39- 72 (34 chapters)

Seckatary Hawkins and the Stranded   73-103 (31 chapters)
Houseboat

The second time the number of writing books was mentioned was in *The Ghost of Lake Tapaho* page 4:

It is my custom to write down not only the minutes of our club meetings, but also everything that happens around this old river bank. It comes natural to me – I just like to do it, that's all – and I always enjoy writing down in my "seckatary" book the happenings of the day. Since our first adventure with Detective Jeckerson, I guess I have written a dozen books full of our exciting times, and these books are stacked under my desk where I am writing this, so that any of the boys in our club can find them and read them over when he wants, and, believe me, they read them over a plenty! The first few of the books are nearly worn ragged!

The first book Detective Jeckerson appeared in was *Knights of the Square Table*. There were nine books in the series from that book up to *The Ghost of Lake Tapaho*. The "guess"

Hawkins made to there being about twelve writing books in this timeframe was roughly correct.

There were two other mentions of there being "several" or "many" writing books, first in *Herman the Fiddler* page 3 (unabridged *Herman the Fiddler* page 3):

> Each day we gathered in this little shack and held a club meeting, and then I would write down the minutes of the meeting, because I was the secretary. And I had been doing this writing for a long time now – ever since the time when I hardly knew how to write – when I spelt the word "seckatary", a nickname which has stuck to me ever since. There had been many exciting times around this old river bank, and I had written several books full – they are all stacked under my desk now, as I write this.

and second in *The Return of the Skinny Guy* pages 8-9:

> There's no use telling tales twice, but just to keep the record clear, I will say that Doc Waters and I accompanied the Skinny Guy to Cuba to claim his inheritance, and it is all written down in one of the many books of my writings which are stacked under my desk here in my writing room, which is a little room the other boys added to our clubhouse while I was down in Cuba with Link.

3. "the fine rifle Larry King had given me several years ago." This refers to an incident related in *The Rejiment Stories Volume II*. In the chapter entitled *Larry the Hunter* that begins on page 444, Larry King arrived on the riverbank wanting to do some hunting. He shot and killed a quail, which got the sheriff upset. Hawkins and the boys got Larry out of his trouble with the law, and in return, on page 454 Larry King gave his rifle to Hawkins as a parting gift. The story was retold with some modifications

in *Trilogy IV: The Nip and Tuck Gang*, where Larry King gave Hawkins his rifle on page 26, but then the rifle changed hands several times, and the boys finally gave it back to Larry King on page 89.

4. "We've been exploring these woods since we were five years old!" There are many passages in the Seckatary Hawkins books where Hawkins mentioned that Johnny McLarren and Bill Darby were his oldest friends, and that they played together in the woods. In a passage found only in the unabridged *The Gray Ghost*, page 113, Hawkins wrote of the woods in the ravine behind the cliffs:

> This is a nice old woods. Seems like every tree in it is a friend of mine. I've been here ever since I was born. When I first started to play, big enough to be on my own legs, and toddle around for myself, these woods were my first playground.

Hawkins and Johnny and Bill thus would have been very young, perhaps five years old as stated in this story, when they first played in the woods.

Hawkins and the other boys formed the Fair and Square Club a few years later, when they were nine years old. This was at the start of the *Rejiment* stories, and the stories progressed in a manner that matched the real calendar for about five years. At that point, Hawkins and the boys were 14 years old, at the beginning of *Knights of the Square Table*. After that, Schulkers stopped the clock and the boys remained 14 years old for the rest of the stories.

That the stories followed the real calendar for about five years (from the start of the *Rejiment* stories in early 1918 to the start of *Knights of the Square Table* in early 1923) is supported by many text passages. These text passages most significantly include many where a prior event is recalled and it is mentioned how long ago it was. These time references are correct up until the beginning of *Knights of the Square Table*, and indicate an even progression of time that matched the real calendar.

The key text passage on the age of the boys in the Seckatary Hawkins books is found in *Knights of the Square Table* page 10 (unabridged *Knights of the Square Table* page 8), originally in the newspaper in May 1923. Herb Acomb is talking to Hawkins:

"How'd you come to get called 'Seckatary' Hawkins? I ain't never heard a fella called that-a-way afore."

"They picked me out," I said, "to write down all that happened in the club. We were only kids, then, I was only nine years old. I didn't know how to spell secretary and so when they put it up to me to write down which was which, I wrote that I was 'seckatary' and the nickname has stuck to me ever since, Herb. I guess it will always stick to me, now. I wish you could have known the others that aren't with us any more. Since we went into our teens, seems like an age. You should have known us when Johnny McLarren was at the head. He was our first captain."

5. Sassafras trees. The sassafras tree (*Sassafras albidum*) was mentioned several times in the Seckatary Hawkins books, namely *Stoner's Boy* page 191 and unabridged *Stoner's Boy* page 354, unabridged *The Gray Ghost* page 22 (this passage omitted from the original edition of *The Gray Ghost*), *The Gray Ghost* page 101 (unabridged *The Gray Ghost* page 113), and *Knights of the Square Table* page 71 (unabridged *Knights of the Square Table* page 89).

6. Cedar tree above opening to Cave of Wonders. In the book *The Chinese Coin*, the entrance to the Cave of Wonders was hidden high up in a cliff in the ravine on the backside of the hill containing the Cliff Cave complex. A tall spruce tree growing on top of the cliff was the landmark Hawkins and the boys

used to remember the spot (the text states "Above the cliff grew the towering spruce." in *The Chinese Coin* page 221, unabridged *The Chinese Coin* page 381; this tree is prominent in the illustration on pages 223 and 382, respectively, of these two books). However, spruce trees are not native to Kentucky; the closest native spruce trees are red spruce (*Picea rubens*) growing in the Appalachian Mountains of North Carolina, Tennessee and West Virginia. For this story, the tree was changed to a red cedar (*Juniperus virginiana*), which is common throughout Kentucky.

7. Beech and walnut trees in woods behind cliffs. In the Seckatary Hawkins books are several passages that mention beech and walnut trees in the woods along the base of the cliffs on the backside of the hill containing the Cliff Cave complex. American beech trees (*Fagus grandifolia*) were mentioned there in *The Red Runners* page 223 (unabridged *The Red Runners* page 228), and *The Lavender Light Mystery* pages 94 and 110. Black walnut trees (*Juglans nigra*) were stated to be growing there in *The Lavender Light Mystery* page 110, *Trilogy I: The Mystery of the Green Light* page 193, and *Trilogy III: The White Bat* page 19.

8. Exit of Cave River. There are several passages in the Seckatary Hawkins books that described the course of Cave River as a branch of the main stream of the river entering the cave system at a hole in the cliffs near the clubhouse and then coming back out into the main stream of the river some distance downstream.

In *Stydle the Strong* page 77:

> "Cave River!" I exclaimed suddenly. "Remember the Cave River! Maybe that will help us all to solve the problem!" So we all got into our canoes, and paddled down to where the willows overhang the water, hiding the great hole in the cliffside, where the water enters and travels in a semicircle for about a mile, and then comes out in the river again.

In *Trilogy II: The Dog Snatchers* page 3:

Today we boys held a club meeting right after school, in our little old houseboat which is fastened to a big log sticking out over the water from the shore, in the mouth of that branch of the stream which we call Cave River. We call it that because about thirty feet farther the branch goes into a hole in the cliff side, which is really the entrance to a cave. The entrance is pretty well hidden by overhanging willows, but we boys have taken canoe rides into it for a good distance, and we knew a whole lot about the insides of that old Cave River, but we have never been able to explore it to the end. Doc Waters told us it flows for a good ways under the cliffs, and then comes out again lower down the river, some miles maybe; but we have never been able to find where it comes out again.

In *Trilogy II: The Dog Snatchers* page 116:

. . . we went down to the branch of our river, as it turns off and flows into a cave in the cliffs – we boys call it Cave River. It flows under the cliffs in the dark, for a mile or two, and then comes out again into the big river.

In *Gander* page 4:

. . . we call this branch "Cave River" because it flows underground for a mile or more and then comes out lower downstream, to join the river again.

In *Trilogy II: Jericho* page 231:

. . . toward the spot where the river branched off to the right into a hole in the cliffs, a branch that we boys had named Cave River, since it ran for some distance underground and came out again to join the main stream at another hole in the cliffy shore.

In *Trilogy III: The Backwater Pool* page 211:

> They took me down to where the river branches off into a hole in the cliffs. We call it the entrance to Cave River, because this little branch flows underground for quite a good way and then comes out again through another hole in the cliffs, to join the main stream. The willows grow thickly in this little bay that forms the mouth of Cave River . . .

In *Trilogy IV: The Gang of Usher* page 206:

> We all knew that the most logical hiding place for anything like a boat was in the rocky tunnel in the cliffs that we called Cave River. Here a branch of the waters of our river flowed underground for several miles, winding through subterranean chambers in the limestone and emerging again into the main stream many miles below.

9. Table Rock. A landmark in Cave River was Table Rock, where they often landed their canoes when entering the Cliff Cave complex by that route. Table Rock was near the bottom of the deep pit in Cliff Cave. It was mentioned by name several times (*The Emperor's Sword* page 143, *Stydle the Strong* page 150, *Trilogy II: The Dog Snatchers* page 68, *Trilogy II: Jericho* page 235, and *Hackbury* page 192).

10. Reuben Muller. There was a single chapter short story entitled *A Wager in the Mill*, which originally ran in the newspaper on 19 July 1925, inserted between the end of *The Chinese Coin* story line and the beginning of *The Yellow Y* story line. Rube Muller featured extensively in that story. At the beginning of the episode, Hawkins greeted Rube and referred to him as Reuben

(this short story was reprinted in the unabridged edition of *The Chinese Coin*, page 468)

Endnotes for Chapter 7.

1. Lion. The William Faulkner book *Go down, Moses* is a collection of seven short stories, loosely connected to each other. The short story entitled *The Bear* is about the hunt for Old Ben, a seemingly invincible bear terrorizing the local community. A huge dog, with extraordinary courage and savagery, is captured and trained to help in the hunt for Old Ben. This dog is named Lion, and he and Old Ben end up in the ultimate showdown, where both are killed.

2. Cheeky. The name was taken from the leader of the Scorpions, a rough gang that wreaked havoc in *The Chinese Coin*. Cheeky even struck Hawkins with a whip one time (*The Chinese Coin* pages 107-108; unabridged *The Chinese Coin* page 199).

3. Lasky. The incident recalled was the capture of Seventh-in-line Lasky of the Red Runners gang. Hawkins, Dick Ferris, Robby Hood and Shadow Loomis encountered Lasky in Cliff Cave, and gave chase. He fled out the back entrance, but was cornered on the riverbank and captured by Jerry Moore, Bill Darby and Perry Stokes (*The Red Runners* pages 176-177; unabridged *The Red Runners* pages 188-189). The back entrance is described as one that "opens out through a little hole in a hillside on the main road where a tree is growing out of the hill" (*The Red Runners* page 174; unabridged *The Red Runners* page 187). The back entrance was well-known to Hawkins and the boys, as Roy Dobel told them about it years earlier (*The Rejiment Stories Volume I* page 244).

4. Sawyer and Quayle. The name Sawyer was taken from a member of the Ching Toy gang, notorious for the time he sawed through the porch posts on the clubhouse. Jeckerson referred to him as being "worse'n a wildcat", and even slapped the boy (*Ching Toy* pages 97-99; unabridged *Ching Toy* pages 99-101).

   The name Quayle was taken from a member of Sadler's

Seven named Joe Quayle. He was exposed as a traitor, secretly helping the Ching Toy gang, and was kicked out of Sadler's Seven. He returned years later as Mopey Quayle, leader of the nasty Mopey's Mob, featured extensively in *The Lavender Light Mystery* and *The Emperor's Sword*. He reformed at the end, and rejoined Sadler (*The Emperor's Sword* page 319).

5. "Cry havoc! And let slip the dogs of war!" An unexpected outburst of culture from The Cincinnati Kid, this is a quote from the William Shakespeare play *Julius Caesar*, Act 3, Scene I, line 273.

6. Perry Stokes shot and killed the dog Lion. This scene was drawn from an earlier incident when Perry shot and killed a dog that was attacking Hawkins on the cliff path. Perry and Hawkins were up on the cliffs, and they saw Link Lambert and Will Standish coming up the river in the launch *Cazanova*. Hawkins and Perry knew Stoner's Boy was in the vicinity with his ugly dog Big Boy, and Hawkins was worried Stoner was planning to ambush Link and Will. Hawkins had Perry fire a warning shot into the air.

> It was the wrong thing to do, but I didn't realize it till too late. As the gun went off we heard the angry barking of the ugly dog, and it was close to us. I turned my head and saw the brute galloping up the rocks toward us. I saw Perry working out the empty cartridge and going through his pockets again –
>
> "Aha," came a voice; oh, how well I knew that voice. "So, my fine Seckatary, you are here. Get him, Big Boy."
>
> I caught first a sight of the gray hat, then the kerchief that hid the lower half of his face. Before I could see more of him, the big dog was upon me. I struck him as he bounded against my chest, and I felt his hot breath on my face, but down I went, and as I fell I managed to drop away from the dog, for there was a step-off to a ledge that hung out over the

side of the cliff. I was more afraid at that minute of falling off that ledge than I was of the dog, but before I had time to realize my greatest danger, I heard Perry's gun bark again – and the howl of a dog and the angry shout of Stoner's Boy –

I pulled myself back upon the top of the cliff again as quickly as I could. As I did so I saw the dead body of the ugly dog flash past me, and I watched it, fascinated as I lay there upon my stomach on the cliff top. With a splash it hit the river fifty feet below, and sank out of sight. There was a red tinge in the circling waves where it had hit the water. That was all.

But I had to leap to my feet quickly, for even as I turned my head I saw the gray ghost spring upon Perry and wrench the rifle from his hands. The next second the gray figure had flung his bulky form upon the slight, freckle-faced boy, and although Perry resisted stoutly, Stoner was slowly but surely bending him back over the edge of the cliff.

I sprang for the fallen rifle and raised it to my shoulder. The gray ghost never missed a thing. He saw me. He must have thought it was loaded, for he suddenly let go of Perry and flew down the rocky path.

This incident is in *The Gray Ghost*, pages 206-207. In the unabridged *The Gray Ghost* this incident, on pages 246-247, is accompanied by a dramatic illustration on page 243 of the moment Perry is about to shoot the dog.

7. Spirit of hartshorn. Another name is salt of hartshorn. An early form of ammonia inhalant, known as "smelling salts". Because they are in a liquid form, they are more properly termed "aromatic spirits of ammonia". Prepared from the hooves and horns of many animals, including the red deer of Europe (hence the name hartshorn), the active ingredient is ammonium

carbonate, which acts by causing an inhalation reflex (making the muscles controlling breathing work faster).

Endnotes for Chapter 8.

1. Stoner's Boy imprisoned Briggen in Cliff Cave. The incident recalled is in *Stoner's Boy* pages 114-117, with an illustration of the prison door (unabridged *Stoner's Boy* pages 271-275). Stoner had imprisoned Briggen in a chamber in the cave, blocked shut with a stout wooden door. Hawkins, Link, and Bill rescued him by sawing the lock out of the door. The sawing was difficult, and they took turns at it. Briggen told them that Stoner hadn't even given him any water.

2. Back entrance to Cliff Cave, with a cucumber magnolia tree. The "back entrance", known to Roy Dobel who calls it "the back way". Described in *The Rejiment Stories Volume I*, page 244: "It was a nice back entrance, but we had to clime up a rock, and then come through the ground where a hole was along side of a big tree coming out of the side of the hill." This is the entrance Lasky got out when they were chasing him, *The Red Runners* page 174 (unabridged *The Red Runners* page 187): "There's another opening," I said, "up above - it opens out through a little hole in a hillside on the main road where a tree is growing out of the hill". This also features in the exciting chase of Androfski in *The Gray Ghost*, pages 98 (unabridged *The Gray Ghost* page 110): "There's a back way," I yelled, "a hole in the hill, by the root of a tree". The "big tree" is never identified in the Seckatary Hawkins books. For this story, the cucumber magnolia was chosen (*Magnolia acuminata*), native to Kentucky and the most magnificent magnolia in the state, growing to a height of 80 feet.

3. There were four clues placed in this chapter that this was the day when the Morgans met Seckatary Hawkins. First, there was the early morning rainstorm that delayed breakfast at the clubhouse, the same storm coming from the south that hit just after the Morgans broke camp and resumed their journey

upstream. Second, when Hawkins, Roy, Robby and Shadow climbed up to the back entrance of Cliff Cave on the rescue mission for Link and Will, they saw the steamboat *Crescent City* headed upstream. Earlier in the day, that steamboat had passed the Morgans coming upstream in their canoes, just before they reached the island. Third, back at the clubhouse, Hudson Lee had stayed behind while the steamboat *Hudson Lee* had continued downstream. When the *Hudson Lee* passed the Morgan canoes as they were leaving the island, they did not see their friend Hudson Lee on board. Fourth, when Hawkins, Dick and Johnny walked up the cliff path under a flag of truce, they saw the small steamboat *City of Clifton* going downstream on an excursion. That same steamboat passed the Morgan canoes shortly before they passed the wreck of the *Smokey City*. It was soon after that the Morgans reached the clubhouse vicinity and met Hawkins.

Also, recall this exchange near the end of Chapter 4. The Morgans were paddling upstream from their breakfast stop on an island, and passed by a ferryboat:

A man was standing on the deck.

He scowled at us. "Where do you fellers think yer goin'?"

Clay answered. "We're going to do some exploring a little further upstream."

The man glared at Clay. "Upstream? Wouldn't go up there if I was you. Nothin' but trouble up there. Some bad trouble right now, even got my boy mixed up in it. He be gone up there for days."

The man, of course, was Mr. Hobbs, and he was referring to his son Lige having gone to help Hawkins and the boys.

Endnotes for Chapter 9.

1. Long distance telephone calling. First set up in limited areas in 1892, it was widespread across the nation by 1914.
2. Carriage turntable. At the time Schulkers was growing up in the Eastside neighborhood of Covington, his home address was 120 13th Street (today, 220 East 13th Street). The house immediately west of the Schulkers home, at 116 13th Street, is shown on old maps as having a carriage house with a turntable.
3. Burgoo. A thick meat and vegetable stew, traditionally served at outdoor functions. There are many recipes for burgoo. Here is the recipe for "Colonel Blanton's Burgoo", taken from a poster at the Buffalo Trace Distillery in Frankfort, Kentucky.

First 16 ingredients

1 4-5 pound hen	1 red pepper pod
1 pound beef flank	2 tablespoons salt
1 pound veal	1 tablespoon lemon juice
2 pounds beef stew bones	1 tablespoon Worcestershire sauce
1 onion, diced	1 tablespoon sugar
5 sprigs parsley	1½ teaspoon black pepper
1 10.5 ounce can tomato puree	½ teaspoon cayenne pepper
1 carrot, diced	4 quarts water

Remaining ingredients

6 onions finely chopped	2 cups thinly sliced celery
8 tomatoes, peeled and chopped	2 cups finely chopped cabbage
1 turnip, peeled and finely chopped	2 cups sliced okra
2 green peppers, finely chopped	2 cups fresh corn, shaved
2 cups fresh butter beans	½ unpeeled lemon, seeded

Combine first 16 ingredients in a large pot and bring to a boil. Cover and simmer four hours; cool. Strain, reserving meat and stock; discard vegetables. Remove bone, skin and gristle from meat. Return meat to stock and refrigerate overnight.

The next day remove fat layer from stock, add remaining ingredients, cover and simmer one hour. Uncover and simmer 2 hours longer, stirring frequently to prevent sticking. Burgoo is ready when it reaches the consistency of a thick stew.

4. Roy's turkeys. There are several passages in the Seckatary Hawkins books about Roy Dobel raising turkeys. In the unabridged *The Red Runners*, there is a collection of short stories from 1920 in the back of the book. Chapter 2, starting on page 336 and entitled *Turkey thief captured*, is all about Roy and his turkeys. They are also mentioned in *Gander* page 206 and *Trilogy III: The White Bat* page 19.

5. The horse names are taken from the names of horses who won the Kentucky Derby, all before 1914 (the year this story is set). Lookout won the Derby in 1893, and Apollo in 1882.

6. Vagrant won the Derby in 1876.

7. Meridian won the Derby in 1911.

8. Steentzen's Mill. The name of the old mill on Banklick Creek was said to be Steentzen's Mill (*Knights of the Square Table* page 33; unabridged *Knights of the Square Table* pages 39, 172, and 185; *The Lavender Light Mystery* page 5).

The old mill is probably based on Taylor's Mill that operated on Banklick Creek from 1795 until about 1860, and which is the basis of the name of the city of Taylor Mill in Kenton County. Hawkins states about the old mill that "many years ago, [it] was used by our grandfathers as the place where they had their grain ground into meal" (*Hackbury* page 371).

The following information is taken from the book *History of Taylor Mill* (an unpublished manuscript written by Michael J. Hammons in 1988), the report *Kenton County, Kentucky, Historic Resources Survey Research Design Report* prepared in 2000 by Taylor and Taylor Associates, Inc. of Brookville, PA, for the Northern Kentucky Area Planning Commission and the

Kentucky Heritage Council, and from Campbell County court records. In May 1795, Campbell County was formed and was much larger than it is today, encompassing the areas that are now Kenton County, along with Boone, Pendleton, Grant, and Bracken counties.

Taylor Mill was originally part of a 5,000-acre patent tract issued in 1790 to Raleigh Colston by Virginia Governor Beverly Randolph. Its earliest settlement dates from 1795, when Jacob Foster and William Smith established a grist mill and sawmill on Banklick Creek. The mill was built about one-half mile upstream from the mouth of the creek. Campbell County court records include a plat of the Colston Banklick property, which shows the mill on the north side of the creek, at a point approximately across the creek from the place where Reidlin Road intersects Grand Avenue today. A milldam, about 11 feet high, was built across the creek. In 1799, Jacob Foster sold the mill to John Crittenden, and it was run by William Wilson who lived at the mill as a tenant until 1810. James Taylor, the founder of the city of Newport, acquired the mill in 1810 and the road leading from the mill to Covington and the Ohio River became known as Taylor's Mill Road. However, Raleigh Colston also claimed title to the land. In 1831, Taylor resolved the title conflict with the Colston family, and obtained clear title to the property. Taylor died in 1848, having willed the mill to his four children, and the mill continued to operate for several more years until it shut down in about 1860.

When Hawkins stated that their grandfathers had used the mill, that would make sense given that the mill was in operation from 1795 to about 1860. While an 1864 Civil War map of Northern Kentucky does not show the mill, this could be because the mill was no longer in operation. How long the old mill continued to stand along Banklick Creek is not known. It is possible that Schulkers had seen the old mill while growing up in the area.

9. See endnote 6 of Chapter 5 for more details on the gnu.

10. Farm of Stringbean Wilson. Stringbean Wilson was a member of the Yellow Y gang. It was mentioned that his father had a farm near Hobbs Ferry (*The Yellow Y* page 50; unabridged *The Yellow Y* page 50).

11. A ford downstream of Hobbs Ferry. There is mention of a ford across the river in *The Rejiment Stories Volume I* pages 324 and 348, and *The Rejiment Stories Volume II* page 45. This ford is stated to be downstream of Hobbs Ferry, close to Finchtown, in *The Mystery of the Red Hand* page 257, and mentioned again in that book on page 291.

12. The Parks Hills water gap. When a river or stream cuts a transverse gap through a ridge, it is termed a water gap. This feature in the landscape of this story was created to deal with some apparent inconsistencies between a few passages in *Ching Toy* and all the other Seckatary Hawkins books. In *Ching Toy*, it is stated that Hobbs Ferry is downstream of the island (it is upstream of the island in all the other books where it is mentioned), that the wreck of the steamboat *Smokey City* is downstream of Parks Hills (it is upstream of Parks Hills in all the other books where it is mentioned), and that Parks Hills are near the island (they are far upstream of the island in all the other books where they are mentioned). The most problematic passage is the one in which the Ching Toy gang took the hidden houseboat from the island across the back channel – "it had been rolled from the river smack up against the side of the hill – one of the branches of the ridge called Park's Hills" (*Ching Toy* pages 82-83; unabridged *Ching Toy* pages 83-85). The phrase "one of the branches of the ridge called Park's Hills" was interpreted to mean that, as stated in this story, the Parks Hills ridge starts upstream on the western side of the river, then is split by the water gap created by the Looking Glass, and continues downstream on the eastern side of the river down to the vicinity of the island.

13. Three summer camps on the island. Since this story is set immediately after the events of *The Yellow Y*, the reference is to the three times they had camped on Seven Willows Island in

The Rejiment Stories Volume II, *The Red Runners*, and *Ching Toy*.

14. Chant won the Derby in 1894, and Donerail in 1913.

15. Mrs. Dobel's apple dumplings, and the Dobel farm spring water. Mrs. Dobel's "fine apple dumplings" are mentioned in *Stormie the Dog Stealer* page 210 (unabridged *Stormie the Dog Stealer* page 241), and the Dobel farm spring is mentioned in *Gideon* page 33.

16. Oscar Koven camp in Cliff Cave; Yella Kid Stevens at the hidden houseboat. The incident with the Koven camp in Cliff Cave is in *The Rejiment Stories Volume II* page 314, and the lunch provided by Mrs. Dobel for the Yella Kid Stevens is in *The Rejiment Stories Volume II* page 340.

17. Four entrances to the tunnel system on the island. At the time this story was set, there were four known entrances to the tunnel system on the island. These tunnels had originally been dug by river pirates, and were later expanded by Stoner's gang, then by Harkinson and the Pelhams, and later still by the Ching Toy gang. The main entrance was inside a hollow tree (later this became a stump, and then a rotted stump) (*Stoner's Boy* page 229, unabridged *Stoner's Boy* page 399). Stoner's gang opened a second entrance on the north end of the island (*Stoner's Boy* page 241, unabridged *Stoner's Boy* page 412). Harkinson and the Pelhams added the third entrance under a trap door in the log house in the stockade (*The Red Runners* page 85; unabridged *The Red Runners* page 115). The Ching Toy gang added the fourth entrance near the main channel of the river (*Ching Toy* page 195; unabridged *Ching Toy* page 194). After this story, a fifth entrance was found, dug by river pirates in the middle of the island (*Trilogy I: The River Pirates* page 176).

Endnotes for Chapter 10.

1. There have been twenty-seven United States flags. The first flag was adopted in 1777, and had 13 stars for the original 13 states (listed in order of ratification of the Constitution:

Delaware, Pennsylvania, New Jersey, Georgia, Connecticut, Massachusetts, Maryland, South Carolina, New Hampshire, Virginia, New York, North Carolina, and Rhode Island). This flag lasted 18 years, until 1795 when two stars were added after the admission of Vermont and Kentucky (this fifteen star flag was known as "the star-spangled banner", featured in the lyrics to the U.S. National Anthem referring to the British bombardment of Fort McHenry in 1812). Since 1818, new stars were added to the flag on the Fourth of July immediately following each new state's admission: 1818 – 20 stars (Tennessee, Ohio, Louisiana, Indiana, Mississippi), 1819 – 21 stars (Illinois), 1820 – 23 stars (Alabama, Maine), 1822 – 24 stars (Missouri) (this was the flag known as "Old Glory"), 1836 – 25 stars (Arkansas), 1837 – 26 stars (Michigan), 1845 – 27 stars (Florida), 1846 – 28 stars (Texas), 1847 – 29 stars (Iowa), 1848 – 30 stars (Wisconsin), 1851 – 31 stars (California), 1858 – 32 stars (Minnesota), 1859 – 33 stars (Oregon), 1861 – 34 stars (Kansas), 1863 – 35 stars (West Virginia), 1865 – 36 stars (Nevada), 1867 – 37 stars (Nebraska), 1877 – 38 stars (Colorado), 1890 – 43 stars (North Dakota, South Dakota, Montana, Washington, Idaho), 1891 – 44 stars (Wyoming), 1896 – 45 stars (Utah), 1908 – 46 stars (Oklahoma), 1912 – 48 stars (New Mexico, Arizona), 1959 – 49 stars (Alaska), and 1960 – 50 stars (Hawaii). The 1912 flag with 48 stars existed for 47 years, longer than any other flag until our current flag with 50 stars, which passed it on the Fourth of July of 2008, and is now in its 58th year of existence.

There were challenges to creating sensible designs for some of the flags, with respect to the arrangement of the stars. Images of these flags are readily available on the internet (see, for example, the Wikipeda article "History of the flags of the United States"). Some of the more startling designs are the 1819 flag with 21 stars, and the 1851 flag with 31 stars.

All these flags remain official United States flags and may be properly flown at any time.

2. Spennenberg's grocery and feedstore. This was a business in Covington, established in about 1860 by Henry Spennenberg. Located at the southwest corner of Bush and 12th Streets, it was just a couple of blocks from the Schulkers home. The original building is still there, and a plaque on the outside states that it is Covington Register No. 108004.

3. Two dogs killed in *Stormie the Dog Stealer*. The two dogs killed were Jerry Moore's water spaniel Shag (*Stormie the Dog Stealer* page 80; unabridged *Stormie the Dog Stealer* page 94) and Briggen's "yella dog" (*Stormie the Dog Stealer* page 83; unabridged *Stormie the Dog Stealer* page 98).

4. Death of Rolling Stone John Loomis. The dramatic incident leading to the fatal fall of John Loomis into the deep pit in Cliff Cave is recounted in *Knights of the Square Table* page 283 (unabridged *Knights of the Square Table* page 421).

Endnotes for Chapter 11.

1. St. Joseph's Church. While never mentioned by name in the Seckatary Hawkins books, St. Joseph's was the church the Schulkers family attended. Located at the northwest corner of Greenup and 12th streets in Covington, the church was a short two blocks from the Schulkers home. The imposing bell tower contained two large bells, with the largest (at 2200 pounds) being named St. Maria, and the other (at 1600 pounds) being named St. Joseph. St. Joseph's School was nearby on 12th Street, with the older boys taught by priests from the Brothers of Mary. This included James Banzer (1863-1939), the Brother Jim referred to in ten of the Seckatary Hawkins books, as well as the principal Francis Laehr (1857-1939), the Brother Francis mentioned twice in the books (see endnote 1 for Chapter 5). Built in 1859, the last Mass at St. Joseph's Church was on 5 July 1970, and the church was demolished later that year. One surviving item from the church is the 1859 Matthias Schwab organ, which today is in the balcony at the back of St. Mary's Cathedral Basilica at Madison and 12th streets in Covington.

Most of the information on St. Joseph's Church was taken from the book *History of the Diocese of Covington, Kentucky* by Reverend Paul E. Ryan, published in 1954 by The Diocese of Covington.

2. The name Stewart Kidd was taken from the name of the first publisher of the original Seckatary Hawkins books. The Ferguson boys, along with Russel Railey and Elijah Craig, have already appeared in this book, in Chapter 2. The other names introduced here for the first time were taken from the actual names (or composites of two names) of teenaged black and white boys listed in the book *Woodford County, Kentucky 1910 Census* compiled by Dona Adams Wilson, and published in 2003 by the Woodford County Historical Society in Versailles, Kentucky. The village of Clifton along the Kentucky River is in Woodford County.

3. The Pelhams named Briggen, Ham Gardner, Dave Burns, and Lanigan were featured in many of the Seck Hawkins books. Booby Warren appeared in *The Rejiment Stories Volume I*, *The Rejiment Stories Volume II*, *The Red Runners*, *Knights of the Square Table*, *Trilogy IV: The Nip and Tuck Gang*, and *Trilogy IV: Goldfish*. Little Tim appeared in *The Rejiment Stories Volume II*, *Stoner's Boy*, and *Gideon*. Jake Grubbs appeared in *The Yellow Y* page 94 (unabridged *The Yellow Y* page 96). Where necessary, they have been given first or last names for this story. The other named Pelhams were added for this story.

4. Steps to Heaven, and The Big Arch. These geological features of the back side of the cliffs and cave complex are mentioned in *The Chinese Coin* pages 176 and 184 (unabridged *The Chinese Coin* pages 313 and 326). The Big Arch is referred to as The Big Stone Arch in *The Red Castle* page 244.

5. Throckmorton Granbery. Old Evan Keys refers to Judge Granbery as Throckmorton Granbery, or "Throcksy" (*Trilogy IV: The Gang of Usher* page 429). Judge Granbery said:

> "You are Montmorency Evan Keys, aren't you? I studied under you at Harvard Law, and know you to

be one of THE authorities on inheritance law as well as historical justice. Welcome to my humble court!"

"Thank you, Throckmorton!" bellowed the old man, "and I am happy to see you still have your wits about you too. We will continue this personal chat later if you will have time for me."

"It will be my honor to have you stay a few days at my humble abode," smiled the judge.

"For a sleepover like the old days, Throcksy, old boy?" replied the old man with a big smile.

"Done, Monte my pal!" chuckled the judge.

What a treat to see the old sour judge turn out his young-boy inner self. You could see the knowing smiles of townsfolk all around the room.

6. Stoner's "cheese hole" in Cliff Cave. This slang term is used for a cavity in a cave system more properly referred to as a tube, and is defined as a structure too small for a person to enter. The descriptions of this part of Cliff Cave, and the items they found that Stoner's Boy had stolen and stashed there, are in *Stoner's Boy* pages 262-264 and 284 (unabridged *Stoner's Boy* pages 436-438 and 458).

Endnotes for Chapter 12.

1. The mummy in Cliff Cave. The mummified body of the old slave that Burney had owned was in a passage that branched off from one of the side walls of the deep pit in Cliff Cave (*The Yellow Y* page 297; unabridged *The Yellow Y* page 319). Mickey Maus had interpreted the treasure map to refer to this passage off the deep pit, and he and the Mudmucks had entered the passage and seen the mummy.

2. The Mokka name. Mokka is a Tamil word, thus for this story the Mokka family were Tamils from Ceylon. Ceylon (today called Sri Lanka) is a small island nation off southern India, in the Indian Ocean.

3. Trot Rice related to Hal Rice. Few slaves had last names. After the Civil War, some ex-slaves took the last names of their former owners. A freed slave child often took the last name of the owner. This was not necessarily an indication of paternity, but could simply indicate previous ownership. In this case, however, the parents and grandparents of Trot Rice would have told him the true story of his ancestry, that he was partially descended from a white slave owner named Rice, and that he had white relatives living in the area.

4. Cincinnati the sixth largest city in the Union. In 1860, the ten largest cities in the United States were (in order of population) New York, Philadelphia, Brooklyn, Baltimore, Boston, New Orleans, Cincinnati, St. Louis, Chicago, and Buffalo. Since New Orleans was not in the Union during the Civil War, the statement by Hawkins is correct. Brooklyn was a separate city at that time, and was not absorbed into New York until 1898.

5. The song *My Old Kentucky Home*. Written in 1852 by Stephen Foster, this anti-slavery ballad was likely inspired by Harriet Beecher Stowe's popular anti-slavery novel *Uncle Tom's Cabin*. Indeed, Foster's original title for the song was *Poor Old Uncle Tom, Good Night!* Foster changed the title before the sheet music was published in 1853 to *My Old Kentucky Home, Good Night!* The tradition of singing the first verse and chorus before the start of the Kentucky Derby started in 1921. It became the Kentucky State Song in 1928. Two changes have been made to the lyrics in recent decades. First, the phrase "the old Kentucky home" that appears multiple times is now sung as "my old Kentucky home". Second, in 1986 the Kentucky State Legislature changed the word "darkies" to "people" for use of the song at all official State events. This nod to political correctness either ignores the meaning of the lyrics, or belies a fundamental misunderstanding of them.

There are at least four mentions of *My Old Kentucky Home* in the Seckatary Hawkins books. On page 14 of *Stormie the Dog Stealer* (both the original and unabridged editions) is the following passage: "Lew Hunter struck into the old favorite tune of *My Old Kentucky Home* and away they went – and, believe me, boys, those fellas knew how to sing it. Even in this old dreary weather of October it would make you feel the warm days of vacation time –

'Tis summer, the darkeys are gay
And the birds make music all the day."

Oddly, a line is left out of this part of the first verse, where the lyrics are:

'Tis summer, the darkies are gay
The corn top's ripe and the meadow's in the bloom
While the birds make music all the day"

On page 79 of *Knights of the Square Table* (pages 97-98 of the unabridged *Knights of the Square Table*), Hawkins hears the boys singing at night at their summer camp on Banklick Creek:
"There had been a lull in the music over at the tent, and now again it started up –

The sun shines bright on my old Kentucky home

It was usually the last song before turning in . . ."

The original first line of the song was:

The sun shines bright in the old Kentucky home.

but is frequently changed to "on my old Kentucky home", again reflecting a lack of understanding of the ballad.
The song is also named and sung (although without lyrics in the text) on page 347 of *Hackbury*, and page 103 of *Trilogy IV: The Harmonica King*.

6.   Twenty-one Club members. Hawkins, Dick Ferris, Lew Hunter, Jerry Moore, Roy Dobel, Bill Darby, Johnny McLarren, Link Lambert, Harold and Oliver Court, Perry Stokes, Shadow

Loomis, Robby Hood, Will Standish, Lige Hobbs, Rube Muller, Hudson Lee, and Scout, Clay, Cliff and Stone Morgan.

7. Hank Hood and Silas Sargent. The grandfathers of Robby Hood and Sargent appeared in *The Yellow Y* pages 271-272 (unabridged *The Yellow Y* pages 294-295) and in an illustration in the unabridged *The Yellow Y* page 296. Sargent was revealed to be a member of The Yellow Y gang, who had infiltrated Sadler's Seventeen. Hawkins and the boys first met Sadler when he was a member of Pooley's gang Knights of the Square Table (*Knights of the Square Table* page 126; unabridged *Knights of the Square Table* page 239). When Sadler reappeared in the next book, *Ching Toy*, he had a club called Sadler's Seven. By the next book, *The Chinese Coin*, they had grown to Sadler's Seventeen. Sargent was taken into Sadler's Seventeen when Sadler dismissed Scraggs for stealing (*The Yellow Y*, page 69; unabridged *The Yellow Y* page 71). Hawkins exposed Sargent as a traitor and member of The Yellow Y gang (*The Yellow Y* pages 166-171; unabridged *The Yellow Y* pages 177-183). However, Sargent had been taken away by his grandfather Silas Sargent, who had just gotten out of prison. Sargent did appear briefly at the end of *The Yellow Y*, but did not appear in any other books. Hawkins and the boys continued to enjoy the friendship and assistance of Sadler's Seventeen in *The Red Castle, Mystery of the Stonewall House, The Lavender Light Mystery, The Emperor's Sword*, and *Little Flower of the Sun*.

8. The iron hook over the deep pit in Cliff Cave. One of the most fascinating objects in the Seckatary Hawkins stories is the mysterious iron hook someone mounted in the cave ceiling directly over the deep pit in Cliff Cave. Stoner's Boy fastened a rope to this hook, and used it to swing back and forth over the pit. This means of crossing the pit is illustrated in *Stoner's Boy* pages 101 and 273 (unabridged *Stoner's Boy* pages 250 and 448). There is one other illustration of the rope in use, this time by Stydle (*Stydle the Strong* page 146). However, and somewhat surprisingly, the hook itself does not appear in these illustrations; the rope stretches up and out of the illustration at

the top. The other three illustrations of the deep pit in Cliff Cave also do not include the hook (unabridged *Knights of the Square Table* pages 422 and 425 [these illustrations did not appear in the original edition of the book], and *Trilogy III: The White Bat* page 157). The iron hook is shown in *Comic Book II: The Yellow Y* page 232.

Endnotes for Chapter 13.

1. "The gold coins were said to have been in carpet bags, which I saw when I first entered that tomb earlier this year, but those bags were empty." In events that past March, late in the book *The Yellow Y*, when Hawkins first entered the chamber in Cliff Cave containing the mummified body of the old slave that Burney had owned, he saw and picked up "an old carpet bag" on the floor of the cave (*The Yellow Y* page 298; unabridged *The Yellow Y* page 320). Hawkins later mentions this to Detective Jeckerson (*The Yellow Y* page 301; unabridged *The Yellow Y* page 323). From the way in which Hawkins described the bag and how it felt when he picked it up, it seemed to be empty. Indeed, Judge Granbery thought Burney "took the treasure away with him" (*The Yellow Y* page 301; unabridged *The Yellow Y* page 323).

2. Jeckerson's officers Danny Columbo and Matt Phillips. There is a mention of one of Jeckerson's officers being named Danny (*The Yellow Y* page 256; unabridged *The Yellow Y* pages 277 and 283). Another of Jeckerson's officers, named Phillips, appears in several books.

3. Judge Montmorency Evan Keys. The name is taken from that of a former professor of Judge Granbery's (*Trilogy IV: The Gang of Usher* pages 427-429).

4. Alvin Jeckerson. The first name of Detective Jeckerson was never mentioned in the Seckatary Hawkins books. Alvin was originally chosen by Club members Dan Kindel and Bernie Knoll for their Seck Hawkins adventure stories.

5. Hamilton County Assistant Prosecuting Attorney Roger Montilla. The name is taken from the Cuban attorney in *Seckatary Hawkins in Cuba*, but with an Anglicized first name indicating he was born and educated in the US. His command of Spanish proves to be useful in his questioning of Ben Gunn.

6. Tunnel from Burney's house to the slave cabin. The tunnel leading from behind the fireplace in Burney's house to the slave cabin is described in *The Yellow Y* pages 267-270 (unabridged *The Yellow Y* pages 289-293).

7. Mr. Montilla looked skeptical. "Hablas muy bien el español?"
Ben Gunn smiled. "Sí, estoy con fluidez en español."

"Qué hiciste cuando estabas viviendo en Cuba?"

"Formé un consorcio de inversión con varios socios, con intereses en la caña de azúcar, tabaco y ron."

The translation is:

"Do you speak Spanish very well?"

"Yes, I am fluent in Spanish."

"What did you do when you were living in Cuba?"

"I formed a consortium with several partners, with interests in sugar cane, tobacco, and rum."

8. Suez Canal. After ten years of construction, the Suez Canal was opened in 1869. The canal is 120 miles in length, connecting the Mediterranean Sea to the Red Sea. This route allows ships to avoid having to sail around the southern tip of Africa, and cuts the length of a sea journey from Europe to South Asia by about 4300 miles. The Suez Canal is the dividing line between Africa and Asia.

9. "Lembacher Burney, grandson of old Legran Burney." The Rat-Faced Man is called Uncle Lem by little Siegfried Wye (*The Yellow Y* page 248; unabridged *The Yellow Y* page 270). He is not the uncle of Siegfried, but instead bears a close resemblance to Burney (*The Yellow Y* page 276; unabridged *The Yellow Y* page 299). Hawkins states that "He is surely the grandson

or some relation of old Burney . . ." (*The Yellow* Y page 278; unabridged *The Yellow* Y page 301).

10. Laird's Military Academy. This military school for young men is mentioned in *The Red Castle* pages 404 and 410, *The Lavender Light Mystery* page 385, and *Trilogy III: The Backwater Pool* pages 218-219, 221, 228, and 363-365; the entry on page 221 states that Laird's Military Academy was in Watertown, so for this story it was placed in Cincinnati.

BIBLIOGRAPHY

Biography of Robert F. Schulkers, author of the "Seckatary Hawkins" stories.

O'Dell, Gary A., and Gregg Bogosian. "Fair and Square. Robert F. Schulkers, Seckatary Hawkins and the Literature of an Ohio Valley Childhood." *Ohio Valley History* 15 (Fall 2015), 43-67.

How Schulkers wove the real Clifton Cave into Cliff Cave in his stories.

O'Dell, Gary A., and Gregg Bogosian. "Seckatary Hawkins and Cliff(ton) Cave: The Subterranean Adventures of Robert F. Schulkers." *National Speleological Society News* 72 (July 2014), 10-20.

The eleven original "Seckatary Hawkins" books of Robert F. Schulkers.

Robert F. Schulkers began writing the "Seckatary Hawkins" stories in early 1918, first published as a regular weekly feature in newspapers. New episodes continued to be published in newspapers until early 1942. After that only reprints of previous stories were published, until the publication of Seckatary Hawkins stories in newspapers came to an end in late 1951. From 1921 to 1930, ten hardback books were published comprised of most of the newspaper episodes from early 1920 to late 1926. In addition, a paperback book was published in 1932 comprised of newspaper episodes from 1930.

Schulkers, Robert F. *Seckatary Hawkins in Cuba*. Stewart Kidd Co., Cincinnati, OH, 1921.

Schulkers, Robert F. *The Red Runners*. Stewart Kidd Co., Cincinnati, OH, 1922.

Schulkers, Robert F. *Stormie the Dog Stealer*. D. Appleton and Co., New York and London, 1925.

Schulkers, Robert F. *Stoner's Boy*. Robert F. Schulkers, Cincinnati, OH, 1926.

Schulkers, Robert F. *The Gray Ghost*. Robert F. Schulkers, Cincinnati, OH, 1926.

Schulkers, Robert F. *Knights of the Square Table*. Robert F. Schulkers, Cincinnati, OH, 1926.

Schulkers, Robert F. *Ching Toy*. Robert F. Schulkers, Cincinnati, OH, 1926.

Schulkers, Robert F. *The Chinese Coin*. Robert F. Schulkers, Cincinnati, OH, 1926.

Schulkers, Robert F. *The Yellow Y*. Robert F. Schulkers, Cincinnati, OH, 1926.

Schulkers, Robert F. *Herman the Fiddler*. Robert F. Schulkers, Cincinnati, OH, 1930.

Schulkers, Robert F. *The Ghost of Lake Tapaho*. Robert F. Schulkers, Cincinnati, OH, 1932.

The later "Seckatary Hawkins" stories published by the Seckatary Hawkins Club (www.seckatary.com)

The newspaper episodes that had not previously been published in book form were issued by the Seckatary Hawkins Club in 19 hardback books. These were comprised of the newspaper episodes from early 1918 to early 1920, and from late 1926 to early 1942. In addition, there was a Seckatary Hawkins comic strip which ran every day (except Sunday) from 3 September 1928 to 26 May 1934, a total of 1794 strips. The Club published two hardback books containing all the comic strips.

Schulkers, Robert F. *The Red Castle*. Charles R. Schulkers, Powhatan, VA, 2007.

Schulkers, Robert F. *Mystery of the Stonewall House*. Charles R. Schulkers, Powhatan, VA, 2007.

Schulkers, Robert F. *Little Gil*. Charles R. Schulkers, Powhatan, VA, 2007.

Schulkers, Robert F. *The Emperor's Sword*. Charles R. Schulkers, Powhatan, VA, 2007.

Schulkers, Robert F. *The Lavender Light Mystery*. Charles R. Schulkers, Powhatan, VA, 2008.

Schulkers, Robert F. *Little Flower of the Sun*. Charles R. Schulkers, Powhatan, VA, 2008.

Schulkers, Robert F. *The Mystery of the Red Hand*. Charles R. Schulkers, Powhatan, VA, 2008.

Schulkers, Robert F. *The Lacquer Fan*. Charles R. Schulkers, Powhatan, VA, 2008.

Schulkers, Robert F. *Gideon*. Charles R. Schulkers, Powhatan, VA, 2009.

Schulkers, Robert F. *Stydle the Strong*. Charles R. Schulkers, Powhatan, VA, 2009.

Schulkers, Robert F. *Trilogy 1: Mystery of Stattenham Manor, The River Pirates, and The Mystery of the Green Light*. Charles R. Schulkers, Powhatan, VA, 2009.

Schulkers, Robert F. *Gander*. Charles R. Schulkers, Powhatan, VA, 2009.

Schulkers, Robert F. *Trilogy 2: The Dog Snatchers, The Dug-Out Trailer, and Jericho*. Charles R. Schulkers, Powhatan, VA, 2009.

Schulkers, Robert F. *Trilogy 3: The White Bat, The Backwater Pool, and The Big Dogs*. Charles R. Schulkers, Powhatan, VA, 2009.

Schulkers, Robert F. *Hackbury*. Charles R. Schulkers, Powhatan, VA, 2010.

Schulkers, Robert F. *Trilogy 4: The Nip and Tuck Gang, Related Stories, and The Gang of Usher*. Charles R. Schulkers, Powhatan, VA, 2010.

Schulkers, Robert F. *The Return of the Skinny Guy*. Charles R. Schulkers, Powhatan, VA, 2010.

Schulkers, Robert F. *The Rejiment, Volume 1*. Charles R. Schulkers, Powhatan, VA, 2011.

Schulkers, Robert F. *The Rejiment, Volume 2*. Charles R. Schulkers, Powhatan, VA, 2012.

Schulkers, Robert F. *Comic Book 1*. Charles R. Schulkers, Powhatan, VA, 2013.

Schulkers, Robert F. *Comic Book 2*. Charles R. Schulkers, Powhatan. VA, 2013.

The eleven original books published as unabridged editions by the Seckatary Hawkins Club.

The stories in the eleven original books had been extensively edited from the episodes that had originally been published in the newspapers. The Seckatary Hawkins Club issued unabridged editions of these books, restoring the original newspaper text and illustrations (including much omitted text and many omitted illustrations). There were also a number of short stories published in newspapers in the 1920 to 1932 timeframe that were published in book form for the first time as addenda to these unabridged editions.

Schulkers, Robert F. *Stoner's Boy*. Unabridged edition. Charles R. Schulkers, Powhatan, VA, 2011.

Schulkers, Robert F. *Seckatary Hawkins in Cuba*. Unabridged edition. Charles R. Schulkers, Powhatan, VA, 2015.

Schulkers, Robert F. *The Red Runners*. Unabridged edition. Charles R. Schulkers, Powhatan, VA, 2012.

Schulkers, Robert F. *The Gray Ghost*. Unabridged edition. Charles R. Schulkers, Powhatan, VA, 2012.

Schulkers, Robert F. *Stormie the Dog Stealer*. Unabridged edition. Charles R. Schulkers, Powhatan, VA, 2012.

Schulkers, Robert F. *Knights of the Square Table*. Unabridged edition. Charles R. Schulkers, Powhatan, VA, 2013.

Schulkers, Robert F. *Ching Toy*. Unabridged edition. Charles R. Schulkers, Powhatan, VA, 2013.

Schulkers, Robert F. *The Chinese Coin*. Unabridged edition. Charles R. Schulkers, Powhatan, VA, 2014.

Schulkers, Robert F. *The Yellow Y*. Unabridged edition. Charles R. Schulkers, Powhatan, VA, 2014.

Schulkers, Robert F. *Herman the Fiddler*. Unabridged edition. Charles R. Schulkers, Powhatan, VA, 2015.

Schulkers, Robert F. *The Ghost of Lake Tapaho*. Unabridged edition. Charles R. Schulkers, Powhatan, VA, 2017.

General reference books.

Gastright, Joseph F. *Gentlemen Farmers to City Folks. A Study of Wallace Woods, Covington, Kentucky*. The Cincinnati Historical Society, Cincinnati, OH, 1980.

Kleber, John E. (editor in chief). *The Kentucky Encyclopedia*. The University Press of Kentucky, Lexington, KY, 1992.

Tenkotte, Paul A., and James C. Claypool (eds.). *The Encyclopedia of Northern Kentucky*. The University Press of Kentucky, Lexington, KY, 2009.

Tenkotte, Paul A., James C. Claypool, and David E. Schroeder (eds.). *Gateway City: Covington, Kentucky 1815-2015*. Clerisy Press, Covington, KY, 2015.

Books and reports cited in the endnotes.

Beers, D.G., and J. Lanagan. *Atlas of Bourbon, Clark, Fayette, Jessamine and Woodford Counties, Kentucky*. D.G. Beers and Co., Philadelphia, PA, 1877.

Hammons, Michael J. *History of Taylor Mill*. An unpublished manuscript written in 1988, and on file at the Taylor Mill, KY, city hall.

Kenton County, Kentucky Historic Resources Survey Research Design Report. Prepared by Taylor and Taylor Associates, Inc., Brookville, PA, 2000. Accessed February 2017 at www.pdskc.org/Portals/pdskc/documents/plan_pdf/redesrpt.pdf

Lake, D.J. *An Atlas of Boone, Kenton and Campbell Counties, Kentucky*. D.J. Lake and Co., Philadelphia, PA, 1883.

Luarca-Shoaf, Nenette, Claire Barry, Nancy Heugh, Elizabeth Mankin Kornhauser, Dorothy Mahon, Andrew J. Walker, and Janeen Turk. *Navigating the West: George Caleb Bingham and the River*. Amon Carter Museum of American Art (Forth Worth, TX) and the Saint Louis Art Museum (Saint Louis, MO), 2014.

Rennick, Robert M. *The Post Offices of Northern Kentucky*. The Depot, Lake Grove, OR, 2004.

Ryan, Paul E. *History of the Diocese of Covington, Kentucky*. The Diocese of Covington, KY, 1954.

Schulkers, Robert F. The Schulkers papers. The Schulkers papers are a loosely organized collection of documents and papers curated by the author's grandson, Charles R. Schulkers, in Powhatan, VA.

Way, Jr., Frederick. *Way's Packet Directory, 1848-1994*. Ohio University Press, Athens, OH, 1994.

Way, Jr., Frekderick and Joseph W. Rutter. *Way's Steam Towboat Directory*. Ohio University Press, Athens, OH, 1990.

Wilson, Dona Adam. *Woodford County, Kentucky 1910 Census*. Woodford County Historical Society, Versailles, KY, 2003.

La Tentación
del
Tejedor de Milagros

"Les aseguro que el que cree en mí hará también las obras que yo hago, y aún mayores, porque yo me voy al Padre. Y yo haré todo lo que ustedes pidan en mi nombre, para que el Padre sea glorificado en el Hijo." (Juan 14:12-13)

El autor, Roberto G. Rosas, creó y escribió todas las historias y personajes del Tejedor de Milagros. El primer libro publicado y registrado en el 2002 fue este, "La Tentación del Tejedor de Milagros" (En Inglés: *The Temptation of the Miracle Weaver*). Todos los demás libros en la serie del Tejedor de Milagros proceden de esta historia original. Este es el quinto libro en el orden cronológico de la saga.

Todas las citas Bíblicas incluidas en esta obra han sido obtenidas con permiso del Sitio de Internet Catholic.net (**http://es.catholic.net**)

ISBN-13: 978-0615420745

ISBN-10: 0615420745

Cuarta Edición – 2018

__Soli Deo Gloria__

"Roberto Rosas ha escrito una historia cautivadora que obliga al lector a pensar. Captura la esencia de la naturaleza humana, de dilemas morales de la vida tal como es con matiz y sabiduría. Su estilo literario mantiene al lector deseando avanzar a la página siguiente y hace muy difícil el dejar de leer el libro."

Dr. Henry Cisneros

Primer alcalde Hispano de una ciudad mayor de los Estados Unidos

Primer alcalde México-Americano de San Antonio desde 1842

10[imo] Secretario de la Vivienda y Desarrollo Urbano de los Estados Unidos

Capítulo I

Reto

Eran las 4:30 a.m. del martes 31 de agosto, cuando el sonido de una pieza instrumental empezó a tocar en el radio/reloj despertador.

"¡Buenos días, Señor! Es hora de comenzar otro día excitante," pensó el hombre, estirando su atlético cuerpo de 1.83 m. sobre su cama individual.

Ya casi tenía 38 años y estaba en excelente condición física. Se levantó, fue al baño, regresó a su cama, encendió la lámpara, y agarró su librito de oraciones. Se arrodilló al pie de su simple camita y recitó la oración matutina. Cuando acabó, besó su librito y lo regresó al buró, tendió su cama y se puso sus pantaloncillos de correr, camiseta, y tenis.

Eran las 4:50 a.m. cuando salió de la casa. La mañana era tibia, típica del Sur de Texas. El área alrededor de la iglesia católica y la escuela de la Santísima Trinidad en el oeste de San Antonio se veía muy pacífica. Gabriel Infante, el pastor de la parroquia y director de la escuela, se empezó a estirar y a calentar los músculos para ir a correr.

El Padre Gabriel saludó a una pareja, los Mendoza; que lo pasaron en una camioneta entregando periódicos. Un perrito se acercó a la cerca del frente de una casa, ladrando feroz. El sacerdote corrió veloz contra el Chihuahua; la pequeña bestia huyó rumbo a su casa, chillando espantado. Una vez que el peligro había pasado, el can regresó a la cerca para ladrarle de nuevo.

Un ligero viento levantó unos papeles enfrente del atleta. Sus alertas ojos discernieron una forma familiar entre ellos. Pescó el papelito, aún en el aire, y lo examinó bajo la luz del poste. ¡Era un billete de diez dólares! Pensó en comprarse un sabroso desayuno esa mañana después de la misa de ocho. Se metió el billete entre los pantaloncillos y la camiseta y se mantuvo corriendo a un paso de ocho-minutos por milla.

En la parada de autobuses, el cura vio un tipo dormido con la cabeza colgando a un lado de la banca. El Padre Gabriel decidió detenerse por un momento y enderezar al borrachito. El hombre se despertó en cuanto sintió al extraño moviéndolo.

"¿Qué demonios estás haciendo?" le gruñó el vagabundo mientras se quitaba de encima las manos del corredor.

"¡Lo siento! Pensé que estabas bien borracho y solo te quería acomodar para que no despertaras con el pescuezo todo torcido," le dijo el presbítero echándose hacia atrás.

"¿Borracho? No traigo ni pa' comida, mucho menos pa' cerveza o vino."

Era un tipo flaco, de la misma edad que el cura, pero se miraba más viejo. El cabello largo y la barba del hombre le recordaron al ministro a San Juan Bautista. Gabriel se conmovió, mirando los ojos sumidos del pordiosero.

"¿Traes una feriecita que me pudieras prestar pa' comer, Camarada?" el flaquito le rogó al extraño.

"Bueno pues..." el sacerdote se acordó del billete que se había hallado cinco cuadras atrás. "¿Qué harías con diez dólares?"

Gabriel le puso una mano al hombre en el hombro y muy discreto se sacó el billete de los pantaloncillos cortos con la otra.

"¡Ah, con diez dólares, podría comer todo un día!" el tipo dijo, sonriendo.

El atlético ministro le metió el billete en el bolsillo del pecho sin que se diera cuenta y levantó al flaquito jalándolo por la camisa.

"Bueno, pues si es así, creo que ya tienes suficiente para comer hoy. ¿Por qué andas pidiéndome dinero cuando ya traes diez dólares en tu bolsillo?" le dijo, fingiendo enojo.

"¡Ey, suéltame, Hombre! Si no me quieres prestar una feria está bien, pero no tienes porque estrujarme, ¡Vaya!"

El Padre Gabriel se sonrió y le guiñó un ojo. Solo estaba jugando con él.

"¡Siempre revisa tus bolsillos primero, mi Amigo!" el cura le dijo al hombre antes de alejarse a paso veloz.

El desconcertado tipo se arregló la camisa jaloneada y sintió algo en el bolsillo. Se sacó el billete y se dio cuenta que el bondadoso extraño se lo había puesto ahí y ni siquiera se esperó a que le diera las gracias. El callejero vio el dinero y luego buscó al tipo aquel en la oscura distancia, pero el corredor estaba ya fuera de vista. El limosnero estaba muy contento y buscó a alguien alrededor con quien compartir su alegría. Los Mendoza venían acercándose aventando sus periódicos mientras el hombre sostenía el billete de a diez en la mano.

"¡Ey! ¿Vieron al fortachón que se fue corriendo por allá?" el limosnero le preguntó a Martín Mendoza al acercársele en la camioneta.

"Sí. ¿Qué tiene?" repuso Mendoza, parándose para ver qué quería.

"¡Bueno, pos' que's bien de aquellas! Me sacó un... sustote; pensé que me iba a dar una friega de perro bailarín. Pero luego me di cuenta que me regaló este billete y ni esperó a que le diera las gracias. Me pregunto quién será," dijo el limosnero, rastreando la oscuridad de la calle.

"¡Está re' facilita! Ese era el Padre Gabriel, el pastor de la iglesia de la Santísima Trinidad, y tienes razón, es bien a toda madre. Me curó de un tumor maligno hace tres meses. Los doctores ni la podían creer. Quesque debían operarme o si no, me iba a llevar la tiznada. Nomás mírame 'hora ¡sano como un gusano! Es un hombre de Dios; la gente le dice el Tejedor de Milagros," Martín le dijo antes de arrancarse para continuar su negocio.

El hombre los vio partir calle abajo y pensó en la última vez que puso pie en una iglesia. Habían sido cinco años, en la boda de su hermana. Quizás necesitaba regresar, y aquella había sido una señal del Señor para que volviera a su fe original. Sintió un suave y tibio viento acariciando su cara como si el Todopoderoso aceptara sus pensamientos y los aprobaba. El hombre se persignó, cerró los ojos, y rezó un Padre Nuestro para agradecerle a Dios antes de irse a comer su muy anticipado desayuno.

El Padre Gabriel estaba ya ejercitando en el Gimnasio del Salvaje Oeste. Había practicado el boxeo desde que estaba en la secundaria. Primero ganó el Torneo Juvenil de Boxeo de la ciudad cuando apenas era estudiante de secundaria jovencito y pesando 55 kilos. Para cuando estaba en los dos últimos años de la preparatoria, Gabriel prefirió el fútbol americano al boxeo, pero luego regresó a él en el seminario.

Tuvo un par de amigos seminaristas, Raphael y Michael, quienes eran de la misma talla que él, ochenta y cuatro kilos para entonces, y le entraron al boxeo para manejar mejor la tensión de los jóvenes que se someten a la vida célibe del sacerdocio. Por sus nombres, ellos tres eran conocidos en el seminario como los Tres Arcángeles. También les gustaba juntarse a tocar música y cantar. Gabriel era el mejor cantante y tocaba un poco la guitarra, Michael era el organista y Raphael tocaba muy bien el bajo. Aquellos dos se volvieron como los hermanos que Gabriel nunca había tenido.

El sacerdote era un buen amigo del dueño del gimnasio, Jaime Bravo, quien le permitía entrenar ahí gratis. El Padre G, como algunos del barrio lo llamaban, trabajó en su cintura; hizo dominadas en la barra y lagartijas. Luego trabajó con el costal pesado. Se movía como un peso medio a pesar de que ya pesaba noventa kilos de músculos sólidos.

Cuando estaba todo bombeado en el gimnasio, era difícil imaginarse que era un bondadoso cura. Gabriel se parecía al Hércules de las películas con su barba recortada y su bien definido físico. Podía levantar ciento treinta y seis kilos en la banca y hacer sentadillas con ciento ochenta y un kilos.

El boxeador amateur terminó sus ejercicios y se fue a dar un duchazo. Gabriel se sintió inspirado a cantar una canción acerca de un ruiseñor. Su potente voz resonó a través del gimnasio. Los versos hablaban del pajarillo pronosticando que la felicidad estaba casi por llegar. Era una canción casi religiosa invitando al oyente a agradecer a Dios por su bondad. Los otros en el centro deportivo se miraron sonriendo mientras escuchaban su canción y seguían ejercitando, casi bailando al ritmo del melodioso sonido.

El primer lenguaje de Gabriel había sido el español porque sus padres habían inmigrado de México. Su nacimiento fue milagroso. Sus papás habían estado casados por varios años, queriendo tener un bebito, pero María de la Luz, su madre, era incapaz de concebir. Sufrió una infección que le dejó los ovarios estériles cuando aún era jovencita. Su marido, José Arturo Infante, había sugerido que adoptaran a un niño, pero la mujercita tenía fe que Dios les iba a conceder tener un hijo propio.

Diez años después que se casaron, María tuvo un sueño acerca del Arcángel Gabriel anunciándole a la Virgen María que ella iba a concebir al Hijo de Dios. Petrita Martínez, una vecina, invitó a María de la Luz a un servicio de sanación en su iglesia al día siguiente. La vecina sufría de artritis, a pesar que solo tenía treinta años.

El Padre Xavier, quien tenía el carisma de sanación del Espíritu Santo, era el celebrante esa tarde. Habló con María en la iglesia y le impuso la mano sobre su abdomen; ella se sintió caliente, contenta, y excitada en ese momento. Su marido se fijó que venía muy chapeteada y se veía radiante cuando regresó de la iglesia. Aquella fue la noche en que su hijo unigénito fue concebido.

Nació el día del cumpleaños número treinta de su mamá. Su madre sabía que él era un regalo de Dios muy especial y lo nombró Gabriel en honor del arcángel. María de la Luz pensó que el bebito había sido su mejor regalo de cumpleaños. Petrita había sido curada de su artritis también, y más tarde se convirtió en madrina de bautismo del niño. Petrita y su esposo, Felipe Martínez tenían una tienda en la esquina de la Calle Guadalupe.

El niño milagro creció en el oeste de la ciudad con una fuerte influencia católica-mexicana. Su padre, José, era un exitoso y habilidoso carpintero con propio taller. Su madre, María, se hacía cargo del hogar y de sus dos hombres muy bien. Manejaba el presupuesto y estiraba el dinero que su esposo ganaba, así que todas sus necesidades estaban cubiertas. Gabriel creció como hijo único, pero tuvo una crianza feliz en una familia amorosa.

El reverendo se tomó un jugo de toronja como desayuno mientras revisaba las últimas noticias en el periódico. Nada nuevo sucedía. La ciudad aún estaba celebrando el campeonato nacional ganado por los

Látigos, el equipo local de básquetbol profesional.

Él había contribuido para traer el trofeo a la ciudad ese año. Ivory Peterson y Daniel Williamson, dos de los estrellas del equipo, habían conocido al Padre Gabriel en una función de beneficencia dos años atrás. Habiendo oído de sus milagros, le pidieron que rezara por ellos para llegar a la final. El sacerdote estuvo de acuerdo porque le cayeron bien los dos atletas cristianos. Pensó que no tendría nada de malo pedirle a Dios por algo como un campeonato aún si parecía una cosa banal.

Al principio sus oraciones parecieron contraproducentes pues los Látigos tuvieron un año terrible. Williamson se lastimó, y el equipo acabó en el sótano. Esto, sin embargo, les permitió ganar la lotería de la liga y obtener a Tom Lincoln como la última adición al plantel. El talentoso novato los llevó a donde habían orado por estar.

Una vez en la liguilla, los Látigos invitaron al cura a que presenciara los juegos locales, junto a la cancha. Estuvo ahí cuando Shawn Scott anotó la canasta ganadora de tres puntos al final del partido por su división. Supo entonces que los Látigos iban a llegar hasta la meta porque sus oraciones habían sido escuchadas. Gabriel recordó como él y Ivory estaban hablando acerca de los extraños modos en que Dios nos concede nuestras peticiones en sus términos, no en los nuestros.

El Padre G miró su reloj: casi eran las 8; dejó el periódico y corrió para la iglesia. Los feligreses estaban ya esperando que empezara la misa.

Mirando al sacerdote en la iglesia, celebrando la misa, predicando el Evangelio, uno podría pensar que era el mismo Jesucristo, con pelo corto, hablando a la audiencia. Hablaba con convicción; sus acciones revelaban su profunda fe en Dios. La gente se sentía en paz solo al escucharlo.

Era muy conocido en el barrio porque había hecho muchos milagros. Siempre negaba recibir crédito y decía a todos que había sido la fe de ellos y Dios quienes les habían concedido los milagros. Trataba de mantenerlo en secreto lo más posible para evitar que se le echaran encima multitudes.

Él mismo no podía explicarles el por qué un milagro podía ocurrir en un caso particular y no en otros, o por qué las cosas pasaban como en el caso de los Látigos. No todos sabían de sus milagros, ni todas las cosas que él hacía eran milagros. Muchas gentes no creían que hacía milagros en lo absoluto. Por causa del enredo de rumores acerca de si sus milagros eran reales o no, la gente lo conocía como El Tejedor de Milagros.

De la iglesia, el cura se fue a la escuela justo al cruzar la calle.

Siempre andaba ocupado, teniendo la responsabilidad sobre la parroquia y la escuela; sin embargo, sabía cómo delegar autoridad y confiaba en su subdirectora con la mayor parte del trabajo en la escuela mientras que un diácono permanente lo asistía en administrar la bulliciosa parroquia.

La vida de Gabriel era excelente; era un hombre realizado. La gente lo amaba, y él amaba a la gente. Algunos lo consideraban un santo; algunos lo criticaban por su estilo de vida. Era un hombre de carne y hueso al cual le gustaba echarse un trago o dos aunque nadie lo había visto borracho. También se deleitaba con un buen puro. Algunas personas no aprobaban su pugilismo, pues lo había usado en varias ocasiones para vapulear a algunos malhechores. Otros tenían problemas con su pasión por las artes.

Gabriel pintaba y disfrutaba del canto y el baile. Sus retratos desnudos artísticos y sus compañeras de baile eran blanco para chismes. Gabriel tenía sentido del humor y no permitía que esos le evitaran el hacer lo que le gustaba. Otra causa para que algunos tuvieran problemas con el sacerdote era su posición política. Era abiertamente republicano y oía programas conservativos por radio; eso no era bien visto en la comunidad hispana demócrata. El hombre no era perfecto, pero sí vivía muy contento.

Después de la escuela y asuntos parroquiales, Gabriel fue a cenar en casa de las hermanas religiosas esa tarde. Tenía cuatro monjitas enseñando en su escuela. Kathryn Cabrini, irlandesa, estaba a cargo del primer año. Era de edad media, flaquita y alta; ella disfrutaba de la poesía y la cerveza. Kathryn era la ministra de música en la parroquia.

Magdalene McKay, otra irlandesa, era una chaparrita exuberante ya grande de edad pero muy alegre a cargo del tercer año quien tenía gran pasión por toda clase de comidas, bebidas, y música clásica. Era la madre superior en la pequeña comunidad y una organista consumada.

Carmen Armienta, argentina, era una piadosa mujer de edad media y talla mediana a cargo del quinto año quien tenía dificultad para manejar problemas disciplinarios en su salón de clases. Era una cantante inspirada que adoraba los cantos gregorianos y toda clase de dulces.

Mary Dáskalos, de ascendencia griega, era la más jovencita de ellas con veintiocho años, y estaba a cargo del séptimo grado. Era una mujercita llena de energía cuya pasión era la educación. Una excelente guitarrista, a Mary le gustaba usar la música popular en celebraciones religiosas.

A pesar que ninguna de las hermanas era particularmente atlética, todas ellas habían hallado gusto en ver los juegos de béisbol en la televisión. Su equipo favorito era el de los Rancheros de Texas, uno de los más malos.

Gabriel disfrutó una deliciosa cena "de oro" con las cuatro hermanas. Comieron pollo frito con puré de papa y granos de elote, acompañado por unas cervezas para el Padre G, Magda, y Kathryn, té helado para el resto. El postre consistió de una taza de café y torta de nueces con una bola de nieve de vainilla. Gabriel, Magdalene, y Carmen limpiaron sus platos; Kathryn y Mary solo comieron un poco del postre, quejándose que no les quedaba ya lugar para más, aunque solo se habían comido la mitad de sus porciones.

Después de dar gracias a Dios por su cena, el grupo se movió al cuarto de música y disfrutó cantando y tocando música cristiana alabando al Señor por una hora. Kathryn tocó el violín mientras que Magda tocaba el órgano y Mary la guitarra; Gabriel y Carmen cantaron los himnos.

El cura cerró la noche con un chiste de un tejano que se fue al infierno. El pastor sabía del interés que las religiosas tenían en el béisbol profesional.

"Un tejano murió y se fue al infierno. Cuando llegó, encontró a todo mundo quejándose del calorón que hacía. ¡Eran 80 grados Fahrenheit y un 80 por ciento de humedad! El tejano se sintió muy a gusto en ese ambiente y andaba siempre sonriendo. El Diablo notó que el recién llegado andaba muy cómodo con su sombrero y sus botas de vaquero en el maldito lugar. Le preguntó si no tenía calor. Él le contestó, '¡Demonios, no! Esto es como Texas en mayo.' El Diablo se dejó ir a subirle al termostato a los 90 grados con un 90 por ciento de humedad. ¡Pronto se oyeron las lamentaciones por todo el infierno! Cuando lo miró de nuevo, el Diablo encontró al tejano aún sonriendo, con su sombrero en la mano. El demonio le preguntó si no tenía calor todavía. Él le contestó, '¡No, no, que va! Esto es justo como Texas en junio.' Satanás fue y le subió otra vez al termostato hasta los 100 grados de calor y 100 por ciento de humedad, pero no encontró un gran cambio de actitud en el tejano. Solo se había quitado las botas y se estaba echando airecito con su sombrero mientras le decía, '¡Hombre, esto es como Texas en julio!' Satanás lo pensó un rato y decidió cambiar de estrategia. Se arrancó de regreso al termostato y le bajó a la temperatura del infierno hasta los 20 grados Fahrenheit. ¡Hielitos comenzaron a colgar por todos lados! Echando vaporcito por la boca y frotándose las garras heladas, el Diablo corrió a la cueva donde tenía al tejano. Lo encontró brincando de gusto como un chiquillo, exclamando, '¡Los Rancheros de Texas finalmente ganaron la liga mundial de béisbol!'"

Las religiosas soltaron la risa al comprender su chiste. Magda se disculpó para arrancarse al baño.

El Padre Gabriel les agradeció por una velada muy agradable y se marchó a su casa a pie. Eran diez cuadras de la casa de las hermanas a la iglesia, donde él tenía su residencia asignada.

Encendió su puro y caminó despacio, absorbiendo los últimos vestigios de luz en el poniente. Otro día exitoso estaba acercándose al fin. Hablaba con Dios al caminar, agradeciéndole por el gran día que había disfrutado.

Una viejita estaba sacando la basura para la acera de enfrente para que se la llevara el camión de la ciudad en la mañana. Lo oyó hablando solo y pensó que había de estar loco, o borracho. Se apuró a regresar para evitar al extraño que se iba acercando a su casa.

Gabriel notó su comportamiento y se sonrió. Entonces empezó a cantar una canción acerca de un borrachito trayéndole serenata a su amada.

La mujer se asomó por la ventana y al escucharlo cantar concluyó, "Es un borracho cantador. ¡Pero qué bonito canta!"

La voz del trovador se fue apagando rumbo al final de la cuadra con su apasionada canción.

Mientras se iba acercando a la iglesia, el sacerdote miró a una elegante viejecita hablando con un hombre en la entrada del templo. Se veía desesperada y estaba enviando a su chofer para que fuera a la rectoría. El Padre Gabriel les preguntó si podía servirles. Notaron su collar de clérigo bajo la luz de la lámpara al salir de la oscuridad del callejón. Él reconoció a la vieja como una nueva parroquiana a quien había visto por primera vez aquella mañana en misa. Podría haber sido una reina de belleza 50 años atrás; ahora era solo una vieja ricachona muy llena de sí misma.

"¡Padre Gabriel, qué gusto verlo!" dijo ella, caminando hasta él para saludarlo con ambas manos.

"Ya veo que no trae su andador que traía esta mañana, Alice. ¿Qué pasó?"

Alguien había convencido a la mujer para que fuera a ver al cura a que la sanara de un dolor de espalda que la había atormentado por años. Tenía gran dificultad al caminar y necesitaba el apoyo de un andador o tenía que ser transportada en silla de ruedas por su chofer. Ella también era muy olvidadiza, y por eso había regresado a la iglesia esa noche.

"Oh, Padre, estoy tan contenta de no tener que usar esa cosa horrible. ¡Debí haber venido a verlo en cuanto empecé a tener este problema!"

"¿Qué hice?" preguntó el Padre Gabriel, interesado en oír los detalles.

Aquella mañana, Alice Silverstone le había pedido que orara para que se curara, pero el cura tuvo la impresión que la fe de la mujer era inexistente. Estuvo de acuerdo en mantenerla en sus oraciones, lo cual había hecho, pero debido a su falta de fe, no esperaba que fuese restaurada como pedía. Él había, sin embargo, recomendado que viera a un quiropráctico amigo suyo con oficina en el norte de la ciudad. Ella le alegó que ya había visto a los mejores doctores especialistas, pero todo lo que ellos querían era operarle la espalda sin ninguna garantía que se iba a componer.

"Fui a ver al quiropráctico que me sugirió. Yo nunca había tratado uno de esos antes, ¡pero funcionó! Me asusté de veras cuando me tronó la espalda; sin embargo, ¡sentí la diferencia inmediatamente! El dolor me dejó en cuanto mi columna vertebral estuvo alineada como debería."

"Qué gusto me da oír eso, Alice. ¡Dios trabaja de maneras misteriosas!"

"¡No sé de eso! Pero su consejo tuvo mucho valor para mí, ya sea que Dios haya tenido algo que ver con ello o no. Lo que me trae por aquí a esta hora es otro asunto. Perdí un anillo esta mañana. Pensé que alguien me lo había robado, así que lo reporté a la policía. Luego tuve un recuerdo. Usted sabe que mi memoria ya no es tan buena como cuando estaba más joven. Me acordé que el último lugar donde traía puesto mi anillo fue aquí en la iglesia esta mañana. Se me hace que me lo estaba yo moviendo y seguro lo perdí en donde estaba sentada. Usted estaba diciendo algo muy bonito en su sermón que me tocó el corazón..."

Gabriel y el chofer se le quedaron viendo a Alice.

Ella pensó por un ratito; luego se rindió y dijo, "¡No me puedo acordar de que se trataba! Como sea, me gustaría buscar en la iglesia para tratar de encontrar ese anillo de diamante. Es invaluable para mí porque era el anillo de bodas de mi abuela. Vale cincuenta mil dólares."

El Padre Gabriel observó a la vieja y sintió lástima. Por como se veía, el valor del anillo no era nada que al perderlo la mandaría a la pobreza. Había venido en una limusina con su chofer y traía puesto un vestido muy caro. Traía también joyería con un valor tres veces lo que costaba el anillo perdido. El dinero y la joyería no eran cosas que excitaran al pastor de la iglesia de la Santísima Trinidad.

"Echémosle un vistazo al interior. Creo que estaba usted en medio a la izquierda..." dijo el sacerdote, abriendo la puerta del templo.

"No. Creo que estaba enfrente a la derecha," alegó ella, muy segura de donde había estado, y se encaminó en esa dirección mientras que el padre iba a encender las luces.

Alice le ordenó a su chofer que buscara por las bancas desde el frente hasta atrás en el lado derecho. El empleado, un hombre negro de edad media, cumplió con la orden de su jefa sin decir palabra. Gabriel se preguntaba si el hombre sería mudo. Parecía que la mujer hablaba suficiente por los dos, y él no tenía chanza de decir nada.

Gabriel pensó, "¡Cincuenta mil dólares por un pedacito de metal y una piedrita!" El cura se preguntó cuánto podría lograrse con esa suma para alimentar hambrientos, vestir necesitados, o educar ignorantes.

Fue a asistir a los dos visitantes con el cateo. Mientras se dirigía a ellos, una luciérnaga le voló por enfrente de la cara. Gabriel se detuvo y siguió el vuelo del pequeño insecto con los ojos. El bichito se paró en una de las bancas en el lado izquierdo. El sacerdote sintió algo dentro de su pecho y decidió seguir al insecto.

La viejita le ordenó al presbítero que los asistiera en su lado, "¡Por acá, Padre! ¿No le dije que estaba en este lado? Puede usted ver junto a la pared en caso de que se me haya caído y haya rodado, o que alguien lo pateó. ¡Espero no lo haya encontrado alguien y decidió quedárselo!"

Él ignoró su orden y miró a la luciérnaga, la cual andaba en vuelo de nuevo, haciendo brillar su lucecita. Voló hacia el piso bajo un asiento de en medio, en el lado izquierdo. Gabriel se sonrió y se arrodilló donde el bicho había aterrizado. El diamante de 5 quilates reflejó la luz de la luciérnaga, iluminando por un instante el oscuro rincón debajo de la banca.

"Lo sabía. Gracias, Criaturita. ¡Gracias, Señor, por mandarme a este guía para ayudar a Alice a recobrar su anillo!"

El pastor se incorporó con el anillo en la mano; el pequeño insecto voló y se reposó sobre su hombro.

"¡Alice, encontramos su anillo!"

La viejita, sonriendo como una niña contenta la mañana de navidad, se apresuró lo más que pudo. El chofer la siguió de cerca, respirando aliviado porque más temprano había sido nombrado como sospechoso. Alice tomó la pieza de joyería y le agradeció al cura. Su chofer estaba contento y, aún sin decir palabra, le estrechó la mano.

"Padre, déjeme darle una recompensa por haber encontrado mi anillo. Le voy a escribir un cheque por quinientos dólares. ¿Qué le parece?"

La mujer se sacó la chequera de la bolsa y una pluma.

"No, no. No puedo aceptarlo. Fue un placer el poder haberle sido útil."

Philip Sanders, el chofer, notó la luciérnaga en el hombro del sacerdote y se la tumbó. A pesar que el cura subió su guardia y se echó para atrás como buen boxeador, no pudo evitar el contacto de la mano de Philip con el insecto.

"¡Oh, no!" Gabriel dijo, volteando a ver al insectito muerto en el piso.

El presbítero se volvió a mirar el sobresaltado rostro de Philip. Solo había tratado de quitarle un animalillo de la ropa, y el ministro había reaccionado como si Philip hubiera matado a un niño. El pastor levantó la luciérnaga muerta y la puso en la palma de su mano izquierda.

"Es curioso cómo valuamos ese anillo en cincuenta mil dólares, una cosa sin vida, una creación del hombre, un objeto de lujo, y símbolo de riqueza; sin embargo, a una luciérnaga, un trabajo viviente de Dios, una pequeñita criatura que puede volar y dar luz, comer, respirar, digerir alimentos y reproducirse, no le asignamos valor alguno."

Philip estaba muy contrito escuchando al ministro. Murmuró, "Lo siento muchísimo, Reverendo, yo nunca pensé..."

"Lo sé. La mayoría nunca nos detenemos a pensar en esto. Tomamos el regalo de la vida como si nada. Yo sé que tú solo trataste de ser amable conmigo sin considerar al animalito."

El Padre Gabriel le puso la mano al chofer sobre el hombro y le sonrió. La viejita le extendió el cheque.

"Acepte este dinero, Padre, si no para usted, al menos para su parroquia."

El pastor tomó el cheque bajo esas circunstancias, como una donación para la iglesia. Los encaminó hacia fuera y los vio partir en la limusina. Esperaba que tal vez su encuentro les hiciera reflexionar un poco en su relación con Dios. El lujoso vehículo dio la vuelta en la esquina y desapareció de su vista.

Gabriel notó un grupito de jóvenes caminando por la banqueta opuesta, empujándose entre ellos e insultándose en inglés y en español. Varios carros iban pasando por la calle, y uno de ellos les pitó a los escandalosos. Uno de entre ellos miró al sacerdote; el pastor le respondió agitando la mano y diciendo, "Shalom, Jorge!" Los inquietos adolescentes dieron vuelta en la esquina; el chico no le contestó el saludo al clérigo.

Gabriel se regresó al interior del templo con su amiguito muerto aún en la mano. Cuando apagó las luces, sintió una sensación en su pecho como había experimentado antes, cuando cosas extrañas ocurrían a su alrededor.

El sacerdote se arrodilló y encaró el altar. Su espalda se le puso chinita tocado por un inmenso poder invisible. Cerró los ojos y empezó a rezar. La sensación se regó por todo su cuerpo. El Padre Gabriel estaba brillando en la oscura iglesia, arrodillado frente al altar. Levantó su mano derecha al cielo e hizo la señal de la cruz sobre la palma de su mano izquierda donde la luciérnaga yacía sin vida. Cuando su dedo índice derecho tocó al pequeño insecto, una chispa de luz le entró al cuerpo y empezó a mover las alitas. Gabriel dejó de brillar y extendió su mano izquierda hacia el altar.

"¡Gracias, Señor, por concederme esta petición! ¡Que tu nombre sea alabado por siempre!"

La luciérnaga voló de su mano y se elevó hasta los recesos del santuario, haciendo su lucecita brillar en la oscuridad. El místico se persignó y se levantó. Salió de la iglesia, cantando uno de los himnos que habían cantado en la casa de las monjitas. Le echó llave al lugar y se fue a su casa a prepararse para dormir.

A pesar de ser una noche tibia y tranquila, un fuerte viento frío llegó a la iglesia levantando tierra, hojas y basura. Las luces exteriores se apagaron, y la oscuridad rodeó el sitio. Un perro callejero que pasaba por ahí sintió la maligna entidad y le gruñó al remolinillo, el cual se iba moviendo alrededor de la iglesia por el callejón. Los pelos de la espalda del perro se le pararon, y huyó de ahí, aullando. El Diablo le estaba haciendo una visita al lugar.

Le gruñó a Dios desde afuera del templo, "¿Por qué siempre concedes a Gabriel, un simple hombre, todo lo que te pide?"

"Porque él es fiel," una suave respuesta emanó del santuario. Una intensa y misteriosa luz brilló intensamente, llenando el interior del templo.

"Eso es porque siempre estás con él y nunca le das oportunidad de probar mi lado."

"¡Eso no es cierto, y tú lo sabes! Gabriel es bueno, y Nosotros estamos contentos con él."

"¿Qué tal una prueba de su 'fidelidad,' ya que estás tan seguro?"

Dios pausó por un instante, y luego estuvo de acuerdo.

"Muy bien, te dejaremos ponerlo a prueba de cualquier modo que puedas concebir, pero no lo mates. Ya verás que él, siendo solo un hombre, es fiel."

El demonio se rió con una risa grave, macabra.

"¿Cuánto tiempo me darás para poner a tu chico a prueba?"

"¡Tres meses!" dijo el Señor en un tono pacífico pero firme.

"No creo que sea suficiente tiempo. Tú te lo has estado trabajando por muchos años ya. ¡Dame un año entero!"

"No un año, te daremos seis meses."

"Si durante ese tiempo te puedo demostrar que él es simplemente otro mortal infiel, si lo hago renunciar a su promesa de servirte como sacerdote, ¿me puedo quedar con él?"

"Si Gabriel abandona su ministerio por tu tentación, será tuyo, pero te daremos únicamente seis meses, de hoy hasta el último día de febrero ¡Ahora, retírate!"

El remolino apestoso se desvaneció, y las luces regresaron a la calle fuera de la iglesia mientras que la luz interior se disipó.

Otro perro vago empezó a ladrar en el callejón; pasó una ambulancia ahogando el ladrido del perro.

El Padre Gabriel se asomó por la ventana, sin imaginarse lo que estaba a punto de acontecerle. La unidad de emergencias se fue hacia el sur con sus luces relampagueando, otra noche típica del lado oeste de la ciudad.

El cura se metió a la cama y apagó la luz. El último día de agosto estaba llegando a su fin.

Capítulo II

Encuentro

La noche después de que tuvieron al Padre Gabriel de invitado, las cuatro religiosas estaban limpiando después de la cena cuando el teléfono timbró. Sor Magdalene le dio el teléfono a Sor Kathryn. Era su primo, Joseph McKloski, en llamada de larga distancia desde Irlanda. Al ver la expresión de Kathryn mientras platicaba con su primo, todas las hermanas supieron que eran malas noticias. Kathryn colgó el teléfono y se sentó, sollozando.

Sor Mary le trajo un vasito de agua. Magdalene y Carmen le pusieron las manos en los hombros para hacerle saber que estaban listas para apoyarla. Mary le tomó la mano a Kathryn y le preguntó qué había pasado.

"Mi mamá está en el hospital. Se está muriendo de un problema del corazón. Los doctores no creen que le quede mucho," Kathy les explicó.

Las tres hermanas expresaron su solidaridad y le ofrecieron orar para que se recuperara. Sor Magda, la superior del grupo, le ofreció, "¿Por qué no vas a ver a tu madre?"

Los ojos de Kathryn se abrieron muy grandes con esperanza, pero luego recordó todos los compromisos que tenía.

"Desearía poder ir, pero tengo trabajo que hacer aquí y en la escuela. Necesitaría tiempo para hacer arreglos y dejar quién se hiciera cargo."

Magdalene la levantó de la silla y le echó su grueso brazo sobre los hombros a la flaquita.

"Lo único que necesitas es preparar tu veliz, Hermana. Nosotras nos haremos cargo de todo por ti, para que puedas abordar un avión mañana y vayas con tu madre."

Magdalene se llevó a Kathryn a su cuarto para que empezara a empacar. Poco después, la mayor regresó a la sala, mirando a Mary.

"Mary, ponte en la computadora y consíguele un boleto para Irlanda en el primer vuelo disponible. Tú eres muy buena para esas cosas." Entonces se volvió a la otra hermana y le dijo, "Carmen, quiero que revises el calendario de trabajo de Kathryn y me digas lo que necesitamos para continuar sus labores en su ausencia. Yo me haré cargo de su ministerio de música en la iglesia y hablaré mañana con el padre acerca de conseguir una maestra sustituta para el primer grado."

El equipo de religiosas se puso en acción y pusieron a Kathryn en un avión a la mañana siguiente con la esperanza que aún pudiera encontrar a su madre con vida.

IRLANDA

Sor Theresa Reynolds, una hermana religiosa de treinta y siete años con un título de maestría en educación, estaba charlando con Sor Rebecca Sterling en un convento en Dublín. Era una mañana fresca y seca, perfecta para sentarse en el patio del convento a disfrutar de una tacita de café con una vieja amiga.

"Todo pasa por alguna razón, Theresa. El Señor quizás te necesita en alguna otra parte. ¡Estoy tan feliz que hayas salido de África con vida!"

Rebecca había entrado a la hermandad con Theresa catorce años atrás, y habían estado en contacto a pesar de siempre haber sido enviadas a diferentes partes del mundo.

"¡Yo también!" dijo Theresa. "¡Fue horrible! Un día todo estaba normal: yo estaba dando clases en la escuela. Al día siguiente, la guerra civil estalló. Se oían balazos por todos lados; había edificios ardiendo. Se nos ordenó que nos fuéramos del país; el nuevo régimen no quería ninguna influencia religiosa. Podíamos haber sido ejecutados. Lo siento mucho por los niños de ahí, quienes aún están pasando por esa terrible experiencia."

Sor Martha se acercó a preguntarles si querían ir con ella a recoger a una hermana proveniente de América quien había venido a ver a su moribunda madre en el hospital. Rebecca estuvo de acuerdo; Theresa declinó la invitación pues tenía una cita con el doctor esa mañana.

Todo se acomodó rápido. La mamá de Kathryn se puso un poco mejor en el hospital; estaba muy alegre de ver a su familia reunida. Sabía que su final se acercaba, pero apreciaba mucho la compañía de su hija mayor.

La Madre Superior del convento decidió enviar a Theresa a sustituir a Kathryn en Texas, por todo lo necesario para permitirle a Kathryn quedarse con su familia. La Superior había hablado con el Padre Gabriel y con Sor Magdalene; acordaron en el repuesto temporal para así mantener a la perturbada Hermana Theresa ocupada en un ambiente estable mientras se recuperaba del trauma de la guerra civil en un país africano.

Antes del fin de semana, Theresa estaba volando sobre el Océano Atlántico para regresar a su tierra natal. La mujer había nacido en Fort Bragg, una instalación militar en Carolina del Norte.

Theresa había crecido como hija única. Su padre era oficial del ejército, y su madre una escritora de ficción neoyorquina. La familia vivió en varios diferentes países y bases militares en los Estados Unidos.

Para cuando ella estaba en el tercer año de preparatoria, su padre había obtenido rango de General Mayor y comandaba el Fuerte Sam Houston en San Antonio, Texas. Theresa tenía dulces memorias de la ciudad a la cual estaba regresando después de veinte años de viajes alrededor del mundo.

Sus padres murieron en un accidente de avioneta después que su papá se había retirado del ejército. Ella había encontrado una vida de actividades al servicio del Señor como hermana católica.

La dama iba ansiosa por envolverse en su nueva misión en la ciudad de su juventud. Pensó en el noviecito que había tenido en la preparatoria y se preguntó si aún viviría ahí, probablemente casado y con hijos adolescentes. Había perdido contacto con él desde que sus padres se la llevaron hasta Alemania sin aviso previo; él nunca le contestó sus cartas. Probablemente había sido solo una aventura juvenil para él, pero ella aún sentía su corazón palpitar más rápido al recordarlo.

SAN ANTONIO, TEXAS

Sor Mary fue en la van de las hermanas a encontrarse con Theresa en el Aeropuerto Internacional. Mary quedó prendada de Theresa. A pesar que la recién arribada era diez años mayor, Mary quedó con la impresión que era una maestra muy dinámica. Se veía inteligente y en buena condición; la forma en que sonreía y hablaba revelaban su carácter amable y cálido.

"¿Tuviste un buen viaje, Hermana Theresa?"

"¡Excelente! Solo que un poco largo, pero me dio oportunidad de leer bastantito."

Mary era una ávida lectora también pero se brincó preguntarle qué era lo que había venido leyendo para moverse a otro tema mientras salían del aeropuerto, conduciendo rumbo a la casa de las religiosas.

"¿Tuviste ocasión de conocer a Sor Kathryn en Irlanda?"

"No. Lamento decirlo. El día que llegó, yo tenía una cita con el médico y no pude ir a recibirla al aeropuerto. Luego ella se ocupó con su familia, y yo me apuré a prepararme para venir a reemplazarla... por un tiempo."

"¡Bienvenida a San Antonio, Hermana! ¿Es tu primera vez por aquí?"

"Oh, no. Yo viví aquí, justo por allá, en el Fuerte Sam Houston." Theresa apuntó el dedo en dirección de la base militar cercana y explicó, "Mi papá era el comandante del fuerte cuando vivíamos aquí."

"¡Entonces debes tener muchos amigos en San Antonio!"

"No realmente. Han pasado veinte años desde que vivíamos aquí. Los que conocí probablemente se han ido o se han olvidado de mí. Yo estuve en esa escuela católica para chicas. (Iban pasando cerca de ella.) Pero no me pude graduar con las de mi clase. Mi papá fue enviado a una plaza importante en Alemania, y nos tuvimos que ir un par de meses después que apenas había empezado mi último año de prepa."

Mary meció la cabeza como que entendía la situación y volvió a cambiar el tema de conversación.

"Oí que apenas te pudiste escapar de África con vida..." Se cubrió la boca, parando su interrogación, acordándose de lo que Sor Magdalene le había advertido más temprano. "¡Lo siento! No se supone que debo preguntarte."

"Está bien, Hermana. Ya me estoy recuperando del choque emocional. Quizás más delante te pueda contar detalles de mis aventuras en los países del tercer mundo. El Señor me ha protegido a todas partes donde he ido a hacer lo que ha preparado para mí."

Mary suspiró, aliviada.

"Tienes una maestría en educación, ¿verdad?" preguntó la joven.

"Sí. ¿Cómo lo supiste?"

"Viniste altamente recomendada. Yo también tengo mi maestría en educación. Pienso que la educación es la clave para resolver la mayoría de los problemas del mundo. Yo trato de infundirles a mis estudiantes un apetito verdadero por el aprendizaje y espero que se lo pasen a otros."

La recién arribada maestra sonrió con admiración y asintió con la cabeza muy de acuerdo antes de inquirir, "¿Cómo es el director?"

El rostro de Sor Mary se iluminó.

"¿El Padre Gabriel? ¡Te vas a enamorar de él! Es un gran hombre, un santo, muy dulce y lleno de energía. También es el pastor de nuestra parroquia, así que está siempre ocupado. ¡Y hermanita mía, canta como un ángel! El Padre es muy carismático y ha hecho muchos milagros."

Theresa abrió los ojos muy grandes.

"¡Guau! Ya estoy ansiosa por conocerlo. ¿De qué clase de milagros estás hablando? ¿Tiene el poder de sanar a los enfermos?"

"Oh sí, eso y mucho más. Nadie sabe en verdad cuántos milagros ha hecho porque siempre trata de mantenerlos en secreto. El Espíritu Santo habita en él."

La maestra sustituta se preguntó como se vería aquel sacerdote; se lo imaginó como San Juan Bosco. Theresa volteó a ver el cielo del anochecer y caviló el por qué habría ella sido enviada a trabajar con aquel santo. El sol ya había desaparecido de vista en el poniente, y la oscuridad estaba comenzando a vencer la luz del día.

Mientras la Hermana Mary procedía por una intersección cuando la luz se había cambiado a verde, una camioneta se pasó la luz roja viniendo del lado derecho. Mary le dio el pisotón al freno y se dio vuelta a la izquierda para evitar chocar. El chofer del otro vehículo les pitó y les hizo un gesto poco amigable con la mano en el aire mientras se alejaba veloz.

"¿Estás bien, Hermana Theresa?" preguntó la chofer a su pasajera.

"Sí. ¡Gracias a Dios por los cintos de seguridad!" dijo la pasajera, aún agarrada del tablero de la van.

"¡Y el hombre ese aún tiene el descaro de pitarnos, como si hubiéramos tenido la culpa!" Mary exclamó, conduciendo para fuera de la intersección.

Cuando acomodó la van en la posición apropiada en la calle, Sor Theresa le dijo, "Perdónalo, Hermana. Él pensó que estaba en lo correcto porque su luz roja está fundida. ¿La ves?" Theresa le apuntó al foco fundido del semáforo para la calle por donde venía la camioneta. "Probablemente sintió que tenía el derecho de pasar y nosotras éramos las que nos debíamos de parar. Debo decir que tus rápidos reflejos nos salvaron. "

Mary asintió y dijo, "Bueno, gracias a Dios que no pasó nada. Imagínate, escapar la muerte en una guerra civil en África para venir a morir en un accidente de tráfico en San Antonio. Ya casi llegamos. ¡Vámonos!"

Theresa se sonrió, se reclinó en su asiento, mirando las calles de la ciudad y comentó, "Espero tener una estancia pacífica y sin más complicaciones que aquellas que me traigan los niños en mi clase."

"Oh, estoy segura que vas a tener tus manos llenas con esos chiquillos, pero no creo que vayas a tener ningún problema serio al estar aquí."

Las otras hermanas vinieron a recibir a Theresa como si fueran viejas amigas. Ella se sintió bienvenida al que sería su hogar por un tiempo. Ya estaba oscuro. Después de instalarla en la recámara con la Hermana Mary, se juntaron a cenar, hacer su oración nocturna, y a cantar alabanzas a Dios antes de acostarse. Theresa durmió como bebé después de su largo vuelo.

Muy temprano al día siguiente, la nueva maestra fue a atender la misa del sábado en la iglesia de la Santísima Trinidad. El celebrante era un padre muy viejito para ser el pastor del que le habían hablado. Theresa esperó el final de la misa para ir a presentarse con él. El presbítero le informó que no era el pastor y que el Padre Gabriel estaba en el gimnasio de box, calle abajo. La hermana religiosa le dio las gracias y se encaminó rumbo al lugar.

Theresa sintió el calor de la mañana del sur de Texas mientras caminaba. Un remolinillo terregoso surgió del callejón y rodeó a la monjita. El viento del remolino se metió por abajo de su falda y se la levantó, exponiendo sus pantorrillas y muslos. Theresa se bajó la falda y caminó rápido, alejándose del remolinillo. Escuchó una risita ahogada pero no volteó a ver quién se estaba riendo. No había visto a nadie más en esa cuadra, solo el remolino desde donde la presencia del demonio la observaba con interés. Había un asqueroso olor en el aire, y la mujer sintió un escalofrío recorrerle toda la espina dorsal. Se persignó mientras caminaba rumbo al gimnasio.

Theresa se asomó al interior del gimnasio por una ventana abierta. Había un grupo de hombres entrenando. Sus ojos se posaron en uno musculoso que golpeaba el costal pesado con energía. Su piel estaba brillosa de sudor. Se movía como un león; no le podía ver la cara porque estaba de espaldas a ella. Él se movió alrededor del costal para continuar vapuleándolo, así que la pesada bolsa se atravesó y no le permitió verle el rostro.

Ella se estremeció con el sonido de los puñetazos, sacudió la cabeza pensando por qué a los hombres les gustaría el boxeo, y se fue a la entrada. Se pasó y buscó a alguien a quien preguntarle por el párroco. Se imaginó que el cura estaría haciendo alguna visita social. El hombre que había visto golpeando el costal se había desaparecido. Había otros, la mayoría jóvenes, algunos negros, otros hispanos, solo un chamaco blanco. Se detuvieron de entrenar para observar a la hermosa visita. Al notar su distintiva ropa de religiosa, se regresaron al ejercicio. Un hombre hispano, propietario del gimnasio, vino a atenderla.

"Buenos días, Hermana. ¿En qué le puedo servir?"

"Buenos días. Estoy buscando al Padre Gabriel. Me dijeron que estaba aquí."

La Hermana Theresa miró alrededor, sin hallar a ninguno que se viera como un sacerdote ahí. El teléfono comenzó a timbrar en la pared.

"Oh, sí. Estaba aquí hace un minuto. Debe haberse ido para allá atrás," le dijo en un tono gentil, y después la hizo pegar un saltito al gritar muy fuerte, "¡Timmy, ve y háblale al Padre G! Dile que lo andan buscando."

El niño de nueve años puso el cepillo de barrer por un lado y pegó carrera a la parte trasera para ir a hablarle al cura. El dueño del gimnasio se volteó a contestar el teléfono.

"¡Padre G... Padre G... Órale, lo buscan allá enfrente... Antes-que-inmediatamente!" el niño gritó.

La hermana pensó que el pequeño estaba poniendo más urgencia en su tono de voz de lo que era necesario. Se oía como una emergencia.

El hombre que había estado golpeando el costal salió apresurado de los vestidores. Se estaba alistando para bañarse, así que se apareció vistiendo solo un suspensor deportivo muy breve para ver qué era tan importante.

Se quedó parado en la puerta de los vestidores, a solo unos pasos de la mujer. Ella trató de cubrirse los ojos pero detuvo su mano antes de llegar a ellos y se tapó la boca.

El sacerdote reconoció aquella hermosa carita de veinte años atrás. Había madurado bastante, pero su lindo rostro era el mismo del que se había enamorado cuando estaba en la preparatoria. Los ojos muy claros como dos gotas de miel con unas pizquitas de verde limón eran los mismísimos que había tenido en sus sueños por muchas noches.

"¡Theresa Reynolds!"

"¡Gabriel Infante!"

La hermana también lo reconoció. Él también había madurado bastante. Traía bigote con barba y había ganado peso muscular, pero el magnetismo de sus oscuros ojos cafés y su luminosa sonrisa eran los mismos que le habían hecho enamorarse de él desde que se conocieron en la preparatoria.

"¡Ja-ja-ja-ja-ja, el Padre G anda encuerado!" dijo Timmy, apuntándole al hombre con solo su suspensor deportivo parado frente a la monjita. Ambos se habían quedado paralizados por la sorpresa hasta que la risotada del chiquillo los regresó al presente.

"Discúlpame." Gabriel corrió al interior del vestidor, avergonzado. Le gritó desde el interior, "¡Enseguida salgo!"

La cara de Theresa cambió de rosa a crema pálido y luego a rojo. No había esperado ver tanto así del pastor, pero le había gustado lo que vio.

"¡Lo esperaré mejor en la rectoría, Padre G!" ella le gritó antes de partir del gimnasio a la carrera.

Su corazón latía muy rápido. Iba corriendo, alejándose del gimnasio y casi fue arrollada por un ciclista al atravesar la calle. El ciclista evitó pegarle a la monjita, pero perdió control de su vehículo y se cayó a la banqueta. Theresa ni siquiera volteó a ver al caído. El desafortunado ciclista murmuró algo entre dientes mientras se levantaba de la banqueta, sacudiéndose el polvo de los pantalones.

La Hermana Theresa se metió al templo y se arrodilló, rezando por poner sus pensamientos y sus sentimientos en orden.

Gabriel por su parte, dándose cuenta que ya se había marchado, se metió al baño. De verdad necesitaba un buen duchazo, y también una cabeza fría. Abrió la llave del agua fría y permaneció ahí por unos minutos, pensando qué estaba ocurriendo en su vida. ¡Aquel no iba a ser un sábado ordinario!

"¡Theresa es monjita, y está aquí! ¿Por qué, después de todos estos años?"

Se sintió más contento que de costumbre y se apuró a vestirse. Regañó al travieso de Timmy por no haberle advertido que se trataba de una dama buscándolo. El chiquillo solo se rió y se fue corriendo.

El Padre amaba al muchachito, Timmy, de forma especial. Lo halló en una caja de zapatos bajo un puente; el niño acababa de nacer cuando su madre lo abandonó. Gabriel andaba corriendo por ahí cuando oyó la vocecita llorando bajo el puente. Recogió al niño y reportó su hallazgo a las autoridades. La madre nunca fue encontrada.

Timmy fue adoptado por el dueño del gimnasio y su esposa cuando el Padre Gabriel les contó del bebé. El cura lo había visto crecer y convertirse en un chicuelo inquieto y travieso pero muy listo. Timmy estaba en tercero en la escuela de la Santísima Trinidad; el sacerdote era padrino del niño.

El presbítero caminó rápido hasta la iglesia con la esperanza que sí era cierto que Theresa, su noviecita de la prepa, estaría ahí esperándolo. Se puso a cavilar sobre las complicaciones que su relación anterior podría traerles, pero decidió despedir aquellos pensamientos y simplemente descubrir por qué lo andaba buscando. La encontró a la entrada de la iglesia. ¡Se veía encantadora aún en su vestimenta religiosa!

Gabriel pensó en actuar profesionalmente, pero ella habló primero, con la misma intención.

"Padre, he sido enviada de Irlanda para sustituir a Sor Kathryn Cabrini cuya madre se encuentra muy enferma."

El Padre Gabriel la llevó hasta su oficina en la rectoría de la parroquia. No había nadie más en la casa ese sábado.

"Hermana es usted muy bienvenida. Estaré encantado de trabajar a su lado. Si hay alguna cosa que pueda hacer para ayudarle a que se sienta cómoda con nosotros, por favor, no titubee en pedírmelo."

"Muchas gracias, Padre. Hice una listita de las cosas que me gustaría tener y que la Hermana Kathryn no usaba en su clase."

Gabriel tomó el papel de su manita, y ambos recibieron una ligera descarga de energía estática cuando se rozaron, muy levemente.

"¡Bien, pues esta sí que es una sorpresa electrizante!" Él se sonrió y le preguntó, "¿Cuánto tiempo lleva de ser una hermana religiosa, Theresa?"

El hombre se sentó detrás de su escritorio mirando a la mujer, incrédulo.

"Decidí entrar a la vida religiosa cuando me convencí de que usted ya me había olvidado."

Aquellas palabras le partieron el corazón; se oía que aún estaba herida.

"¡Pero si nunca te olvidé! Tú desapareciste de mi vida un día y nunca te pusiste en contacto conmigo. Tenías mi dirección y número de teléfono; no supe a dónde te fuiste. ¿Por qué no me llamaste o me escribiste?"

La formalidad se había disipado y él le estaba hablando como a su noviecita perdida hacía muchos años. Ella trató de explicarle lo que pasó.

"Mis padres me llevaron a Alemania con la excusa que mi papá había sido asignado a una plaza muy importante. No querían que tuviera más contacto contigo. Me dijeron que tú y yo no éramos de la misma clase."

"¿Y tú se los creíste?"

"¡No, por supuesto que no! Te escribí cartas, pero parece que mi mamá. . intercepto todo mi correo y nunca lo dejó salir. Yo concluí que ya que no contestabas mis cartas, era cierto lo que ella me decía: que tú ya tenías otra novia por acá y te habías olvidado de mí. Yo realmente creí que ella estaba de mi lado cuando mi papá me prohibió usar el teléfono."

Gabriel apretó el descansabrazos de su silla al oír aquello.

"Ella me advirtió de ti pero me dijo que podía escribirte y ver que pasaba. Ahora veo que nunca mandó ninguna de mis cartas."

Fue como si una cortina oscura hubiera caído y la luz del sol entrara a un cuarto que había estado en la penumbra por años. Hubo un momento de silencio en lo que los que fueran amantes juveniles ponían en orden sus sentimientos. Tuvieron que reprimir un ardiente deseo de abrazarse.

"¿Cómo están tus papás?"

Theresa volvió la cara al piso al decirle, "Murieron en un accidente de avioneta un año después de que mi papá se retiró, hace dieciséis años."

"Verdaderamente lo siento, Theresa."

Theresa lo vio de nuevo y le sonrió, aceptando sus sinceras palabras; luego se volvió al cielo para contener una lágrima en sus ojos.

"Ahora comprendo que mi mamá pensó que me estaba haciendo un favor al dejar que mi amor por ti muriera con el tiempo y la distancia. En su mente eso era lo mejor para mí."

"¿Murió en verdad tu amor por mí, Theresa?"

La hermana se levantó de la silla y caminó a la ventana. Caviló en su pregunta y luego regresó a decirle, "No estoy segura, pero cuéntame de ti. ¿Cuándo decidiste convertirte en sacerdote? Creí que te iba a encontrar felizmente casado y con un montón de criaturas, como habías deseado."

"La única mujer con la quería casarme fue arrancada de mi vida, así que busqué nueva dirección y encontré a Dios," Gabriel le explicó. "Un día sentí su presencia como una fuerza invisible que sin palabras me llamó a la iglesia. ¿Te acuerdas que había yo aplicado para la academia militar de West Point para impresionar a tu papá? ¡Bueno, pues decliné el atender esa escuela y acabé en el seminario en vez de eso!"

Él siguió hablando y tratando de convencerse a sí mismo que el llamado al sacerdocio era lo mejor que le había podido suceder.

"Descubrí la llave de la felicidad eterna y decidí dedicar mi vida y energía a ello. He descubierto que mientras más doy, más recibo. Es como un tesoro inagotable el cual me siento obligado a compartir con toda la gente a mi alrededor. No me habré casado ni tenido niños propios, pero tengo un montón de criaturas para educar y cuidar. ¡Todos ellos me llaman Padre!"

Ella lo miró a los ojos y le susurró, "¿Murió tu amor por mí cuando decidiste convertirte en sacerdote?"

Entonces fue turno de él de levantarse e ir a la ventana para cavilar sobre aquella pregunta. Se volvió para mirarla a los ojos y se estremeció dándose cuenta que su amor por ella estaba realmente aún muy vivo.

"No. No lo creo. Solo se fue a dormir. Se convirtió en un hermoso sueño, parte de mi pasado. Tuve que batallar con tu imagen en mis recuerdos, pero pensé que mi destino era ser sacerdote. Yo no tenía los medios para irte a buscar alrededor del mundo. A mí también me aconsejaron que tú te habías olvidado de mí, como una aventura juvenil, y de seguro te habías casado con alguien de la alta sociedad, como tus padres querían."

"A ambos nos mintieron y nos dieron mal consejo; sin embargo, Dios tenía otros planes para nosotros y así fue como nos llamó a su servicio."

"Sí. ¡Tienes razón! ¿Eres feliz, Sor Theresa?"

"Sí. Tengo una carrera muy satisfactoria. Me siento útil y bendecida. ¿Eres feliz tú, Padre Gabriel?"

"Sí, pero me siento especialmente feliz de verte de nuevo, mi Vieja Amiga. Creo que esta es una bendición, un regalo de Dios, al menos para mí."

"Estoy de acuerdo, Padre Gabriel. Es grandioso el verte de nuevo. Estoy encantada de trabajar a tu lado. Me han dicho cosas increíbles acerca de ti y de los milagros que haces."

"No creas todo lo que dicen las gentes. Ya sabes como les gusta exagerar las cosas, pero Dios es muy grande, y aún hace milagros en nuestros días, en formas misteriosas."

Sor Theresa se levantó y le extendió la manita. Él se la estrechó, dándole la bienvenida como maestra del primer año. Ella besó la mano del hombre en reverencia a su posición oficial como el pastor de la parroquia.

Theresa declinó su oferta de llevarla a la casa de las hermanas, diciendo que necesitaba caminar y volverse a familiarizar con la ciudad. También sintió que necesitaba estar a solas. Su corazón estaba acelerado como cuando era adolescente. Se alejó, temiendo que él pudiera darse cuenta de lo afectada que había quedado con su encuentro.

Él la siguió con los ojos hasta que desapareció en la esquina. Entonces se fue a su oficina a meditar en el significado de su encuentro. Un vaso de vino le ayudó a humedecer su seca garganta.

El domingo en la mañana el Padre Gabriel encontró a Sor Theresa lista para tocar el órgano para la primera misa. Estaba entusiasmado por verla de nuevo. Theresa rechazó la oferta de Magdalene de tocar ella para la celebración y así dejar a Theresa dormir tarde. Estaba deseosa de atender la misa del Padre Gabriel y verlo en acción.

Ver a Gabriel sirviendo en el altar era inspirante. El evangelio hablaba del reino de los cielos siendo como un tesoro en un campo o una rara perla que cuando uno lo encontraba, dejaría todo por poseerlo. Gabriel invitó a la congregación a imaginarse que el hombre en la parábola era Jesús mismo, y la perla preciosa representaba a cada uno de nosotros. Él dejó el cielo y lo dio todo por su gran amor a nosotros.

Theresa disfrutó de esa misa como ninguna. Cuando fue el tiempo de compartir la paz, el Padre Gabriel anduvo estrechando manos y abrazando a aquellos más cercanos al altar. Se encontró con Theresa no lejos de él, así que se le acercó y la abrazó por un momento. Sintieron como que el tiempo se hubiera detenido en el instante que la sostuvo en sus brazos.

"¡La paz del Señor esté contigo, Hermana Theresa!"

Se sintió cargada de energía y se puso a tocar el himno para la comunión con gusto, a pesar de que le temblaban un poco las rodillas. Se concentró en la música, tratando de evitar ponerle mucha atención a sus sentimientos mezclados. ¡Había sido sensacional estar en sus brazos de nuevo!

Al fin de la misa, el cura despidió a sus feligreses estrechando sus manos y charlando un poco al salir, mientras la organista tocaba el último himno.

Una de las parejas, un gordito y una gordita, ambos más jóvenes que él, preguntaron, "¿Cómo le hace para mantenerse tan bien, Padre?"

El pastor miró a Sandra y Eric Jones, los dos chaparritos pero pesando noventa y tantos kilos cada uno.

"No he dejado de hacer ejercicio desde joven, corriendo, nadando, levantando pesas, y un poco de boxeo para mantenerme al tiro."

"Sandra y yo vamos a empezar un programa. ¿Qué nos recomendaría usted? ¿Cree que ya es muy tarde para que empecemos?"

"Les recomiendo que empiecen a caminar juntos, luego agreguen un poco de correr si pueden, y después una nadadita. Se van a divertir y mejorarán su salud. No es muy tarde para que empiecen, pero tengan mucho cuidado. Mi abuelita empezó a correr cuando cumplió los sesenta y cinco años, ¡y nadie sabe dónde está ahora!"

La pareja de pesos completos se marchó riéndose; a Gabriel le encantaba hacer reír a la gente.

Para la hora que se regresó a la sacristía, Sor Theresa se había ido. La buscó, pero ya se había desaparecido. Le quería dar las gracias por la hermosa música que proveyó. Quizás la podría llamar más tarde.

El pastor se encontró la piernita de plástico de una muñeca en una de las bancas y la recogió. Acomodó los himnos y misales en otras bancas.

Una mujer regresó a la iglesia con su niña de cinco años llorando porque su muñeca había perdido una pierna. El Padre Gabriel le cerró un ojo a la joven madre y le hizo señas para que le trajera a la niña. Se sentó en cuclillas para estar al nivel de la criatura y le preguntó qué pasaba.

"Elizabeth perdió su pierna y ya no va a poder jugar fútbol."

"Vamos a pedirle a Dios que alivie a tu amiguita." El sacerdote tomó la muñeca y les pidió que cerraran los ojos. "Señor, Dios Todopoderoso, concédenos que Elizabeth recupere su piernita, para que pueda volver a jugar al fútbol. Te lo pedimos en el nombre de Jesucristo, tu Hijo amado.'

"¡Amén!" la niña y su madre dijeron en respuesta a su oración.

Cuando la mujer y su hija abrieron los ojos, encontraron que la muñeca tenía las dos piernas de nuevo. La chiquilla estaba feliz entonces. Se estiró y le dio un besito al padre en la mejilla.

"Gracias, Padre Gabriel."

"De nada, Pequeña. ¿Cómo te llamas?"

"¡Tammy!"

"Bien, Tammy, cuida mucho a Elizabeth de ahora en adelante."

La madre tomó la mano del sacerdote entre las de ella. Se daba cuenta de que el cura había hallado la piernita en la banca donde se habían sentado y se la puso a la muñeca cuando tenían los ojos cerrados, pero apreciaba lo que el gesto significaba para su hijita.

"Muchas gracias, Padre. Tammy estaba bien angustiada porque esa es su muñeca favorita."

El pastor se mantuvo ocupado con las siguientes misas como siempre.

En la tarde se fue al hospital a visitar a un parroquiano quien había tenido un accidente en el trabajo. Le llevó la comunión y se quedó a platicar un rato con la familia. El hombre se iba a recuperar; era solo cuestión de tiempo para recobrarse de sus heridas. Para hacer que el herido se sintiera mejor, Gabriel le contó un chistecillo.

"Un señor le aconsejó a su hijo que si quería una vida larga, el secreto era echarle un poco de pólvora en vez de pimienta en sus tacos del desayuno cada mañana. El hijo siguió el consejo del papá y vivió hasta la edad de noventa y tres años. Cuando murió, dejó siete hijos, veintiún nietos, doce bisnietos y un tremendo agujero de cinco metros de diámetro en el techo del crematorio."

El parroquiano herido se quejó de que le dolía mucho el reírse fuerte, así que Gabriel se guardó sus chistes para después.

Para cuando el cura regresaba a casa, ya era hora de la cena. Tenía hambre pues no había almorzado. A Gabriel no le atraía la idea de tener que cocinarse su propia cena ese domingo. Estaba tratando de decidir qué comer. Cualquier cosa que se le venía a la mente sonaba apetitoso pero requeriría algo de trabajo en la cocina.

El ama de llaves, la Señora Black, estaba libre los domingos; era una viuda tailandesa que se había casado con un miembro del ejército y que había venido a vivir con él en Estados Unidos después del conflicto de Vietnam. Era una excelente cocinera y una persona muy pulcra y sabia. Su marido había fallecido de cáncer de los pulmones diez años atrás.

Cuando el muy viejo sedán negro iba rodando por una calle donde unos muchachos estaban jugando básquetbol, uno reconoció el vehículo del Padre G. No había otro en el barrio tan viejito ni tan bien cuidado. Los estudiantes de mecánica en la preparatoria técnica se las habían arreglado por varios años para restaurar y mantener ese carro conocido como el Curimóvil. El instructor, el Señor Ramiro Vega, era un amigo personal desde sus días en la escuela preparatoria católica para muchachos. Ramiro sabía la historia del viejo sedán, y él mismo era parte de ella.

Un cartero llamado Joseph Smith había comprado el carro nuevecito en 1935. Joe mantuvo su poco usado vehículo por 20 años en perfectas condiciones. Él murió y se lo dejó a su esposa, pero ella nunca manejó un auto. La vieja Señora Smith le dio el carro a José Alfredo Infante como pago por un nuevo juego de gabinetes que le hizo para su cocina en 1960. El carro no había sido manejado en cinco años, pero no necesitaba mucho para reingresar a la carretera.

José y María Infante ya se estaban estableciendo en San Antonio para entonces. Compraron una casita en el oeste y José abrió su negocio de carpintería. Se consiguieron el sedán modelo 1935, el cual en aquel tiempo era color azul metálico, cuando Gabriel iba apenas a cumplir un año.

José mantuvo el carro tan bien como Joseph Smith lo había hecho antes; así que cuando Gabriel graduó de la preparatoria, José le dio el muy viejo pero muy bien cuidadito carro como regalo de graduación.

Al joven Gabriel le encantaba manejarlo, pero odiaba lidiar con la mecánica. Afortunadamente, su amigo Ramiro Vega era un excelente mecánico aún de adolescente. Ramiro quería comprarle el carro a Gabriel, pero él no quería vendérselo porque temía que a su papá no le gustaría que vendiera el regalo que le había heredado. Hicieron un acuerdo que si Ramiro podía contribuir al mantenimiento del viejo automóvil, tenía derecho a sacarlo prestado cuando lo necesitara para salir a dar la vuelta.

Ramiro había manejado ese carro con por lo menos veinte diferentes noviecitas a través de su juventud. Solo dejó de usar el auto cuando su esposa le exigió que se consiguiera su propio carro y dejara que Gabriel, ya un seminarista para entonces, fuera el único chofer.

Ramiro se convirtió en maestro y usaba el carro para darles a sus estudiantes entrenamiento en mecánica. Ellos también se hacían cargo de las llantas, batería, luces, carrocería, interior, todo. Le instalaron un buen sistema estéreo donado por un estudiante. Le agregaron sistemas hidráulicos modernos y partes nuevas cromadas para reemplazar las acabadas. La máquina era nueva y mucho más potente que la original.

El dueño de una tienda de llantas, amigo del sacerdote, donó las ruedas y llantas. Gabriel milagrosamente había regresado la salud a la única hija del hombre. Ella sufría de continuos y muy intensos dolores de cabeza; todo lo que hizo el cura fue imponerle las manos y orar sobre ella para que se curara. El impresionante carro era la única posesión de valor de Gabriel.

Jerry Collins brincó enfrente del Curimóvil, moviendo los brazos como un pajarillo aprendiendo a volar.

"¡Padre G, Padre G, debe ayudarnos!"

Gabriel detuvo su auto y salió de él.

"¿Qué sucede, Jerry?"

El cura miró a su alrededor, tratando de discernir el problema. No había nada más que un grupo de adolescentes, muchachos y muchachas, en la cancha de básquetbol alistándose para un partidito.

"Estos cuates dicen que nos van a dar una paliza en el juego. A uno de nuestros jugadores se lo llevó su abuelita a la casa, así que necesitamos un suplente. ¿Podría usted jugar con nosotros?"

"¡Déjenme estacionar mi cabalgadura, y cuenten conmigo!"

Gabriel se metió de nuevo a su carro y lo estacionó cerca de la banqueta. Abrió la cajuela y sacó sus tenis de ahí. Entonces se quitó la camisa para deleite de las chicas quienes le empezaron a chiflar y a decir jugando que se sentían muy acaloradas.

Una vez listo con sus pantalones negros, camiseta blanca sin mangas y sus tenis, procedió a la cancha. El Padre G era muy bien conocido en el barrio como un hombre de acción. La mayoría de ellos lo respetaban, pero se había hecho de algunos enemigos también.

El equipo oponente tenía un par de drogadictos rateros, a quien Gabriel había ayudado a poner en la cárcel, un tiempecito atrás. Se sonrieron ante la oportunidad de ponerle las manos encima al cura durante el juego.

Tenían la asistencia de un muchachote hispano de uno noventa y tres, y de dos negritos que se movían como que eran muy buenos en la cancha. El Padre G tenía hispanos de estatura media en su equipo. Jerry Collins era una mezcla de blanco, negro, e hispano; era el más corto de estatura en su equipo con solo uno setenta. Los otros tres eran tan parecidos que uno podía pensar que eran trillizos mexicanos, un metro setenta y cinco, delgaditos y veloces, Javier, Jacinto, y Jorge. El Padre Gabriel era el más alto de su equipo con uno ochenta y tres de estatura.

"¿Por qué nos la estamos rifando?" el cura le preguntó a Jerry mientras practicaban sus tiros a la canasta.

"¡Una cena! Si les ganamos, vamos ir a comer barbacoa estilo vaquero."

"¿Cuánto dinero tiene uno que poner?"

"Yo lo cubro, Padre G. Nomás denos su bendición y haga lo mejor que pueda en el juego. No creo que podamos perder con usted de nuestro lado."

El juego empezó. El Padre G sabía que iba a estar duro; aquellos tipos jugaban muy agresivamente. Se persignó y recibió la bola de Jorge. El primer equipo que llegara a los treinta puntos ganaría.

Gabriel le pasó la bola a Jacinto quien se la pasó a Javier. Javier se metió hasta debajo de la canasta con dos oponentes encima. Él rebotó la pelota en el piso hacia atrás para Jerry, que saltó y lanzó un tiro desde 3 metros. El balón entró a la canasta; el equipo del cura se colocó arriba dos a cero.

Damián el centro grandulón del otro equipo, le pegó al clérigo con el hombro al pasar cerca de él. Antoine, uno de los morenos, que se parecía a Ivory Peterson de Los Látigos, iba botando la pelota rumbo a la canasta.

Walter y Clint, los dos raterillos blancos, se pararon a las orillas pidiendo el balón. Antoine se la pasó a su mejor jugador, Scottie. El garrudo negrito se metió rebotando la pelota entre tres oponentes como un jugador estrella y se coló hasta adentro para igualar el marcador dos a dos.

Los muchachos empezaron a echar habladas presumiendo que ellos eran mejores que los otros. El Padre G les tronó las palmas de las manos y los animó a que jugaran en vez de estar de habladores.

Era un partido muy parejo. El Padre G consiguió diez puntos combinando el colarse hasta la canasta y tirando desde afuera del área. Tenía dos tiros de tres puntos y dos anotaciones de cerca. Jorge tenía solo una canasta; Jacinto hizo dos, igual que Javier; Jerry tenía una canasta y cuatro tiros de castigo para un total de 26 puntos para su equipo.

El equipo de los raterillos tenía 27 puntos; Scottie los estaba dominando con 17. Era un jugador personalista a quien le gustaba crear sus propias jugadas y raramente pasaba el balón pero siempre estaba gritando que se lo pasaran. Antoine tenía 6 puntos, Walter y Clint solo una canasta cada uno.

Damián no tenía puntos pero había acumulado 5 faltas; era un demoledor muy rudo. El clérigo ya había sido golpeado por todos los contrarios pero también les había dado con sus hombros, codos y rodillas para mantener el juego parejo y no permitirles pensar que lo podían intimidar. Estaba duro como una roca, así que los chicos optaron por jugar un poco más limpio.

Los raterillos planearon acabar al equipo del presbítero con un tiro de 3 puntos. Iban a dejar que Scottie lo tirara. Tenían la pelota y se comenzaron a mover hacia la canasta. Clint le pasó la bola a Antoine. Él avanzó botando el balón alrededor de Damián y pasó la bola al lado opuesto donde Walter la atrapó. En cuanto la tuvo, la pasó hacia atrás en donde Scottie estaba ya esperando en la distancia apropiada para tirar por los tres puntos.

Gabriel dejó a Damián solo en el centro y se arrancó contra Scottie; el negrito ya estaba doblando las rodillas y apuntando a la canasta. Scottie se elevó en el aire con mucha confianza. La bola partió de sus manos en la dirección exacta de la canasta. La mano del cura bloqueó su tiro a un metro de la mano de Scottie. El balón se elevó y trazó una curva para atrás del tirador. Gabriel siguió corriendo y agarró el balón que había bloqueado.

No había nadie entre él y la canasta opuesta. Se metió hasta el área y clavó la bola en la canasta para poner a su equipo arriba, 28-27. Los raterillos aún tenían chanza porque tenían el balón de nuevo. El Padre G les gritaba a sus jugadores que apretaran la defensa y levantaran los brazos.

Cubrieron a cada jugador, hombre a hombre, por toda la cancha. Antoine burló a Jerry quien lo estaba marcando. Gabriel vio que Antoine iba a tratar de anotar, así que se le paró enfrente para evitarle que tirara sin obstrucciones. El jugador más joven se la pasó a su centro, Damián, quien acabó solo bajo la canasta cuando el sacerdote se dejó ir a tapar a Antoine. El grandulón clavó la pelota en la canasta para delicia de sus compañeros de equipo quienes por un momento creyeron que habían ganado el juego y comenzaron a levantar las manos triunfalmente. Jerry les recordó que aún les faltaba un punto; el marcador era ahora 28-29.

Jerry jaló al Padre G cerca de él y le susurró algo, luego le sirvió la bola a Javier. Scottie atravesó la mano y casi se robaba el balón, pero se le escapó y salió de la cancha.

Jorge la metió desde un lado, dándosela a Jerry. Él le hizo seña a Gabriel; el sacerdote emprendió carrera hasta el rincón de la derecha como para tirar desde la esquina. Damián y Antoine fueron a marcar al cura en el rincón, pero Jerry le lanzó la bola a Jacinto quien estaba en la esquina de la izquierda. Scottie y Clint saltaron enfrente de él para no dejarlo tirar.

Jacinto le tiró un pasecito corto a Jorge. Él se metió con la pelota rumbo a la canasta donde Walter ya lo estaba esperando. Jorge rebotó la pelota en medio de sus piernas para dársela al Padre G quien venía cruzando la cancha de derecha a izquierda. El cura se llevó a sus marcadores en aquella dirección y le pasó la bola a Jerry quien se había quedado atrás solito.

Jerry se elevó en el aire y disparó un tiro de tres puntos. Scottie llegó a él ya muy tarde pero lo empujó, derribándolo de espaldas al piso al tiempo que su tiro entraba en la canasta. Jerry rebotó jubiloso del suelo, feliz de haber hecho la canasta ganadora para un marcador final de 31-29.

Luego de unas habladas e intercambio de insultos, los dos equipos se dieron las manos, Jerry fue con Trisha, novia de Antoine, y cobró el dinero que les habían ganado para la cena. Los cuatro jugadores y sus novias le pidieron al padre que fuera con ellos al restaurante para celebrar.

El presbítero pidió que unieran sus manos en un círculo para dar gracias a Dios. Antes de comenzar, llamó a los otros a que se unieran con ellos. Clint se dio la vuelta y se marchó; el cura solo meneó la cabeza, triste.

"Oh, Padre Celestial, te damos gracias por la vida que nos has dado, todas las bendiciones que nos has otorgado, nuestras familias, nuestros amigos. Te pedimos que nos mantengas a salvo y unidos a ti toda la vida. Guíanos y cuídanos mientras seguimos la jornada que nos has preparado. Permítenos disfrutar del juego tanto en la victoria como en la derrota porque la única victoria que importa es el haberte encontrado a ti y haberte aceptado como nuestro Dios y a Jesucristo como nuestro salvador. Te damos gracias, te alabamos y te glorificamos por los siglos de los siglos."

Todos los jóvenes respondieron, "¡Amén!"

"¡Muy bien, a comer, que me muero de hambre!" Gabriel los exhortó.

Todos se metieron en el Curimóvil, Jerry y Sandra enfrente con el Padre G, Jorge con Jessica, Jacinto con Rita, y Javier con Tina. Las chicas se sentaron sobre las piernas de los chicos. Gabriel les pidió que abrieran las ventanas para que entrara aire fresco pues andaban todos sudados.

Sandra le preguntó al sacerdote si podría poner algo de música. El Padre G prendió su estéreo con un disco compacto que empezó a tocar la obertura de William Tell, la cual los llevó hasta llegar al restaurante.

Se la pasaron muy bien hablando del juego durante la cena. Las parejitas se estaban portando de la mejor manera por tener al sacerdote con ellos. Gabriel estaba agradecido de haber calmado su apetito y al mismo tiempo compartir un rato con los chicos. A Sandra le gustaba el cura como hombre.

"¿Ha tenido alguna vez una novia usted, Padre?" ella le preguntó.

"Sí, cuando tenía más o menos tu edad que fue... hace casi un siglo."

"¿Y qué tal ahora, tiene alguna amiguita por ahí?" Sandra inquirió con una sonrisita pícara.

"¡No, no tengo una... tengo muchas! Y tú eres una de ellas ¿Verdad?" fue la rápida respuesta del cura.

"Usted sabe que Jerry es mi novio," dijo Sandra, echándole el brazo al cuello a Jerry.

"Está bien, al cabo yo no soy celoso," dijo Gabriel, sonriendo y guiñándole un ojo a Sandra. El ministro se levantó y volteó a ver a Jerry diciéndole, "Más te vale que me cuides a mi amiguita Sandra. ¿Entiendes? Me tengo que ir, pero ya nos veremos más delante."

Jerry se paró a estrecharle la mano y le dijo. "¡Gracias Padre G, usted sí que es bien de aquellas!"

Sandra se le acercó y le dio un abrazo y un beso en la mejilla. Jerry se sonrió y les hizo señas a sus amigos para que le pararan de hacerle burla por haber "perdido a Sandra con el sacerdote." El cura levantó la mano y les mandó su bendición antes de marcharse.

Cuando Gabriel llegó a casa, el teléfono estaba timbrando. Lo levantó y escuchó la voz de Theresa. El corazón le saltó jubiloso.

"¿Padre Gabriel?"

"Sí, ¿Quién habla?" Fingió no reconocer su voz, pero lucía una sonrisota de gusto.

"La Hermana Theresa."

"Oh, sí, sí... ¿En qué le puedo servir, Hermana?"

"Llamé para decirte que disfruté tu misa. Eres un gran predicador."

"¡Muchas gracias; eres muy amable! Te busqué después de la misa para darte las gracias; eres una organista estupenda. La gente me comentó qué alegre se había puesto la celebración contigo en el órgano esta mañana."

"Tenía varias cosas que hacer, y yo sé que tú estás muy ocupado los domingos. No quise interferir con tus deberes; por eso fue que me marché. Nos vemos mañana."

"¡Espera!" Gabriel le imploró.

"Dígame, Padre..."

"Quería decirte que..." Gabriel batalló, buscando algún tema que tocar para alargar su conversación. Le dijo, "Me puse a jugar un partidito de básquetbol con unos chicos. Venía de vuelta del hospital; fui a visitar a uno de mis feligreses que se cayó del techo de su casa. Va a ponerse bien. Me venía muriendo de hambre y pensando qué comer. No quería cocinar nada yo mismo en domingo por la noche. Entonces Jerry, un muchacho que trabaja en una gasolinera y siempre me da gasolina gratis, saltó enfrente de mi carro para reclutarme para su equipo en contra de unos tipos rudos. Habían apostado una cena, así que les ayudé a ganar y me senté a cenar con ellos una barbacoa. El juego estuvo medio violento; probablemente voy a amanecer adolorido. Me hace falta un buen baño, pero me divertí mucho con los muchachos y sus noviecitas. Una de las chicas me preguntó si había yo tenido novia y le dije de ti."

"¿Le dijiste que soy tu novia?"

"¡No! Que habías sido, hace como cien años."

"¡Un momento, no soy tan vieja! Hace veinte años de eso, no cien."

"Sí. Tienes razón... Aún no puedo creer que estés de nuevo en mi vida."

"Estas son circunstancias muy diferentes ahora, Padre Gabriel."

"Tienes razón de nuevo, pero es lindo poder verte y hablarte otra vez."

"A mí también me gusta hablar contigo y escuchar tu voz. ¿Aún cantas aquellas canciones románticas que me cantabas?"

El Padre Gabriel cerró los ojos y revisó su repertorio de canciones. Aspiró aire y comenzó a cantar una que se le vino a la mente. La canción habla del poeta clamando ser un ave de paso, una mariposa de mil flores quien se encuentra sintiendo la nostalgia de los brazos y los ojos de su amada, un amor del pasado. El sacerdote cantó con inspiración por el teléfono mientras la que fuera su novia capturaba las emociones y sentimientos expresados en la canción en el otro lado de la línea.

Al estar cantando Gabriel el último verso, escuchó a Theresa decirle, "¡Gracias!" y luego el teléfono le dio un tono de marcar.

La hermana religiosa oyó a alguien entrando al cuarto en ese momento así que le colgó abruptamente al cura. Ella se sintió como que había sido pillada haciendo algo malo.

"¿Con quién hablabas, Hermana Theresa?" inquirió Sor Mary.

"¡Con... una vieja amistad mía! Si me perdonas, necesito... ir al baño."

Sor Mary se sentó frente a su computadora y la prendió, sin poner atención a la cara ruborizada de Theresa quien se encaminó al baño.

En el otro lado de la línea, el Padre Gabriel se le quedó viendo al teléfono, intrigado. El cura se preguntó que pasaría, pero colgó pensando que le serviría de excusa para enganchar a la hermana en conversación al día siguiente.

Era hora de su oración vespertina y tomarse un buen baño. Se recorrió el cuerpo con las manos y descubrió algunos puntos tiernos donde había sido codeado durante el juego. Se rió, recordando la tarde que había pasado, abrió su librito de oraciones, y comenzó a rezar frente a su crucifijo.

El domingo 5 de septiembre se estaba convirtiendo en historia para la hora en que se metió a su cama. ¡Qué diferente se había vuelto su vida en menos de una semana! Había pensado que era feliz el domingo anterior, pero no se podía comparar con la felicidad presente. Gabriel estaba convencido que aquel era definitivamente un regalo de Dios, así que le agradeció por ello y se quedó bien dormido en cuestión de minutos.

Capítulo III

Secuestro

La primer semana de Theresa en la escuela fue muy buena para todos. Los niños de primero estaban felices de tenerla sustituyendo a Sor Kathryn. Magda, Mary, y Carmen estaban contentas de tenerla en casa. Sin tratar de compararlas, se fijaron que Theresa era superior a Kathryn como maestra, trabajadora, y organista. Theresa tenía gran energía y entusiasmo mientras que Kathryn era una mujer de edad, dulce, cansada, y con muchos años de enseñanza para crédito suyo. Kathryn era buena; Theresa era excelente.

El Padre Gabriel andaba más contento que de costumbre y esperaba ansioso ver a la nueva maestra a la hora del almuerzo o en las juntas del plantel educativo. No le habían mencionado a nadie que ellos ya se conocían desde antes: era su pequeño secretito. Actuaban diferente uno con el otro cuando estaban solos que cuando alguien más estaba presente. Ninguno de los dos lo planeó; solo que así se acomodaron las cosas.

El jueves en la noche, el Padre Gabriel iba regresando de una recepción para recaudar fondos; había hablado a favor de que el gobernador de Texas buscara la candidatura para la presidencia de los Estados Unidos. Gabriel iba pensando qué bueno era que él no estaba involucrado en el sucio mundo de la política sino en el campo espiritual. Como sacerdote católico, tenía prohibido buscar oficina pública, pero él concluyó que ya tenía una oficina pública en su capacidad como pastor de la parroquia.

Gabriel se acabó el puro que iba fumando y apachurró lo que le quedaba en el cenicero del auto. Se detuvo en una luz roja; había otro carro delante de él con una chica al volante. Camino a una cita, la muchacha hablaba por teléfono mientras escuchaba sonora música contemporánea. Se estaba viendo en el espejo, aplicándose otra capa de lápiz labial, y jugando con su largo cabello.

La luz del semáforo cambió de roja a verde, pero a la chica, sumida en su mundo del chisme y belleza, no pareció importarle. El Padre G le iba a pitar para que se arrancara, pero algo le llamó la atención en el rabillo del ojo.

Seis pandilleros iban cargando a una joven a una casa abandonada. La pobre chica iba pataleando y tratando de gritar, pero le iban cubriendo la boca. Uno de sus zapatitos se le cayó en su lucha por liberarse. El grupo se desapareció en la oscuridad de la casa.

El Padre Gabriel se dio cuenta que la mujercita estaba en gran peligro, y pensó que debería hacer algo para ayudarle.

El presbítero salió de su viejo auto y corrió hacia la chofer del carro enfrente del suyo. Le arrancó el teléfono de la mano; ella ahogó un grito. Gabriel le dijo a la persona en el otro lado de la línea que la chica le llamaría otra vez. Entonces colgó y marcó el nueve-uno-uno.

La hembra al volante pensó en arrancarse en su carro, pero se fijó que el hombre aquel era un sacerdote cuando le vio el collar romano. Lo escuchó haciendo la llamada de emergencia a la policía.

"¡Esta es una emergencia! Es un secuestro en la calle Calaveras, número 666. Una chica fue acarreada a la fuerza por varios hombres al interior de una casa abandonada. ¡Por favor manden oficiales lo más pronto posible!"

El cura le regresó el teléfono celular a la muchacha y corrió de vuelta a su auto, buscando algún arma. Lo único que tenía en el asiento de enfrente era un crucifijo metálico de buen tamaño, 25 centímetros. Se estiró al interior y agarró la cruz. Gabriel miró hacia la oscura casa a donde los hombres se habían llevado a la jovencita; su pecho empezó a arderle con furia.

Odiaba el crimen, en especial crímenes violentos. El sacerdote se persignó y empezó a correr rumbo a la casa abandonada, con la cruz en la mano, recitando parte del Salmo 92.

"Si los impíos crecen como la hierba y florecen los que hacen el mal, es para ser destruidos eternamente: tú, en cambio, eres el Excelso para siempre. Mira, Señor, cómo perecen tus enemigos y se dispersan los que hacen el mal."

La intrigada automovilista se estacionó junto a la banqueta y volvió a marcar el número del hombre con el que había estado hablando antes, para decirle lo que estaba sucediendo. Se sentó ahí a ver lo que iba a pasar. El sacerdote se acercó a la vieja casa, aún recitando el salmo.

"Pero a mí me das la fuerza de un toro salvaje y me unges con óleo purísimo. Mis ojos han desafiado a mis calumniadores, mis oídos han escuchado la derrota de los malvados."

El místico escuchó los sonidos de lucha en el interior, llanto, gemidos, bofetadas, desgarrar de ropa, risas malignas, y voces de hombres alegando.

El sacerdote irrumpió en la casa gritando, "¡Deténganse en el nombre del Señor! Dejen ir a la muchacha y no les haré ningún daño."

"¿Quién eres tú? Es mejor que te largues de aquí o tú también la vas a llevar," el líder le gruñó entre una multitud de palabras soeces.

Tres maleantes estaban deteniendo a la chica, ya desnuda, en el piso.

"No me voy a ir hasta que me entreguen a la niña," declaró el religioso en voz firme.

El más grandote de los pandilleros de ojos enrojecidos se le echó encima al cura, puñal en mano y gritando profanidades. Había algo de luz entrando por las ventanas sin cortinas; el Padre Gabriel miró la reflexión de la luz en la hoja del cuchillo que se le aproximaba y se preparó para la batalla.

El sacerdote bloqueó con el crucifijo el filoso puñal que venía a su pecho. La cruz pescó el cuchillo; el Padre G torció la cruz y le arrebató el puñal al pandillero. Crucifijo y puñal cayeron al suelo. Con la base de la palma de su mano, el boxeador le pegó al malhechor, un tipo enorme, justo en el mentón. El criminal se elevó en el aire y cayó de espaldas, inconsciente.

El furioso místico avanzó hacia adelante y miró a su derecha; había uno con un bate de béisbol acercándosele. Otro que venía de su lado izquierdo le echó los brazos alrededor al intruso por detrás, para inmovilizarlo. El Padre G veía la maldad en sus enrojecidos ojos.

El del bate se acercó y preparó un buen batazo para el cura; Gabriel se resbaló hacia abajo para zafarse del que lo abrazó. El bate le pegó al otro pandillero en la cabeza en lugar de Gabriel. Él pateó al bateador con fuerza explosiva. El dolor de una rodilla dislocada hizo al criminal soltar el bate y caer al piso berreando, agarrándose su rodilla malherida.

El místico saltó a continuar la pelea contra los otros tres, los cuales aún estaban deteniendo a la chica, observando todo incrédulos. Uno se levantó y se sacó una navaja de muelle; se abalanzó contra el sacerdote. Gabriel dio un pasito a un lado y lo pescó de la muñeca. Giró, sosteniendo el brazo armado y lanzó al atacante a través de la ventana cerrada hasta el jardín de enfrente entre pedazos de vidrio.

El ministro continuó dando la vuelta y le dio una patada en la cabeza al otro pandillero como pelota de fútbol. Ese cayó al suelo como un costal de estiércol. El último se levantó para enfrentarse al presbítero; Gabriel levantó el bate. El aterrorizado malhechor corrió para atrás de la casa.

El sacerdote se quitó la camisa y cubrió a la temblorosa muchacha desnuda. Sus ojos estaban muy abiertos, pero no podía decir ni una palabra. La tomó por los hombros.

"Todo va a estar bien, pequeña. Ya se acabó todo; estás bien."

El Padre G se inclinó para ayudarle a la muchacha a levantarse de estar arrodillada; en ese momento la policía entró a la casa.

"¡Deténganse; pongan las manos en alto en donde yo las pueda ver!"

Gabriel obedeció la orden, sabiendo muy bien que el oficial le estaba apuntando con una pistola. Oyó algo en la parte trasera de la casa. Habían pescado al que trató de escapar por atrás.

"¿Qué demonios pasó aquí?" preguntó el oficial, mirando a los cuatro pandilleros en el piso iluminados por su lámpara de mano, uno gimiendo y agarrándose la pierna, los otros tres inconscientes.

"¡Tengo uno en el jardín de enfrente!" dijo otro policía afuera.

La joven abrazó al sacerdote quien aún tenía las manos en alto, esperando que el oficial se convenciera que él no era uno de los maloras.

"Yo soy el que los llamó, Oficial. Mire, pregúntele a la chica. Ella le puede decir lo que sucedió. Habla con el oficial, Muchachita."

La víctima no podía decir palabra y estaba cambiando de color. El presbítero le dio una fuerte nalgada.

"¡Respira, Chiquilla, toma aire!"

La chica empezó a llorar a grito abierto sobre el pecho del párroco. Otro oficial entró y reconoció al ministro. El segundo oficial le bajó la mano armada a su compañero para que ya no le apuntara la pistola al sacerdote y le dijo que todo estaba bien, que enfundara su arma.

"¡Les dio una buena revolcada a estos peladitos, Padre G!" el segundo oficial le dijo, palmeándole la espalda.

"Es que estaban tratando de revolcarse a esta mujercita. No podía yo permitírselos. Traté de detenerlos sin violencia, pero no me hicieron caso."

Los policías esposaron a los prisioneros, y el cura se llevó a la chica con su camisa a su carro. Les pidió que llamaran a una ambulancia para la joven.

"¿Cómo te llamas, Chiquilla?"

"Aurora... Aurora Fuentes, Padre."

"¿Te sientes mejor ya, Aurora?"

"Sí, creo que sí. Oh, Padre, muchísimas gracias. ¡Temí que iba a morir esta noche!"

Ella comenzó a sollozar de nuevo y se abrazó de él.

46

Él le acarició la cabeza y le alisó su largo cabello negro diciendo, "Gracias a Dios que estuvimos ahí a tiempo de detenerlos. Ya vas a estar bien ahora. ¿Estás herida?"

"No. No estoy herida, solo perturbada. Me siento débil y mareada, como con ganas de vomitar."

"Acuéstate en el asiento de atrás y levanta los pies. Déjame cubrirte con mi saco para mantenerte calientita. Respira profundamente y bajo control, reza una pequeña oración y trata de relajarte."

El Padre Gabriel le explicó al Oficial Vega que la chica no necesitaba un viaje al hospital porque no había sido violada sexualmente. Iba a necesitar consejo profesional, pero eso se podría hacer fuera del hospital. Los sospechosos, sin embargo, sí necesitaban ir a la sala de urgencias. Uno tenía el cráneo fracturado, otro una rodilla dislocada. Uno iba a necesitar puntadas por las cortadas profundas que sostuvo al salir volando por la ventana, y dos tenían conmociones cerebrales de los golpes que les propinó el sacerdote. Todos ellos enfrentaban cargos por secuestro agravado.

El Padre G se quedó con Aurora a través de la investigación hasta que ambos dieron sus declaraciones a los detectives nocturnos.

La familia de Aurora la fue a encontrar en el cuartel general de policía y le llevaron ropa limpia para que se pusiera; la muchacha le regresó al padre su camisa. Ella lo abrazó y lo besó para agradecerle de nuevo.

El novio de Aurora, James Woodland, también le dio un abrazo y le estrechó la mano. James era un exitoso contratista de construcción.

"Escúcheme, Padre, lo que se le ofrezca, nomás me dice... No sé cómo le podría pagar por lo que hizo por mi Aurorita esta noche."

"¡Ni lo menciones! Fue la mano de Dios la que me llevó a ese lugar. Yo no soy más que un instrumento del Señor. A Él hay que darle las gracias y alabanzas."

"¡Tiene usted toda la razón! ¿Sabe qué? Aurora y yo estábamos pensando en casarnos. ¿Estaría dispuesto a celebrar nuestra boda?"

"Sería un honor para mí; como quiera, hay algunos requerimientos que deben cumplir antes de que podamos casarlos. Llámenme la semana que viene y hablaremos de cómo prepararlos a ustedes dos."

El padre y la madre de la chica abrazaron agradecidos al cura antes de irse de la estación de policía. Ya era medianoche para cuando Gabriel llegó a casa, muy tarde para llamar a Theresa y contarle su aventurilla.

El viernes fue un día ocupado en la escuela. Sor Theresa les dio exámenes a sus niños en todas las materias y preparó a sus pupilos para que actuaran, cantaran, y bailaran en el festival de otoño. No vio al Padre Gabriel en lo absoluto; ni en el almuerzo. El cura tenía varios asuntos parroquiales, pero se dio tiempo para conseguir los materiales educativos que Theresa le había pedido, para que ella los revisara durante el fin de semana.

Ya era después de horas de escuela cuando Gabriel regresó con aquellos materiales. Las hermanas ya se habían ido, así que el sacerdote fue a casa de las monjitas a entregarle los útiles a Theresa antes de ir a cenar.

Magdalene y Theresa eran las únicas dos en casa porque Carmen y Mary se habían ido a Austin a una conferencia por todo el fin de semana.

Magda iba a ir a recoger pollo frito para su cena. Había encontrado un restaurante cuya dueña había sido educada por monjitas y le proveía con pollo gratis en cualquier ocasión que se lo solicitara. El sitio quedaba a unos buenos 30 minutos de distancia en carro, pero Magda consideraba que valía la pena el viaje. En el camino podía oír música clásica en la radio.

Además le encantaba platicar con la dueña, Francis Schott, una exitosa mujer de negocios que estaba considerando unirse a las religiosas después de diez años de viuda. Francis tenía tres hijas y un hijo así como siete nietos; ella andaba buscando un reto mayor en su vida, algo más satisfactorio que el negocio que ella y su esposo habían administrado por los pasados treinta y tres años. Eran propietarios de siete restaurantes en la ciudad para el tiempo en que el viejo Steven Schott falleció.

Mientras Magda iba para su van, Theresa estaba bañándose después de un día caluroso. No sospechaba que no estaba sola en el baño. Si se hubiera asomado para afuera de la cortina, quizás podría haber notado la entidad maligna transparente que estaba causando daños.

El demonio tiró la bata de baño del gancho del que colgaba en la puerta y después rasguñó la manguerita de abajo del tanque del escusado de tal manera que inundó el piso y empapó la bata.

El Padre Gabriel arribó a la casa de las religiosas al mismo tiempo que Magda salía de su cochera. El cura pitó e hizo una maniobra exagerada con su carro como tratando de evitar estrellarse contra la van de las hermanas. Se dio la vuelta y pisó el freno, levantando los brazos para cubrirse la cara, pretendiendo un tremendo pánico frente a la ya detenida van.

Magda sabía que solo estaba jugando, así que se rió y le siguió el juego, pitándole y gritándole que se quitara de en medio. El presbítero salió de su auto y se acercó a la van.

"Shalom, Magda. Le traigo a la Hermana Theresa los materiales que me pidió para su clase."

"Bueno, pero fíjese que se está bañando ahorita, Padre. Yo recibiré sus cosas y las meteré. Le puedo avisar a Theresa que está aquí."

La hermana apagó su van para salirse y regresarse a la casa, pero Gabriel la detuvo.

"No. Eso no será necesario. No necesito hablar con ella. Usted váyase a donde iba, y yo le dejaré la caja en la puerta."

La religiosa mayor le susurró, "Si quiere mejor metérsela hasta adentro, la puerta de atrás no está atrancada. Voy a ir a traer algo de pollo frito ¿Le gustaría comer con nosotras?"

"No, muchas gracias. No quiero molestarlas. Ya tengo mi propia cena esperándome. Nomas voy a meter la caja y la dejaré en el comedor."

La bañista se dio cuenta que solo había traído una toalla con ella al baño pero iba a necesitar dos porque se había lavado el cabello. Elevó su voz para pedirle a Magda si le podría traer una segunda toalla de su cuarto, pero la madre superior no le respondió.

Theresa se secó el cabello y se enredó la toalla en la cabeza. Llamó de nuevo a Magda, pero pudo escuchar el motor de la van arrancando afuera de la casa. Se dio cuenta entonces que Magda ya se iba.

La Madre Magda se despidió de Gabriel y se arrancó. Encendió el radio y escuchó a Brahms como el primer compositor de su concierto móvil.

Cuando Theresa abrió la cortina de la regadera, sintió mucho frío. También sintió como que alguien la estaba observando. La piel de sus brazos y espalda se le puso chinita; se cruzó de brazos y miró alrededor del cuarto. No había otro ser humano ahí, y no había otra toalla tampoco.

Theresa volteó para todos lados, oyendo que el agua seguía corriendo en alguna parte a pesar que ella ya había cerrado la regadera. Su bata de baño estaba empapada en el piso mojado; la manguerita del escusado estaba rota y el agua estaba inundando todo el piso del baño. Se agachó a cerrar la llave de paso para detener el flujo de agua. Aquella casa estaba muy viejita y necesitaba reparaciones, pensó ella.

La bata de baño había acabado en el piso, aparentemente porque el gancho de la puerta se zafó. El escusado necesitaría otra manguerita, y el gancho para la ropa en la puerta debía de ser reforzado con algunos tornillos. Theresa pensó en llamar al señor de mantenimiento de la escuela para pedirle su ayuda con aquellas cositas. Él le había ofrecido su ayuda cuando se conocieron, y parecía ser un simpático caballero.

Gabriel se metió a la cocina y escribió una notita para Theresa acerca de los materiales que había pedido, esperando que encontrara todo como lo necesitaba. Se encaminó hacia la puerta de atrás de la vieja casa de un piso.

Theresa aún necesitaba otra toalla para secarse el cuerpo. Decidió ir a conseguirla ella misma ya que pensó estar sola en la casa. Preocupada con el pequeño problema que enfrentaba en ese momento, no le puso atención ya a la sensación de que alguien la estaba observando.

La casi invisible entidad se deslizó bajo la puerta y salió al pasillo rozando ligeramente a la mujer; Theresa sintió que toda la piel se le erizaba de nuevo pero pensó que era por estar mojada en el baño aquel tan frío.

Sor Theresa salió del baño con solo la toalla que traía enredada en la cabeza. Se dio vuelta para ir a su cuarto y se encontró frente a frente con el sacerdote en medio del pasillo.

Los dos se quedaron pasmados por un instante como cuando se habían visto el otro día en el gimnasio en circunstancias similares. Antes que ninguno dijera algo, Theresa corrió a su recámara y cerró la puerta.

"Yo... lo siento... Theresa," Gabriel dijo, titubeante, "Solo vine a dejarte los materiales que me habías pedido."

"Muchas gracias, Padre. No sabía que usted estaba aquí. Creí que Magda se había marchado y que estaba yo sola en la casa. No fue mi intención..."

"Yo tampoco había planeado verte tampoco. Te dejé una notita en la mesa con los materiales."

Estaban hablando en ambos lados de la puerta. Luego hubo un incómodo momento de silencio. Gabriel decidió que era mejor marcharse.

"Ya me voy, si quieres andar retozando alrededor de la casa desnuda, nada más cierra las cortinas. Fue un placer verte de nuevo... ¡Especialmente en tu lindo trajecito de recién-nacida!"

Gabriel partió. Theresa se rió sola dentro de su alcoba. Agarró la toalla que andaba buscando y se fue a la ventana de enfrente.

Gabriel abordaba su Chevy modelo 1935. La cortina estaba abierta. El cura volvió la cara hacia la casa y la vio en la ventana. Ella le dijo adiós con la mano. Él fingió tomarle una foto poniéndose las manos frente al ojo. Theresa, ya enredada en la otra toalla, le sonrió y cerró las cortinas.

"¡Creo que así estamos a mano ahora, Amigo mío!" dijo ella medio divertida por el incidente y recordando lo que les pasó en el gimnasio.

La entidad diabólica estaba parada cerca de ella. Theresa sintió la presencia maligna y rápido se dio la vuelta, pero solo se encontró con su propia imagen reflejada en el espejo de la pared. Se sobresaltó con su propia reflexión al principio, pero después se carcajeó.

"¡Qué tonta!"

Theresa se paró frente al espejo despojándose de las toallas. No había puesto mucha atención a su apariencia en mucho tiempo. De pronto se preguntaba si ella aún era atractiva. ¡Definitivamente lo era! Se veía de no más de unos treinta años aunque ya casi cumplía los treinta y ocho.

El ser instructora de baile en la escuela le proveía un magnífico ejercicio aeróbico y le mantenía el tono muscular. La mayoría de las hermanas encontraban muy práctico el mantener el cabello corto, Theresa había decidido dejárselo largo, aunque lo traía agarrado en un chonguito. Era color café rojizo, lacio, y sedoso. Le llegaba a los hombros. Se sintió muy satisfecha con la forma en que se veía... como Gabriel la había encontrado en el pasillo. Pensó que probablemente se llevó una buena impresión.

La mujer se dejó caer en la cama preguntándose por qué se sentía como una adolescente enamorada, excitada, deseando llamarlo por teléfono y oír su canto. ¿Por qué esos sentimientos si ella había estado tan segura de su vocación por la última década o aún más? Era mujer madura, realizada, inteligente, educada, positiva, y espiritualmente rica.

¿Podría estar algo mal con enamorarse de un hombre de nuevo, un sacerdote, en este periodo de su vida? La entidad invisible le soplaba en el oído para excitar su sexualidad. Ella se avergonzó, sintiéndose culpable de algún pecado. Se arrodilló a la orilla de la cama y comenzó a orar, pidiendo a Dios orientación. La entidad maligna la dejó en ese momento, pero sus oraciones no le consiguieron respuesta alguna. La imagen de Gabriel sonriéndole reapareció en su mente.

Mientras tanto en una biblioteca pública, no lejos de la casa de las religiosas, el grupo de delincuentes juveniles llamados los Apóstoles de Satanás andaba explorando la biblioteca, escogiendo libros de ocultismo.

Jorge, el líder, les mostró uno que encontró. Era grueso como una Biblia, con una cubierta que se sentía y parecía piel humana; la escritura tenía un color que era muy semejante a sangre seca.

"¡Órale, batos, echen ojo! Este libro de veras que está de aquellas. Me lo voy a llevar," Jorge les susurró, excitado.

"Está escrito en un lenguaje extranjero, Jorge. ¿Cómo le vas a hacer para poder leerlo?" comentó Cindy Lowe, su novia.

"Ey, ya me las arreglaré. Acuérdate que soy bilingüe," replicó el muchacho, arrebatándole el libro de las manos a Cindy.

"Pos sí, pero ese no es maldito español, Menso," la chica declaró, encogiéndose de hombros.

Un oscuro tipo con ojos rojos observaba desde un rincón de la biblioteca a los chamacos examinando el raro libro. Uno no podía decir si se trataba de un hombre o una mujer pues la luz que entraba por la ventana ocultaba los detalles de su negra silueta. Cindy volteó a verlo y sintió que se le ponía la carne de gallina. Se frotó la piel erizada de su brazo y volvió los ojos al rincón, buscando al extraño, pero ya se había desvanecido.

El Padre Gabriel cenó y se salió a dar una caminadita disfrutando de un buen puro. Se detuvo en un bar y se asomó. Un viejo amigo de su infancia, Mario Arámbula, estaba ahí con unos amigos bebiendo, celebrando el inicio de un fin de semana después de una larga jornada de trabajo arduo como techeros. Gabriel entró al lugar y elevó su mano en saludo.

"Shalom, Mario ¿Cómo te va?"

"¡Padre G, qué gusto verlo! Venga, siéntese, y échese un trago," Mario respondió, levantándose de su silla para estrechar su mano y abrazarlo.

Mario le presentó a sus amigos techeros, Jay Sanders y Philip Johnson, uno negrito y otro blanco, quienes compartían la ocupación y el bajo nivel económico del hispano viviendo en el oeste de la ciudad. Los tres eran casados y con hijos; el viernes en la noche era su tiempo de relajarse y echarse un trago o dos... o tres, y olvidarse un poco de la vida del hombre pobre y sus problemas.

El grupito estaba apostando veinte dólares por cabeza en el dominó y bebiendo cerveza helada. El ministro sacó algo de dinero para jugar y tomarse una fría también. Los dos amigos habían oído a Mario hablar de ese sacerdote antes.

"Oiga, Reverendo, he oído que usté' hace milagros. ¿Es cierto?" preguntó Jay, el negrón de uno ochenta y ocho con ciento nueve kilos de peso.

"¡Órale, Jay! ¿Qué clase de pregunta es esa para nuestro invitado?" protestó Mario, sintiéndose avergonzado por su amigo.

"Está bien la pregunta; no me molesta," el cura lo interrumpió, poniendo su puro en el cenicero. "Dios hace milagros todo el tiempo. Yo he tenido la bendición de ser utilizado como su instrumento en algunas ocasiones, así que la respuesta es, no, yo no hago milagros. Es Dios quien los hace."

"¿Pero cómo trabaja eso, Padre? ¿Usted nomás se lo pide y ya?" preguntó Philip después de darle un trago a su cerveza.

"Le vas a tener que preguntar eso a Dios. Todo lo que te puedo decir es que la fe de la persona que busca el milagro hace la diferencia. Cuando siento que va a ocurrir un milagro, me siento como turbo-cargado. Se me duerme todo el cuerpo. No siento como que soy yo mismo ni que estoy en donde estoy. Es muy difícil de explicar, pero es una sensación grandiosa. Me siento muy excitado, con ganas de cantar y bailar."

El Padre G bebió un buen trago de su botella. Los mariachis se les acercaron a la mesa a ver si querían alguna canción.

"¡Guau, se oye fenomenal!" dijo Mario, agarrándole el musculoso brazo al cura, "Ey, ahora que menciona el canto. ¿Podría cantar una canción para mis amigos? Les he dicho qué bien canta usted."

"¡Seguro! ¿Por qué no?" respondió Gabriel, levantándose a hablar con la banda, "Ey, mariachis, vamos a echarnos una canción bonita."

Agarró prestado un sombrero de charro y se lo puso. El grupo de mariachis estaban familiarizados con el cura y algunas veces habían tocado para sus misas. La banda tocó una vieja canción romántica, y algunos hombres gritaron de gusto, escuchando la tradicional música mexicana.

En uno de los versos el poeta le pide a Dios olvidar el objeto de su afección cada noche que se acuesta a dormir, solo para despertar al día siguiente dándose cuenta que debe adorarla aún más. Los tres hombres fueron criados en el área hispana de la ciudad y hablaban español tan bien como el inglés a pesar de sus diferentes colores y linaje.

El Padre Gabriel estaba cantando con inspiración especial esa noche. La imagen de Sor Theresa permanecía en su mente al cantar. Toda la clientela del bar estalló en aplauso por su interpretación del bolero romántico. El cantante le dio las gracias a su audiencia, le regresó el sombrero al músico, y se sentó a seguir jugando dominós con el trío de amigos.

"¡Hombre sí que se avienta usté' pa' cantar, Reverendo! Se oye como un hombre enamorado," Jay comentó como un cumplido.

"Estoy enamorado, de la vida, Jay. ¡Gracias!"

"Oiga Padre, también he oído a Mario decir que usté' es re' bueno con los puños," comentó Philip, levantando su guardia y moviendo el torso como un pugilista.

"¡Sí! ¿Quieres que nos salgamos allá afuera para demostrártelo, Philip?" dijo el cura, levantándose como si estuviera listo para pelear.

"¡No, no, yo le creo!" contestó el hombre blanco más pequeño, de solo un metro sesenta y siete y pesando sesenta y ocho kilos.

"Reverendo, si usté' es tan bueno con los puños como con su voz, podría ser campeón del mundo," dijo Jay mientras levantaba su cerveza para brindar alegremente con su nuevo amigo.

"No la amuele, Padre G. Les dije a estos cuates que usté' era casi como Jesucristo mismo, y aquí lo tengo a punto de darles en toda la torre," Mario protestó también jugando, sabía que el padre estaba solo vacilando.

"Bueno, pero aún Jesús tuvo su momento de furia," Gabriel les recordó. "¿Se acuerdan del pasaje del evangelio donde hablan de esa ocasión en que Jesús se enojó con los cambiadores de dinero en el templo de Jerusalén? Les volteó las mesas y los chicoteó. Les dijo que la casa de su Padre era una casa de oración y que ellos la habían convertido en una cueva de ladrones. Estaba más enojado con los líderes religiosos que con los cambiadores de dinero porque eran los responsables por la corrupción de la fe judía. Yo trato de ser lo más paciente que puedo, pero este temperamento mío algunas veces no puede ser contenido. Por eso fue que empecé a boxear: para soltar algo de energía golpeando algo sin lastimar a nadie. En verdad les puedo decir que yo nunca he golpeado a nadie... que no se lo merecía."

Jay y Philip se le quedaron viendo al sacerdote, sorprendidos que un ministro del Señor se viera envuelto en pleitos, pero lo podían entender. Los cuatro bebieron al mismo tiempo y comenzaron su juego. Gabriel recordó una pequeña broma que compartió con ellos.

"Un día en nuestra escuelita, la maestra les estaba diciendo a los niños que deberían ser buenos y generosos, les dijo, 'Recuerden niños que es mejor dar que recibir.' Uno de los estudiantes levantó su manita y dijo muy orgulloso, 'Eso es lo que siempre dice mi papá.' La maestra se sonrió y comentó, 'Obviamente tu papi es un hombre bueno y generoso. ¿A qué se dedica?' El niño le respondió, '¡Es boxeador profesional!'"

El cura se tomó varias cervezas y les ganó en los juegos que tuvieron Ya había recogido cien dólares de cada jugador para el final de la velada. Aquello era casi la mitad de su salario semanal. Cuando salieron del bar, el sacerdote les regresó el dinero a todos. Ellos rehusaron aceptarlo, diciendo que les había ganado limpiamente, pero él les dijo que era un regalo que les quería mandar a sus familias.

"La próxima vez, asegúrense de dejarles a sus esposas suficiente para el gasto de la semana antes de venir a tirarlo en apuestas. Acuérdense que tienen chiquitos; eso debe ser lo primero y no este templo de tentaciones."

Los tres hombres agacharon las cabezas, avergonzados, y tomaron el dinero que el pastor les estaba regresando para sus familias.

"Que el Señor los bendiga y los proteja siempre. Espero volver a verlos otra vez, pero en la casa de nuestro Padre, este domingo."

El sacerdote les echó la bendición y empezó a caminar a casa. Su paso era firme; su mente estaba clara. Le gustaba tomar pero nunca en exceso.

Cuando llegó a casa, Gabriel levantó el teléfono y marcó el número de las monjitas sin pensarlo. Se dio cuenta lo tarde que era y pensó en colgar, pero Theresa levantó el teléfono en cuanto timbró la primera vez.

"¡Hola, Padre Gabriel!"

"¿Cómo supiste que era yo?"

"Es una cosita del teléfono que se llama identificador de llamadas. Enseña el número y el nombre del que está llamándonos."

"¡Ah, es cierto! Por un momento pensé que estabas esperando mi llamada y tenías poderes telepáticos."

"¿Sabe usted que horas son, Padre Gabriel?"

"La una de la mañana, de acuerdo con esta cosita alrededor de mi muñeca que se llama reloj, enseña la hora y también la fecha."

"¿Alguna razón particular para llamar a esta hora de la noche?"

"Pues, acabo de volver de una cantina. Me tomé unas cervezas y jugué dominós con unos amigos," Gabriel titubeó, buscando algún tema de conversación que pudiera justificar la tardía llamada.

"¡Estás borracho!" dijo Sor Theresa, sonando como una esposa.

"No, no, absolutamente no. No sé lo que es estar borracho; quiero decir: nunca he estado. Solo sentí la urgencia de hablarte en cuanto entré a casa."

"Fue bueno que estaba yo despierta y cerca del teléfono. Magdalene está dormida pero la podías haber despertado."

"¿Y cómo es que tú no estabas ya dormida también?" le reclamó Gabriel, sonando como un marido.

"Estaba esperando tu llamada. Quería que me llamaras. No podría dormir hasta hablar contigo. No preguntes por qué. Solo sé que me ibas a llamar."

"¡Entonces tenía yo razón! Fue telepatía. Me enviaste el mensaje, y yo tuve que levantar el teléfono para llamarte. ¿Te acuerdas que pasamos por unas cosas así varias veces cuando éramos jóvenes? Tú me llamaste una vez a casa de Mario aún cuando no te había dicho que estaba ahí."

"¡Sí! Y aquella vez que tú me llamaste a la casa de Bárbara cuando yo no sabía donde andabas y quería hablar contigo urgentemente."

"Ey, aún tenemos esa conexión. Quizás no necesitamos siquiera el teléfono," dijo el ministro en un tono juguetón.

"Es extraño... Bueno, me quería disculpar contigo por el vergonzoso espectáculo que te di hoy, más bien ayer. Ya es sábado en la mañana."

"Oh, por favor... Fue un placer verte así."

Gabriel cerró los ojos para re-visitar aquel momento en su mente.

"¿No te escandalizaste ni te espantaste?"

"Quedé encantado. ¡Te ves muy bien! Estoy acostumbrado al nudismo. Tú sabes como los artistas practicamos dibujar modelos desnudos. Mantengo mis habilidades atendiendo sesiones de arte una vez al mes. Quizás podrías tú modelar para la próxima. Podría hacerte un grandioso retrato."

"¡Oh, no, en absoluto! Yo nunca podría desnudarme enfrente de un grupo de gente para que me dibujaran o me pintaran."

"Solo estoy bromeando, Theresa. No me gustaría compartirte con el resto del grupo."

"Ahora que para ti solito, pueda que me anime a posar un día de estos," ella le susurró en tono pícaro.

"¿De veras? ¡Eso sería sensacional!"

"Estoy bromeando, Padre Gabriel. Fue un accidente. Yo sí me espanté de encontrarte en el pasillo de esa manera." Theresa fingió ponerse seria.

"¿Qué tal el otro día, en el gimnasio?" Gabriel la tanteó.

"También me espanté, pero por diferente motivo. Nunca soñé que te iba a volver a encontrar, y menos con solo... ¿Qué era lo que traías puesto?"

"Prácticamente nada, un suspensor deportivo. Apenas me iba a meter a bañar cuando me habló Timmy con gran urgencia."

El tono pícaro regresó a la voz de la mujer cuando le dijo, "Bueno, pues te veías muy bien tú también. Me gustó lo que vi."

Él le contó de su día y de la canción que cantó en el bar pensando en ella. Ella le agradeció por los materiales que le había llevado. Así se la pasaron charlando un par de horas hablando del ayer. Fueron transportados por su conversación al baile de gala de la prepa en que se la pasaron bailando casi toda la noche. Ambos habían acabado adoloridos al día siguiente.

Finalmente Gabriel miró su reloj; eran las tres de la mañana. No había rezado su oración nocturna. Sor Theresa necesitaba dormir, así que el cura decidió terminar su conversación con un chistecillo bobo.

"Dos convictos iban a ser ejecutados en un país de Centroamérica el mismo día. Las autoridades trajeron al primer condenado a muerte y le dijeron que podía escoger si quería morir colgado o en la silla eléctrica. El prisionero pensó que al colgarlo le iba a doler mucho el pescuezo, así que optó por la silla eléctrica que por lo menos le ofrecía la comodidad de sentarse. Lo amarraron a la silla y le prendieron al aparato, pero la silla no funcionó. La apagaron y la prendieron otra vez, pero la silla no le hizo ni cosquillitas. El circuito no funcionaba, así que dejaron ir al prisionero. Cuando iba en camino rumbo a su libertad, le susurró al siguiente condenado, 'La silla eléctrica está descompuesta.' Trajeron al segundo convicto, y para ser parejos, le ofrecieron la oportunidad de elegir si quería morir ahorcado o en la silla eléctrica. El condenado les dijo, 'Creo que va a tener que ser ahorcado pues supe que la silla eléctrica está descompuesta.'"

Gabriel fue recompensado con la risa de Theresa que para él sonaba como música pura.

"Buenas noches, es decir, días, Gabrielín."

"Buenos días para ti también, Tere. Duérmete aunque sea un ratito."

Ninguno de los dos fue capaz de dormir en lo absoluto aquella noche, repasando su conversación una y otra vez. Sentían emociones mezcladas por haberse encontrado de nuevo, pero ambos racionalizaban que había sido la voluntad de Dios la cual los juntó.

El siguiente domingo, durante la misa de mediodía, el Padre Gabriel estaba dando su sermón. Mientras caminaba al frente de la congregación y les explicaba la palabra de Dios, sintió como un ligero dolor de cabeza. Su olfato percibió el olor de algo quemándose. Continúo su homilía mientras que al mismo tiempo buscaba alguna señal de fuego o humo en la iglesia pero solo había el fuego de las velas. Sus ojos se posaron en una mujer y sus dos pequeños en medio de la congregación; sintió un escalofrío recorrerle la espalda al mirarlos. Terminó su sermón y los volvió a mirar. Se veían como cuerpos achicharrados en una visión que le duró solo un segundo. La mujer se preguntó qué lo haría verse tan alarmado.

El Padre Gabriel continúo con la preparación de la Eucaristía, tratando de no mirar más a la madre aquella. Sabía que estaba teniendo una visión acerca de ella, pero aún no comprendía qué se suponía que debía hacer. Rezó en silencio por tener la sabiduría necesaria para interpretar la señal y al mismo tiempo celebrar la misa sin interrupción.

Durante el canto del Padre Nuestro, toda la congregación se unió de manos. Todos estaban tocando a dos personas, una con cada mano. El sacerdote cerró sus ojos mientras cantaba con el coro y los feligreses.

"Padre Nuestro que estás en los cielos santificado sea tu nombre."

La energía de la mujer y sus niños le llegó a través de la cadena humana que habían formado; Gabriel sintió algo como un ligero choque eléctrico. Abrió los ojos y encontró los de la madre observándolo muy atenta.

"Vénganos tu reino. Hágase tu voluntad, en la tierra como en el cielo."

La cara de la mujer ardía, poniéndose negra con el fuego, así también las caritas de sus hijos, un niño y una niña de siete y ocho años de edad.

"Danos hoy nuestro pan de cada día. Perdona nuestras ofensas."

El ministro cerró los ojos y tuvo una visión de una casa ardiendo en la noche. Había una familia atrapada mientras dos tipos huían de la escena.

"Así como nosotros perdonamos a los que nos ofenden. No nos dejes caer en tentación y líbranos del mal."

Los guitarristas siguieron tocando, esperando que el padre cantara su parte él solo. El Padre sacudió la testa para escapar de la visión y recuperar la perspectiva. Finalmente, para alivio de los músicos, comenzó a cantar.

"Líbranos Señor de todos los males y concédenos la paz en nuestros días, para que, ayudados por tu misericordia, vivamos siempre libres de pecado y protegidos de toda perturbación, mientras esperamos la gloriosa venida de nuestro salvador, Jesucristo."

Toda la gente levantó las manos en alto para la conclusión de la oración cantada. El sacerdote cerró de nuevo los ojos y se sintió conectado otra vez con la mujer y sus dos niños en la asamblea.

"Tuyo es el reino, tuyo el poder, y la gloria por siempre Señor, ¡Amén!"

El Padre Gabriel abrió los ojos después de la oración como si al fin hubiera entendido el mensaje. Rezó, "Señor Jesucristo, que dijiste a tus Apóstoles, mi paz les dejo; mi paz les doy. No tengas en cuenta nuestros pecados, sino la fe de tu iglesia, y conforme a tu palabra concédele la paz y la unidad. Tú que vives y reinas por los siglos de los siglos."

"¡Amén!" contestó la gente de nuevo.

Después de una breve pausa el cura le dijo a la congregación, "La paz del Señor esté siempre con ustedes."

"Y con tu espíritu," contestaron ellos.

"¡Compartamos unos con otros una señal de la paz!"

Todos los feligreses se volvieron unos a los otros para abrazarse, besarse o saludarse, deseándose la paz. Sor Theresa se encaminó al Padre Gabriel para abrazarlo, pero él se fue caminando al centro de la iglesia en donde la mujer y sus niños estaban. Theresa lo vio alejándose y se sintió ignorada, aunque notó que también había ignorado a otras gentes que le trataron de dar la mano al pasar caminando hacia alguien en las bancas de en medio.

Theresa estrechó las manos de las gentes a su alrededor y observó fijamente al sacerdote abrazando a una mujer muy bonita, joven, de no más de veinticinco años. Gabriel le dijo algo al oído, y la mujer se alarmó. El pastor abrazó a ambos niños y les impuso las manos en la cabeza antes de regresarse al altar. La hermana se puso al órgano y tocó para que el coro cantara el "Cordero de Dios."

Al final de la misa, el celebrante dijo, "Que el Señor esté con ustedes."

La gente respondió como siempre, "Y con tu espíritu."

El presbítero se sonrió y les relató algo que se le vino a la mente antes de darles la bendición final.

El arzobispo, Trinidad Rosales, iba a leer el evangelio en la catedral cierto domingo, pero el micrófono no estaba funcionando. Se le acercó y lo examinó, le dio unos golpecitos con el dedo, lo prendió y lo apagó del botón. El arzobispo dijo, 'Algo está mal con este micrófono.' Y la gente le respondió, '¡Y con tu espíritu!'"

La congregación se rió con su chiste. Él les dio tiempo de recuperarse y luego les dio la bendición para terminar la misa.

Cuando la celebración hubo terminado, Sor Theresa vio a la mujer bonita conversando con el Padre Gabriel en la entrada de la iglesia. El Padre se bajó al nivel de los niños y los besó a ambos. Abrazó y besó a la mujercita también y les dio su bendición. La joven madre le besó la mano y se fue con sus niños tras de ella. La hermana religiosa se esperó a que el sacerdote regresara.

"¿Qué te traías con esa muchacha?" le preguntó, celosa.

"Tuve una visión de ella," respondió él impasiblemente.

"¿Quién es ella? ¿Cuánto tiempo tienes de conocerla?"

"Se llama Gloria Vásquez, pero nunca la había visto antes."

El Padre G se encaminó a la sacristía para despojarse de las vestiduras; la hermana fue con él.

"¿De qué se trataba la visión?"

"Le tenía que decir que se saliera de su casa esta noche y que se fuera a quedar en alguna otra parte por unos cuantos días. Tuve una premonición de que si no lo hace, su familia entera va a morir una muerte horrorosa," explicó el pastor, colgando sus vestimentas.

"¿Piensas que te haya creído?"

"Pienso que ella sí me creyó. El problema va a ser convencer a su marido. No es un hombre de fe, y probablemente no acepte la sugestión de un sacerdote," dijo Gabriel con preocupación en su rostro.

"¡Oh, qué bueno!" exclamó Theresa con alivio. "Por la forma en que vi que los abrazaste y besaste, tuve la terrible idea que esos niños pudieran ser tuyos y que ella podría ser una amante secreta que tú tenías."

Theresa se detuvo y bajó la cabeza, apenada.

"Yo te perdono y te absuelvo en el nombre del Padre, y del Hijo..." Gabriel se sonrió y, jugando, hizo como si hubiera estado oyendo su confesión. Le dijo, "Nos vemos mañana en la escuela, Hermana Theresa."

Ella se encaminó rumbo a la puerta y se detuvo antes de salir.

"Sí, Padre. ¡Que tengas un buen día!" Pausó un instante y luego le preguntó, "¿Me vas a llamar a la noche?"

"Lo pensaré," respondió él como si no hubiera considerado la idea. Se sonrió de nuevo y le guiñó un ojo. Ella sabía que la iba a llamar. Estaban encontrando mucho placer en sus nocturnas conversaciones telefónicas.

Al día siguiente, Theresa oyó a unas mujeres dejando a sus niños en la escuela comentar acerca de un incendio de casa el domingo en la noche. Unos tipos habían iniciado el fuego para vengarse de un hombre que había estado envuelto en un pleito con ellos una semana atrás. Afortunadamente, la familia había decidido ir a pasar la noche con un hermano en Austin, así que nadie salió lastimado. Dijeron que había sido la casa de los Vásquez la que se había quemado. La policía ya buscaba a los responsables por el incendio. Una de las mujeres mencionó que ella conocía a la señora de esa casa, su nombre era Gloria Vásquez y tenía dos hijos pequeños.

Theresa se volteó hacia la iglesia al cruzar la calle y vio al Padre Gabriel caminando rumbo a la escuela. Ella le sonrió, lo tomó del brazo y lo jaló cerca para decirle lo que acababa de escuchar.

"¡Qué bueno! Me alegra que haya sido capaz de convencer a su marido de dejar su casa."

"¿Qué tal si no lo hubiera podido hacer, Gabriel?"

"Entonces estaríamos celebrando un funeral múltiple, Theresa."

"¿No habrías tratado de detenerlo?" ella dijo, sorprendida.

"Yo lo vi. Iba a pasar. Fui aconsejado que le advirtiera a la familia pues no era aún su tiempo. Creo..." replicó él, encogiendo sus hombros.

Se metió a la escuela en lo que Theresa daba la bienvenida a los niños.

Ella se preguntaba cómo funcionaban aquellas cosas sobrenaturales y cómo era que su amigo no estaba preocupado por ellas. Él simplemente estaba disfrutando de otro día como si nada extraordinario hubiera sucedido, pero en realidad, para él aquel había sido uno más en una larga serie de eventos sobrenaturales. Ya estaba acostumbrado y no parecía andar buscando una explicación.

Era lunes trece de septiembre. En unos pocos días, Theresa se había puesto celosa de todas las mujeres quienes tenían acceso a la amistad y bondad de Gabriel. Desechó sus propios sentimientos y decidió sumergirse en su trabajo en lugar de preocuparse por su relación con el pastor.

Capítulo IV

Cumpleaños

Sor Magdalene se empezó a fijar en la forma en que el Padre miraba a la Hermana Theresa y también la forma en que ella lo miraba a él. Magda rechazó la idea de un romance entre los religiosos. Eran amables y muy amantes personas; sus conversaciones parecían gentiles y profesionales.

El padre era conocido como un juguetón y muy chistoso todo el tiempo, así pues, el hacer reír a Sor Theresa no era nada raro. Él hacía reír también a todas las hermanas, maestros, trabajadores, y estudiantes. Aún así, algo en su percepción femenina le decía que lo que estaba ocurriendo entre el cura y la hermana era más intenso que las relaciones que él tenía con el resto de las personas en la escuela o en la parroquia.

Por un momento se imaginó a Theresa y Gabriel como una pareja; se veían perfectos. Magda pensó que le hubiera gustado tener una hija como Theresa, y de ser así, Gabriel constituiría un magnífico yerno. La hermana religiosa sacudió la cabeza para borrar aquellas imágenes y se santiguó, pensando que iba a ofender al Señor con sus pensamientos.

Agarró una rebanada de pizza de la cafetería para dar su aprobación al almuerzo de los niños ese día. Irma, una de las trabajadoras de la cafetería, se le quedó viendo muy atenta, esperando su reacción.

"¡No está mal! Dame el botecito de chile seco quebradito y el de queso seco desboronado para mejorarla un poco."

La cocinera le dio los dos botecitos.

"No creo que a los niños les guste agregarle el chile, Hermana."

"¡Qué mal, porque sabe mucho mejor así! Ahora que si pudiéramos tener una cerveza con esta pizza picosa, ¡estaría simplemente perfecta!"

"¡Madre Magda!" exclamó Irma, mirando a la gordita religiosa como si hubiera sugerido algo pecaminoso, pero sabía que la hermana bromeaba acerca de tomar cerveza en la escuela, no de beberse una con su pizza.

"Mira, Irma, los niños no usan el chile picante, el cual es para adultos. ¡Nosotras podríamos tener cerveza únicamente para adultos también!"

"Ya me imagino a las maestras con sus cervezas a la hora del almuerzo."

"Algunas veces, con estos chiquillos, ¡te caería bien una con el almuerzo."

El Padre Gabriel sentía necesidad de ver a Sor Theresa por cualquier excusa. Estaban hablando por teléfono ya todas las noches para entonces. Siempre tenían explicación para sus frecuentes conversaciones, música para las misas, el desarrollo del festival de otoño, o la implementación de cambios en la técnica de enseñanza del primer grado.

Theresa se hizo cargo del grupo de estudios bíblicos que Kathryn había tenido. Se encontraban en la rectoría una noche por semana. Aquello le daba otra oportunidad de ver al cura en su casa. Ambos racionalizaban lo bueno de que siendo viejos amigos, ellos pudieran ahora trabajar juntos y disfrutar la compañía uno del otro en el servicio del Señor. Aún no le habían dicho a nadie en la parroquia el hecho que ya se conocían desde antes; aún era su pequeño secreto.

Un día que la Hermana Theresa enseñaba a su clase cómo usar letras mayúsculas, el Padre Gabriel fue a visitar la clase como el director de la escuela, para revisar el progreso de la nueva maestra. La hermana hizo que se levantaran los niños de sus pupitres para saludar al cura.

"¡Buenos días, Padre Gabriel!" dijeron todas las vocecitas en coro.

"¡Buenos días niños y niñas, shalom! Por favor tomen asiento."

Los pequeñuelos se sentaron y le pusieron atención. Theresa se fue a sentar en una silla en el rincón de atrás.

"Bien, ¿qué les parece su nueva maestra, la encantadora Sor Theresa?"

Las voces infantiles dijeron mucho al mismo tiempo, en aprobación.

"¿Es muy dura con ustedes?"

"¡Nooo!" todos contestaron en unísono, moviendo sus cabecitas.

"¿Alguno de ustedes tiene algún problema...?" empezó a decir el cura.

Una niñita pelirroja de seis años levantó la mano de inmediato, interrumpiéndolo. El presbítero levantó las cejas, asombrado. Theresa se cubrió la sonrisa con una mano porque ella ya sabía que Amanda Southwell siempre levantaba la mano y quería decir algo, aún si no tenía nada que ver con el tema que se estaba tratando.

"¿Cuál es el problema, Jovencita?"

La nena se paró como una soldadita en posición de firmes.

"Yo tengo miedo del Diablo. Es muy espantoso y muy malo."

"Estoy de acuerdo contigo, gracias por compartir eso con nosotros. Por favor siéntate," le dijo Gabriel, palmeándole la cabecita colorada.

El cura se sonrió, mirando alrededor del salón las caritas de los chiquillos que empezaron a hacer comentarios acerca del demonio. Un chico se estaba poniendo los dedos en los lados de su frente para pretender tener cuernos mientras le susurraba a su amigo cercano cómo se ve el Diablo.

"Quise decir problemas con su nueva maestra. ¿Alguien aquí tiene algún problema con su maestra? ¡Sean honestos conmigo! Yo soy el director y la puedo correr de inmediato si es necesario."

"¡Noooo!" gritaron todos.

"¿Entonces están contentos con ella?"

"¡Síííííí, Padre Gabriel!" replicó el coro de voces infantiles.

"Muy bien entonces, déjenme contarles una historia acerca del demonio, para que no le tengan miedo."

El ministro cerró los ojos por un momento para revisar un pasaje de las escrituras en su memoria. Les habló del capítulo dos del evangelio de San Marcos donde dice la historia de un endemoniado que entró a la sinagoga un sábado, cuando Jesús estaba enseñando en Cafarnaúm. Puso la historia en términos muy simples para que entendieran los niños y demostrarles que Jesús fue capaz de echar fuera el espíritu maligno del hombre poseído. Les afirmó a los niños que Jesús estaba con ellos y que podían siempre contar con Él para defenderlos contra el demonio.

Los pequeños se regocijaron con sus palabras. Una niñita con lentes le pidió que les cantara una canción porque a ella le gustaba como cantaba. Gabriel se volvió a ver a Sor Theresa la cual estaba muy sonriente y le guiñó un ojo en aprobación de que cantara.

"Se me hace que ustedes ya se saben esta. Canten conmigo si quieren."

Su poderosa y melodiosa voz resonó en el salón de clases para delicia de todos los chiquillos y Theresa. Su canción hablaba de la misericordia y el poder de Dios; les dio confianza a los pequeños creyentes de que no ser maligno podría vencerlos con el Señor cerca de ellos. Los estudiantes y aún la maestra se le unieron a cantar el coro de la canción.

Los niños y Sor Theresa aplaudieron al final de su interpretación.

El Padre G agarró el borrador del pizarrón como si fuera un micrófono y les agradeció al estilo de Elvis Presley, "¡Gracias, muchas gracias! Bueno, es hora de que se pongan a trabajar de nuevo."

Gabriel puso el borrador de vuelta y le echó ojitos a la maestra en la esquina para que se regresara y se hiciera cargo de su grupo. Una manita se elevó entre ellos dos. El director reconoció al negrito que quería decir algo. Él se levantó y se puso en posición de firmes.

"¿Padre Gabriel, nos podría contar un chiste antes de irse?"

El Padre miró su reloj y luego a Theresa; ella se volvió a sentar.

"¡Seguro! Déjame ver de cual me acuerdo que no hayan oído. ¡Oh, ya sé! Estaba un rancherito mexicano en un lado de la carretera no muy lejos de un pueblecito en México. Estaba parado ahí con una vaca muy gordota pidiendo que alguno de los carros que iban pasando le diera un aventoncito al pueblo. Nadie se quería parar por causa de la vaca parada junto a él."

Los niños se rieron, imaginándose aquella chusca escena de la vaca gorda.

"Venía un turista americano viajando por México en un carrito chiquito deportivo, convertible, para dos personas. Se detuvo junto al rancherito y le preguntó, 'Buenos días hombre, ¿a donde ir tú?' El rancherito le dijo, 'Pos nomás quería ver si me podía dar un aventoncito aquí al pueblo, Patrón.' El turista le dijo en su mejor español, 'Bueno, mí puede darte un raid por ti, pero no a tu vaca, ella es muy gordota por mi pequeño automóvil.' El mexicano se metió de un brinco al carrito y le dijo al gringo que no se apurara, que la vaca los iba a seguir corriendo por sí misma."

Los chiquitines se rieron, tratando de adivinar lo que pasaría enseguida.

"El americano se quedó picado pero se arrancó quedito, a 10 millas por hora. La vaca, justo como su dueño había dicho, iba siguiendo al carrito de cerca. El chofer le aceleró un poco, 20 millas, pero la vaca iba aún pegadita atrás de ellos. El turista estaba asombrado de la velocidad de la vaca cuando le subió a 30 y aún podía mirar su cara, fresca como pepino, en su espejo retrovisor. El chofer se preguntó que tan rápido podría correr aquel animal, así que le subió, a 40, y vio el espejo. La vaca aún estaba ahí. A 50, aún estaba ahí. El rancherito iba disfrutando el paseíto muy contento agarrándose el sombrero para que no se le volara. A las 60 millas por hora, el americano finalmente se alegró cuando vio en el espejo que la vaquita iba sacando la lengua. 'Ah!' le dijo al pasajero, 'Su vaca estar cansándose, Señor. Estar sacando lengua para afuera.'"

Los jovencitos estaba encantados con la complicación de la historia.

"El rancherito le preguntó, '¿Pa'onde está sacando la lengua, Patroncito?' El americano le contestó, 'Por el izquierda, dentro y fueras al izquierdo.' El mexicano le dijo, 'Tonces, hágase usté' un poquito pa' la orilla porque nos va a rebasar.' Y ¡ruuuuum! Que los pasa la vaca y les ganó al pueblito.'

Las pequeñas gentes se carcajearon con su chistecillo, imaginándose una rápida vaca gorda pasando a un carrito deportivo.

Theresa lo acompañó a la puerta para despedirlo y agradecerle la visita. Se quedaron quietos por un rato cuando sus ojos se encontraron. Un ligero choquecito eléctrico les pegó en sus corazones y les hizo sonreír con placer. La maestra sacudió la cabeza, recordando que su clase los estaba viendo.

"Es bienvenido a cualquier hora que decida pararse por aquí, Padre."

"Fue un placer estar con usted y con su clase, Hermana. Siga trabajando tan bien como lo ha estado haciendo."

Cuando Theresa estaba alistándose para irse esa tarde, se encontró afuera de la escuela con una pareja muy simpática de negritos. Le preguntaron si podrían ver al Padre Gabriel; la hermana les dijo que había ido a visitar a los prisioneros en la cárcel y no regresaría hasta más tarde.

"¿Hay algo con lo que pudiera yo ayudarles?"

"Queremos ver al reverendo porque le queremos dar las gracias por haber aliviado a nuestro hijito, Johnny," la linda dama morena le explicó a Sor Theresa mientras estaban parados enfrente de la escuela.

"¿Cuándo pasó eso?" inquirió Theresa, caminando con ellos hacia la sombra de un gran árbol, cubriéndose de los rayos del ardiente sol.

"El año pasado," dijo el caballero moreno que traía collar de clérigo protestante.

"Sé que debíamos haber hecho esto hace mucho, pero no estábamos seguros. Fíjese que nuestro hijo sufría de ataques de epilepsia desde que estaba chiquito. No hay mucho que se pueda hacer cuando a un epiléptico le da un ataque. Sufríamos, pensando que nuestro hijito iba a padecer eso toda su vida," Janie Atkinson le relató a Theresa, compartiendo su alegría.

El marido continuó la historia para la hermana religiosa. "El año pasado, conocimos al Padre Gabriel en un partido de fútbol. Yo era el entrenador del equipo de mi hijo porque los otros entrenadores no querían tomar la responsabilidad de tener un epiléptico en su equipo."

Theresa sonrió al enterarse de los demás detalles del sorprendente caso.

"El Padre Gabriel era el entrenador del otro equipo ese día. Era un juego muy apretado. Estábamos empatados a dos en la segunda mitad. Mi hijo era el mejor jugador de nuestro equipo, pero de repente cayó en el campo y empezó a convulsionarse. Sabía que se recuperaría, pero el árbitro detuvo el juego. Me metí y sostuve a mi niño. Lo saqué cargado para la orilla y preparé a otro jugador para reemplazarlo hasta que se recuperara. Pensé que ya no iba a poder regresar porque solo quedaban diez minutos. Nunca había tenido un ataque en un juego. Cuando lo tenía en mis brazos, con mis ojos al cielo pidiendo ayuda de Dios, me fijé que el entrenador del otro equipo, el Padre Gabriel, se dejó venir corriendo a través de la cancha antes que el árbitro volviera a reanudar el partido."

La religiosa meneó la cabeza, imaginando al cura corriendo por la cancha.

"El Padre Gabriel me dijo que mis oraciones habían sido escuchadas. Le impuso las manos a mi hijo. Yo sentí algo como una ola de tibia energía corriendo por el cuerpo de mi hijo y pasándome a mí también cuando le puso las manos encima y rezó sobre el chiquillo. Me sentí débil y caí de rodillas aún sosteniendo a mi hijo. El Padre Gabriel le dijo a Johnny que se levantara y le extendió la mano. ¡Ahí estaba yo, de rodillas, presenciando un milagro! Johnny se recuperó como si nunca le hubiera dado un ataque. Me preguntó por qué lo había sacado del juego. Se veía alerta y bien vivillo, no adormilado y confuso como usualmente se veía después de un ataque."

"¡Alabado sea el Señor!" exclamó Theresa con una mano en su pecho.

"Le di las gracias al sacerdote por su ayuda, pero, para decirle la verdad, no quería creer que había sido milagro. Johnny había tenido convulsiones antes y luego seguía viviendo su vida como cualquier otro chico hasta que se le venía otro episodio. Nos llevó un año para asegurarnos que Johnny estaba curado. Lo hicimos examinar por varios doctores. No encontraron absolutamente nada mal con él. Antes le daban ataques casi una vez al mes, pero desde ese día el año pasado, no ha tenido ni uno solo, aún después que dejamos de darle la medicina."

Theresa se fijó que los ojos de John Atkinson se rasaron de lágrimas.

"Ahora me doy cuenta que estaba envidioso de que Dios le dio a Gabriel el poder de sanación y no a mí. Hubiera querido ser yo el que tocó al niño y lo curó, así pues no quería conceder que el chico fue curado por Gabriel."

"¿Pero, John, no había dicho el Padre Gabriel que sus oraciones habían sido escuchadas antes de imponerle las manos a su hijo?" preguntó Sor Theresa, tratando de darle crédito a la fe del hombre.

"Sí, sí lo hizo. Al pasar del tiempo, me di cuenta que Dios estaba obrando de manera misteriosa para abrir mis ojos. Me puse más consciente de mi propia fe y mi ministerio. Soy predicador, no curador. Esta es mi vocación. Vinimos a darle las gracias a Gabriel. Le conseguimos este certificado para la tienda SoccerPro para su equipo, como muestra de agradecimiento."

"¿Y cómo terminó su juego esa vez? Dijo usted que estaban empatados cuando Johnny cayó."

"Eso fue lo chistoso. Cuando vi que Johnny estaba listo para jugar de nuevo, lo mandé de vuelta al campo, y él anotó el gol ganador. Los del equipo de Gabriel no estaban contentos con él por haber aliviado al que les metió el gol definitivo. Mientras nos íbamos de la cancha, lo oí hablando con sus jugadores y los padres de ellos acerca del amor a los enemigos. Pero les explicó que no somos enemigos, aún cuando estábamos en equipos diferentes y pertenecemos a diferentes denominaciones, teníamos más en común que las diferencias que nos dividían. Dijo que algo más importante que un juego había tomado lugar en aquel campo ese día: Dios había estado presente y había otorgado salud y alegría a una familia."

John le echó el brazo sobre los hombros a su esposa, le entregó a Theresa un sobre y le dijo, "¿Le podría usted entregar esto al Padre Gabriel? Lo podríamos invitar a cenar uno de estos días, y a usted también, Hermana."

"Tengo una idea aún mejor," Theresa dijo, "El cumpleaños del Padre Gabriel se viene en un par de días. ¿Por qué no le preparamos una fiesta sorpresa en donde lo puedan ustedes tener de invitado para una cena y le den el regalo? He estado buscando quien me ayudara a hacer esto."

"Eso suena bien, Hermana; ¡puede contar conmigo!" Janie se volvió y le preguntó a su esposo, "¿John, tenemos el salón disponible?"

"De hecho, lo tenemos," contestó John con una gran sonrisa, "La recepción que teníamos planeada ha sido cancelada. La novia decidió irse con otro hombre antes de la boda."

"¿Qué era lo que tenía pensado, Hermana Theresa?"

Se pusieron de acuerdo a grandes rasgos para organizar la fiesta sorpresa.

Theresa fue con ellos a su iglesia y visitó su acogedor saloncito. Ambos, John y Janie, eran muy fieles a su credo. Theresa fácilmente podía identificarse con gente tan espiritual. Ellos también encontraron a la hermana religiosa adorable; invitaron a Theresa a su casa y compartieron una cena con ella antes de regresarla a casa.

Esa noche Theresa estaba pensando que ella y Gabriel podrían ser como los Atkinson, una pareja felizmente casada con tres adorables pequeños, sirviendo a Dios. Janie era activa en su iglesia. La diferencia era que eran bautistas; para fin que Gabriel y Theresa hicieran lo mismo, tendrían que renunciar a su fe católica. ¿Qué tendría eso de malo? Theresa se dio en la frente con la palma de su mano. Se fue mejor a rezar un rosario para aclarar su mente de lo que consideraba pecaminoso.

El día que Gabriel cumplió los treinta y ocho años, jueves treinta de septiembre, actuó como si fuera un día ordinario. Se levantó temprano, fue a correr y nadar, celebró la misa matutina y trabajó en su oficina en asuntos de la escuela y la parroquia toda la mañana.

A la hora del almuerzo, el Diácono Andrés García acompañó al sacerdote a comerse una sopa y ensalada. Theresa se presentó a comer con ellos. Ella lo que quería era evitar que el Padre G regresara a la escuela donde el plantel estaba haciendo planes para su fiesta de cumpleaños aquella tarde.

"Será un gran honor y un placer el que nos engracie con su presencia, Hermana," dijo el Padre Gabriel, sacando una silla para Theresa.

El sacerdote tomó asiento y les contó a los amigos religiosos un chiste.

"Los diáconos de una iglesia protestante estaban entrevistando a un joven quien había aplicado para pastor. Le preguntaron si sabía la Biblia; él les dijo que la sabía bien. Le pidieron que les dijera cuál era su parte favorita, y él les respondió que era la historia del hijo pródigo. Los diáconos le pidieron que les contara la historia, así pues el joven les relató, 'Había un hombre leproso, ciego y sordo de los fariseos llamado Nicodemo quien bajo a Jericó por la noche y cayó en tierra rocosa, y las espinas plantadas por un enemigo lo ahorcaron casi a muerte. Él luchó contra ellos con la quijada de un burro hasta que se lastimó el nervio ciático en su cadera."

Theresa se cubrió la boca y miró a Andrés que se estaba riendo bajito.

"Por la mañana, Sodoma y su esposa, Gomorra, lo llevaron cargado al arca para que Moisés lo cuidara, pero cuando entró en el arco del este del arca, se le atoró la cabellera en una rama, y quedó colgado ahí por 40 días y 40 noches. Después de eso tuvo mucho hambre y unos cuervos le dieron de comer maná y codornices. Vio un ángel agitar las aguas mientras comía. Al día siguiente 3 reyes magos montados en una manada de puercos vinieron y partieron las aguas junto a las tumbas con una plaga de langostas."

Andrés palmeó la mesa, incapaz de controlar una risotada. Theresa se rió con él, pero el Padre G les dijo que se esperaran pues aún había más.

"Ellos agarraron al hombre y se lo llevaron hasta el puerto donde agarró un barco rumbo a Nínive; encontró a Dalila sentada en la pared vendiendo su harina y aceite. El hombre gritó, '¡Échensela, muchachos! ¡Échensela!' ellos dijeron, '¿Cuántas veces nos la echaremos... siete veces siete?' Y él les dijo, '¡No! Setenta veces setenta.' Se la echaron cuatro mil novecientas veces, y ella se reventó en medio de todos. Recogieron doce canastas llenas de los fragmentos. Y en la resurrección de los justos en el último día, ¿de quién será esposa ella, Hijo Pródigo?' El presidente de los diáconos dijo, 'Compañeros, creo que debemos aceptarlo. Es muy joven, ¡pero de veras que sí se sabe muy bien su Biblia!"

Theresa y Andrés se estaban carcajeando.

El diácono recuperó la compostura y declaró, "Como las chinches, voy a tener que comer y correr. Mi esposa está volando de regreso después de ver a su hermana en Las Vegas. Va a llegar en una hora."

Theresa estaba encantada de compartir un tiempecito sola con Gabriel.

"Oh, no hay problema, Diácono García. Es mejor que esté ahí a tiempo para que recoja a esa mujer. Usted ya sabe que no nos gusta que nos tengan esperando," dijo Theresa, mirando a Gabriel discretamente.

Gabriel pescó el significado de sus palabras, pero solo le sonrió con cara de inocencia. El almuerzo consistía en sopa de crema de champiñones, ensalada de camarones, pan negro tostado y un vasito de vino blanco.

Después del almuerzo, la hermana recogió los trastes sucios de la mesa y se fue a lavarlos en el fregadero. El Padre G encaminó a su diácono a la puerta y regresó a la cocina.

"Oh, no, por favor, Theresa deja ahí esos trastes. Yo me haré cargo de ellos más tarde, o la Señora Black lo hará. Tú no tienes que hacer eso; además, ya es hora que regreses a tu clase."

Gabriel la agarró de la cintura, tratando de alejarla del fregadero. Ella se aferró a la orilla, rehusando moverse pero disfrutando del contacto.

"No me iré hasta que no haya hecho esto. Ahora, si quieres, los puedes enjuagar en lo que yo los tallo. Mi clase está en educación física ahorita, así que tengo tiempo." Puso sus manos sobre las de él, aún tomándola por la cintura, volteó su cara atrás, y suavemente le sopló las palabras, "Además, me gustaría que me cantaras una canción, bonita, romántica."

El sacerdote se dobló las mangas de la camisa y se acercó al fregadero.

Gabriel se acabó lo que le quedaba de vino y aclaró su garganta para comenzar su canción.

La letra hablaba de las cosas que la amada aprendería una vez que se diera cuenta del amor del poeta, que ella era su vida, su cielo, y su Dios. Theresa se volvió a ver a Gabriel con sus ojos claros muy abiertos.

"¡Eso es sacrilegio!"

"Solo es una canción, Hermana. Yo no la escribí; yo solo la canto. Si no te gusta le paro."

"No, sí me encanta, pero tengo un problema con eso que 'eres-mi-Dios.'"

"Entonces piensa que se la estoy cantando a Dios y no a ti."

"Bueno, así sí. Eso tiene más sentido. Continúa con la canción por favor," Theresa le suplicó mientras regresaban a lavar trastes.

El cantante repitió el último verso para concluir la canción mientras que terminaban su labor. Ella le agradeció por el almuerzo; él le agradeció por lavar los trastes. Ella le dio las gracias por la canción; él le dio las gracias por pedirle que cantara. Se miraron a los ojos, parados junto a la puerta.

"¡Ahora vete de aquí y vuelve a tu trabajo!" el cura le dijo con una gran sonrisa mientras le abría la puerta para mandarla a la escuela.

Theresa se apresuró para llegar allá; Gabriel la fue siguiendo con sus ojos hasta que desapareció dentro del edificio.

El cura se metió a su cuarto a sacar un puro nuevo. Lo encendió y caminó afuera, alrededor de la casa, mirando a los niños jugar en el patio de la escuela. Era un día grandioso, ¡su trigésimo octavo aniversario de vida! Nadie lo había mencionado todavía, y no pensaba mencionárselo a nadie. Ya había disfrutado su cumpleaños por ese momento solito con Theresa.

Un representante de una compañía editora vino a encontrarlo ahí afuera. Lo había estado esperando en la escuela pues tenían cita para revisar unos nuevos libros de texto que el director pensaba ordenar. El Padre G se disculpó por haber olvidado que tenían esa cita y se llevó al hombre con él a la oficina para hacerse cargo de su asunto.

Esa tarde, el Padre Gabriel fue a visitar a una viejecita en las casas de gobierno. Estacionó su carro cerca del patio de juegos.

Había unos chicos jugando básquetbol ahí. El clérigo se coló en la cancha y le arrebató la pelota a un distraído. Se fue botándola con habilidad y saltó para meter la bola por el aro. Los chicos lo conocían y se rieron con él. Les pidió le echaran un ojito a su carcacha y siguieran practicando su deporte.

Uno de los muchachillos agarró la pelota y la aventó fuerte hacia el sacerdote. Él la atrapó, se volteó y saltó en el aire y encestar un tiro largo.

"¡Pura red!" dijo él viendo la bola entrar a la canasta.

Martin Davis, el chiquillo de catorce años con la mala actitud, fue y recogió el balón de nuevo. Parecía ser el único en la cancha a quien no le había caído bien que el presbítero les interrumpiera el partido.

"¡Vamos a seguirle al partido, chavos!" el adolescente les gritó, despidiendo al cura con desdén.

Gabriel decidió alejarse y hacer lo que había ido a hacer ahí. Los otros chicos le dijeron al corajudo que se calmara porque el Padre era bien chido. El sacerdote sabía que ellos eran pandilleros juveniles pero esperaba hacerse amigo de ellos y poder salvar por lo menos a alguno.

El ministro rezó con Doña Mariquita y le dio la comunión. Escuchó a la vieja hablar orgullosamente de su nieto, Henry, quien estaba en el Cuerpo de Marina. La anciana estaba confinada a una silla de ruedas y vivía sola. Había criado al muchacho y lo mantuvo en la escuela. La madre había muerto de una sobre-dosis de heroína; el padre de Henry, quien nunca había reconocido ser su padre, estaba aún en la prisión por asesinato.

Mariquita misma había sido víctima de una venganza. Una noche que pasaron disparando de un vehículo, le dieron en la espalda baja al dormir en la sala. Un grupito opuesto a los amigos de Henry buscó vengarse luego que estos le habían disparado a uno de los de ellos. Henry era solo asociado y nunca había sido iniciado en la pandilla. Los otros no lo sabían; eso ni les importó. Henry ni siquiera estaba en la casa cuando le dieron el balazo a Mariquita. Ese día decidió que se iba a meter a la Marina para conseguir un mejor sitio para llevarse a vivir a su abuelita. Aún estaba trabajando en ese plan; Mariquita tenía la esperanza que se la llevara a San Diego.

En el lado opuesto de la manzana en la que el Padre G daba ministerio a la mujer, una van iba pasando con estruendosa música metálica pesada. Unos Apóstoles de Satanás iban en la van, fumando drogas. Jorge Ramírez conducía el vehículo. El pasajero de enfrente llevaba una bomba molotov y se iba asomando por la ventana buscando su blanco.

"Se me hace que ahí es donde vive ese bato. Dales en toda la torre, Chucky!" dijo Jorge entre obscenidades.

El adolescente lanzó el proyectil encendido; quebró el vidrio de una ventana trasera, penetrando el departamento e iniciando un fuego. Los chicos en la van vitorearon mientras Jorge aceleraba la van.

"¡Buen tiro, Camarada! Ahora esos tipos sabrán que no nos andamos con cuentos. ¡Van a tener que pensar dos veces antes de volvernos a insultar!" exclamó Jorge Ramírez entre maldiciones, dándole a su "artillero" una palmada por alto.

"¡Apóstoles de Satanás son reyes! ¡Apóstoles de Satanás son reyes!" cantaron en coro los de la van al dar la vuelta en la esquina y se fugaron.

Unos minutos después, una mujer en puro fondo salió del departamento en llamas; iba tosiendo y gritando, rodeada de un humo negrísimo.

Al ir caminando de vuelta a su carro, Gabriel oyó los gritos y olió el humo saliendo del edificio de departamentos en el otro lado del complejo habitacional. El sacerdote volvió los ojos y miró el cielo nocturno iluminado por el techo del edificio ardiendo. Corrió a ver qué podía hacer.

La angustiada mujer en fondo de nylon estaba siendo detenida por su hijo adolescente, el mismo chico que le había tirado el pelotazo en la cancha. Ella estaba gritando y llorando porque su bebito aún estaba dentro del departamento, en el segundo piso. Su hijo luchaba por detenerla para evitar que tratara de meterse en el departamento en llamas.

El clérigo evaluó la situación. Medio edificio ya estaba ardiendo. Lleno de misericordia por la mujer y su bebito, se arrancó a la puerta sacándose su botellita de agua bendita. Murmuró una oración, se santiguó, y se roció algo de agua bendita sobre su cabeza y hombros. Estaba recitando una oración de memoria.

"Señor, por tu sagrado nombre protégeme. Dame fuerza para defender tu causa. Dios Todopoderoso escucha mi oración. Atiende a mis súplicas."

El místico se metió en el departamento ardiendo, orando, *"El maligno se ha levantado en contra mía; el despiadado busca mi ruina."*

Estaba muy caliente y oscuro en el lugar. El sacerdote pudo escuchar una risa muy profunda y gruesa; él continuó con su oración.

"Siempre estás presente como mi ayuda; eres tú quien sostiene mi vida."

El clérigo sintió una presencia maligna observándolo en el fuego.

Los cabellos de la nuca se le pararon de punta como si hubieran sido atraídos por energía magnética. Gabriel rezó más intensamente.

"Protégeme del maligno; por tu fidelidad, aléjame de cualquier daño."

Algo de humo le entró por la nariz; empezó a toser. Se agazapó a seguir su camino, buscando la escalera, y oyó una voz muy ronca en el fuego.

"¡Eres... mío!"

Gabriel miró alrededor; la puerta por la que entró estaba ardiendo. Escaló en sus manos y rodillas al segundo piso; el bebito estaba llorando.

"Te ofreceré como mi único sacrificio, mi humilde y contrito corazón, y te daré alabanza a ti, O Señor, porque tú me has rescatado del peligro."

Una lengüeta de fuego rodeó el tobillo del sacerdote como una zarpa y le quemó la punta de los pantalones y el calcetín. Gabriel se volteó a ver su tobillo ardiendo y oyó la profunda voz otra vez.

"¡Eres mío, Gabriel!"

El cura se roció el tobillo con el agua bendita que le quedaba en la botellita. Increíblemente el fuego retrocedió, y su pierna se refrescó.

"¡En el nombre de Jesús te lo ordeno; retírate de mí, Satanás!"

El bebito estaba llorando y tosiendo dentro de la recámara. El Padre Gabriel llegó hasta el cuarto arrastrándose y localizó al pequeño bajo la cuna. El fuego ya llegaba hasta la puerta de la recámara; no había modo que saliera por el mismo camino que había entrado.

Gabriel envolvió al bebé en una cobijita de la cuna y miró que las cortinas de la ventana estaban ardiendo. Se incorporó y lanzó un buró a través de la ventana haciéndola estallar en miles de fragmentitos.

Los espectadores afuera gritaron cuando el buró salió volando. Casi le pegaba a uno que se encontraba ojeando a la semidesnuda madre.

Gabriel se dejó caer al suelo y cubrió al niño con su cuerpo. La corriente de aire mandó largas llamaradas afuera a través de la ventana quebrada. Los mirones afuera gritaron de nuevo.

El místico se levantó con el pequeñito en sus brazos y saltó por la ventana de cabeza como disparado por un cañón. La gente gritó por tercera vez mirándolo volar por el aire.

El viaje al suelo era como de cuatro metros. Enroscó su cuerpo para aterrizar sobre su espalda y rodar sobre el pasto con el bebito entre sus brazos. Los bomberos llegaron cuando el sacerdote salió por la ventana. La camisa del clérigo ardía; un bombero con manguera en mano lo roció con bastante agua sobre el pasto. El cura se paró y le entregó la criaturita a Violeta Ojeda, la desesperada madre.

"¡Mi niño! ¡Gracias a Dios, mi niño está bien! ¡Gracias señor, por haber salvado a mi bebito! ¡Alabado sea el Señor, bendito sea Dios!"

La madre examinó a su niñito quien estaba llorando pero no herido. Lo abrazó y se lo echó al brazo izquierdo para acercarse a abrazar al sacerdote con su brazo derecho, llorando por tener a su bebé vivo. Gabriel todavía emanaba vapor de su parcialmente quemada y empapada camisa.

"Bendito sea el Señor, en verdad, Hija mía. Él fue quien nos salvó a los dos allá adentro."

El Padre Gabriel le besó las frentes a la mujer y a su criatura. Se le quedó viendo a Martin, el hermano mayor, parado detrás de su mamá y su hermanito. El muchachito se adelantó, abrazó al sacerdote y le agradeció por salvar a su hermano menor.

"Le puedes ir a dar gracias a Dios personalmente viniendo a la iglesia este domingo," él le dijo al adolescente, poniéndole las manos en los hombros para verlo directamente a los ojos.

"¡Seguro! Ahí estaremos, Padre G... ¿Sabe una cosa? ¡Usted sí que es un bato bien chido!" replicó el chico.

Gabriel se sonrió y le palmeó el hombro al muchacho en reconocimiento de su nueva amistad.

"¡Este es de los míos! Lleva a tu mami y tu hermanito también, ¿Sí?"

Un paramédico vino a examinar al cura mientras que los bomberos batallaban con las flamas para evitar que se extendieran a otros edificios.

"¿Cómo se siente, Reverendo?" le preguntó el paramédico.

"Oh, me siento como un campeón que acaba de ganar el título mundial, adolorido y cansado, pero muy contento."

El Padre G se quitó su camisa negra y la observó, estaba arruinada completamente. La hizo bola y la lanzó a un cercano tambo de basura abierto. La garra mojada echa bola cayó en el centro del tambo.

"¡Pura red!" dijo Martin Davis, guiñándole un ojo al sacerdote al tiempo que sostenía a su hermanito en los brazos.

"¿Sabe que lo que hizo usted ahí fue muy estúpido? Meterse a una casa en llamas, como lo hizo, sin ningún equipo, nunca es recomendado," el paramédico le comentó al héroe.

"Tienes razón pero estás equivocado, Hijo mío."

"¿Por qué dice eso?"

"Tienes razón que meterse a una casa ardiendo es estúpido; sin embargo, salvarle la vida a un bebito no lo es," Gabriel explicó, agregando, "Y eso de que no tenía ningún equipo... ¡Esto es todo lo que necesito para enfrentar cualquier problema, cualquier enemigo, a cualquier hora!"

El ministro le mostró su crucifijo colgando alrededor de su cuello.

Los bomberos estaban ganándole el pleito al fuego, pero cuando Gabriel volteó a ver el incendio, pudo oír una voz entre las llamas.

"A la próxima, Sacerdote."

"¡Cuando quieras, Satanás! ¡No te tengo miedo porque el Todopoderoso está de mi lado!" el Padre G dijo y giró sobre sus talones.

Se encaminó hacia su auto antes que los miembros de la media trataran de entrevistarlo. El paramédico se quedó intrigado, pensando que el héroe le había estado hablando a él cuando respondió la amenaza del Diablo.

Cuando el párroco llegó a casa, encontró una nota grapada en su puerta.

"Padre Gabriel, por favor venga a verme a la calle Delgado número veintiocho quince. Es muy importante. ¡Necesito verlo esta noche!" Estaba firmado por, "Un Alma Desesperada."

El ministro se preguntó quién podía ser. Decidió que quien fuera, parecía desesperada y necesitada ayuda. Iba a dejar la cena para más tarde, hasta que supiera de qué se trataba aquello.

Se metió y se cambió de ropa, se cepilló el cabello, rellenó su botella de agua bendita, y puso sus cosas en orden en caso de que necesitara oír una confesión o dar la unción de los enfermos.

Se regresó a su carro y se dirigió a aquel sitio.

La dirección era la del salón de una iglesia bautista, el cual estaba todo oscuro. El cura revisó el número de nuevo en la nota y en el edificio. Decidió ir a tocar a la puerta. Para su sorpresa, la puerta no estaba atrancada y había un papel grapado en ella con una nota.

"Pásale, si te atreves, Padre Gabriel."

Gabriel se asomó cauteloso al interior a través de la puerta ligeramente abierta. Había solo oscuridad y silencio en su interior. La escritura en ambas notas era la misma. Se acordó de su reciente encuentro con el maligno y se preguntó si aquella sería una trampa. En ese instante Gabriel escuchó una tos apagada; así que se metió al lugar.

"¡Hola! ¿Hay alguien aquí? Soy el Padre Gabriel; recibí un mensaje..."

Las luces se encendieron, y un sistema estereofónico comenzó a tocar la canción de cumpleaños.

"¡Bienvenido, Padre Gabriel, y muy feliz trigésimo-octavo cumpleaños!" dijo Theresa por un micrófono y comenzó a liderar al grupo a cantar.

"Un cumpleaños feliz..."

Gabriel miró a su alrededor y encontró muchas caras conocidas de la parroquia y la escuela, algunas no conocidas, y una familia de la que se acordaba muy bien desde el juego de campeonato de fútbol el año anterior. La canción terminó, y todo mundo vino a abrazarlo.

La última persona en línea fue Theresa quien le preguntó, "¿Dónde había estado? ¡Lo hemos estado esperando una hora! ...Huele a humo."

"Bueno, obviamente, como puede usted oler, andaba en el infierno, peleándome con Satanás por la vida de un bebito."

"¡Está usted bromeando como siempre! ¿Qué fue lo que pasó en verdad?"

"Es la verdad. ¿A poco cree que le voy a decir mentiras, Hermana?"

John, el anfitrión, agarró al cura para llevarlo al asiento de honor. Un grupo de damas comenzaron a servir para todas las mesas. Suave música instrumental empezó a llenar el ambiente. Theresa aún se estaba preguntando qué le habría pasado a Gabriel. Ya lo interrogaría más delante cuando hablaran por teléfono antes de acostarse. ¡Obviamente no podía él haber ido al infierno y regresar de allá esa noche! ¿O sería posible?

La cena fue excelente, bistec con papas al horno y vegetales por un lado. No se sirvieron bebidas alcohólicas; sin embargo, el ponche y el té helado estuvieron sabrosos. A pesar que tenían un sistema de sonido tocando música movidita, era obvio que no iba a haber baile pues las mesas tenían el espacio lleno. Había unos estandartes en las paredes que decían, "¡Que Dios lo bendiga Padre Gabriel!" "¡Todos te queremos, Amigo!" "¡Feliz cumpleaños, Viejito!" "¡Que Dios te mantenga con vida otros cien años!"

Para comenzar la presentación de los regalos, John Atkinson tomó el micrófono para agradecer al del cumpleaños por haber curado a Johnny de su epilepsia por el poder de Dios, aún si le costó el campeonato a su equipo. Le presentó al Tejedor de Milagros el certificado de regalo.

El Padre G fue bañado de regalos, libros, camisas, suéteres, tenis, una petaca para gimnasio, guantes de box, otros para pesas, y un muy pequeño traje de baño, el cual les levantó las cejas a muchos. Algunos siguieron al Diácono García y su esposa cantándole al sacerdote que se los pusiera. El Padre G agarró el bikini y se lo puso en la cabeza; alguien tomó una foto.

Abrió otros regalos, un sombrero blanco de vaquero, un maletín negro de cuero, discos compactos de Beethoven, una rasuradora eléctrica con cabeza ajustable, ¡una chaqueta negra de cuero y unos lentes oscuros! Se puso la chamarra y los lentes, luego agarró los guantes de levantar pesas y se los puso también para completar su atuendo de hombre rudo.

"¿Alguien me compró una moto para irme a pasear? ¡Estoy listo!"

Se montó en un banco pretendiendo que se iba manejando una moto; luego regresó a la mesa por su último regalo.

Sor Theresa le regaló una estola multicolor de México. Siempre había querido una como esa pero nunca la había comprado ni nadie había pensado en dársela. Ella de veras sabía lo que él quería y lo que le gustaba.

Después de la fiesta, cuando la mayoría se había marchado, Gabriel y Theresa se quedaron a ayudarles a los Atkinson. Sor Theresa le dijo a Magda que se iba a quedar a limpiar ya que había sido idea suya el hacer la fiesta. Theresa declinó usar la ayuda de las otras hermanas, diciendo que no era mucho de cualquier manera. Ya fuera el Padre Gabriel o los Atkinson la podían llevar a su casa más tarde.

John y Gabriel compararon notas. Ambos eran pastores de congregación y tenían una escuelita bajo su supervisión. Eran solo un par de años aparte. John ya tenía cuarenta. Theresa y Janie tenían deberes similares. Ambas enseñaban el primer año, lideraban un grupo bíblico, y tenían el ministerio de música. La diferencia era que los Atkinson tenían dieciocho años de casados y tenían un hijo, Matthew, en la preparatoria, una hija, Rebecca, en secundaria, y el niño que antes era epiléptico, Johnny, en la primaria.

Janie comentó, "Ustedes dos se ven tan bien juntos. Creo que harían una hermosa pareja."

"Vamos, Cariño, los religiosos católicos son célibes; no se pueden casar," su esposo interpuso.

"Es muy cierto eso; estamos casados con nuestro Señor y nuestro ministerio," dijo la hermana religiosa, volteando los ojos a ver al sacerdote.

"Bueno, pues respeto eso, Hermana, pero estoy contenta de no ser católica y poder servir al Señor y ser casada con hijos al mismo tiempo," dijo Janie, contenta de su posición como esposa de un predicador.

"Hay diferentes caminos en la vida. Debemos solo de identificar cuál es el que Dios ha reservado para nosotros," Theresa explicó, agregando, "Para cada bendición, hay una responsabilidad. Lo más importante es permitir el Espíritu de Dios nos guíe en nuestra jornada y aceptar ambas, bendiciones y responsabilidades como se nos conceden."

Las dos parejas iban rumbo a la puerta mientras Sor Theresa les decía, "Ha sido un gran placer conocerlos, Reverendo John y Janie. Espero que podamos compartir más tiempo juntos en el futuro. ¡Quizás podrían traer a su coro a una de nuestras celebraciones!"

Se iban aproximando al carro del Padre Gabriel.

"¡Hombre! ¿Qué tan vieja es esta cosa?" Preguntó John, mirando al viejo pero bien cuidado vehículo.

"Es más viejo que tú y yo. Es de 1935, no un clásico. Es más bien como un mutante. Los muchachos de mecánica en la preparatoria técnica lo han transformado; le dicen el Curimóvil. Mira el interior renovado por una tapicería en mi parroquia, las ruedas deportivas donadas por un amigo, el estéreo donado por un ladrón reformado. Escucha la potente máquina que los chicos sacaron de un carro volteado que estaba en un deshuesadero."

Gabriel encendió la máquina del Curimóvil y le pisó al acelerador.

"¡Se oye muy bien! ¿Cuánto dinero has invertido en él?"

"¡Ni un centavo! Es mantenido por la gracia de Dios y la bondad de mis muchos amigos. Otro amigo aún me provee con gasolina gratis. Es cierto lo que dicen que el que tiene amigos no sufre; ¡los que sufren son los amigos!"

Se rieron y dijeron adiós mientras el Curimóvil desaparecía en la noche.

Gabriel tuvo tiempo de relatar su aventura de rescate en el incendio a la Hermana Theresa en el camino a casa. Ella estaba asombrada de las cosas en las que su amigo se veía envuelto y cómo siempre salía victorioso.

Cuando iban comentando acerca de los Atkinson, Gabriel recordó otra historia y se la contó a Theresa para ver su encantadora sonrisa de nuevo.

"En una de las recientes conferencias teológicas en el Vaticano, el grupo reunido ahí estuvo de acuerdo en tres verdades indisputables."

Theresa volteó a verlo con interés, pensando que estaba compartiendo importantes puntos teológicos con ella.

"Primero, concluyeron que los judíos jamás reconocerían a Jesús como el Hijo de Dios. Segundo, estuvieron de acuerdo que los protestantes jamás reconocerían al Papa como el verdadero sucesor de San Pedro, y tercero, que los bautistas jamás se reconocerían uno al otro en la tienda de licores."

Theresa repitió las últimas dos oraciones y le dio un manazo en el hombro, riéndose.

"Ya me tenías pensando que estabas compartiendo alguna información importante y seria pero luego me di cuenta que estabas saliendo con otra de tus payasadas. Fue chistoso, eso sí."

"Me encanta verte sonreír, Tere. Adoro escuchar tu risa, verte cerca, oírte hablar, olerte, sentirte junto a mí. Simplemente me encanta tenerte a mi alrededor, mi Querida Tere."

"Me siento igual yo también, mi Querido Gabrielín."

Se miraron a los ojos por un ratito sin decir palabra. Ya habían llegado al frente de la casa de las monjitas. La luz del portal se prendió para iluminar la entrada, así que se dieron cuenta de que las hermanas ahí adentro ya los habían visto llegar. Él fue a abrirle la puerta del auto.

"Muchísimas gracias por la fiestecita sorpresa. ¡Estuvo sensacional!"

"Me alegra que la hayas disfrutado. ¿Te gustó mi regalo?" ella preguntó mientras caminaban rumbo a la puerta de la casa.

"¡Oh, esa estola mexicana fue mi regalo favorito!"

"¿De veras? Pensé que había sido la chamarra," ella comentó con desdén.

"¡Quizás las pueda usar las dos al mismo tiempo!" declaró él con una expresión infantil en su rostro. "¿Qué crees?"

"¡Buenas noches, Padre Gabriel!" le dijo ella, sonriendo al agarrar la perilla de la puerta.

Era el final de septiembre, el primero de los seis meses que el Diablo había recibido. Los dos amantes estaban disfrutando volverse a enamorar, sin darse cuenta que el alma de Gabriel estaba en juego. Después de todo ¿Qué tenía aquello de malo? Eran perfectos uno para el otro, y no estaban lastimando a nadie con su romance. Aún pretendían que no era ningún "romance," solo una "amistad muy cercana" de tiempo atrás.

El sucio remolinillo corrió a través del jardín de enfrente y desapareció atrás del Curimóvil cuando el auto daba vuelta en la esquina.

"¿Qué es ese olor tan feo?" preguntó Theresa a Magda al entrar a la casa.

Magda cerró la puerta detrás de ellas diciendo, "No sé, pero viene de allá afuera. ¡Huele como a huevos podridos, uggh!"

Capítulo V

Aniversario

El Padre Gabriel estaba discutiendo los detalles de una misa para el vigésimo quinto aniversario de bodas con una pareja y sus hijos adultos en la oficina de la rectoría. Ya estaba todo preparado para ese sábado en la tarde. La pareja no quería una misa especial sino solo celebrar con la congregación que atendía la misa a la que ellos iban regularmente.

Gabriel no había tenido ocasión de sentarse y charlar con la familia por un rato. Aquella era su oportunidad para poderlos conocer un poco mejor y aprender algo que pudiera ser útil para mencionar durante la celebración. Tenían dos hijos y dos hijas. El hijo mayor, Peter, y las dos muchachas, Leticia y Patricia estaban presentes en el encuentro. El hijo menor, Paul, era la oveja negra de la familia y no estaba con ellos. Gabriel notó que cuando los padres empezaron a hablar acerca de la situación con Paul, Peter se disculpó y se salió de la oficina para irse a fumar un cigarrillo.

El año anterior, Paul se había robado un dinero del negocio. Tenían una empresa de camiones de transporte que era administrado por Peter, quien había adquirido un título en administración de empresas con ese propósito. Paul se hizo adicto a las drogas, empezó a juntarse con malas compañías, llenó varias tarjetas de crédito hasta el tope, se llevó uno de los camiones y lo vendió, luego huyó a California y perdió contacto con la familia.

Los papás estaban muy preocupados por que se encontrara en problemas o quizás estuviera muerto. Don Santiago Córdoba, el padre, tenía diabetes, y Peter le echaba la culpa a Paul, diciendo que había sido por el tremendo choque y disgusto que sufrió cuando oyó acerca de las actividades de Paul antes de huir. La madre, Doña Angelita, decía que le rezaba a la Virgen por que cuidara a su hijo, para que aún estuviera vivo y pudiera regresar.

Las hermanas estaban de lado del hermano mayor y también habían echado fuera de la familia a su hermano más chico. Para ellos era como si su hermano hubiera muerto cuando se fue. Ese problema le preocupó al Padre Gabriel quien lo vio como un cáncer en la familia Córdoba.

Sor Theresa tomó la responsabilidad de proveer la música para la misa de aniversario y organizó al coro de niños de la escuela. La familia insistió que el sacerdote y la hermana religiosa atendieran la recepción en el salón de la parroquia; ellos aceptaron atender el evento social para aprovechar la ocasión y estar juntitos otra vez. Cuando los Córdoba dejaron la oficina, Gabriel llamó a su amigo, el Detective Pablo Hernández del Departamento de Policía, y le rogó que investigara el paradero de Paul Córdoba.

"¿Ha cometido él algún crimen aquí?" inquirió el detective antes de aceptar la petición.

"Sí. Ha estado usando cocaína con sus amigos. Llenó las tarjetas de crédito del negocio de su familia, y también se robó un camión-tractor grande y dinero antes de huir a California," le explicó el cura al oficial.

"Bien, parece que la familia no le hizo cargos. No hay caso pendiente ni reporte de esos robos. Veo que fue arrestado por posesión de substancias ilegales, pero los cargos fueron descartados. Quizás tuvo un buen abogado. Está limpio aquí. Voy a tratar un reviso de sus archivos a nivel nacional y lo buscaré a través del Internet. ¿Por qué lo quiere encontrar, Padre G?"

"Sus padres van a celebrar su veinticinco aniversario de bodas este sábado, y han perdido todo contacto con él. Deseo hablar con el muchacho y tratar de hacerlo que atienda la celebración, tal vez, alisar un poco sus diferencias y hacer la paz entre ellos."

"¡Vamos, Padre! ¿Qué le hace pensar que un tipo como ese le va a hacer caso a usted?"

"No lo sabremos hasta que no hable con él. Ahí es donde tú me puedes ser muy útil. Solo dime en dónde lo puedo encontrar, ya que eres tan bueno para encontrar gentes. Probablemente esté en Los Ángeles."

"Está bueno, Padre Gabriel. Lo haré por usted ya que le debo una."

Pablo hablaba de una vez cuando trabajaba en patrulla y el sacerdote lo ayudó en una lucha con tres adictos a oler pintura aerosol. Uno de ellos agarró a Pablo por detrás, otro le empezó a pegar y el tercero le quitó la pistola. El clérigo los agarró a los dos del cuello antes que pudieran usar el arma contra el policía, les chocó las cabezas, y los derribó. Pablo trabó al que lo estaba deteniendo y le cayó encima sofocándolo con el impacto. Entonces el policía esposó al asaltante y pidió ayuda de otros colegas para asistirlo a llevarse a los tres prisioneros. Pablo había quedado muy agradecido con el presbítero por haberle salvado la vida esa tarde.

"Hazlo por ser mi amigo y te interesa hacer el bien; no me debes."

"¡Está bien, mi Amigo! Lo haré por usted y también porque me interesa hacer el bien!" dijo el detective.

"¡Así se habla, Pablito! Espero oír de ti muy pronto," exclamó el sacerdote y colgó el auricular, dándole gracias a Dios en silencio por la ayuda que el viejo amigo le podría brindar.

Como una hora más tarde el Detective Hernández llamó al Padre Gabriel de nuevo con la información. Los rumores eran acertados. Paul Córdoba estaba en la cárcel del Condado de Los Ángeles, por prostitución. Ya tenía una ficha como criminal en California acumulada apenas durante ese año anterior. Ese último era ya su cuarto arresto en ese estado.

"No se ve como alguien en quien valga la pena gastar su tiempo, Padre G."

"Pablito, tienes prejuicios en contra de los criminales. Debes aprender a darle a la gente una segunda oportunidad. Ellos aún son hijos de Dios."

"Usted perdónelos y deles una segunda oportunidad. Yo los perdonaré pero aún los voy a tener que poner en la cárcel para darles chanza que recapaciten sobre el mal que hicieron," replicó Pablo.

"¡Bueno! Creo que no durarías mucho en tu trabajo si perdonaras a todos los criminales y los dejaras ir todas las veces. ¿Eh?"

"Es cierto eso, pero lo voy a tener que dejar ir a usted. Tengo que tomar una declaración de un testigo que acaba de llegar. Hablaremos más tarde."

"Gracias, mi Amigo. Que el Señor te bendiga y te proteja todos los días de tu vida."

Tan pronto como colgó, Gabriel pensó cómo ponerse en contacto con Paul Córdoba en la cárcel del Condado de Los Ángeles. No había modo que pudiera cruzar el país y traerlo de vuelta para el sábado. Necesitaría enviar a un mensajero que lo representara. Se acordó del Padre Raphael Sanguedulce, uno de los "tres arcángeles" de sus días en el seminario, quien estaba trabajando con las pandillas de Los Ángeles. Era el hombre perfecto para la misión. Gabriel sacó su archivo de números de teléfono y buscó el de la oficina de su viejo amigo en L.A. para llamarlo de inmediato.

LOS ÁNGELES, CALIFORNIA

El Padre Raphael se estaba yendo de la oficina cuando la secretaria de la iglesia lo llamó porque tenía una llamada importante.

"¿Quién es? Ya voy tarde a una presentación que tengo que dar en la Escuela Saint Anthony. Tome su número y dígales que les llamaré esta tarde."

Se volvió rumbo a la puerta de nuevo como que ya había decidido no tomar la llamada, pero se quedó paralizado cuando oyó que era un tal Padre Gabriel de San Antonio, Texas, y que era muy urgente. Giró sobre sus talones y se metió en su oficina con una sonrisa en su rostro, olvidándose de la presentación para la cual ya iba tarde.

"¡Gabriel, viejo! No había oído de ti en..." Raphael empezó a decir.

"¡Tres años, tres meses, y tres días, Ralph!"

"Yo creí... ¡Oh, olvídalo! ¡Es bueno oír tu voz! ¿Qué te traes ahora?"

"Necesito tu ayuda."

"¡Sí, como siempre! Necesitas ayuda. Dios no escucha tus súplicas; entonces vienes conmigo. ¿Verdad?"

"Algo así. Necesito mandarte a la cárcel."

"¡Ey! ¿Qué hice? ¡El último pleito que tuvimos lo gané limpiamente!"

"Si me acuerdo bien, mi Amigo, tú fuiste el que acabó en la lona la última vez que nos subimos al ring," el cura en San Antonio le recordó, "No, en serio, necesito que visites a un joven en la cárcel y hables con él por mí."

El Padre Gabriel le explicó la situación con la familia y lo que necesitaba saber del muchacho en la cárcel. Raphael entendió perfectamente lo que su hermano espiritual estaba tratando de hacer y le prometió que se iba a hacer cargo del asunto esa misma tarde. Gabriel le relató a su viejo amigo un chiste que le acababa de oír a un camarada.

"Cuatro madres católicas bebían tecito y discutían qué importantes sus hijos se habían convertido. La primera les dijo a sus amigas, 'Mi hijo es un sacerdote, cuando entra a un cuarto, todo mundo lo llama Padre.' La segunda replicó, 'Bien, pues mi hijo es obispo. Cuando entra a un cuarto, la gente le dice, su Excelencia.' La tercera dice muy presumida, 'No es por ponerlas abajo, pero mi hijo es cardenal, cuando entra a un cuarto la gente dice, su Eminencia.' La cuarta tomaba su tecito en silencio, oyéndolas. Las primeras tres se le quedaron viendo y le dijeron, 'Bueno, ¿y el tuyo?' Ella les contestó muy tranquila, mi hijo es un musculoso bailarín de Chippendales de 1.95, cuando entra al cuarto la gente dice, ¡Dios mío!'"

"Creo que sacaron ese chiste cuando alguien me vio en mi trajecito de baño," dijo Raphael, riéndose.

El presbítero en Los Ángeles entonces volteó a ver su reloj y dejó de reírse. La conferencia que se suponía debía atender iba a empezar en diez minutos, y él estaba por lo menos a treinta minutos de distancia.

"¡Dios mío, no la voy a hacer a esa conferencia en la escuela de Saint Anthony! Me tengo que ir, pero te llamo de regreso a la noche con los resultados de mi entrevista con Paul."

"Ralph, no vayas a la conferencia; ha sido cancelada. Vete a la cárcel mejor."

El cura en California se quedó paralizado antes de colgar el teléfono aunque ya estaba parado y listo para correr a su auto.

"¿Qué quieres decir con que fue cancelada? ¿Cómo sabes eso?"

"¿Era la preparatoria de Saint Anthony a donde ibas?"

"Sí."

"Confía en mí. Ve a la cárcel y olvida la conferencia. Si no me lo crees, nada más prende la televisión y ponla en las noticias. ¡Ciao, Bambino!"

Raphael estaba intrigado, pensando si Gabriel estaría bromeando. Encendió su televisor en la oficina y cambió los canales hasta que encontró las noticias locales. ¡Era verdad! Hubo un incendio en la cafetería de la escuela y todas las actividades habían sido canceladas. Los bomberos aún estaban tratando de apagar la lumbre que había empezado en la cocina. Todos los estudiantes fueron enviados a casa. Nadie había salido lastimado.

"¿Cómo lo supo?"

Mientras tanto en Texas, Gabriel apagaba su televisor. Su teléfono timbró en ese momento, y él lo levantó.

"Estabas viendo las noticias... ¿No es así?" preguntó Raphael.

"Debí dejar que te fueras echo la cochinilla a esa conferencia, pero no quería que te pasara nada antes que cumplieras con la misión que te he asignado. ¡Por supuesto que estaba viendo las noticias del incendio! ¿Qué creías, que el Señor me había mandado a un ángel para decírmelo?"

"¡Tú...! Tú me dejaste picado por un momento. Me acuerdo como tenías aquellas visiones antes y siempre salían ciertas."

"Esto es tecnología moderna, no clarividencia. Ahora márchate, y que Dios te guíe por el camino correcto, con menos congestionamientos."

Gabriel y Raphael se rieron, colgaron sus teléfonos y movieron la cabeza al mismo tiempo recordándose uno al otro. Raphael era un nativo de Philadelphia, un par de años mayor que Gabriel, y el más viejo de los tres arcángeles. Los tres eran de la misma talla, uno ochenta y tres de alto por noventa kilos de peso. Ralph tenía cabello castaño y ojos azules; su principal característica era su grueso bigote.

Su ministerio era con adolescentes y adultos jóvenes. Raphael había estado en la cárcel muchas veces, visitando a su rebaño de jóvenes perdidos. Había desarrollado contactos en el sistema judicial y también era conocido por los oficiales en las áreas llenas de pandillas. Conoció muchos detectives investigando casos envolviendo a la gente que él frecuentaba.

Sus habilidades pugilísticas le habían sido útiles en su ministerio. Era respetado como un hombre en el cual podían confiar ambos lados.

Su capacidad de oír confesiones lo había puesto en posición complicada con las autoridades muchas veces; sin embargo, cuando le era posible, él trataba de convencer a los criminales a rendirse y entregarse por sí mismos a la ley. Su costumbre era decirle al penitente que aquello era una señal de los cielos, que Dios los llamaba para que se arrepintieran y cambiaran, para ponerle fin a su vida de crímenes y volverse a Él, por ellos y sus familias. Eso funcionaba la mayor parte del tiempo, pero él no los presionaba cuando los criminales se rehusaban a cambiar.

El sacerdote bigotón se encontró con Paul Córdoba en el área de visita. El muchacho de diecinueve años se le quedó viendo al presbítero. Estaba perplejo porque no había pedido hablar con ningún clérigo, y nunca antes había visto a aquel cura en su vida.

"Paul, soy el Padre Raphael Sanguedulce. Tengo noticias de tu familia."

El sacerdote estiró su mano, por la rendija debajo del vidrio dividiendo el área en la celda, para tocar la del joven. Estaba fría comparada con la suya.

"¿Usted conoce a mi familia?"

Paul se sentó y abrió los ojos muy grandes, interesado.

"No, no personalmente. Soy un mensajero del Padre Gabriel de San Antonio."

"¡Ah, el Padre G!"

Paul se sonrió. El joven había oído hablar del cura en su ciudad a pesar que él nunca fue a su iglesia.

"Sí. El Padre G me pidió que viniera a hablar contigo. Tus papás van a celebrar su 25 aniversario de bodas en su iglesia este sábado que viene. Le gustaría que atendieras la ceremonia."

"¡Sí como no, eso estaría muy bien! ¿Cómo demonios voy a ir si estoy encerrado aquí?" Paul le gritó, "Además, mi familia no me quiere cerca de ellos. Hice algunas cosas muy estúpidas. No los culpo por no querer verme. ¿Sabe qué? Mi hermano sabe que estoy aquí, pero no me quiere ayudar en absoluto. No aceptan mis llamadas tampoco. Les hice la vida difícil..." la voz de Paul se convirtió en un triste susurro.

"Te ves como que has pasado por tiempos difíciles tú también, Hijo."

"Bueno, creo que ya toqué fondo, Padre Raphael. A veces siento ganas de regresar a casa y decirle a mi padre que me acepte como empleado, lavando los camiones, o barriendo la oficina. ¡Lo que sea! Aquí, mis días están contados. Déjeme decirle. Maté a uno... en defensa propia, el mes pasado. Su familia es de pandilla y venden drogas; me quieren matar. Oí que ofrecieron dinero para que alguien lo hiciera aquí adentro. No estoy seguro ni en la cárcel. Mi abogado dijo que iba a tratar de conseguirme libertad condicional por todos los cargos que tengo pendientes, pero estoy seguro que en cuanto salga a la calle, esos tipos me van a andar buscando."

Raphael estudió las expresiones faciales de Paul; parecía sincero y se veía muy atemorizado. El cura se sintió conmovido por el joven y pensó en ayudarlo.

"Puede que yo sea capaz de ayudarte a que regreses a casa, pero debes cooperar conmigo, ser bien honesto y no decepcionarme."

Los ojos de Paul se agrandaron, llenos de esperanza, y le prometió al ministro que haría lo que fuera necesario para regresar a su familia. Tuvieron una conversación muy larga. Raphael escuchó su triste historia y luego lo absolvió de sus pecados, animándolo a empezar de nuevo.

El presbítero fue a ver a un juez amigo de él y arregló para que el joven fuera puesto en libertad y transferido al Departamento de Supervisión Adulta en el Condado de Bexar. Raphael llamó a Gabriel esa noche con las buenas noticias. Le iba a conseguir un boleto de autobús a Paul el día siguiente para ponerlo en camino en cuanto lo dejaran salir de la cárcel. El joven sería capaz de llegar a la ciudad el sábado para la celebración.

SAN ANTONIO, TEXAS

El Padre Gabriel acabó su oración vespertina y se salió afuera a disfrutar de la tibia noche y a estar en la presencia de Dios bajo el cielo estrellado.

El sonido de sirenas de policía y luces de emergencia reflejadas por el vecindario perturbaron la paz del momento; entonces un helicóptero de la policía pasó volando sobre la iglesia y los terrenos de la escuela con su lámpara rastreadora. Por el número de unidades de patrulla envueltas, el sacerdote se imaginó que algo muy serio debía haber pasado.

Un equipo canino (K-9) se apareció de repente con el feroz animal ladrando como si se quisiera comer vivo al pastor de la parroquia quien se sobresaltó un poco. El oficial sostuvo al animal y le preguntó al ministro si había visto a alguien corriendo por ahí.

"No, en absoluto. He estado aquí por diez minutos más o menos, Oficial."

"Estamos buscando a un sospechoso en un asalto a mano armada; trae una pistola y es muy peligroso."

"Me aseguraré que todos los edificios estén atrancados con llave."

Gabriel dejó de hablar cuando el radio del policía empezó a relatar información de un posible sospechoso que estaba siendo perseguido a pie por otros oficiales como a tres cuadras de ahí.

"Discúlpeme, Padre, tenemos que ir allá."

El can y su manejador se arrancaron rumbo al arroyo y dejaron al sacerdote solo de nuevo.

"Espero que lo atrapen," se dijo a sí mismo el pastor, al ir a revisar los edificios.

Para su sorpresa, la puerta de un lado de la iglesia estaba desatrancada. La abrió y se asomó. No vio ningún movimiento en el interior de la iglesia ni oyó ningún ruido, pero sintió la presencia de alguien ahí adentro.

Se pasó al interior y cerró la puerta detrás de él. El leve sonido de algo pequeño cayendo al piso lo alertó. Caminó rumbo al confesionario y abrió la puerta de un lado.

Había un hombre ahí adentro a punto de inyectarse heroína en la vena de su brazo. El sonido que el cura había oído era la cubierta de plástico de la aguja de la jeringa, la cual estaba tirada entre los pies del hombre. El intruso, un hispano en sus treintas, agarró la pistola que tenía a un lado.

"Termina lo que estabas haciendo, Hijo mío. No necesitas el arma; yo no represento ningún peligro para ti. La policía ya se fue. Me voy a sentar aquí a esperar a que acabes. Tenemos tiempo," Gabriel le dijo con calma.

El sacerdote se metió al viejo confesionario como si fuera a oír una confesión. El fugitivo traía manchas frescas de sangre en los pantalones. Optó por creer que el presbítero no lo iba a entregar a las autoridades y se inyectó la droga en su vena. Gabriel pensó que era mejor dejarlo que se calmara inyectándose porque se miraba como un hombre desesperado.

El Padre se sentó orando en silencio, preguntándose qué hacer con él. La droga lo iba a relajar lo suficiente para quedarse y platicar. El cura se sintió inspirado y empezó a cantar una canción acerca de traerle a Dios todo lo que tenemos mientras le pedimos todo lo que necesitamos. Los versos parecían dirigidos al criminal que escuchaba muy atento la canción mientras la heroína lo empezaba a calmar.

El drogadicto, fugitivo de la justicia, simplemente se quedó sentado ahí, oyendo las palabras de la canción desde su lado del confesionario.

Había sido católico practicante de su fe hasta los veinte años cuando se metió a la Naval de Estados Unidos. Comenzó a usar marihuana ahí. Lo dieron de baja con descarga general después que se metió en problemas por no seguir órdenes. Cuando regresó a Texas, empezó a divertirse con los tecatos del vecindario quienes lo introdujeron a la heroína. Ya había estado en la prisión un par de veces por hurto y robo con allanamiento de morada. Su matrimonio había fracasado; tenía dos pequeñas quienes vivían con la madre. Él y su esposa se separaron dos años atrás.

"Padre quiero confesarme. ¿Podría oír mi confesión?"

"¡Sí! Sabía que lo harías. ¿Puedes verlo? Dios te trajo aquí por un motivo. Podrías haberte escondido abajo del puente o en la casa de alguien, pero viniste a la casa de tu Padre. Él te trajo hasta aquí porque quiere que le pongas fin a esa vida miserable que estás viviendo ahora, y que empieces una vida nueva desde este momento. Esta es tu oportunidad, Hijo mío, de dar vuelta a tu vida y regresar a Dios. ¡Empezar de nuevo, en limpio!"

El párroco escuchó su confesión y le dio la absolución de sus pecados. Lo convenció que le diera la pistola y que hablara con la policía. Le dijo que no tuviera miedo de ir a la cárcel a pagar por sus crímenes, que aprovechara el tiempo que iba a estar encerrado para ponerse en paz con Dios y consigo mismo, para liberarse de la drogadicción y alejarse de su estilo de vida.

Lo retó a actuar como hombre de verdad y a encarar las consecuencias de sus acciones, pero le aseguró que Dios estaría con él a cada paso del camino hasta el final de sus días. El hombre, Eleazar Gutiérrez, le dio las gracias al sacerdote y le prometió que lo iba a venir a visitar cuando saliera, para mostrarle que había cambiado con el favor de Dios.

El cura llevó a Eleazar a su casa y llamó a la policía. Un minuto después, un par de patrullas arribaban. Los oficiales brincaron pistola en mano, listos para atrapar al criminal. El sacerdote les pidió que guardaran sus armas porque Eleazar se iba a ir con ellos pacíficamente. Gabriel llevó del brazo al hombre hasta el primer carro de policía y se lo entregó al oficial. Les dio a los policías la pistola que Eleazar había andado portando.

"No sé como le hace, Padre G, ¡pero muchas gracias por su ayuda!" dijo el agente de policía, mirando al peligroso criminal entrando a la patrulla.

Ellos pensaron que iban a tener que pelear con Eleazar para capturarlo. El Padre Gabriel les dio su bendición mientras las dos patrullas se alejaban.

Se fue luego a dormir, satisfecho.

La Escuela de la Santísima Trinidad estaba celebrando su día de campo anual ese viernes. Los estudiantes de la Hermana Theresa entretuvieron a la audiencia con una pequeña obra teatral que incluía actuación, bailable, y cantos. Sor Magda probó la mayoría de las comidas que se ofrecían en el evento. El Padre G jugó un partidito de fútbol con los muchachitos del nivel secundario. Las gentes disfrutaron del bingo y juegos infantiles.

Gabriel y Theresa juntaron sus piernas en un costal para entrar en una carrera de tres piernas; perdieron pues se cayeron antes de llegar a la meta.

La Hermana Magda casi se ahogó con un pedazo de pastel, viendo a Theresa rodar en el pasto en los brazos del párroco después que se cayeron. Se echó un trago de refresco y se calmó al ver que fue un accidente.

Todos se estaban riendo de la caída de los dos religiosos. Ya que Magda no había visto más que lo último del incidente, se puso sospechosa de lo que estaba sucediendo. La madre superiora se llevó a Theresa a un lado.

"Sor Theresa, deberíamos ser más prudentes. Sé que eres mujer sociable y amistosa, pero se espera que nos comportemos más... apropiadamente."

"No pienso que estoy actuando inapropiadamente, Madre. ¿Qué es lo que he hecho que usted piensa que no está bien?"

"Bueno, no es una sola cosa. Es la impresión general que estás causando. Mírate nomás en esos pantalones cortos, y corriendo como una chiquilla. Además me parece que te le estás acercando demasiado al Padre Gabriel. Sabes como la gente tiende a chismear con los más pequeños detalles," le aconsejó Magda, tomándola del brazo y alejándose de la gente.

"Le agradezco su interés, Madre, pero le garantizo que no está ocurriendo nada inapropiado. La gente siempre anda buscando algo para chismear."

"No les demos motivo para que lo hagan, Sor Theresa," dijo la Madre Superior, haciéndole una señal cortante con la mano como reproche.

La superior dio por terminada su conversación y se volvió para saludar a unas viejitas que estaban llegando al día de campo. Theresa se miró los pantaloncillos y luego volteó a ver al Padre Gabriel correteando tras unos chiquillos en el jardín de juegos.

"Quizás Magda tiene razón. Algunas gentes podrían mal entender mi comportamiento, pero estoy segura que no estamos haciendo nada malo... ¿O sí?" Theresa murmuró para sí misma.

Ella notó que tres maestras estaban cuchicheando entre ellas y mirando al pastor, el cual pescó a un niñito y, para delicia del chiquillo, lo levantó muy alto en el aire. Las maestras luego vieron a Theresa pero se hicieron las disimuladas cuando notaron que ella las estaba observando.

Theresa decidió irse a cambiar a su ropa de religiosa, prometiéndose mantener su distancia entre ella y Gabriel, para evitar escándalo.

Cuando regresó se encontró al pastor contando un chiste a las maestras.

"Una viejita leía su Biblia en un avión. El hombre sentado junto a ella decidió interrogarla ya que él era un ateo. '¿Usted cree todo lo que está escrito en ese libro?' le preguntó con una sonrisita burlona. 'Sí, Señor. Yo lo creo porque es la palabra de Dios,' ella le contestó sin pensarlo dos veces. '¿Qué tal la historia esa de Jonás y el pescadote? ¿Cree que estuvo adentro de un pescado por tres días y tres noches?' 'Sí, Señor. La Biblia lo dice así, y yo lo creo,' fue su rápida respuesta. 'Bueno. ¿Qué cree que haya él comido y bebido mientras estaba ahí? ¿Cómo podía respirar?' El tipo la arrinconó con duras preguntas. 'Esas son buenas preguntas. Le voy a preguntar a Jonás cuando lo encuentre en el cielo,' ella le respondió y regresó a su lectura. '¿Qué tal si Jonás no se fue al cielo?' le preguntó el hombre aún con su sonrisita. Sin quitarle los ojos de encima a su Biblia, la viejecita le contestó, '¡Entonces usted mismo se lo podrá preguntar!'"

Las viejitas, las maestras, y las hermanas se rieron con el chistecito.

Theresa no fue con los estudiantes al juego de béisbol esa tarde-noche para evitar pasar mucho tiempo cerca del director. El juego fue muy bueno; el equipo local ganó esa noche. Los chicos se divirtieron.

La decisión de la hermana religiosa de mantenerse alejada de su querido amigo iba a ser solo un atentado muy débil e inútil. Se estaba sintiendo más apasionada cada día; se dio cuenta que lo necesitaba casi tanto como necesitaba el aire para respirar.

El sábado en la tarde, el autobús llegó a San Antonio con Paul Córdoba. Venía lleno de esperanza y ya traía preparado un pequeño discurso que había compuesto por el camino de regreso. Le iba a hablar a su familia y pedirles perdón. Les rogaría que lo tomaran aunque fuera como empleado y le permitieran pagar por todo. Iba a mantenerse limpio de las drogas y trabajaría muy duro para volver a ganarse su confianza.

Con sus últimas monedas, Paul llamó a su casa. Peter levantó el teléfono.

"Hola Peter, soy yo, Paul... Estoy de nuevo en San Antón... Necesito hablar con todos ustedes."

"¡Espérate! No queremos oír una sola palabra de ti. Has causado mucho dolor a esta familia. Es muy mal momento para que te presentes. Si te queda algo de decencia, no te vayas a parar por la casa. Tú ya sabes que no eres bienvenido nunca más. Te llevaste tu parte y la despilfarraste en drogas y mujerzuelas. No te queda ya nada por aquí. Considera que ya no eres miembro de esta familia. Si te veo por aquí, yo mismo me encargaré de que te zambutan de nuevo a la cárcel."

Peter, muy enfurecido, colgó el teléfono. Volteó a ver a su alrededor, esperando que sus padres no lo hubieran oído hablar. Ellos ya estaban afuera, metiéndose al carro para ir a la iglesia. Encendió un cigarrillo y se dirigió a su propia camioneta. Su prometida estaba ahí esperándolo.

"¿Qué pasó? Te vez muy alterado, Cariñito," ella le preguntó.

"¡No es nada!" Peter le gritó en respuesta a la chica.

Él no le quería decir de la llamada, pero ella sabía que tenía algo que ver con su hermano. Siempre se ponía así con solo hablar acerca de Paul. La camioneta siguió al carro de los papás a la iglesia para la celebración. La muchacha no le preguntó nada más a Peter.

Paul se sentó en la estación, frustrado. ¿Por qué lo tenía que tratar su hermano así? Necesitaba hablar con sus padres y oírlo de ellos mismos.

Se buscó en los bolsillos y no encontró más dinero. Le pidió a una dama si traía algo de cambio que le pudiera dar para hacer una llamada; ella lo miró con disgusto e ignoró su petición. La mujer se fue acercando a un policía en la estación de autobuses; le empezó a hablar al oficial y le apuntó a Paul. El joven decidió irse de ahí antes que lo arrestaran por pedir limosna. Salió corriendo y volteó para atrás desde ya una cuadra. El oficial salió del edificio, buscándolo; volteó para los dos lados, pero no vio a Paul, quien presuroso se metió por un callejón.

Se sentía muy bien, caminando libre, y decidió que iba a irse a casa caminando a encarar a su familia en lugar de llamarlos. Iba a ser una caminata larga, pero había venido de muy lejos para dejar que su hermano lo desanimara. Se ató la mochila sobre los hombros y se encaminó a casa a paso rápido. ¡Se sentía muy bien estar de regreso en su ciudad natal!

Paul llegó y no encontró a nadie en la casa. Se acordó que estaban celebrando su aniversario en la iglesia de la Santísima Trinidad, como a diez cuadras de la casa. Empezó a caminar más rápido a pesar que estaba cansado después de su caminata de una hora desde el centro.

Cuando llegó a la iglesia, estaba ya cerrada. Eran las 6:30; la misa había sido a las 5:00 según el anuncio afuera del templo. Paul no sabía que la recepción era en el salón, a la vuelta de la esquina. Se sentó en las gradas de la iglesia, cansado y frustrado. Levantó los ojos al cielo, pidiendo ayuda.

"¿Te puedo ayudar, Joven?" un tipo alto que le recordó a Jesús, con pelo corto, le preguntó a Paul.

"¿Sabe usted en dónde es la recepción del aniversario de bodas de la familia Córdoba?"

"¡Seguro! Tú has de ser Paul."

El Padre Gabriel le ofreció su mano para que se levantara del escalón.

"Sí. Soy Paul Córdoba ¿Cómo lo supo? ¿Quién es usted?"

"Tu mamá me enseñó tu foto. Te ves algo diferente ahora. Yo soy el Padre Gabriel Infante, el que te mandó al Padre Raphael en Los Ángeles."

"¡Oh, gracias, Padre G! Ya había oído hablar de usted antes. Realmente aprecio que me haya mandado a ese sacerdote tan chido. Él fue quien hizo posible que pudiera venir."

Paul saludó de mano al párroco y caminó con él rumbo al salón.

"¿Sabe tu familia que ya estás en San Antonio?"

"Bueno, pues les llamé y le dije a mi hermano, Peter, pero él me advirtió que no viniera o él se iba a asegurar que me echaran a la cárcel."

Gabriel se paró y pensó por un momento, sobándose la recortada barba y mirándose preocupado. Se le quedó viendo a Paul directamente a los ojos.

"¿Qué quieres hacer, Paul?"

"He venido a pedirle a mis padres que me perdonen, aún si no me perdonan. Tengo que hablar con ellos y decirles que me arrepiento por todas las cosas que les hice pasar. Ya sé que mi hermano y mis hermanas no me perdonarán, pero tengo que hablar con mi papá y mi mamá."

El sacerdote percibió un corazón contrito y sincero, así que decidió que valía la pena intentar ayudarlo.

"¡Yo te ayudaré! Acompáñame."

El Señor y la Señora Córdoba estaban en la entrada, hablando con unos parientes e invitándolos a pasar. Paul los vio y corrió hacia sus padres. El Padre G observó la escena de cerca. Antes que Paul pudiera abrazar a su madre, Peter lo jaló de la camisa para alejarlo de ellos. Comenzaron a forcejear frente a sus padres quienes trataron de separarlos, y se formó una alegata tremenda. Leticia y Patricia salieron a apoyar a Peter regañando a Paul. Los padres estaban muy angustiados con la escena.

El Padre Gabriel se les acercó e intervino para poner fin al argumento.

"¡Por favor, por favor, párenle de tonterías, todos ustedes!"

Todos se quedaron parados en silencio, escuchando al pastor.

"¡Ya oí suficientes riñas! Vengan todos conmigo a la oficina. Tengo algo que decirles."

El cura tomó a Paul del brazo y los guió a todos a una pequeña oficina cerca de la entrada del salón de fiestas. Cerró la puerta después que entraron todos y les pidió que se sentaran.

Doña Angelita estaba llorando. Don Santiago estaba también conteniendo lágrimas, sonándose la nariz. Peter, Leticia, y Patricia estaban enfurecidos y con los labios apretados. Paul tenía los ojos llorosos, muy contrito.

"Pueden pensar que este problema es demasiado para sobrepasarlo, que consideren que su hermano es el peor hombre en la faz de la tierra, y que sería mejor si se hubiera quedado lejos evitándoles esta amargura. Puede que se pregunten cómo vino a pasar esto. Bien, déjenme decirles que fui yo quien lo trajo a encararlos a ustedes y a sus corazones de piedra."

"Padre, no puedo creer que usted nos haría algo así," protestó Peter, dando un paso adelante sin querer creer lo que había oído.

"¡Silencio! Siéntate y escúchame, Peter," dijo con tal convicción que el joven tuvo que obedecerle sin decir palabra.

El pastor bajó una Biblia de un librerito en la pared y rápidamente localizó un pasaje del Evangelio de San Lucas que le quería leer a todo el clan de los Córdoba.

"Un hombre tenía dos hijos; y el menor de ellos dijo al padre: 'Padre, dame la parte de la hacienda que me corresponde.' Y él les repartió la hacienda. Pocos días después el hijo menor lo reunió todo y se marchó a un país lejano donde malgastó su hacienda viviendo como un libertino."

El místico pausó y volteó a ver a Paul quien bajó la cabeza. Luego vio a Peter que estaba cruzado de brazos y con los labios muy apretados.

"Cuando hubo gastado todo, sobrevino un hambre extrema en aquel país, y comenzó a pasar necesidad. Entonces, fue y se ajustó con uno de los ciudadanos de aquel país, que le envió a sus fincas a apacentar puercos. Y deseaba llenar su vientre con las algarrobas que comían los puercos, pero nadie se las daba. Y entrando en sí mismo, dijo: '¡Cuántos jornaleros de mi padre tienen pan en abundancia, mientras que yo aquí me muero de hambre! Me levantaré, iré a mi padre y le diré: Padre, pequé contra el cielo y ante ti. Ya no merezco ser llamado hijo tuyo, trátame como a uno de tus jornaleros.' Y, levantándose, partió hacia su padre. Estando él todavía lejos, le vio su padre y, conmovido, corrió, se echó a su cuello y le besó efusivamente. El hijo le dijo: 'Padre, pequé contra el cielo y ante ti; ya no merezco ser llamado hijo tuyo.' Pero el padre dijo a sus siervos: 'Traed aprisa el mejor vestido y vestidle, ponedle un anillo en su mano y unas sandalias en los pies. Traed el novillo cebado, matadlo, y comamos y celebremos una fiesta, porque este hijo mío estaba muerto y ha vuelto a la vida; estaba perdido y ha sido hallado.' Y comenzaron la fiesta. Su hijo mayor estaba en el campo y, al volver, cuando se acercó a la casa, oyó la música y las danzas; y llamando a uno de los criados, le preguntó qué era aquello. Él le dijo: 'Ha vuelto tu hermano y tu padre ha matado el novillo cebado, porque le ha recobrado sano.' Él se irritó y no quería entrar. Salió su padre, y le suplicaba. Pero él replicó a su padre: 'Hace tantos años que te sirvo, y jamás dejé de cumplir una orden tuya, pero nunca me has dado un cabrito para tener una fiesta con mis amigos; y ¡ahora que ha venido ese hijo tuyo, que ha devorado tu hacienda con prostitutas, has matado para él el novillo cebado!' Pero él le dijo: 'Hijo, tú siempre estás conmigo, y todo lo mío es tuyo; pero convenía celebrar una fiesta y alegrarse, porque este hermano tuyo estaba muerto, y ha vuelto a la vida; estaba perdido, y ha sido hallado.'" (Lucas 15:11-32)

Se quedaron sentados en silencio escuchando toda la historia; el Padre Gabriel se volvió al hijo menor.

"Ahora, Paul, dile a tus padres, hermanas, y hermano lo que viniste hasta aquí a decirles hoy, Hijo."

Paul cayó de rodillas y comenzó a sollozar. Les pidió a sus padres que lo perdonaran por todo el mal que le había hecho a la familia. Ambos lo levantaron y lo abrazaron; los tres estaban bañados en lágrimas.

El ministro tomó a Paul y lo volteó a encarar a sus hermanas; ellas se rindieron pronto y lo abrazaron también, con el apoyo y ánimo de su mamá y su papá. Al último, el Padre Gabriel paró a Paul frente a Peter.

"Perdóname, Peter. Sé que te lastimé a ti y a la familia. Lo siento mucho."

Peter pasó saliva duramente, mirando a los ojos a su hermano menor. Gabriel le susurró a Peter muy cerca del oído.

"¿Qué haría Jesús, Peter? ¿Qué crees que Él quiere que hagas? ¿Cuántas veces te ha perdonado a ti?"

Poco después, Peter abrazó a su hermano y le dijo, "Yo te perdono, Paul. Bienvenido de vuelta a la familia. Perdóname tú a mí, por ser tan necio."

Todos los miembros de la familia estaban llorando, abrazando a Paul. Al Padre G se le rasaron los ojos y se les unió en el abrazo de grupo.

"Por culpa suya, aquí tiene a toda mi familia llorando," Paul le dijo al cura, riendo y llorando.

"Ya lo sé," dijo Gabriel sonriendo. "Déjenme arreglar la situación. Séquense los ojos y suénense las narices. ¡Tenemos una fiesta que atender! Ya escucho a los mariachis allá afuera. Vamos a darles la cara a los invitados, y déjenme cantarles una canción por su feliz aniversario."

Con ojos rojos y amplias sonrisas, Peter al frente, todos los miembros de la familia Córdoba salieron de la oficina. Paul salió con su papá en un lado y su mamá en el otro. Leticia y Patricia estaban atrás de él, poniéndole una mano cada una en sus hombros.

El Padre Gabriel llamó a los mariachis para pedirles cierta canción mientras que los miembros de la familia tomaban la mesa de honor ante el aplauso de todos los invitados. Gabriel se acercó al micrófono en el estrado con los mariachis atrás de él.

"Queridos hermanos y hermanas, hoy es un día muy especial en la vida de la familia Córdoba. No solamente están Angelita y Santiago celebrando 25 años de bendiciones matrimoniales, sino que también acaban de recibir de regreso al hijo pródigo. Vamos uniéndonos en su regocijo y en darle gracias a Dios, quien les ha concedido estas bendiciones. Quiero dedicarles la siguiente canción a la novia y al novio, desde el fondo de mi corazón."

Se volvió a los mariachis y agarró prestado un sombrero del más grande. Se lo puso al tiempo que la música llenaba el salón.

Gabriel vio a Theresa en una mesa en el centro del salón. Le cerró un ojo y empezó a cantar una canción acerca del pasar de los años y de cómo van cambiando las cosas.

El poeta y su amada se encuentran lado a lado como dos adolescentes que se miran sin hablar, como la primera vez que se conocieron. La potente voz de Gabriel les hizo cosquillitas en los oídos y corazones a la audiencia.

La pareja estaba sintiendo el significado de la canción dedicado a su amor perdurable, pero Theresa también estaba interpretando la canción como si la estuviera cantando para ella, acerca de su vieja relación siendo removida.

La canción dice que a pesar de que el tiempo ha pasado, su amor no ha sido disminuido por los años. Theresa recordó el baile de gala de la prepa, veinte años atrás, cuando hicieron promesas que no cumplieron. Dejó escapar un suspiro y miró a Gabriel jalando a Angelita para bailar con ella unos cuantos pasos con él antes de cantar el último verso. Le regresó la novia al novio y acabó la canción para el aplauso de toda la concurrencia.

Gabriel dejó que los mariachis siguieran entreteniendo mientras él se iba a sentar con Theresa. Ella le sonrió y le dio la bienvenida. Se sentó y puso su cálida mano encima de la de ella, haciéndola que se le pusiera la piel chinita en el brazo. Sin decir palabra, se quedaron mirándose a los ojos.

Luego vino el brindis. Peter era el escolta de honor y pronunció unas elocuentes palabras. La familia le pidió al Padre G que dijera algo. El ministro los bendijo y les deseó felicidad. Sor Theresa los alabó como un ejemplo de fidelidad y de amor para las nuevas generaciones. Todos bebieron champaña, y luego empezó el baile. Un animador con su sistema de sonido les brindó una buena variedad de música.

En cuanto los novios abrieron el baile, el Padre Gabriel jaló a Sor Theresa para en medio de la pista. Ella se resistió un poquito al principio, pero acabó cediendo y comenzó a bailar una melodía lenta. Las gentes se estaban riendo bajito, viendo al sacerdote y la hermana bailando, pero luego se les unieron en la pista y dejaron de ponerles atención. Las luces fueron reducidas de intensidad para permitir que se formara un ambiente más íntimo.

"Te quiero felicitar por tu último milagro del hijo pródigo," Theresa le susurró cerca del oído a Gabriel.

"Es el trabajo de nuestro Señor; yo solo soy un humilde instrumento," contestó Gabriel en su orejita, excitándola con su cálido aliento.

"Si tienes todo tan bien figurado, dime: ¿Por qué nos juntó el Señor ahora, bajo estas circunstancias?"

"El instante que pensamos tener a Dios figurado, hemos cometido un gran error. ¿Por qué pasan las cosas? Puede que no lleguemos a saber nunca en esta vida. No presumo saber por qué estamos aquí, así. Quiero creer que es un regalo de Dios. Todo amor viene del Eterno; Él quiere que nos amemos los unos a los otros, ¿verdad?"

Theresa asintió con la cabeza, tratando de seguir su discernimiento.

Él continuó, "Muy bien, yo te amo, Theresa... ¡Nunca dejé de amarte! ¿A quién podemos lastimar con amarnos ahora? ¿Quién se puede oponer a nuestro amor? ¿Qué podría estar mal con amarnos?"

La hermana religiosa sintió el rostro y pecho ardiendo. Quizás era el efecto de la champaña, o la sensación de Gabriel sosteniéndola al bailar, o su cálido aliento soplándole en el oído mientras le declaraba su amor. Era en verdad muy lindo escucharlo decir aquellas palabras y confirmar que ella no era la única que se sentía enamorada como una adolescente.

La música se detuvo. Theresa se disculpó y le informó que debía irse. La música comenzó de nuevo con una pieza tejana. Theresa le pidió a Gabriel que no saliera del salón con ella, para evitar los chismes.

Antes de soltarle la mano, Gabriel le preguntó en un susurro, "¿Aún me amas, aunque sea un poquito?"

Ella le apretó la mano y le susurró, "¡Sí!"

Él la dejó partir. Ella tomó su bolsa, le fue a dar las gracias a la familia por haberla invitado y se fue del salón para irse a acostar temprano.

Sintió que iba caminando entre las nubes hasta llegar a su casa y ni siquiera se dio cuenta cómo llegó. Theresa se acostó temprano pero no pudo dormir, pensando en Gabriel. Se levantó, se dio un baño helado para refrescarse, y rezó un rosario antes de regresar a su cama.

Gabriel se quedó en el salón cuando Theresa se fue. No quería que nadie sospechara que era la única mujer a la cual quería como mujer, así que se puso a bailar con tantas de las damas en el salón como pudo, tejano con Doña Angelita, cumbia con Leticia, y salsa con Patricia. Disfrutó de un vals con la vieja Raquelita, rock-and-roll con Dorothy, vaquera con Alice, polka con María Fernanda, y tango con Amparito.

Aún cuando estaba bailando con diferentes damas, la carita de Theresa se le quedó grabada en su mente. Se sentía tan contento como la primera vez que ella le había dicho, veinte años atrás, que lo quería. Él bailó y bailó en secreta celebración de su renovado y apasionado amor.

El sacerdote estaba tan contento que no se fijó en un hombre oscuro, alto, con un bigote y barbita de chivo, bebiendo en el rincón más oscuro y viéndolo bailar. A pesar de la oscuridad, sus ojos se podían ver como dos trocitos de carbón encendido. Pero cuando alguien volteaba a verlo, el miraba hacia abajo, y su sombrero negro le cubría la cara.

Dos mujeres ladinas sentadas del otro lado de la pista, bebiendo y esperando que alguien las sacara a bailar, notaron al misterioso personaje vestido en un elegante traje negrísimo. Se rieron, mirándolo mientras bebían sus margaritas. Entonces se levantaron y comenzaron a cruzar la pista en cuanto había empezado otra canción. Ellas habían decidido invitar al atractivo sujeto a que bailara con una de ellas o con las dos.

La tenebrosa figura las miró acercándose entre los bailadores; se sonrió y se empinó su bebida. Cuando las excitadas mujeres llegaron a su mesa, ¡ya no estaba ahí! Las damas se vieron una a la otra, intrigadas, y luego vieron por todo el salón. No había modo que aquel tipo se hubiera ido sin que lo vieran. Las desilusionadas hembras regresaron a sus sillas, riéndose y culpándose por haber asustado al misterioso tipo y hacer que se esfumara.

El sábado, nueve de octubre, llegó a su fin.

Capítulo VI

Regalo

La noche del domingo 10 al lunes 11 de octubre, Gabriel tuvo un sueño muy extraño. Andaba bailando con Theresa solos, se abrazaron y besaron Se sonrieron y se declararon mutuamente su amor. Enseguida se vieron caminando por el pasillo central de una iglesia rumbo al altar como novios. Él vestía un elegante traje negro de gala pero aún traía su collar romano; ella vestía un hábito religioso todo blanco.

Al momento en que el celebrante los declaró marido y mujer, ¡el altar se encendió! Miraron el altar ardiendo y al celebrante carcajeándose mientras ardía, alcanzado por las llamas. ¡Era Satanás mismo quien los había casado! Una alarma se oyó, y las gentes en la congregación corrieron hacia fuera. El fuego envolvió a los recién casados. La alarma seguía sonando.

El Padre G despertó sudando. Su radio-reloj-despertador timbraba; eran las cuatro a.m. Lo tenía siempre en la estación de música clásica. Pero esa vez seleccionó el timbre sin fijarse la noche anterior cuando lo ajustó.

Gabriel planeaba ir de pesca esa mañana. Otro sacerdote se iba a hacer cargo de dar la misa matutina. Era un día de fiesta para la escuela, el día de Cristóbal Colón. No tenía cita ni asunto de negocios ese día. Gabriel se levantó pensando en su sueño, pero lo descartó como una pesadilla loca. Se puso a recitar su oración matutina y se preparó para su viaje al lago.

El Padre G fue a pescar con un par de adolescentes que estaba tratando de alejar de una pandilla. Uno de los pandillerillos, Martin Davis, se había hecho amigo del sacerdote después de que este rescatara a su hermanito de su departamento en llamas. Shawn Aguilar era el mejor amigo de Martin y también su primo lejano quien vivía en el lado este de la ciudad.

Los tres entusiastas pescadores no habían pescado nada después de dos horas, pero el Padre G les había estado platicando a los dos adolescentes acerca de Jesús y sus apóstoles que eran pescadores. Les relató a los chicos el pasaje donde Jesús se fue de pesca con unos de sus apóstoles y les ayudó a atrapar tantos pescados que las redes ya casi se les reventaban.

"Estaba Jesús a la orilla del Lago Genesaret y la gente se agolpaba sobre Él para oír la Palabra de Dios, cuando vio dos barcas que estaban a la orilla del lago. Los pescadores habían bajado de ellas, y lavaban las redes. Subiendo a una de las barcas, que era de Simón, le rogó que se alejara un poco de tierra; y, sentándose, enseñaba desde la barca a la muchedumbre. Cuando acabó de hablar, dijo a Simón: 'Boga mar

adentro, y echad vuestras redes para pescar.' Simón le respondió: 'Maestro, hemos estado bregando toda la noche y no hemos pescado nada; pero, en tu palabra, echaré las redes.' Y, haciéndolo así, pescaron gran cantidad de peces, de modo que las redes amenazaban romperse. Hicieron señas a los compañeros de la otra barca para que vinieran en su ayuda. Vinieron, pues, y llenaron tanto las dos barcas que casi se hundían." (Lucas 5:1-7)*

Los chamacos le preguntaron al cura si le podría rezar a Dios, así como Jesús, para que les ayudara a atrapar muchos peces a ellos también.

"Se me hace que eso sería hacer trampa," él les dijo. "Vamos a ver si con habilidad y paciencia podemos pescar algo. No estoy tan desesperado."

"¿A poco usted de veras cree que Dios le va dar cualquier cosa que le pida?" inquirió Martin quien no tenía mucha fe en la existencia de Dios.

"¡Cualquier cosa! Si se lo pides con fe verdadera," dijo Gabriel, poniendo su mano en el hombro del jovencito y mirándolo a los ojos.

"Me gustaría conseguir algo de dinero para comprarle a mi mamá un regalo porque ya se viene su cumpleaños," rezó Martin, viendo al cielo.

"¿A poco esperas que te caiga dinero del cielo y te pegue en la cabeza?" Shawn le dijo, burlándose.

"Nuestro Señor tiene diferentes y misteriosas formas de obrar, Shawn. Es un camarada medio chistoso, así como tú. Déjenme contarles de una vez que los cobradores de impuestos del templo le preguntaron a los discípulos de Jesús si su maestro no pagaba impuestos."

Entonces les contó la cita bíblica a los chicos.

"Al llegar a Cafarnaún, los cobradores del impuesto del Templo se acercaron a Pedro y le preguntaron: '¿El Maestro de ustedes no paga el impuesto?' 'Sí, lo paga,' respondió. Cuando Pedro llegó a la casa, Jesús se adelantó a preguntarle: '¿Qué te parece, Simón? ¿De quiénes perciben los impuestos y las tasas los reyes de la tierra, de sus hijos o de los extraños?' Y como Pedro respondió: 'De los extraños', Jesús le dijo: 'Eso quiere decir que los hijos están exentos. Sin embargo, para no escandalizar a esta gente, ve al lago, echa el anzuelo, toma el primer pez que salga y ábrele la boca. Encontrarás en ella una moneda de plata: tómala, y paga por mí y por ti.'" (Mateo 17:24-27)

Los dos chamacos escuchaban al Padre, esperando el chiste de la historia.

"Pedro fue, hizo lo que el Maestro le dijo y pronto sacó un pescadote con una moneda dentro de la boca," concluyó el pastor, sonriendo.

"Es una buena historieta de pescadores, Padre G. ¿Cómo le hizo Jesús para saber que había un pescadote que traía una moneda y además que iba a ser pescado por Pedro?" Martin le preguntó.

El Padre G se encogió de hombros diciéndole, "Eso sí que no lo sé, pero de que pasó, ¡pasó! Jesús es Dios y lo sabe todo.

Burlándose de él por creer lo que el párroco le estaba diciendo, Shawn le dijo a Martin, "Si pescamos algo, deberías examinar la boca del pescado a ver si trae algo de dinero adentro."

"En ese momento, el celular de Martin sonó. Era su mamá. Martin rodó sus ojos, asumiendo que su madre estaba apurada por él, aunque sabía que andaba con el Padre Gabriel y con Shawn en el lago.

"Creo que mi mamá ha oído muchas cosas malas acerca de los sacerdotes abusando de chicos. Probablemente quiere asegurarse que todo está bien."

Martin abrió su celular, pero se le acabó la batería. El chico echó unas maldiciones y trató de volver a encender el telefonito sin éxito.

"Ve y llámala," le sugirió el cura, "Hay un teléfono público por allá, cerca de la tienda de carnadas. ¿Traes feria para hacer la llamada?"

Martin le dijo que sí traía dinero, dejó su caña de pescar y se llevó a Shawn con él para llamar a su madre. El Padre G se quedó ahí, cuidando las tres cañas de pescar en caso que algo mordiera.

Un momento después que los chicos desaparecieran, el Padre G se volvió a ver su caña sacudiéndose. Levantó la caña y empezó a trabajarse al pescado. ¡Parecía grande! Pensó que ya lo tenía y comenzó a jalarlo a tierra. ¡Mala suerte que los chamacos se lo hubieran perdido!

Para desaliento suyo, el hilo perdió la tensión. Se le había escapado el pez. No muy contento, enrolló su hilo de pescar. Para hacer las cosas peores, la línea se le atoró. El pescador jaló para la izquierda y la derecha, arriba y abajo, hasta que se le soltó, pero se trajo algo de hierba enganchada.

El sol estaba apareciendo. El decepcionado pescador agarró las hierbas para desenredar su hilo. Algo brillante estaba entre las hierbitas, reflejando los rayos del sol. Era un hermosísimo reloj de mujer con diamantitos. Pensó que debía haberse perdido en el lago recientemente. Porque aún trabajaba y se veía en buenas condiciones. Gabriel notó la fecha y recordó algo. ¡Era el cumpleaños de Theresa!

Algo más se le vino a la memoria. Habían pasado ya 20 años de aquello. Había guardado dinero de cortar zacates en su vecindario para comprarle a su novia un reloj cuando cumpliera dieciocho años. Fue cuando se enteró que se había marchado, así que no tuvo oportunidad de dárselo.

Cuando se enteró que había sido llevada a Europa por sus padres para alejarla de él por ser solo un pobre méxico-americano del oeste de la ciudad, hijo de un carpintero y un ama de casa oriundos de México, se enfureció y se la pasó caminando por mucho rato, vagando sin rumbo por la ciudad. Acabó en la orilla de un laguito cerca de una universidad católica en el oeste de la ciudad. Lleno de frustración, Gabriel desenvolvió el regalo y lo tiró al lago tan lejos como pudo.

¿Por qué designio celestial había él pescado un reloj para dama en esa fecha en particular, veinte años más tarde en otro lago? ¿Acaso era aquel un signo incentivo de un nuevo destino, juntos? Ambos habían sido atormentados por las últimas cinco semanas por la idea de abandonar sus ministerios para dedicar sus vidas el uno al otro, renunciando a sus votos.

Las voces excitadas de los chicos corriendo de vuelta al sitio lo sacaron de sus pensamientos. Sepultó el reloj en su bolsillo.

"¡Padre G, Padre G, mi mamá dijo que un tal Señor Peters nos quiere llevar a trabajar a su rancho el fin de semana, pagándonos seis dólares por hora!" dijo Martin, sacando su caña de pescar para regresar a su casa.

"Eso quiere decir que nuestro día de pesca se acabó. ¡Qué bueno! No íbamos a pescar nada como quiera. Pero, ahí está el dinerito que estabas pidiendo, Martin," Gabriel le dijo, palmeando su espalda.

Martin y Shawn se miraron uno al otro.

"Sí, pero vamos a tener que trabajar para conseguirlo, Padre," alegó Shawn, queriendo poner el evento como no-por-intervención-de-Dios.

"Es verdad. Ya te había dicho que Él opera en formas diferentes de las que imaginamos. El hecho es que van a tener algo de lana, la cual van a poder apreciar mucho más que si se la hubieran encontrado. ¡La mejor forma de hacer dinero es el trabajar por él honestamente!"

Una semana antes, el Padre Gabriel había hablado con David Peters de darles trabajo a los muchachos para alejarlos de la pandilla durante los días que no tenían que ir a la escuela. El rancherón aquel, de 2 metros de altura y 145 kilos de peso le había prometido al pastor que trataría de conseguirles algo que hacer en su rancho en cuanto tuviera oportunidad. A David le gustó la idea de ayudar al Padre G a enderezar a aquellos chicos.

El ranchero le dijo a Violeta Ojeda, la madre de Martin Davis, que iba a volver por ellos a las siete de la mañana. Por eso fue que la mujer le había llamado a su hijo. David le ofreció que los ocuparía ese lunes y el siguiente fin de semana también.

El Padre Gabriel llevaba a los jóvenes de regreso a su casa, felices, pensando en todo el dinero que podrían ganar en esos tres días, y ya iban pensando cómo gastar lo que aún no habían ganado.

"¿Cuántos son tres días por ocho horas? Shawn le preguntó a Martin, tratando de hacer las cuentas.

"¡Veinticuatro horas!" les dijo el sacerdote al ver que tenían problemas sacando la respuesta.

"Entonces, veinticuatro horas a seis dólares la hora es. . ¿Cuánto?"

Martin se miró los dedos, pero no tenía suficientes. Shawn cerró los ojos apretados y se arrepintió no haber puesto atención a sus maestros de matemáticas durante las clases.

"¡Ciento cuarenta y cuatro dólares!" el Padre Gabriel les dijo.

"¡Guau, más de cien dolaritos por tres días para cada uno!" exclamó Martin.

Los chamacos empezaron a mencionar las cosas que podrían comprar con todo ese dinero.

Gabriel les hizo una sugerencia, "Acuérdense de dar el diezmo a la iglesia. Les sugiero que les den 50 por ciento de lo que quede a sus madres. Pueden poner alguna parte en ahorros, digamos el 10 por ciento, y se gastan lo que quede en lo que se les pegue la gana."

Shawn y Martin se miraron entre ellos, y decidieron que no iban ni siquiera a intentar lidiar con el problema de figurar porcentajes.

"¿Tienen una calculadora a la mano?" preguntó Shawn mirando primero a Martin y luego al sacerdote.

"Mejor vamos a verlo a usted luego que nos paguen, y entonces decidimos como repartirnos la lana, Padre," dijo Martin, agarrando la salida fácil.

El cura se rió de su inhabilidad para trabajar con los números y su facilidad para gastar lo que aún no ganaban. Pensó en darles tutoría a los dos algunas tardes para motivarlos a aprender más acerca de matemáticas, ciencias, religión, lenguaje y cosas así. Aquel era el comienzo de su relación con los chicos; solo el tiempo diría si tendría algún impacto en sus vidas. Se acordó de un chistecillo y se los contó a sus pasajeros mientras conducía.

"Iba un cuate caminando por un lado del manicomio. Había una pared muy grande entre el jardín del manicomio y la calle. Mientras el tipo caminaba por la banqueta, escuchó un cántico en el otro lado de la pared. '¡Oochoo, oochoo, oochoo, oochoo!' Se oía como que se estaban divirtiendo mucho los loquitos. El hombre se quedó picado y quiso saber de qué se trataba. Adentro los loquitos seguían en friega, cantando felices, '¡Oochoo, oochoo, oochoo, oochoo!' Se encontró un agujerito en la pared, así que el curioso fue y echó un vistazo. En cuanto se asomó, uno de los loquitos le picó el ojo con una vara. El pobre se retiró agarrándose el ojo adolorido y echando madres. Adentro del jardín el canto se detuvo por un momento pero luego empezó de nuevo con una canción diferente, '¡Nueve, nueve, nueve, nueve, nueve!'"

Llegaron al hogar de Martin aún riéndose. Violeta salió a recibirlos y se le acercó al párroco por el lado del chofer antes que se fuera. Le besó la mano y le dio las gracias por ayudar a su hijo. Él la bendijo y se alejó en su auto con una sonrisa de satisfacción. Las cosas iban funcionando bien, como siempre. Violeta dejó ir un suspiro mientras veía al sacerdote alejarse.

"¿No podría el papá de Martin ser, siquiera un poquito, como el Padre Gabriel?" se preguntó ella, viendo el Curimóvil dar la vuelta en la esquina.

Gabriel estacionó su carro y fue caminando a la tienda de empeños de Don Pedrito ahí cerca, para saludarlo y preguntarle algo acerca del reloj que había pescado en el lago. Pedro Mireles se puso muy contento de ver al sacerdote y fue a abrirle la puerta.

"Pásese, Padre G; qué bueno verlo de nuevo. ¿Qué milagro que desciende usted a visitar a los pobres?" preguntó el comerciante, jugando.

"Si tú eres uno de los pobres, entonces voy a tener que agregar a Bill Gates, Steve Forbes y Donald Trump a esa lista."

Aunque el lugar aún estaba cerrado al público a esa hora de la mañana, al viejo le gustaba estar ahí desde temprano y leer el periódico en la oficina. Luego se tomaba un café y se comía unos tamales o pan dulce antes de arreglar los exhibidores para el día de trabajo. A Don Pedrito le encantaba alegar con Gabriel de política. Mientras que el viejo presumía de ser puro demócrata, el presbítero solo podía defender ideas republicanas. Esa mañana, Pedro tenía unos tacos de barbacoa para desayunar. El inesperado huésped estuvo de acuerdo en compartir los alimentos con su amigo.

"¡Ándele sí, Padre! si usted sabe que yo muy apenas la hago para ir malviviendo en este desgraciado negocio."

"No te vine a pedir donaciones esta vez. Solo quiero decirte, shalom, y hacerte una pregunta profesional acerca de algo que me encontré."

"Bueno, shalom a usted. ¿En qué le puedo servir, mi Santo Amigo?"

"Móchale lo de santo. ¡Yo soy un pecador, casi tan grande como tú! Échale un ojito a este reloj, y dime como cuánto vale."

El cura sacó el reloj de dama de su bolsillo y se lo entregó a Pedro. Mientras que él fue a traer su lupa de joyero, Gabriel se sirvió una taza de fuerte café negro y agarró uno de los tacos del escritorio de su amigo.

"¡Ey! ¿Dónde se encontró esta cosita, Padre G?" le preguntó el dueño del negocio, viendo con interés los diamantes, asegurándose que eran reales.

Gabriel le estaba echando salsa picante a su taco.

"Lo pesqué en un lago esta mañana. Me fui de pesca con Martin y Shawn, un par de chicos de las casas del gobierno con los que estoy trabajando para alejarlos de su pandilla. No pescamos pescados, pero me ganché ese relojito. Mis dos jóvenes amigos fueron llamados de regreso a casa para ir a trabajar con otro amigo mío. Tú lo conoces, Don David Peters."

"Oh, sí, sí, el vaquero grandote. Me compró un rifle de cacería el mes pasado... Este relojito no está muy mal que digamos. Le podría dar quinientos dólares por él ahorita mismo, Padre."

El sacerdote sabía que el reloj valía por lo menos cinco mil dólares si Pedro estaba dispuesto a darle quinientos. Gabriel se bebió un buen trago de su café.

"No lo vendo. ¿Cuánto me cobrarías por darle una buena limpiadita?"

"Ummm, por ser usted... ¿Qué le parecen veinticinco dólares? A menos que... se me enfrentara, y me ganara usted a las vencidas, en cuyo caso sería gratis. Si se atreve, hasta le daría un lindo estuchito para el reloj."

El hombre de 60 años se empezó a enrollar la manga de la camisa mientras el ministro pensaba en la sabiduría de tomar tal reto. Pedro tenía unos brazos como de gorila pues levantaba pesas todos los días. Gabriel decidió aceptar; no tenía nada que perder de cualquier manera. Se acomodaron en lados opuestos en la esquina de una mesa después que hicieron a un lado los tacos que quedaban.

Se agarraron de la mano derecha, contaron hasta tres, y empujaron el brazo del oponente con gran poder. Pedro, que era el campeón de vencidas del barrio, le empezó a ganar a Gabriel. El cura regresó su brazo de nuevo hasta arriba con un grito gutural. Pedro estaba sorprendido de que no pudo acabar al clérigo tan pronto como había pensado. Los brazos de los dos se estaban hinchando de sangre, con las venas saltadas. Por varios segundos, sus manos permanecieron entrelazadas y estáticas en la posición inicial. Los luchadores de vencidas se miraron a los ojos con gran determinación.

"¿Está usted listo para rendirse, Padre?"

"¿Quiere decir eso que ya te cansaste y no puedes aguantar más, Pedrito?"

Se sonrieron uno al otro, fingiendo facilidad para mantener su posición. Los brazos les temblaban con el esfuerzo titánico. La frente de Pedro se empezó a perlar de sudor. Una de las gotas de sudor se le metió en un ojo, haciéndolo que parpadeara y rompiera su concentración. Gabriel rugió como un león y empujó el grueso antebrazo de Pedro hasta la mesa.

"¡El que parpadea pierde, mi Amigo!" Gabriel le dijo, levantándose y al mismo tiempo sobándose el brazo como si se hubiera lastimado. "Oye, Viejecito, creo que te debía de haber pagado los veinticinco dólares. No sospechaba que fuera tan difícil vencerte. ¿Estás hecho de acero o qué?"

Pedro Mireles flexionó su musculoso brazo y dijo con orgullo, "Me mantengo en forma. Uno nunca sabe cuando tenga que luchar con algún ratero o algún otro malhechor."

"¡Amén!"

Después de su desayuno y la limpieza, Gabriel puso el brilloso reloj en un bonito estuche de terciopelo rojo que el viejo le dio, se lo echó al bolsillo y dejó la tienda de empeños, dirigiéndose de nuevo rumbo a su casa.

Una camioneta se acercó a un lado de él, rodando despacio.

"¡Ey, Padre Gabriel! ¿Cómo le va? Oí que fue de pesca esta mañana."

Era David Peters con los dos chicos en la camioneta.

"Shalom, Amigo mío, muchas gracias por darles trabajo a mis cuates."

Después de intercambiar algunas palabras, el chofer de la camioneta se sacó un par de boletos de la bolsa de su camisa y se los dio al peatón.

"Tenga, Padre, acepte estos boletos como muestra de mi agradecimiento por conseguirme estos dos trabajadores. Parece que tienen muchas ganas de talonearle duro."

"Oh, no, no necesitas darme nada. Soy yo el que está endeudado contigo por tu bondad para con mis amigos."

"Por favor, Padre, agárrelos. Fíjese que mi vieja cayó enferma de repente con un virus y no va a poder ir al tiatro. Yo, pos' no soy de los que les gusta el tiatro, usté' sabe. He oído que a usté' le gusta el arte, así que pos' vaya usté' y diviértase. Nomás le pido, por favor, que rece por mi pobre vieja."

El ranchero le metió los boletos en la bolsa de la camisa al ministro y se alejó, diciéndole adiós con la mano y sonriéndole por el espejo retrovisor.

Gabriel elevó sus ojos al cielo y le rogó a Dios por la salud de la Señora Peters. En ese preciso instante la fiebre la dejó.

Ella se levantó de su cama y se sorprendió de ya no sentirse enferma, no le dolía la garganta, y su voz estaba normal. Se sirvió una taza de café y se preguntó qué pudo haber ocurrido para que ella recuperara su salud así. No había tomado ninguna medicina. Llamó a su esposo al celular para decirle que siempre sí iban a poder ir al teatro esa noche.

David no la podía creer, pero le dijo a su esposa que le había pedido al místico que rezara por ella. Ella le confirmó la hora en que se había curado, lo cual había sido justo después que David dejó al sacerdote. También le tuvo que decir que le había dado los boletos para el teatro al cura. Habían oído hablar de los milagros de Gabriel, pero no lo habían creído hasta ese día. Martin y Shawn se miraron uno al otro sorprendidos, escuchando la conversación. Shawn nomás se encogió de hombros.

El Padre G se subió a su Chevrolet modelo treinta y cinco sin pensar en el rumbo que se iba a dirigir ni lo que hacía. Se fue a darse un paseíto para escuchar algo de música clásica y disfrutar del hermoso día, su día libre, antes que alguien viniera y lo agarrara para algún asunto. Se la pasó vagando sin rumbo por su parroquia, saludando a las gentes al pasar.

Vio a un muchachote negro leyéndoles una historia a unos niños afuera de una tienda, bajo la sombra de un árbol. Era Dominique Watkins, el Toro. El Padre G le pitó y saludó al grupo agitando la mano desde su carro. Dominique le otorgó al presbítero una amplia y blanquísima sonrisa.

"Ese, Padre G, ¿cómo le va?"

"Espléndidamente bien, Nicky. Eres narrador de historias. ¡Qué bueno!"

"Sí, y usted sabe que tuvo mucho que ver con esto que estoy haciendo ahora. ¡Gracias, Amigo mío!"

"¡De nada! Ahí nos vemos luego, chavos; ando pachangueándomela."

Gabriel se alejó mientras que el peso pesado se sentaba para continuar leyéndoles la historia a los chiquillos de escuela primaria alrededor suyo.

Habían sido varios meses de que Nicky había cambiado. De ser amenaza del vecindario pasó a ser el protector del mismo. Gabriel había oído que Nicky había lastimado a golpes a muchos. Dominique era un fortachón que jugaba fútbol americano en la preparatoria antes de dejar sus estudios para dedicarse a manejar prostitutas, vender drogas, y aterrorizar el área.

El Padre G se acordó de cuando se enteró que Dominique estaba usando pequeños como entregadores de cocaína-crack. Los pequeños iban a entregar la droga escondida en los manubrios de sus bicicletas.

Timmy, el hijo adoptivo de James Bravo, fue reclutado para eso. El ministro pescó al niño haciendo una entrega cerca del gimnasio y le preguntó qué estaba haciendo. Timmy le explicó al cura que él solo estaba haciendo un trabajito para su amigo Dominique. Le iba a pagar bien si iba a entregar el crack, o le daría una buena paliza si no lo hacía.

Gabriel sintió la sangre hervirle por las venas, pensando en tal descaro: usar un niño para vender su veneno. El Toro estaba consciente de que si pescaban al niño con drogas, no le podían hacer cargos por su edad; así que le gustaba usar menores de diez años para distribuir sus drogas.

El clérigo le preguntó a Timmy en dónde estaba el Toro y se dirigió en esa dirección a encontrarlo.

En ese momento el Toro tenía un par de chicas y un par de camaradas con él adentro de un departamento en el complejo de casas de asistencia pública. El Padre G sabía que estarían armados, pero no tenía miedo.

"¡Aquí se acaba el camino para ti, Dominique!" dijo el cura, entrando a empujones hasta el departamento para enfrentarse al vendedor de drogas.

"¿Quién eres tú? ¿De qué estás hablando?" preguntó el narcotraficante entre una lluvia de palabras vulgares y obscenas.

Dominique levantó su mano para indicarles a sus pistoleros que se detuvieran de sacar sus pistolas cuando se fijó que era solo un ministro religioso. Gabriel traía puesto su camisa negra con collar romano.

Las dos chicas se jalaron un poco los atrevidos vestiditos y se cruzaron de piernas, tratando de verse más modestas y apropiadas. El cura las miró y sintió piedad por su obviamente pecaminosa y desviada forma de vida.

"Soy el Padre Gabriel Infante, pastor de la iglesia de la Santísima Trinidad. Ya sé lo que haces para ganarte la vida, y he venido a decirte que debes pararle a todo esto, o tendrás que encarar las consecuencias."

El musculoso negro se levantó del sofá y le sopló humo de marihuana en la cara del presbítero.

"¿Quién demonios te crees para venir a decirme que hacer, Desgraciado? Ni siquiera soy católico. ¿Qué te hace pensar que puedes detenerme de vivir como me dé la gana?"

El puño del Toro se apretó, como listo para darle un golpe al intruso.

Continuó diciendo entre vulgaridades, "Vienes sin que nadie te invite, a mi propio hogar, me insultas enfrente de mis amigos, y me amenazas. Creo que te debería de dar en toda la madre aquí mismo, Reverendo."

Dominique agarró al cura por la camisa y se lo acercó a la cara, tratando de intimidarlo. Sus cuatro amigos estaban muy sonrientes, pensando que iban a presenciar otra vapuleada por su rudo líder. A pesar que el Toro era un poco más grande que el ministro, el hombre más chico le mantuvo la mirada clavada en sus ojos sin mostrarle miedo. Fue Dominique quien se sintió avergonzado, mirando al interior de los calmados ojos del sacerdote.

"¿Sabes que puedo ordenar que te maten ahora mismo? ¿Qué demonios quieres conmigo?" el joven preguntó, soltando al clérigo.

Sus seguidores se sorprendieron al verlo echarse atrás y bajar los brazos.

"Quiero que cambies tu forma de vida. Estás arrastrando a mi gente al caño. Hoy me enteré que reclutaste a mi amiguito, Timmy Bravo, el hijo del dueño del gimnasio. No te permitiré corromperlo a él, ni a nadie más."

Uno de los hombres sacó la pistola y se la puso en la nuca al Padre G.

"¿Quieres que me eche al padrecillo este, Toro?"

Las chicas se asustaron, pensando que Joshua iba a jalar el gatillo; había matado a tres hombres a pesar de su tierna edad de 18 años. Toro le miró la cara al presbítero. No mostraba miedo. Gabriel se mantuvo mirando al Toro intensamente e ignorando al pistolero con el arma en su nuca.

"¿Qué te hace pensar que te voy a escuchar?" gruñó el rudo pandillero.

Había algo en los intensos ojos cafés de Gabriel que, nada más con verlo, le llegó hasta el tuétano al criminal. Era como si el ministro pudiera mirar el alma manchada del muchacho. Nick sintió un escalofrío correrle por la espalda, así que se volteó para ya no verle los ojos. Se le ocurrió algo.

"Déjame decirte algo, Curita. Si me puedes vencer en una pelea, te haré caso. ¿Que dices, le entras?"

El Toro creyó que el santo hombre nunca aceptaría el reto y se retiraría a su negocio eclesiástico.

"Está bien, vamos al gimnasio. No quiero ser arrestado por pelearme contigo en la calle, y aquí, en tu guarida, estoy en desventaja."

Gabriel se dio media vuelta y se encaminó rumbo al gimnasio de boxeo, ignorando al pistolero, quien solo regresó su arma a la funda.

Los seguidores del Toro lo miraron y le preguntaron, "¿Hablas en serio? ¿Por qué quieres darle en la madre al ministro, Hombre?"

Una de las chicas lo animó, "¡Qué bueno, Papi, pártele el hocico para que les enseñes a todos que tú eres el mero-mero del barrio!"

El pistolero había oído hablar del místico antes, así que le advirtió al Toro, "Ten cuidado, Toro, este no es un sacerdote ordinario."

El Toro se acabó su cigarrillo de marihuana y se quitó la camisa.

"Nomás vean como manejo a ese desgraciado. ¡Este es mi barrio, y nadie me dice lo que tengo que hacer!" rugió entre maldiciones el muchacho.

Los abultados músculos de Dominique se veían duros como una roca. Caminó aprisa con sus amigos detrás de él. Las chicas invitaron a otros que fueran a mirar al Toro "partirle el hocico a uno" en el gimnasio.

Gabriel le aventó un par de guantes a Dominique cuando entró al gimnasio. El cura ya estaba listo sobre el cuadrilátero sin su camisa. No parecía un sacerdote allá arriba. Tenía un cuerpo cincelado que se veía tan poderoso como el del Toro.

Dominique se puso los guantes con la ayuda de sus amigos y se subió al ring, mirando a su oponente. Gabriel lo miró a los ojos sin ningún temor; Dominique volteó los ojos para evitar su mirada. El líder de la pandilla se enfureció que el hombre no se vencía ante sus miradas amenazantes. Antes era el Toro quien sentía debilidad mirando a los tranquilos ojos de Gabriel.

Timmy, el protegido de Gabriel, sonó la campana.

"El pleito se acaba cuando te rindas o caigas noqueado," anunció el clérigo, moviéndose alrededor con la gracia de un consumado pugilista.

"¡No! el pleito se va a acabar cuando TÚ te rindas, después que te dé una buena paliza, Sacerdote."

El Toro lanzó varios golpes con toda su fuerza. Gabriel los evadió todos resbalándoselos, moviéndose a un lado, o inclinando su cuerpo arriba, abajo, o de lado a lado. El Toro se enfureció más al no poder conectar. Estaba acostumbrado a trabar y empujar, no a boxear. El pugilista bailó alrededor del oponente y le tiró un par de golpes rectos de izquierda que le abrieron el labio inferior y lo hicieron sangrar.

"¡Chin...! ¡Te voy a matar, Desgraciado!" gruñó el muchacho con palabras vulgares, viendo su sangre correrle por la barbilla y manchando el guante cuando se tocó la boca.

Dominique se le abalanzó al cura quien simplemente se movió a un lado para evitar su empujón. El Toro se tropezó en el pie derecho del ministro y cayó a la lona. Se paró de inmediato, más furioso, y le tiró un par de golpes con intenciones asesinas. El Padre G bloqueó uno y se agachó evitando el otro. El Toro le quería arrancar la cabeza con sus explosivos pero inútiles atentados.

Gabriel lanzó un recto seguido por un gancho que le sacudieron la cabeza al Toro. El joven abrazó al sacerdote para evitar caerse. El Padre Gabriel lo empujó contra las cuerdas. Cuando rebotó, la cara del Toro se encontró con los puños de su oponente seis veces, tamborileándole la cabeza a gran velocidad. Todo se tornó oscuridad para él.

Los seguidores del Toro no podían creer lo fácil que el sacerdote había acabado con su líder. Nadie en el vecindario se atrevía siquiera a hablarle mal al Toro; había vencido a todos en pleitos callejeros. Pero ahora aquel tipo duro se hallaba inconsciente, tendido de espaldas en la lona.

Sus desanimados seguidores lo dejaron ahí tirado y se regresaron a sus casas. El Padre Gabriel le ayudó a Dominique a recuperarse.

"¿Estás ya de vuelta, Nicky?" le preguntó el cura, cacheteándole la cara ligeramente al joven sentado sobre un banquillo en el cuadrilátero.

"Sí... ¿Qué pasó?" el aún atontado maleante le preguntó al clérigo.

"El poder de Dios te ha tocado, para traerte a donde perteneces."

El Padre Gabriel sintió una onda cálida cubriéndolo. Sabía que algo estaba a punto de pasar, así que le impuso las manos al maleante en la cabeza y oró sobre él.

"Oh, Padre Celestial, te imploro que abras los ojos de este hijo tuyo, para que pueda ver el futuro que le espera en el camino por el que va."

Dominique tuvo una visión del infierno. Su padre y su madre estaban ahí. Sus prostitutas estaban ahí, sus amigos también. Le estaban extendiendo los brazos, tratando de hundirlo en la oscuridad junto con ellos. El lugar era oscurísimo y frígido a pesar de arder en llamas. El Toro escuchó lamentos y una multitud de gritos angustiados. Experimentó el miedo más grande de su vida. Entonces oyó la voz de Gabriel de nuevo.

"¡Gracias Señor! Te suplico que abras tus brazos y recibas a Dominique de nuevo en tu reino. Toca su corazón y llámalo a ti, para que pueda vivir su vida solo para alabar tu nombre y hacer tu voluntad por el resto de sus días. Te lo pido en el nombre de Jesús, tu Hijo, quien vive y reina contigo y el Espíritu Santo, un Dios por los siglos de los siglos."

Dominique cayó del banquillo de rodillas sobre la lona del cuadrilátero a los pies de Gabriel.

"¡Perdóneme, Padre!" susurró él y luego comenzó a sollozar, abrazando al clérigo por la cintura.

Gabriel lo abrazó por los hombros y le impuso la mano en la cabeza diciendo, "¡Bienvenido a casa, Hijo!"

Le ayudó a Dominique a que se pusiera de pie y luego lo acompañó hacia fuera del gimnasio. El pequeño Timmy, que había visto todo desde fuera del ring, estaba boquiabierto y extático acerca del resultado de aquel pleito.

"Tú sabes que es lo que tienes que hacer, Nicky. Ve y hazlo ahora."

El místico palmeó la musculosa espalda de Dominique y lo mandó a su casa sin más instrucciones. Gabriel estaba seguro que el Espíritu Santo iba a guiar al hombre reformado.

Regresando de aquella memoria, el Padre G se encontró manejando en dirección de la casa de las hermanas religiosas. Cuando ya estaba a dos cuadras de distancia, detuvo su auto y se preguntó a dónde iba. Cuestionó a su subconsciente y se dio cuenta que quería darle el regalo a Theresa por su cumpleaños, el regalo que él había querido darle veinte años atrás. ¡Aquel era el día de hacerlo! Soltó el freno y se continuó acercando a la dirección de las monjitas.

Paró el carro de nuevo, desechando la idea como absurda. Pensó que podía hacer mejor uso del valioso reloj para alimentar hambrientos con el dinero que podría sacarle. De nuevo se convenció a sí mismo que todas las indicaciones estaban ahí para que le diera el reloj a Theresa y la invitara al teatro con los boletos que le dio David. Él no lo había planeado; ¡así quería el destino! Puso el carro en movimiento, muy seguro que debía de hacerlo, pero se detuvo de nuevo a media cuadra de la casa de las monjitas.

El chofer que iba atrás de él se cansó de sus paradas y lo pasó, pitándole el claxon y enseñándole el dedo al sacerdote. Gabriel sonrió y le envio al iracundo chofer una bendición en respuesta. Decidió entonces alejarse de ahí, pero Sor Theresa se acercó corriendo a su vehículo. Estaba regando las plantitas cuando el claxon del iracundo motorista le llamó la atención.

"Padre Gabriel, ¿Qué anda haciendo hoy por aquí?"

"Pues... ando paseándome y escuchando música clásica."

"¡Qué lindo! Oye, me alegra verte. Necesito ir a comprar el mandado, y las hermanas se llevaron la van a Corpus Christi a una conferencia por el fin de semana largo. ¿Me podrías tú llevar a la tienda en tu carro, por favorcito?"

La hermana religiosa hizo una carita angelical como una chiquilla, suplicándole que la ayudara. Él no se podía rehusar.

"Trépate, Theresa. Será un placer ayudarte a traer el mandado."

"¡Magnífico! Déjame ir a cerrar la llave del agua y traer mi bolsa."

Ella corrió hasta dentro de la casa después de cortar el agua. El Padre G se salió de su auto. Volvió el rostro al cielo, sonriendo y meneando la testa.

Theresa regresó vestida con un vestido floreado que la hacía verse como una hermosa florecita. Gabriel le abrió la puerta para que se subiera al carro; disfrutó el aspirar su perfume al entrar al vehículo.

"¿Cómo fue que las hermanas no se quedaron a celebrar tu cumpleaños?" preguntó Gabriel mientras se alejaban de la casa.

"Oh, no se los mencioné. Dejé de celebrar mi cumpleaños hace tiempo," Theresa replicó, descartando el evento como algo sin importancia.

"¡Qué bien! Pues te está funcionando. Te ves preciosa y muy joven a los... ¿Qué, 28 años?" dijo el ministro con sonrisa pícara, admirando su belleza.

"¡Sí, como no! Tú sabes mi edad, así que ni para qué pretenda contigo.

Ambos nos estamos haciendo viejos. Me acuerdo cuando mi mami tenía esta edad; creí que ya estaba ancianita. Ahora que estoy aquí, siento que en los sesentas sería vieja, no en los treintas, pero gracias por el cumplido."

Pasaron dos horas en el supermercado. El Padre G se encontró una nena tendida en uno de los pasillos, coloreando un caballo en un librito que había agarrado. Él se detuvo a admirar el trabajo de la pequeña; ella se levantó con una paletita en la boca y le mostró al hombre su obra de arte.

"¡Es muy bonito... Ey, Theresa, mira esto!"

El cura pidió a la hermana religiosa que dejara las latas de champiñones para que viera el colorido caballo. La nena continuaba chupando su paletita, disfrutando de la crítica positiva sobre su trabajo.

"¡Oh, guau! ¿Tú solita coloreaste a ese caballito?"

Theresa se sentó en cuclillas para estar al nivel de la niña; la pequeña artista se llenó de orgullo y movió la cabecita, admitiendo que así fue.

"¿Cómo te llamas?" Theresa le preguntó a la criatura, echándole el cabello a un lado de la carita y tras de su oreja.

"Dorothy."

"Bueno, Dorothy, mucho gusto en conocerte. Yo me llamo Theresa y él es el Padre Gabriel."

El cura extendió su mano a Dorothy y le dijo, "Creo que eres una gran artista. Sigue practicando para que le puedas dar al mundo muchas imágenes bonitas de caballitos y flores y toda clase de cosas coloridas."

En ese momento, un nuevo asistente del gerente, aún en entrenamiento, se dejó venir sobre el trío con una caja abierta de galletas y una bolsa desgarrada de paletitas como la que Dorothy traía en la boca.

"Por favor, no dejen a su hija sin supervisión. ¡Miren lo que ha hecho!"

Dorothy se asustó porque el hombre se oía muy serio; ella se fue a esconder atrás de sus dos nuevos amigos y se asomó por un lado de Theresa para mirar al hombre enojado.

"Espero que vayan a pagar por esos crayones y también por el libro de colorear."

El empleado del negocio hizo una cara muy seria como si los hubiera descubierto cometiendo un crimen mayor. El Padre Gabriel le puso la mano en el hombro al empleado y le explicó que ellos no eran los padres de la niña. Invitó al hombre a que lo confirmara preguntándole a la pequeña.

"Ven para acá niña. Dime ¿quiénes son estas dos gentes?"

Dorothy titubeó y no quería muy bien acercársele al hombre, aún cuando le estaba sonriendo. Theresa le ayudó a la nena, empujándola gentilmente hacia delante para que le explicara al hombre quienes eran ellos.

"Ella es... Theresa, y el es... Padre."

Dorothy se escondió de nuevo. Gabriel miró a ver a Theresa, y ambos vieron al asistente del gerente meneando su cabeza. Gabriel traía pantalón vaquero negro y una camiseta de cuello blanca; Theresa andaba con su vestido floreado y sandalias. No se veían como un par de religiosos.

"¡Hombre, no la puedo creer que negaras a tu propia criatura!"

Gabriel iba a explicarle, pero en ese momento la madre verdadera se dejó venir corriendo tras la chiquilla. Había alivio y ansiedad en su voz.

"¡Dorothy Marie Parker! ¿Por qué nunca me haces caso? Te dije que te quedaras en el baño conmigo." La mujer se volvió a ver a los tres adultos junto a su niña y les preguntó, "¿Qué fue lo que hizo ahora?"

El asistente de gerente se disculpó con Theresa y Gabriel y se volvió hacia la madre, mostrándole los paquetes que la niña había abierto. El empleado y la mujer se fueron rumbo a las registradoras. Dorothy se volteó a decirles adiós y les mandó un besito. Gabriel pretendió que lo pescaba en el aire y se lo plantaba a Theresa en la mejilla, para deleite de la pequeña.

"¡Bueno, esa sí que fue una pequeña aventura!" comentó la hermana religiosa, regresándose a donde estaban las latas de champiñones.

"Sí, fue muy bonito por un instante imaginar que era de nosotros. Ella se parece un poco a ti, el mismo color de cabello y también tu linda sonrisa."

Theresa no contestó nada pero se quedó pensando que hubiera sido muy lindo si la chiquilla fuera de ellos en verdad y estuvieran comprando el mandado para su hogar. Se preguntó qué habría sido la vida si se hubieran quedado juntos como lo habían planeado cuando estaban en la prepa. Acabaron con las compras y volvieron a casa.

Cuando arribaron, Gabriel le ayudó a Theresa a descargar el mandado y a ponerlo sobre la mesa de la cocina. Al ir entrando, la puerta de tela de enfrente se zafó al caérsele la bisagra superior.

El caballero le ofreció arreglarla en lo que ella guardaba los comestibles. Ella lo envió a un armario por herramientas; él pronto se puso a trabajar.

Las monjitas tenían una buena caja de herramientas bien equipada, la cual Gabriel sacó para arreglar la bisagra de arriba y también la de abajo que ya estaba muy floja.

Mientras estaba ocupado en el trabajo de carpintería para reparar la puerta, se acordó de una canción y empezó a cantarla lo suficientemente recio para que Theresa lo escuchara adentro de la cocina. Su fuerte y melodiosa voz reverberó a través de la casa y le tocó el corazón a la mujer.

En la canción, el poeta le dice a su amada que ella es la culpable de todas sus angustias y sus quebrantos, de llenar su vida de dulces inquietudes y amargos desencantos al mismo tiempo. Uno de los versos dice que el poeta daría toda su vida por vencer el miedo de besarla. Él disfrutó diciéndole aquellas cosas en la canción; ella disfrutó mucho escuchándolas.

Gabriel silbó el intermedio de la canción y se asomó a la cocina. Theresa ya estaba cocinando. El delicioso aroma de la comida le entró por la nariz y le cosquilleó el estómago. Con el último verso de la canción, acabó con su trabajo de reparación. Guardó las herramientas. Llamó a Theresa para que fuera a examinar los resultados de su trabajo y diera su aprobación.

"¡Guau! Hiciste un trabajo fantástico. Has sido bendecido con muchos talentos," ella dijo, abriendo y cerrando la firme puerta de tela.

"Acuérdate que soy hijo de un carpintero. Le aprendí una o dos cositas a mi papá."

Ella se sonrió y lo miró a los ojos diciendo, "¡Ah, sí! Te debían de haber puesto Jesús, hijo de un carpintero, hacedor de milagros."

"¿Sabes? Ahora que lo mencionas, es algo chistoso. Mi papá se llama José Arturo y mi mamá es María de la Luz, ¡José y María!" Gabriel le dijo, "Nomás que no son judíos."

Riéndose se encaminaron a la cocina. Él se lavó las manos y ya se iba a marchar; sin embargo, Theresa le anunció que el almuerzo estaba servido. Le dijo que era lo mínimo que podría ella hacer por él por toda su ayuda.

"Digo, si no te importa comer sobras de lasaña que cociné ayer."

"¡Pero si me encanta la lasaña!" le dijo, a sabiendas de que si hubieran sido frijoles negros fríos, también le encantarían.

Su almuerzo estuvo calmado pero lo empezaron un poco formal. Él actuó como párroco y director de la escuela mientras ella actuó como maestra de primero y ministra de música. Mantuvieron una conversación diplomática acerca del clima, la escuela, Europa, comidas, música, arte y el teatro. Ella se acordó haber visto la obra, "La Dama de San Luis," en el periódico.

"Siempre he querido ir a ver esa obra musical. Leí que va a estar en la ciudad toda esta semana."

Gabriel se empinó lo último de su vino tinto y se sonrió.

"Hermana, creo que debería de rezarle a nuestro Señor para que le permita ir a ver esa obra musical por su cumpleaños."

"Oh, por favor, Padre..."

"Por favor, cree en milagros, Theresa, cerremos los ojos por un momento y pidámosle a Dios por lo que quiere tu corazón en tu cumpleaños."

Ella cumplió con lo que le pedía y cerró sus claros ojos. Gabriel se aseguró que no lo estaba mirando y se sacó los dos boletos de su bolsillo para ponerlos en la mesa enfrente de la mujer.

"Abre los ojos, Criatura. El Señor sabe lo que quieres aún antes de que se lo pidas."

Theresa recogió los boletos, incrédula.

"Pero, Padre... ¿Cómo?"

Él se puso el dedo sobre los labios para que dejara de interrogarlo.

"No digas nada por favor, ¡Feliz cumpleaños, Tere! Acepta los boletos y también este otro regalito."

Sacó el estuchito de terciopelo rojo y lo abrió.

Theresa en verdad necesitaba un reloj porque le había regalado el de ella a la Hermana Rebecca Sterling antes de partir de Irlanda. Titubeó a aceptar el caro reloj, aunque le encantó desde el instante que lo miró.

"Por favor, acéptalo, Tere, estaba destinado a ser tu regalo hoy. Me esperé veinte años para regalarte un reloj. He oído que para un buen tiempo, necesitas un buen reloj. Fíjate, yo no tuve ni que comprar los boletos ni el reloj."

"¿Te los robaste, Gabrielin?"

"¡Ja-ja-ja-ja-ja! No, yo solo soy el mandadero. Dios te mandó estos regalitos, Tere."

Sin fijarse, se estaban llamando uno al otro con sus sobrenombres de cariño como cuando eran adolescentes, Tere y Gabrielín. La formalidad del almuerzo se había disipado. Él acercó su silla junto a ella para ayudarle a ponerse el reloj de oro que le sentó a la perfección.

Le contó cómo había pescado el relojito del lago y se había enfrentado a Don Pedro a las vencidas para que lo limpiara y le agregara el estuche. Y le explicó de los boletos que David le dio por los ayudantes que le consiguió.

"¡Está bien, de acuerdo! Los acepto pero con una condición."

Ella le agarró las manos y se le quedó viendo a sus oscuros ojos.

"¿Qué condición, Tere?"

"Me vas a tener que llevar tú al teatro esta noche porque no tengo a nadie más con quien ir. No tengo siquiera medio de transporte, y además estoy bien segura que vas a disfrutar mucho del espectáculo."

"¡Su deseo es una orden para mí, su alteza!" Gabriel le besó la mano como si fuera una reina y se levantó para partir. "Me voy a ir a dar un regaderazo y cambiarme. Regresaré por ti en un par de horas, o ¿necesitas más tiempo... para retozar encueradita por la casa?"

Theresa se cubrió la cara, recordando cuando la encontró desnuda en el pasillo saliendo de bañarse. Agarró una servilleta y se la aventó jugando.

"No, no necesito más tiempo 'para retozar encueradita por la casa.' Voy a estar lista en dos horas."

Un gato negro con ojos rojos pareció sonreírse desde la ventana donde observaba a los dos religiosos caminando rumbo a la puerta de enfrente.

Después que Gabriel se marchó, Theresa se volteó a ver al gato al entrar de nuevo al comedor. El felino saltó de la ventana afuera de la casa.

Theresa se acercó a la ventana abierta buscando al animal, pero se había desaparecido. La religiosa se preguntó si en verdad le había visto los ojos rojos al gato o había sido su imaginación. Pensando en el gato sintió un escalofrío y se le puso la piel del brazo chinita, pero cuando se lo frotó, se encontró su nuevo relojito en la muñeca y lo admiró con gran placer.

"¡Gabriel es tan dulce y bueno para saber lo que necesito!" pensó ella.

Recogió los trastes de la mesa del comedor y se fue a alistar para su cita. Theresa se excitó muchísimo con la idea de salir con su antiguo novio en su cumpleaños. Se preguntó si él era aún su antiguo novio o si podrían nomás cortarle lo de antiguo.

Al meterse al baño, Theresa pensó que estaban jugando con fuego y que sería mejor terminar con eso, pero luego recordó la canción que Gabriel le cantó y se convenció que no tenía nada de malo amarlo tanto. Tarareando la canción que él le ofrendó, abrió las llaves de la regadera y se metió a bañar, habiendo decidido continuar con sus planes para esa noche.

Capítulo VII

Cita

Gabriel regresó a la casa de las monjitas demasiado pronto. Aunque Theresa ya estaba lista, la obra de teatro empezaría tres horas más tarde.

Decidieron irse al centro a matar un tiempo ahí. La pareja pasó por la biblioteca central y se paseó alrededor de la Plaza Principal, viendo la vieja Catedral y la Corte del Condado. Cuando iban pasando por el River-Center Mall, Gabriel recordó un buen lugar en el cual podían pasarse un par de horas agradables antes que empezara la obra de teatro, el Museo de Arte. A Theresa le gustó la idea y estuvo de acuerdo en que fueran.

"¿Has pintado algo últimamente?" ella le preguntó, recordando que él acostumbraba pintar cuando era jovencito.

"No tengo mucho tiempo. Tú sabes, con esto de andar sacando a las maestras al teatro y a cenar no me deja tiempo para el arte."

"¿A poco? ¿Quieres decir que sacas a todas tus maestras como a mí hoy?"

"¡Por supuesto que no! Estoy explorando nuevo territorio contigo!"

Arribaron al museo y estuvieron de acuerdo que era interesante visitar tales sitios. Theresa se interesó en una pintura abstracta y se paró enfrente de ella, tratando de entenderla. Declaró que era linda pero que aquella pieza tenía algo extraño. Gabriel se puso detrás de ella para tener el mismo punto de vista; acercó tanto su cara a la de ella que su cabello le acarició el oído a él. Inhaló el perfume de violetas que emanaba de su cuello. Ella sintió su espacio personal siendo invadido pero no se opuso.

"Vamos a verla muy de cerca, tan cerca de la pintura como podamos," sugirió Gabriel. La tomó de los hombros y suavemente la empujó hacia delante hasta que su nariz casi tocaba la pintura, y le dijo, "Relaja tus ojitos enfrente de la obra y mira que impresión consigues en esta distancia."

Con las manos en sus hombros, la empezó a jalar pasito a pasito hacia atrás, deteniéndose y echándole un vistazo a la pieza entera en cada paso. Le explicó los punto más finos de la composición y el ritmo de la pintura; le habló de la relación entre la media utilizada por la artista y el título de la obra. Mientras tanto él se estaba embriagando con su aroma y su proximidad. Ella se sintió muy excitada también, así que para romper el encanto en el cual estaba cayendo, se dio media vuelta para alabarlo por su profunda percepción artística y su entendimiento de la pintura abstracta.

"¡Sabes mucho de arte abstracto!"

"A decir verdad, te estaba leyendo los comentarios de la boletita de información que agarré en el mostrador de la entrada. Yo la veo como una pieza medio extraña también," le confesó él con una amplia sonrisa.

"¡Tramposo!" exclamó Theresa, dándole un leve puñetazo en el hombro.

Continuaron con su exploración del museo hasta que ya casi era hora que se fueran al teatro. Cuando iban bajando por las escaleras, el tacón de un zapato de Theresa se le atoró en la alfombra, y ella perdió el equilibrio. Gabriel la atrapó entre sus brazos.

"¡Gracias! Pensé que me iba a ir rodando por las escaleras y quebrarme el cuello."

"Yo no podía permitir eso porque los boletos son buenos para la función de esta noche solamente. ¡No me gustaría desperdiciarlos! Además, imagínate tener que estar en la sala de urgencias en lugar de ir al teatro... No suena muy divertido. ¿O sí?" él le dijo sin soltarla.

Un guardia de seguridad los volteó a ver desde la planta baja y se aclaró la garganta. Gabriel soltó a Theresa y solo le tomó la mano mientras bajaban por los últimos escalones. A Theresa no le desagradaba estar entre sus brazos, pero se contentó con solo irse tomados de la mano.

La pareja de viejos amigos disfrutaron de la obra musical desde el principio hasta el final. Fue una interesante y muy bien actuada obra, pero lo principal era que estaban juntos. Eso hacía una simple caminata por la calle una experiencia muy agradable.

Después del teatro, Gabriel y Theresa se fueron al Paseo del Río a estirar las piernas un ratito y a buscar un buen lugar para cenar. Las otras hermanas iban a volver a casa hasta el día siguiente, así que no había razón para que Theresa regresara a su casa temprano.

Gabriel se sintió caminando en las nubes, pero pensó en lo que estaban haciendo. Su conciencia cuestionó su comportamiento. Andaban en cita como cualquier hombre y mujer. Su lado conservativo le ordenó que le pusiera fin a aquello para evitar más tentación, pero se encontró queriendo oler su perfume, respirar su aliento, tocar su carita y su cabello, escuchar su risa, tomar su mano, y caminar toda la noche así. Su débil lado humano desobedeció la orden de su conciencia y racionalizó que no estaba pasando nada malo. Decidió seguir disfrutando la noche y proveerle a la chica del cumpleaños con la velada más agradable que fuera posible.

Theresa iba pensando exactamente lo mismo. Ambos llegaron a la misma conclusión de dejar caer las cosas donde cayeran y deleitarse con su cita.

Se sonrieron, parados en un área oscura del Paseo del Río, preguntándose qué decir para romper el silencio momentáneo. Theresa dijo que tenía antojo de comida mexicana y le gustaría ir a un restaurante donde tuvieran música en vivo. El tronó los dedos y le dijo que sabía de un buen lugar no muy lejos de ahí.

Una figura oscura emergió de entre las sombras y agarró la bolsa de Theresa. Ella reaccionó agarrándola más fuerte. El ladrón le dio un tirón violento y se arrancó corriendo ya con el botín en las manos, derribándola al piso en el proceso.

Gabriel, lleno de amorosa preocupación, le ayudó a incorporarse.

"¿Estás bien, Tere?"

"Sí, estoy bien, pero él se llevó mi bolsa."

Ella se arregló la falda y miró en la dirección en la cual el ladrón había huido. Como un corredor olímpico, Gabriel se lanzó tras el criminal.

"¡Noooo, Gabrielín, déjalo que se vaya!" le gritó Theresa, preocupada de que pudiera salir lastimado.

El ratero iba muy adelante del sacerdote. Para hacer las cosas más difíciles, un borrachito salió de un bar tambaleándose enfrente del ministro corredor. El Padre G giró como un trompo para evitar aventar al borracho al río. Gabriel rodó de espaldas sobre una mesa a la orilla del río y aterrizó sobre sus dos pies para continuar la persecución. El ebrio giró, mirando al corredor y preguntándose qué era lo que estaba pasando.

Gabriel se fijó que el ladrón cruzó el río por un puentecito y se regresó por el otro lado del río, dirigiéndose a las escaleras que llevan al nivel de la calle. El clérigo miró muy enojado que el joven bandido le estaba enseñando la bolsa y burlándose de él.

No había tiempo para que Gabriel corriera por el puente para alcanzar al raterillo antes que llegara a la calle y se perdiera entre la muchedumbre.

El ladrón se rió y empezó a subir los escalones hacia la calle. El Padre G levantó los ojos al cielo estrellado y le pidió ayuda a Dios. ¡Se persignó y comenzó a correr a toda velocidad sobre las aguas del río sin hundirse!

Sor Theresa lo vio haciendo eso y se puso la mano en la boca.

Gabriel aceleró, saltó sobre tres escalones a la vez, y alcanzó al criminal. El tipo sintió una poderosa mano agarrándole el talón al tiempo que estaba poniendo pie en la calle. El muchacho cayó al suelo de cara, perdiendo un par de dientes con el impacto contra la banqueta.

Dos policías en bicicleta parados a una cuadra vieron cuando cayó al piso.

Con gran furia, el Padre G saltó sobre él como un tigre. Lo agarró con las dos manos y lo levantó en vilo.

Los oficiales pedalearon hasta donde estaban los dos hombres mientras avisaban a la despachadora que tenían un pleito en acción.

El cura estrelló al ratero contra la pared y demandó que le regresara la bolsa. Gabriel lo estaba sosteniendo en lo alto, los pies colgándole en el aire y su cuerpo apretado contra la pared del edificio. Sintiendo la increíble fuerza del hombre que lo estaba sosteniendo, el ladrón sintió mucho miedo. Se sacó la bolsa de adentro de la camisa y la dejó caer.

"¡Por favor, por favor... ya no me pegues!" el ratero gritó mientras los dos policías saltaban sobre el presbítero y lo sujetaban de los brazos.

Viendo que aquellos eran policías, el cura se relajó en sus manos. Uno de los agentes se sacó las esposas para sujetar al musculoso. El raterillo vio su chanza de escapar, se arrancó corriendo, y dio vuelta por un callejón.

"Muchas gracias, Oficiales. ¡Dejaron escapar a un ladrón de bolsas!"

Los dos policías miraron la bolsa tirada en el piso, y luego se vieron uno al otro. Le quitaron las esposas al sacerdote y se montaron en sus bicicletas mientras ponían la descripción del ladrón por el radio.

Theresa subió los escalones, buscando a Gabriel y se sintió aliviada de verlo en cuanto emergió del Paseo del Río al nivel de la calle.

"¿Gabrielín, estás bien? ¡Oh, recuperaste mi bolsa, gracias! ¿En dónde está el muchacho?"

"Sí, estoy bien. Recuperé tu bolsa, y el muchachillo... anda corriendo por las calles del centro, jugando a las escondidas con la policía," Gabriel le respondió, regresándole su bolsa.

Mientras caminaban de regreso al estacionamiento, Theresa le tuvo que preguntar, "¿Te vi caminar sobre el agua?"

"No Tere, Jesús caminó sobre el agua; yo tuve que correr para no hundirme. ¡Ja-ja-ja! No lo podía creer, ¡pero funcionó! Le pedí a Dios que me permitiera alcanzar al ladrón para recuperar tu bolsa, y me concedió mi petición. Vámonos al carro. Me dio mucho hambre con tanta emoción."

Se fueron a un popular restaurante en la parte oeste cercana al centro, para cenar y beberse unas margaritas mientras escuchaban una banda de mariachis en vivo. La anfitriona los llevó hasta una cabina contra la pared. Había bastante gente comiendo, bebiendo, y divirtiéndose ahí. El aroma de la deliciosa cocina mexicana flotaba en el ambiente mientras que la música mexicana tradicional resonaba en el lugar.

"Gracias por traerme aquí. El día entero ha sido un placer en tu compañía," dijo Theresa, poniéndole la mano sobre la de él mientras revisaban los menús.

"Tere, el placer ha sido todo mío. Nunca, en mis más atrevidos sueños, me imaginé que íbamos a estar así, divirtiéndonos juntos en esta etapa de nuestras vidas."

Él la miró profundo a los ojos mientras le cogía la mano. Gabriel se volteó a ver un chiquitín que estaba paradito en una silla inclinándola hacia atrás, balanceándola en las dos patas traseras. Estaba tratando de mantener el balance en lo que sus padres decidían que ordenar. El cura tuvo que estirarse para pescarlo cuando el nene se fue para abajo con todo y silla.

"¡Epa! Ya te tengo, Muchachote. Será mejor que te voltees al otro lado y te sientes. Guarda las acrobacias para tu casa," Gabriel le aconsejó al chicuelo.

El clérigo levantó la silla, con el chiquillo colgando en su cuello como un changuito. Gabriel lo puso de vuelta en su silla y les sonrió a los papás.

"¡Gracias, Señor!" ambos padres le dijeron a Gabriel al mismo tiempo y se voltearon a ver al niño muy serios.

"¡Ya te lo he dicho que no andes jugando en la mesa, Justin! ¡Podías pegarle a alguien, o te podías haber lastimado!" la madre regañó al niñito.

El Padre Gabriel le regresó su atención a Sor Theresa, e inspirado por aquel pequeño incidente le contó otro de sus chistecillos.

"Había un excelente acróbata de circo que tenía una debilidad terrible por el vino. Un día en un pueblito, el circo tuvo una función de un día. Al final del espectáculo, el acróbata, llamado Duffus, se fue a buscar algún bar. Solo tenían una escuelita y una iglesita en el pueblo, pero tenían seis cantinas con bastante clientela. Duffus encontró que su vino era excelente y sus precios muy razonables. Se puso a beber hasta que se le acabó el dinero y perdió el conocimiento. El gerente del circo ya estaba cansado de sus constantes borracheras y sus desapariciones, así que decidió mover el circo esa noche, dejando atrás a Duffus para que se las arreglara por sí solo."

Gabriel interrumpió su historia porque un mesero les trajo vasos de agua con hielo, tostaditas, y salsa, en lo que su comida estaba lista. Theresa ordenó una margarita congelada de fresa; Gabriel una margarita congelada regular. Ella pidió unas enchiladas verdes de pollo mientras que el pidió un platillo de fajitas de res. El mesero tomó su orden y se fue. El Padre G continuó su historia después de morderle a una tostadita con salsa picante.

"Bien, a la mañana siguiente, Duffus el acróbata, se despertó con un dolor de cabeza, hambriento, sediento, y adolorido, tirado en la dura banqueta. Una viejita andaba barriendo la calle y lo miró con disgusto. Duffus le preguntó si le podría dar algo de beber. Ella levantó su escoba para que se alejara. Duffus se paró y se fue, echo la mocha, antes que la viejita le diera en la chirimoya. Sin un quinto, se fijó que el campito en donde estaba el circo estaba vacío; sabía a donde iban a ir. Solo debía alcanzarlos, pero necesitaba dinero para el camión. En eso oyó las campanas de la iglesia llamando a los fieles y pensó que el párroco, siendo hombre de Dios, le podría prestar un dinerito. Duffus fue a la iglesia y llegó al tiempo que el pastor salía a oír confesiones. El acróbata le suplicó al ministro que le ayudara, explicándole su precaria situación. El cura tuvo piedad, le dio el dinero, y le pidió a su ama de llaves que le diera unos chilaquiles al pobre crudo y lo dejara lavarse. ¡Nombre, Duffus quedó muy contento! Decidió ir a darle las gracias al presbítero antes de dirigirse a la parada de autobuses."

El mesero les trajo las bebidas. Sor Theresa se echó un buen trago de su margarita porque la salsa estaba muy picosa, ¡pero muy buena! La helada bebida le alivió el ardor de los labios y lengua.

"¡Újule, ni te esperaste para el brindis!" dijo Gabriel como un reproche, aunque se dio muy bien cuenta de su situación.

"¡Lo lamento, la salsa está muy caliente!" ella se disculpó, ruborizándose.

"Podríamos pedir una salsa fría, pero se me hace que no estaría tan buena. ¡Ja-ja-ja-ja! No se dice salsa caliente, sino picante, Gringuita."

"¡Oh, sácate por allá! Tú sabes lo que quiero decir. Caliente o picante, me estaban ardiendo bastante la lengua y los labios, por eso le tuve que tomar a la margarita de inmediato," ella le contestó, riéndose.

"Sí, te comprendo. Bueno, brindemos por nuestra amistad y que el Señor te conceda muchos otros felices cumpleaños," dijo Gabriel, levantando su copa de Margarita para tocar el de ella.

"¡Por nuestro amor, que el Señor lo bendiga y lo haga eterno!" ella respondió, para delicia de él, "¿Entonces, qué fue lo que pasó con Duffus, Gabrielín?" preguntó Theresa, remojando otra tostadita en la salsa picante.

"¿En dónde estaba? ¡Oh, sí! Duffus se metió al templo y vio que había dos líneas largas de gente en ambos lados del confesionario, la mayoría viejitas. No quería esperar hasta que el cura acabara, así que se acercó frente al sacerdote. La gente se le quedó mirando y pensaron que estaba empezando una tercera fila; sin embargo, solo lo miraron con disgusto acercársele al presbítero en cuanto terminó con la persona a la que estaba confesando. Duffus le dijo al padre en un tono apagado, 'Padre, estoy muy agradecido por lo que usted ha hecho por mí. ¡Prácticamente me salvó usted la vida! Le quiero demostrar mi aprecio haciéndole algunos de los truquitos que hago en mi trabajo.' El párroco, por supuesto, le dijo que no sería necesario y lo dejó ir con su bendición. Duffus le rogó que le permitiera enseñarle, y el cura decidió aceptar para así poder continuar con su labor."

Theresa le dio otro sorbito a su rica bebida alcohólica y le sonrió a él.

"El confesor llamó a la siguiente persona a su derecha. El cirquero volteó alrededor y decidió hacer su numerito ahí frente al clérigo. Duffus se paró de manos en una de las bancas. Le dio vuelta a sus piernas por entre sus brazos y comenzó a girarlas alrededor como un gimnasta olímpico. Se echó varias maromas, y para terminar el número hizo unas cuantas vueltas de carreta encima de las bancas. Dos viejecitas lo observaban con los ojos muy pelones. Una le dijo a la otra, '¡Ay, Dios mío! Se me hace que mejor me voy pa' mi casa. El Padrecito está rete' duro esta mañana. Mire nomás que está dando saltos y maromas de penitencia... ¡Y yo no traigo calzones!'"

Theresa se carcajeó con su chiste. Se cubrió la boca y sacudió la cabeza.

"¿De dónde sacas todos estos chistecillos bobos?"

"¡Ey, esta es una historia verdadera! Bueno, el borrachín que nos la contó en la cantina de Rosita nos aseguró que era cierta."

"¿Así que vas a las cantinas a recoger material para tus sermones?"

"Eso, y también para echarme unas frías, mirar a las chicas, cantar una canción o dos, jugar a las barajas o dominós, platicar con la gente, y a mover el bote un poquito," explicó él, sumiendo otro totopo en la salsa.

"¿Dónde aprendiste que así es como debe vivir un respetable párroco? ¿Era parte del currículo en el seminario que atendiste?"

"Sí, Señorita. Este es el modo en que Jesús vivía. Era un pachanguero a quien le gustaba disfrutar la vida con sus amigos. Algunos no me creen buen ejemplo para sus hijos, pero no creo ser tan malo. ¿Qué crees tú?"

"¿Cómo puede ser malo alguien que puede correr sobre el agua?"

Chocaron sus vasos y bebieron. La suculenta comida fue servida; ellos le dieron gracias a Dios por los alimentos que iban a tomar y luego continuaron disfrutando de su conversación y de su cena.

Cuando acabaron de comer, el mariachi se les acercó y les preguntaron si les gustaría oír alguna canción en particular. El Padre Gabriel les pidió que lo acompañaran a cantar para la hermosa dama en su mesa. Se levantó y agarró prestado uno de sus sombreros de charro para empezar a cantar.

"Que vivas siempre dichosa y llena de bendiciones..."

Luego de cantar un par de versos, Gabriel tomó la mano de Theresa y la paró a bailar con él el intermedio musical; después continuó cantando, aún bailando con la del cumpleaños frente a la banda de alegres mariachis.

"Quisiera yo ser un ángel. Quisiera ser un San Pedro..."

Al final, los clientes del restaurante aplaudieron al cantante. Gabriel les pagó a los músicos y les regresó el sombrero. Los mariachis le exigieron en coro a la del cumpleaños que le pagara al cantante con un besito.

Ella les obedeció y le dio en beso en la mejilla. Gabriel la levantó del piso en un apretado abrazo y susurró en su oído, "Feliz cumpleaños, Amor!"

Los mariachis le cantaron, "Felicidades," por su propia cuenta, de pilón, antes de dejarlos solos de nuevo.

La reportera local de televisión, Leslie McCoy, andaba entrevistando turistas y visitantes. Un camarógrafo la seguía, filmando todo lo que estaba pasando en el lugar. Habían filmado las actividades de la pareja en la cabina de en medio, la cena, las bebidas, la canción, el baile, el beso, y el abrazo fueron todos capturados por la cámara sin que se dieran cuenta. Cuando los mariachis se retiraron, Leslie se acercó a Gabriel y Theresa.

"¿Son ustedes recién casados, o están celebrando algún aniversario?"

"No," los dos dijeron, sorprendidos.

"¿Son visitantes de fueras? ¿O Son clientes regulares de este negocio?"

"Ni una cosa ni la otra," le dijo Gabriel preguntándose cómo podría, gentilmente, terminar aquella indeseable entrevista.

"Bueno, andamos preguntando qué es lo que piensan que el condado pague una nueva arena para Los Látigos subiendo los impuestos de hoteles y renta de carros. ¿Cuál es su opinión?" Leslie les extendió el micrófono.

Theresa le dijo, "No tenemos ningún comentario que hacer. Por favor, nos gustaría tener algo de privacidad, si no le es muy inconveniente."

No contenta con su respuesta, Leslie preguntó, "Muy bien, ¿les gustaría mandar saludos a alguien mientras los tenemos frente a la cámara?"

Gabriel cubrió el lente de la cámara con la mano y se paró. El camarógrafo se echó para atrás y se tropezó con la pierna extendida del cliente que estaba sentado en la mesa de atrás. Mientras caía, el de la cámara trató de agarrarse de algo y se llevó el mantel con todo y los platos, bebidas, y utensilios de una mesa cercana. Ni la cámara ni el camarógrafo se lastimaron mucho; sin embargo, pareció como que el sacerdote había empujado al hombre para terminar con la entrevista.

Gabriel trató de ayudarle a levantarse, pero el hombre se enardeció y le gritó que no lo tocara. Leslie estaba contenta por cómo habían resultado las cosas y pensó que podría usar la filmación para darle un poco de sabor a su reporte. Gabriel le pidió a Theresa que se fueran de ahí.

Theresa se iba riendo por todo el camino hasta llegar al carro. Gabriel le abrió la puerta y le preguntó qué le parecía tan chistoso.

"¿Por qué tuviste que aventar por allá al pobre camarógrafo?"

"No lo aventé. Fue un accidente, ¡y tú lo sabes! Ya me imagino las noticias: 'Sacerdote y monjita católicos en cita de amores en restaurante local se vieron envueltos en un pleito, resultando en una cámara rota y un hombre malherido. La estación de televisión y los reporteros han iniciado una demanda contra de la arquidiócesis por daños no especificados.'"

"¡Eso sería incorrecto!" dijo Sor Theresa en lo que el Padre Gabriel se subía a su carro por el lado del chofer.

"Sí, pero podría pasar," él le dijo serio, encendiendo la máquina y manejando hacia fuera del estacionamiento del restaurante.

"Quiero decir, no es 'un sacerdote y una monjita.' Soy hermana religiosa no monjita. Las monjas se quedan en un convento; las hermanas salen a la comunidad a servir," Theresa le explicó, sacándolo de enfoque.

"¿Sabes una cosa, Hermanita Theresa? Eres una chica muy chistosa. Me sorprende lo campante que te encuentras acerca de todo el incidente."

"¡Bah, no te preocupes! Estoy segura que no va a tener ninguna consecuencia seria," Theresa le dijo, descartando el incidente entero con un movimiento de su mano.

La mujer abrió la ventana para sentir la brisa de la noche volándole el cabello castaño rojizo. Gabriel prendió el radio en música clásica y se dirigió a la casa de las hermanas a muy baja velocidad. Theresa lo observó mientras conducía. Decidió que le gustaba muchísimo más que veinte años atrás. Dejó ir un suspiro y se recostó sobre el hombro de él.

"¿Qué te pasa, Tere? ¿Te falta el aire? ¿O estás enamorada?"

"Estoy enamorada de ti, pero me pregunto ¿a dónde vamos?"

"Ahorita solo vamos para tu casa."

"Tú sabes lo que quiero decir, Gabrielín."

"Si, sé lo que quieres decir, pero no sé la respuesta a esa pregunta," susurró Gabriel, encogiéndose de hombros.

Theresa se sintió un poco molesta por su evasiva respuesta. Quería oírlo decir que la amaba y que estaba considerando seriamente dejar el sacerdocio por ella.

Cuando llegaron a su casa, Gabriel la encaminó hasta la puerta. Ella le agradeció por una noche encantadora. Él admitió que se habían divertido bastante juntos y sugirió que deberían hacerlo de nuevo. Ella mencionó que tal vez sería mejor que no. Él se le acercó a la cara. Ella lo detuvo, poniéndole la mano en la boca para evitar que la besara.

"Buenas noches, Padre Gabriel."

Él le besó la palma de la mano.

"Buenas noches, Hermana Theresa."

En cuanto llegó a su casa, se acordó que no había estado recitando sus oraciones regulares cada vez que andaba con Theresa. Se arrodilló junto a su cama y recitó su oración vespertina.

Gabriel sentía algo raro por dentro, como si se estuviera enfermando, como que le iba a dar una gripa o algo así. No se acordaba la última vez que había estado enfermo. No se había enfermado de adulto, ¡jamás! Aquella sensación era extraña, debilitante pero placentera. Estaba ansioso y excitado, cansado y listo para enfrentarse al mundo al mismo tiempo.

Fue afuera de la casa a fumarse un puro y beberse una copita de coñac.

"¡Qué manera de terminar con un día grandioso! Gracias Señor por todo lo que me has dado en esta vida. ¿Me podrías dar entendimiento del por qué Theresa ha regresado a mi vida ahora?" preguntó él, mirando a la luna y las estrellas, buscando una respuesta, pero ninguna le llegó.

En otras ocasiones, una visión o un pasaje de las escrituras venían a su mente, pero cuando preguntaba de Theresa, el silencio era su respuesta. Gabriel se dio por vencido, se acabó su bebida y su puro para irse a acostar. Normalmente se dormía rápido, pero ahora tenía problemas. Su mente se quedó re-viviendo la romántica tarde-noche que había disfrutado. Abrazó su almohada recordando como bailó con su amada.

Ya era la 1:00 a.m. cuando el teléfono junto a la cama de Gabriel timbró. Lo levantó, sospechando que era Theresa. Ella le dijo que no podía dormir tampoco y que había estado orando por la respuesta al por qué habían sido reunidos pero que no había recibido respuesta, ni siquiera una pista.

"Yo he estado haciendo la misma pregunta, y también recibí la misma respuesta, ¡ninguna!" Pausó un segundo y dijo, "Qué bueno que llamaste porque... Debo confesarte que deseaba quedarme contigo toda la noche."

"Bueno, no quería que te fueras. No sé ni que fue lo que me hizo detenerte cuando me trataste de besar, pero al tiempo que te marchabas, me tuve que recargar sobre la puerta para mantenerme adentro de la casa y no salir corriendo tras de ti. Besé el beso que me dejaste en la mano como mi único consuelo, pero necesitaba al menos oír tu voz de nuevo."

¡Se sentía tan placentero oírla decir aquellas cosas! Gabriel estuvo tentado a correr a su casa. Podría llegar allá en cinco minutos, pero decidió relajarse y contentarse con solo disfrutar de su conversación telefónica. Ella le contó que la noche anterior había tenido un sueño muy extraño.

"Estábamos bailando como en el aniversario de bodas hace dos semanas. Nos abrazamos y nos besamos, planeando nuestro futuro. Ya ves cómo son los sueños, de repente íbamos caminando rumbo al altar por el pasillo de una hermosa iglesia con nuestros parientes y amigos presentes. Mis papás y tus papás estaban ahí. El celebrante era un sacerdote muy extraño con una barbita y bigote agudos. Tú vestías un traje muy elegante de fiesta pero aún traías puesto tu collar de clérigo; yo traía un hábito todo blanco como vestido de novia. Nos casamos, pero en cuanto nos pronunciaron marido y mujer, las velas de los lados cayeron sobre el altar, el cual se encendió en llamas. El sacerdote se empezó a quemar y a carcajear como un loco."

Gabriel estaba estupefacto, escuchando la descripción de su sueño.

"¡Nos dimos cuenta que había sido el mismo Diablo quien nos había casado! Tenía una risa horrible, profunda. Yo me agarré de ti, aterrada. Una alarma sonó, y tú desapareciste. No supe a dónde fuiste. El demonio me pescó del brazo. Yo lo sentí quemándose en su garra. Me jalé para zafarme y me caí por las escaleras que llevaban al altar. En eso desperté. Me había caído de la cama y tenía el brazo dormido. Probablemente había estado durmiendo encima de él. Eran exactamente las cuatro de la mañana cuando desperté. Te llamé a las cuatro y media cuando sé que te levantas normalmente, pero nadie me contestó. Adiviné que ya te habías ido de pesca."

Un escalofrío le recorrió la espina dorsal al presbítero oyendo el sueño de Theresa. ¡Era el mismo que él tuvo la noche anterior! También se había despertado a las cuatro de la mañana, cuando sonó la alarma.

"¡Dios mío! Fue exactamente el mismo sueño que yo tuve anoche y la misma hora en la que desperté. ¿Cómo puede ser eso?"

"¡Estás bromeando! ¿Verdad?" ella jadeó, boquiabierta.

"No, Tere. Te estoy diciendo la verdad. Sentí un escalofrío escuchándote a ti contándome mi sueño y diciendo que tú lo soñaste. Pienso que Satanás nos está tendiendo una trampa, pero no puedo comprender de qué se trata. Vamos a rezar por la fuerza necesaria para evitar caer en ella."

Rezaron un rosario cada uno y se pudieron dormir. La oscurísima sombra del maligno se alejó de la ventana del párroco y se escurrió por la pared de afuera de la rectoría; un perrito callejero le empezó a ladrar a la sombra y después pegó carrera, aullando aterrorizado por la entidad invisible.

Durante los siguientes días, el Padre Gabriel siguió predicando, manejando sus deberes, dando consejos, curando, y haciendo milagros. Sor Theresa estaba enseñando, liderando el grupo de estudios bíblicos, tocando, y organizando la música para las celebraciones litúrgicas.

Cuando se encontraban juntos, sin embargo, sus mentes se sentían como empañadas con deseos contradictorios. Por un lado querían continuar con sus ministerios para gloria de Dios, mientras que por el otro, querían abandonar esos ministerios para pasar más tiempo cerca uno del otro, ser felices juntos, como marido y mujer, ser uno. Por esto, ambos se estaban sintiendo enfermos, la dulce enfermedad de estar enamorados.

Capítulo VIII

SIDA

El martes 12 de octubre en la noche, el Padre Gabriel estaba en la casa de Felipe Martínez en el corazón del barrio. Felipe había sido un amigo de muchos años. Él fue el que había ayudado a José Arturo Infante y María de la Luz Negrete de Infante a acomodarse en San Antonio cuando acababan de llegar de México. Felipe y su ya finada esposa, Petrita, habían sido los padrinos de bautizo de Gabriel; cuando era niño había trabajado con ellos, barriendo la tienda y acomodando productos en los estantes.

Felipe le enseñó a Gabriel ajedrez; tenían encuentros que a veces duraban semanas. También había animado al joven Gabriel a que se enlistara en las reservas del Ejército mientras aún estaba en la preparatoria, creyendo que le ayudaría a Gabriel a ser aceptado por el papá de su novia, un general. También le aconsejó que tratara de atender la academia militar West Point.

Las cosas no habían salido como habían planeado, y Gabriel acabó en el seminario en lugar de la academia militar. Sirvió seis años en la reserva del ejército como especialista médico, acabando su breve carrera militar esa vez como sargento de las reservas del ejército. Mas delante sirvió cuatro años como capellán del Ejercito y hasta fue a la Primera Guerra del Golfo.

Ahora, años más tarde, el pupilo podía vencer al maestro cuatro de cinco veces. Pero esta era una de las cinco que Felipe podía vencer al pupilo en el juego. Usó una letal combinación de reina, torre, obispo, y caballo.

El sacerdote, cuya mente parecía estar en algo aparte del juego, concedió su derrota y trató de disculparse para irse a acostar temprano. Felipe estaba tan feliz con su victoria que no le permitió irse.

"¿Por qué no te quedas y cantas unas viejas canciones conmigo?"

"¡Bueno, está bien! ¿Como en los viejos tiempos, eh, Don Pipi?"

Cuando Gabriel tenía menos de dos años de edad y estaba aprendiendo a hablar, le decía a su padrino Pipi en lugar de Felipe. Petrita, su esposa, empezó a llamar a su esposo con ese sobrenombre también y se le quedó.

El viejo dueño de la tiendita cerró su negocio por esa noche y se llevo al Padre Gabriel a su casa, la cual estaba en la parte de atrás de la tienda

Felipe sacó su guitarra y la empezó a afinar; le pidió a Gabriel que sacara un par de cervezas del refrigerador.

137

Ya tenía unos nachos listos para salir del horno. Eran los favoritos de Gabriel, no solo con queso y jalapeños sino también frijoles refritos y tocino, además de cebolla y tomate frescos, ¡perfectos para la cerveza!

Felipe sacó un viejo cancionero de un librero y se lo aventó al joven.

"Fíjate a ver si te acuerdas de alguna de esas canciones, Gabrielín... Quiero decir, Venerable Padre."

"¡Aguzado, Viejo Mollejón...! Digo, Señor Martínez, mi Padrino del alma."

Gabriel abrió el cancionero en la página que traía una canción de serenata, lo cual le trajo recuerdos de veinte años atrás.

Pipi le había sugerido en ese tiempo que llevara sus mariachis y le diera una serenata a Theresa. Ya que la chica había pasado diez años en países de habla hispana cuando estaba creciendo, era fluente en el lenguaje y las costumbres. Ella disfrutó mucho de la serenata, pero el General Reynolds, su padre, mandó a los policías militares para que escoltaran a los músicos y al cantante hacia fuera de la instalación militar. Ni el general ni su esposa aprobaban al novio de su hija por causa de su etnicidad y humilde origen.

"Vamos a empezar con esta, Pipi," dijo el cura después de darle un buen trago a su cerveza helada.

Felipe silbó la introducción que normalmente se toca con un violín y comenzó a tocar el guapango con su guitarra.

Gabriel empezó a cantar como si estuviera bajo la ventana, dándole serenata a su amada, haciéndole saber de su amor, y quejándose de su desdén. El cantante se levantó y bailó un poco de zapateado mientras que Felipe pegaba un grito de gusto.

El viejo admiraba la manera en que la voz de Gabriel se había madurado y desarrollado. Su estilo de canto le daba énfasis al sentimiento de los versos. Continuó cantando el segundo verso, expresando tristeza por ser pobre y no merecer el amor de la señorita, pero prometiendo que lo conseguiría en contra de todo.

Gabriel se aprovechó del intermedio musical para comerse otro nacho y beberse otro trago de cerveza para aclararse la garganta y continuar cantando. El último verso hablaba de su obsesión con esa mujer y ninguna otra, con la esperanza de que ella le corresponderá. Felipe tocó la guitarra y chifló la parte del violín para acabar la canción.

Le aplaudió al cantante, y Gabriel le aplaudió al guitarrista. Los dos atacaron la charola de nachos y las cheves con gusto.

Felipe buscó en el cancionero otra de sus favoritas. Se cantaron unas más, hasta que los nachos se terminaron entre canción y canción. El seis de cervezas también se acabó, así que fue hora que Gabriel se fuera, una hora después de lo que había dicho que ya se iba. Pero fue un rato muy ameno.

"Gracias por una tardeada espléndida, mi Amigo. ¡Que el Señor te bendiga y te socorra todos los días de tu vida!"

"Gracias, Padre. Necesitas venir a verme más seguido. Puedo traer a un par de mis amigos para que nos acompañen y tengamos un concierto de a de veras, con violín, corneta y guitarrón.

Sharon McKenzie era una prostituta muy bien conocida en el oeste de la ciudad. Era una de las pocas blancas trabajando esa área; la mayoría eran mexicanas o méxico-americanas, unas negritas, y algunos transvestistas.

No siempre fue así para Sharon. Había graduado de una preparatoria del Distrito del Norte, se casó joven y tenía una familia con un tornero que tenía buen empleo en la Fuerza Aérea. Tuvieron un hijo y una hija. Después que sus hijos nacieron, ella se convirtió en chofer de camiones pesados.

Entre ella y su esposo, estaban ganando más de ochenta mil dólares al año. La vida era buena entonces. Su marido era hombre bueno y honesto así como un padre amoroso, pero un poco débil de personalidad. A Steven McKenzie era muy fácil convencerlo de que hiciera cosas, como comprar un bote para ir a pescar con los amigos cuando no era en realidad pescador.

Steve quería caerle bien a la gente, así que seguido tenía pachanguitas en casa para sus compañeros de trabajo. En una de esas, un tipo nuevo en el grupo, llamado Fernando Galán, los introdujo al uso de la heroína.

Fernando era nacido y criado en California. Nadie sabía la historia de su vida, pero sus tatuajes y sus acerados músculos denotaban algún tiempo en la prisión. Sharon se sintió atraída hacia Fernando desde el principio, tan diferente a su esposo. Había algo magnético en aquel hombre, y no pasó mucho tiempo antes que Sharon estaba copulando con Fernando en su propia cama, mientras que Steven estaba tirado en el suelo bajo el efecto de la heroína combinada con un número de cervezas.

Desde el momento en que Sharon se vio por vez primera en los verdes ojos de Fernando, las cosas se fueron derrumbando cada vez más rápido para ella. Sharon se hizo adicta a la droga. Steve se divorció de ella cuando se enteró que lo andaba engañando. La corte le quitó a los niños y le dio custodia de ellos a Steve porque ella fue declarada madre irresponsable.

Mientras andaba manejando bajo la influencia de la droga, Sharon atropelló a una viejita. Acumuló una ficha incluyendo narcóticos, manejar bajo influencia de drogas, hurto, falsificación de cheques, y prostitución. Perdió su hogar, su trabajo, su licencia de chofer comercial, y su dignidad; acabó como prostituta adicta a la heroína trabajando para Fernando. Él tenía controladas así a otras cinco mujeres. Para hacer las cosas peores, Sharon había sido diagnosticada con SIDA. Estaba muy asustada.

La mujerzuela enferma estaba bebiendo en un bar cerca de la tienda de Don Felipe, preguntándose qué podría hacer. Fernando estaba a punto de ir a verla y recogerle el dinero que le correspondía. Siempre se llevaba la mayor parte de lo que Sharon ganaba y le proveía a cambio con una casilla vieja. Le daba también heroína, alcohol, y protección. ¡Lo odiaba!

Sharon traía en su bolsa el dinero de sus últimos clientes. Por un rato se sintió culpable, preocupada que aquellos hombres pudieran infectarse, pero luego racionalizó que si se enfermaban, ¡se lo tenían bien merecido! Uno de sus muchos clientes le había pasado el virus; ella se iba a morir por culpa de eso. Todos ellos merecían morirse con ella, fue lo que se dijo a sí misma. Sharon no se estaba sintiendo bien esa noche, y el güisqui que estaba tomando no le estaba ayudando en absoluto.

Lágrimas rodaban de sus ojos claros al acordarse de su hogar, su familia, y sus niños. Pensó que todo era culpa de Fernando. Si él nunca hubiera aparecido en su vida, ella aún lo tendría todo. ¡Tendría que pagar por eso! Ni siquiera tenía ya ningún interés por ella.

Al principio, Fernando le había prometido que se iba a hacer cargo de ella. Se iban a casar después que se divorció de Steve. ¡Puras mentiras! Él nunca había tenido intenciones de nada más que seducirla y humillarla para que se convirtiera en una de sus esclavas. La droga le daba un gran poder sobre ella y las otras.

No pasó mucho tiempo después que ella se fue a vivir con Fernando que despertó la mañana después de una parranda en la cama con tres hombres a quien jamás había visto. Fernando le dijo que había hecho "muy buen trabajo" y le dio algo de dinero además de un poquito de la droga. Se dio cuenta que se había convertido en esclava de Fernando y su heroína.

Sharon conoció a otras dos que también trabajaban para Fernando, y que habían muerto tratando de dejarlo. La muerte era su única salida. Todas las mujeres bajo su control sabían que él las había matado, pero sabían que a nadie le importa si otra prostituta acababa muerta en el oeste de la ciudad.

Gina murió de una sobredosis en una casucha abandonada; Shenika se había "cortado las venas" de acuerdo con las noticias. Sharon sabía que fue Fernando quien le inyectó la sobredosis de droga a Gina y le cortó las venas a Shenika para hacerlo parecer como suicidio. Había hecho aquello como ejemplos de lo que les pasaba a las que trataban de dejarlo. Ya había amasado una pequeña fortuna del sexo y las drogas.

Fernando nunca usaba heroína. Fumaba marihuana y esporádicamente aspiraba cocaína. Cultivaba imagen de hombre de mundo y practicaba artes marciales. Tenía un condominio en una comunidad muy exclusiva, manejaba un carro deportivo, disfrutaba fumar puros caros, cenar en buenos lugares, beber buenos vinos, y vestir ropa de diseñador.

Mantenía un ojo abierto buscando prospectas empleadas para reemplazar las que había perdido. Fernando estaba algo preocupado por su reporte de impuestos; así pues, inició un negocio de consulta para Internet que le sirviera de frente para justificar su estilo de vida tan caro.

Ocupó a un gerente para que le administrara el negocio porque él sabía muy poco acerca de computadoras o negocios en el Internet. El gerente del negocio ocupó a un pequeño grupo de jóvenes expertos y estaba haciendo la pequeña empresa progresar. Pronto Fernando iba a tener problemas lavando su dinero. El tener aquel negocio le quitaba tiempo para supervisar de cerca a sus chicas. El ex-convicto se había mantenido fuera de la cárcel desde que se había cambiado a Texas, y planeaba seguir así.

Fernando llegó al bar de la esquina en donde le había dicho a Sharon que la iba a recoger. Ella estaba ahí esperándolo afuera.

"Métete al carro Sharon," dijo él, abriéndole la puerta desde adentro.

Ella abordó el auto y trató de besarlo, pero él le dio una bofetada tan tremenda que ella comenzó a sangrar profusamente por la boca. Él se raspó un poco la parte posterior de la mano con los dientes de ella.

"Con una..." le gritó entre palabras vulgares, "Ya te he dicho que esto es exclusivamente negocio. ¡Nunca más trates de besarme!"

Sacó unas toallas de papel de la cajuelita, se las aventó y tomó otra para limpiarse su propia mano.

"¡Limpia ese atascadero, Perra! Me estás manchando el carro de sangre. ¡Límpiate el hocico!" continuó gritándole con hirientes maldiciones.

Sharon obedeció sin decir palabra. Luego metió la mano a su bolsa y le dio a Fernando cinco billetes de veinte dólares.

Él los contó y le preguntó, "¿Dónde está el resto de la lana?"

"El negocio está lento," dijo ella, "Es todo lo tengo para darte ahorita."

Fernando aspiró profundo, impaciente, mirando a la distancia. Sharon sabía que él estaba a punto de explotar. La agarró de los cabellos y le estrelló la cara en el tablero, quebrándole la nariz. Su sangre se derramó por doquier y manchó el tablero. La situación hizo que el alcahuete se enfureciera más. Salió de su carro, maldiciendo, y fue al lado del pasajero.

"¡Salte de mi carro!" le ordenó entre maldiciones.

Fernando abrió la puerta del lado del pasajero, jaló a Sharon hacia fuera cogiéndola por el pelo de nuevo, la sostuvo con una mano y le apuñeteó el estómago un par de veces; después la lanzó violentamente contra la pared. Ella rebotó y cayó al suelo, tratando de aspirar aire.

Fernando metió la mano al carro deportivo y agarró la bolsa de Sharon. Sacó otros doscientos dólares y volteó a verla.

"¿Por qué me estabas ocultando este dinero, Sharon? ¿Qué intentabas hacer con esta lana, eh?"

Tiró la bolsa a la banqueta. Sharon estaba llorando y sangrando profusamente a través de su nariz fracturada. Sus pantimedias estaban rotas y sus rodillas raspadas. Trató de incorporarse de la banqueta.

"Necesito ese dinero para mis medicinas y para hacer mis pagos."

Fernando la pateó en el abdomen, derribándola de nuevo. El Padre Gabriel venía saliendo de la tienda al cruzar la calle cuando vio aquello.

El cura le gritó, "¡Detente en nombre de Cristo Rey!"

El excitado Fernando oyó al hombre gritándole la orden a sus espaldas y pensó que podría ser un policía diciendo, ¡Detente en nombre de la ley! así que saltó a su carro para escaparse. Vio una silueta oscura cruzando la calle, corriendo hacia él.

"¡Un desgraciado polizonte!"

Fernando maldijo entre dientes mientras ponía el carro en movimiento. ¿Quién más se atrevería a interferir entre un alcahuete y su prostituta?

El sacerdote miró a la mujer ensangrentada, tirada en la banqueta; le recordó a nuestro Señor en el camino al Calvario. Gabriel se enfureció, y corrió tras el fugitivo. El auto deportivo ya iba zumbando calle abajo.

El Padre G volvió sus ojos al cielo y rugió frustrado, "¡Aaargh, Señor, permíteme ponerle la mano encima!"

El carrito deportivo se tuvo que dar un frenón para evitar chocar con un camionzote que salía de un taller mecánico. El Padre Gabriel se dejó ir a toda velocidad en dirección del carro detenido.

Fernando vio la cara enojada del corredor aparecer en su espejo retrovisor. Aún sin saber quién era el que lo iba persiguiendo, vio tal determinación en su rostro que decidió mejor darse la vuelta y huir de ahí en dirección opuesta antes que el sujeto pudiera alcanzarlo.

Al tiempo que hacía una vuelta en U, su carro pasó muy cerca del Padre G. El místico estaba cargado de furia. A pesar de darse cuenta que aquel no era un oficial de la ley, Fernando siguió en su huida.

Gabriel le dio un puñetazo a la ventana del chofer y agarró al hombre por el cabello. El alcahuete le dio el acelerón al vehículo, haciendo al presbítero girar como un trompo antes de caer al pavimento.

El auto desapareció en la esquina cuando dio vuelta a la derecha. El Padre G sintió un dolor agudo en su hombro derecho donde el carro lo había golpeado. La mano derecha de Gabriel estaba un poco cortada y sangrando. Traía algo del cabello negro de Fernando en su mano.

"¡Dios mío! ¿Qué he hecho?"

Se sobó el hombro derecho y empezó a caminar de regreso a donde Sharon estaba reponiendo sus cosas en su bolsa. El sacerdote se inclinó y levantó algo del suelo. Luego ayudó a la mujer a levantarse.

"¿Estás bien, Sharon?"

Ella miró al extraño y notó su blanco collar romano de clérigo.

"¿Usted me conoce?" le preguntó ella, sorprendida.

"Bueno," él le sonrió al decirle, "sé tu nombre, fecha de nacimiento y dirección, pero no creo que nos hayamos encontrado antes."

"Usted es un predicador. ¿Cómo sabe mi nombre y...?"

"Está todo aquí, en tu tarjeta de identificación."

Le dio su identificación que se la había salido de la bolsa. El Padre G le tocó levemente la nariz, y ella se hizo hacia atrás adolorida.

"Creo que te quebró tu linda naricita."

"¡Me quebró la vida entera!" dijo ella, sollozando.

"Hija mía, estas heridas van a sanar, y tu vida se va a recomponer," el cura le dijo para darle esperanza mientras acariciaba su carita sangrada.

Se sacó el pañuelo blanco de su bolsillo y se lo ofreció a la mujer.

"Soy el Padre Gabriel," le dijo, estrechando su mano, "Debíamos llamar a una ambulancia para que te lleven al hospital. No se te vayan a infectar tus heridas."

"¡Ay, Padre!" Sharon dijo horrorizada, mirando su sangre en las manos del ministro y en su camisa.

"¿Cuál es el problema, Niña?" Gabriel le preguntó, notando la alarma en el tono de su voz.

Fernando Galán regresó en su auto. Pensó que un sacerdote no era peligro para él; aún más, estaba muy enojado que aquel tipo le había quebrado la ventana del carro, le arrancó unos cabellos de la cabeza, y le sacó un buen susto. Fernando siempre traía una pistola automática de nueve milímetros cargada bajo el asiento de su carro. Había decidido enseñarle al intruso una buena lección, así que regresó a la escena.

El carrito deportivo bajó de velocidad frente a la pareja. La ventana del pasajero estaba abierta. El alcahuete tenía la pistola apuntándoles. Gabriel cubrió a la mujer con su cuerpo mientras imploraba ayuda de Dios.

"¡Padre Eterno protégenos del enemigo!"

Fernando saboreó el momento al apretar el gatillo, riéndose, pero ¡la pistola no disparó!

Detuvo el carro, y amartilló de nuevo el arma. Una bala con casquillo saltó de la cámara. El enojado alcahuete le apuntó a la pareja una vez más y apretó el gatillo de nuevo, pero ¡la pistola no disparó esa vez tampoco!

El Padre Gabriel se dio la vuelta y encaró al pistolero; lo miró fijamente a los ojos con un gesto grave.

"¡Lárgate!" le ordenó con voz muy firme y potente.

Al oír el tono tan autoritario del místico, Fernando sintió un escalofrío hasta el tuétano y un profundo temor en su corazón. Soltó la pistola y se arrancó. Sharon miró las luces traseras del carrito dorado desvanecerse en la distancia y se sintió aliviada. Volteó a ver el rostro de Gabriel. El enojo ya se le había pasado, y se veía lleno de amorosa preocupación por ella.

"Tengo SIDA, Padre. Lo siento mucho que no le dije inmediatamente. Mire sus manos. Está todo embarrado de mi sangre infectada, y luego trae cortadas abiertas en la mano. ¡Lo siento tanto!"

Sharon estaba llorando. Infectar a uno de sus clientes era una cosa, pero infectar a un hombre inocente que estaba tratando de ayudarla era muy diferente. El presbítero la abrazó y recargó su cabeza contra el pecho de él.

"Siempre confía en el Señor con tu vida, Sharon; Él tiene un plan para ti y para mí. Por eso fue que nos encontramos aquí esta noche."

El Padre G trató de darle ánimo a ella, y a sí mismo, pero por un segundo sintió sus rodillas débiles, pensando que podría adquirir SIDA con ese encuentro. Antes que Theresa reapareciera en su vida, estaba listo para morir cualquier día en el servicio del Señor. Esa noche, temió morir y no volver a ver a Theresa. Sharon era de la misma talla que ella. Gabriel sostuvo a Sharon en sus brazos, pensando en Theresa.

Una voz en su mente le dijo, "Confía en el Señor siempre."

Fernando no paró hasta llegar a casa. Había ido manejando como si el mismo Diablo lo fuera persiguiendo.

Salió del carro con la pistola en la mano; confundido y enojado, apretó el gatillo rápidamente tres veces apuntándole al suelo. La pistola disparó tres tiros, uno de los cuales atravesó el pie derecho del alcahuete.

Fernando cayó al suelo, berreando de dolor. Los vecinos, al oír los tiros, llamaron a la policía.

En la calle Guadalupe, un policía salió de su carro de patrullas con el radio en una mano y su pistola en la otra, apuntándole al Padre Gabriel.

"¡Retírate de la mujer y pon las manos arriba en donde las pueda ver ahora mismo!"

Gabriel reconoció al oficial Lara pero aún así obedeció su orden.

"¿Qué demonios pasó aquí, Padre G?" el oficial inquirió, mirando la cara ensangrentada de la mujer y las manos llenas de sangre del cura.

El sacerdote le explicó al policía mientras mantenía las manos en alto, "No es lo que parece, Oficial Lara."

"Él no me golpeó, Oficial. Fue mi novio, Fernando Galán, quien también trató de matarnos a los dos después que el Padre Gabriel vino a salvarme."

Sharon se interpuso entre el cura y el policía para defender a su salvador. El oficial guardó su pistola. Ya estaba familiarizado con Fernando y sus actividades.

"¿Dónde está Fernando?" preguntó el Oficial Lara. Antes que Sharon pudiera replicar, él le dijo a la despachadora por su radio, "Veintitrés cuarenta, vamos a necesitar una ambulancia para una persona herida."

"Diez cuatro, Veintitrés Cuarenta," la despachadora le contestó.

"¿Anda a pie o en su carrito dorado?" el oficial continuó haciendo preguntas, tratando de ganar información para avisar a los otros policías.

"Anda en su carro. Ya debe estar llegando a su casa," dijo Sharon.

El policía puso la información por el radio para que sus colegas se alertaran en caso que vieran el carrito dorado. Incluso tenía el número de las placas del carro porque ya había lidiado con el alcahuete antes.

La semana anterior, Lara le había dado una infracción a Fernando por exceso de velocidad en la calle Zarzamora. Todo había estado bien, así que no pudo arrestarlo ni catear su vehículo. Tuvo que dejarlo ir con solo una infracción. Lara sabía que una vez que arrestara al hombre, podría encontrar la pistola y las drogas que se suponía andaba siempre cargando con él. El patrullero pensó que aquella sería su oportunidad de ponerle las manos encima y erradicarlo de las calles.

El Oficial Lara había andado con Gina Zamarripa, la chica a quien Fernando había dado una sobredosis de heroína. Había sido la novia de Lara en la preparatoria. Roger Lara se hizo policía mientras que Gina Zamarripa se convirtió en prostituta; sin embargo, Roger aún guardaba amor por Gina. Le rompió el corazón oír de su muerte y el hecho que su asesino no fue siquiera acusado por falta de evidencia.

"Padre déjeme decirle la verdad," Sharon le dijo a Gabriel mientras iban sentados en la ambulancia camino al hospital.

"Ya me la dijiste, Sharon. No es culpa tuya; no te preocupes por eso. No estoy enojado contigo. Las cosas siempre ocurren por algún motivo," el cura le dijo sonriéndole, comprendiendo su preocupación.

"Ya había oído hablar de usted," ella le dijo, mirando al piso, buscando las palabras apropiadas. "Hasta fui a uno de sus servicios. La gente dice que hace milagros. Yo quería dejar de usar drogas, pero no creía en milagros."

146

El Padre Gabriel le levantó la cara con su dedo índice en la barbilla de la mujer y la miró a los hermosos ojos claros. Eran parte azul, parte verde y parte café clarito. Gabriel le pidió que continuara.

"Esta noche, que lo vi defenderme, me acordé de lo que había hablado el día que fui a su servicio. Dijo la historia de una mujer que había andado con hemorragias por muchos años. Solo tocó el manto de Jesús y se curó. Yo lo vi a usted y me imaginé que era Jesús quien venía a mi rescate. No me pregunte por qué. Por eso no lo detuve que me tocara, porque esperaba que Dios me curara a través de su toque. Me sentí tan bien en sus brazos aún cuando estaba llorando; me sentí como una bebita en los brazos de mi madre. Por un momento creí con todo mi corazón que esto era posible, pero más tarde me di cuenta que lo más seguro sería que lo haya yo condenado a muerte por intentar salvar mi vida miserable. Perdóneme, Padre. Sé que voy a morir pronto, y he sido la peor de las pecadoras."

Sharon descansó su cabeza en el hombro del ministro, llorando. Le recordó a María Magdalena. Sus lágrimas le mojaron la pierna del pantalón; se conmovió por ella y la bendijo.

"Yo te perdono y te absuelvo de todos tus muchos pecados, en el nombre del Padre y del Hijo y del Espíritu Santo."

Gabriel le dio un beso en la cabeza a Sharon y le alisó el cabello.

El sacerdote recibió un par de puntadas en su mano derecha. A Sharon la admitieron para observación y estudios de la sangre cuando se enteraron que había sido diagnosticada con el virus del SIDA. El equipo médico también tomó unas muestras de sangre y de saliva de Gabriel.

Cuando llegó a casa, Gabriel se fue al teléfono a llamar a Theresa, pero no queriendo alarmarla, decidió no hacerlo. Después de todo, no estaba seguro de haberse infectado. Si había sido infectado, su fantasía de dejar el sacerdocio y casarse con Theresa de seguro que se desvanecería. Preferiría morirse que pasarle la mortal enfermedad a su amada Theresa.

Se sirvió un vaso de brandy con hielo y Pepsi Cola, encendió un puro y se sentó afuera de la casa a contemplar el cielo estrellado. Era una noche cálida. Se quitó la camisa embarrada de sangre y la aventó en una cubeta con agua y jabón para dejarla que se remojara toda la noche. Gabriel se recorrió el musculoso tórax con la mano y pensó que inútil era toda aquella potencia muscular ante una enfermedad como el SIDA.

"Señor, te necesito más que nunca. No entiendo qué está pasando en mi vida. ¿Por qué me mandaste a Theresa de vuelta? ¿Voy a morir ya pronto? ¿Ya se está acabando mi misión en este mundo? ¿Quieres que siga sirviéndote como sacerdote? ¿Me estás poniendo a prueba? ¿Por qué no oigo tu voz en mi mente para contestar mis preguntas cuando me has ayudado en otras cosas? ¿Por qué siento miedo de la muerte esta noche?"

Se tomó su bebida mezclada, fumó su puro, y escuchó el suave viento moviendo las ramas y las hojas de los árboles. Gabriel se rindió de estar esperando una respuesta y decidió irse a dormir.

Antes de entrar a la casa, volvió los ojos al cielo y dijo, "Buenas noches, mi Señor. Entre tus manos encomiendo mi vida y mi alma. Que se haga tu voluntad y no la mía."

El suave y tibio viento le acarició la cara moviéndole levemente el negro cabello y la barba.

Al siguiente día, Gabriel fue al hospital a visitar a Sharon. El doctor vino a su cuarto para hablar con los dos. Escucharon con gran ansiedad las palabras del doctor.

"Bien, pues los exámenes rápidos de sangre y saliva han sido hechos, y los resultados fueron confirmados un par de veces."

Sharon y Gabriel se tomaron de la mano y se voltearon a ver a los ojos mientras el doctor continuaba su reporte.

"¡Ninguno de ustedes dos muestra traza de VIH ni SIDA en su sangre!"

El Doctor Snow no la podía creer. Estaba comparando los resultados con el archivo médico de Sharon en donde se confirmaba que ella tenía SIDA. Esta vez, sin embargo, su sangre era perfectamente normal, así como la de Gabriel. El doctor trató de explicar las posibilidades.

"Es posible que haya habido algún tipo de error en su diagnosis de la sangre la última vez, aunque no parece muy obvio con solo mirar los récords. No tengo en realidad ninguna explicación del por qué puedas haber tenido SIDA un día y nada el día siguiente."

"Yo sí," dijo Sharon mientras abrazaba al Padre Gabriel. "¡Fue un milagro! ¡En verdad, en verdad funcionó! ¡Gracias Padre!"

"Dale gracias a Dios. Fue ese momento de fe que tuviste anoche, lo cual te salvó," le dijo Gabriel, sosteniéndola en sus brazos.

El médico solo se sonrió. Aún pensaba que había habido algún error en la primera diagnosis porque él estaba muy seguro que el segundo, que los mostraba saludables, estaba correcto pues él mismo lo había revisado.

Estaba contento de ver que su paciente se iba a poner bien. Sería solo cuestión de tiempo para que su nariz sanara.

"Me gustaría que vinieran luego para hacerles otros exámenes. Los otros resultados estarán de vuelta en dos semanas, y pudiera ser que no tuvieran síntomas por meses o años después," explicó el galeno.

Estuvieron de acuerdo en tomar otros exámenes más delante, pero no tenían duda en sus mentes que Dios ya había limpiado a Sharon, y que Gabriel no podía estar infectado ya que Sharon no tenía la enfermedad.

Aliviado e inspirado por las buenas noticias, el Padre Gabriel empezó a cantar en el cuarto del hospital una canción de fe en inglés.

"Sorprendente gracia, dulce sonido que salvó a un miserable como yo."

Sharon se le unió en el canto, sintiéndose que debía unírsele también en agradecimiento a Dios.

"Andaba perdido, pero he sido rescatado, estaba ciego, pero ahora puedo ver. Fue tu gracia la que me enseñó a temer, y la gracia me quitó el miedo. ¡Qué preciosa apareció esa gracia la hora en que creí por vez primera!"

Conmovido por su canción, el viejo doctor se les unió también.

"A través de muchos peligros, luchas y trampas ya he pasado. Es tu gracia la que me ha traído hasta aquí con seguridad, y esa gracia me llevará a casa. El Señor me ha prometido solo lo bueno. Su palabra asegura mi esperanza; Él será mi escudo y mi porción mientras haya vida."

Oyendo su canto, una enfermera vino al cuarto, pero en lugar de detenerlos, se les unió también.

"Estando ahí diez mil años, radiantes brillando como el sol, tendremos no menos días para cantar la gracia de Dios que cuando apenas empezamos."

El improvisado coro aplaudió calurosamente al terminar su himno.

"¡Alabado sea el Señor! Dijo Sharon, abrazando a todo mundo.

Lleno de alegría, el Padre Gabriel exclamó, "¡Amén!"

Un hombre de traje café claro entró al cuarto. El presbítero lo reconoció como detective de homicidios con quien había lidiado en el pasado.

Sharon dijo, "Padre, definitivamente me voy a meter a un programa de ayuda para dejar de usar heroína. Solo espero que Fernando no me encuentre antes que ya esté yo limpia del vicio."

"¡Eso es grandioso, Sharon!" le dijo el cura, volteando a ver al recién llegado. Gabriel lo saludó, "Bienvenido a la fiesta, Detective O'Hara. Estamos celebrando la vida y alabando al Buen Señor."

Le extendió la mano vendada al oficial. Él se la estrechó.

"Bueno, pues les traigo buenas noticias para agregar a su celebración. Anoche agarramos a Fernando en donde vive. Después que Lara puso la descripción del hombre y su carro, recibimos una llamada en su área por un tiroteo. Parece que Fernando se dio un balazo por accidente mientras estaba jugando con su pistola. Cuando los policías llegaron, lo encontraron en posesión de drogas, además de la pistola. Los de evidencias encontraron las dos balas que intentó dispararles, estaban aún intactas en el interior de su auto. No sabemos por qué fue que no estallaron, las dos tenían la marca de la aguja de percusión, y no se veía nada defectuoso en ellas hasta donde sabemos. Creo que los dos tuvieron mucha suerte anoche."

"¡Por supuesto! Es que el ángel del Señor nos protegió; por eso fue que la pistola no disparó," dijo Sharon, interrumpiendo el reporte del detective.

El Padre Gabriel la miró, preguntándose de dónde había sacado eso. Ella se encogió de hombros y le hizo seña al investigador para que continuara.

"Bueno, Fernando enfrenta cargos por intento de asesinato capital de dos personas, posesión de heroína y cocaína, portar armas ilegalmente, y posesión de la medicina prescrita para Sharon. La oficina de impuestos federales está investigando sus reportes; le van a hacer una auditoría. La unidad que investiga el vicio está juntando a sus prostitutas para hacer un caso por promoción agravada de prostitución. Van a necesitar declaración tuya, Sharon. La unidad de narcóticos tenía un par de casos por heroína en contra de él los cuales van a llevar a la fiscalía del distrito. Estoy seguro que nuestro amiguito se va a pasar buen tiempo en prisión, si sobrevive."

"¿Qué quiere decir?" preguntó Sharon.

"¡Me acabo de enterar por el hospital donde fue tratado que los exámenes de su sangre resultaron positivos de tener SIDA!"

Sharon miró al cura para ver si tenía alguna explicación, pero él solo se encogió de hombros y levantó las cejas, asombrado.

Para alivianar la atmósfera en el cuarto, la cual se había tornado muy sombría de repente al haber oído lo que le esperaba al criminal, Gabriel se acordó de un chiste y se los contó.

"Un día un peluquero estaba platicando con uno de sus clientes mientras le cortaba el cabello. El cliente, que era de los regulares ahí, era vendedor de seguros. El agente le comenzó a decir al peluquero acerca de un día en el que le dio un dolor de cabeza tan terrible que no podía ya ni trabajar. No les podía hablar por teléfono a los clientes ni se podía concentrar en el papeleo. Se sentía nauseado..."

"¡Un dolor de cabeza migraña!" interrumpió el doctor al oír los síntomas, pero luego se cubrió la boca e hizo seña para que el ministro continuara.

"Probablemente..." Gabriel estuvo de acuerdo y continuó, "El agente de seguros le dijo al barbero, 'No podía trabajar, y decidí irme a casa. Cuando llegué, ¡encontré a mi esposa en la cama con otro!' El barbero boquiabierto quiso saber más detalles. Le preguntó al agente, '¿Y qué estaban haciendo cuando los hallaste? ¿Estaban desnudos?' El agente dijo indignado, '¡Ey, encontré a mi mujer en la cama con otro dolor de cabeza, no con otro hombre!' Ambos se carcajearon. El peluquero le dijo, 'Estuvo muy buena. La voy a tener que usar yo.' Tan pronto como un nuevo cliente vino a la peluquería, después que el agente ya se había ido, el barbero le contó la historia al cliente en lo que le cortaba el pelo. "Sabes, José, el otro día me dio un terrible dolor de cabeza... migraña, y ya no pude trabajar. Cerré la peluquería y me fui a casa. Cuando llegué, ¡que me encuentro a mi mujer en la cama con otro! El cliente se quedó callado pero luego le dijo, 'Sí, ya todos sabíamos lo que estaba pasando pero no te habíamos querido decir. Al menos ya te enteraste. ¿Qué le hiciste al vendedor de seguros ese?'"

El doctor y la enfermera se salieron del cuarto risa y risa. O'Hara solo se rió poquito porque ya lo había oído antes. Sharon se estaba riendo como una chiquilla. El sacerdote se disculpó y dijo que tenía que partir.

"Aún necesito una declaración de su parte, Padre," dijo el detective, dándole un par de formas para llenar.

"Lo escribiré y se lo enviaré por fax de mi oficina, como la última vez," Gabriel le dijo, tomando las formas con las que ya estaba familiarizado.

"Magnífico, usted ya sabe lo que necesitamos en su declaración. Creo que ha estado escribiendo más reportes para la policía que algunos de nuestros oficiales. ¿Cómo es que siempre se ve envuelto entre tanto argüende?"

"Es porque me envuelvo en los asuntos de mi comunidad. Su negocio y el mío envuelven a las mismas gentes."

Sharon le dio un beso a Gabriel y le dio las gracias. El cura dejó el hospital muy aliviado, como si hubiera dejado caer una tonelada de acero de sus hombros. Estaba sano... ¿Debería contarle a Theresa?

Otro día, Gabriel y Theresa les estaban leyendo un libro a un grupo de niños en la Biblioteca Pública Principal en el centro de la ciudad. Theresa leía las partes del narrador y partes femeninas o de niños mientras que el clérigo leía las partes correspondientes a hombres o a bestias. Cuando acabaron su lectura, caminaron rumbo a la catedral.

"¿Me vas a contar qué fue lo que le pasó a tu mano, Gabrielín?"

"No creo que quieras saberlo, Tere," replicó él para picar su curiosidad.

"¿Has estado envuelto en pleitos otra vez?" inquirió ella, actuando como una madre, con las manos en la cintura.

"Sí," contestó él. Luego, pretendiendo como que había hecho algo malo, agregó, "¡Y por una prostituta!"

Theresa paró de caminar y se volteó a ver su rostro.

"¡Estás bromeando! Sé que fumas esos puros apestosos y tomas bebidas alcohólicas. Vas a las cantinas a apostar, bailas con cuanta vieja te lo pide. Pintas modelos desnudas, te metes en pleitos, y enamoras religiosas, ¡pero no me imaginaba que también te metías con prostitutas!"

El Padre G se sonrió con una viejita que iba pasando y oyó lo que Theresa le dijo; tomó a la religiosa del brazo y la forzó a que siguiera caminando.

"Te ves bien chula cuando te enojas; sin embargo, te estás enojando basada en lo que asumes. Déjame explicarte lo que pasó. Yo no ando promoviendo la prostitución ni uso esos servicios. Nunca lo he hecho. Esta fue una historia de misericordia divina. ¡Fue otro maravilloso milagro!"

El Padre Gabriel le relató la historia completa a la Hermana Theresa. Fueron y se sentaron en una banquita en la plaza principal enfrente de la catedral. Gabriel compró un par de raspas en conos y le dio uno a Theresa.

"¡De fresa, mi favorito!"

Ella comió del dulce helado. Sus labios se tornaron rojos y húmedos. Gabriel quedó embelesado y sintió un deseo de besarlos y aún morderlos.

"Bueno, ¿te la vas a pasar ahí nomás paradote como un bobo, mirándome comer mi raspa, o te vas a sentar en la banca a comerte la tuya, Gabrielín?"

"Esta raspa no es en lo que me gustaría poner mis labios."

"¡Sí, como no, enfrente de la mera catedral!" ella le dijo, apuntándole al histórico edificio.

Justo entonces, el Arzobispo Rosales salió de la catedral y, reconociendo al Padre Gabriel, los saludó desde el otro lado de la calle. Nunca había visto a Sor Theresa. El arzobispo se metió a su carro y partió. El sacerdote y la hermana le dijeron adiós y se siguieron comiendo sus ricas raspas.

Un par de días más tarde, en octubre quince, Sharon fue a visitar al Padre Gabriel después de la misa del viernes por la mañana. Él se sentó en una de las bancas de atrás de la iglesia con ella a platicar por un rato.

"Qué gusto volverte a ver, Sharon. ¿Cómo has estado?"

"Estoy mucho mejor, Padre. Lo vine a ver acerca de Fernando."

"Oh, sí. Necesitas perdonarlo con todo tu corazón por el mal que te hizo, así podrás encontrar la paz. Estaba pensando en irlo a visitar. Él ya debe de estar fuera del hospital, en la cárcel."

"¿No oyó lo que pasó?" dijo la mujer, sacudiendo la cabeza.

"No oí... ¿qué?"

"Fernando está muerto. Trató de escaparse de la policía esta mañana cuando lo iban a trasladar a la cárcel. Decía que jamás regresaría a prisión. Se peleó con los oficiales que lo iban a transportar del hospital a la cárcel. Él era un cinta negra en Tae-Kwan-Do, así que se les zafó a los agentes del sheriff y le sacó la pistola a uno de ellos. El otro le tuvo que disparar y lo mató antes que pudiera usar el arma. A pesar que me lastimó mucho, me sentí mal cuando oí lo que pasó," explicó ella, conteniendo una lágrima.

"Lamento mucho oír eso," Gabriel le dijo. "Ni siquiera tuve chanza de ir a hablar con él e invitarlo a cambiar. Aún así, quiero que lo perdones en tu corazoncito, así como el Señor te ha perdonado a ti."

"Tiene usted mucha razón, Padre, pero es que es tan duro perdonar a aquellos en quienes pusimos nuestra confianza y nos traicionaron."

"¡A ellos son a los que debes perdonar! Tú tienes el poder de perdonar. ¡Ejercítalo! Si no, siempre vas a andar cargando con ese rencor contra él en tu corazón. ¡Perdona y sé libre! ¡Perdona y encuentra la paz! El perdón es la mejor medicina del mundo."

El Padre G caminó con Sharon hacia la puerta. Ella le agradeció, lo abrazó, y lo besó en la mejilla antes de marcharse. Él le dijo adiós con la mano al tiempo que se alejaba y luego volvió sus ojos a la escuela.

Sor Theresa lo estaba observando. Él le sopló un besito, le guiñó un ojo, y le obsequió una gran sonrisa. Ella se metió de nuevo al edificio escolar, preguntándose por qué sentía tanto coraje al ver a otras mujeres demostrándole afecto al bondadoso sacerdote. Sus sentimientos posesivos por el pastor se estaban haciendo más fuertes con el pasar del tiempo.

Gabriel recordó lo que Theresa había mencionado acerca de fumar "puros apestosos" y se prometió a sí mismo dejar de fumarlos. Pensó que le daría gusto saber del sacrificio que pensaba hacer por ella. Había fumado puros desde diez años atrás y realmente los disfrutaba. Hizo un puño con la derecha y se golpeó la palma de la mano izquierda para sellar su promesa.

Capítulo IX

Revivida

Era la tarde del domingo 17 de octubre. Tan pronto como el Padre Gabriel terminó con su misa de mediodía, se trepó a su Curimóvil y se fue al centro a encontrarse con Mary y Theresa para comer. Unas palabras del pasaje del evangelio le venían resonando en la mente mientras manejaba.

"No es de muerte, es para la gloria de Dios." (Juan 11:4)

La lectura había sido del Evangelio de San Juan capítulo once donde habla de la resurrección de Lázaro. El cura puso atención a aquellas palabras reverberando en su cerebro.

Pensó que aquella podría ser la respuesta a sus confundidos sentimientos, aunque no estaba muy clara. Él no estaba enfermo, solo se sentía ansioso y caliente. Había perdido su buen apetito y no estaba durmiendo bien. Se dio cuenta que eran síntomas de cualquiera que se encontraba enamorado.

El párroco se rió y se dio una cachetada, pensando que pondría en orden esos sentimientos y controlaría sus emociones. Se fijó que iba a casi 90 en una zona de 50, ansioso por llegar al centro y ver a Theresa. Miró un juego de luces rojas y azules en su espejo retrovisor, relampagueando en el toldo de una patrulla detrás de él. Gabriel se hizo a un lado de inmediato.

"¡Grandioso! Esto me pasa por ir soñando al manejar."

"Buenas tardes, soy el Oficial Calderón del Departamento de Policía de San Antonio. El motivo por el que lo he detenido es porque iba usted conduciendo a ochenta y ocho kilómetros por hora en una calle de cincuenta. Permítame ver su licencia de manejar y su prueba de seguro."

Gabriel cumplió con las órdenes del policía y le sonrió, recordando lo que otros policías amigos le habían recomendado de mantener actitud positiva cuando fuera detenido por los representantes de la ley. El oficial notó su collar de clérigo al tiempo que le recogía los documentos.

"¿Es usted el famoso Padre G de la iglesia de la Santísima Trinidad?" Calderón le preguntó, examinando su licencia.

"Sí, Señor. No sé si sea famoso, pero algunos me conocen como Padre G en lugar de Padre Gabriel. ¿Nos habíamos encontrado antes?"

"Sí y no. Mi mamá me contó de usted. El año pasado, caí al hospital con una grave pulmonía e infección que yo pensé me iba a llevar a la muerte.

Mi madre le pidió que rezara por mí. Era viernes al anochecer cuando me admitieron al hospital. El doctor me recetó toda clase de medicinas, pero me sentí muy bien antes que me las empezaran a dar. Solo me habían empezado una infusión intravenosa, y me dijeron que ya estaba yo bien."

El Padre Gabriel tronó los dedos, acordándose de ese incidente que el policía le estaba relatando, pero dejó que continuara su emotivo relato.

"El doctor estaba orgulloso que su receta había hecho efecto tan rápido, hasta que las enfermeras le informaron que aún no me habían dado nada. Un psicólogo de ahí atribuyó mi recuperación a un choque psicológico, diciendo que mi mente creó una sobrecarga de anticuerpos para prevenir el quedarme en el hospital. Mi mamá vino y me dijo que había sido un milagro, y que usted había rezado a Dios con ella por mi salud. Yo no lo quería creer, pero así fue como sucedió. Había tenido ganas de agradecerle en persona, pero no soy de esos que van a la iglesia seguido."

"¡Eres el hijo de Ofelia Calderón! Me acuerdo bien de tu madre; es una mujer de fe. Yo sabía que el Señor le concedería lo que pidiera, y ella mencionó que tú no eras uno de esos que van seguido a la iglesia. Andas siempre ocupado con tu trabajo de policía y cosas en las que estás envuelto. Entrenas un equipo de béisbol de niños. Además, estás en el programa de tutelaje de chicos y el de construir Habitaciones para la Humanidad. ¿No?"

"Parece que mi mamá le contó todo acerca de mí. ¿Eh?"

"Estaba muy preocupada que te podrías morir en el hospital porque estabas muy grave. Quería darme a saber lo valiosa que es tu vida, para que yo le implorara a Dios por ti."

"¡Bueno, pues muchísimas gracias, Padre G!" exclamó el policía, sonriéndole y extendiéndole la mano al sacerdote.

"Dale gracias a Dios y a tu madre cuya fe te salvó. Yo solo me le uní en la oración."

Se saludaron de mano y se miraron sonrientes como nuevos amigos.

"¿Me vas a dar esa infracción por ir a exceso de velocidad?" preguntó el cura, acordándose que aún necesitaba llegar al centro a encontrarse con sus amigas para comer.

"¡Con un demonio, claro que no! Oh, discúlpeme, quise decir: ¡Por supuesto que no, Padre! Le daré una advertencia escrita. ¿Qué le parece?"

"Una decisión excelente, Oficial Calderón. Prometo ser más cuidadoso."

El oficial le escribió una boleta de advertencia. La cual él quería guardar como un suvenir. El Padre G la firmó.

"Ahora yo te voy a dar una advertencia a ti por no ir a la iglesia. Si haces todas esas obras buenas, sin hacerlas para alabanza y gloria de Dios, estás perdiendo tu tiempo. Ven a la iglesia y revívete en la fe."

"Tiene usted toda la razón, Padre. Lo veré en la iglesia muy pronto."

"Aún tengo una misa de seis de la tarde hoy."

"¡Le prometo que ahí estaré! Ahora sí, váyase y tenga mucho cuidado. Muchas gracias de nuevo," el policía le dijo, despidiendo al sacerdote.

Gabriel manejó al este rumbo al centro, contento que su encuentro fue fructífero para ambos. Aún en una situación estresante podía ver la mano de Dios usándolo para hablar con su gente. Había tenido que ir más recio de lo permitido para que el oficial lo detuviera y tener aquella charla.

Pensó en el pasaje que había tenido en mente y se preguntó si por eso fue que le había reverberado en el cerebro, *"No es de muerte, es para la gloria de Dios." (Juan 11:4)* Gabriel volteó a ver su velocímetro de nuevo; iba a cincuenta entonces.

Sor Theresa y Sor Mary tuvieron que orillarse en el camino cuando escucharon un tronido. La llanta derecha de enfrente se reventó cuando iban rumbo a un café del centro; ya estaban a una distancia que podrían cubrir caminando para llegar al sitio acordado.

"Podríamos irnos caminando desde aquí y venir después de comer a componer la llanta ponchada, Hermana," dijo Theresa, ansiosa que Gabriel podría ya estar allá esperándolas.

"Oh, no, Hermana. Puede que no encontráramos la van si la dejamos aquí. He oído que hay mucho ladrón en esta área, en esos departamentos. No quiero que Sor Magda se vaya a enojar porque su precioso estéreo fue robado de la van. Vamos cambiando la llanta. ¿Qué tan difícil puede ser?" La más joven le dijo, saliéndose de su vehículo y buscando la extra.

"¿Has cambiado tú antes una llanta, Mary?" le preguntó Theresa quien nunca antes había tenido que lidiar con tal problema.

"No, pero creo que podemos figurar cómo hacerlo, ¿No crees tú?"

Mary estaba estudiando el dibujo sobre la cubierta de la llanta y empezó a desatornillar la tuerca de mariposa que sostenía la extra.

"Busca el manual del propietario en la cajuelita, Theresa. Se me hace que hay unas instrucciones ahí de cómo cambiar una llanta."

Mientras Theresa buscaba el manual, el Oficial Calderón llegó a donde estaban. Puso sus luces de emergencia y se estacionó atrás de la van.

"¿Cuál parece ser el problema, Hermana?" el oficial dijo muy sonriente al acercarse a la joven religiosa en su distintivo atuendo.

"Oh, se nos reventó una llanta, y estamos figurando cómo reemplazarla."

"¿Le gustaría que les ayudara?"

Mary iba a declinar su oferta porque quería hacerlo ella, pues le gustaba valerse por sí misma, pero Theresa saltó del interior de la van.

"¡Sí, sí, Señor Oficial! Le estaríamos muy agradecidas. Tenemos a un amigo esperándonos en el centro y ya vamos tarde."

El policía sacó la rueda extra de la parte trasera de la van.

"Todos ustedes, los religiosos, andan a la carrera hoy. Acabo de parar a un sacerdote que iba hecho la mocha a unas cuantas cuadras de aquí."

Theresa y Mary se miraron una a la otra, así que la hermana mayor le preguntó, "¿Quién era el sacerdote al que detuvo?"

"El Padre G, iba volado al centro. ¿Qué está sucediendo allá?"

Ambas hermanas se cubrieron las bocas y se rieron bajito. Mary le ayudó al policía, trayéndole las herramientas y le explicó el asunto.

"Él es el amigo que vamos a encontrar para comer. Creímos que ya iba a estar cansado de estarnos esperando, pero creo que usted nos lo detuvo por un ratito. ¿Cuánto hace que lo vio?"

"Apenas lo acabo de dejar ir, hace unos minutos."

El patrullero le tocó la manita a Mary cuando tomó el gato hidráulico. Ella recogió su mano de inmediato, sintiendo una pequeña descarga estática. El Oficial Calderón y Sor Mary eran de la misma edad. Ella notó que el policía era muy amable y bien parecido; él notó que la religiosa era muy vivaracha y también muy bonita.

Theresa percibió las miradas entre ellos y los dejó solos. Se fue a observar el interior del carro de patrullas sin meterse a él. Tenía una como jaula para transportar a los prisioneros atrás. Enfrente, había una computadora y botones para luces de emergencia y sirena. El oficial cargaba varios libros y formas. El lado del pasajero parecía una pequeña biblioteca móvil.

En cuanto el oficial terminó de reemplazar la llanta ponchada, la despachadora le dio una llamada.

"Me tengo que ir, hermanas. ¡Que pasen muy buen día!"

"Muchas gracias, Oficial..." Theresa dijo mientras él se arrancaba raudo en su crucero con las luces de emergencia aún encendidas rumbo al centro.

Mary le completó la expresión a Theresa, "Calderón, Oficial Antonio Calderón."

Theresa se metió a la van y dijo, "Parece ser un buen hombre, muy simpático, y también me pareció que le gustaste, Mary."

"Sí! Él me gustó a mí también. Me enseñó como cambiar la llanta yo la próxima vez. ¿A dónde te fuiste, dejándome ahí solita con ese hombre?"

"Me fui a ver su patrulla. Pensé que no te importaría."

Las dos soltaron unas risitas. Ambas sabían que probablemente ni el oficial ni Mary se volverían a encontrar. Aún si se volvieran a encontrar, su situación y la de Theresa con Gabriel eran mucho muy diferentes. Se metieron en su van y se encaminaron rumbo a su destino.

"¿Alguna vez has estado enamorada, Mary?"

Mary la volteó a ver con ojos tristes y le respondió, "Sí. Cuando estaba en la universidad. Salía con un chico bien guapo llamado Eric. Era jugador de fútbol. En Grecia el soccer es muy popular. Se iba a hacer profesional en España. Estábamos pensando en casarnos. Decidimos posponer nuestros planes hasta que él consiguiera su contrato y yo terminara la carrera. Eric era muy audaz; con el dinero que le dieron de adelanto, compró una moto. Murió al poco tiempo en un accidente en su nueva moto. Sentí que había yo muerto también; todos nuestros planes fueron enterrados con él. Un par de años más tarde, el Señor me llamó a su servicio, y aquí me tienes."

"Siento mucho oír eso. Yo también sé lo que es perder seres amados en un accidente. Mis padres murieron en un accidente de avioneta."

"¿Que tal tú, Theresa, alguna vez has estado enamorada?"

"¡Padre Gabriel!" exclamó Theresa.

"¿Estás enamorada de él?"

"¡No! Quise decir... Míralo ahí entre esa muchedumbre. ¿Qué será lo que anda haciendo? Detén la van, Mary."

UN POCO ANTES DE ESO

Cuando Gabriel había llegado a la orilla del centro, una muchedumbre le llamó la atención. Había algo grave pasando ahí. La gente hacía señas para que otros consiguieran ayuda y llamaran una ambulancia. Una mujer se estaba cubriendo la cara y alejándose del grupo, obviamente alterada.

El sacerdote detuvo su carro y se salió de él. Vio un cuerpo tendido en la banqueta. Un hombre usaba un palo para mover un cable y alejarlo del cuerpo. El ministro se acercó más y se enteró que una mujer había sido electrocutada cuando pisó un cable de alta tensión.

Se trataba de una mujer joven. Un niño de cinco años lloraba a su lado y le movía el hombro, tratando de despertar a su mami. El corazón de Gabriel se conmovió por el pequeño. La dama no parecía estar respirando; Su pecho no se movía. Gabriel evaluó la situación al acercarse junto al cuerpo de la mujercita. Se arrodilló y le buscó el pulso; no tenía ninguno. Le pidió a una mujer mayor, y pasadita de peso, que detuviera al niño.

El místico se santiguó y oró a Dios, pidiéndole alumbramiento. Aquella joven madre ya estaba muerta, no tenía pulso ni respiración. Su corazón se había detenido cuando recibió el choque de alto voltaje.

Gabriel Infante se había enlistado en las Reservas del Ejército a los 17 años, cuando aún atendía la preparatoria. Planeaba conseguir tanto entrenamiento militar como pudiera antes de ir a West Point. No sabía aún si iba a poder conseguir aceptación cuando atendió entrenamiento básico. Más tarde fue entrenado como especialista médico militar. Para entonces, ya había rechazado la posición en West Point. Se hallaba confuso acerca de su futuro después de perder a Theresa, el amor de su vida. Su entrenamiento médico le llevó a considerar una vida de servicio, lo cual lo guió al seminario. Como médico de combate, aprendió cómo hacer algunos procedimientos salvavidas, como el de resucitación cardiopulmonar.

El ministro sintió la energía del Espíritu Santo llegándole mientras oraba sobre el cuerpo y visitaba la memoria de su entrenamiento militar. Colocó a la mujer plana sobre su espalda y le extendió el cuello.

Todo el ruido a su alrededor se convirtió en una cosa borrosa mientras él se concentraba en su acción elegida. Por un segundo, miró a la misma mujer parada entre las gentes, a su derecha y tras del niño, quien aún estaba llorando y tratando de regresarse al lado de su mami.

Gabriel le desabrochó el sostén que tenía broche enfrente. Colocó su boca sobre la de la mujer, le pinchó la nariz y le sopló un par de alientos en los pulmones. Entonces puso las manos, con los dedos entrelazados, en el centro de su pecho y comenzó a presionarlo rítmicamente, contando

"Uno, y dos, y tres, y cuatro..."

Cuando contó quince, se inclinó a soplarle otra vez aire. Luego reanudó las compresiones. La tercera vez que le ventiló los pulmones, ¡ella tosió!

Gabriel se detuvo, le puso el dedo en el cuello y sintió el pulso; se llenó de entusiasmo. La mujer apretó los ojos y luego los abrió; eran azul celeste.

Gabriel volteó a la derecha a ver al niño. La mujer que había visto detrás de él ya no estaba ahí. Le pidió a la gordita que dejara al niño venir con su mami. La muchedumbre le aplaudió y vitoreó al presenciar su proeza.

La ambulancia se estaba aproximando en ese momento.

El Padre G le habló a la revivida; ella se hallaba aún confusa y tratando de entender la situación. Preguntó por Pedrito, su hijo, y se quejó de que le dolía el pecho. La mujer preguntó quien le había abierto el sostén. El sacerdote le aconsejó que se quedara tendida y les permitiera a los médicos ponerla en una camilla. Ellos le explicarían todo más tarde.

Gabriel se levantó y habló con los paramédicos acerca de lo que había hecho.

La van de las hermanas religiosas iba pasando por ahí muy despacito y se detuvo. El Padre Gabriel corrió hacia ellas.

"Hermana Theresa, Hermana Mary, ya las alcanzaré en el restaurante en un par de minutos."

"¿Padre Gabriel, qué estaba usted haciendo?" Theresa le preguntó, mirándolo a él y luego a la muchedumbre.

"Solo estaba ayudando a una damisela en apuros."

"¿Y tuvo que besar a la damisela para ayudarla?" Theresa le preguntó, aventándole un par de toallitas de papel para que se limpiara la boca roja.

Se miró en el espejo de la van y se limpió las manchas de lápiz labial

"Les explicaré luego," Gabriel le dijo, "Váyanse al restaurante y ordenen para todos; pidan para mí un platillo de carne guisada."

El Oficial Calderón les hizo una seña a las hermanas para que movieran su vehículo. El sacerdote regresó al lado de la mujer electrocutada y su niño. La gente ya se estaba empezando a marchar, hablando entre ellos acerca de lo que habían presenciado.

"Me quiero disculpar contigo; puede que te haya quebrado las costillas cuando estaba tratando de revivirte."

"No sé si estarán quebradas, pero si sé que estoy viva gracias a usted."

"Agradécele a Dios por darte otra oportunidad. ¿Cómo te llamas?"

"Linda, Linda Richards, ¿y usted?"

"Yo soy el Padre Gabriel Infante. ¿Tienes a alguien que se pueda hacer cargo de tu niño mientras estás en el hospital?"

"No, Señor Infante. Soy recién llegada a la ciudad, una madre soltera buscando trabajo. No tengo parientes ni amigos aquí. ¿Podría usted ayudarme o referirme a alguien que me pueda ayudar?" Linda le explicó, no queriendo perder contacto con el hombre que le había salvado la vida.

Los paramédicos pusieron a la mujer en la ambulancia y se alistaron para transportarla al salón de emergencias más cercano.

"Yo me haré cargo de tu hijito. ¿Cómo se llama?"

"Pedrito. Es un niño muy inteligente a sus cinco años."

"Muy bien. Lo voy a mantener conmigo, y te iremos a visitar al hospital en un rato. ¿Ya comió?" Gabriel le preguntó a la mujer en la ambulancia.

"No. Andábamos buscando dónde comer cuando todo esto pasó."

"No te preocupes por nada, Linda. Yo me aseguraré que coma algo y luego lo llevaré a visitarte. Tú nada más ponte mejor."

El sacerdote le dio su tarjeta de negocios y cargó al niño en sus brazos. El pequeño quería irse con su madre. Gabriel le dijo, hombre a hombre, que estaba lastimada y necesitaba ir al hospital para descansar y ver al doctor. El chiquillo debía venirse con él y dejar que su mami se pusiera mejor. Le prometió llevarlo a comer y a comprar algo para su mamá. Pedrito miró a su madre, quien le dio su aprobación.

"Vete con nuestro amigo, Cariñito. Te va a traer luego a verme en el hospital. ¿De acuerdo?"

Le dio un beso a su hijo y se lo soltó al sacerdote. El Padre se salió de la ambulancia con el pequeño en sus brazos.

Linda le dijo al paramédico, "¡Ese hombre es muy bueno! Es justamente lo que andamos buscando, y le gusta a mi hijito también."

Fuera de la ambulancia, el presbítero habló con el policía, el mismo que lo había parado anteriormente.

"¡Padre G, ya anda metido en líos otra vez! Creí que le había dicho que tuviera cuidado."

"¡Ey, voy a donde Dios me necesita!"

"Sí, así es. Hizo muy buen trabajo aquí, Padre. Creo que esa mujer estaría muerta de seguro si no hubiera sido por usted. Ya con eso somos por lo menos dos que le debemos la vida, creo yo."

"Oficial Calderón, creo que ya tiene toda mi información para su reporte en la boleta de advertencia que me dio. A menos que necesite algo más de mi parte, me gustaría alcanzar a mis amigas para comer."

Oh, sí, Conocí a sus amiguitas también. Salúdeme a la Hermana Mary de mi parte. Es una mujercita muy linda."

Gabriel se alejó caminando con el niño agarrado de su mano. El oficial alcanzó al cura y le dio la maleta de Linda.

Unos minutos más tarde, Gabriel y Pedrito entraron al restaurante buscando a las dos hermanas religiosas.

"¡Parece que este va a ser nuestra almuena, almuerzo y cena al mismo tiempo!" el Padre les dijo mientras él y su pequeño amigo se les acercaban.

"Sí. Así parece," dijo la Hermana Theresa, mirando su reloj regalo de cumpleaños, ya eran las dos y media de la tarde; luego, mirando al recién llegado le preguntó al cura, "¿Quién es este guapo jovencito?"

Era un niño hermoso, con pelo negro y ojos azules.

"Estimadas damas, él es Pedrito Richards, de cinco años de edad. Su madre pisó un cable de alta tensión y murió electrocutada. Fui capaz de revivirla dándole RCP, gracias al entrenamiento que recibí en el Ejército, y por supuesto, gracias a Dios que me puso ahí, justo a tiempo."

"Mi nombre es Pedrito Sifuentes, no Pedrito Richards," el pequeño invitado lo corrigió, y Gabriel se disculpó de inmediato.

"¿Revivió a la mujer después que murió electrocutada?" exclamó Sor Mary, anonadada, mientras los recién llegados tomaban sus asientos.

"Sí. ¡Parece que así fue! Lo chistoso es que en la misa de hoy, había yo leído el pasaje del evangelio en el cual Jesús resucitó a Lázaro después de cuatro días. Un pedacito de las escrituras se me quedó pegado que decía, *"No es de muerte, es para la gloria de Dios." (Juan 11:4)* Pensaba por qué se me había pegado. Creo que era una advertencia que esto iba a ocurrir."

"¡Guau! hizo usted un trabajo realmente fantástico, Padre Gabriel. ¡Alabado sea el Señor!" dijo Sor Mary.

"¡Alabado sea el Señor, de veras! Otra cosa interesante que ocurrió fue que pensé haber visto a la muerta parada detrás del niño al tiempo que estaba tendida en la banqueta, antes que le empezara a dar la resucitación."

Las dos mujeres se miraron entre ellas, incapaces de salir con alguna buena explicación. El místico les dio su propia opinión del evento.

"Se me hace que su alma se rehusaba a dejar este mundo por su deber de madre con Pedrito. Estaba yo en uno de esos trances cuando todo parece surrealista. Sabía que había mucha gente a mi alrededor diciendo cosas, pero no entendía nada de lo que hablaban. Era como si se movieran a una velocidad mucho más lenta que yo. Me sentí lleno del Espíritu Santo y tuve un recuerdo de mi entrenamiento médico militar. Sabía lo que tenía que hacer y lo empecé a hacer. A decir verdad, tenía esperanzas que podría imponerle las manos y despertarla, pero como he dicho antes, el Señor trabaja en modos misteriosos. La mujer parada detrás de Pedrito parecía decirme, '¡Hazlo, hazlo!' como si supiera lo que iba a tratar de hacer."

El mesero trajo la comida que las hermanas ordenaron. El Padre Gabriel bendijo la comida antes de empezar a comer. Compartieron sus platillos con el niño, quien parecía no haber comido en un par de días. Estuvo muy quietecito y gentil durante todo el rato que comieron su almuena.

El cura les contó a las religiosas lo que sabía de la madre soltera, que acababa de llegar al pueblo y que andaba buscando trabajo. También le pasó a la Sor Mary el saludo afectuoso que el Oficial Calderón le había mandado y la interrogó acerca de lo que había tomado lugar entre ellos.

Mary le explicó que el oficial solo les había ayudado a cambiar una llanta reventada y le había enseñado cómo hacerlo ella misma. Reiteró además que Antonio era un hombre muy simpático.

Theresa concibió una idea.

"Padre, sabe que Laura, la de la cocina, está a punto de marcharse para Alemania porque su esposo recibió órdenes del Ejército. Se van en una semana. Tal vez usted le podría ofrecer ese empleo a la mamá de Pedrito."

El clérigo se acabó su carne guisada, dejando su plato limpio, se bebió lo último de su té helado, y estuvo de acuerdo con Theresa.

"¡Es cierto, qué buena idea! No sé que clase de trabajo ande buscando Linda, pero le podríamos ofrecer esa posición."

Linda Richards comenzó a trabajar en la escuela de la Santísima Trinidad en cuanto se recuperó, el miércoles 20 de octubre. Sus costillas habían sido magulladas durante la resucitación, pero ninguna quebrada. No había ya nada mal con ella, de acuerdo con los doctores en el hospital. La única evidencia de su suplicio era una marca de quemadura del cable eléctrico en su tobillo derecho donde la había tocado el alambre de alta tensión.

Linda vivió un tórrido romance con Leonardo Sifuentes en Milwaukee, Wisconsin, donde vivía. El tejano, Leo, había ido al norte en busca de fortuna. Presumía ser inventor de productos químicos como detergentes, desodorantes, limpiadores y cosas así; en realidad, había comprado un libro grueso de fórmulas químicas de esos productos. Leo andaba buscando una compañía que se interesara en manufacturar sus inventos, o socios para iniciar una nueva compañía de productos químicos.

A Linda le gustó el soñador de Texas y se entregó a él por completo aquel verano, pero para el invierno, Leo se había marchado a New York, Chicago o California en búsqueda del éxito. Para primavera del año siguiente, Linda tuvo a su bebito sin haber oído más de Leo, ni una llamada, ni una carta. La única clave que tenía para buscar a Leo era una tarjeta postal de Texas. Un amigo llamado Eliseo Reyes se la había mandado a la dirección de Linda en donde Leo se la había pasado todo el verano sin pagar renta.

Cuando a Linda la desocuparon del trabajo que tuvo por diez años, pues la planta estaba cerrando en Milwaukee, decidió ir a Texas a buscar a Leo para que conociera a su hijo. Eliseo Reyes había vivido tiempo atrás en la casa en donde los Hinojosa estaban viviendo en el presente, pero no había quedado traza de él ni de ningún Leonardo Sifuentes.

Fernando y Rocío Hinojosa sintieron pena por la madre soltera cuando les dijo la razón de su visita. Tenían una hija, Jennifer, quien se había ido sin permiso de la casa cuando cumplió 17 años, y no habían oído nada de ella en un año. Rocío ofreció dejar a Linda y Pedrito quedarse en el cuarto de Jennifer, hasta que pudiera conseguir su propio hogar en San Antonio.

Linda se había sentido honrada con la oferta, pero no podía aceptar su generosidad. Se llevó su maleta y se fue al centro a buscar trabajo.

Los Hinojosa oyeron las noticias de lo que le sucedió a Linda y fueron a visitarla al hospital. Ella entonces sí aceptó su invitación a quedarse en su hogar, el cual no estaba muy lejos de la iglesia y escuela de la Santísima Trinidad. La simpática pareja en sus tempranos cuarenta también le presentaron a un abogado llamado Scott Anderson quien la representaría en una demanda en contra de la compañía constructora responsable por dejar el cable de alta tensión expuesto a los peatones.

Sor Theresa estaba muy contenta que las cosas estaban funcionando bien para la madre soltera. Era buena trabajadora y parecía contenta a pesar que el pago era mínimo. Le permitieron que metiera a Pedrito en el kínder sin costo alguno, gracias al Padre Gabriel.

Lo único que empezó a molestar a Theresa era lo agradecida que la mujer de Milwaukee estaba con el carismático presbítero por haberla resucitado, haberle dado trabajo, y haber aceptado a su niño en la escuela gratis. Linda iba y abrazaba al sacerdote, presionando su alto y bien formado cuerpo contra el del cura en manera provocativa. Luego también le tomaba las manos y se las besaba en demasía, en la opinión de Theresa.

Linda no solo era alta y de prominente busto, era más joven, tenía labios muy sensuales y blanca sonrisa como la de una modelo para comerciales de pasta dental, una cascada de cabello dorado, y brillantes ojos azules. El Padre Gabriel parecía disfrutar sus frecuentes demostraciones de gratitud.

Un día, la maestra de primero traía a sus niños a la cafetería para el almuerzo cuando escuchó la distintiva voz del director cantando en la cocina de la escuela. Era una canción romántica, un bolero que hablaba de un romance que deja el sabor de un amante en los labios del otro, un sabor que permanecería en ellos por más de mil años.

Su voz melodiosa resonaba a través de la cocina y por toda la cafetería escolar. Cuando acabó su canción, Linda se le dejó ir a abrazarlo y le plantó un buen besote muy cerquita de la boca. Theresa lo vio y se enceló mucho.

Linda le echó un brazo al cuello, tomó la mano del cura y se la puso en su cadera para anunciarles, jugando, al resto de las mujeres en la cafetería, "¡Este va a ser el nuevo Elvis! Se va a retirar de ser sacerdote para meterse al mundo del espectáculo. Me casaré con él y le daré seis chiquitines."

Todas alrededor se rieron de su ocurrencia excepto Sor Theresa quien entró a la cocina con el semblante muy serio, mirando al cantante. Agarró un trapo de cocina y se lo aventó.

"Hasta que renuncie a sus votos, le sugiero actúe con más recato en frente de los niños. ¡Y límpiese ese lápiz labial de la cara, Padre Gabriel!"

Todo el grupito de trabajadoras se volteó a ocuparse con sus labores de servir el almuerzo de los niños, asombradas por la firmeza de la religiosa.

Linda se alejó de Gabriel y se fue a ayudarles a las otras. Había crecido sin ninguna religión, así que estaba ignorante de las reglas y tradiciones católicas. Linda les echó un vistazo de reojo a los dos religiosos y pudo observar como Theresa estaba castigando a Gabriel al voltear sus ojos lejos de su mirada suplicante. No se necesitaban palabras. Si quería conseguirse al sacerdote, iba a tener que lidiar con la maestrita del primer año.

Cuando acabaron de limpiar, Linda le preguntó a la Señora Williams, la supervisora, si los sacerdotes solo se podían casar con monjitas. La mujer le explicó que los sacerdotes no se podían casar en absoluto. Linda había dicho la verdad cuando dijo que para casarse con ella, el Padre tendría que renunciar a su ministerio, su vocación de servir a Dios como sacerdote.

"Quizás renuncie por la mujer apropiada," comentó la alta norteña.

"No este sacerdote. ¡Es un santo! No sabes ni cuántos milagros a hecho," dijo la negrita, defendiendo a su patrón.

"Bueno, sé que es un obrador de milagros: ¡me trajo de regreso a la vida!"

"No te atrevas a tentar al buen párroco, muchacha. ¡Busca por otro lado!" Williams le aconsejó muy seria.

Pero Linda continuó diciendo, "Parece que le gusto. Quiero decir, no parece molestarle mi aprecio en lo absoluto."

La Señora Williams le quiso cortar las alas, diciéndole, "El Padre Gabriel ama a todo mundo. Lo que ha hecho por ti, lo haría por mí, aún que estoy vieja, gorda, y fea. Para él no hay gente fea; cada uno de nosotros es una adorable y hermosa criatura del Señor."

La supervisora agarró su suéter y se fue afuera a su carro, dejando a la nueva empleada sola. Linda se asomó por la ventana y miró a Gabriel jugando fútbol con los chicos del octavo grado. Su equipo había recibido el primer gol, así que se tuvieron que quitar las camisas. El cura se movía y se veía muy bien para tener 38 años. Se reía como un chicuelo y miraba a la gente directo a los ojos. Linda se puso la mano en la cara y la deslizó por su cuello, busto, abdomen, vientre, y muslo mientras se imaginaba fantásticas escenas envolviéndolos a ella y al atlético ministro.

"Gabriel, debes ser mío. Yo puedo completar tu vida. ¡Ya lo verás!" Linda susurró para sí misma antes de retirarse de la ventana.

Al final del día de escuela, el pastor estaba en la puerta de la institución despidiendo a los niños por el fin de semana. Linda mandó a Pedrito a que le diera un beso al Padre.

El chiquillo corrió hacia el clérigo con sus bracitos muy abiertos; el ministro lo levantó en sus brazos y recibió un gran beso en la mejilla de parte del niño. Gabriel se volteó a ver a Linda y le cerró un ojo para hacerle saber que el chiquillo se estaba sintiendo a gusto en su nueva escuela.

Ella pensó que el cura sería muy buen padrastro para Pedrito. Era maduro, inteligente, guapo, educado, fuerte, lleno de energía positiva, un maestro, atleta, cantante, y ninguna mujer lo había reclamado aún. Linda se daba cuenta que la Hermana Theresa era muy bonita, pero Linda se sintió segura que Gabriel la escogería a ella una vez que llegara a conocer mejor todos sus atributos femeninos.

Linda Richards decidió envolverse en las actividades del Padre Gabriel para demostrarle que era la mujer que necesitaba para hacerlo feliz. Lo llamó, invitándolo a que fuera a casa de los Hinojosa de visita ese viernes por la noche; mandó a Pedrito con los Hinojosa al cine mientras ella se quedaba en casa a descansar después de una "dura semana de trabajo."

Fuera de la casa de los Hinojosa, perchado en un árbol, Satanás estaba observando al místico cuando llegó al lugar. El maligno estaba en la forma de una urraca con plumaje negrísimo y ojillos rojos. El Padre G volteó a ver el ave después que tocó el timbre. Se sintió nauseado mientras observaba al pajarraco sobre la rama. Gabriel se preguntó si algo que había almorzado le había revuelto el estómago. La puerta se abrió, y una voz familiar hizo que Gabriel se volteara. Mirando a la hermosa mujer que le abrió la puerta para darle la bienvenida, se le olvidó la náusea y la extraña ave negra.

"¡Hola, Padre Gabriel! Muchísimas gracias por aceptar mi invitación. Por favorcito, pásese," le dijo Linda Richards, tomándolo de la mano y jalándolo al interior de la casa.

"No. Gracias a ti por invitarme, Linda," Gabriel le respondió, "¿Dónde están los demás?" preguntó él, notando que nadie más vino a saludarlo.

"Oh, los Hinojosa decidieron llevarse a mi hijo al cine esta noche," explicó ella en tono casual, "Adoran a mi hijo... y me lo chiflan mucho."

Linda traía puesto un vestidito que caía sobre su ondulado cuerpo exaltando su figura. El ministro se sintió incómodo en esa situación.

"Tal vez sería mejor que pospusiéramos esta visita para otra ocasión, cuando la familia Hinojosa pueda estar presente. ¿No crees, Linda?"

La mujer se le acercó y lo retó.

"¿Por qué se quiere ir, Padre Gabriel? ¿Le disgusta tanto mi compañía? ¿Le ofendo con mi presencia? ¿No le importa que quiero convertirme en católica?"

Le hizo una desarmante carita de niña triste, con su labio inferior protruyéndole con fingida tristeza. El Padre G pensó que tal vez estaba siendo más cauteloso de lo necesario. Estaba seguro que nada malo podría suceder, así que decidió quedarse. Linda se regocijó.

"¿Qué te hizo tomar la decisión de convertirte en católica, Criatura?" le preguntó él mientras se iba a sentar a la mesa.

Ella caminó rumbo a la cocina, meciendo sus caderas mientras le explicaba la razón. Gabriel no podía dejar de admirar su voluptuosa figura.

"¡Usted, por supuesto! Dios me lo mandó, para darme una segunda oportunidad. Podía haber sido alguien más; ¡o tal vez me podía haber muerto! Pienso que usted fue mi mensaje de Dios, que quiere que haga yo esto. ¿Le gustaría tomar algo bien helado y relajante, Reverendo?"

Ella había puesto el termostato del control de clima en treinta grados centígrados así que la casa se sentía caliente.

"¡Sí, por favor!"

El sacerdote le contó un chiste a la anfitriona mientras servía su bebida.

"Un sacerdote novato estaba tan nervioso en su primera misa que casi ni podía hablar. Le preguntó al monseñor, '¿Cómo hago para relajarme?' el monseñor, un viejón experto en su trabajo, le dijo, 'Hijo mío, puede que te ayude poner tequila en el frasco en vez del agua. Con unos traguitos, vas a ver como todo saldrá bien.' El joven hizo lo que el monseñor le sugirió. Creyó que todo le había salido bien suave esa vez. Después del sermón, el joven le preguntó al monseñor qué tal había hecho. El viejo le dijo, 'Muy bien, pero antes de dirigirte a la congregación, debías darle sorbitos al frasco de tequila, no empinártelo. Acuérdate que son diez mandamientos no doce; fueron doce los discípulos, no diez. David mató a Goliat, no le dio en toda la madre. No nos referimos a nuestro salvador Jesucristo y a sus discípulos como Chucho y la pandilla. La Santísima Trinidad son Padre,

Hijo y Espíritu Santo, no Papo, Chico y el Fantasma. Y por último, la madre de Jesús es la Santísima Virgen María, no Mariquita la del Quinto.'"

Linda se estaba riendo abiertamente en la cocina. Realmente le encantaba el presbítero, su sentido del humor, su canto, y toda su personalidad en general. Definitivamente tenía que ser suyo y pronto. Regresó de la cocina con un vaso largo conteniendo algo que parecía té helado.

Se agachó a poner el vaso enfrente de Gabriel, y su escote abierto reveló bastante. Gabriel sentía mucho calor. Agarró su bebida y le dio un buen trago. Sus ojos se le agrandaron de la sorpresa en cuanto saboreó la bebida.

"¿Qué es esto?" preguntó, observando su vaso, tratando de identificar la bebida color café.

"¿Le gusta? Es una bebida mezclada, jugo de tamarindo, ron, hielo, agua mineral y un poco de azúcar."

La hermosa ojiazul se echó un buen trago para demostrarle que la bebida estaba buena. Él iba a mencionarle que se sentía fuerte, pero decidió no hacerlo, viendo que ella se la bebió muy fácil.

"Sí! Me gusta. Se siente penetrante y refrescante."

Linda le volvió a llenar el vaso y se sentó a un lado de él.

"¿Qué pasos debo tomar para hacerme católica?"

Ella parecía brillar, y su perfume estaba intoxicando a Gabriel, esparciendo una sensación excitante por todo su cuerpo.

"Pues, bien, a-jum... Necesitarías entrar al Rito de Iniciación Católica para Adultos, el cual es el programa que lleva a la comunión con nosotros."

La luz de la ventana detrás de ella iluminaba su pelo. Tenía una hermosa cabellera, larga, espesa, de ondulado pelo dorado que le caía como cascada sobre los hombros desnudos. La boca del Padre Gabriel estaba seca porque el corazón le palpitaba más rápido al tener a tan tentadora criatura juntito a él, invadiendo su espacio personal, así que bebió más de la misteriosa y fuerte bebida. Sintió el helado líquido acariciando su interior.

"¿Me ayudaría usted a aprender todo lo que necesito?" ella le preguntó con sus labios a solo unos cuantos centímetros de los de él.

Su aliento era como una brisa de primavera. Sus ojos celestes le estaban suplicando como si su vida dependiera de aquello.

"¡Seguro que sí! Es mi deber como pastor."

El cura sintió el suave busto de Linda reposándose sobre su antebrazo al beber otro trago. Linda se le acerco aún más y le sopló unas palabras en el rostro, mirándolo profundamente en sus oscuros ojos cafés.

"¿Me podría usted dar lecciones personalmente, Padre Gabriel?"

El cura se sintió ligeramente embriagado por su perfume, su proximidad, y la fuerte bebida alcohólica que le había servido. Con gran esfuerzo de conciencia, se levantó del asiento para romper el embrujo.

"Bueno, no. Hay otras personas que te pueden brindar esa atención personal. ¿Comprendes que no puedo dedicar mucho tiempo a una de mis feligreses, especialmente una joven tan hermosa como tú?"

"¿Y por qué no?"

Ella se levantó buscando sus ojos, tratando de leerle el pensamiento. Él se volvió a un lado, hacia la ventana de enfrente de la casa. En ese preciso momento, vio el vehículo de las monjitas pasando por enfrente de la casa.

Sor Theresa iba mirando al viejo Curimóvil que estaba estacionado en el camino a la cochera, y luego miró hacia la ventana. Ella iba sentada en el lado del pasajero; Sor Carmen iba manejando. Su casa quedaba a solo unas cuadras. A pesar que no podía ver a Gabriel a través de las cortinas de encaje, Theresa adivinó que estaba visitando a alguien en aquella casa. Desde su posición ventajosa, la malévola urraca aún estaba perchada sobre la rama observando a través de las entreabiertas cortinas a Gabriel y Linda charlando adentro; el ave parecía satisfecha con la situación.

"¡Hermana Theresa!" dijo el Padre Gabriel, al verla pasar.

La religiosa trató de penetrar la ventana con sus ojos, pero las ramas del árbol y las cortinas no la dejaron ver al interior. Gabriel sintió su corazón saltar en su pecho como si hubiera sido pillado haciendo algo prohibido.

"¿Qué tiene ella que ver con esto?" Linda le preguntó, desconcertada, poniéndose entre Gabriel y la ventana.

"Nada. Es que la acabo de ver pasar. Viven en este vecindario."

El Padre Gabriel le apuntó a la ventana y se tomó otro trago de su bebida mientras que buscaba otro lugar donde sentarse en la sala.

"Un sacerdote se debe abstener del matrimonio, criar una familia, tener aventuras amorosas, o dedicar demasiado tiempo a unas cuantas gentes porque eso le causaría dejar el resto de su rebaño desatendido."

"¿Qué tiene que ver el que yo sea una mujer joven y hermosa como usted dice?" Linda le preguntó, pretendiendo no entender.

¡Ella olía tan rico y se veía tan hermosísima! Gabriel sabía que nomás lo estaba tanteando. Él se sentó en el sofá.

"Nomás imagínate lo que pensaría la gente de la parroquia si me vieran aquí todas las noches así como estamos ahora, los dos solitos. Tú sabes cómo es la gente. Les gusta inventar chismes aún si no está pasando nada."

Linda se movió como gata, con los ojos muy abiertos; se sentó pegadita a él, su cadera presionando la de él, su mano en el antebrazo del pastor.

"¡Ay Padre! ¿Se metería en problemas, y a la mejor lo corren del trabajo sus superiores, si la gente empezara a decir chismes sobre nosotros dos?"

"No, Linda, pero somos figuras públicas, vivimos en el ojo de la gente. Somos líderes morales y no debemos dar ocasión para tales escándalos."

"No quiero que se vaya a meter en problemas por mi culpa, Padrecito. Yo solo haré todo lo que usted me diga... sea lo que sea, y estaré feliz de verlo nomás en la escuela o en la iglesia si quiere. Le estoy tan agradecida por lo que ha hecho por mí y por mi hijito. No tiene idea lo que significa para mí."

Su linda cara se acercó aún más a él; su aliento le acarició los labios. Aquellos suculentos labios de mujer estaban a muy corta distancia de los de él, pronunciando palabras de sumisión a cualquier cosa que él le pidiera que hiciera. Gabriel tragó saliva y cerró los ojos por un segundo para juntar fuerzas desde su interior. Súbitamente, se paró del sillón.

"¡Me tengo que ir!"

Linda se sobresaltó. Ella se levantó también y por accidente, le tumbó el vaso de la mano al chocarlo con su hombro. La helada bebida de tamarindo se derramó sobre su vestido blanco, volviéndolo casi transparente. Quedó empapada del cuello hasta la cintura. Ambos se disculparon profusamente.

Linda se excusó para ir a cambiarse el revelador vestido mojado. Él se puso a secar el líquido de la mesita y el piso con unas toallas de papel.

Antes que Linda regresara, Gabriel se fue a su auto y huyó, rezando por mantener la serenidad. Rodó abajo el vidrio de la ventana de su carro y dejó que el aire del atardecer le aclarara los pulmones que estaban llenos del perfume de Linda. Con mano temblorosa, encendió el radio para oír música clásica y borrar las incitantes palabras de su mente.

"Gracias, Señor, por ayudarme a alejarme de esa tentación."

Después que vio que el presbítero se había alejado a la carrera, la uraca negra voló del árbol frente a la residencia de los Hinojosa y se desapareció en la distancia con unos macabros chillidos.

Gabriel siguió rezando mientras manejaba a la iglesia. Una vez que llegó, se metió al templo y se arrodilló frente al altar para orar más. Sintió su debilidad y buscó fuerza espiritual. Había encontrado fuerza a través de la oración y la meditación antes; tenía que encontrarla de nuevo. Solo, en la iglesia, de rodillas, rezó hasta que la imagen de Linda se le desapareció y su cuerpo volvió a sentir la paz. Perdió la noción del tiempo y del espacio.

Ya era la medianoche cunado terminó de rezar y se fue a acostar. Se preguntaba cómo manejar la situación. El correrla del trabajo no era una opción. Gabriel, sin embargo, se prometió el evitar ocasiones similares de tentación sexual. Pensó que debía guiar a Linda en la dirección apropiada. Después de todo, ella tenía gran necesidad de amor. Iba a rezar para que Dios le mandara un buen hombre que llenara todas sus necesidades.

Linda estaba convencida que el sacerdote la quería. Se dio cuenta lo trastornado que estuvo por su cercanía. Ya casi no se podía contener; ¡le atraía mucho como hembra! Era, después de todo, un hombre normal, y lo había excitado. Solo necesitaba algún tiempecito para que se decidiera. Una vez que la conociera, muy íntimamente, él sabría que hacer.

Si Linda pudiera conseguir tener sexo con él una vez, estaba segura que jamás querría regresar a su estilo de vida célibe. Lo haría más feliz de lo que había sido. Linda estaba obsesionada con el que consideraba había sido enviado por Dios para ser el compañero de su vida. Tendría que metérsele en el corazón, pero muy sutilmente.

El 31 de octubre, la noche de brujas, el grupo de Los Doce Apóstoles de Satanás se reunió en un cementerio alrededor de un diseño fosforescente redondo en el suelo con una estrella de cinco picos. Jorge Ramírez estaba parado en medio, pronunciando palabras en un lenguaje ininteligible que estaba leyendo del viejo y grueso libro que había sacado de la biblioteca el otro día. Se oía como una oración. Todos los adolescentes parecían estar en trance. Repetían las frases que Jorge proclamaba.

"Jaght maul sorvit satanachi..." entonó Jorge Ramírez, y los ojos se le empezaron a tornar blancos.

"Jaght maul sorvit satanachi..." repitieron los otros apóstoles.

La luna se cubrió de gruesas nubes y una tormenta eléctrica se comenzó a aproximar al cementerio en lo que los chicos continuaban su canto.

"Quezt terrani chaul diabolos," Jorge proclamó.

"Quezt terrani chaul diabolos," los demás le respondieron.

Un fuerte viento llenó el cementerio, levantando tierra y envolviendo al grupito en inmensa oscuridad. Un estruendoso rayo le pegó a Jorge. El círculo y la estrella se encendieron en llamas, iluminando la tétrica escena. Los espantados jóvenes detuvieron su cántico. El sitio se tornó silencioso como sepulcro. Una garra de fuego surgió de entre las llamas de la estrella y agarró a Jorge. No podía moverse pero estaba berreando de dolor.

"¡Trágame!" una profunda voz inhumana gruñó.

Todo el polvo, fuego y viento se concentraron en un chorro que se metió en la boca de Jorge, quien cayó al suelo como muerto.

"¡Ya eres mío!" la voz satánica declaró triunfante.

Jorge se puso de pie con un salto anormal, como una marioneta. Sus ojos eran como carbones encendidos.

Los aterrorizados apóstoles huyeron despavoridos, pero Jorge agarró a Cindy de un tobillo y la derribó al suelo.

Ahí la abofeteó repetidamente con gran fuerza, le arrancó la ropa a tirones, y brutalmente la sodomizó.

Luego que acabó con ella, arrojó la aturdida chica a una tumba recién excavada y se alejó del cementerio, gruñendo como fiera rabiosa.

El siguiente lunes, 1 de noviembre, Sor Theresa vio a Linda dándole al Padre Gabriel una torta que horneó para él. La alta norteña interrumpió una pequeña conferencia que la maestra estaba teniendo con el director en el pasillo. Linda le dijo que esperaba que le gustara y se marchó. Gabriel observó a la mujer meciendo sus caderas al caminar rumbo a la cafetería. Theresa sintió el piquete de los celos de nuevo.

"¿Qué hay entre tú y esa... mujer?"

"¡Nada! Me dijo el viernes pasado que quiere convertirse a católica. ¿No crees que es sensacional?" Gabriel le dijo, pretendiendo inocencia.

"¿Entonces, por eso estabas en esa casa el viernes?"

"Oh sí. Te vi pasando por ahí con la Hermana Carmen en la van."

"¿Estabas tú solo con ella?"

Tenía el presentimiento que así era, pero deseaba que él dijera que no.

"Sí. El resto de la familia había salido esa tarde," le explicó como si fuera una cosa sin importancia.

"¡Qué conveniente! ¿De quién fue la idea?" dijo ella, poco disgustada.

"¿Qué es lo que quieres decir?"

"¿Resultó que fuiste a verla así, nomás porque sí, solita en su casa?"

"¡No, no, no! Ella me había invitado a cenar en la casa de los Hinojosa."

"¡Sí, mira que casualidad, cuando los Hinojosa no estaban en casa!"

Los orificios nasales de Theresa estaban muy abiertos, imaginándose lo que podía haber pasado entre ellos.

"¡Si ni siquiera me quedé a cenar!" Gabriel le susurró, dándose cuenta que el tono de sus voces se había elevado al avanzar la interrogación.

"¿Y por qué?"

Theresa bajó también el tono de su voz, casi deslizando en un susurro la pregunta cuando vio su mano señalándole que bajara el tono de su voz. Sus ojos claros estaban clavados en los de él.

"Bueno... Pensé que era inapropiado, así que me marché poco después."

No muy convencida, ella le pidió más detalles, "¿Qué pasó?"

"¡Nada! Platicamos, tomamos una copa, y me marché." Gabriel la miró y le regaló una pícara sonrisa. Entonces le preguntó, "¿Estás celosa?"

"¡No! ¡Por supuesto que no!" Theresa sabía que estaba bien celosa.

"¡Sí lo estás!" Gabriel le dijo triunfante.

El Padre G le trató de ver los ojos, y ella se volteó de lado.

"¿Y por qué debía estarlo? ¡Ya sé que tú amas a todo mundo!"

"Pero temes que pudiera gustarme Linda Richards más que tú."

"Bueno, ¿a poco no? ¿Quién podría culparte a ti o a cualquiera? Es tan alta, tan hermosa, tan dulce, tan necesitada de amor y compañía. Aún más, viene equipada con un precioso niño y además de eso, ¡hasta sabe cocinar!"

El Padre Gabriel sintió gran alegría al confirmar que Theresa realmente lo amaba y que estaba siendo atormentada por las apariencias externas que él podría estar interesado en otra mujer.

"Nuestra relación es algo único. No te cambiaría a ti por nadie," le dijo bajando aún más la voz.

El corazoncito de Theresa sintió alivio al escuchar sus palabras, pero buscó más afirmación. Él le tocó la mano para asegurarle que era verdad.

"Pues no parece muy claro como yo lo veo," Theresa dijo tocando la superficie de la torta de queso con su dedo.

"¿Qué es lo que no parece claro?" preguntó Sor Magdalene, acercándose a la pareja después de haber escuchado la última parte de su conversación.

"¿Es esta torta de queso con piña o torta de queso simple?" fue la rápida respuesta del clérigo para la intrusa.

Magda agarró un pedacito del postre y lo probó. Theresa y Gabriel se miraron entre ellos y sonrieron mientras Magda cerraba los ojos para paladear la deliciosa torta.

"¡Mmmmmh! Torta de queso sencilla, pero ¡requete-buena! Guárdenme una rebanada para mi hora del cafecito."

Magda tomó a Sor Theresa del brazo y se la llevó hacia los salones de clases, hablando de sus asuntos escolares. Theresa volteó la cabeza antes de meterse al salón y le guiñó un ojo a Gabriel. Él le respondió de la misma manera y se metió a la oficina probando él también el postre.

"¡Está delicioso!"

"¿Quién le dio esa torta, Padre?" le preguntó la subdirectora, la Señora Gray, mirando el dulce trabajo de repostería.

"Linda Richards, la nueva damita que trabaja en la cafetería. ¿Le gustaría una rebanada?"

"Nombre no. Ya no me queda mi ropa. Necesito menos, no más, de esos antojitos. Tenga cuidado con eso, Padre," la asistente le aconsejó al cura.

"Usted sabe que no me preocupo por mi peso; yo nomás voy al gimnasio y lo quemo todito."

"No estoy hablando de eso," dijo la Señora Gray, "Usted sabe lo que dicen por ahí, que el camino al corazón de un hombre es por el estómago. Cuídese de esa mujer bonita. No me le vaya a dar un toloache para que se enamore de ella."

"¡Ya estoy enamorado de ella! ¿Quién no lo estaría? Pero no se preocupe, mi Querida Sharon, aún la adoro a usted tanto como antes y su lugar en mi corazón está asegurado para siempre," el sacerdote dijo dramáticamente.

El Padre Gabriel se puso a juguetear con su asistente, tomándola de la mano y llevándosela al pecho para que sintiera palpitar su corazón.

"¡Padre Gabriel, soy mujer casada!"

"Sí. Lo sé, pero no soy celoso, mi Preciosa Perla."

La tomó por la cintura para bailar con ella en la oficina y guiarla danzando hasta su escritorio mientras tarareaba una vieja canción romántica acerca de dos extraños que se enamoraron una noche.

Capítulo X

Lotería

Linda Richards fue enviada a la casa del párroco a ayudar a la Sra. Black a limpiar el horno. Linda aprovechó para ojear alrededor de la casa del Padre Gabriel. Se metió a un cuarto que contenía bastantes pinturas, dibujos, esculturas, fotos, e impresiones. Admiró los paisajes, naturalezas muertas, obras abstractas, encolados, temas religiosos y un buen número de cuadros con desnudos artísticos. Todas las obras tenían las iniciales PGI en la parte posterior, seguidas por las letras S.D.G.

"¡Padre Gabriel Infante!" ella dijo su nombre, dándose cuenta que aquella era la colección de arte privada de las propias obras del sacerdote.

"No le vayas a dañar sus pinturas al Padre porque las cuida como si fueran sus propios hijitos. ¡Le encanta el arte!" le dijo el ama de llaves a Linda desde la puerta del cuarto.

Linda se les quedó viendo a las tres letras de enseguida pero no pudo descifrar su significado. Se le ocurrió una idea al observar las pinturas de desnudos, salió del cuarto y fue a hablar con la Señora Black.

"¿Cuándo tiene tiempo el Padre Gabriel de pintar, si siempre está ocupado con la escuela y la parroquia?"

La tailandesa se le quedó viendo a la alta norteña, sospechándola de tener un interés personal en el cura. Las mujeres de la cocina ya le habían hablado de ella. Poco se les escapaba de su red de chismes.

"El Padre Gabriel pinta cuando puede. A veces encuentro sus pinturas en la mañana cuando llego. Se me hace que lo hace en la noche después de las horas de oficina. También va a un estudio de artistas en la Calle Culebra, cerca de la carretera estatal donde dibujan y pintan figuras de modelos en vivo cada lunes en la noche. El Padre va para allá una o dos veces al mes."

"¿Has modelado para él alguna vez?" Linda le preguntó a la mujer mayor mientras regresaban las parrillas del horno a su lugar.

"De hecho que sí. Una vez él hizo un retrato mío. En realidad hizo dos, uno para su colección y otro para mi casa. Lo tengo en mi sala."

"¿Posaste desnuda?" Linda inquirió con una sonrisa pícara.

"¡Por supuesto que no! Yo ya estoy vieja. La mayoría de las modelos que usan son jóvenes, como tú. Yo posé en un traje típico de Tailandia."

"¿Sabes lo que quieren decir las iniciales en la parte posterior de las pinturas?" preguntó Linda, apuntándoles. "Me imaginé que PGI quiere decir Padre Gabriel Infante, pero ¿qué significa SDG?"

"No sé lo que quiera decir SDG..." replicó el ama de llaves, encogiéndose de hombros. Volteó hacia la puerta en donde Theresa se apareció con una jovial sonrisa. La saludó, "¡Buenos días, Hermana!"

Ambas, Theresa y Linda se examinaron discretamente una a la otra, considerándose rivales por la atención del Tejedor de Milagros.

"¡Buenos días, damas!" la religiosa respondió y les preguntó, "¿De qué estaban hablando?"

Se sintió algo molesta por la idea que hubiesen estado hablando acerca de su Gabriel.

Linda le dijo acerca de las pinturas del pastor y las letras en ellas; le preguntó si la hermana religiosa sabía el significado de SDG.

"¿Es algún tipo de código religioso secreto o qué?"

Theresa lo pensó por un momento y después tronó los dedos antes de explicarles el significado de las iniciales a las dos mujeres.

"Johann Sebastian Bach, el famoso compositor clásico y organista alemán, acostumbraba escribir esas letras sobre los títulos de algunas de sus composiciones. S.D.G. quiere decir Soli Deo Gloria que en latín significa Solo a Dios dar Gloria; así pues, tienes toda la razón, Linda, se trata de una expresión religiosa, aunque no necesariamente secreta. Tiene mucho sentido que el párroco les ponga eso a sus obras de arte también."

La ojiazul se le quedó viendo a la maestra con algo de envidia por su superior educación; Linda únicamente había terminado la preparatoria.

"Ah, ya veo... ¡Que lindo!" la Señora Black comentó y después le preguntó a la hermana, "¿En qué le puedo servir, Sor Theresa?"

La profesora inquirió si el ama de llaves sabía en dónde se encontraban las cajas de velas porque necesitaba unas para su clase. Ella le dijo que sí sabía y le pidió que la acompañara. Ambas se encaminaron a un armario y consiguieron lo que la religiosa necesitaba llevar a su salón de clases.

Linda terminó el trabajo de limpieza con el ama de llaves y se regresó a la escuela a recoger sus cosas. Aún tenía un par de horas antes de tener que ir por su niño al kínder, así que se fue a buscar el estudio artístico al que iba el sacerdote pintor los lunes en la noche. Platicó con Meredith Olsen, la artista que manejaba el estudio, y Linda fue empleada inmediatamente como modelo para empezar esa misma noche.

El párroco tuvo un día estresante, con multitud de problemas y quejas con qué lidiar en la escuela y en la parroquia. Estaba ansiando la noche para retirarse a atender su sesión de dibujo en el estudio de arte. Pensaba solo dibujar con carboncillo esa vez en su libreta grande de dibujo, así que llevó pocos utensilios de arte para su trabajo esa noche.

Un amigo psicólogo le dijo que era buena idea tener un pasatiempo como el arte para manejar el estrés; Gabriel lo tomó como una receta y se apuntó en el círculo de artistas que se reunían a dibujar modelos al natural. Era una buena forma de mantener sus habilidades artísticas bien pulidas. Él ya había hecho algunos frescos para iglesias en diferentes ciudades. A pesar que no se consideraba un Miguel Ángel, su trabajo era en verdad excelente, especialmente en el estilo realista convencional.

El pastor notó una carta de África sobre su escritorio entre varias otras. Se detuvo para leerla antes de irse a su sesión de dibujo. Era del que fue su hermano seminarista, el Padre Michael Frost. Él había elegido convertirse en misionero en el continente negro.

Michael era el tercero del grupo de seminaristas boxeadores a los que apodaron los arcángeles. Era un mulato de Luisiana con pelo negro rizado y ojos cafés claros, el único de los tres que mantenía su rostro siempre bien afeitado, un excelente organista. Gabriel lo recordaba con gran cariño.

El místico abrió su carta, esperando fueran buenas nuevas; en vez de eso, eran terribles. Michael pedía ayuda. Su misión había sido devastada por calamidades duales. Primero un incendio forestal causado por la larga sequía había quemado la mayor parte de la misión; después, cuando las lluvias torrenciales llegaron, las inundaciones arrasaron lo que quedaba.

Michael quería volver a empezar, pero necesitaba fondos para reconstruir lo más pronto posible. Tenía una comunidad de dos mil gentes en su misión. Necesitaban de todo. A pesar de saber que Gabriel no tenía dinero, confiaba que podría pedirle a sus parroquianos que les enviaran de lo que pudieran disponer.

"Sé que puedes hallar forma de ayudarnos, Hermano," escribió Michael, "Fuiste la primer persona que vino a mi mente al pedir a Dios ayuda." La carta terminaba diciendo, "Esperando tu respuesta, concluyo, enviándote amor filial y bendiciones." Firmada por Michael Frost, traía una posdata que decía, "¿Me podrías mandar salsa picante de Texas? No he tenido chanza de comerla en mucho tiempo. Es solo para mí, y no es prioridad.

Pero si la puedes mandar, te agradeceré y te mantendré entre mis héroes."

Gabriel cerró la carta y se sonrió, acordándose de Michael. Levantó los ojos al cielo y le pidió a Dios que le proveyera con los medios para ayudar a su hermano necesitado.

Meredith Elizabeth Olsen dio la bienvenida a los veinte artistas a la vieja bodega, convertida en estudio de arte gracias a su visión empresarial. Les anunció que tenían a una nueva modelo llamada Linda esa noche, lo cual fue de suerte para Meredith porque ningún otro modelo había estado disponible. Linda había aparecido súbitamente, resolviéndole el problema.

"Pensé que iba a tener que posar esta noche ya que no podía conseguir a nadie," Meredith les dijo a los miembros del grupo que reaccionaron silbando con entusiasmo. Los calmó y dijo, "Por favor denle la bienvenida a Linda a nuestra sesión y sean gentiles con ella porque es su primera vez."

Meredith llamó a Linda para que se pusiera en medio del salón entre todos los artistas. Había diez hombres y diez mujeres en el estudio esa noche. Linda Richards solo miró al Padre Gabriel en lo que se salió de su esquina y se quitó la bata para erguirse sobre una plataforma de madera que la puso sobre un pedestal como una escultura viviente.

Linda se miraba monumental, alta y bien formada, el cabello recogido encima de su cabeza. Ella se sonrió al estar totalmente desnuda frente al sacerdote-artista. Gabriel se sorprendió de ver a alguien tan familiar posando, pero le sonrió de regreso a la modelo y se alistó para dibujar. Meredith los detuvo antes que empezaran. La maestra de arte fue y acomodó las luces para realzar la figura con áreas de sombras.

El Padre Gabriel oyó a dos de los artistas hablando acerca de su juego de golf en lo que esperaban. Se acordó de un chiste y lo compartió con ellos mientras preparaban sus utensilios para dibujar.

"Un famoso jugador de golf que era muy malhablado cuando se enojaba fue puesto en pareja con el Papa en un torneo de caridad con jugadores profesionales y celebridades. El golfista malhablado no estaba teniendo un buen día en su juego, así que comenzó a soltar maldiciones. Cuando tuvo un mal golpe, exclamó, '¡Chin... me falló!' y luego se volteó a ver al Papa quien le dio una mirada seria. El golfista se disculpó diciendo, 'Lo lamento su Santidad.' El Santo Padre lo absolvió y siguieron adelante sin decir más. En el siguiente hoyo, el golfista tuvo otro golpe terrible y volvió a gritar muy enojado, '¡Chin... me falló!' El Papa le dio una amonestación, 'Hijo mío, debes tener más cuidado con tu lenguaje. Dios te podría castigar.' El golfista se veía contrito cuando se disculpó, 'Lo siento, su Santidad. Le prometo que voy a tener más cuidado.' Se movieron al siguiente hoyo; el golfista volvió a dar un mal golpe y gritó emberrinchado, 'iChin... me falló!' Un rayo cayó del cielo y le pegó al Papa, quien cayó fulminado, patas pa'rriba. Una voz del cielo se oyó diciendo, 'iChin... me falló!'"

Todos se estaban riendo, listos para empezar. Meredith volteó a ver a la modelo y le dijo, "Linda, quiero que voltees a los cuatro lados del salón y asumas diferentes posiciones de pie primero, luego harás cuatro de rodillas o sentada. En las últimas cuatro te puedes reclinar o acostar, pero solo asegúrate que encaras los cuatro lados del salón. ¿Está bien?"

Linda afirmó que entendía las instrucciones y trató de seguirlas. Iba a ser más difícil de lo que pensaba, el mantener el cuerpo inmóvil mientras estaba desnuda en un salón lleno de gente no era tan fácil como parecía. Le iban a pagar cien dólares por la sesión. Ella necesitaba el dinero extra para poder sostener a su niño. ¡Eso sonaba como una buena excusa!

Durante el descanso, Linda se puso su bata y se acercó al Padre Gabriel a ver sus bosquejos. Eran bonitos, rápidos dibujos de su figura. Se podía reconocer a sí misma, a pesar que no tenían mucho detalle.

"¡Padre G, qué sorpresa verlo aquí! Me da mucha vergüenza que me haya usted visto de este modo." mintió ella, pretendiendo que no sabía que él era uno de los artistas en el grupo.

"No te preocupes por mí," él le dijo. "Estás haciendo muy buen trabajo para ser tu primera vez; eres muy hermosa y te ves monumental."

"Ay, pues es que... Estaba buscando modo de ganar un poco extra. Usted sabe que no gano mucho en la cafetería," Pausó un momento y luego dijo. "¿Padre, cree que me podría usted llevar a mi casa después de la sesión?"

"¡Seguro que sí! Lamento que no te pagamos mucho en esa posición en la cocina. Este trabajito extra no está tan mal. ¿Qué son, como treinta dólares la hora por posar?"

"Cien dólares por sesión; ha de suplementar algo mi sueldito."

Linda estaba parada junto a Gabriel, su suave cadera apretada contra su hombro mientras él pulía un poco su último dibujo. Los otros regresaron del descanso. Meredith les dijo que iban a hacer dos de treinta minutos con un pequeño descanso entre cada uno. Linda dejó caer su bata junto a Gabriel y se subió a la plataforma. La instructora cambió las luces e hizo a la modelo reclinarse sobre una cobija. Linda estaba contenta que la había colocado viendo hacia el lado donde estaba el ministro para la primer pose.

Linda se sintió muy agotada de "no hacer nada" esa noche. Después de la sesión se subió al carro del presbítero.

"¿Cree que la hice bien como modelo de arte, Padre Gabriel?"

"Oh, sí," replicó él. "Lo hiciste espléndidamente bien. Todos estuvimos contentos de tener nueva modelo, especialmente una tan hermosa."

"Estoy agotada. No sabía que quedarse inmóvil por un rato era tan difícil. Tengo ganas de un trago. ¿Le gustaría uno? ¡Al cabo que yo pago!"

Gabriel lo pensó por un momento. No tenía en realidad nada que hacer excepto ir y meterse en su cama, así que aceptó su invitación.

"¿A dónde te gustaría ir a tomarte ese trago?"

"No conozco ningún buen lugar en esta ciudad. Acuérdese que apenas vine de Milwaukee," Linda le dijo. Luego agregó sugestivamente, "Lléveme a donde usted quiera."

"Entonces vamos por unas margaritas congeladas," decidió él, y se encaminó rumbo a un restaurante mexicano cercano.

El plan de Linda estaba trabajando perfectamente. Le había podido mostrar lo que tenía para ofrecerle, aún cuando se lo tuvo que mostrar a todos los demás en el salón también. ¡Y ahora iban a tomarse unas copas!

Linda se fijó que el clérigo estaba un poco distante mientras se tomaban su bebida en el restaurante. No podía lograr que la mirara por más de unos cuantos segundos. Él le contestó todas sus preguntas muy amablemente pero sin mucho entusiasmo, no dándole muchos detalles. Ella le preguntó de su educación y su origen, sus gustos y disgustos, sus milagros y aventuras, las cuales él trató como sin importancia. Ella sí le contó acerca de su vida, pero la mente del cura parecía estar en otro lugar.

Linda le agarró los hombros y los antebrazos unas cuantas veces sin que él le pusiera mucha atención. En cuanto se acabaron sus bebidas, él se levantó y la condujo hacia fuera del restaurante. Gabriel tendría otro día lleno de actividades por delante, empezando temprano en la mañana.

Gabriel sintió su corazón detenerse cuando iban para afuera del lugar. Una van, justo como la de las monjitas estaba entrando al estacionamiento. Dándose cuenta que no era la de ellas, el cura dejó ir un suspiro de alivio. Linda lo tomó del brazo mientras iban al carro y lo volteó a ver.

"¿Qué fue eso?"

"Se siente muy a gusto aquí, ¿no te parece?" comentó él. "Es increíble que

184

estamos en otoño y no se ha puesto frío. Me pregunto si vamos a tener clima realmente frío este año."

En el camino a casa, el Padre G puso su estación favorita de radio con música clásica. Linda se esperó a que él le platicara algo, pero él manejó en silencio, pensando en algo o alguien más. Antes que se diera cuenta, ya estaban estacionándose frente a la residencia de los Hinojosa. La chica de los ojos azules estaba un poco decepcionada de no haber avanzado mucho en esa cita, y se dio cuenta que iba a tomarle algún tiempo.

Con un sorpresivo movimiento rápido, se estiró hasta Gabriel y lo besó en los labios para agradecerle por el buen rato. Se salió del auto y se fue caminando a la casa, dejando al sacerdote con el sabor de su besito.

Un maligno gato negro con ojos rojos brillándole en la oscuridad estaba observando la escena desde encima del buzón de los Hinojosa. El felino pareció sonreírse cuando Linda le pasó cerca sin ponerle atención; sin embargo, la mujer experimentó un escalofrío al pasar junto al gato. Se le puso la piel chinita en la espalda. Ella pensó que había sido por el beso que le había plantado al sacerdote. Linda se volvió desde la entrada de la casa y, con una gran sonrisa le dijo adiós a Gabriel, agitando su mano.

El cura se esperó ahí hasta que la vio meterse a la casa. Se rascó la barba y se lamió los labios al alejarse. Linda estaba decidida a ganarse su atención. Él lo entendía, pero no quería engancharse en ese tipo de relación con ella. Era muy atrevida a hacer lo que fuera necesario por conseguir su propósito y satisfacer sus deseos. Por el otro lado, no quería lastimarla, empujándola lejos de él. Rezó por encontrar forma de mantenerla en su círculo pero a distancia segura. Siendo hombre de carne y hueso, no era fácil despreciar tanta belleza. Era halagador saber que esa preciosa hembra lo deseaba.

Gabriel se fue a casa y se apuró a agarrar el teléfono para llamarle a Tere. Ella levantó el teléfono al primer timbre.

"¿Dónde has estado esta noche, Amigo mío? Había estado esperando tu llamada por mucho rato. Todas las hermanas ya están dormiditas."

"Lamento estar llamándote tan tarde. Fui a mi sesión de dibujo de figura; tuvimos una nueva modelo. Adivina quien decidió ganar un poco de dinero extra modelando."

"No tengo la menor idea quien, de los que conozco, se atrevería a desvestirse frente a un puño de extraños."

"¡Linda Richards!"

"¿Nuestra Linda Richards a la cual rescataste del más allá? Theresa le preguntó, pasmada.

"La misma! Realmente lo hizo muy bien para ser su primera vez."

"¿Sabía ella que tú atiendes sesiones en ese lugar?" inquirió Theresa, sospechando que ahí había algo muy sospechoso.

"No lo sé. Yo nunca se lo mencioné, pero ahí estaba..." Pausó un instante. "Linda dijo que el trabajo de posar es más duro de lo que había pensado."

"Yo creía que una vez que una ha pasado por una experiencia como la de Lázaro, una se convertiría en una gran seguidora de Cristo, llena de modestia y principios morales."

"No es inmoral el que pose por amor al arte; además, necesita el dinerito," Gabriel dijo, tratando de justificarla. "Tú sabes que no gana gran cosa en la cocina."

"Ya no estoy segura que fue tan buena idea ocuparla después de todo. ¿Te pidió que la llevaras a su casa después de la sesión?"

"Pues... Sí. ¿Cómo lo supiste?"

"Es lo que yo haría si estuviera en su lugar y quisiera que me conocieras un poco mejor para gustarte un poco más. ¿Así que te mostró su bien torneada figura primero y luego salió contigo?"

"Solo tomamos una margarita, y luego me la llevé derechito a su casa."

"¿Qué más pasó?"

Theresa se puso ansiosa mientras él confesaba lo que ella sospechaba.

"Nomás me dio... un besito de buenas noches y se metió a su casa. Entonces me vine a la carrera a llamarte a ti. Te extrañaba. No puedo dormir en paz si no escucho tu voz."

"¡Te besó! ¿Y tú también la besaste a ella?" El tono de su voz se elevó.

"No, realmente no. Solo me besuqueó en la boca de repente. Fue como un besito de gracias, nada más."

Casi podía ver la naricilla de Tere abriéndose de ira.

"Voy a tener que dar una buena platicada con esa... mujer."

Gabriel se sonrío de que se estuviera enojando ella por tan poca cosa.

"¿Y qué le piensas decir, Tere?" le preguntó. "¿Le vas a ir a decir, 'Más vale que dejes a mi hombre en paz?'" Pausó y le dijo. "Acuérdate que soy un hombre público, dedicado a mi rebaño. Ya te dije que no ando buscando una aventura con Linda, no importa que tan seductora sea."

"Aún así, ella anda saliendo contigo y haciendo cosas que yo no puedo hacer," se quejó Tere.

"¿Quisieras tú posar para mi grupo?" Gabriel la retó muy pícaro.

"¡No! ¿A ti te gustaría que lo hiciera?"

"¡No!" admitió él. "¿Qué otra cosa quisieras hacer conmigo?"

"Bueno… No puedo realmente correr a tu paso porque no estoy acostumbrada, pero ¿me llevarías a caminar contigo en las mañanas cuando haces tus ejercicios?"

"¿Hablas en serio? ¿A poco de veras quieres venir a ejercitar conmigo?" preguntó Gabriel, excitado con su idea.

"¿Es muy loco? ¿Temes que te vaya a hacer reducir mucho el paso?"

"No, no, no. ¡Sería fenomenal! ¿Cuándo te gustaría empezar?"

"Mañana en la mañana. ¿A qué hora quieres que esté lista?"

"Podría correr a tu casa y encontrarte a las cinco en punto."

"¡De acuerdo! Vámonos a dormir. Te veré a las cinco."

"¡Buenas noches, mi dulce Tere!" dijo Gabriel en un tono amoroso.

"¡Buenas noches, Don Juan!"

Theresa ya estaba trabajando en un plan para eliminar a Linda. No iba a permitirle a la entrometida que siguiera tentando a su amigo… su novio… ¿su amante? ¡Lo que fuera! Iba a encontrar el modo de mantener a la madre soltera ocupada con alguien más. Theresa pensó en conseguirle un trabajo mejor pagado y presentársela a algún soltero atractivo. ¡Tenía que encontrar algo!

En el lado opuesto de la ciudad, se iba desarrollando una tragedia.

James Hickey, un joven negro, estaba celebrando esa noche con dos de sus cercanos amigos en el departamento de su hermana, Lorraine. Larry y Antoine habían sido amigos de James desde la preparatoria. James los invitó a beber cerveza. Muy contento les informó que había terminado con su novia, Ruby Maldonado.

"¿Por qué terminaste con ella, Hombre? ¡Si es un mangazo!" le preguntó Larry, quien creía que Ruby era la mexicana más hermosa que había visto.

"Larry, no te imaginas el problemón que es esa muñeca. Estoy celebrando mi libertad. Si a ti te interesa ella, este es el momento de que te avientes, mi Amigo," fue la explicación de James, adornada con vulgaridades.

"Ey, si James no la quiere, tiene que haber algo mal ahí. Yo no querría estar envuelto con ella tampoco," dijo Antoine, el otro amigo. "Yo sé que su familia está en la maldita Mafia Texicana. Esos tipos son malos; ni te metas con ellos. Te pueden matar aún sin motivo, si acaso nomás por que te les quedaste viendo feo. La vida no vale nada para ellos," Antoine le advirtió a Larry, se bebió la mitad de su cerveza, y se estiró por más tostaditas.

"¿Así que esta vez sí es de verdad, Carnal? ¿O vas a regresar con ella la próxima semana, cuando te venga a buscar de nuevo?" le preguntó Lorraine después de haber puesto a sus niñas a dormir en su cuarto.

James se paró y abrazó a su hermana. Eran muy apegados, los únicos sobrevivientes de los Hickey. Lorraine tenía 24 años y James 26. Su padre había muerto en un accidente de tráfico; su madre había fallecido de cáncer cuando Lorraine recién había tenido su tercer bebita. Su hermano mayor, un allanador de moradas, fue asesinado en prisión. La menor se había ido de la casa seis años atrás, cuando murió su madre. No lo sabían, pero la hermanita había muerto en san Francisco dos años atrás, entre los desamparados sin hogar, y fue enterrada en una fosa común.

"¡Esta vez sí es de seguro, Carnalita! Te garantizo que las cosas ya se están viendo mejor. No tengo intención de regresar con esa mujer. Pensé que quizás tú y las niñas se podrían venir a vivir conmigo a Denver."

"¿Qué, acaso te sacaste la lotería, James? Porque no sé de que otro modo nos podrías llevar a ningún lado. Ya ni siquiera estás trabajando. ¿Qué pasó con la chambita que tuviste por años en la imprenta del Señor Jackson? Dejaste todo cuando conociste a la vieja esa, Ruby. Yo sabía que no te convenía desde un principio. Espero que hables en serio esta vez y no vuelvas con ella. Esas gentes, Ruby y su familia, me dan escalofríos. Son asesinos, James, y tú lo sabes."

"¡Hablo en serio, Manita! Además tengo un secretito del que te enterarás a su debido tiempo," dijo James, levantó a su hermana, y le besó la mejilla.

Antoine, quien deseaba a Lorraine, se paró.

"¿Puedo formarme para recibir un abrazo de ella también?"

Al Antoine le encantaría abrazar y besar a la madre soltera de tres niñas, de primero, segundo, y tercer año. Los tres diferentes padres de las niñas estaban fuera de contacto y ni siquiera le pagaban por sostenimiento de las criaturas. Antoine aspiraba a ser el padre del cuarto bebé de Lorraine.

"¡Tú te aplastas en tu asiento, Negro; esta es mi hermana!" James le gritó, entre insultos, depositando a Lorraine en el piso para voltear a ver a Antoine con un gesto amenazante en su rostro.

"Serénate, mi Hermano," Antoine le dijo entre palabras soeces, "Nomás estoy tratando de ser amigable, nada más. ¡No la... amueles!"

Antoine se sentó mientras Larry se carcajeaba y aplaudía. A Lorraine le gustaba Antoine, pero estaba harta de su tipo. Sus tres amantes anteriores habían sido justo como él, listos para embarazarla y desaparecer de su vida. Estaba tratando muy duro de hacerse cargo de su destino, trabajando como conserje en la primaria que sus niñas atendían. Había conseguido diploma equivalente a la preparatoria y atendía clases nocturnas de universidad.

"Ey, Antoine, si de verdad deseas parte de esto, tendrías que estar dispuesto a cambiar un poco."

Lorraine lo provocó, apuntándole a su exuberante cuerpo.

"¡Yo me haría un cristiano vuelto a nacer por ti, Chiquilla!"

Antoine miró a James para asegurarse que no se le iba a echar encima. James dejó que su hermana manejara la situación.

"Eso sería lo primero, pero también necesitarías conseguirte un trabajo."

"¡Ey, yo trabajo! Cuando me cae algo... de vez en cuando, pero yo trabajo. Tú sabes bien que yo soy un empresario auto-empleado."

"No considero un hombre de 25 años con una vieja podadora de zacate un empresario. Aún vives con tu mamá pues no puedes ni pagar renta. Yo ya estoy harta de vivir en estas malditas casas de asistencia pública."

"¡Está bueno! Te prometo conseguir una chambita. Siempre ocupan gente en la barbacoa o las hamburguesas. ¿Es todo lo que quieres? Carajo, las viejas nomás están interesadas en dinero, dinero, dinero," dijo Antoine, pensando tener una chancita de meterse en las pantaletas de Lorraine.

Se acabó su cerveza después de chocar su botella con la de Larry. James aún lo estaba mirando con una cara muy seria.

"Pues, vamos a ver: Te haces un buen cristiano, te consigues un título de colegio, un buen empleo, una casita de verse, y un carro, entonces me traes un anillo de bodas, y seré tuya para siempre."

"¡Uuh, que la...! Tas' soñando 'ora si, Chavala. Tú sabes que yo no serví pa' la escuela. Me reprobaron del noveno después de tres años ahí, y así quieres que saque un título de universidá'. ¿Quién puede hacer eso?"

"Yo lo estoy haciendo. Les quiero enseñar a mis niñas el modo de triunfar. Tú sabes que trabajo y además voy a la escuela en la noche. No quiero ser voltea-hamburguesas. Yo sí voy a tener mi propio negocio."

"Ta' bueno, Chiquilla. Si te prometo tratar, ¿me darías un adelantito?"

Antoine se estiró para agarrar la mano de Lorraine. James le atrapó la muñeca y le aventó la mano de vuelta sobre sus muslos. Estaban sentados alrededor de la mesita de centro en la sala. James amenazó a Antoine, quien estaba tratando de defender su posición. Lorraine les estaba gritando a los dos. Larry solo se reía y aplaudía, muy divertido con su alegato.

"¡Ya, párenle! Me van a despertar a mis pequeñas. Me voy a acostar. Sé que ustedes, inútiles, no se tienen que levantar temprano, pero yo sí. Más les vale que limpien el mugrero que hagan, o nunca los voy a volver a dejar entrar," Lorraine les advirtió en lo que se encaminaba a su recámara.

"¿Puedo ir contigo?" preguntó Antoine. Las cervezas le habían bajado las inhibiciones, así que se sentía valiente para retar al rudo James.

"Solo si haces lo que te dije," la mujer le recordó a Antoine de la puerta de su recámara, se metió a su cuarto, cerró la puerta y la atrancó por dentro.

James meneó la cabeza; estaba contento que su hermana había manejado al tipo bien. No era que no le cayera bien Antoine, James se consideraba el hombre de la casa. Era la única figura varonil en la vida de sus sobrinas. Tenía grandes planes para ellas. James se levantó, fue y agarró otras tres cervezas. Se sacó una baraja e invitó a los amigos a jugar póquer.

Los tres estaban jugando cartas y acordándose de sus días de escuela. James había sido el único de los tres que se había graduado. James había sido un gran atleta en la escuela, jugando fútbol americano y como miembro del equipo de pista y campo. Ganó una carrera de 10 Km en su último año, y ganó el campeonato estatal como receptor ala abierta.

Al graduar, James se sintió responsable por Lorraine, su única hermana que le quedaba. Natalie la más chica, se había ido de la casa y su madre había muerto, así que en lugar de continuar sus estudios en la universidad, decidió quedarse en la ciudad y conseguirse un empleo para ayudar a Lorraine a mantener a sus tres chiquillas, como si él fuera su padre.

"¿James, no le tienes miedo al hermano de Ruby? ¿Cómo se llama?" preguntó Larry después de jugar, alistándose a ver una película.

"Julián Maldonado. Se cree mucha pieza, pero yo no le tengo miedo," dijo James, entre maldiciones. Sabía que Julián había asesinado varios hombres y que tenía rudos pistoleros bajo sus órdenes.

"¿Y qué te dijo la Ruby cuando la cortaste?" preguntó Antoine, echándose hacia atrás en el sofá reclinable.

Antoine deseaba haber estado en su lugar cuando Ruby conoció a James. A ella le encantó James por ser buen bailarín. Estaban en la boda de una amiga mutua. Después de bailar una vez con James, Ruby se quedó bailando con él toda la noche. Antoine creía que se podía haber conseguido a la linda mexicanita si Ruby hubiera empezado a bailar con él. Antoine, sin embargo, no era tan bueno para bailar como James, ni tan apuesto.

"Me echó madres hasta donde ya no, y me amenazó quesque le iba a ir con el chisme a su hermano de que yo la había golpeado y violado y que iba yo a darle información a la policía de sus actividades."

"¡A ca...rajo! ¿Qué piensas hacer si de veras va y le dice eso?" Antoine se paró de su sillón y se fue a asomar por la ventana para revisar el área de estacionamiento de los departamentos.

"Yo no estoy preocupado por eso. Siéntate a ver la película, Negro," fue la relajada respuesta de James.

Las cervezas habían logrado su mágico efecto, disolviendo el miedo real de James que la familia Maldonado se quisiera vengar de él.

Vieron la película, pero al final, unos pandilleros mataron al personaje principal. La posibilidad de venganza contra James retornó a sus mentes.

"¿James, tienes pistola aquí?" preguntó Larry, reclinado en el sofá. Se daba cuenta que las cosas se podrían poner serias si la chica realmente le había dicho aquellas mentiras a su hermano.

"¡No! Tú sabes cómo es mi hermana. No quiere tener nada de pistolas en la casa por sus niñas. Yo vendí la que mi papá me dejó y no he vuelto a comprar una desde entonces," James le dijo entre obscenidades.

James puso otra película y se fue de nuevo al sillón doble a continuar bebiéndose su sexta cerveza. Las cosas se podrían poner muy duras si Ruby en realidad le había mentido a su hermano acerca de James.

Por todo un año él y la hermosa mexicanita habían tenido una relación con altibajos. Ella lo había tenido como un trofeo. James era un magnífico espécimen de hombre, voz gruesa, alto, musculoso, guapo, honesto, con buen sentido del humor, y gran ritmo en la pista. Ella, sin embargo, estaba metida en la venta de las drogas y envolvió a James en el negocio. Aquella era la razón por la que él había dejado el taller de imprenta donde trabajaba desde que graduó de la preparatoria.

El celular de James empezó a timbrar. Vio el número. Era Ruby.

"Parece que esta vieja no me la creyó cuando dije que ya no quería nada con ella."

Contestó su llamada, pensando ponerla en su lugar de una vez por todas.

"Ya te dije que terminamos, Ruby... ¿Qué?"

La ex-novia interrumpió su declaración.

"Y yo te dije que no habíamos terminado, Querido Amante. Le dije a mi hermano que me golpeaste, me violaste frente a tus amigos, y amenazaste que ibas a hablar de nosotros con los detectives de narcóticos. No necesito decirte que se enfureció. Ya mandó a unos amigos a darte un mensajito."

James se dejó caer sentado sobre un banco alto en el bar entre la cocina y el comedor. Las piernas le flaquearon. Sabía lo que aquello quería decir, y lo dejó sin habla.

"¡Adiós, Chaguito, considérate carne para zopilotes, Desgraciado!" Ruby le dijo entre palabras vulgares y riéndose como una loca.

Los dos amigos miraron a James y se dieron cuenta lo que había pasado con solo leer el lenguaje de su cuerpo. Ruby se carcajeó más recio antes de colgarle.

"Creo que ahora sí estoy en problemas. Será mejor que me vaya a quedar en donde no me puedan encontrar. ¿Larry, está jalando tu camionetita?"

"Esa carcacha ha estado fuera de comisión por más de un mes. No tengo pa'reglarla. Necesita un chifladal de cosas, transmisión y otras madres."

¡Bam, bam, bam, bam!

Unos golpes a la puerta los sobresaltaron a todos. Los tres amigos se vieron unos a los otros con ojos muy abiertos. Los golpes sobre la puerta se repitieron, más fuertes esa vez.

¡Bam, bam, bam, bam!

Lorraine salió de su cuarto amarrándose la bata de dormir.

"¡Demonios! ¿Por qué no abren la puerta?" les gritó enfadada.

La mujer se detuvo de pronto y comprendió la situación con solo verles las caras a los tres hombres paralizados en el área de la sala, mirándose unos a los otros.

"¡Mejor me pelo! Me buscan a mí. Nomás deténganmelos tantito. No creo que les hagan nada a ustedes si yo ya me fui. Díganles que no me han visto hoy," James les susurró a su hermana y amigos.

James corrió a la ventana de la recámara trasera. Lorraine vivía en un departamento en el segundo piso, el cual solo tenía una puerta. En cuanto James saltó de la ventana del segundo piso, Lorraine fue y abrió la puerta. Tres hispanos irrumpieron, pistola en mano.

"¿En dónde está James?" uno de ellos demandó saber.

El mismo empujó a Lorraine al sofá junto a Antoine y Larry. Los tres estaban fingiendo haber sido despertados por sus toques a la puerta.

"Ni lo hemos visto..." Lorraine dijo, temblando.

El tipo que la empujó le dio un fuerte revés, maldiciendo.

"¡Perra mentirosa! Sabemos que está aquí. ¡Muchachos busquen en los cuartos!"

Antoine trató de defender a Lorraine, pero cayó de nuevo sentado al sofá con la punta de un pistolón apuntándole entre los ojos.

"¿Te quieres morir esta noche, Negro?" lo amenazó el pistolero.

"No..."

"Bien, puede que decida no matarlos, si solo nos dicen dónde está."

"Ya se fue," Lorraine dijo. "Se me hace que iba para Corpus Christi."

El celular del pistolero timbró en su cintura. Lo levantó y escuchó la llamada. Era Ruby. Le dijo que James ya se había marchado del lugar.

"Vámonos, compañeros, el gorrión voló por la ventana de atrás. Vamos a alcanzarlo," el mayor de los tres pistoleros les gritó a los otros.

Las niñas de Lorraine despertaron y comenzaron a llorar, espantadas por los dos extraños en su cuarto. Lorraine se levantó para ir a ver qué pasaba. El más viejo de los mafiosos la pescó del cuello y le puso la pistola en sien.

"Nos vamos. Si llamas a la policía, volveremos."

Los tres maleantes salieron disparados y se metieron a un carro.

James "agarró prestado" un carro que halló con la máquina en marcha. Había sido dejado desatendido por un hombre que estaba despidiéndose de su novia en uno de los departamentos. Cuando el hombre acabó de besar a su novia, se volteó y vio a James huyendo en su carro. El dueño le gritó y corrió tras de él, pero no lo alcanzó. Su novia lo dejó llamar a la policía.

Ruby alertó a los matones de la Mafia Texicana por teléfono que James se había subido al sedán deportivo rojo. Vieron al carro pasar a alta velocidad y lo empezaron a perseguir con su poderoso carro blanco de lujo.

James agarró rumbo a la carretera inter-estatal. Ganó velocidad en el carrito deportivo, 160 kilómetros por hora. Agarró la salida al periférico, esperando que ellos siguieran derecho por la estatal; sin embargo, lo vieron y lo siguieron al periférico. El carro de lujo se le fue acercando al deportivo al aproximarse al siguiente intercambio. James bajó su velocidad porque quería dar vuelta al oeste, con la esperanza que ellos se fueran de largo al sur. Uno de los pistoleros le tiró un par de balazos mientras el carro blanco se acercaba al rojo. James se agachó y le dio el jalón al volante. El vehículo se salió por la rampa de acceso en las dos ruedas del lado izquierdo.

Cuando el vehículo volvió a caer sobre las cuatro ruedas, James le aceleró y se encaminó rumbo al centro. Mirando el espejo retrovisor, vio humo de las llantas del carro blanco; los mafiosos se detuvieron y se regresaron en reversa para continuar su persecución en lugar de irse a rodear.

James tomó la primera salida que encontró. Se escondió bajo el puente por un par de minutos. Eran las 4:15 de la mañana. Pudo escuchar el carro blanco pasar a toda velocidad rumbo al oeste.

Pensó ir a la sub-estación de policía ahí cerca, pero se dio cuenta que sería arrestado por andar manejando auto robado. No quería ir a la cárcel.

No sería más seguro para él ahí. Julián tenía gente en la cárcel que podía llevar a cabo lo que estos estaban tratando de lograr. Decidió salirse del vecindario aquel. El carro grande se había ya esfumado.

James fue a su vieja preparatoria, pensando que sería un lugar seguro para esconderse a esa hora de la mañana; sin embargo, Ruby pudo deducir a dónde se había ido; fue a confirmar sus sospechas. Era malévola y sagaz. Una vez que vio el carrito de dos puertas, escondió su propio convertible plateado y le llamó a Miguel Salinas, el asesino.

"Ya encontré a tu hombre, Mike," le dijo Ruby a Miguel en su celular, "Se está escondiendo atrás del estadio de fútbol. Ven a terminar el trabajo. Ya me quiero ir a acostar."

En diez minutos el carro blanco arribó. James los pudo ver antes que lo hallaran, así que se alejó veloz. ¡La persecución volvió a empezar!

"¿Cómo demonios me encontraron?" exclamó James, frustrado.

James tomó la carretera al centro, pero los pistoleros lo persiguieron de nuevo hasta el periférico a mas de 160 kilómetros por hora. El tráfico era ralo ese martes por la madrugada; el aroma a muerte se percibía en el aire. El carro rojo tenía poco combustible. Cuando James entraba en el área del centro con sus enemigos pisándole los talones, la lucecita de advertencia se anunció que la gasolina en el tanque estaba a punto de acabarse.

Cada vez que se le acercaban al carrito deportivo, uno de los pistoleros se asomaba y le disparaba a James. Se vio forzado a manejar en zigzag, para evitar que le dieran. El condenado a muerte se salió de la carretera. No quería que se le fuera a terminar el combustible en la supercarretera donde sería un blanco fácil. Dio la vuelta al oeste en cuanto salió de la carretera. Le pegó a otro carro en la intersección, pero siguió avanzando.

El choque lo hizo reducir su velocidad. La llanta de adelante iba rozando metal y se reventó. Entonces los mafiosos ya estaban encima de él. Le dispararon un par de balazos. James se agachó adentro del vehículo y perdió control del auto. El carrito deportivo se volteó y fue a caer a un arroyo. Todo se le oscureció a James con el tremendo impacto.

El hombre de 26 años no sintió ya ningún dolor; se sentía flotar en el aire. James se sacó el boleto de lotería que traía en su bolsillo de la camisa y se rió. Luego se miró a sí mismo corriendo muy asustado.

¿Cómo podía estar en dos lugares al mismo tiempo? Desde su posición flotante en el aire, siguió a su otro yo, corriendo a través de callejones oscuros, seguido del ladrido de muchos perros caseros. Vio que el carro blanco de lujo ya lo iba alcanzando. Al final del callejón lo vio acercársele.

Un tipo le disparó tres balazos y le dijo algo. Su yo corredor cayó al suelo como un muñeco de trapo.

Cuando oyó hombres hablando en español, bajando por la ladera del arroyo, su instinto de conservación despertó a James Hickey del estupor en el que estaba. Se escurrió por la ventana del auto y salió disparado como si fuera a recibir un pase largo en un partido de fútbol. Su vida dependía de su velocidad.

Miguel lo alcanzó a ver primero y le disparó, pero los pilares del puente proveyeron a James con defensa contra las balas. Los asesinos se volvieron a subir a donde estaba su auto para perseguir al corredor. Estaban muy familiarizados con aquella parte de la ciudad.

James aún tenía la imagen de su muerte e iba corriendo más rápido que nunca en su vida. Antes que llegara al área del centro, vio al carro blanco acercándosele. Se acordó de Dios en ese momento. Un periodo de su vida relampagueó ante sus ojos.

Los Hickey se habían convertido al catolicismo cuando vivían en Chicago. Todos los niños habían sido bautizados, celebraron reconciliación, primera comunión, y confirmación. James había sido un acólito cuando tenía once y doce años. Había esporádicamente practicado su fe hasta que conoció a Ruby el año anterior.

James rezó como Pedro lo había hecho al comenzar a hundirse en las aguas cuando se estaba acercando a Jesús quien caminaba en el mar.

"¡Señor sálvame!" (Mateo 14:30)

El sedán de lujo ya estaba frente a él, bloqueándole el camino. Los tres pistoleros le dispararon al mismo tiempo desde menos de un metro.

¡PUM! ¡PUM! ¡PUM!

Miguel le gritó a James entre vulgaridades, "¡Este es el mensaje de Julián por lo que le hiciste a su hermana!"

James cayó como un muñeco de trapo sobre el pavimento, sintiendo que la vida se le escapaba por los hoyos de las balas. Quemando llanta, los pandilleros desaparecieron calle abajo. Eran las cinco y media.

MAS TEMPRANO ESA MADRUGADA

Cuando Gabriel llegó corriendo a la casa de las monjitas, Theresa ya se estaba estirando en el porche. Traía puestos una camiseta, pantaloncillos cortos, y tenis. Salió bostezando pero determinada a dar una caminata de potencia. Eran las cinco como él le había prometido.

"Buenos días, Gabrielín. ¿Estás listo?"

"¡Vámonos, Tere!"

"¿Qué tan lejos vamos?" ella le preguntó, caminando a su lado.

"Oh, pensaba que como unos seis kilómetros," replicó él, muy sonriente.

"¡Seis kilómetros! ¿Me quieres matar? ¡Es mi primer día!"

"¡Ja-ja-ja-ja! Lo se, Tere. Vamos a ver qué tan lejos llegamos."

Se arrancaron caminando rumbo al centro a buen paso. Theresa iba hablando más que él mientras que Gabriel solo la escuchaba y disfrutaba su voz y su compañía. Era mejor que platicar por teléfono. La podía ver y disfrutar de su presencia. Ella se veía muy bonita, aún así de temprano.

Gabriel estaba sorprendido que ya iba sudando mientras Theresa iba fresca como lechuga. Ella le contó algunas de las cosas por las que había pasado en Europa, en Latinoamérica, y en África. Gabriel admiró el cuerpo de Theresa; se estaba convirtiendo en una mujer de edad media con una figura más llenita. Le contó un chiste en lo que iban caminando.

"Una nena de 4 años se comía un panecito con crema en la peluquería viendo al peluquero cortarle el pelo a su papá. Estaba paradita muy cerca de la silla, así que el barbero la miró y le dijo con una benévola sonrisa, 'se te va a llenar de pelos tu panecito, Nena.' La niña se sonrió ampliamente y le dijo al viejito, 'Si, ya sé. ¡También me van a salir tetas!'"

Theresa se rió y le dio un manazo en el hombro mientras caminaban en la oscuridad de la madrugada. Antes que se dieran cuenta, ya estaban cerca del área del centro. Ya se iban a devolver, cuando escucharon tres disparos y luego un carro alejándose a gran velocidad. Eran las cinco y media.

"¡Vámonos de aquí, Gabriel. ¡Esos fueron balazos!"

"¡No, Tere! ¡Vamos a investigar!"

Gabriel trató de convencerla que fuera con él. Le tomó la mano y siguió andando rumbo a la víctima.

"Escucha. Quien haya tirado los balazos ya huyó. Ni puedo oír al carro que se arrancó quemando llanta. Creo que eso pasó a la vuelta de la esquina. Oigo a alguien pidiendo ayuda. ¿Lo puedes oír?"

"Sí, oigo a alguien gimiendo... ¡Ahí, en el callejón!" dijo Theresa caminando rápidamente tomada de la mano de Gabriel.

Había un joven gimiendo y rodando en su propia sangre en el callejón, a una cuadra del albergue para desamparados, a unas cuadras del hospital.

El Padre G lo volteó y se fijó que el hombre había recibido tres tiros mortales. El sacerdote le impuso las manos al caído; Theresa se le quedó viendo al místico, preguntándose si acaso iba a hacer un milagro y salvarle la vida al hombre. El ministro la miró a ella y sacudió la cabeza indicándole, "No." Levantó en vilo al herido.

"El hospital solo queda a unas cuadras de aquí. Vamos llevándolo para allá. Será más rápido que llamar a una ambulancia."

Theresa lo siguió, rezando por que pudieran conseguir ayuda médica lo suficientemente rápido para salvarle la vida al hombre.

Comenzó a hablarles cuando llegaron a la sala de emergencias. El cura pidió una camilla para poner a la víctima del tiroteo. Mientras esperaban que el cuerpo médico viniera a verlo, el agonizante hombre les agradeció por su ayuda en una voz muy débil.

"¿Quiénes son ustedes que se detuvieron a ayudar a un extraño?"

"Yo soy el Padre Gabriel, y ella es la Hermana Theresa."

"¡Aaah, dos servidores del Señor! Creo que me los mandó a ayudarme en mi último aliento."

"No diga eso. Ya está usted en el hospital. Mientras hay vida hay esperanza," Theresa le dijo con una sonrisa para darle ánimo.

El moribundo se rió dolorosamente y siguió hablando.

"Yo... tuve una visión... anoche. Vi los números ganadores de la lotería... 1, 3, 7, 12, 40... y 50. Fui a comprar un billete de la suerte... ¡y me salieron exactamente esos números! Yo... estaba muy emocionado... porque sabía que tenía en mis manos el... boleto ganador."

La Hermana Theresa notó que se estaba esforzando mucho para hablar y tosió algo de sangre. Ella se volteó, buscando asistencia.

"Debería de ahorrarse su fuerza... Dios mío, ¿Dónde están metidos los doctores o las enfermeras?" exclamó ella, volteando a su alrededor.

Gabriel puso su mano en el hombro del muchacho para que continuara.

"Estaba seguro que me iba a hacer rico... Terminé con mi novia... Ella no era nada buena... Tiene un hermano... en la Mafia Texicana... Es hermosa... pero tiene corazón maligno. Padre... yo era un buen católico... hasta que me junté con Ruby... Ella me tendió... esta trampa... Julián Maldonado, su... hermano... mandó a sus pis... toleros... a matarme... Me... dijeron... antes de... disparar... Julián... te man...dó... esto... hijo de... ¡Cof... cof... cof!"

Jaime empezó a toser. Parecía como si nadie estuviera disponible en la sala de urgencias mientras que la vida del hombre se le escapaba. El Padre Gabriel se le acercó más a James escuchando su voz ya muy apagada.

El joven ya tenía los ojos cerrados y hablaba muy quedito, como en una confesión. Theresa se retiró un paso atrás. James le dio algo al clérigo.

El equipo de emergencia finalmente apareció y tomó control de la camilla mientras el cura bendecía a James, absolviéndolo de sus pecados.

Lo conectaron a un monitor y comenzaron una infusión intravenosa. El monitor daba una línea recta. El corazón del paciente había dejado de latir. El plantel se puso a tratar de revivirlo con todo su equipo médico. El traumatólogo del lugar, el Doctor Arcángel, les ordenó que se detuvieran y no intentaran nada más. Les apuntó a las heridas del hombre.

"Este hombre recibió tres heridas mortales, al corazón, hígado, y el riñón derecho. No entiendo como alcanzó a llegar vivo al hospital. Debía haber muerto en donde cayó. No hay nada que podamos hacer para resucitarlo. ¡Se ha marchado de este mundo!" el doctor declaró en voz solemne.

Gabriel y Theresa aún estaban viendo la escena de cerca. Entonces, se fueron a sentar por un ratito. Theresa sentía curiosidad de saber lo demás que el moribundo le había contado a Gabriel.

"¿Me puedes contar lo que te estaba diciendo el muchacho?"

"Sí, sí puedo," Gabriel respondió. "Estoy sorprendido que me alcanzó a decir tanto. Siento como si lo hubiera conocido por los detalles que me dio de su corta vida. Su nombre era James Hickey. Ruby Maldonado, su novia, estaba muy enojada que él la había dejado, así que llamó a su hermano, Julián Maldonado, el tipo ese de la mafia Texicana. Ella acusó a James de golpearla y violarla antes de marcharse. James se suponía que iba a dar información a la policía concerniente a los Maldonado, lo cual no era cierto. Todo lo que James quería era alejarse de ellos y vivir para cobrar el premio de la lotería. Tiene una hermana, Lorraine Hickey, viviendo en el este de la ciudad, a quien planeaba ayudar con el dinero. Me dio el boleto."

El Padre Gabriel le enseñó a la Hermana Theresa el billete.

"Sí. Me fijé que te había dado algo. ¿Qué fue lo que dijo del billete?"

"Me dijo que dejara su mitad para mis necesidades y que le diera la otra mitad a Lorraine. Confió en que yo lo haría así. También me dijo que había visto su muerte pronosticada en una visión exactamente como pasó."

"¡Diez millones de dólares es el premio estimado para este miércoles!" exclamó Theresa, leyendo el billete de lotería.

"¡La mitad de eso le ayudaría bastante al Padre Michael a reconstruir su misión en África!" comentó el clérigo, preguntándose si por eso fue que habían encontrado al moribundo.

"¿Quién es el Padre Michael?"

"Estuvo en el seminario conmigo. Fuimos ordenados juntos. Él y el Padre Raphael, de quien te he hablado antes, eran íntimos amigos míos. Tenemos mucho en común. Raphael se fue a Los Ángeles a trabajar un área infestada de pandillas. Yo regresé a predicarle a mi gente, y Michael decidió ser como tú y convertirse en un misionero en el continente negro. Debías conocerlos a ambos uno de estos días; son como hermanos para mí. Practicamos el boxeo juntos mientras cursábamos los estudios en el seminario; los dos son bien rudos y bien dulces al mismo tiempo."

"Como tú," Tere comentó. "En verdad los debo conocer."

Un oficial de policía llegó a tomar el reporte del tiroteo. Después de hablar con los dos religiosos, el Oficial Vaughn les informó que necesitaban ir a la Oficina de Homicidios y dar su declaración. El Padre G se fijó en su reloj. Debía regresar a celebrar la misa de la mañana y regresar a la Hermana Theresa a su casa para que se alistara para ir a la escuela.

"Oficial, iremos a la Oficina de Homicidios más tarde. Tenemos que volver a nuestra parroquia ahorita mismo."

"Lo siento, Reverendo, es muy importante que hablen ustedes dos con los detectives en este momento," insistió el policía.

"Ya le di toda la información. Comprendo la necesidad de una declaración a los detectives; sin embargo, debo regresar a mi iglesia para celebrar la misa. Pregúntele al supervisor de Homicidios. Me conocen y le dirán que soy de confiar. Volveré a la estación más tarde y traeré a Sor Theresa."

El agente habló con el Sargento Villarreal quien le dijo que estaba bien que dejara ir a los religiosos. El Padre Gabriel les había ayudado antes en otros casos y estaba familiarizado con los procedimientos.

El Oficial Vaughn llevó a los religiosos a sus casas en el carro de patrullas. Dejaron primero a la monjita y luego al sacerdote.

Durante el evangelio en la misa, Gabriel recordó a James Hickey

"Había un hombre rico, cuyas tierras habían producido mucho, y se preguntaba a sí mismo '¿Qué voy a hacer? No tengo dónde guardar mi cosecha'. Después pensó: 'voy a hacer esto: demoleré mis graneros, construiré otros más grandes y amontonaré allí todo mi trigo y mis bienes, entonces yo conmigo hablaré: alma mía tienes aquí muchas cosas guardadas para muchos años: descansa, come, bebe, pásalo bien.' Pero Dios le dijo: 'Insensato, esta misma noche vas a morir. ¿Y para quién será lo que has amontonado?'" (Lucas 12:16-20)

El Padre G pensó en el premio de lotería, ¡diez millones de dólares! Si la visión de James de ganarse la lotería era tan acertada como la visión de su propia muerte, Gabriel se podría convertir en millonario, llevarse a Theresa con él, y desaparecer en una remota isla paradisíaca del Caribe. Sacudió la cabeza para borrar aquella tentadora fantasía y pronunció el nombre de su amigo en su mente.

"Michael, Michael, creo que Dios te va a proveer con lo que le pediste a través de mí."

Así continuó la celebración sin más interrupciones.

En cuanto Gabriel pudo ir a la estación de policía para dar su declaración concerniente al asesinato, fue y se llevó a Theresa con él. Era una buena excusa para ir al centro con su chica.

Cuando llegaron, un detective de homicidios les dio la bienvenida y se llevó a Theresa a dar su declaración. Mientras el Padre G esperaba, vio a una mujer llegar a la estación bañada en lágrimas. Asumió que se trataba de Lorraine; había cierto parecido en su carita con la del fallecido James.

"¿Eres Lorraine Hickey?" el sacerdote le preguntó.

"Sí. ¿Quien es usted?" ella replicó, estudiando al extraño.

"Soy el Padre Gabriel. ¿Te explicaron los policías...?"

"¡Sí, sí, y no lo puedo creer! ¿Están seguros que es la persona correcta?"

"Creo que así es." Pausó un momento. "Yo estuve ahí cuando James falleció. Te amó mucho y sus últimas palabras fueron precisamente del amor que tenía por ti y por tus niñas."

El Padre Gabriel le tomó las manos para proveerle apoyo moral. Ella estaba devastada. Lorraine abrazó al cura, buscando alivio mientras irrumpía de nuevo en llanto.

"James ahora descansa en el Señor. Estoy seguro que continuará cuidándolas a ustedes desde el cielo. Piensa en que él se ha ido a preparar un lugar para ti en el cielo para cuando se vuelvan a encontrar. Yo sé que tú eres una mujer de fe."

Lorraine se retiró un paso del presbítero y se sentó, limpiándose los ojos con una servilletita de papel.

"¿Cuánto tiempo tenía de conocer a James? Nunca me lo mencionó."

"Lo suficiente para saber que no vivió en vano. Yo le ayudé a hacer la paz con nuestro Señor antes que expirara."

Otro detective fue asignado a llevar a Lorraine a que identificara el cuerpo de su hermano. Antes de irse, ella se volvió al Padre Gabriel.

"¿Me podría ayudar con el funeral, Padre?"

El ministro le tomó las manos y le sonrió diciendo, "Por supuesto que sí, Lorraine. Puedes contar conmigo."

Un tercer detective salió e invitó al clérigo a que pasara a su oficina a dar su declaración. El Detective Johnny Correa no solo le estrechó la mano sino que también le dio un abrazo como a un viejo amigo. Gabriel había presidido durante su boda. El oficial era muy amable y también eficiente. Terminó antes que el otro detective completara el de Theresa.

Cuando Gabriel salió a esperar a la religiosa, se encontró a una hermosísima mexicana en la sala de espera de la Oficina de Homicidios. Estaba seguro que se trataba de Ruby, así que la llamó por su nombre.

"¿Ruby Maldonado?"

Su abogado estaba a un lado de ella. La mujer, quien se veía como una estrella de cine, y su abogado se volvieron a ver al sacerdote, intrigados.

"¿Quién es usted?" preguntó el abogado, mirando el collar romano de Gabriel y colocándose entre ellos dos.

"El Padre Gabriel, pero eso no importa. Tengo un mensaje para Ruby."

Gabriel dio un pasito a un lado para encarar a la cliente

"James me dijo que te amó mucho. Es muy triste que vayas a tener que vivir el resto de tus días sabiendo que causaste su muerte."

"¡Espere un segundo! Protesto en contra de esta acusación infundada en contra de mi cliente ¿Quién demonios es usted? ¿Y bajo qué autoridad se atreve a hacer esa acusación?"

El abogado de Ruby se interpuso de nuevo. El presbítero apostó sus potentes manos sobre los hombros del abogado y lo miró a los ojos.

"Yo actúo bajo la autoridad del Todo-Poderoso. Lo que digo es la verdad."

Lo quitó de en medio para volver a encarar a Ruby una vez más.

"Ven a verme, sola, cuando estés lista para hablar de este asunto, Ruby."

La mujer estiró su mano para ponérsela al clérigo en el pecho y le sonrió seductivamente.

"¿Está usted interesado en la apertura que dejó la desafortunada muerte de mi novio?"

Él le quitó la mano de su pecho y le respondió, "Estoy más interesado en el vacío de tu vida que en cualquier apertura que tú tengas. ¡Que Dios te perdone!"

Gabriel salió del cuarto rápidamente, dejándolos intrigados. El abogado se acordó por qué estaban en la estación de policía cuando el Detective Correa fue a llamar a Ruby para dar su declaración. El abogado asaltó al policía con preguntas.

"¿Tienen orden de arresto para mi cliente? ¿Por qué la quieren interrogar si ella ha sido victimizada también? Su queridísimo novio fue asesinado a sangre fría esta mañana y ustedes están interrogando a la gente inocente cuando deberían andar en búsqueda de los culpables," vociferó el abogado.

Correa miró a los dos, sacudió la cabeza, y se los llevó a su oficina para tomar la declaración. Sabía que el abogado no le permitiría responder mas que su identidad y su información personal. Como actriz consumada, Ruby entró a la oficina, llorando a mares, aparentando gran dolor y angustia.

Gabriel estaba afuera de la estación esperando a Theresa. La vio salir, riéndose con el joven detective. Se detuvieron en la puerta del edificio para despedirse. Sor Theresa lo abrazó; él le dio un beso en la mejilla.

"¿Qué fue eso?" la cuestionó Gabriel, un poco molesto por la demostración de afecto de aquel joven policía.

"¿Qué cosa?" Theresa le preguntó, fingiendo ignorancia.

"Acabas de conocer al tipo ese, y lo dejas que te abrace y te bese como..."

"¿Como todas esas mujeres que te abrazan y te besan a ti?"

"¡Bueno, pero eso es muy diferente!"

"¡No, no lo es!"

"¿Quién es él? ¡Sea como sea!"

"Es Charlie, Charles Ross. Su hermana mayor, Alice, fue a la escuela conmigo. Se casó con un banquero y tiene seis niños ahora. Era muy amiga mía la mayor parte del tiempo que viví aquí. Pasé la noche en su casa varias veces. Por eso conozco a Charlie. Era un niño entonces. Cuando empezamos a platicar, me preguntó si había estado en la preparatoria que atendió su hermana. Así fue que nos enteramos que ya nos conocíamos. Me confesó que estaba enamorado de mí en aquel entonces."

"¿Ah, sí?" dijo el Padre G, sonriendo en lo que caminaban a su carro.

"¡Sí! Claro que él solo tenía diez años entonces. ¿Estás celosito?"

"¡No!" él mintió, pero luego lo admitió: "Bueno, quizás un poquito. Esto es extraño. Nunca me había sentido así antes, que yo me acuerde."

"¡Oh, ya cálmate! Si es casado y tienen dos bebitos. Ahora que si se divorciara, o de repente se quedara viudo..."

"¡Métete al carro y deja de estar torturándome, Mujer!"

Gabriel le abrió la puerta del auto y la nalgueó de pasada como castigo al entrar al vehículo.

"¡Ey, me dolió!" ella protestó, pero se metió al auto con una sonrisa.

Gabriel se fue alrededor del auto muy satisfecho con el contacto aquel.

"¿Estás enojado conmigo?" preguntó Theresa, en lo iban a su casa.

"No me puedo enojar contigo; te amo demasiado."

"¿Me podrías entonces cantar una canción?"

Gabriel pensó en una canción, tomó aire, y comenzó a cantar.

El compositor de la canción le pide a Dios perdón por amar tan apasionadamente que aún el matar no le importa. Es atormentado cuando alguien más habla, ve, o toca a su amada. Ella se ha convertido en su infierno y su gloria.

"¿Cómo puedes salir con la canción apropiada al tiempo propicio?"

"No lo sé... inspiración, combinada con amplio repertorio, diría yo."

En verdad no lo sabía, pero canciones se le venían a la mente de su niñez y juventud. Se sabía varios cientos de canciones, así que tenía bastante de dónde escoger. una palabra era suficiente para recordarle una canción.

Dentro de la casa de los Ramírez esa noche, Lupe, la mamá de Jorge, se despertó al escuchar unos ruidos extraños provenientes de la alcoba de su hija de trece años. Se levantó y fue a investigar. Era como un gruñido de león mezclado con unos gritos ahogados de muchachita.

Lupe abrió la puerta de la alcoba de Rosita y horrorizada se cubrió la boca cuando, a pesar de la oscuridad de la habitación, vio que su hijo estaba violando a su hermanita en la cama. Jorge se había marchado de la casa y no había vuelto en muchos días.

"¿Qué demonios estás haciendo, Jorge? ¡Párale!" gritó la enardecida madre, metiéndose a la carrera a la recámara.

Raúl Ramírez, un hombrón, entró al cuarto en calzoncillos en ese instante y miró a su hijo dándole un revés a su madre. Se le echó encima a su chico.

"No. ¡Párale a esas tarugadas, ahora mismo, Chamaco!" le gruñó Raúl.

Jorge golpeó a su padre tan fuerte que el hombrón voló a través del cuarto y se fue a estrellar contra la pared, cayendo al piso, inconsciente.

Lupe Ramírez le suplicó entre sollozos y lágrimas, "¡Noooo, por favor, Jorge, detente... Déjala en paz, por Dios Santísimo!"

Jorge le replicó con obscenidades en una voz muy profunda "Tú eres la que sigue, Perra!" Sus ojos estaban rojos como carbones encendidos.

Lupe quedó paralizada de miedo. El demoníaco se le acercó a la mujer y la pescó del cuello.

"¡Dios mío, ayúdame!" rezó Lupe.

Se sacó el bendito rosario con crucifijo, el que el Padre Gabriel le había bendecido durante su fiesta de ordenación años atrás, y se lo mostró al poseído. Este se volteó y se fue corriendo para afuera, espantado.

"Rosita, mi 'ja, estás lastimada?" le preguntó Lupe, tosiendo y sobándose la garganta.

La pequeña no podía ni hablar. Estaba temblorosa, bañada en lágrimas, al tiempo que buscaba refugio en los brazos de su madre. Al pie de la pared opuesta, Raúl se comenzó a incorporar, examinándose la cabeza.

Al poco rato dos policías entraron a la casa y hablaron con la familia.

Los oficiales revisaron alrededor de la casa pero no pudieron encontrar al joven. Una ambulancia se llevó a la madre e hija al hospital. Raúl y uno de los agentes se iban también a ir de la casa cuando escucharon unos ruidos procedentes del techo. Raúl corrió alrededor, hacia el patio trasero.

"Jorge, mi 'jo, bájate y ven a hablar con nosotros, Muchacho. Necesitas ayuda," gritó Raúl, viendo hacia el techo.

El oficial que estaba enfrente de la casa, mirando también hacia el techo, se sorprendió cuando de repente un cuerpo cayó desde lo alto, gruñendo como bestia y derribándolo sobre el pavimento en la entrada de la cochera.

Jorge le dio puñetazos al policía hasta que el hombre quedó inconsciente; entonces el muchacho poseído le sacó la pistola de la funda al hombre de la ley, carcajeándose como un maniático.

"Jorge, detente. No lo hagas, Hijo!" le gritó Raúl, acercándose a donde Jorge estaba parado, apuntándole con la pistola a la cabeza del oficial.

"Échatelo, ahora mismo. ¡Ja-ja-ja-ja-ja-ja! Ándale, Jorge, hazlo ya!" la voz satánica saliendo de la boca del muchacho lo incitaba.

Raúl se sacó su rosario bendito de adentro de la camisa y se le acercó al demoníaco con el crucifijo por delante. La mano del muchacho temblaba pero empezó a apretar el gatillo; se detuvo y miró a Raúl que se le aproximaba. El joven poseído se tapó la cara y se echó hacia atrás al ver el crucifijo. Jorge se metió a la patrulla que tenía la máquina en marcha y se alejó veloz.

El jueves por la mañana, el 4 de noviembre, el Padre Gabriel estaba leyendo el periódico en la oficina de la escuela y se acordó del boleto de lotería que traía en su cartera desde que James se lo dio.

No se lo había mencionado a nadie más. Solo Theresa y él sabían acerca de aquel billetito. Los números ganadores eran el 1, 3, 7, 12, 40 y 50; todos aquellos eran significativos números bíblicos, ¡los mismos números que en el ticket de James! Gabriel abrió los ojos muy grandes y revisó los números en el periódico dos veces contra los del boleto. James había tenido la razón: ¡tenía el boleto ganador de diez millones de dólares!

El presbítero se recargó en su silla. Sintió un poder oscuro cubriéndolo por completo. Nunca antes había experimentado esa sensación; nunca le había importado el dinero antes. Dios siempre le había proveído con todo lo que necesitaba.

La escena que se le vino a la mente durante la misa regresó a él. Theresa había estado en sus brazos vestida en un pequeño bikini, jugando con él en las claras y tibias aguas del Caribe. El místico cerró los ojos y disfrutó de la deleitosa fantasía.

El poder oscuro envolviéndolo se movió a la ventana y tomó la forma de un gato negro con ojos rojos encendidos como brazas de carbón ardiendo. El felino parecía sonreír mientras observaba al sacerdote frotando el billete ganador de diez millones de dólares con sus dedos.

"¿En que está soñando despierto, Padre Gabriel?" la Hermana Theresa lo regresó a la realidad al entrar a su oficina sin anunciarse.

"Cierre la puerta Hermana, y siéntese por favor."

Gabriel le sonrió y le enseñó el boletito. Ella comprendió.

"¡Ay Dios mío! ¿Siempre sí salió ganador?"

"¡Sí! ¡James estaba en lo correcto!"

Theresa cerró la puerta y se acercó a preguntarle en un susurro, "¿Qué piensas hacer ahora, Gabriel?"

"Tenemos dos opciones, Querida Amiga: uno," el cura dijo, levantándose de su asiento y yendo alrededor de su escritorio para susurrarle, muy cerca de su linda cara, "Nos quedamos con los diez millones y huimos al Caribe donde nadie nos encuentre, y viviremos muy felices para siempre."

La religiosa abrió los ojos muy grandes y se ruborizó.

"¿O...?" ella dijo, mirándolo a los ojos fijamente.

"O... le decimos a Lorraine acerca de el último deseo de su hermano. Esto la convertiría a ella y sus niñas en millonarias, una misión entera en África próspera para muchas familias, el Padre Michael muy feliz... y tú y yo que nos quedáramos como estamos ahorita."

"¡Definitivamente la segunda opción!" dijo Theresa, emocionadísima que un milagro había ocurrido de nuevo.

"¡Por supuesto! ¡Bendito sea el Señor quien siempre provee con todo a aquellos que confían en Él!" exclamó el sacerdote, regresando a su asiento. Fue como si sus palabras lo hubieran liberado del embrujo del poder oscuro que se había apoderado de él cuando vio que era el boleto ganador.

"Le diremos hoy, después del entierro. Pero... ¿Qué fue lo que te trajo a mi oficina, Theresa?"

"Vine a... Lo siento mucho... ¡Se me olvidó a lo que había venido!"

"Bien, pienso que ya cumplió con su misión, Hermana, ahora regrésese a su salón a desquitar el sueldo," dijo él, abriéndole la puerta de su oficina.

Una vez que ella se marchó, él se volteó a ver el crucifijo sobre la pared.

"Gracias, Señor, por mandarla a ayudarme a hacer la decisión apropiada."

Afuera de la oficina del director, el gato negro de ojos rojos saltó de la ventana desde donde había estado mirando a la pareja. La criatura se desvaneció y cambió de apariencia, pasando a ser el remolinillo apestoso. Levantó velocidad y hojas secas, corriendo a través del campo de fútbol soccer y derribando a un par de niños que se atravesaron en su camino.

El remolino desapareció mientras los futbolistas se preguntaban qué les había sucedido a los caídos y les ayudaban a levantarse. Había un olor extraño y muy fuerte en el aire. Los niños se empezaron a acusar unos a los otros de ser responsables por el apestoso aroma.

Después que toda la gente se marchó del cementerio, el Padre Gabriel y la Hermana Theresa caminaron con Lorraine de regreso a la limusina que la iba a llevar a su casa. Theresa se llevó a las tres nenas a un lado en lo que Gabriel hablaba con Lorraine a solas por un momento.

Le explicó lo que había pasado en los últimos minutos de vida de su hermano y de las visiones que tuvo. El cura le dio el boleto ganador a la madre soltera después de describirle el último deseo de James.

"James me dijo que mantuviera su mitad para mis necesidades y que te diera la otra mitad a ti y a tus hijitas. ¡Yo no necesito nada, gracias a Dios! pero tengo un amigo en África que necesita ayuda, el Padre Michael. Él es un misionero por allá. Su misión fue destruida por fuego e inundación; van a tener que empezar a construir todo desde el principio. Él me había pedido ayuda justo antes que conociera yo a tu hermano."

Gabriel le extendió un papel con la información del misionero en África. A Lorraine le pareció increíble que el sacerdote le estuviera entregando diez millones de dólares sin querer dejar nada de dinero para él.

"Padre, puede contar con ese dinero para la misión africana de su amigo. De hecho, yo misma iré personalmente a ver que consiga toda la ayuda que necesite, aún si es más de la mitad de lo que James nos dejó. Yo estaba pensando en marcharme de esta ciudad de todos modos, ¡y siempre había tenido muchas ganas de ir a África!"

Llamaron a las niñas y se enlazaron en un abrazo de grupo. Entonces formaron un círculo y comenzaron a bailar, cantando alabanzas al Señor.

Con lágrimas en los ojos, Lorraine abrazó al cura; él la levantó un poco y le dio unas vueltas con los pies en el aire, como su hermano lo hacía. Cuando la puso de nuevo en el suelo, ella lo besó en ambas mejillas y llamó a sus niñas para que lo besaran también.

Lorraine fue a besar a Theresa mientras las tres niñas vapuleaban a Gabriel a besos. Se subieron a la limusina para irse a su casa. El chofer estaba sorprendido de lo contentas que estaban aquellas gentes después de haber enterrado a un pariente cercano, pero no dijo una palabra.

"Oh, espera, Lorraine," Gabriel le gritó cuando ya se iban. "¿Podrías llevarle al Padre Michael de mi parte, un buen frasco de la salsa más picante que puedas hallar?"

"Seguro, Padre Gabriel," ella le respondió desde la ventana abierta de la limusina, "Le voy a llevar una caja llena de diferentes salsas, a ver cual le gusta más. ¿Lo veremos a usted algún día en la misión del Padre Michael?"

"Tal vez... Manténganme informado de su progreso. La Hermana Theresa ha trabajado en África antes; podría servirme como guía."

"¡Se oye como un buen plan!" estuvo de acuerdo Theresa, imaginándose que podrían viajar juntos.

La limo se marchó, llevándose a las nuevas millonarias.

Gabriel y Theresa se quedaron parados solos, viendo el auto desaparecer al salir del cementerio. Theresa lo abrazó y lo besó en las dos mejillas.

"¡Eres tan bueno! Hiciste lo correcto. ¡Estoy muy orgullosa de ti!"

Él le ofreció su brazo izquierdo y se fueron caminando rumbo al Curimóvil. Se sentía muy bien caminar al lado de su amada amiga.

Satanás, en forma de urraca negra con ojillos rojos, estaba viéndolos desde lo alto de un poste de electricidad fuera del cementerio mientras salían de ahí en el viejo auto.

"No eres tan bueno, Gabriel. Ya caerás tarde o temprano."

Capítulo XI

Exorcismo

Don Pedro Mireles fue a la misa matutina del Padre Gabriel el miércoles para invitarlo a desayunar y a jugar ajedrez. El cura aceptó ir, pero le dijo que primero tenía que platicar con una pareja que había visto en la iglesia con un chiquito de tres años que se quedó rezando después de la misa.

"¡Shalom! (Paz) ¿Cómo están ustedes?" dijo el pastor, acercándoseles al ver que terminaron sus oraciones.

El padre del niño, Leopoldo Cárdenas, le explicó al pastor, "Nosotros bien, gracias, Padre. Es nuestro niño el que está muy enfermo. Oímos que ocurren milagros en esta iglesia. Por eso vinimos hoy. Benito necesita un trasplante. Nació con un defecto en el corazón. Los doctores dicen que solo se puede curar con una operación. Necesitaríamos medio millón de dólares para tal operación; nosotros no tenemos manera de conseguir tanto dinero así. Yo trabajo en mi propio negocito de reparar llantas ponchadas. No tenemos ni siquiera seguro médico. Si Benito no tiene esa operación, se nos va a morir muy pronto. Es nuestro único hijo,"

Lleno de compasión el párroco se le acercó al chamaquito. Le impuso las manos sobre su cabecita y oró. En lugar de sentir la energía sanadora del Espíritu Santo, Gabriel empezó a tener una visión. Vio a un demonio dorado clavándole la mano en el pecho al niñito para apretarle el corazón. El demonio volteó a ver al sacerdote y se rió.

"¿Quieres este niño, Gabriel? Me vas a tener que vencer en batalla, mano a mano, si quieres ayudarlo."

Gabriel miró al niño en su visión. El aterrorizado pequeñito empezó a llorar. El llanto del niño regresó al místico de su visión. Le quitó las manos de la cabecita, se puso en cuclillas para estar a su nivel y lo miró a los ojos. El chiquillo había visto la visión también. Gabriel le tocó el rostro.

"No temas, Benito. Yo te protegeré de ese grandulón y muy malo demonio dorado."

La madre de Benito volvió sus ojos hacia su marido, muy sorprendida, y luego volteó a ver al presbítero.

"¿Cómo se enteró usted acerca del demonio dorado? Benito nos había hablado acerca de él, pero creímos que era porque se había asustado un día que vio una lucha en la televisión. Había un enmascarado llamado el Demonio Dorado, quien medio-mató a otro luchador."

211

El Padre G se encontró temblando y sudando después de la terrible visión. No sabía que hacer.

"Vayan en paz. Dios nos proveerá los medios para salvar a su niño. Voy a rezar por Benito. Regresen el domingo."

La pareja hizo como se los indicó y no cuestionaron al clérigo. Les echó la bendición y besó a Benito en la cabeza.

Gabriel estaba trastornado por la experiencia. Caminó al restaurante con Pedro pero se negó a desayunar. Solo se bebió un poco de agua para humedecerse la garganta. El viejo amigo dispuso de unos huevos rancheros con tocino, tortillas de harina, y un café. El Padre G estaba revisando su versión de bolsillo del Nuevo Testamento en lo que Pedro comía.

"¡Oración y ayuno!" murmuró Gabriel, cerrando su libro como si hubiera encontrado lo que había estado buscando.

"¿De qué está usted hablando, Padre?"

El párroco abrió su librito de nuevo y leyó parte del Evangelio según San Marcos.

"Uno de ellos le dijo: 'Maestro, te he traído a mi hijo, que está poseído de un espíritu mudo. Cuando se apodera de él, lo tira al suelo y le hace echar espuma por la boca; entonces le crujen sus dientes y se queda rígido. Le pedí a tus discípulos que lo expulsaran pero no pudieron'. 'Generación incrédula,' respondió Jesús, '¿hasta cuándo estaré con ustedes? ¿Hasta cuándo tendré que soportarlos? Tráiganmelo'. Y ellos se lo trajeron. En cuanto vio a Jesús, el espíritu sacudió violentamente al niño, que cayó al suelo y se revolcaba, echando espuma por la boca. Jesús le preguntó al padre: '¿Cuánto tiempo hace que está así?' 'Desde la infancia, le respondió, y a menudo lo hace caer en el fuego o en el agua para matarlo. Si puedes hacer algo, ten piedad de nosotros y ayúdanos. ¡Si puedes...!' respondió Jesús. 'Todo es posible para el que cree'. Inmediatamente el padre del niño exclamó: 'Creo, ayúdame porque tengo poca fe'. Al ver que llegaba más gente, Jesús increpó al espíritu impuro, diciéndole: 'Espíritu mudo y sordo, yo te lo ordeno, sal de él y no vuelvas más'. El demonio gritó, sacudió violentamente al niño y salió de él, dejándolo como muerto, tanto que muchos decían: 'Está muerto'. Pero Jesús, tomándolo de la mano, lo levantó, y el niño se puso de pie. Cuando entró en la casa y quedaron solos, los discípulos le preguntaron: '¿Por qué nosotros no pudimos expulsarlo?' Él les respondió: 'Esta clase de demonios se expulsa sólo con la oración.'" (Marcos 9:17-29)

Pedro miró a su amigo religioso sin entender de lo que estaba hablando ya que el sacerdote no había compartido con él nada del problema de la familia Cárdenas, ni la visión que experimentó esa mañana.

Pedro cambió el tema a algo que acababa de encontrar en el periódico en ese momento. Gabriel, entonces, no pudo explicarle que algunas traducciones del evangelio dicen "oración y ayuno" o "ayuno y oración" como la prescripción para lidiar con demonios difíciles de expulsar.

"¿Qué no es este, Jorge Ramírez, uno de sus chamacos?"

El viejo le mostró una foto del criminal más buscado en el condado El joven había sido un acólito, estudiante bíblico, cantor, lector, candidato al seminario, buen estudiante de preparatoria y orgullo de su familia. Ese joven tenía órdenes de arresto por asalto sexual de una menor de edad, asalto a mano armada, y asalto físico en contra de un oficial de policía. También era sospechoso en varios otros crímenes violentos.

"El periódico dice que se le debe considerar muy peligroso porque se llevó el arma del policía y la ha estado usando en los robos. Hay una recompensa de cincuenta mil dólares por la captura o información que lleve a la captura del muchacho," Pedro leyó en voz alta.

La policía lo andaba buscando febrilmente. El Padre Gabriel se talló la frente incrédulo.

"¡Dios mío! ¿Cómo puede ser?"

Pedro se fijó que el cura se entristeció con las noticias acerca de su joven amigo, así que buscó algún otro tema para discutir con él. Abrió la página de deportes.

"Mire esto, Padre. ¡Están ofreciendo 500,000 dólares a quien venza al Demonio Dorado en el cuadrilátero! El reto está abierto para todos, ya sean profesionales o amateurs, luchadores, boxeadores, peleadores de judo o karate, o cualquier valiente que se anime enfrentarse a este gigante."

El título del luchador le llamó la atención al ministro. Comenzó a cavilar acerca de la coincidencia del anuncio, la cantidad del premio, y la visión que había tenido. Don Pedro se tomó otro trago de café.

"¿Sabe qué, Padre? Fui luchador profesional hace muchos años. Si tuviera veinte años menos, me atrevería a pelear con este tipo. Ha matado a varios hombres en el ring y ha dejado a otros lisiados de por vida."

El cura parecía en trance, murmurando, pero sí oyó lo que el viejo le dijo.

"Quinientos mil dólares... Demonio Dorado... Lucha... Operación de corazón... Oración y ayuno."

Acordándose luego de la familia de Jorge Ramírez, el Padre G sacudió su cabeza y se despidió de su amigo.

"Me debo marchar, Pedro, gracias por invitarme a desayunar."

"¡Pero si solo se bebió un trago de agua, Padre!"

"La intención es la que cuenta, mi Amigo. ¡Nos vemos!"

El sacerdote casi corrió para salir del restaurante después de estrecharle la mano a Pedro y se dirigió a su oficina.

La Señora Greene, la secretaria de la parroquia, le informó que la familia Ramírez le acababa de llamar por teléfono. Pedían que fuera a su casa.

"¿Jorge?" dijo el cura, adivinando de qué se trataba el asunto.

"Sí. Regresó a su casa. Ya llamaron a la policía también," explicó la Señora Greene mientras que el presbítero ponía sus cosas en el maletincito, un crucifijo, agua bendita, libro de oraciones, y su estola morada.

"Regresaré en cuanto pueda. Dígale por favor al Diácono García que se haga cargo de mis citas de esta mañana, y notifíquele a la Señora Gray que voy a salir, para que se haga cargo ella de la escuela."

El sacerdote se trepó a su carro y manejó rumbo a la casa de los Ramírez.

Un par de patrullas de policía y un carro de detectives ya estaban ahí.

Lupe Ramírez, la madre de Jorge, salió llorando a recibir al pastor con un abrazo. Raúl Ramírez, el padre, se quitó el sombrero y le apretó la mano al cura para saludarlo.

Los policías estaban revisando la casa y los alrededores, pero Jorge ya se había desaparecido.

Gabriel se fijó que los dos padres traían señas de heridas recientes. Raúl traía un ojo morado y un labio reventado; Lupe tenía moretones en su cuello. Los uniformados enfundaron sus armas y les informaron a los papás que el muchacho ya no estaba. Dieron la descripción del fugitivo por radio para avisarles a todos los agentes en la sección que estuvieran alertas.

Los patrulleros se fueron, pero los detectives, uno de crímenes sexuales y el otro de robos, se quedaron a hablar con los padres.

Los Ramírez estaban muy desconsolados; habían estado llorando mucho. El Padre G les pidió que se sentaran y le contaran lo que había sucedido. Se pasaron a la sala a platicar.

Los detectives le preguntaron al sacerdote si se podían quedar a escuchar. Gabriel les preguntó a los Ramírez si ellos tenían algún problema con eso. Estuvieron de acuerdo en permitir que se quedaran.

"Todo había ido muy bien para Jorge. Estaba más seguro cada día que se quería hacer sacerdote como usted, Padre Gabriel. Pero se empezó a juntar con un grupito de estudiantes de la preparatoria, y empezó a cambiar. Se comenzó a desvelar, a fumar, a tomar, a experimentar con las drogas y el sexo," la madre le estaba platicando al cura, quien le tomó la mano para consolarla. Ella continuó "Ese grupito de muchachos y muchachas estaban muy interesados en brujería, santería, adoración satánica, música pesada de rock, películas de horror y vestirse con ropa negra. Se reunían por las noches y se iban al cementerio a hacer no sé qué."

En ese momento, alguien estaba entrando por la puerta de enfrente. Los detectives sacaron sus pistolas, preparados para enfrentarse al sospechoso que habían ido a buscar; sin embargo, se trataba de una chica, Cindy Lowe, quien entró preguntando en voz alta si había alguien en casa.

Lupe le dijo, "Pásate, Cindy. Estamos acá en la sala."

El papá de Jorge se levantó a recibir a la joven. Ella también traía unos moretones en la cara y los brazos.

"¿En dónde está?" preguntó la muchacha.

"Ya se fue otra vez, Cindy. Siéntate con nosotros y ayúdanos a aclarar la situación," Lupe le dijo al tiempo que la tomaba del brazo para que se sentara junto a ella en el sofá y luego le preguntó, "¿Qué hacían en su grupo que hizo a mi Jorge cambiar? Ya ni lo reconozco, ¡en absoluto!"

"Al principio era solo juego y diversión; buscábamos nuevas emociones y profundas sensaciones," la chica confesó. "Nos metimos en música pesada y películas de terror. Alguien trajo cigarrillos y cerveza; pensamos que éramos la gran cosa. Ya de ahí, probamos a oler pegamento y pintura metálica. Fumábamos marihuana; uno conocía a alguien que nos podía conseguir crack, cocaína, o heroína. Lo probamos todo. Con esas cosas, también empezamos a tener sexo con todos los miembros del grupo, seis chicas y seis chavos; nos pusimos los Apóstoles de Satanás para asustar a los bravucones de la escuela. Teníamos nuestras orgías en el cementerio, cantándoles a los espíritus malignos y aturdiéndonos con las drogas."

Los apenados padres bajaron la cabeza y se cubrieron la cara, escuchando lo que ya sospechaban que había estado pasando.

La muchachita continúo su triste historia. Les relató todo lo que había presenciado, aún los detalles del incidente en el cementerio. Cindy tenía lágrimas rodando por sus mejillas y estaba meciendo el cuerpo atrás y adelante sobre el sofá mientras recordaba la terrible escena. Lupe le echó el brazo sobre los hombros.

La chica miró a las gentes a su alrededor. Los papás de Jorge se estaban cubriendo el rostro; los detectives estaban mirando a Cindy con ojos de incredulidad. El cura la tomó de la mano y le dio un apretoncito.

"¿Qué clase de drogas andaban usando esa noche, Cindy?" preguntó el Detective García de la Unidad de Crímenes Sexuales.

"No me acuerdo que hallamos usado drogas esa noche. Fue el libro que habíamos estado leyendo el que nos puso como bajo un encanto."

"¿Qué le pasó al libro?" preguntó el Padre Gabriel.

"Cuando el rayo le pegó a Jorge, el libro se quemó hasta que no quedaron más que cenizas, pero aún las cenizas fueron recogidas por el ventarrón y se le metieron en la boca a Jorge," Cindy luego murmuró, "Me golpeó y me violó como bestia enloquecida... ¡Se me hace que se le metió el Diablo!"

"¿Hiciste un reporte de policía acerca de lo que pasó, acerca de tu novio violándote?" preguntó el Detective García, aún sin creerle.

"¿Quién me lo iba a creer?" respondió irritada la joven al incrédulo detective, "Solo me fui a mi casa y me di un baño. No he podido dormir mucho desde esa noche."

"¿Qué pasó con tus otros amigos?" continuó García interrogándola.

"No nos hemos vuelto a juntar. Dos chavas se fueron de la ciudad. Dos de los muchachos están en una clínica mental bajo terapia. Los demás se están quedando con parientes, creyendo que el Diablo los anda buscando. Un par de chicos y una chica fueron a su iglesia a buscar protección."

"Vamos a necesitar declaraciones de todos ellos. Quiero que me des sus nombres, direcciones, y números de teléfono para poder hablar con ellos," García le dijo a Cindy.

Después que la chica había terminado su historia, fue el turno de los Ramírez de describirles al cura y a los oficiales lo que ellos sabían.

Les describieron las horrorosas acciones de su hijo y la fuerza descomunal que demostró la noche que los atacó.

El Detective Gresham de la Unidad de Robos mencionó, "Algunas veces las drogas hacen a la gente más fuerte de lo que son y los hace comportarse de manera realmente anormal."

Los padres del muchacho escucharon su explicación, pero ellos no creían que había sido una droga la que alteró la personalidad de su hijo a tal extremo. Raúl les contó como Jorge atacó al patrullero y le quitó la pistola. Los dos detectives se estaban tallando la frente, afectados por la historia. Raúl continuó con lo que había pasado después.

"Más policías vinieron. Buscaron al chamaco toda la noche, pero lo único que encontraron fue la patrulla abandonada en un arroyo."

"En qué biblioteca consiguieron el libro ese, Cindy?" Gabriel preguntó.

La chica le dijo que ella les enseñaría el sitio. Pensando que el libro nada tenía que ver con su investigación, los detectives se fueron por su cuenta.

El párroco llevó a Raúl, Lupe, y Cindy a la biblioteca pública de donde habían sacado los libros.

Una amable viejita bibliotecaria los atendió y les dijo que recordaba al extraño grupo de chicos sacando libros muy raros. Dijo que sí se acordaba del libro en cuestión, uno grueso como una Biblia, con una cubierta como piel morena y escrito en tinta roja. En verdad era un libro muy viejo, ella estuvo de acuerdo, pero no se podía acordar de su nombre.

Revisó los archivos de los chicos que habían sacado libros ese día; todos, excepto Jorge, estaban en la lista. La bibliotecaria se echó la culpa por no haber anotado la transacción bajo el nombre de Jorge Ramírez. No había comprobante que sacó libros. También, ya que no se acordaba del nombre del libro, no podía buscarlo en los archivos para verificar que existía. El Padre Gabriel le agradeció su ayuda, y se regresaron a casa de los Ramírez.

Una vez en su oficina parroquial, Gabriel pensó cuál sería la mejor forma de manejar la situación, y decidió ir a la iglesia a rezar. Estaba vacía, así que el cura se hincó frente al altar y se sumergió en una oración profunda.

Creía que el maligno estaba envuelto. Las historias que aquellas gentes le contaron no habían sido inventadas. Gabriel se preguntó cómo se ataban los eventos más recientes, Benito, operación, Jorge, posesión, el Demonio Dorado, dinero, fe, ayuno, oración, y pelear contra el Diablo.

Necesitaba fuerza, fe, valor, entendimiento, y guía divina; así pues, oró por horas sin darse cuenta del transcurso del tiempo.

Timmy Bravo, hijo adoptivo de James Bravo, el dueño del gimnasio, salió de la escuela de la Santísima Trinidad y se asomó a la iglesia camino a casa. Decidió meterse a rezar como de costumbre antes de un examen grande. Algunas veces el pastor había encontrado a Timmy rezando por sí solo y le había regalado algo, un dulce, una fruta, un juguetito, o alguna otra cosita que sabría-Dios-de-dónde había sacado el misterioso cura. El chiquillo sospechaba que su padrino-sacerdote era un mago.

El niño del tercer año entró de la brillante luz de afuera a la penumbra del interior y vio a su padrino rezando ahí. Timmy se le quedó viendo por un rato al místico arrodillado. Había algo diferente acerca de él; tenía un halo como fosforescente alrededor del cuerpo entero. Lo que más le sorprendió al niño fue el hecho que el cura sumido en su oración ¡estaba flotando en el aire! Sus rodillas estaban a unos treinta centímetros por encima del piso.

Timmy sonrió, acercándose al clérigo.

"¿Padre G, cómo puede hacer eso?"

Gabriel abrió los ojos y le sonrió a su ahijado, volvió los ojos a la imagen de Cristo y se santiguó para terminar. Timmy vio las rodillas del sacerdote de nuevo, pero ya estaban descansando sobre el escalón del altar.

"¿Cuál era tu pregunta, mi Viejo Amigo, Don Timoteo el Bravo?" preguntó el presbítero, echándole el brazo sobre los hombros al pequeño y caminando hacia fuera de la iglesia con él.

"Quiero saber cómo le hace para volar," dijo Timmy. "Lo vi volando en el aire cuando rezaba. Sus rodillas estaban arriba del piso como tanto así."

Timmy le mostró con sus manos un espacio de treinta centímetros.

"¡Ja-ja-ja-ja-ja-ja, sí que tienes una gran imaginación, mi Viejo Amiguito! Yo diría que no podías ver muy bien, ya que entraste de la intensa luz del sol de afuera a la oscuridad de la iglesia; sin embargo, yo también te quiero hacer una pregunta. ¿Cómo es que no te lavas bien las orejas?"

"¿Qué es lo que quiere decir, Padre G?" preguntó intrigado el chico.

El místico le frotó la orejita al niño y pretendió jalarle una moneda de un dólar de atrás del oído.

Se la había encontrado abajo del altar cuando terminó su oración, y la recogió cuando Timmy le estaba revisando las rodillas. El chamaquito estaba sorprendido de los poderes mágicos de su amigo mayor.

"Mira, Timmy: tú no le dices a nadie que me viste volando, y yo no le digo a nadie que tú traes dólares pegados en las orejas. ¡Además, te podrás quedar con el dólar!"

Timmy le sonrió y le cerró un ojo en complicidad. El chiquillo se echó el dólar al bolsillo y saludó de mano a su padrino para cerrar su pacto, luego se echó a correr muy contento hasta su casa, a solo tres cuadras de distancia. El sacerdote mandó su bendición tras el veloz corredor.

Gabriel se acordó de Jorge. Cerca de nueve años atrás, Jorge era como Timmy ahora. El Padre G había sido asignado a esa parroquia como pastor asociado entonces. Jorge era acólito como Timmy. Ambos muchachitos admiraban al párroco y andaban diciendo que querían ser como él.

El muchacho mayor estaba en peligro mortal. Toda la bondad que había demostrado al crecer se había perdido en poco tiempo. Había cometido el pecado más grande, traicionar a Dios invocando al Diablo. Gabriel se preguntó qué sería lo que desvió al muchacho; aún tenía esperanza que no fuera muy tarde para salvar al joven de perder su alma eternamente.

Gabriel tenía mucho hambre, pero le dio instrucciones a su ama de llaves, la Señora Black, que le diera la comida que había preparado para él a la familia pobre que vivía en la misma cuadra que ella. Debería darles su comida diario hasta que él le indicara lo contrario.

"¿Qué es lo que le pasa, Padre G? ¿Ya no le gusta mi comida?"

"No... Quiero decir, sí: me encanta la comida que tan gentilmente preparas para mí. Confía en mí y cumple con lo que te pido. Continúa haciendo lo que haces normalmente como si me estuvieras alimentando a mí, pero llévales esa comida a tus vecinos, la joven viuda y sus niños."

"¿Quiere usted decir a Maricela y sus tres diab... chiquillos?"

La tailandesa puso cara de disgusto porque Maricela Alva tenía mala reputación. Sus hijos eran un gran problema para todos los vecinos.

"Sí. Creo que ahí es a donde debe ir mi comida por unos días."

"¿Qué es lo que va usted a comer entonces?"

"Dios proveerá, mi Querida Amiga, Dios proveerá. Tú no te preocupes por mí, pero solo ayúdame con esta misión. ¿De acuerdo?"

"Está bien, Jefe, pero esa piruja no se merece que se preocupe por ella."

"Vamos, Hija mía. ¿Qué hemos aprendido acerca de juzgar a los demás?"

"Lo lamento, Padre. Tiene usted razón. Haré lo que me pide."

El Padre Gabriel se masajeó el estómago para que dejara de gruñirle. Estaba seguro que su hambre iba a pasar. Pensó en las instrucciones que le dio a la criada; habían sido pronunciadas con intención de prevenirla de saber que iba a estar ayunando. Solo había visto a Maricela una sola vez pero había oído bastante acerca de ella y de su cuestionable moralidad. Ni sabía por qué le sugirió a la Señora Black que le llevara su comida, pero confiaba que había sido inspiración divina.

Ese anochecer, el Padre Gabriel platicaba con los miembros del grupo de estudios bíblicos, dirigido por la Hermana Theresa desde que asumió los deberes de la Hermana Kathryn. Habían terminado su junta esa noche y disfrutaban unas piececitas de repostería con café en la biblioteca. Habían estudiado la parábola de la oveja perdida. Un caballero ya grande de edad invitó al pastor a que se les uniera a paladear los deliciosos bocadillos.

"¡Ándele, Padre! Éntrele a estos deliciosos panecillos que mi vieja nos preparó para esta noche. Nos los tenemos que acabar toditos."

El hombre se puso una galletita en la boca y cerró los ojos para demostrarle al cura qué buenas estaban. El delicioso aroma del café recién hecho tentó el estómago vacío de Gabriel. Rezó por fuerza para resistir la tentación y mantener su ayuno. No había comido ni bebido nada desde el último trago de agua que se había tomado aquella mañana con Don Pedro.

"Estoy seguro que están deliciosos, pero debo de pasar por esta noche. De todos modos, ¡muchísimas gracias!"

El clérigo se acercó a abrazar a una de las más antiguas parroquianas.

"Padre Gabriel, que gusto verlo entre nosotros esta noche. Usted siempre anda tan ocupado. ¿Cuándo va a venir a cenar conmigo? Ya sabe que mi casa siempre está abierta para usted. ¿Cuándo fue la última vez que vino a visitarme, hace un año...? ¡No! ¿Dos?"

"Lo siento mucho. Debemos formalizarlo y ponerlo en mi agenda mañana mismo. De esa manera no me olvidaré de volver a visitar tu hogar sin dejar pasar tanto tiempo, Grace. Solo llámale a la Señora Greene y dile que te apunte para el día que estoy disponible. Ella es la que me guía en lo que tengo que hacer todo el día."

Gabriel se hizo para atrás y chocó contra un cuerpo suave a sus espaldas. Se volteó, disculpándose, y se encontró cara a cara con Theresa.

"Discúlpeme que lo empujé, Padre Gabriel. Estaba agarrando este pastelito y no lo vi."

Theresa le dio una mordida a su pieza de pastel. Gabriel se encontró fascinado al observarla comérselo. Ella le dio un traguito a su café; él se le quedó viendo fijamente, encantado.

La mujer le obsequió una hermosa sonrisa, adornada con una embarradita de chocolate en sus suaves labios color de rosa. Gabriel se imaginó a sí mismo lamiendo el chocolate de esos labios.

"¡Padre!" Grace le llamó en voz alta, notando que no se había volteado a atenderla a ella después de intercambiar disculpas con la hermana.

"Sí, Grace," dijo el sobresaltado cura, volteándose a ver a la viejita.

"¿Tenía Jesús en verdad cabello largo y barba? ¿O se veía como en la imagen del buen pastor que usaban en la iglesia antigua, usted sabe, con pelo corto y sin barba?"

"¿Cómo crees tú que se veía, Grace?"

"Yo personalmente creo que tenía el pelo largo y usaba barba como el actor en la película de Jesús de Nazaret."

"El Sudario de Turín y yo estamos de acuerdo contigo, mi Amiga."

El presbítero se la pasó platicando con la mayoría de los estudiantes de Biblia. Parecían contentos de tener a Sor Theresa de líder del grupo.

Después que todos los miembros del grupo de estudios bíblicos se fueron de la rectoría, los dos religiosos acabaron solitos en la casa. Theresa recogió la basura y la puso en una bolsa para sacarla. El Padre G encendió el televisor para ver las noticias de las diez.

Theresa entró a la sala y se sentó junto a él a ver la televisión; él le ofreció llevarla a casa. Ella le dijo que Sor Carmen ya venía en camino a recogerla. Gabrielín tomó las manos de Tere entre las suyas, sentados en el sofá. Se miraron a los ojos sin hablar. Gabriel cantó parte de la canción que había cantado en la recepción del vigésimo-quinto aniversario de bodas de los Córdoba; la parte que habla de dos amantes que se miran frente a frente como cuando eran jovencitos, incapaces de decir palabra.

¡Piiiiiiiip-piiiiiiiip!

Tere y Gabrielín saltaron, turbados por el pito de la van, avisándoles que Sor Carmen estaba afuera. Se sonrieron uno al otro e intercambiaron amorosas miradas en silencio antes de encaminarse a la puerta.

Ella le besó las manos; él le besó las de ella. Se abrazaron para desearse buenas noches. Theresa se marchó con Carmen. Gabriel observó a la van desaparecer en la noche, calle abajo.

"Buenas noches, mi Amor," dijo quedito y luego cerró la puerta.

Cuando regresó a la sala, se fijó que Theresa le había dejado media tacita de café y media rebanada de su pastel. Sabía exactamente lo que aquello quería decir.

Cuando andaban de novios en su adolescencia, el dinero de él nunca era suficiente para hacer todas las cosas que querían hacer, ir al cine, a cenar, al baile, juegos mecánicos, o conciertos.

Una de esas ocasiones, cuando se fueron caminando al centro después de un partido de fútbol americano en su escuela, fueron a un restaurante a comerse una rebanada de pastel con café. No era un lugar barato, y Gabriel sabía que no le alcanzaba el dinero más que para comprar una rebanada de pastel y una taza del café tan caro que vendían ahí. También sucedió que Theresa había dejado su bolsa en el carro de su mejor amiga. Decidieron compartir el café y el pastel a la mitad; pensaron que sería más romántico.

Esa tarde, Gabriel metió el touchdown ganador en una jugada defensiva. Estaba jugando como esquinero e interceptó la pelota; luego corrió ochenta yardas para el touchdown. Se sintió que estaba en la gloria, el héroe del partido, y compartiendo una placentera cita con un ángel como Theresa.

Entonces, ella le había prometido que él lograría "anotar" la próxima vez que compartieran café con pastel como esa noche. Tenían ahora chanza de compartir tiempo juntos, pero "anotar" con ella era algo muy diferente.

Las noticias de las diez empezaron y lo sacaron de sus pensamientos.

"El criminal más buscado en la ciudad es un joven llamado Jorge Ramírez. Solo es estudiante de preparatoria pero tiene varias órdenes de arresto por felonías. Si usted sabe en dónde se encuentra, llame a la policía o a la oficina del sheriff. Este tipo ha llevando a cabo una ola de crímenes en el lado oeste de la ciudad, robos, asaltos, y violaciones. No se vayan a enfrentar a este muchacho porque anda armado y es extremadamente peligroso," el anunciador, muy serio, le advirtió a la audiencia.

El Padre G olfateó el pastel y el café. Se volteó para todos lados. No había nadie que lo pudiera ver comerse una mordidita y darle un traguito al café, pero sus ojos descansaron en el crucifijo de la pared. Gabriel tiró el pastel a la basura y vació el café en el fregadero.

"Ayuno y oración... ¡Ayuno y oración!" se recordó en voz alta.

Gabriel se sentó a escuchar las noticias acerca del fugitivo.

"Algunas gentes en la ciudad creen que este criminal está poseído por un demonio. Entrevistamos a algunos para preguntarles por qué."

Mostraron a una chica en la oscuridad para evitar revelar su identidad. El Padre G reconoció la figura y voz como las de Cindy.

"Jorge Ramírez está poseído por un demonio. Él nunca haría lo que ha hecho si no lo estuviera. Yo estuve ahí cuando el demonio mismo se apoderó de él. ¡Vi cuando eso pasó!"

La imagen de la televisión cambió para mostrar al Detective Gresham haciendo sus comentarios acerca del caso.

"Este joven era miembro de un grupo que usaba drogas y estaba interesado en el ocultismo. Experimentaron con drogas diferentes y luego usaron la posesión diabólica para evitar responsabilidad por sus crímenes. El demonio en este caso es la droga que usaron para alterar su mente."

La pantalla entonces mostró al papá, Raúl Ramírez, también en la oscuridad para proteger su identidad.

"Les puedo decir que mi hijo está poseído. Lo único que lo detuvo de matarnos a todos fue el crucifijo que tenemos mi esposa y yo en nuestros rosarios. No teme a ningún hombre, solo a Dios Todo Poderoso. ¿Por qué iba a huir de una imagen de Cristo si solo anda bajo influencia de drogas?"

La reportera, Leslie McCoy, miró a la cámara y le dijo a la audiencia, "¿Posesión diabólica o criminal bajo drogas? Consideren si este muchacho quien anda violando, robando, y lastimando a la gente es una víctima de posesión diabólica, o solo otro depravado predador cuyas inhibiciones han desaparecido por la influencia de las drogas estupefacientes."

Gabriel meditó por un momento. Sabía de alguna manera que tendría que encarar al demonio en Jorge tarde o temprano. Se preguntó si acaso podría estar listo para tal encuentro. El sacerdote volteó a ver el crucifijo de nuevo y sintió confianza de que lo estaría.

El anunciador de noticias continuó diciendo, "Hay un demonio en San

Antonio en estos días, efectivamente, un demonio dorado retando a todos los hombres del área a pelear contra él en el ring mano a mano para un encuentro televisado a través de la nación. Hay un premio de 500,000 dólares para el hombre que se atreva a vencer este demonio enmascarado en el ring, pero hasta ahora no hay quien se atreva, y por buen motivo."

El Padre G puso atención a lo que tenían que decir del luchador. Había una conexión entre ese evento y los crímenes que estaban ocurriendo. Solo necesitaba figurar cómo estaban relacionados.

"Este gigantón de seis pies y seis pulgadas quien pesa trescientas treinta libras de acerados músculos, ya ha matado a dos hombres y a enviado al hospital varias docenas. Algunos de sus oponentes han terminado con las espaldas fracturadas, daño cerebral, u otros daños físicos permanentes."

La televisión enseñó unos videos del luchador en acción, vapuleando y destrozando a los oponentes uno tras otro sin misericordia.

"Algunos sospechan que el misterioso enmascarado fue profesional de fútbol americano. Otros dicen que era un asesino entrenado en la súper-secreta Fuerza Delta. Nos paseamos por la ciudad, viendo a este fenómeno entrenar. Puede levantar 230 kilos en la banca. Puede correr 100 metros en 12 segundos. Jamás ha perdido un pleito en su vida. ¡Es un destructor! Boxeadores, luchadores, peleadores de judo o karate no pueden con él."

La televisión mostró al luchador flexionando sus enormes músculos, rodeado por cuatro mujeres, rubia, pelirroja, oriental, y una negrita.

El gigante gritó en el micrófono con una voz áspera, "¡Soy el hombre más peligroso del mundo! ¡El mejor! ¡Busco a un hombre que me pueda vencer, pero creo que no hay ninguno aquí! ¡Este es un pueblucho lleno de gallinas! Lo que sí tengo que admitir es que... ¡Me encantan sus preciosas hembras!"

Agarró a cada una de las chicas y las besó enfrente de la cámara. Terminó su entrevista con una demostración de su poder. Rompió un montón de bloques de cemento con un golpe de karate y otro con un golpe de cabeza. Se alejó caminando con las cuatro mujeres en sus brazos, dos sentadas en sus amplios hombros y una en cada antebrazo.

"¡Nunca, y de ninguna manera!" dijo un hombre a quien la reportera entrevistó en la calle, "¡No pelearía yo con él ni por cien millones!"

Luego mostraron una voluptuosa mujer en sus treintas.

"A mí me parece muy sexy. Yo me le enfrentaría a cualquier hora, ¡pero no en el ring sino en mi recámara!"

Al último mostraron a un viejecito caminando con la ayuda de un bastón afuera de un asilo de ancianos.

"Seguro que sí me le enfrentaría a ese mugre de Demonio Dorado. Yo no le tengo miedo!"

El viejito levantó su bastón como para golpear a un oponente imaginario, abanicó con el arma y cayó estrepitosamente al pasto.

"Yo me le enfrentaré... tan pronto como salga del hospital," dijo el viejito mientras que lo ayudaban a levantarse.

El conductor del programa dio información de cómo ponerse en contacto con los promotores para enfrentarse al Demonio Dorado por medio millón de dólares. Gabriel se preguntó si aquel era el dinero que Benito necesitaba para su operación. Se fue a dormir, para decidir eso después.

Al día siguiente, el Padre Gabriel llamó al Detective García y le preguntó si podría notificarle cuando Jorge fuera localizado. Ofreció su ayuda ya que Jorge había sido su amigo cercano. El detective le dijo que no tenían aún buenas pistas pero que le mantendrían informado.

Timmy estaba afuera de la oficina del director oyendo la conversación del sacerdote con el policía porque la puerta estaba entreabierta. La Señora White entró a la oficina cuando el cura colgó el teléfono.

"Padre, Sor Magdalene le mandó un estudiante de tercero con problemas de disciplina. Timmy Bravo le pegó con el puño a John Clark en clase."

"¡Que pasen al acusado!" dijo el director en un tono solemne.

La Señora White le dijo al niño que pasara, y cerró la puerta tras él. El Padre G estaba dándole palmaditas al escritorio con la mano mientras miraba al cielo de la oficina, preguntándose qué hacer con el travieso muchachito. Antes que pudiera decirle nada, el acusado habló.

"¿Padre G, usted cree que Jorge tiene al Diablo metido?"

"¿En dónde oíste eso?"

"Lo vi en las noticias."

"Bueno, pues no sé acerca de él, pero cuéntame de ti. ¿Se te metió el Diablo a ti para hacerte que le pegaras a Johnny?"

"¡Oh, no, Padre! Ese fui nomás yo. Le tuve que dar una trompada porque me desobedeció."

"¿Cómo estuvo eso?"

"Estaba haciendo trampa," dijo el chiquillo. "¿Se acuerda que fui a rezar a la iglesia ayer porque tenía un examen hoy? Bueno, estaba yo haciendo bien, y luego... Que me pesco al Johnny copiando mis respuestas. Le dije que le parara, pero le siguió. ¡Tuve que disciplinar a ese muchachito!"

El director fingió toser y se cubrió la cara para taparse la sonrisa. Volvió a ganar la compostura y le explicó a Timmy que no era su prerrogativa ejecutar la justicia en el salón de clases. Iba a tener que disculparse con Johnny por haberle pegado y debería escribir, "Debo de amar a mi prójimo como a mí mismo; no debo de castigar a mi prójimo," cien veces en un papel que debería entregar al día siguiente a la oficina.

"¿Le explicaste a la Hermana Magda el por qué golpeaste a Johnny?"

"Sí, y ella ya le dio un cero en el examen y una nota para sus papás."

"¡Muy bien! Eso era todo lo que se necesitaba en este caso."

El director escribió una nota para la maestra y la mandó de regreso al salón con el niño. Antes de marcharse, Timmy se volteó.

"Voy a mantener los ojos bien pelones por si aparece Jorge por algún lugar y le aviso cuando venga por el vecindario, Padre G."

"Haz eso, después que hayas terminado con tu tarea esta tarde."

El director miró al inquieto muchachito encaminándose de regreso a su salón; Gabriel sacudió la cabeza y se sonrió, recordando sus palabras.

Timmy era uno de los jugadores en el equipo de básquetbol que Jorge Ramírez había estado ayudando a su padre a entrenar, así que el chiquillo estaba preocupado que el asistente de su entrenador podría estar poseído. El sacerdote no quería a Timmy envuelto en ese asunto.

El viernes, Gabriel se quedó en la iglesia en oración después de la misa de la mañana. No había comido nada excepto la Eucaristía desde el miércoles. Su hambre y sed se estaban comenzando a hacer dolorosos ese tercer día de ayuno, pero su oración parecía ayudarle a ignorar sus necesidades físicas.

Gabriel se levantó de sus oraciones y se persignó. Se fijó en su reloj de pulsera; ya eran las doce treinta de la tarde. Pensó que había estado orando por unos diez minutos, ¡pero había estado en oración por cuatro horas!

La Hermana Theresa entró a la iglesia buscándolo.

"¿Padre, en dónde ha estado toda la mañana?"

"Aquí."

"¿Desde la misa?"

"Sí."

"¿Qué estuvo haciendo aquí toda la mañana?"

"Orando."

"¿Ya almorzaste?" Theresa lo empezó a tutear al ver que estaban solos.

"No."

"Vamos a tu casa y te prepararé algo de comer. Te ves con hambre."

"No quiero..."

"¿No quieres... que te me acerque en mi descanso de las clases? ¡Anímate! Tengo tiempo en lo que mis niños andan en su clase de educación física."

Theresa lo agarró del brazo y lo jaló rumbo a la puerta.

"¡Está bien!" Gabriel dijo, cediendo a su jaloneo juguetón.

El sacerdote se preguntaba cómo podría evitar que Theresa lo obligara a comer, pero sin tener que decirle que estaba ayunando.

La Señora Black se había ido a llevarle su almuerzo a Maricela y sus niños. Se estaban convirtiendo en amigas rápidamente después que la vieja le empezó a llevar la comida del Padre G.

Maricela acababa de ser desempleada del cabaret donde trabajaba como bailarina; el lugar había sido clausurado por presión que la comunidad ejerció sobre el Concilio Municipal. La desempleada madre de tres no tenía ahorros y no recibía ayuda de programas de gobierno. La bondad de la que le llevó la comida en el momento más apropiado, cuando no tenían que comer, hizo que Maricela recapacitara y considerara cambiar la dirección de su vida. La Señora Black le dijo que le podría preguntar a su cuñado si le daría trabajo a Maricela en su negocio de construcción como recepcionista.

Gabriel estuvo encantado de oír las buenas noticias de parte de la Señora

Black, y el ama de llaves se sentía orgullosa de haber hecho una diferencia.

Gabriel y Theresa entraron a la rectoría.

"Theresa, me dijiste la otra noche que posarías para mí solito. ¿Verdad?"

"¿Quieres decir aquí mismo? ¿Justo ahora...? ¿Desnuda?"

"Sí, sí, y no. Déjame hacer un retrato tuyo en lugar de mi almuerzo, aquí mismo, justo ahora, pero no te tienes que despojar de tu ropa. Toda clase de gentes vienen a visitar durante el día, y no querríamos escandalizarlos. ¿Qué dices? ¿Me concederás este antojo de dejarme comer tu imagen como mi almuerzo? ¿Por favorcito?"

"Está bien, Picasso. ¿Qué tanto te llevará?"

"Vamos a hacerte un retrato de treinta minutos. Siéntate en el sofá en una pose cómoda mientras consigo lápiz y papel."

Theresa se acomodó en el sofá en una posición que pensó poder sostener por media hora, una que le permitiría estarlo viendo a él mientras la dibujaba. Gabriel regresó corriendo, excitado como chiquillo con un juguete nuevo y puso dos sillas enfrente de la modelo, una para su tableta de dibujo y la otra para sentarse él. Fue y prendió el radio para oír un programa de plática conservativa mientras trabajaba en el retrato.

"¿Por qué escuchas a ese hombre? Tiene una voz que molesta y se oye como muy orgulloso y lleno de sí mismo," se quejó Tere.

"Estoy de acuerdo con él acerca de muchas cosas. Ofrece una perspectiva diferente a la de la media, la cual está inclinada a la izquierda. A mucha gente no le cae bien, pero creo que es un hombre que busca la verdad, que predica auto-confianza, y el asumir responsabilidad por los actos propios."

"Bueno, por lo menos por esta vez, ¿podrías poner algo de música en lugar de ese programa? No me quiero interesar mucho acerca de lo que está hablando porque tendré que regresar pronto a mi clase."

"Tú eres la que manda, Tere. Deseo que mis modelos se sientan tan cómodas como sea posible."

"Sí. Ya he oído acerca de eso."

Cambió la estación a una con música clásica en FM y comenzó a dibujar. Su hambre no le importaba mientras estaba haciendo algo tan excitante como hablar con Dios en la oración o dibujar la amada figura de Theresa.

Trabajó febrilmente, poniéndole tanto detalle como fuera posible en el poco tiempo que tenía. Theresa estaba disfrutando la experiencia de tener los ojos de él recorriéndola de pies a cabeza, absorbiendo cada detallito, cada curva, cada sombra. También le encantó verlo a él sin que nadie los interrumpiera, mirarlo trabajando y sonriendo nada más para ella.

"¿Te gustaría ir a un partido de básquetbol esta noche conmigo?" el artista le preguntó a la modelo reclinada.

"¿Están jugando de nuevo los Látigos de San Antonio?"

"No. Me invitaron a ir a ver un juego de nuestro equipo del tercer año en la liga católica de deportes. ¿Te acuerdas de Timmy, el niño del gimnasio que me llamó cuando tú me andabas buscando el primer día?"

"Oh, sí. Está en la clase de la Hermana Magda. ¿Verdad?"

"Así es. Está en el equipo y quiere que lo vaya a ver jugar esta noche."

"Seguro. ¿Tú me recogerás?"

"¡Por supuesto!" él exclamó. "Nuestro tiempo se ha terminado. Creo que le puse suficiente detalle; voy a trabajar en él un poco más, luego, en la noche. Mira." La invitó a ver el dibujo preguntando, "¿Te gusta?"

"Es hermoso, pero no se parece a mí. Se ve como que dibujaste a un ángel, no a una ajetreada hermana religiosa de edad media."

"Eso es porque te veo casi como a un ángel y no como a una ajetreada hermana religiosa de edad media, Tere."

"Déjame verlo cuando lo hayas terminado. Luego platicamos. ¿A qué horas quieres que esté lista para irnos al juego?"

"Estaré en tu casa a las 6:30. ¿Crees que la Hermana Magda se oponga?"

"Las invitaré a todas ellas a ir con nosotros, pero dudo que vayan. A ellas les gusta el béisbol, no el básquetbol."

"Muchas gracias por este excelente almuerzo, mi Querida Amiga," Gabriel le dijo, poniéndole la mano en la espalda baja.

"Fue... un placer para mí," ella dijo, disfrutando su contacto al andar.

La acompañó a la puerta y la miró atravesar la calle hasta desaparecer en el interior de la escuela. Luego suspiró y se metió de nuevo a casa.

El pastor hizo varias llamadas y abrió piezas de correo. Sorteó las cosas que necesitaban hacerse, las que podían ser delegadas, y aquellas que podían dejarse para más delante. Trabajó rápido y furiosamente tratando de completar todo lo que fuera posible antes de salir con Theresa esa tarde.

Lo bueno era que tenía tiempo porque no iba a cenar; lo malo era que se andaba casi muriendo de tanta hambre que sentía. Cuando ya era hora de cenar y su estómago le empezó a rugir otra vez demandando alimento, él se metió a la privacidad de su recámara a rezar de nuevo.

Gabriel y Theresa fueron solos al partido, como ella había pronosticado. Todas las otras hermanas religiosas estaban ocupadas con sus agendas de actividades y declinaron atender. Magda ya había notado que su nueva subordinada se había hecho muy amiga del pastor, pero eso no tenía nada de malo. Todas las hermanas estaban un poco enamoradas de él, y él continuaba llevando a cabo sus deberes sin ninguna indicación que las cosas habían cambiado en su vida.

"¿Has estado ayunando?" Theresa le preguntó a su amigo en el auto.

"¿Por qué dices eso?"

"Te ves un poco más delgado. Escuché que te gruñía el estómago como un león, y te rehusaste a dejarme que te diera de almorzar. Además, veo que te lavaste la cara y te peinaste el cabello. Yo también he leído los evangelios, y se que eso fue lo que Jesús nos instruyó que hiciéramos al ayunar."

"Sí."

"¿Por qué? ¿Estás siendo atormentado por algo específico?"

"Tengo algunos demonios que enfrentar en batalla. Necesito más oración y ayuno para ganar fuerza en mi fe."

"¡Guau! ¿Hay algo con lo que te pueda ayudar?"

"Reza por mí."

"Desde luego, pero ya lo he estado haciendo, todo el tiempo."

"¡Ajá! me preguntaba yo de dónde venía toda esta energía extra. ¡Ahora lo entiendo!"

Ella solo le sonrió. Gabriel era un hombre de gran fe. Theresa se preguntaba qué quiso decir con enfrentar demonios pero decidió dejarlo que le dijera cuando él estuviera listo.

Era muy bueno pasar tiempo con él, solos en su carro, en su casa, o en cualquier parte, pero con él, ¡era grandioso! Iría hasta el fin del mundo y de vuelta tomada de su mano. ¡Era sensacional estar enamorada de nuevo!

James Bravo le dio la bienvenida al Padre con un fuerte abrazo al llegar al gimnasio de la parroquia de la Santa Cruz. Saludó de mano a la Hermana Theresa y le dio las gracias por ir a apoyar a los chiquillos de su equipo.

James se había hecho cargo de dirigir el equipo de su hijo adoptivo pues Raúl Ramírez estaba pasando un rato muy duro con Jorge. Timmy y sus compañeritos de equipo corrieron a abrazar al Padre G, cantándole.

"¡Padre G, Padre G, vamos a ganar porque vino usté'!"

"Más vale que le echen ganas y jueguen bien o si no van a perder. Aún si vine a verlos esta vez," Gabriel les advirtió.

Theresa estaba observando al sacerdote saludando de mano a todos los pequeños jugadores. James fue a hablar con el otro entrenador y le dijo algo; luego regresó y habló con el Padre Gabriel.

"¿Padre, nos podría empezar el partido con una oración?"

"¡Seguro!"

El presbítero se encaminó al centro de la cancha y pensó en una oración.

Antes que empezara, uno de los niños le gritó, "¡Cántenos una canción!"

"Muy bien, vamos haciendo las dos cosas entonces. ¿Sabían ustedes que cuando le cantamos a Dios estamos rezando el doble?"

El místico les hizo señas que se sentaran todos. Los dos equipos se sentaron alrededor de él con sus directores técnicos. Los árbitros se sentaron en su banca para ver qué era lo que iba a hacer.

Gabriel recitó el principio de una canción en inglés y en español. Los versos describen a Jesús de Nazaret, su edad, origen, profesión y cosas así; la parte cantada habla del amor de Cristo e invita a la audiencia a buscarlo para encontrar la paz. Cuando terminó la canción animó a los jugadores.

"¡Vamos ahora a jugar básquetbol del bueno, muchachos!"

Gabriel tomó asiento junto a Theresa. Su canción la había conmovido.

"Aún no entiendo cómo puedes pararte ahí en medio de todos y, de repente y de la nada, salir con una canción que nos toque el corazón."

"Tú me inspiras a cantar desde el fondo de mi corazón," le susurro él en el oído.

El equipo de Timmy ganó, pero fue reñido. La Santísima Trinidad iba adelante, pero luego La Santa Cruz aventajó. Los visitantes recuperaron la superioridad solo para perderla de nuevo. Así estuvo todo el tiempo, lo cual mantuvo a los excitados papás vitoreando y animando a sus chiquillos.

El marcador estaba a favor de La Santa Cruz, 36-35 con solo 5 segundos de tiempo en el reloj en el último cuarto. Timmy botó la pelota entre tres oponentes y se coló para encestar de rebote en el tablero al tiempo que sonaba el timbre final, dándole a la Santísima Trinidad la victoria, 36-37.

Gabriel llevó a Theresa a casa y entró con ella para oírla relatarles a las otras religiosas los pormenores del partido. Ellas voltearon a verlo y lo acusaron de haberle rezado a Dios para que ganara su equipo.

"Yo diría que eso es hacer trampa, Padre," dijo Sor Mary Dáskalos jugueteando.

"¡Yo no estoy de acuerdo con eso! Lo que pasó es que nuestro equipo tenía una fe más grande que la de ellos," dijo Sor Carmen Armienta.

"Ese es buen punto porque el Señor no iba a mostrar favoritismo de una iglesia sobre la otra. Todos somos cristianos, hijos del mismo Dios. Creo que el Señor dejó que ganara el mejor equipo," concedió Mary.

"¡Yo no creo que Dios interviene en esos juegos en lo absoluto!" exclamó Sor Magdalene.

El Padre Gabriel les contó una pequeña historia a las hermanas.

"Hablando de fe. Había un hombre de mucha fe viviendo cerca del Río Mississippi. Un día la lluvia hizo que el río se desbordara e inundara el área. Los pronósticos del tiempo eran que la lluvia iba a continuar, así que las autoridades recomendaron a todas las gentes de aquel valle que evacuaran sus casas y se movieran a tierra más elevada."

"Es cierto. Estuve en Nueva Orleans una vez que se inundó..." dijo Magda.

La religiosa superior se tapó la boca, así que el cura continuó: "Nuestro fiel hombre, Joshua, decidió quedarse en casa. Sus vecinos se marcharon cuando tenían el agua hasta los tobillos. El departamento de bomberos mandó un camión a rescatar al único que se quedó en el valle cuando el agua ya le llegaba a las rodillas, pero él les dijo que se fueran. Le explicaron que la lluvia iba continuar y que el río iba a crecer aún más. Joshua les dijo, 'El Señor me ayudará', y se rehusó a irse con ellos."

"No fue muy sabio..." Magda interrumpió de nuevo. Se detuvo cuando todos voltearon a verla. Le hizo señas para que continuara su historia.

"Más tarde, un equipo de rescate fue en una lancha cuando Joshua tenía el agua al pescuezo. Le rogaron que se subiera a la lancha, que la lluvia iba a continuar y que el río iba a seguir subiendo. Les dijo lo mismo, 'El Señor me ayudará', y los mandó de regreso. El agua siguió subiendo como había sido predicho. Joshua se trepó al techo de su casa. Ya estaba parado en la chimenea, en las puntitas de los dedos de sus pies, cuando el agua le estaba salpicando la cara. Un equipo de rescate de la Guardia Nacional en un helicóptero vino y lo localizó. Le lanzaron una escalera de mecate y le gritaron que se subiera a bordo porque la lluvia iba a continuar y el río iba a aumentar aún más su nivel. Joshua les gritó, 'Váyanse de aquí. ¡El Señor me ayudará!' El helicóptero entonces se alejó de ahí, y Joshua se ahogó..."

"¡Que tonto, ya sabía yo!" exclamó Magda, alzando las manos.

"Joshua se murió y, por supuesto, se fue al cielo. Al llegar a la puerta celestial, habló con San Pedro, molesto, '¿Dónde está el Señor, Pedro? ¡Necesito hablar con Él!' Pedro lo condujo hasta Dios para una audiencia. Joshua se dirigió al Señor diciéndole, 'Señor, yo siempre te fui fiel. ¿Por qué me dejaste morir? ¿Dime qué pasó con esto, pues?' El Señor le contestó, 'No sé. Te mandé un camión, una lancha, y un helicóptero.'"

Las hermanas se carcajearon. El Padre les deseó buenas noches y se fue a su casa.

Cuando el sacerdote llegó a su casa, se sorprendió de encontrarse a la hermosa Linda Richards en su cama, bajo las cobijas, esperándolo.

"¿Qué haces aquí, Linda? ¿Cómo pudiste entrar?"

"La puerta estaba sin atrancar. Vine a platicar con usted. Como no estaba, decidí esperarlo. Me encontraba cansada, así que me metí en su cama."

Ella decía la verdad. Él no se preocupaba por atrancar la puerta a pesar que sabía debería de hacerlo. Muchas veces la dejaba desatrancada, especialmente si había salido ansioso por ir a recoger a su amada Theresa.

"¿De qué querías hablar conmigo, Criatura?"

"Bueno, es muy íntimo, pero creo que puedo confiar en usted. ¿Sabe cómo... se supone que usted como sacerdote debe ser célibe?"

"Sí, así es."

"Bien, pues... He estado en la misma situación desde que el papá de Pedrito me dejó embarazada, hace seis años. Ha sido mucho tiempo desde la última vez que hice el amor. Entiendo perfectamente como se debe usted de sentir... teniendo que aguantarse por tantos años sin sexo."

"¿Entonces?" preguntó el pastor, viendo toda la ropa de ella en el piso.

"Entonces... he venido para que los dos cojamos un poquito de alivio. Yo sé que es discreto, y yo sé mantener un secretito. Ven Gabriel, métete a la cama... está rica y calientita."

Ella sonrió y le estiró los brazos. El Padre Gabriel se quedó ahí, paralizado, preguntándose qué hacer. La oferta era muy tentadora. Le estaría haciendo un favor y proveyéndola de consuelo físico. Él mismo podría usar alivio a su incrementada tensión sexual como ella había dicho.

"¿Qué pasa? ¿No te gusto?" Linda le preguntó, muy triste.

"No es eso."

El cura se sentó en la cama junto a ella. Linda pretendió estar muy lastimada con su desaire, así que se sentó para salirse de la cama.

"Lo siento... ¡Qué vergüenza! Debe pensar que soy una mujerzuela, ofreciéndomele de este modo. Debí haberlo pensado mejor."

Linda estaba empezando a derramar lágrimas en lo que se estiraba para alcanzar su ropa, medio-cubriendo su desnudez con la sábana. Gabriel caminó alrededor de la cama y le tocó la hermosa carita.

"Me siento de verdad muy, muy halagado de que una mujer como tú quisiera compartir su cuerpo conmigo, pero esto no sería correcto."

"¿Quién saldría lastimado, Gabriel? ¿Tú? ¿Yo? ¿Dios? ¿La Hermana Theresa?" Linda le dijo muy airada.

¡Riiiinnnngggg... Riiiinnnngggg... Riiiinnnngggg!

El teléfono personal de Gabriel sobre el buró comenzó a timbrar. Era un número que muy pocas gentes tenían. El ministro presintió que era algo importante, así que levantó el auricular.

"Padre G. Soy yo, Timmy. ¡Jorge está robando la tienda de la esquina!"

El presbítero miró a Linda y colgó el teléfono aprisa.

"¡Lo siento mucho, Linda. Debo irme!"

Agarró su estola, crucifijo, y una botellita de agua bendita que tenía encima de su mueble de cajones antes de salir apresuradamente de su recámara y de la rectoría.

Linda estaba perpleja. No tenía idea por qué se había ido como si la vida de alguien dependiera de él. Se decidió a regresar a casa. Aunque estaba frustrada, Linda pensó en tratar de nuevo, de una manera diferente.

El atlético ministro corrió tres cuadras en menos de 30 segundos. Chocó con una camioneta al cruzar la esquina, pero rodó sobre el cofre y siguió corriendo hasta llegar a la tienda.

Podía ver a Jorge dentro de la tienda, alegando con el encargado mientras le apuntaba una pistola. Jorge mostraba señas en todo su cuerpo de la dura semana que había pasado. Su ropa estaba sucia y rota. Tenía sangre seca y heridas infectadas; su pelo era un desastre. Sus ojos se veían como brazas ardiendo; su cara sin afeitar, estaba rasguñada e hinchada. Era Jorge, en verdad, y podría estar bajo la influencia de las drogas, o... ¡poseído!

El místico entró a la tienda y le llamó la atención.

"¡Jorge, en el nombre de Dios, tira la pistola y déjalo en paz!"

La horrible criatura volteó los ojos rojos encendidos a ver al intruso.

"¡Padre Gabriel Infante, criatura favorecida del Señor, al fin vienes a mí! He esperado esta oportunidad para tener una pequeña charla contigo. ¿Ya acabaste con esa mujerzuela, Linda Richards, tan pronto? Oh, no tuviste tiempo, pero estaba muy tentadora. ¿No? La deberías haber tomado y hacerla feliz. ¿En dónde está tu compasión por la pobre mujercita?"

¿Cómo se podía haber enterado Jorge? El cura trató de ganar control.

"Jorge ven conmigo afuera para platicar."

"¡Jorge está muerto y ardiendo en el infierno!" la bestia le dijo en una voz rasposa; luego, tratando de sonar muy dulce agregó, "Te manda saludar."

"Vamos afuera, Jorge. Deja ese hombre en paz; esto es entre tú y yo."

El Padre G se le quedó viendo a los ojos encendidos. ¡Aquellos no eran ojos humanos! Gabriel supo que estaba en la presencia del maligno: todo estaba muy confuso y él se sentía nauseado.

"Aaah, Gabriel, esta noche Jorge tiene que matar a alguien. Pensé que sería este empleadillo de tienda, pero un piadoso sacerdote como tú sería muchísimo mejor. ¡Ja-ja-ja-ja-ja-ja!"

Jorge golpeó al encargado con la pistola; el hombre cayó al suelo como un costal de papas. Gabriel reaccionó saltando sobre el empistolado, tratando de desarmarlo. La bestia movió su brazo con sorprendente potencia y lanzó al cura hasta el otro lado de la tienda, derribando una parrilla con revistas y algunos productos de abarrotes de los escaparates con el impacto.

Jorge se agazapó como bestia a punto de abalanzarse contra su víctima. El Padre G se levantó del piso y volvió a ver al poseído a los ojos. Mirando aquellos malévolos ojos, tuvo una visión.

Vio a Jorge tratando de mantenerse a flote en un mar de lava, gritando de profundo dolor. El cura tembló al ver que estaba encarando maldad pura.

"Jorge encontró poder, placer, y sabiduría en mí, Gabriel."

El Ministro decidió comenzar a rezar en voz alta.

"¡El Señor es mi pastor, nada me falta!"

"Si te inclinas ante mí, tendrás todo lo que quieres tener, Gabriel."

La bestia apuntó al mostrador junto a la caja registradora. Gabriel vio a Theresa ahí sentada sobre el mostrador con un vestidito rojo muy cortito y con maquillaje que la hacía ver como a una supermodelo. Ella estaba sonriéndole, mandándole un beso y extendiéndole los brazos.

"¡El Señor es mi roca en la cual confío!"

Gabriel tuvo que cerrar los ojos para borrar la tentadora visión.

"¡Inclínate ante mí, Sacerdote, o morirás esta misma noche!"

El poseído levantó su pistola y se la apuntó al cura.

"¡Señor Jesucristo, ten compasión de mí, un pobre pecador!"

Gabriel se sacó el crucifijo del interior de su camisa y empezó a caminar hacia el empistolado. La bestia hizo gestos al ver la audacia del ministro.

La presencia del bendito crucifijo tuvo un efecto en él. Se cubrió la cara con la mano izquierda y apretó el gatillo de la pistola con la mano derecha.

El Padre G pisó un charco de mostaza tirada y perdió el balance al tiempo que la pistola vomitaba la bala. El proyectil le pasó muy cerca del pecho.

El místico recuperó su balance y continuó avanzando y orando. La oración le estaba dando más confianza; dejó de temblar.

"¡El Señor, creador del universo, me salvará de todos mis enemigos porque mi confianza descansa solamente en Él!"

El Demonio disparó de nuevo al tiempo que el sacerdote avanzaba.

Gabriel sintió el impacto en su pecho y casi cayó de espaldas. El crucifijo colgando en su pecho había recibido el tiro directamente y había protegido su cuerpo. El Padre Gabriel recuperó el balance y continuó acercándosele.

La bestia disparó un tercer tiro. El tiempo pareció reducir su marcha. Gabriel pudo ver la bala girando al salir de la pistola, dirigiéndose a su cabeza. Se inclinó a la izquierda y sintió la bala rozar su oído derecho.

Los ojos rojos estaban abiertos con furia e incredulidad. El poseído trató de disparar de nuevo, pero ya Gabriel estaba encima de él. El clérigo agarró la pistola con su mano izquierda y se la torció en la mano para arrancársela al sorprendido demonio. Con su puño derecho, el cura boxeador le dio un puñetazo a Jorge justo bajo del mentón, derribándolo sobre su espalda.

La pistola cayó al suelo al mismo tiempo que el cuerpo de Jorge.

Con gran aplomo, el Padre Gabriel se sacó la botella de agua bendita y le roció algo de su contenido formando una cruz sobre el caído.

"En el nombre del Padre, y del Hijo, y del Espíritu Santo."

La criatura se empezó a retorcer en el suelo y gritó muy fuerte.

"¡Noooooooo!"

El Padre G se arrodilló junto a Jorge y le impuso el crucifijo metálico sobre el pecho.

"¡Gloria al Padre, gloria al Hijo y gloria al Espíritu Santo! ¡Como era en un principio, ahora y siempre, por los siglos de los siglos, amén!"

Las luces de la tienda empezaron a relampaguear y se apagaron. Los escaparates de mercancía se sacudieron violentamente y se cayeron. Una voz terrible, inhumana, salió del interior de Jorge.

"¡Aléjate de mí!"

El exorcista hizo la señal de la cruz sobre el joven poseído quien empezó a sacudirse en convulsiones.

"¡El poder del Dios eterno, tu Señor, te domina. Dime tu nombre!" Gabriel dijo en voz firme.

"¡Yo soy Satanás!"

La mano izquierda de Jorge pareció adquirir vida propia y comenzó a moverse como una araña hacia la pistola que estaba en el piso, no muy lejos de ellos. La mano agarró la pistola y metió el dedo índice en la apertura del gatillo. Gabriel habló con una voz de trueno.

"¡En el nombre de nuestro Señor Jesucristo, te ordeno, Satanás, deja este hombre y regrésate al infierno! Es el Padre quien te lo ordena. Es el Hijo quien te lo ordena. Es el Espíritu Santo quien te lo ordena, y no te puedes rehusar. ¡Abandona a esta criatura del Señor en el nombre de Jesús!"

Las ventanas de la tienda se reventaron con tremendo estallido cuando el maligno espíritu, con un horroroso chillido, abandonó el cuerpo del joven. En ese instante, todas las luces de la tienda volvieron a encenderse.

El tendero recuperó el sentido y agarró su revólver de abajo de la caja registradora. Se levantó atrás del mostrador y miró a Jorge con la pistola en la mano izquierda, apuntándole al sacerdote.

Gabriel estaba de rodillas, rezando y mirando a Jorge en lo que el muchacho se levantaba, un poco atontado y tambaleándose.

El empleado, Walter Simmons, no dudó. Para defender al presbítero, apuntó su revólver 357 magnum y disparó dos tiros en la dirección del bandido armado. Los ojos de Walter se volvieron rojos por un instante y una maligna sonrisa apareció en su rostro. Los disparos le pegaron al ladrón en el pecho y en el abdomen.

"¡Noooooo!" gritó Gabriel, recibiendo el mortalmente herido cuerpo de Jorge en sus brazos.

El místico sintió la sangre tibia del joven escurriéndole por el pecho y el abdomen. Los ojos de Jorge eran color café de nuevo y miraron al párroco con multitud de preguntas. El sacerdote y el muchacho sabían que no había tiempo para preguntas ni explicaciones. La vida de Jorge se le estaba escapando tan rápido como la sangre estaba abandonando su cuerpo.

"Paa...dre Ga... briel... ¿Por... qué?"

"Hijo mío, no tenemos mucho tiempo."

Gabriel acomodó la cabeza del moribundo sobre sus muslos.

"¿Padre G, está usted bien?" preguntó Walter, viendo que el cura estaba bañado en sangre.

"Estoy bien, pero llama a una ambulancia para él," dijo el presbítero, para que los dejara solos.

"Jorge, sé que pecaste al traicionar a nuestro Señor, pero aún tienes tiempo de arrepentirte y regresar a Él. Te está esperando, como el padre del hijo pródigo. ¿Te acuerdas?"

"Siií..." Jorge dijo mientras su voz se iba haciendo más leve.

"¿Aceptas a Jesucristo como tu salvador y rechazas a Satanás?

"Sss... íhhh..."

El cuello de Jorge se soltó al tiempo que expiró. El Padre Gabriel hizo la señal de la cruz sobre el muerto, absolviéndolo de todos sus pecados. Gabriel miró sus propias lágrimas cayendo sobre el rostro de Jorge. Le cerró los ojos con su mano y gentilmente lo recostó en el piso de la tienda.

Llegó la policía, pistola en mano; los paramédicos en su ambulancia los siguieron al interior de la tienda en cuanto les dieron la señal. El clérigo se levantó con las manos abiertas y levantadas.

El Padre G dejó que los paramédicos lo examinaran. Solo tenía unos moretoncitos menores en su cara y espalda, pero no fue herido de bala.

Sus pensamientos estaban en la familia de Jorge y lo que les iba a decir acerca de lo ocurrido ahí esa noche. Walter les contaba a los oficiales lo que podía recordar, pero había mucho que permanecía inexplicable.

El Detective Gresham también se apareció por la escena del crimen.

"Pues, bien, Padre, ¿Qué piensa usted?" Gresham le preguntó, "¿Estaba el Jorge poseído como la chica aquella, Cindy, alegaba?"

El Padre G lo miró directo a los ojos.

"Sí."

El detective no esperaba que le respondiera tan decisivamente.

"¡Bueno, eso ya no tiene importancia; el pobre bastardo está muerto!"

Al místico le molestó el comentario insensible del policía.

"Escuche, Detective, Jorge Ramírez fue buen muchacho hasta que buscó la amistad del maligno. Fue responsable por haber convocado al Demonio, sí, pero todos sus crímenes fueron cometidos mientras estaba poseído por una entidad mucho más poderosa que él. Después que expulsé al Diablo que traía, Jorge no sabía lo que había hecho mientras estuvo poseído. Al menos tuvo oportunidad de arrepentirse de sus pecados antes de morir."

"¿Quiere decir que se va a ir al cielo después de todo lo que hizo, violando, robando, y asaltando gentes?"

"Estoy muy seguro de eso."

Gresham estalló con unas palabrotas pero luego se tapó la boca.

"Oh, discúlpeme Padre. ¿Pero cómo puede eso ser justo?"

El Padre Gabriel le sonrió y puso la mano sobre el hombro musculoso del detective. Gresham era uno de los hombres más fuertes en todo el estado.

"¿Ha oído alguna vez la parábola de los trabajadores?"

El enorme detective admitió que no y se sentó en la ambulancia mientras el ministro se la contaba.

Porque el Reino de los Cielos se parece a un propietario que salió muy de madrugada a contratar obreros para trabajar en su viña. Trató con ellos un denario por día y los envió a su viña. Volvió a salir a media mañana y, al ver a otros desocupados en la plaza, les dijo: 'Vayan ustedes también a mi viña y les pagaré lo que sea justo.' Y ellos fueron. Volvió a salir al mediodía y a media tarde, e hizo lo mismo. Al caer la tarde salió de nuevo y, encontrando todavía a otros, les dijo: '¿Cómo se han quedado todo el día aquí, sin hacer nada?' Ellos le respondieron: 'Nadie nos ha contratado.' Entonces les dijo: 'Vayan también ustedes a mi viña.' Al terminar el día, el propietario llamó a su mayordomo y le dijo: 'Llama a los obreros y págales el jornal, comenzando por los últimos y terminando por los primeros.' Fueron entonces los que habían llegado al caer la tarde y recibieron cada uno un denario. Llegaron después los primeros, creyendo que iban a recibir algo más, pero recibieron igualmente un denario. Y al recibirlo, protestaban contra el propietario, diciendo: 'Estos últimos trabajaron nada más que una hora, y tú les das lo mismo que a nosotros, que hemos soportado el peso del trabajo y el calor durante toda la jornada.' El propietario respondió a uno de ellos: 'Amigo, no soy injusto contigo, ¿acaso no habíamos tratado en un denario? Toma lo que es tuyo y vete. Quiero dar a este que llega último lo mismo que a ti. ¿No tengo derecho a disponer de mis bienes como me parece? ¿Por qué tomas a mal que yo sea bueno?' Así, los últimos serán los primeros y los primeros serán los últimos." (Mateo 20:1-16)

El fortachón detective estaba asintiendo al escuchar la parábola.

Gabriel le explicó, "Jorge tuvo oportunidad de cambiar su condición pecadora antes de morir, y estoy seguro que fue bienvenido en el cielo porque se arrepintió de sus pecados antes de morir."

"Bueno, ahora que lo pone de esa manera, lo puedo entender, Padre Gabriel. Se me hace que es como el ladrón aquel que fue crucificado junto al Señor. ¿Cómo se llamaba, Dimas?"

"Así es, Detective, San Dimas se arrepintió en el último momento de su vida criminal y le rogó a Jesús por su misericordia. Eso fue suficiente para que el Señor le dijera, *'¡Hoy estarás conmigo en el paraíso!'*"

Entonces el sacerdote y el policía se pusieron de acuerdo en ir a notificar a la familia acerca de la muerte de su hijo. A pesar de estar entristecido por la forma en que resultaron las cosas, Gabriel se sentía aliviado que ya se había terminado. Había aprendido a aceptar la voluntad de Dios y no cuestionarla cuando pasaban cosas así.

Capítulo XII

Pleito

Al día siguiente, sábado 13 de noviembre, el Padre Gabriel se levantó a las 4:30 a.m., después de haber dormido solo una hora de profundo sueño. Se fue a correr unas millas y luego al gimnasio donde le pegó al costal pesado de boxeo hasta que quedó exhausto. Enseguida se dio un regaderazo con agua fría y regresó a la iglesia a celebrar la misa matutina del sábado.

Theresa lo encontró en la sacristía.

"Buenos días, Padre," dijo ella, asegurándose que estaban solos.

"Buenos días, Hermana. ¡Shalom!"

"¿Pasaste bien la noche?"

"¡Oh! fue una noche brutal, excitante, e increíble, pero solo alcancé a dormir una hora," le respondió, meneando la cabeza.

"¡Sí, apuesto que fue una noche muy excitante!" asintió Theresa con la cabeza. "Fui a tu casa a ver si querías caminar conmigo, pero ya te habías ido. Me encontré estos en un lado de tu cama."

Theresa le enseñó unas sedosas pantaletitas de encaje color de rosa

"¡Oh! Pues no son mías. Probablemente le pertenecen a Linda Richards."

"Eso fue lo que sospeché. Pude oler su perfume en tu cama."

Theresa se volteó y le dio la espalda para evitar verlo a la cara, se cruzó de brazos, y comenzó a golpetear el piso con la punta del pie, esperando su explicación de cómo habían acabado las pantaletas de Linda bajo su cama.

"No es lo que te imaginas... Bueno, casi, pero no exactamente," declaró Gabriel con una sonrisa pícara en su rostro.

"¿No acabas de decirme tú mismo que fue una noche brutal, excitante, e increíble? ¿Ahora me vas a negar que te acostaste con Linda?"

A Gabriel le divertía ver a Theresa celosa. Ya era hora de comenzar la misa, así que se le acercó al oído por detrás para susurrarle, "Te lo explicaré todo después de la misa. ¿Vas a tocar algo de música para la celebración?"

"¡NO!" le contestó, molesta. "Te voy a esperar, aquí sentada."

El clérigo se sonrió al ver su berrinchito y le besó la cabeza antes de encaminarse al altar a empezar la misa.

Theresa se arrodilló frente al crucifijo en la sacristía y rezó que no fuera cierto que Gabriel pasó la noche con Linda. Su relación se estaba haciendo cada vez más física; deseaba tenerlo y estar en sus brazos. Theresa cambió su oración para decidir qué hacer con el hombre de su vida. ¿Los estaba llamando Dios para una vida de casados? ¿O solo era una tentación?

Después de misa, el cura regresó a la sacristía con una enorme sonrisa a encarar a la aún seria hermana religiosa.

"¿Bien...?" le dijo ella, ayudándole a salir de sus vestiduras religiosas.

"Linda me estaba esperando en la cama cuando llegué a la casa anoche. Quería serme útil, para aliviar la tensión de una vida célibe. Me dijo que también ella había vivido una vida célibe por los últimos seis años, así que sería muy bueno para los dos. Es muy agresiva y se veía muy tentadora."

"¿Y...?" inquirió Theresa, su corazón acelerado.

"Recibí una llamada de un ángel del Señor, Timmy, quien me dijo que Jorge estaba asaltando la tienda de la esquina. Me arranqué tan pronto como pude para enfrentarme al Demonio que había poseído a Jorge. Linda se quedó en la casa. Debe haber creído que me espantó con su propuesta."

"¿Y por qué te dejó sus pantaletas?"

"No lo sé. Puede que se le hayan perdido, o quizás quería dejarme un suvenir de anoche para que reconsiderara su oferta."

"¿Lo vas a reconsiderar?" Theresa preguntó con preocupación.

"No lo sé," replicó Gabriel, fingiendo duda. "Es muy hermosa."

El labio inferior de Theresa comenzó a protruirle como el de una niña enojada. El místico la abrazó y le aseguró que solo bromeaba.

"¡No, no, no, no, y no! Ya te dije antes que no tengo intenciones de enredarme en una relación íntima con Linda. Tú sabes lo mucho que te amo, Tere."

"¿Estarías dispuesto a dejar el sacerdocio por mí?"

"¿Estarías dispuesta a dejar de ser una hermana religiosa por mí?"

"Sí, sí estoy," ella le dijo firmemente. "Si tú estás dispuesto a abandonar también tus votos eclesiásticos. He estado rezando por la sabiduría para decidir lo que debemos hacer. Estoy empezando a pensar que deberíamos considerar el matrimonio como una opción."

"¿Por qué no dejamos que las cosas sigan su rumbo y buscamos otras señales en el camino antes de tirarnos de clavado en esa decisión? Yo he estado muy contento de la forma en que estamos hasta ahorita."

"Sí. Yo también estoy contenta, ¿pero no desearías tener más?"

Theresa se le acercó con los labios entreabiertos. Estiró su boquita buscando la de él. Gabriel la tomó por las mejillas y, para sorpresa suya, le sopló en un ojo cuando él oyó que se abría la puerta de la sacristía.

"¡Ándele, Hermana! Creo que ya se le salió."

Sor Magdalene entró a la sacristía buscando a Theresa. Las otras estaban en la van esperándolas para ir a la casa de campo de una amiga; Francis Schott, la dueña de los restaurantes, las había invitado a desayunar.

Theresa se talló el ojo y entendió lo que Gabriel había hecho para cubrir las apariencias. Magda los habría pescado en el acto si él la hubiera besado, pero Theresa había deseado que la besara, aún si los hubieran pescado.

"Gracias Padre Gabriel! Ya me tengo que ir. Hasta luego."

El clérigo las acompañó a la puerta y les dijo adiós a todas. Luego se encaminó con paso rápido a la tienda de empeños de Don Pedro.

Los amigos fueron al restaurante donde estuvieron el miércoles anterior, pero esa vez, el párroco devoró un desayuno pesado: bistec con tres huevos, papas ralladas, jugo de frutas, panqueques, café, y ensalada de fruta. El viejo lo vio comer como si fuera un náufrago recién rescatado.

"¡Dios mío! ¿Cuándo fue la última vez que comió, Padre?"

"El martes en la tarde. ¿Te acuerdas lo que te mencioné del ayuno y oración el miércoles en la mañana?"

"Sí," dijo Don Pedro; luego, sacudiendo la cabeza, agregó, "Yo me hubiera muerto sin comer nada desde el martes pasado."

"Casi me moría, no por falta de comida sino por falta de fe."

"¿Falta de fe? ¿Usted? ¡Sáquese por allá, Hombre!"

"Tuve una prueba de fe anoche, mi Viejo Amigo."

"¿Y cómo le fue, Padre?"

"¡Pasé!"

"¿Pos' qué pasó?"

Al amigo le entró curiosidad. Algunas de las cosas en las que se envolvía el ministro eran en verdad increíbles.

"Jorge estaba poseído por el Demonio, pero con la ayuda del Todo-poderoso, fui capaz de expulsarlo."

"¡Magnífico! ¿Así que ya Jorge está bien?"

"Bueno... Está muerto, pero confío que descansa en el Señor. Tuve chanza de darle la absolución después que lo dejó el Demonio. Fue balaceado de muerte por el empleado de la tienda que había estado robando. Se me hace que fue mejor así. Casi nadie cree en posesión diabólica estos días. Habría tenido grandes dificultades con el sistema judicial."

Pedro pensó si en realidad sería mejor estar muerto que vivo con los problemas que el chico enfrentaría por los crímenes que cometió estando poseído. Sacudió la cabeza, no queriendo pensar más en aquello. Abrió el periódico mientras el clérigo continuaba devorando su gran desayuno.

"Hablando de demonios, nadie ha aceptado el reto del Demonio Dorado para pelear. Hoy es el último día para aceptar su reto. Se van a tener que ir a Houston enseguida si no le sale contrincante aquí."

El corazón le saltó a Gabriel en el pecho. Se volvió a ver a Pedro.

"¿Me ayudarías tú a pelear contra el Demonio Dorado, Amigo mío?"

"¿Quiere decir los dos, juntos contra él?"

Por un segundo la expresión del viejo se vio muy animada; sin embargo, volteó a ver la foto del gigante y decidió declinar la oferta. Puso el periódico sobre la mesa y le enseñó a Gabriel la foto.

"Nomás échele un ojo. Pesa tanto como nosotros dos juntos. Es imposible ganarle a una fiera como esa en el cuadrilátero," declaró el viejo, apuntándole a la imagen del enorme enmascarado.

"¡Con Dios, nada es imposible!" afirmó Gabriel.

"Pero, Padre, usted mide 1.83 y pesa 90 kilos. ¡Este asesino es 15 centímetros más alto, 60 kilos más pesado y el doble de fuerte que usted!" Don Pedrito le recordó a Gabriel, meneando la testa. El viejo pensó que era su deber detener al sacerdote de considerar esa peligrosa posibilidad. Le preguntó, "¿Acaso quiere morirse joven? ¿Eso es lo que anda buscando?"

"Anoche, con la ayuda de Dios, me enfrenté y vencí al verdadero Demonio. Este otro no es más que un hombre como tú y yo."

El cura se acabó el último trago de su taza de café. Sus platos estaban ya todos limpios. Estaba confiado que lo podría lograr.

"¿Se atrevería de veras, de-a-de-veras, a pelear con este mastodonte?"

El viejo amigo puso la mano en el hombro del cura y lo vio a los ojos.

"¡Sí!" el Padre G exclamó con una sonrisa, sobándose el estómago lleno.

"Pero, Padre, ¿por qué?" preguntó Pedro, encogiéndose de hombros.

El ministro le apuntó al periódico donde mencionaba el premio en efectivo. Pedro no la podía creer.

"¿Quiere dinero? Escúcheme, yo le podría prestar, darle si es necesario, algo de dinero si lo necesita con tanta urgencia... Quizás no tanto así, pero ¿cuánto necesita?"

"Lo necesito todo, pero no es para mí. Es para pagar por un milagro."

"¿Milagro? Yo pensé que usted siempre hacía esos gratis."

"El Señor trabaja de modos muy misteriosos, Don Pedro. Sé que voy a tener que pelear con este Demonio Dorado, y estoy seguro que lo voy a vencer, pero siento que necesito tu ayuda por algún motivo. Creo que tú, con tu experiencia, me puedes decir cómo derrotar a este tipo en el ring."

El amigo se sintió halagado por su comentario, pero se puso a vacilar. Le dijo, "Padre, lo siento mucho, pero no quiero tener parte en su muerte."

Pedro se acabó su taza de café para dar su desayuno por concluido.

"Antes, dijiste que si fueras 20 años más joven, podrías enfrentártele. Bien, pues digamos que yo soy ese tú, 20 años más joven... Dime, ¿qué harías, como luchador, para vencer a tan formidable enemigo?"

Pagaron, se fueron del restaurante, y caminaron al negocio de Don Pedro. El viejo concibió una idea, tronó los dedos y se volteó a ver al presbítero, muy emocionado.

"¡Ya lo tengo! Necesita tener alguna ventaja. Físicamente él es superior, y nada podemos hacer para cambiarlo. Psicológicamente, se ha puesto en ventaja, con su máscara, récords, y su espectáculo de invencible. Yo digo que debemos lanzarle una curva psicológica, la cual combinada con esa gran determinación suya, ¡lo va a derribar a la lona, vencido!"

Pedro se empezó a emocionar con los detalles de su propio plan.

"Tengo una idea brillante. Vamos consiguiendo una máscara para ponerlo al mismo nivel, pero ya que él es un demonio, usted debe ser un ángel, un santo, o... ¡un exorcista! ¡Sí, eso es! Le conseguiré una máscara como la del famoso luchador mexicano, El Santo. Entonces le pegamos una cruz azul para convertirlo en El Exorcista de Plata. Voy a hacer una investigación en el Internet para reunir tanta información sobre este hombre como sea posible; estoy seguro que debe tener alguna debilidad en alguna parte."

"¡Mujeres!" dijo el cura, uniéndose al plan entusiasta que su amigo iba desarrollando.

"No. Bueno, sí, pero ando buscando algo como su tendón de Aquiles. Debe tener alguna debilidad física la cual podamos explotar, pero necesito saber primero de dónde viene él originalmente."

El viejo entró a su oficina y encendió su computadora para empezar su investigación.

El Padre Gabriel ya iba de salida de la tienda cuando el negociante le preguntó, "¿Está usted seguro de esto, Padre?"

El Padre G se detuvo en la puerta y le explicó la situación.

"¿Te acuerdas de las gentes esas que estaban en la iglesia el miércoles con las cuales me paré a platicar antes de irnos a desayunar?"

"Sí: una pareja joven con un chiquito muy mono."

"Ellos necesitan todo ese dinero para el trasplante de corazón de su hijo, así que la respuesta es: No solo sí, sino: ¡Con un demonio que sí!"

"¡Amén!" dijo Pedro mientras el cura se iba, cerrando la puerta tras él.

El viejo comerciante se rió y aplaudió, a pesar de que no estaba muy seguro que podrían lograr lo que el sacerdote quería. Decidió seguir el plan que acababa de concebir para ayudar al intrépido Tejedor de Milagros.

Pedro quería a Gabriel como si fuera su propio hijo. El hombre había tenido un hijo, Rogelio, quien murió en combate. Gabriel parecía tener el mismo espíritu temerario.

El manejador-de-estrella-de-lucha-libre llamó al promotor para aceptar el reto del Demonio Dorado y hacer una cita para encontrarse a firmar el contrato. Dejó a sus empleados a cargo del negocio de empeños mientras él se apuraba a conseguir la máscara plateada alterada como la quería.

También fue capaz de obtener bastante información útil a través de la Internet acerca del misterioso Demonio Dorado. Era solo cuestión de saber dónde buscar, y estar dispuesto a tirar unos cuantos dólares por la información en los lugares apropiados y espacios de charlas.

El Demonio Dorado, había sido miembro del Fuerza Delta después de unos años en las Fuerzas Especiales en Fort Bragg, Carolina del Norte.

Cuando dejó el servicio, había sido cortado de Los Centauros, un equipo profesional de fútbol americano, porque se lastimó una rodilla durante un entrenamiento antes de comenzar la temporada, así que no pudo jugar. Era conocido en el círculo de físico-culturismo y levantamiento pesado de pesas por haber ganado más de 20 kilos usando esteroides anabólicos ilegales. Ya era un tipo grandote cuando salió de la Fuerza Delta, pero agregó esos kilos extras tratando de hacerla en el mercado del fútbol profesional.

Su nombre verdadero era Charles O'Hara. Su padre fue un alcohólico que abusaba físicamente de él cuando era un niño; él murió en un accidente de tráfico manejando ebrio. Su madre, muy estricta, llevaba a Charlie a la iglesia todos los días. Ella nunca le permitió salir con muchachas. Cuando el chico terminó la preparatoria se enlistó en el Ejército.

Sus viejos conocidos no lo conocían como el Demonio Dorado porque Charles había cambiado demasiado y ya no se asociaba con ellos, pero eso sí, tenían mucha información acerca del Charles O'Hara que conocían, de Manhattan, Nueva York.

La madre de Charles fue hallada muerta un día. Se había quebrado el cuello en lo que parecía ser una caída del segundo piso. Los rumores eran que Charlie la había matado y lo hizo ver como un accidente.

Pedro consiguió mucha información del gigante de parte de mujeres que habían salido con el luchador. Entonces ya tenía suficiente material para usar, física y también psicológicamente, en contra del oponente, lo que le dio más confianza que triunfarían.

Theresa Reynolds hizo un par de llamadas durante el fin de semana a algunos viejos amigos de su familia; el retirado General McKennan era uno de ellos. El viejo era presidente de una compañía de seguros e inversiones. Theresa arregló las cosas para obtener una buena oferta de trabajo ahí para Linda Richards. Si la aceptaba, la madre soltera ganaría el triple del salario que estaba recibiendo en el trabajo de la cocina de la escuela.

Theresa también le pidió a Scott Anderson, el abogado de Linda, que se encontrara con ella en la escuela después de las clases el lunes.

Durante su junta, Theresa le preguntó al abogado algunas cosas y se enteró que era soltero y muy próspero. A él le gustaba Linda, pero, como su abogado, mantenía solo una relación profesional con ella.

Theresa le dijo que Linda había andado hablando muy excitada acerca de alguien a quien acababa de conocer, pero que no podía estar con él debido a su profesión. El hombre se decía ser un tipo apuesto, inteligente, bien educado, y de éxito. La astuta religiosa no elaboró en los detalles del verdadero interés romántico de Linda, Gabriel, y lo hizo aparecer como que la norteña estaba muy interesada en el abogado.

Theresa le sugirió a Scott ir al estudio artístico donde Linda trabajaba, y que le ofreciera llevarla a su casa porque la pobre chica tenía que caminar en la noche, después de la sesión, a menos que le dieran un aventoncito.

Sor Theresa expresó admiración por Linda por su dedicación a su hijito, hasta el punto de desnudarse como modelo de arte para poder sostenerse.

El abogado se excitó con las posibilidades y le agradeció a Theresa por su ayuda. Ella le dijo que le había conseguido a Linda una oferta de trabajo, pero preferiría que Scott le pasara la información sin mencionar que la hermana religiosa había tenido algo que ver con ello. No quería que Linda fuera a pensar que ya no era apreciada en la escuelita.

Scott le prometió que le haría saber a Linda de la oportunidad de trabajo sin revelar su fuente de información.

Ese mismo lunes por la noche, el 15 de noviembre, Don Pedro organizó una rueda de prensa para anunciar el gran pleito. A su lado estaba sentado un encapuchado, como un monje, con máscara plateada. Los periodistas se entusiasmaron con el pleito del Demonio Dorado y el Exorcista Plateado. Todo estaba listo para el evento el cual se iba a llevar a cabo el siguiente domingo en la tarde en el coliseo local. El Demonio hizo un escándalo, como se esperaba, durante la conferencia de prensa.

"Voy a torturar a este insecto insignificante hasta que le rece a su Dios, pidiendo que le mande la muerte para aliviar su dolor. ¡Es audaz, pero se va a arrepentir una vez que nos encontremos dentro del ring!"

El Padre G estaba callado, escuchando al gigante echar sus habladas. El sacerdote tenía una cruz grande de madera en sus manos, como si estuviera orando. Ni siquiera volteó a ver a su oponente. El mastodonte se burló de él, pero no consiguió reacción del misterioso retador.

"¿Lo ven? Ya está comenzando a ponerse en paz con su Dios, pero es muy tarde para él. ¡Ni siquiera Dios puede ayudar al hombre que se atreve a retar al campeón del universo!"

El gigantesco luchador se acercó al lado de la mesa donde Gabriel seguía sentado en oración mientras que Pedro hacía sus declaraciones a la prensa. El Demonio Dorado quería intimidar al retador.

"Este ratoncillo es un cobarde inútil que ni siquiera tiene el valor de hablar enfrente del todopoderoso campeón del universo."

El luchador de la máscara dorada le dio un manazo en la nuca al sacerdote para llamarle la atención. El hombre vestido de monje le respondió pegándole al bruto sobre la rodilla derecha con la cruz de madera. El agudo dolor de su rodilla débil hizo que el gigante perdiera el balance. Golpeó la mesa con ambas manos, muy duro, para recuperar el balance y pretender ferocidad. Gruñó de dolor e ira.

"¡Aaaaaargh! Puede que no aguante hasta el domingo para hacerte trizas. ¡Anda, Cobarde, levántate! ¡Aquí mismo, muéstrame lo que tienes!"

Cuatro guardias se le echaron encima al gigantón. Las cuatro glamorosas chicas de su equipo se unieron a los guardias para alejarlo del retador quien permanecía en su silla. Don Pedro se interpuso para proteger a Gabriel del ataque del Demonio Dorado, sabiendo muy bien que el asesino no iba a hacer nada ahí. Era un escándalo de publicidad; sin embargo, el golpecito en la rodilla había confirmado lo que Pedro le dijo a Gabriel. El Demonio Dorado había sufrido una lesión en su rodilla que terminó con sus aspiraciones en el fútbol americano profesional con Los Centauros, y era su punto débil. Tendrían que explotar esa debilidad durante el pleito.

"¿Qué clase de comportamiento profesional es este? Demando respeto y protección para mi peleador quien es un verdadero caballero... ¡No un payaso bravucón como ese diablillo amarillo!" Pedro anunció. "¡Sus días están contados! ¡Necesita revisar sus opciones de retiro!"

Las cámaras de TV capturaron la protesta de Pedro Mireles y siguieron al Demonio Dorado escoltado rumbo a su cuarto de hotel.

Pedro y Gabriel salieron por otra puerta y se metieron a una limusina que los llevó de regreso al gimnasio de boxeo del Salvaje Oeste.

El evento estaba dispuesto y despertó gran interés del público. Un grupo de reporteros siguieron la limusina al gimnasio a pesar de sus intentos de perderlos; James Bravo dejó entrar al enmascarado retador y a su manejador pero cerró las puertas a los reporteros, para proteger la identidad del Exorcista Plateado. Gabriel se quitó su disfraz, se trepó al techo del negocio y se marchó por el callejón de atrás.

Pedro se encontró afuera con los periodistas y les pidió su cooperación y comprensión en mantener secreta la identidad del peleador. Estuvieron de acuerdo y se marcharon. Pedro sabía que iban a tratar de descubrir quién era el retador, pero estaba determinado a no dejárselos saber.

El Pastor de la Iglesia de la Santísima Trinidad fue a la casa de Leopoldo y Alma Cárdenas a informarles de su plan.

"Quiero que confíen en mí. Dejen que Benito mire esta pelea. Puede que se asuste un poco, pero le ayudará a sobreponerse a sus pesadillas una vez que me vea vencer al Demonio Dorado. Pero si no quiere ver, no lo forcen."

"Que Dios lo bendiga Padre, ¿pero en verdad cree que pueda ganarle a ese gigante?" preguntó Alma quien tenía sus dudas.

"No hay nada imposible con Dios, Alma. De este modo tendrán el dinero que necesitan para la operación de Benito."

"¿Va a pelear con ese asesino y nos va a dar todo el dinero que gane para la operación?" preguntó Leopoldo, segurísimo que era imposible.

"Sí. Es solo cuestión de fe, tiempo... y quizás algo de dolor," explicó el sacerdote, levantando a Benito en sus brazos.

El chiquito lo abrazó muy apretadamente y le besó la mejilla como si entendiera lo que iba a hacer por él.

"Rezaremos por usted, Padre," le dijo Alma, tomando a su niño de vuelta.

"Gracias, mis amigos. Solo recuerden mantener su fe muy firme."

Después que les advirtió no contarle a nadie que él era el Exorcista Plateado, el ministro los dejó con un rayito de esperanza.

Una vez que se alejó, Leopoldo le dijo a su esposa, "Fuimos a rezar por un milagro. Si el Padre Gabriel puede vencerlo, será un milagro verdadero."

"Yo siento que sí puede. He oído que Dios está junto al Padre Gabriel. ¿Te acuerdas de la historia de David contra Goliat?" Alma le recordó a su esposo mientras abrazaba a su pequeñín. Sacó ella la Biblia del buró junto a su cama y le leyó el pasaje que le había mencionado.

El Padre Gabriel iba por el estudio de arte de Meredith. Se fijó que era tarde para atender su sesión de arte, la cual debía estar terminándose para entonces, pero pensó que Linda quizás necesitaría transporte. El cura bajó su velocidad. Miró a Linda metiéndose en el carro de Scott Anderson, así que se alejó de ahí muy contento, dándole gracias a Dios.

El martes, 16 de noviembre, Linda Richards renunció a su trabajo en la cafetería de la escuela y fue a agradecerle al Padre Gabriel por su ayuda. Se disculpó por tratar de hacerlo que se interesara en ella como mujer. El pastor le dijo que se había sentido halagado que tan hermosa damita lo considerara digno de ser su pareja. Linda le explicó que aún lo consideraba capaz de hacer feliz a cualquier mujer con su bondad, integridad, su actitud positiva, sabiduría, su hermosa voz, y su arrolladora presencia. Era el sacerdote más sexy que jamás había visto, y todavía le debía la vida.

"Fue Dios quien te dio la vida para empezar, y Él mismo fue quien te dio una segunda oportunidad," le dijo Gabriel, tratando de enviar la atención lejos de sí. "¿Qué piensas hacer con tu vida ahora, Chica?"

Estaban sentados a ambos lados de su escritorio en la oficina escolar.

"Bueno, conseguí un trabajo en relaciones públicas con una compañía de seguros y finanzas. Además, mi abogado, Scott Anderson, me consiguió un acuerdo con la compañía eléctrica por 250,000 dólares, pero parece estar interesado en mí. Le encanta mi niño, y Pedrito se siente a gusto con él. Scott rehusó tomar su parte en la demanda. Eso es muy raro de parte de un abogado. ¿No cree? Dejó que me quedara con todo el dinero para que me pueda establecer por mi propia cuenta. Empezamos a salir juntos anoche. Es un hombre estupendo."

"Estoy seguro que serás feliz con él. Conozco a Scott y pienso que será un excelente modelo y un buen padre para tu hijo. ¡Qué suertudo!" El Padre Gabriel cerró los ojos como viendo al futuro. "Le vas a dar hijas gemelitas el año que entra."

Gabriel le soltó la mano y admiró su figura, imaginándola embarazada.

"¡Ándele, Padre! Si apenas empezamos a salir juntos, ¡y usted ya me anda cargando con dos chilpayates suyos!" ella protestó, riéndose.

Gabriel fue alrededor del escritorio para abrazarla.

"Vas a ser muy feliz con tu nueva familia."

Linda le besó la mejilla y se marchó de su oficina. El cura elevó los ojos al cielo y le dio gracias a Dios.

El Padre Gabriel llamó a Sor Theresa a su oficina después de clases. Estaba agotado después de entrenar muy duro en el gimnasio, todo ese día.

Pedro le había enseñado unos trucos de lucha libre y lo tuvo practicando llaves, candados, y lanzamientos, caídas, y rodadas. Hicieron un enorme muñeco de entrenamiento relleno de arena y pesando ciento sesenta kilos. Gabriel lo había estado manipulando, golpeándolo, rodando con él y levantándolo. Perdió algo de peso por causa del extraordinario ejercicio, pero sintió que había aprovechado la experiencia.

El director le dijo a la maestra su plan y le rogó que lo mantuviera en secreto. Solamente le quedaban cuatro días para prepararse para el gran pleito. Aún cuando tenía fe que prevalecería en el combate, presentía que necesitaba hacer su parte. Afortunadamente estaba en una estupenda condición física; solo necesitaba practicar movimientos de lucha.

"Es muy loco, Gabrielín; deberías cancelarlo. ¿Qué tal si sales lisiado?"

Ella le puso las manitas sobre el musculoso pecho.

"Te puedo asegurar que no solamente voy a salir bien, voy a ganar y a conseguir el dinero que necesita el pequeño Benito para su operación."

No había siquiera sombra de una duda en su determinada apariencia. Theresa se paró, cara a cara frente a él. Todos los demás ya se habían ido a sus casas.

"Eres tan valiente y tan bueno, Gabrielín."

"Quiero que, por favor, reces por mí."

"Siempre lo hago."

"¡Gracias, Tere!"

"¡Es un gusto para mí!"

Se estaban acercando cada vez más con cada intercambio de palabras, perdidos en los ojos del otro. Con su mano en el pecho de él, podía sentir su corazón latiendo más fuerte y rápido. Él la cogió de los hombros.

"Gabriel, podrías morir luchando con ese hombre."

"Si es así, ¡recuerda que te amé siempre!"

Sus manos se resbalaron a la cintura de ella para repegársela; ella lo agarró de la camisa y lo jaló más cerca. Sus bocas se unieron en un ardiente, largo, profundo, y prohibido beso de amor.

Después de un largo y delicioso beso Francés, Gabriel abrió los ojos, la soltó, dio un paso atrás, y se fue a sentar del otro lado de su escritorio.

"¡Oh, Dios, mío! ¡Eso fue tan... rico y al mismo tiempo tan... inapropiado!" Gabriel dijo en un susurro, y se cubrió la cara.

Theresa se sentó en el sofá y dijo, "De acuerdo... en ambos puntos."

Él cambió el tema de la conversación.

"¿Te gustaría ayudarme con este pleito, Theresa?"

"¿Me quieres en tu esquina, en bikini, como las chicas del Demonio Dorado?"

"¡Sería sensacional! pero en realidad lo que quisiera es que reclutaras unas personas para que atiendan la pelea y les distribuyas unos cartelones. ¿En quién puedes confiar para mantener este asunto secreto?"

"¿Mantener cuál asunto secreto, el pleito... o nosotros?"

"El pleito, mi identidad secreta como el Exorcista Plateado."

"Algunos miembros de mi clase de estudios bíblicos son confiables, pero por el otro lado se me hace que, ya todos sospechan lo que está pasando entre tú y yo. Se está convirtiendo en una fuente de chismes, un escándalo."

"¡Escándalo!"

"¡Sí! Tenemos que llegar a una decisión más pronto de lo que crees."

Gabriel se le quedó viendo. Recordó lo que le había dicho en la sacristía el sábado anterior. Una melodía se le vino a la mente con la palabra que ella le sugirió, así que le empezó a cantar otra vieja canción romántica en la cual un romance se dice ser un escándalo, pero el poeta aconseja a su amada no poner atención en lo que diga la gente y pide que lo ame aún más porque el escándalo verdadero es no saber amar.

Ella le aplaudió, aprobando su canción, y le aseguró que podía contar con ella para cualquier cosa que le pidiera.

El pequeño Timmy llegó buscando al Padre G en ese momento, así que los dos religiosos tuvieron que despedirse por esa tarde. Gabriel encaminó a Theresa hasta la puerta con Timmy siguiéndolos muy cerquita, observándolos como se miraban a los ojos.

"¿Ama usted a la Hermana Theresa, Padre G?" preguntó Timmy, volteando a ver a su padrino después que se fue la mujer.

"Por supuesto que la amo, mi amiguito. A ti también te amo. ¡Yo amo a todo mundo!" el sacerdote dijo, sintiéndose expuesto.

"Usted sabe lo que quiero decir, Padre G. No se haga. ¿Anda saliendo con ella, como novios?"

"¿Qué crees tú?"

El presbítero se sentó en una banca, encarando al inquisidor.

"¡Yo diría que sí! Todo mundo los ha visto. Un día los vi en la televisión cuando usted le cantó y bailó con ella, y la besó en un restaurante en el centro. Lo pasaron en las noticias la semana pasada. Dijeron que usted se enojó y empujó por allá al de la cámara. Yo no sabía que los sacerdotes podían hacer eso. ¿A los Padres solo los dejan salir con monjitas?"

"Estaban mintiendo. No me enojé; fue un accidente. El camarógrafo se tropezó y se cayó solo," dijo el párroco, "Los sacerdotes podemos salir con nuestros amigos y amigas, como todos. Podemos bailar, cantar, divertirnos, ir a patinar, jugar boliche... todo. Solo no tenemos la opción de casarnos y tener familias propias."

"¿Entonces puede agasajarse a las monjitas pero no se tiene que casar con ellas?" dijo el chiquillo con una malévola sonrisilla, cerrándole un ojo.

"¡Ey, eso no fue lo que dije! ¿Qué sabes tú de andar agasajándose?" Gabriel exclamó, dándole un manacito en la cabeza.

"¿Usted conoce a Susan, la niña pelirroja de mi clase?"

"Sí..."

El cura se inclinó hacia delante para escuchar mejor.

"¡Yo le di un besito el otro día!"

El Padre Gabriel le sonrió a Timmy y decidió mejor cambiar el tema de la conversación en ese punto. Se acordó de un chiste.

"¿Sabes qué, Tim? me recordaste una historia. Estaba un hombre en una plaza vendiendo un perro. Cuando otro se le acercó, él le ofreció venderle el perro, el cual estaba ahí sentado cerca de su pie. '¿Y cuánto está pidiendo por su perro?' el segundo preguntó. '¡Mil dólares!' fue la respuesta del dueño. '¿Por qué tanto dinero por un animal tan corriente?' el segundo preguntó, mirando al perro. 'Este perro habla,' explicó el vendedor. '¡No, no la puedo creer! Si así fuera, entonces mil dólares no sería nada por un perro parlante.' Entonces el perro le habló al posible comprador, 'Señor, por favor, cómpreme y lléveme lejos de este tipo. ¿Sabe qué? Me vende de pura envidia. Yo gané una medalla de honor en combate y un premio Nobel de literatura. Tengo un doctorado en física y la Reina de Inglaterra me hizo un Caballero. ¡Cómpreme y aléjeme de esta miserable excusa de hombre!' El prospecto estaba sorprendido y le dijo al dueño, '¡Esto es increíble. ¿Por qué quiere usted vender tan maravilloso animal?' El dueño del perro le contestó, "¡Ya no aguanto al infeliz, por mentiroso!'"

Timmy se carcajeó, imaginándose al perro parlante y mentiroso. El Padre G se acordó que Timmy había ido a buscarlo.

"Muy bien, mi Carcajeante Amiguito, ¿por qué me viniste a buscar?'

"¡Híjole, ya hasta se me había olvidado! Don Pedro me mandó a que le hablara para que vaya a su tienda porque le quiere enseñar algo.

"Muy bien. Ahora voy para allá. Vete a tu casa a hacer tu tarea. Guárdate las cosas de las que hablamos en privado, y yo no le diré a los papás de Susan que tú te andas agasajando a su hija."

"¿Les puedo contar el chiste del perro a mis cuates?"

"Seguro, pero solo el chiste. ¿De acuerdo?"

"¡De acuerdo!"

El chico estrechó la mano del cura y luego se fue corriendo.

El domingo en la tarde, noviembre 21, en el Coliseo, la arena estaba llena. Gabriel estaba sorprendido de ver cuánta gente se hallaba interesada en ver a un hombre (posiblemente) ser despedazado por un gigante. El promotor del evento había organizado otros pleitos preliminares para crear el ambiente apropiado para el evento principal.

El primer evento era una lucha de sumo entre dos enormes luchadores orientales. Theresa se preguntaba por qué aquellos grandulones tenían que luchar casi sin ropa, pero observó el tremendo choque con gran interés. Había un cierto magnetismo animal en aquel antiguo arte marcial.

El segundo pleito de la noche era de karate. Aquellos peleadores eran de tamaño normal pero parecían capaces de volar. Intercambiaron puñetazos y patadas a través de los seis rounds a los que estaba programada la pelea. Uno recibió la victoria, pero ambos acabaron sangrantes e hinchados.

El tercero fue una lucha greco-romana entre dos jóvenes universitarios. Tenían la gracia y velocidad de los peleadores de karate pero se empujaban y se agarraban uno al otro como los luchadores de sumo. Al menos en ese encuentro no hubo sangre derramada por ninguno de los dos luchadores. Era un pleito más limpio, envolviendo habilidad y fuerza.

Uno de los luchadores era negro y el otro blanco, ambos de la misma talla y musculatura. El choque era visualmente atractivo, casi como un baile para los ojos de Theresa. Ella nunca había atendido un evento como aquel, pero se estaba divirtiendo bastante presenciando los brutales deportes.

El último pleito preliminar fue entre dos boxeadores de peso medio, un negrito contra un hispano. Se dieron puñetazos como si quisieran matar al contrincante. Ellos, como los karatekas, acabaron hinchados y sangrando. Los jueces les dieron un empate, para disgusto de partes del público que pensaba que ya fuera el negrito o el hispano había ganado, dependiendo de su propio grupo étnico o racial.

Un pleito estalló entre dos disidentes espectadores. Los guardias de seguridad de la Oficina del Sheriff descendieron sobre los peleadores no programados en la cartelera oficial y los echaron de la arena.

Un hombre sentado atrás de Theresa le ofreció una cerveza, viendo que era una dama muy atractiva y sola. Theresa gentilmente declinó su oferta, explicándole que cumplía con un deber relacionado con el evento principal. Otra mujer quien estaba atrás del tomador de cerveza se entrometió en la conversación y aceptó la cerveza que él andaba ofreciendo gratis, así que el hombre tuvo alguien con quien compartir su cerveza y con quien poder conversar. Theresa volvió los ojos al cielo y le agradeció a Dios.

Las luces principales se apagaron. Un órgano comenzó a tocar, y un coro empezó a cantar un himno eclesiástico. Entonces una luz azul llenó la arena mientras se escuchaba la voz del anunciador.

"¡Damas y caballeros, bienvenidos al Coliseo de Texas! Producciones Cartwright tienen el honor y el placer de traerles el evento principal de la noche: una batalla que nos promete ser realmente apocalíptica. Estamos a punto de presenciar las fuerzas del bien contra las fuerzas del mal, en el ring, enfrente de nuestros propios ojos, una pelea por el título del Campeón Luchador del Universo. Damas y caballeros, únanseme en darle la bienvenida, primero al retador, de esta gran ciudad de San Antonio, Texas, con uno ochenta y tres de estatura y pesando noventa kilos de músculos de acero inoxidable. Él es el representante del bien y la justicia, el enigmático, ¡El Exorcista Plateado!"

Una ovación resonó a través del Coliseo por el desconocido retador local mientras la gente se levantaba y aplaudía para darle la bienvenida al luchador a la arena. El coro cantó de nuevo un himno casi angelical hasta que el Exorcista se trepó al cuadrilátero enlonado y saludó a la audiencia.

Las luces azules se apagaron. Luego, luces rojas iluminaron la arena. Una serie de quemadores de gas se prendieron, creando un camino con bordes de fuego hasta el ring. El sistema de sonido tocaba una tenebrosa obertura pesada. El anunciador volvió al micrófono para recibir al campeón.

"¡Damas y caballeros, agarren bien sus almas! Con nosotros esta noche, desde las profundidades del oscuro abismo, con 1.98 de estatura y pesando 150 kilos de pura furia hirviente, el invicto, el increíble, el poderoso Campeón del Universo... ¡El Demonio Dorado!"

Algunas gentes le aplaudieron, otros lo abuchearon, algunos le gritaron obscenidades, otros vitorearon para recibir al imponente campeón.

Un adolescente trató de conseguir un autógrafo mientras el enmascarado avanzaba al ring; el coro cantaba un himno satánico. El gigante levantó al chico y lo lanzó por encima de otros fanáticos; el Demonio Dorado le gruñó al atrevido muchacho y amenazó a los miembros de la audiencia que desaprobaban de su trato al chico.

Los guardias le aconsejaron al luchador que siguiera adelante en lo que empujaban al público para alejarlos del atleta. El muchacho rechazado se incorporó de entre unas gentes y vio que estaba sangrando por la nariz después de haberse estrellado contra la cabeza de alguien.

"¡Estuvo chido, camaradas, formidable de veras!" exclamó el chico.

El Demonio Dorado se trepó al ring y se paseó contoneándose, ignorando a su oponente. Sus cuatro muchachas lo escoltaron en lo que él desfilaba con los poderosos brazos en alto. Una de las chicas se detuvo y miró al retador. A pesar que el Padre Gabriel se veía muy atlético cuando se quitó el poncho negro, se veía pequeño comparado con el gigante.

El Exorcista traía puestos una máscara plateada, trusa y zapatillas de luchador todas plateadas también con vivos azules igual que la cruz diseñada en la frente de la máscara. La negrita amiga del Demonio Dorado se le acercó al Exorcista y le puso las manos sobre el musculoso torso.

"Si pudieras ganarle a mi hombre, me podrías tener a mí como parte del premio también," le susurró.

Se lamió los labios y lo miró con ojos de deseo. Luego se alejó meciendo sus amplias caderas y columpiando su cola diabólica que traía cocida atrás de su calzón del bikini.

Gabriel la siguió con los ojos y luego volteó a ver al público. Sus ojos se encontraron con los de Theresa no muy lejos a su izquierda. Le guiñó un ojo; ella le dio una señal positiva con el pulgar elevado.

"Padre, yo le puedo ayudar con esa diablita después que haya derrotado a su novio," susurró Don Pedro a quien le encantó la exuberante hembra.

"Seguro. Te agradecería si me ayudas tú con eso, Amigo mío; aunque podría ser tu nieta. ¿No crees?" Gabriel bromeó en voz bajita con Pedro, quien levantó las cejas y asintió con resignación.

Theresa tembló al ver a los peleadores lado a lado. El Demonio Dorado se veía enorme en comparación con Gabriel (o cualquier otro). Entonces notó algo como un halo alrededor del cuerpo entero del retador. Se acordó que algunos santos habían sido vistos con halos así. Descartó la idea, pensando que era la reflexión de las luces sobre el plateado trajecito del Exorcista.

Theresa hizo contacto con los ojos de los otros siete feligreses a quienes había reclutado para ayudar al Padre G con su plan. Había dos en cada lado del ring en la tercera fila cerca de la orilla. Finalmente cuando el pleito ya iba a comenzar, el réferi llamó a los dos gladiadores al centro para decirles las reglas de la contienda.

"Yo seré quien dé por terminado el pleito. Solo será detenido si uno de ustedes se rinde o es incapaz de continuar la pelea. No hay límite de tiempo. Yo les diré si tienen que hacer alguna pausa al hacer que suene la campana. No pueden usar ningún arma. Si veo que introducen algún arma, detendré el encuentro y descalificaré al peleador armado. ¿Está claro?"

Ambos peleadores estuvieron de acuerdo con las reglas. El Exorcista Plateado extendió su mano hacia el Demonio Dorado, quien se la manoteó lejos con un gruñido gutural. El retador se fue a su esquina y se arrodilló a rezar una última vez, esperando que sonara la campana.

En cuanto sonó la campana, el demonio enmascarado se abalanzó sobre el retador como un toro furioso. El Padre G apenas se iba levantando.

El Demonio le pegó al Exorcista en la nuca con ambas manos formando un martillo, luego agarró el antebrazo de Gabriel y lanzó al religioso contra las cuerdas al otro lado del ring. Cuando el retador rebotó de las cuerdas elásticas, el campeón lo recibió con el brazo extendido como tendedero.

El Padre G pudo ver sus pies elevarse en el aire y cayó de espalda en el blanco enlonado. Volteó a un lado y vio la angustiada expresión en el rostro de Theresa, con las manos en la cara. Volvió su atención al gigante quien se estaba trepando al poste para echarse de clavado sobre su caído retador.

La gente estaba gritando. Gabriel aspiró aire para recuperar el aliento y rodó rápido a un lado, saliéndose de la ruta del demonio volando. El mastodonte aterrizó de nalgas en el enlonado; el retador saltó sobre él para sujetarlo con un candado al cuello, para delicia de la multitud.

El gigante se levantó con el retador pescado de su cuello. Gabriel sintió sus pies elevarse cuando el enorme luchador se irguió, batallando para quitarse del cuello al retador. El Exorcista apretó aún más fuerte el grueso cuello del campeón. El Demonio Dorado se dejó caer hacia atrás con todo su peso y apachurró al Exorcista Plateado contra el enlonado.

Gabriel quedó sofocado, así que dejó ir al enemigo. Ambos peleadores rodaron alejándose uno del otro para recuperar sus fuerzas. Se levantaron y caminaron en círculo, mirándose a la cara. El campeón volvió a gruñir.

El Demonio le tiró el agarrón y atrapó la muñeca del Exorcista. Gabriel se metió bajo el gigante y lo arrojó sobre su hombro con un movimiento de judo. El enmascarado de oro rebotó en la lona y se levantó. ¡Estaba furioso! Saltó al frente y trabó de las rodillas al gladiador enmascarado de plata.

Gabriel se le resbaló de entre las manos al oponente y rodó hacia fuera del ring. El Demonio rugió más fuerte y lo retó a que se regresara. El Exorcista miró al enardecido público. Sus ojos buscaron a Theresa en la tercera fila. Le guiñó un ojo y le sonrió, con una señal del dedo pulgar para hacerle saber que se encontraba bien.

Theresa y una viejecita a su lado se pusieron de pie y levantaron los cartelones que juntos decían, "¡ARREPIÉNTETE CHARLIE!" El gigante miró los anuncios y maldijo a las mujeres. ¡Había funcionado!

El Padre G se aprovechó de la distracción y se metió de nuevo al ring por detrás del Demonio para taclearlo por las rodillas. El Demonio Dorado cayó de cara al piso y golpeó la lona con las palmas.

El Exorcista le desabrochó el cierre de la bota derecha y se la sacó. Se levantó y se alejó del derribado campeón quien estaba intrigado por sus acciones. El Padre G lanzó la larga bota hacia el público, a la derecha de donde Theresa había levantado los dos primeros anuncios.

El gigante volteó a ver en donde cayó su bota y miró a otras dos gentes levantando cartelones que decían, "¡CHARLIE, TU MADRE TE AMA!" El gigante vio al Exorcista, deduciendo que aquello era idea suya. Fue y agarró al contrincante del cuello y de un muslo para levantarlo en alto sobre su cabeza, como si no pesara. El Demonio Dorado lanzó al Exorcista Plateado sobre la audiencia y le ordenó que le trajera su bota.

El Padre G se levantó de entre las gentes y les pidió la bota. Cuando se la dieron, la lanzó más allá, a otra sección de la arena. Cuando los ojos del luchador endemoniado la siguieron, se encontró con otro par de anuncios elevados que le decían, "¡ARREPIÉNTETE, ASESINO!"

El Demonio Dorado se agarró enfurecido de las cuerdas del ring, y amenazó a los dos jóvenes con los anuncios. No se dio cuenta que el retador ya estaba encima de él. Esa vez, el Exorcista pateó al Demonio en la ahora desnuda rodilla derecha.

Durante la preparación para el pleito Pedro y Gabriel se fijaron que el Demonio Dorado usaba bastante protección en su bota para cubrir su rodilla débil, así que habían diseñado un plan para exponer la rodilla y golpearlo ahí.

Un sonoro grito de dolor silenció a la multitud cuando el gigante se dobló sobre su rodilla izquierda y se agarró la derecha. El enfurecido campeón agarró al retador de un tobillo. Le torció el pie y lo hizo caer a la lona. El Demonio, gateando, se echó encima del caído Exorcista, y comenzaron a luchar, rodando en el piso del cuadrilátero.

El enmascarado dorado se le encimó al plateado y lo comenzó a ahorcar con sus gigantescas manos. El Padre G rezó en voz alta.

"¡El Señor es mi roca en quien confío!"

Aún cuando estaba tratando con toda su fuerza de quitarse las tenazas de la garganta, no podía. Su visión se oscureció por falta de oxígeno. Gabriel dejó caer sus brazos, sueltos, como si se hubiera desmayado. El Demonio Dorado sonrió triunfante y relajó sus manos un poco.

Theresa miraba horrorizada pensando que Gabriel ya estaba muerto. El Exorcista le dio un par de manazos al Demonio al mismo tiempo en los dos oídos. El mastodonte lo soltó y se llevó las manos a los lastimados oídos, gimiendo. El Padre G aspiró y rodó hacia atrás para alejarse del gigante.

El Demonio Dorado estaba hincado en su rodilla izquierda con las manos en los oídos. El Exorcista lanzó su ataque, pateando al endemoniado en la cara como a una pelota de fútbol. El grandulón cayó de espaldas; su máscara se ensangrentó. Como quiera, se las arregló para levantarse, agarrándose de las cuerdas y se volteó a encarar al atrevido retador.

Con un grito furioso, el campeón se abalanzó contra el sacerdote. Gabriel se hizo a un ladito, pero le dio una patada en la rodilla derecha de nuevo cuando pasó. El gigante aulló de dolor una vez más y se cayó sobre su rodilla izquierda, pidiendo misericordia con la mano levantada.

Sus ojos se encontraron. El cura le apuntó al último par de cartelones que decían, "¡MAMI TE PERDONA, CHARLIE!" El gigante se volvió como loco y saltó sobre su pierna buena, cojeando un poco, empujó al oponente muy fuerte contra las cuerdas y trató de golpearlo cuando rebotó.

El maestro boxeador se agachó y evitó su golpe elevado; sin embargo, le propinó al gigante una serie de seis puñetazos al abdomen. Sofocado, el Demonio Dorado abrazó al sacerdote y se recargó con todo su peso sobre él. Los dos cayeron a la lona, pero el gigante había perdido fuerza.

Gabriel se le zafó y se encaramó al poste de la esquina del cuadrilátero. El Demonio Dorado se pudo levantar del enlonado, aún tratando de recuperar el aliento. Mientras el hombrón estaba en el centro del ring, el Exorcista se lanzó como un misil y golpeó al gigante con la cabeza entre el pecho y el abdomen. Cualquier otro hubiera quedado derribado e inconsciente con el tremendo impacto, pero el Demonio Dorado se incorporó de nuevo y encaró al Exorcista.

Se pusieron a moverse en círculos en el centro del cuadrilátero. El Padre G dio la señal con ambas manos para que subieran todos los cartelones, mientras hacía al Demonio Dorado mirar hacia los cuatro lados del ring. "¡ARREPIÉNTETE CHARLIE!" "¡CHARLIE, TU MADRE TE AMA!" "¡ARREPIÉNTETE, ASESINO!" "¡MAMI TE PERDONA, CHARLIE!" El sacerdote le apuntaba a los anuncios, y el luchador no podía evitar verlos.

"Yo sé quién eres, Charles O'Hara, y sé también lo que le hiciste a tu madre," Gabriel le susurró mientras continuaban moviéndose en círculos.

"¡Cállate el hocico! ¡Te mataré a ti también!"

El Demonio Dorado se le echó encima al Exorcista Plateado quien se quitó del camino y lo trastabilló, mandándolo a las cuerdas.

"¡El matarme a mí no te va a dar la paz que andas buscando, Hijo mío!"

El cura se agazapó y caminó en círculo una vez más para seguir la charla con los anuncios en alto.

"¡Tú no eres nada! ¡No sabes nada!"

El mastodonte lanzó su ataque, tirándole un potente puñetazo a la cabeza del Exorcista. El Padre G se movió hacia atrás, fuera del alcance del enorme puño, pero se adelantó rápidamente para contestarle con dos golpes al cuerpo y dos a la cara. Era mucho más veloz que el gigante.

El Exorcista se echó atrás en las puntas de sus zapatillas, como boxeador, para moverse alrededor del centro y mostrarle otra vez los anuncios.

"¡Este es el fin del Demonio Dorado! Ya es tiempo que Charles O'Hara regrese y encare la justicia por su crimen. ¡Esa será la única forma en que puedas encontrar el perdón y la paz!"

Con un rugido intimidante, el luchador pescó la cabeza del Padre G y la puso bajo su brazo derecho en un candado. El cura estaba ya más lleno de confianza, así que se relajó bajo la presión que le estaba imponiendo el campeón y le dio un puñetazo en la expuesta y lastimada rodilla derecha.

El gigante lo soltó y se arrodilló, aullando de dolor y rabia. Estaba sobre su rodilla izquierda y protegiendo la derecha con ambas manos.

El Exorcista caminó con gran aplomo frente al gigante arrodillado y dijo en voz de trueno, "¡Yo te exorcizo, Charles O'Hara, en el nombre del Padre, y del Hijo, y del Espíritu Santo!"

Hizo la señal de la cruz sobre el anonadado luchador. Al descender su mano, la audiencia respondió en coro, "¡Amén!"

La mano derecha del Padre Gabriel se elevó de nuevo hecha un sólido puño y se encontró con el mentón del Demonio Dorado como un marro. El gigante cayó de espaldas, fulminado.

El Exorcista Plateado lo volteó boca abajo y le removió la máscara, como David le había cortado la cabeza a Goliat. Se irguió y levantó la máscara al aire para mostrársela al público que irrumpió en una tremenda ovación. El réferi se acercó y le levantó el brazo derecho, declarándolo el ganador.

Las chicas fueron a ayudar al caído gigante que se empezaba a recobrar.

"¿Quién... eres tú?" el desenmascarado luchador preguntó a su oponente.

"Soy un mensajero del Señor. ¡Él me ha enviado a decirte que el perdón es tuyo si tan solo lo pides desde el fondo de tu corazón arrepentido!"

"¿Eres en verdad un ministro... o algo así?"

"¿Qué importancia tiene quién, o qué, soy yo? Tú eres quien tiene que lidiar con tu vida y con tu relación con Dios. Lo que importa ahora, Charles, O'Hara, es el que ya no eres un demonio, solo un hombre."

"¡Tienes razón! Pero aún necesito saber a nombre de quién voy a escribir el cheque por el medio millón de dólares que has ganado."

"Hazlo a nombre de una pareja llamados Leopoldo y Alma Cárdenas. Ya se los había prometido a ellos."

El Padre G se le acercó al gigantesco luchador y lo abrazó.

"No te has dado cuenta, pero esta noche te convertiste en un instrumento del Señor en hacer un milagro. Haz la paz con Él y haz lo que sabes que es correcto, Hijo mío."

El gigante estaba parado escuchando las palabras, sin saber muy bien qué pensar. El Exorcista Plateado se volvió a los lados y levantó los brazos para despedirse de la audiencia.

Theresa le lanzó un besito discretamente; Gabriel le sonrió en respuesta

Varios reporteros se le acercaron al Exorcista Plateado cuando descendía del ring, pero él los refirió a su manejador.

El Demonio Dorado, sentado en su esquina, se dio cuenta que debería entregarse a la ley por el asesinato de su madre. El Exorcista había tenido un efecto muy profundo y extraño sobre él. Charles había cambiado con aquel pleito, como si el demonio dentro de él se hubiera desvanecido. Se sentía aliviado y creía que aún había esperanza en su vida. Empezó a llorar.

Sus chicas se sorprendieron de ver el torrente de lágrimas. Le echaron encima de la cabeza una toalla, y él les pidió que lo guiaran a su vestidor.

Pedro y Gabriel se fueron al gimnasio en la limusina para hacer su acto de desaparición y evitar que la prensa se enterara quién era realmente el Exorcista Plateado. Pedro les dio a los reporteros su declaración desde la puerta del gimnasio y se fue a casa.

El Padre Gabriel se sorprendió de encontrar una fiestecita en la rectoría. Theresa y los cargadores de los cartelones estaban reunidos para felicitar al Exorcista Plateado por la victoria sobre el Demonio Dorado. Theresa lo abrazó y lo besó en la mejilla. Luego todos también fueron y lo abrazaron.

Abrieron una botella de champaña y brindaron por el nuevo Campeón del Universo, Padre Gabriel, el enmascarado Exorcista Plateado.

"Quiero darles las gracias a cada uno de ustedes. Fue trabajo estupendo de equipo, y todos contribuyeron. Por encima de todo, démosle gracias a Dios quien me protegió y me ayudó a serle útil a Benito Cárdenas."

Gabriel se tocó la espalda adolorida e hizo muecas.

"¿Saben? La Madre Teresa de Calcuta una vez dijo que la caridad para ser verdadera tiene que doler... Yo puedo verificar que eso es cierto. Estoy adolorido en sitios que ni sabía que tenía, pero estamos aquí para celebrar nuestra victoria no para oír quejas del viejo cura. ¿Me podrían ayudar a cantarle una canción al Señor, el verdadero Campeón del Universo?"

Sor Theresa se sentó al órgano y comenzó a tocar. El himno trataba de que debe uno confiar en Dios sin importar las circunstancias. Las palabras eran un recordatorio de no tener miedo de nada ya que Dios siempre va delante de nosotros; lo que tenemos que hacer es seguirlo.

Una oscura sombra cruzó la ventana, asomándose a la rectoría. El sucio remolinillo entonces se fue por el callejón y pronunció una advertencia.

"Aún no he terminado, Gabriel. ¡Vas a caer! ¡No eres tan fuerte!"

Una gata blanca que estaba observando al remolinillo apestoso, arqueó la espalda con los pelos de punta y huyó espantada, incapaz de maullar. El felino desapareció tras de una casa. La entidad maligna se perdió rumbo al arroyo, y la noche se volvió apacible una vez más.

Capítulo XIII

Seducción

Ya era diciembre. Todo parecía color de rosa para Gabriel y Theresa. Estaban ejercitando juntos todas las mañanas; Theresa había empezado a correr además de caminar. Ella también empezó a levantar pesas ligeras en el gimnasio mientras que Gabriel levantaba pesas o le pegaba al costal.

Compartían el almuerzo en la escuela. Ella estaba tocando la música de varias misas el fin de semana. Salían a jugar boliche con las otras monjitas. Gabriel la llamaba o Theresa lo llamaba a él en la noche para charlar. La parejita de religiosos se apuntó y ganó un concurso de baile el cinco de diciembre. Habían tenido que practicar varios ritmos diferentes, lo cual les dio una buena excusa para reunirse un par de noches a practicar la danza y estar en los brazos uno del otro.

Theresa posó para el artista un par de veces; cocinó para él los domingos. El otoño se sentía como verano en el sur de Texas. Las noches se habían comenzado a refrescar, pero los días aún estaban calientes. Los chismes acerca del cura y la monjita se habían regado más allá de los límites de la parroquia; sin embargo, no había queja específica en contra de ellos.

Su romance se había desarrollado del momento en que se reencontraron en el gimnasio de boxeo el 5 de septiembre a cuando se besaron en la oficina del director en noviembre 16. Se enamoraron, sintiendo una pasión física y un deseo cada vez más ardiente.

Sus sueños también se hicieron más sexuales. El tiempo de tomar una decisión se acercaba. Mientras Theresa estaba convencida que Dios quería que se casaran, Gabriel se hallaba torturado por la idea de abandonar su ministerio. Él quería creer lo que Theresa decía: que todas las indicaciones estaban ahí para que pudieran disfrutar de su amor, pero aún tenía duda. Solo le pedía que fuera paciente y le diera un poco más de tiempo. Estaba esperando una señal definitiva que aquello sería lo más apropiado.

En esos días, un personaje de su pasado reapareció en sus vidas.

Era sábado en la mañana, el 11 de diciembre. Theresa retó a Gabriel a un juego de tenis. Él no había jugado ese deporte muy seguido pero aceptó su reto. El sábado era un buen día para eso. Solo tenía dos misas, una temprano en la mañana y la otra ya tarde, casi en la noche.

"¿Dónde está Sor Mary? Creí que iba a venir contigo," preguntó Gabriel, dándole la bienvenida a Theresa a la cancha con un abrazo y un discreto besito cerca de los labios.

267

"Decidió quedarse en la computadora en vez de venir conmigo. Dijo que hacia mucho calor para andar afuera."

"Bueno, ¿qué vamos a apostar?"

"¿Qué estás dispuesto a perder?"

"¿Contigo? Podría perderlo todo y no arrepentirme."

"¡Pues, no estoy segura! Vamos a apostar un almuerzo. ¿Qué te parece?"

"Pienso que podría manejar el que tú pagaras por mi almuerzo... o más bien, que pague por el tuyo."

"¡Muy bien, vamos entonces! A ver si eres tan bueno en la cancha de tenis como en el púlpito, el ring, la cancha de básquetbol, la de fútbol, o..."

"¡Ya, ya estuvo bueno, párale!" Gabriel le suplicó, "Estoy seguro que estás a punto de darme una reverenda paliza, pero defenderé mi honor hasta donde pueda, con la ayuda de Dios Todopoderoso."

"Deja a Dios fuera de este asunto, y a ver cómo te va a ti solito."

"Ya me llevó la... corriente entonces." Gabriel dijo en voz alta, moviéndose cabizbajo hacia su posición en la cancha de tenis.

Empezaron a calentarse. Gabriel pensó que no iba a ser tan difícil después de todo. Podía alcanzar la bola y pegarle con la raqueta con una habilidad más o menos decente. Se fijó, sin embargo, que tenía que correr mucho más que Theresa. Aunque estaba en gran forma física, empezó a sudar mientras que ella se mantenía fresca y relajada, pegándole a la pelotita bien, sobre la red y dentro de la cancha, sin dificultad.

El juego estuvo muy disparejo a favor de Theresa. Le ganó a su amigo en ambos sets, seis a cero y seis a cero respectivamente.

"¡Juego para la Señorita Theresa Navratilova!" exclamó el místico luego de tirarle un raquetazo sin esperanza a una bola fuera de su alcance en el último juego. "¿Sabes algo? Eres realmente muy buena para este deporte... además de ser y estar, muy buena, física y espiritualmente," el cura felicitó a su rival de tenis, estrechándole la mano por encima de la red.

"Gracias Gabriel. Eres tan gentil en la derrota como en la victoria."

"¿A dónde quieres que te lleve a comer ese almuerzo?"

"¿Conoces algún buen lugar donde sirvan mariscos frescos por aquí?"

"Hay uno en el corazón del oeste donde podemos comer un rico coctel de camarones frescos con ostiones y beber una cerveza bien helada."

"Se oye bien. Vamos a darnos un buen baño primero," la dama le dijo, levantando la cubierta de su raqueta del piso.

"¡Eso se oye aún mejor!" Gabriel exclamó. "¿Mi casa o tu casa?"

"Yo me voy a bañar en mi casa y tú te me vas a tener que bañar en la tuya hasta que te decidas qué quieres conmigo," Theresa le dijo, apuntándole al pecho con el mango de la raqueta en lo que caminaban al estacionamiento.

Ella le dio un caderazo antes de meterse al carro; él le estaba sosteniendo la puerta. Gabriel solo se rió y no dijo nada. Aún no estaba seguro que estaba listo para abandonar su ministerio para buscar vida matrimonial con su amada amiga, pero era más tentador cada día.

"Adivina a quien me encontré en el centro comercial el otro día." Theresa le dijo mientras él conducía rumbo a la casa de las hermanas.

"¿Bárbara Ann Williams?"

"¡Sí! ¿Cómo lo supiste?" Ella se volteó a verlo, sorprendida.

"Unos dicen que tengo poderes psíquicos," explicó Gabriel muy serio. Luego de una pausa, confesó, "Pero a decir verdad, Bárbara me llamó para invitarnos a los dos a su residencia mañana. Va a tener una recepción íntima en su propiedad en la Tierra de Colinas para revisar una exhibición con veinte años de sus trabajos artísticos."

"¡Ay, esa... chica! ¡Le dije que yo quería ser la que te extendiera la invitación!" dijo Theresa fingiendo enojo. "¿Vas a poder ir?"

"Ya hasta lo puse en mi calendario, y con pluma, no con lápiz," Gabriel le dijo sonriente. "¿Crees que voy a dejar pasar una oportunidad de agarrar gratis queso y vino?"

Gabriel dejó a Theresa en su casa, prometiéndole que regresaría a recogerla en una hora.

Disfrutaron su almuerzo como lo planearon. No se imaginaban lo que la presencia de Bárbara Ann Williams significaría para ambos en aquella etapa de su relación.

Bárbara era una persona muy creativa. Nunca había podido concebir un bebé, pero exploró su creatividad artística en la poesía, danza, pintura, fotografía, y música. Tocaba el piano desde una edad muy temprana y tomó clases de baile a través de sus años formativos.

Se convirtió en una hermosa, creativa, mujer madura acostumbrada a conseguir todo lo que quería. Era rica, famosa, y muy sabia en las cosas del mundo. Bárbara tenía maestría en literatura y también en artes plásticas. Se había divorciado de su primer esposo y había tenido que enterrar al segundo, quien la dejó mucho más acaudalada.

Barbie había sido la mejor amiga de Theresa en la prepa. A pesar que Barbie se enamoró de Gabriel al conocerlo en un baile de escuela, nunca se interpuso entre su mejor amiga y él. Luego que Tere se fue, sin embargo, Barbie y Gabriel tuvieron una muy breve aventura íntima una noche. Las chicas perdieron contacto. Theresa le escribió después de leer el primer libro de poesías que Bárbara publicó. Ya Theresa era para entonces hermana religiosa. Se escribieron una a la otra solo un par de veces.

Cuando Barbie volvió a Texas con su segundo marido, se encontró a Gabriel en la apertura de una exhibición de un artista local. Gabriel ya era un sacerdote. Bárbara asumió en ese entonces que Gabriel, siendo cura, ya sabía que Theresa era una religiosa, y que ella sabría acerca de él porque ambos pertenecían a la iglesia católica. Cuando Barbie se encontró con Gabriel, no le mencionó a Theresa y cuando le escribió a ella, no mencionó que había encontrado a Gabriel, ya hecho un respetable párroco en Texas.

Ella había perdido contacto con los dos desde entonces hasta que Barbie y Tere se encontraron por casualidad en un centro comercial.

Las otras tres religiosas llevaron a Theresa al centro comercial para comprarle un regalito tardío luego que supieron que había cumplido años en su casa sin decirles. Barbie andaba buscando nuevo guardarropa para el invierno. Las monjitas le compraron a Theresa un buen par de zapatos tenis ya que sabían de sus caminatas y carreras en las mañanas, para las cuales había andado usando unos tenis viejitos y ya muy acabados.

Después que se toparon con la hermosa artista, las monjitas decidieron dejar que Barbie se hiciera cargo de Theresa mientras ellas se devolvían a seguir sus propias actividades. Las dos viejas amigas de la preparatoria se fueron a comer a un exclusivo restaurante a recordar los viejos tiempos.

Cuando Tere le informó a Barbie acerca de la situación en la que se encontraba con el que había sido su novio y ahora era clérigo, Barbie la convenció que estaban hechos el uno para el otro. Se admiró que Tere no hubiera aprovechado aún la oportunidad de pescarse bien al Gabrielín.

Barbie le aseguró a su amiga que ella ya lo hubiera hecho si estuviera en su lugar. La amiga le prometió que le iba a ayudar en eso. Aún había tiempo para los dos; Tere aún podía darle a Gabriel un hijo o dos.

Barbie fraguó un pícaro plan para juntarlos en su rancho, El Jardín del Edén, el siguiente domingo con la excusa de la pre-exposición de sus obras de arte. Gabriel estaría interesado en algo así. Bárbara no se esperó a que Theresa lo invitara; temió que se iba a arrepentir y abandonar sus planes. Por eso ella misma lo invitó. Gabriel estaba muy emocionado por la oportunidad de ver la colección de arte de Barbie y compartir un tiempo con las dos amigas, allá en el tranquilo Hill Country (Tierra de Colinas).

El Rancho El Jardín del Edén en la Tierra de Colinas, a una hora en auto desde la parroquia, era en verdad, un paraíso terrenal. Tenía bastantes árboles frutales, entre ellos duraznos, naranjos, mandarinos, toronjos, plátanos, cocos; había piñas, papayas, nogales, aún un buen viñedo. Los campos estaban tan bien atendidos como campo de golf profesional.

En la propiedad había un lago artificial con una islita en el centro. La mansión estaba edificada en aquella isla. Los árboles del perímetro de la propiedad formaban un espeso bosque que encerraba aquel paraíso.

Bárbara Williams tenía un equipo de veinte hombres a su servicio, todos escogidos por ella misma, hombres de entre veintiuno y cuarenta años de edad. Ellos compartían un dormitorio en el bosque separados de la isla.

Sus rancheros, cocineros, mayordomos, choferes, guardias, secretarios, y un gerente constituían un pequeño ejército de admiradores a sus ordenes. La hacían sentir como diosa. Le cortaban el pelo, le arreglaban las uñas, le masajeaban el cuerpo, la alimentaban, la protegían, y respondían a sus más pequeños deseos. Se le había oído decir a sus amigas que no necesitaba volverse a casar porque tenía veinte hombres a su disposición.

Barbie, sin embargo, mantenía una barrera entre ella y sus empleados. A pesar que los trataba bien en sueldo y beneficios, les había advertido desde un principio no pretender poseerla. Si alguno sentía enamorarse de ella, se iba a tener que ir. La mujer se había acostado con cada uno y no quería ver a ninguno celoso. Decía quererlos a todos por igual cuando en realidad los utilizaba como objetos. Barbie se describía a sí misma como una mujer independiente, liberada, moderna, con pensamiento abierto; sin embargo, muy profundo en su interior se sentía infeliz.

El domingo en la tarde, Gabriel dejó su casa después de haber acabado con la misa de mediodía. Una parte de las escrituras se le vino a la mente.

"Después de estos acontecimientos, Dios puso a prueba a Abraham, le

dijo, '¡Abraham!' Él respondió: 'Aquí estoy'. Entonces Dios le siguió diciendo: 'Toma a tu hijo único, el que tanto amas, a Isaac; ve a la región de Moria, y ofrécelo en holocausto sobre la montaña que yo te indicaré'. A la madrugada del día siguiente, ensilló su asno, tomó consigo a dos de sus servidores y a su hijo Isaac, y después de cortar la leña para el holocausto, se dirigió hacia el lugar que Dios le había indicado. Al tercer día, alzando los ojos, divisó el lugar desde lejos, y dijo a sus servidores: 'Quédense aquí con el asno, mientras yo y el muchacho seguimos adelante. Daremos culto a Dios, y después volveremos a reunirnos con ustedes'. Recogió la leña para el holocausto y la cargó sobre su hijo Isaac; él, por su parte, tomó en sus manos el fuego y el cuchillo, y siguieron caminando los dos juntos. Isaac rompió el silencio y dijo a su padre: '¡Padre!'. Él respondió: 'Sí, hijo mío'. 'Tenemos el fuego y la leña, continuó Isaac, pero ¿dónde está el cordero para el holocausto?' 'Dios proveerá el cordero para el holocausto', respondió. Y siguieron caminando los dos juntos. Cuando llegaron al lugar que Dios le había indicado, erigió un altar, dispuso la leña, ató a su hijo Isaac, y lo puso sobre el altar encima de la leña. Luego extendió su mano y tomó el cuchillo para inmolar a su hijo. Pero el Ángel del Señor lo llamó desde el cielo: '¡Abraham!'. 'Aquí estoy', respondió él. Y el Ángel le dijo: 'No pongas tu mano sobre el muchacho ni le hagas ningún daño. Ahora sé que temes a Dios, porque no me has negado ni siquiera a tu hijo único'. Al levantar la vista, vio un carnero que tenía los cuernos enredados en una zarza. Entonces fue a tomar el carnero, y lo ofreció en holocausto en lugar de su hijo. Llamó a ese lugar: 'El Señor proveerá', y de allí se origina el siguiente dicho: 'En la montaña del Señor se proveerá'. Luego el Ángel del Señor llamó por segunda vez a Abraham desde el cielo, y le dijo: 'Juro por mí mismo — oráculo del Señor—: porque has obrado de esa manera y no me has negado a tu hijo único, yo te colmaré de bendiciones y multiplicaré tu descendencia como las estrellas del cielo y como la arena que está a la orilla del mar. Tus descendientes conquistarán las ciudades de sus enemigos, y por tu descendencia se bendecirán todas las naciones de la tierra, ya que has obedecido mi voz'". (Génesis 22:1-18)

El místico recordó tener una pequeña charla con una estudiante de prepa antes de la misa de doce acerca de una tarea sobre la obra de Lorenzo Ghiberti, El Sacrificio de Isaac, un famoso relieve de bronce del Siglo XV que se halla en Florencia, Italia. Gabriel le dijo a la chica donde podría encontrar el pasaje bíblico referente a esa obra maestra del arte italiano.

"Fue creada por el maestro de Donatello," le dijo a la colegiala y también le comentó de otros puntos interesantes acerca de la obra de arte.

Gabriel caviló sobre el pasaje, pero la presencia de un venadito que iba cruzando la carretera enfrente de su carro lo saco de sus pensamientos.

El clérigo apachurró el pedal del freno y torció su vehículo a la derecha para evitar arrollar al animalito. Se sintió aliviado al mirar por el espejo retrovisor y ver que el venadito estaba bien al tiempo que se reunía con su madre del otro lado del camino. El cura se olvidó de lo que iba pensando y encendió el radio en su estación favorita de música clásica.

Gabriel arribó al rancho de Bárbara a las 2:30 de la tarde. Ella abrió el portón de entrada a control remoto. Después que manejó a lo largo de un serpenteante caminito de asfalto hasta el lago, el ministro estacionó su auto cerca de un embarcadero y admiró la belleza de aquel paraíso artificial.

Era otra cálida tarde de otoño con unas cuantas nubes proveyendo alivio contra el ardiente sol de Texas. Barbie vino a recibirlo en una lancha.

Mientras Gabriel caminaba rumbo al bote, se fijó que había varios carros lujosos en el estacionamiento con techo en donde dejó su Curimóvil, una limusina, un carísimo carro deportivo, un exclusivo sedán de cuatro puertas, un lujoso y enorme vehículo deportivo, y una camioneta nuevecita. El sacerdote le sonrió a Barbie quien agitaba su mano desde la lancha.

En cuanto abordó, la mujer lo abrazó y lo besó. Él notó que su largo vestido rojo era de un material muy delgadito y suave, el cual revelaba que no traía ninguna otra prenda abajo. El Padre Gabriel se volteó alrededor a admirar el bello paisaje.

"Es un sitio en verdad muy hermoso, Barb."

"Gracias Gabrielín. Mi finado esposo y yo lo construimos justo del modo que lo queríamos. Es muy triste que él no alcanzó a disfrutarlo."

"¿Te falta servidumbre? ¿Por qué no enviaste a alguien por mí?"

"Oh, dejé ir a todo mi personal libre por el fin de semana. Quería que esta pequeña recepción fuera muy íntima."

"¿Ya están todos los invitados aquí?" preguntó Gabriel, tratando de adivinar quien más podía haber sido invitado.

"¡Sí, Señor! Usted es el último de la lista."

El viajecito a la isla fue breve. El cura saltó de la lancha y le ofreció la mano a Barbie. Cuando ella salió del bote, el vestido se le abrió y expuso sus torneados muslos. El Padre G mejor volvió sus ojos a la mansión y sus jardines. Ella mantuvo su mano agarrada y caminó junto a él colina arriba.

"¿Qué te parece mi humilde casita?" preguntó ella con gran orgullo.

"¡Magnífica! ¡Es en verdad un palacio en medio del paraíso!"

"Por eso le pusimos el Jardín del Edén. Tenemos una variedad muy amplia de frutas y flores, animalillos, agua en abundancia... ¡solo lo mejor!"

Ella le apuntó a unos ejemplos mientras subían por el camino empedrado con un arroyito por un lado. El ministro escuchó música emanando de la imponente mansión. Había una deliciosa fragancia en el aire; el panorama alrededor era precioso. La atractiva mujer sosteniendo la mano de Gabriel era muy hermosa; su manita se sentía cálida y suave. El sacerdote no podía menos que apreciar el estar rodeado de tanta belleza sensual.

El místico se detuvo un segundo al tener una visión. Un hombre se estaba disparando en la boca y luego cayó sobre una mesa junto a una nota que él dejó, explicando su suicidio. Tenía escrito el nombre de Bárbara.

"¿Qué te pasa Gabriel?" preguntó Bárbara al ver que se detuvo de caminar y pareció de repente encontrarse lejos de ahí.

"¿Cómo murió tu marido?" le preguntó él al comenzar a andar de nuevo.

"Le creció un tumor canceroso en el cerebro. Se retiró de sus negocios como inversionista y se vino conmigo para Texas para construir este lugar donde pudiera vivir sus últimos días. Vivió otros dos años después que se lo hallaron, pero su condición se empeoró después que le dio una embolia. Tres meses después murió al estar dormido. Más delante me enteré que haces milagros. Lástima que no sabía, o te hubiera pedido que lo curaras."

"Yo solo hago la voluntad de Dios," explicó Gabriel. "Él es el sanador y el hacedor de milagros. Solo soy instrumento de su amor y misericordia, pero lo que tiene que pasar va a pasar, sin importar que tanto tratemos de cambiarlo o evitarlo. Debemos aprender a interpretar las señales del camino y estar dispuestos a cumplir con nuestro destino."

Llegaron a la entrada de la mansión.

"Hablando de destino..." Bárbara comentó al tiempo que entraban al suntuoso interior.

"¡Hola, Gabrielín!" una voz familiar le dijo en bienvenida.

Tere estaba ahí, en un espléndido vestido blanco. La hermana religiosa se veía como una hermosa novia; su cabello castaño rojizo estaba atado encima de su cabeza, exponiendo la tersa piel de su cuello. Aún desde unos metros Gabriel percibió que Tere había sido ungida con un perfume muy caro. ¡Hasta andaba maquillada!

274

"¡Hola, Tere! ¡Guau, te ves sensacional!"

Bárbara notó cómo se miraron, y se sonrió con picardía. Parecía que la hubieran borrado de la escena, así que se aclaró la garganta para romper el encanto bajo el cual había hecho Tere caer a Gabrielín.

"¡Ajem... ajum!"

Ambos, Gabriel y Theresa voltearon a ver a Bárbara.

"¿Se podría usted, por favor, despojar de sus zapatos y calcetines, Señor... Padre Gabriel Infante?"

Barbie le mostró sus pies descalzos y también los de Theresa en la alfombra blanca. Él inmediatamente cumplió con su petición.

"¡Oh, seguro! No sabía que observabas esa vieja costumbre oriental."

"También arráncale el saco y ese collar de clérigo, ¿Me haces favor, Tere? Mientras que voy a traer algo para beber," dijo Barbie dirigiéndose al bar.

Tere le ayudó a Gabriel a quitarse el saco y el collar romano.

"¿En donde están todos los demás?" preguntó Gabriel mientras que Tere ponía su ropa en un armario cercano.

"¡Somos todos, Amigo!" Barbie anunció, ofreciéndole una copa de vino tinto. "Somos solo mis dos mejores amigos en el mundo, y yo, ¡le artiste!"

La anfitriona sonrió, pasándole su copa de vino a Tere.

El Padre Gabriel miró su copa y recordó que había bebido bastantito del vino consagrado en las tres misas de esa mañana. Menos gente que de costumbre había participado del cáliz, así que él acabó bebiéndose lo que quedaba. Siempre estaba consciente de la cantidad de alcohol que ingería, pero pensó que no sería problema beber un poco más.

Barbie ofreció el brindis mientras chocaban sus copas, "Por viejos amigos que se han vuelto a reunir, ¡que sigamos siendo siempre amigos! ¡Salud!"

¿Cómo podía Gabriel rehusarse a beber con tan encantadora compañía? Paladeó el vino y lo encontró excelente. El sistema musical estaba tocando "Pequeña Serenata Nocturna" de Mozart. Gabriel cerró los ojos para saborear el vino y escuchar la pieza. El dulce perfume emanando de las dos mujeres lo engolfó y armonizó con la música y el sabor del excelente vino.

Abrió de nuevo los ojos y miró a las dos bellezas esperando que dijera algo. Se sonrió, colmado de placer sensual, y recorrió con sus ojos el ricamente decorado interior de la mansión.

"¡Todo esto es estupendo! ¡Gracias Señor por darnos la vida para que disfrutemos de estas cosas, especialmente el amor de nuestros amigos!"

"¡Amén!" Sor Theresa dijo y le chocó la copa de vino.

"Escúchenme, muchachos, aliviánense un poco de su religión," Barbie les dijo. Empezó a caminar a otro salón, haciéndoles señas que la siguieran. "Están aquí para divertirse. Ya sé que ustedes son religiosos profesionales, pero por esta tarde, limítense a ser simplemente un hombre y una mujer, Gabrielín y Tere, mis queridísimos viejos amigos. Vamos a empezar un gran viaje a través del tiempo. Tenemos tanto de que platicar, y les he preparado una noche inolvidable."

La anfitriona se detuvo a la entrada de otro espacioso salón.

"Déjenme ser su guía. Bienvenidos al Jardín del Edén, en donde los sueños se convierten en realidad."

Chocaron las copas de vino otra vez y bebieron más del exquisito vino tinto. En el salón había una mesa con galletitas tostadas, carnes frías, quesos, fruta picada, otros vinos, agua, hielo, vasos de cristal, servilletas y utensilios de plata. El hambriento sacerdote agarró algo de comida.

Barbie les mostró una galería con veinte años de sus obras, dibujos, pinturas, fotografías, esculturas, poemas, y una serie de fotos de unos años antes con ella posando desnuda para una revista popular.

El estilo artístico de Barbie era sensual y muy rico. Sus arreglos y composiciones contrastantes eran bien definidos y llenos de energía. Les explicó sus piezas favoritas con gran detalle mientras la música de Chopin, Beethoven, y Brahms se escuchaban en su magnífico sistema acústico.

Cuando terminó su presentación, Barbie se volvió hacia su diminuta audiencia y se inclinó.

"¡Bravo!" Gabriel la vitoreó.

Theresa se le unió en el aplauso y le dijo, "¡Eres de veras muy buena artista, Barbie!"

Gabrielín miró a Tere y meció la cabeza en desacuerdo.

"¿Buena? ¡Es grandiosa!"

El hombre caminó hacia la pared y le apuntó a una pintura de una flor, la cual le recordaba el trabajo de Georgia O'Keeffe.

"¡Mira nada más esto! Algunas veces quisiera tener la sensibilidad de una mujer para poder pintar de esta manera, y esos poemas... ¡Dios Santo! No puedo imaginarme a mí mismo tratando de crear tal belleza."

Barbie estaba halagada con sus comentarios y les llenó las copas de nuevo. El ambiente era muy excitante mientras ellos bebían y comían sus bocadillos muy contentos. Luego se trasladaron al salón de música.

Barbie fue a apagar el sistema de sonido. El Padre Gabriel se le acercó a la Hermana Theresa para susurrarle al oído.

"En verdad te ves fantástica esta tarde, mi Amor."

"¡Gracias!" ella le dijo, sonrojándose.

Tere se sentó al piano para tocar un animado tango argentino de memoria. Barbie entró de nuevo al salón, excitada.

"¡Sí, sí, me encanta ese!" Bárbara tomó la mano derecha de Gabriel y se la acomodó en su cinturita diciendo, "¿Bailamos?"

Gabriel volteó a ver a Tere. Ella le asintió con la cabeza, aprobando que bailara con la amiga en lo que ella seguía tocando. Al final de la melodía, Gabriel hizo girar a Bárbara, la sostuvo de la cintura y la reclinó hacia atrás espectacularmente para un gran final. Ella se rió.

"Me gusta esa posición, es tan... ¡dramática!"

Mientras Gabriel bebía un poco más de su vino, se acordó de un chiste y se los contó a las amigas.

"Una mujer fue a ver al dentista porque le dolía mucho un diente. El doctor examinó la picadura y le informó a la mujer, 'Me temo que vamos a tener que sacarle ese diente, Señorita.' La mujer, horrorizada con la idea de la dolorosa extracción dijo, '¡Ay, no, prefiero tener un bebé!' Así que el dentista le dijo, 'Bueno, decídase porque tendría yo que ajustar la silla '"

Las mujeres se cubrieron la boca y se rieron. Entonces Tere le pidió a Barbie que cambiara de lugares con ella. Tere se acercó a Gabriel e hizo una reverencia antes de empezar; él se inclinó ante ella como si fuera realeza y la tomó de la mano y la cintura. Barbie tocó una vieja canción romántica. Gabriel reconoció la melodía y empezó a cantarla.

La acústica del salón era tan buena que aún él quedó impresionado con el sonido de su propia voz. La canción romántica habla acerca de dos extraños que se convirtieron en amantes una noche, durante un baile.

Barbie tocó el piano con pasión, excitada de verlos bailando como si fueran los únicos seres vivientes en el mundo entero, perdidos en los ojos uno del otro. Se sintió un poco envidiosa de su profundo amor.

Gabriel aspiró el perfume de Theresa y sintió su suave carne en sus manos mientras disfrutaba la música y el baile. El vino ya ejercía efecto en su pensamiento; se sentía relajado y muy contento. Gabriel continúo la canción hasta el final. Theresa reposó la cabeza en su pecho mientras que Bárbara tocaba las últimas notas de la pieza.

"Gracias, Gabriel, estuvo muy hermosa."

"Vamos a darle las gracias a Barbie por la música y el gran ambiente," sugirió Gabriel, llevando a su compañera de la mano hasta la pianista.

Los tres amigos se abrazaron y se besaron entre ellos, muy alegres.

"¡Creo que morí y he llegado al cielo!" exclamó Gabriel.

"¡Oh, no te has muerto, Amigo mío, y aún no has visto nada!" Barbie le comentó, saliendo del salón de música con los dos amigos detrás de ella.

"¿Soy yo, o es que de veras está haciendo mucho calor?" Bárbara dijo, abriendo las puertas dobles que daban a un patio en la parte de atrás.

"¡Yo me siento bien!" declaró Gabriel, empinándose lo que le quedaba de su tercera... ¿o cuarta? copa.

"¡Yo también!" Tere les dijo, imitando a Gabriel en empinarse el resto de su vino.

Barbie se les acercó para volver a llenarles las copas. El cura se rehusó pues ya estaba "demasiado contento." Tere sí aceptó que se la rellenara. Gabrielín pidió que le sirviera agua helada en lugar del vino.

"¿Puedes transformar el agua en vino?" preguntó Bárbara, dándole un vaso de agua con hielo.

"¡No! ¿Qué clase de pregunta es esa?" Gabriel le dijo, bebiendo un poco de su agua.

"¿Qué no hizo Jesús eso en una fiesta?" preguntó la anfitriona, jugando.

"Sí, en una boda en Cana, pero fue porque había necesidad de evitar una vergüenza para la familia. Además, hay mucho más acerca del significado de sus acciones al transformar el agua a vino. No fue solo por presumirles sus poderes," el ministro explicó mientras caminaban hacia el patio.

Había una pequeña cascada, una piscina con deslumbrante agua cristalina, una tina con agua caliente burbujeante y un hermoso jardín.

"Bueno, ando ardiendo, así que me voy a tirar un clavadito. ¡Vénganse!"

Barbie se desabotonó su largo vestido y lo dejó caer al piso. Se volvió hacia ellos toda desnuda y los trató de animar a seguir su ejemplo.

"¡Vamos, muchachos! ¿A qué le tienen miedo? El agua está deliciosa y no hay nadie más que los vaya a ver echarse un chapuzón al natural."

Theresa se tomó un trago de vino y comenzó a desabotonarse el vestido.

Pasmado, Gabriel se le quedó viendo dejar resbalar su vestido al piso como Barbie lo había hecho y luego lanzarse a la piscina. Él puso su vaso de agua sobre la mesita del patio y se disculpó.

"¿En dónde está el baño?" preguntó Gabriel, entrando a la casa.

"En la puerta de la izquierda en cuanto entras," le informó Barbie al tiempo que se metía al agua por los escalones, "¡Apúrale, Gabrielín!"

Tere nadó suavemente, cruzando la piscina. El sacerdote se metió al baño por unos minutos. Cuando regresó, traía únicamente una toalla blanca enredada alrededor de la cintura.

"¿Qué te pasa, Gabriel? Tú también eres artista, no me digas que tienes problemas con la desnudez," dijo Bárbara, tanteando a su amigo.

Se quitó la toalla y agarró su vaso de la mesita para meterse a la alberca usando los escalones.

"No. Tienes toda la razón. Lo que pasa es que yo..."

"¿Nunca has hecho esto antes?" adivinó la anfitriona, completando su expresión.

Las dos se rieron bajito, paradas con el agua hasta los hombros en lugares opuestos de la alberca, observándolo entrar al agua por la escalinata. El Padre G caminó por el agua y se detuvo cuando le llegó al pecho.

"La verdad, ya había hecho algo así antes, una vez."

Las mujeres se rieron otra vez, sorprendidas por su declaración.

"¿Cuándo fue eso?" Tere le preguntó, intrigada.

"Una vez que estaba en Múnich, Alemania. Me detuvieron ahí por un día porque mi avión tuvo problemas mecánicos, así que me salí a ver la ciudad a pie. Era un día caluroso; por eso, decidí ir a unos baños públicos. Para mi sorpresa, era un baño mixto. No me di cuenta hasta que ya estaba adentro y miré a todas las mujeres que había ahí. No hablo alemán, así que no había entendido el anuncio del frente. Tengo que admitir que estaba sorprendido al principio, pero luego vi que todo mundo estaba actuando muy natural. Así que decidí mezclarme entre la gente. Me bañé, me dieron un masaje, y una afeitada. Hasta me lavaron mi ropa. ¡Salí como nuevo, refrescado y enriquecido! Déjenme decirles que fue toda una experiencia para mí."

Los tres se rieron.

"¡Tienes razón!" Barbie le dijo para darle credibilidad a su relato. "Yo he estado en esos lugares en Europa. La gente de allá es mucho más liberal en cuanto al nudismo, la sexualidad, y el cuerpo humano."

"¿Y que tal tú, Tere?" preguntó Barbie, volteando a ver a su amiga con curiosidad.

"Bueno, ¡sí! algo así... Fue en Europa también, en España."

La monjita se ruborizó y sonrió, avergonzada. El Padre G le dio un buen trago a su bebida y esperó escuchar su historia. Se fijó que su agua sabía sospechosamente como vino. Miró su vaso más de cerca.

"¡Ey, esta no es agua; es vino blanco!"

"¡Un milagro!" exclamó Barbie. "Creí que habías dicho que no podías convertir el agua en vino."

Gabriel bebió de su copa y volteó alrededor buscando la respuesta. Sus ojos descansaron en una botella abierta de vino blanco que estaba sobre la mesita donde había dejado su vaso antes de ir a meterse al baño.

"¡Tú... infeliz, Chiquilla Traviesa!" él gritó, salpicando de agua a Bárbara en la cara. "Tú fuiste la que me cambiaste mi agua por vino."

Todos se rieron de nuevo.

"¡Lo que sí, es un magnífico vino!" admitió Gabriel, echándose otro poco. "Lo siento mucho, Tere, nos ibas a contar de tu escapada en España."

"¡Oh, sí! Bien, pues, pasó hace mucho. Yo todavía estaba joven."

Se detuvo por un momento y sintió los ojos de sus dos amigos clavados en ella, esperando el resto de los detalles.

"Decidí ir a una playa nudista en Barcelona. Me sentí rara. Yo no soy una artista como ustedes. Traía al principio una toalla de playa amarrada como bata cubriéndome. Me la quité y corrí al mar. La playa estaba llena de gente. No creí que nadie se hubiera fijado en mí, pero un guapo español se me acercó nadando y comenzó a hacerme plática. Me invitó a salir con él, pero yo le mostré mi anillo y le dije que no podría. Fue muy amable y me piropeó antes de irse nadando a buscar a alguna otra chica."

Barbie se sonrió y le preguntó, "¿Eso fue todo?"

"¿Andabas completamente desnuda entonces, como ahorita?" intervino Gabriel antes que Theresa dijera nada.

"No, solo con el pecho descubierto."

Theresa comenzó a nadar rumbo al lado hondo de la piscina.

"¿Cómo se llamaba?" Gabriel le preguntó en voz alta.

Tere dejó de nadar, volteó a verlo, y le preguntó, "¿Quién?"

"El peladito ese, el español."

"¡Rodrigo!" contestó Tere, sorprendida del tono celoso de Gabriel.

"Rodrigo es un bonito nombre de hombre," Bárbara comentó.

"Yo no dije que era un pelado. ¡Fue todo un caballero!"

Tere se jaló sobre la orilla de la alberca para salir del agua, dio unos pasos y se tiró otro clavado graciosamente. Gabriel se acabó su vino blanco. Tere nadó bajo el agua y fue a salir de nuevo a la superficie junto a él.

"¿Cómo se llamaba la vieja esa que te dio el masaje en Múnich?"

"Mónika... y no estaba tan vieja."

"He oído cosas acerca de esas Mónikas," Tere le dijo con los ojos entrecerrados.

"¡Solo fue un masajito!" protestó él, con una amplia sonrisa, fingiendo inocencia. Gabriel tomó el rostro de Theresa entre sus manos y la jaló cerca de él para decirle, "¡Que hermosa eres, Tere!"

Bárbara interrumpió el momento.

"Pensé que Gabriel podía caminar sobre el agua. ¿Cómo fue que se hundió igual que nosotras al meterse a la alberca?"

Gabriel se volteó a ver a Tere, sorprendido. Theresa solo se encogió de hombros en respuesta a su mirada.

"Jesús podía andar sobre el agua, Barbie. ¡Yo corrí para no hundirme!"

Los tres se rieron de nuevo.

"¡Ay muchachos, se ven tan bonitos juntos!" dijo Barbie, acabándose su vino. "Me estoy inspirando al verlos. ¿Posarían para mí? Creo que podría hacer una serie de imágenes mezcladas con poesías... acerca de amor perdurable, eterno, invencible, apasionado y tierno amor, pero necesito su ayuda. ¿Por favor? ¿Sí? ¿Por favorcito?" ella les suplicó al verlos titubear.

Los dos amantes se miraron entre ellos y se sonrieron de acuerdo.

"¡Vamos haciéndolo!" anunció Tere con una enorme sonrisa. Se estaba sintiendo bien relajada para entonces.

"Somos tuyos," dijo Gabriel de acuerdo con Tere, "¿Qué quieres que hagamos?"

"Este no es buen sitio," dijo Barbie, saliéndose de la piscina, buscando el lugar adecuado. "¡Ya sé, ya lo tengo! Vamos al lago," dijo ella mientras sus ojos seguían el arroyito que corría hasta el lago. "Quiero solo naturaleza. No objetos artificiales, solo agua, árboles, flores, sol, nubes, aves... y ustedes dos. Déjenme ir por mi cámara. No se me vayan a ir a ningún lado."

Bárbara se secó un poco con la toalla de Gabriel antes de entrar a la casa.

Tere abrazó a Gabriel; todavía estaban en el agua.

"¿Qué te parece, Gabrielín?"

"¡Muy tarde para echarnos atrás! Pero ella es una gran artista. Estoy seguro que va a hacer algo hermoso; ya lo verás."

Gabriel le acarició la carita; ella corrió las manos sobre sus hombros.

Aprovechando la situación, se enlazaron en un largo, apasionado beso. Sintieron como que sus almas se habían fundido en aquel dulce momento.

Barbie regresó con un sombrero y una bolsa de lona atravesada por su tórax, pero aún sin ropa. Le aventó una manzana a Gabriel.

"Es todo el equipo que necesitarán para esta sesión de fotografías."

Los tres se fueron hacia la orilla del lago a trabajar en su proyecto.

"Ay, me siento como Eva en el Jardín del Edén," dijo Theresa, agarrada de la mano de Gabriel.

"Sí, y yo me siento como Adán. Debe haber sido lindo estar ahí," Gabriel dijo, tratando de mantenerse relajado.

"¿Y yo quién soy entonces, muchachos?" preguntó Barbie al oír su conversación, "Se me hace que entonces yo vengo siendo la serpiente en el jardín, ofreciéndoles que coman del fruto prohibido. ¿No?"

Los tres se carcajearon.

"¡Lo que sí te tengo que decir es que eres una serpiente muy bonita, Barbie!" bromeó Gabriel, viéndola contonear las amplias caderas al descender hasta la orilla del agua, aún buscando el mejor lugar.

Había ahí tres caballos atados a un árbol cerca del agua, uno blanco, uno negro, y uno dorado. Barbie invitó a los amigos a pasearse a caballo a puro pelo. Los animales no tenían sillas, solo riendas.

Los dos amantes se vieron y estuvieron de acuerdo con su amiga quien les iba a servir de guía. Barbie montó el semental blanco que era inquieto y solo escuchaba la voz de su ama. Tere se paseó en la vieja yegua negra y Gabriel en la joven yegua dorada.

Se fueron a admirar los paisajes alrededor de la propiedad. Tere se sentía un poco atemorizada que alguien los fuera a ver desnudos, pero Barbie le aseguró que no había ningún otro ser humano en su propiedad. Todo el personal estaba fuera por el fin de semana.

El sitio era increíble; y los colores del otoño hacían los paisajes más excitantes. Era el último de los días cálidos del otoño. El clima más fresco había ya sido pronosticado para la siguiente semana. El agua del lago estaba fría, pero la aguantaron diciendo que estaba refrescante.

La artista llenó varios rollos de película con fotos esa tarde.

Hizo que la pareja se abrazara y se besara y se tocaran el uno al otro de muchas maneras. Corrieron y rodaron por el pasto como niños.

Entonces los llevó a un lugar donde el suelo estaba muy suave, y los hizo que se cubrieran de lodo hasta que acabaron como dos figuras de barro. Después se metieron al agua fría y se lavaron la mayor parte del lodo que se habían embarrado antes de regresar a la mansión.

El sol ya estaba desapareciendo.

"Vamos a la casa a darnos un buen baño. ¡Después cenaremos!" Bárbara les dijo a los amantes que estaban aún en el lago, limpiándose uno al otro las manchas de barro de la cara.

Dejaron libres los corceles, sabiendo bien que se regresarían a su caballeriza en donde tenían su comida.

Los dos amigos religiosos empezaron a escalar el caminito rumbo a la mansión, tomados de la mano, siguiendo a Barbie.

Desde la casa, la vista del ocaso era imponente. Las luces automáticas se encendieron a través de la propiedad, controladas por un reloj, al tiempo que la noche comenzaba a caer sobre la Tierra de Colinas de Texas.

Bárbara llevó a la pareja a una lujosa alcoba para invitados con bañera de hidromasaje y regadera. Les dijo que usaran lo que necesitaran y que la encontraran para cenar en la planta baja en una hora.

Los dejó solos en aquel cuarto y se fue a su propia recámara a darse un relajante baño en tina.

Gabriel levantó a Tere en sus fuertes brazos.

"¡Es hora de tu baño, Niña Mugrosa!"

Ella pataleó y gritó como una niña malcriada, jugando con él.

"¡No, no, no quiero!"

"¡Oh, sí! ¿Cómo que no? ¡Te voy a dar uno muy bueno ahorita mismo!"

La metió a la regadera y le abrió a la llave del agua fría.

"¡Aaaaaaaah!" gritó Tere, sintiendo el agua helada en el pecho.

Ella lo pescó de la barba y lo jaló al interior con ella.

"¡Aaaaaaaah!" grito él también al sentir el frío líquido sobre su espalda.

Barbie los oyó riéndose, gritando, y divirtiéndose. Sonrió, pensando en lo bien que su plan había funcionado. Brindó ante su imagen en el espejo antes de meterse a la tina del baño con agua caliente. Cerró los ojos y se imaginó que aquellos dos ya estarían haciendo el amor.

Barbie había estado con muchos, pero Gabriel había sido el primero. Suspiró, recordando aquella cálida noche en la casa de sus papás cuando Gabriel había ido a preguntarle a ella de la desaparición de Theresa.

Afuera, el viento se comenzó a juntar en un grueso, oscuro y sucio remolino, el cual se acercó a la mansión.

Bárbara se salió de la tina y fue a cerrar la ventana. Hizo cara de disgusto percibiendo el olor a podrido que acarreaba el remolino. Cerró las cortinas de la ventana y se volvió a meter al agua; se le erizó toda la piel del cuerpo y se sintió nauseada, pero solo se encogió de hombros y se sirvió más vino.

Gabriel y Theresa estaban disfrutando la nueva experiencia de darse un baño uno al otro, lavándose el cabello, y después, muy despacio, secándose el cuerpo. Cuando acabaron, Tere fue al armario y agarró un par de batas de baño. Se las pusieron, se sentaron en la cómoda cama y se quedaron viéndose a los ojos por un rato en silencio. Gabriel fue el primero en hablar.

"Gracias por dejarme bañarte, Tere. ¡Fue sensacional!"

"¡Soy toda tuya, y tú lo sabes, Gabriel!"

Ella le ofreció sus labios. Él la besó en la boca con gran pasión. Se recostaron en la cama, y ella le acarició la cara. La miró a los ojos y le tomó la mano. Ella se había puesto su anillo de nuevo, sin pensar. El anillo que indicaba que se había prometido entera al Señor.

Los ojos del cura se posaron en el anillo. La ventana estaba abierta, y la luna se reflejaba en la simple banda dorada. Podía ver estrellas reflejadas en ella. Sintió como un choque eléctrico correrle de arriba para abajo de su espina dorsal, dándose cuenta que era una mujer de Dios a quien estaba a punto de hacer suya. Bajó la cabeza y se alejó de la dama.

"¡NO!"

Gabriel puso las manos en sus oídos donde aquellas palabras resonaban como un eco, "¡Soy toda tuya!" Se volvió y la miró, bajándose de la cama.

"Prometiste tu vida a nuestro Señor. No puedes ser mía."

"Pero yo te amo, y tú me amas... ¿Qué tiene eso de malo, Cariño?"

Él le dio la espalda. Ella lo abrazó por detrás. Gabriel estaba llorando como no lo había hecho desde que ella había desaparecido de su vida.

"Estoy comprometido con nuestro Señor primero que todo, ¡y tú también lo estás! Podemos amarnos uno al otro, pero no nos podemos tener, no de esta manera... Sería una traición a nuestro Dios," le dijo, y cayó de rodillas.

"Pero Él quiere que nos amemos uno al otro," ella alegó, caminando alrededor de él para tomar su cara entre sus manos.

"No es lo mismo que tener sexo uno con el otro."

Ella lo soltó y dejó caer sus manos a los costados; luego se alejó de él, mostrando su frustración. Se volvió airada.

"¿Entonces qué, mi Amor? Quiero decir... ¿Qué estamos haciendo aquí?"

"¡Estamos siendo tentados por el Diablo!"

Tere caminó de vuelta junto a él, quien seguía de rodillas.

"¡Vamos, Gabrielín! Esto fue planeado por Barbie después que le conté que nos habíamos vuelto a encontrar y que aún nos amábamos tanto, o más, que hace veinte años. ¿Qué tiene de malo tratar de ser feliz? ¡Barb dice que no es muy tarde! Muchos han dejado la vida religiosa por razones más pequeñas... ¡Podemos casarnos como habíamos soñado y tener niños! Tú puedes hacer toda clase de cosas; yo soy maestra. Estoy segura que podríamos hacerlo funcionar. No tendríamos que abandonar nuestra fe en Dios. Quizás fue Él mismo que nos volvió a juntar por ese propósito."

Tere estaba suplicándole, con ojos enrojecidos y húmedos de lágrimas, parcialmente por el vino y también porque estaba a punto de llorar, mirando su oportunidad escapársele de las manos.

"¿Barbie fue la que preparó esta trampa?" preguntó Gabriel, sentándose en la alfombra, asombrado por la información.

"Bueno, ella salió con el plan, pero yo estuve de acuerdo... porque te amo tanto. Estoy convencida de que quiero vivir contigo por el resto de mi vida, aún si requiere abandonar mi carrera religiosa y retractarme de mis votos."

Ella se sentó en la alfombra junto a él; él le besó la frente.

"Estarías dejando a Dios por un hombre que no vale nada."

"¡El hombre a quien quiero con todo mi corazón!"

"No soy digno de tal amor, pero me preocupa pensar que has estado recibiendo consejo del enemigo."

"¡Barbie es mi mejor amiga, no Satanás!"

No estoy hablando de Barbie, aunque me temo que ella ha sido utilizada como su instrumento."

El remolino con la entidad demoníaca se retiró furioso de la mansión y derribó un árbol de mandarinas y otro de duraznos en su camino al lago. El remolino se desvaneció a la orilla de las aguas con un gruñido ahogado.

El Padre Gabriel le puso las manos a la Hermana Theresa en los hombros y la miró a los ojos.

"Cuando acababa de llegar y venía agarrado de la mano de Barbie, tuve una visión de la muerte de un hombre. Me fijé que, sutilmente, Barbie se estaba mofando de mí acerca de salvar a su marido de la muerte, cambiar el agua en vino, y acerca de caminar sobre las aguas. ¿Por qué le contaste que había yo corrido sobre el río la otra noche?"

"Lo siento mucho."

"Siento una presencia maligna en este lugar, Theresa. Reza conmigo mi oración vespertina, para que podamos acabar con esta prueba sin rendirnos ante el plan del enemigo."

Los dos amigos se levantaron, abrieron las puertas dobles y se arrodillaron en el balcón, volteando al cielo estrellado.

"En el nombre del Padre, y del Hijo, y del Espíritu Santo," rezó el Padre Gabriel, haciendo la señal de la cruz.

"¡Amén!" respondió la Hermana Theresa.

Juntos oraron bajo la luz de la luna, pidiéndole a Dios protección, pidiéndole que bendijera a su amiga mutua, y también por que los guiara a hacer la decisión apropiada acerca de su relación amorosa.

La voz de Bárbara se oyó por el sistema de intercomunicación al tiempo que ellos terminaban sus oraciones.

"Ey, chicos, la cena está lista. ¡Vengan a comer mientras está caliente!"

Los religiosos se sintieron mejor después de su oración, así que bajaron a cenar tomados de la mano, vestidos con sus batas blancas de baño.

Las palabras del pasaje de la Biblia que había recordado más temprano ese día, acerca de la obediencia de Abraham, reverberaron en su mente.

"Juro por mí mismo –oráculo del Señor–: porque has obrado de esa manera y no me has negado a tu hijo único, yo te colmaré de bendiciones y multiplicaré tu descendencia como las estrellas del cielo y como la arena que está a la orilla del mar. Tus descendientes conquistarán las ciudades de sus enemigos, y por tu descendencia se bendecirán todas las naciones de la tierra, ya que has obedecido mi voz."
(Génesis 22:16-18)

Barbie traía una bata de seda negra y les dio una igual a cada uno de ellos.

Todos con elegantes batas, se sentaron a la mesa con porcelana china, cubiertos de plata, candelabros y copas elegantes de cristal cortado. La cena fue de carne de res en rebanadas al estilo del oeste, elote, puré de papa, ensalada verde, pan negro, vino rojo, torta de queso con fresas y café.

Barbie estaba muy parlanchina. También había ingerido más que su parte razonable del finísimo vino. Les contó cómo se había marchado de Texas a estudiar arte en Chicago. Se casó con un jugador de básquetbol llamado James Jackson, pero aquello acabó en divorcio después de tres años.

Barb se cambió a Nueva York donde consiguió maestría en literatura. Ahí se encontró a Brian Fleming que era de la edad de su padre; sin embargo, era un hombre inteligente, dulce, y muy exitoso como manejador de inversiones en Wall Street. La convenció que se casara con él.

Theresa le preguntó a Bárbara acerca de sus padres y sus hermanos.

"Mis viejos aún tienen su restaurante de barbacoa vaquera y servicio de banquetes en el este de San Antonio. Mi hermana, Laura, está felizmente casada con un miembro del servicio militar; ellos viven en Alemania. Mi hermano, Leonard, es psicólogo; vive en Portland con su esposa. Tienen un niño y una niña. Yo iba a ver a mis papás cada mes, pero ya casi no voy porque critican mucho mi forma de vida. Ustedes saben. Siempre me andan tratando de llevar a la iglesia con ellos. Son bautistas muy arraigados y quieren que le de mi vida a Jesús."

Theresa se terminó su café y trató de concentrarse en las cosas buenas que Barbie había compartido con ellos.

"¡Guau, eres toda una mujer de éxito! Nomás mírate a ti misma, madura, liberada, independiente, inteligente, con mucho talento, hermosísima, saludable, rica, y famosa. ¡Has sido bendecida, Chica!"

"¿Entonces por qué no soy feliz?"

"Tienes un buen corazón, Bárbara Ann Williams, y el Señor tiene planes para ti. Lo que falta en tu vida es Dios," Gabriel le dijo.

Barbie levantó la mano para detener a Gabriel.

"Espérate, Gabriel. Ya les había pedido que dejaran su profesión en la puerta. Recibo suficientes sermones de esos de parte de mis padres."

Se levantó y se alejó de la mesa. Gabriel fue tras de ella. Se detuvieron en el pasillo. El sacerdote le puso la mano en el hombro.

"Está bien. Lo siento si te insulté con mis comentarios, pero te estoy hablando como tu amigo."

Bárbara le puso la mano encima de la suya.

"Lo sé, y tienes razón. Solo que este no es el momento para hablar de eso. ¿Les gustaría ver una película?"

Cuando Barb puso la mano sobre la de él, el místico tuvo otra visión. Vio al inquieto semental blanco relinchando y pateando. Derribó la barra de un portón del corral y saltó por encima de la barra de abajo, escapándose del rancho.

"¿Qué te pasa, Gabrielín?" inquirió Barbie. "Esta es la segunda vez que te me desvaneces."

Gabriel abrió los ojos muy grandes, tratando de enfocarse en la pregunta de su amiga. No la había oído. Tere se les unió entonces.

"¿Qué?" le preguntó el místico.

Ella se sonrió, pensando que el vino lo había ya afectado.

"¿Quieres ver una película con nosotras? Es una cinta para chicas, así que no sé si a ti te gusten esas."

Gabriel se sonrió y abrazó a Barbie con su brazo izquierdo y a Tere con su brazo derecho. Dentro de su mente estaba tratando de interpretar su segunda visión y preguntándose si tenía algo que ver con la primera.

"Me encantan, ¡especialmente en compañía de tan adorables chicas!"

Bárbara los guió hasta un pequeño auditorio. Las mujeres iban cada una agarrada de uno de los brazos de Gabriel.

"¡Que bárbaro, Gabrielín, tienes músculos de acero! ¿Cómo le haces para mantenerte en forma si estás tan ocupado?" preguntó Barb, palpando el musculoso brazo de Gabriel y manoseándole el pecho y el hombro.

"Él corre, nada, levanta pesas, y practica boxeo," explicó Tere.

"¿Cuándo encuentras tiempo para todo eso?" se maravilló Bárbara.

"A las cinco de la mañana, entre mi oración matinal y mi desayuno."

"¡Ugh! ¿Quién se quiere levantar tan temprano? Soy ave nocturna y que no me vengan a tratar de levantar antes de las diez, ¡jamás!" comentó la anfitriona, sentándolos en unos cómodos asientos para ver la película.

"Tere ya empezó a levantarse temprano a entrenar conmigo."

"Ustedes, loquitos, se pueden parar a las cinco, pero no me despierten antes de las diez. ¿Entienden?" Barbie les dijo, "Disfrutemos la película."

Bárbara oprimió un botón del remoto. Las luces se desvanecieron. Una cortina roja se recorrió, dejando ver una pantalla plateada, y la película comenzó. El pequeño auditorio tenía un excelente sistema de sonido.

Se relajaron y disfrutaron del espectáculo. Ya que Gabriel se sentó en medio de las dos, sintió sus manos durante la película. Cuando Barbie le tocaba la mano izquierda, se le venía una visión, un funeral, un hombre apuesto, alto, y de piel oscura, una boda, y un bebé. Cuando Tere le apretaba la derecha, Gabriel sentía que se le erizaba la piel de ese lado.

Para cuando acabó la película, era medianoche. Barb estaba animada y alerta mientras Gabriel y Theresa estaban empezando a bostezar, agotados.

La anfitriona los llevó del auditorio a una cómoda sala para oír discos viejos, ver unas fotos de sus álbumes de fotografías, y seguir charlando.

Barbie les mostró unas fotos que tenía de ellos en el zoológico y el parque municipal, evidencia de un día en el cual los tres se echaron la pinta y faltaron a la escuela. Habían estado en detención escolar el siguiente sábado por aquello, pero pensaron que había valido la pena el servir detención por haber pasado un día entero juntos.

"¿Saben? Me acuerdo que ese día les quería proponer que nos fuéramos a vivir a Utah, y convertirnos en mormones. De ese modo Gabriel podría tenernos a las dos como esposas, y así los tres podríamos vivir juntos, felices para siempre."

Los amigos se rieron.

Bárbara continuó con su confesión, "Yo estaba enamorada de ti, Gabriel, pero Tere era, y aún sigue siendo, mi mejor amiga, así que me sacrifiqué para que fuera feliz contigo. Luego nos fuimos por caminos diferentes, y ya ven lo que pasó. Afortunadamente ya estamos juntos de nuevo, y lo vamos a lograr esta vez. ¿Verdad que sí, Amiga mía?" Le guiñó un ojo a Tere y continuó diciendo, "Yo quiero ser tu dama de honor en la boda, pero si tienen una nena, me tienen que prometer que la nombrarán Bárbara."

La anfitriona estaba llena de entusiasmo y anticipación. Gabriel la detuvo, meciendo la cabeza negativamente.

"No va a haber ninguna boda, mi Amiga. Ya estamos casados con nuestras vocaciones," le explicó el párroco.

"Después de lo que pasó aquí hoy, ¿aún van a continuar con sus mismos trabajos? ¿Van a ser solamente... amantes secretos? ¡Ey, cuenten con mi silencio; mis labios están sellados! Pueden usar mi casa cuanto quieran, pero... ¿qué tal si Tere sale embarazada? ¿Cambiaría eso las cosas?"

"Si salgo embarazada, sería un acto del Espíritu Santo, ¡una concepción virginal!" Theresa dijo con liviandad.

"¿Quieres decir que...? empezó a decir la sorprendida Barbie.

"Nada sucedió en esa recámara," Tere le dijo, poniendo la mano sobre la de su amiga. "Gabriel fue todo un hombre para resistir la tentación, pero me hizo ver mi error al tratar de alejarlo de su ministerio y también en abandonar el mío."

"No lo comprendo, Tere," dijo Bárbara, incapaz de creerlo.

"Yo tampoco, Barb, pero así va a tener que ser para nosotros," Tere le replicó, encogiéndose de hombros. "Lo que sí te tengo que decir es que... ¡nos la pasamos de lo más lindo hoy!" Tere se estiró a abrazar a su amiga y luego se volvió a Gabriel diciendo, "¿No estás de acuerdo, mi Amor?"

"Este fue, sin duda, el día más sensualmente satisfactorio de mi vida," él le contestó. "Me embriagué con tanta belleza a mi alrededor. Disfruté cada segundo. No cambiaría ni una cosita si lo tuviera que hacer de nuevo, pero sé que eso nunca volverá a suceder. Por siempre les estaré agradecido a las dos por el gran placer, la alegría, la amistad, y el amor que me han dado."

Continuaron hablando, escuchando música y mirando las fotografías. Tere se quedó dormida en los brazos de Gabriel, reclinados en el sofá. Bárbara fue a traerle una cobija.

"Se pueden dormir en ese cuarto de huéspedes si quieres, Gabrielín," le dijo ella, apuntando a la alcoba donde se habían bañado.

"Gracias, pero no. Debo volver a mi parroquia. Tengo que celebrar la misa matutina y también muchos asuntos de escuela que arreglar. Es mejor que me vaya arrancando porque aún me falta un largo tramo que manejar."

Theresa se veía como un angelito dormido. Había consumido más vino ese día que cualquier otro en su vida. Gabriel le besó los labios suavemente y la acostó, poniéndole una almohada mientras él se levantaba del sofá. Bárbara arropó bien con la cobija a Theresa.

Recogiendo su collar de clérigo y su saco negro, Gabriel fue al baño a vestirse. Salió viéndose como un sacerdote otra vez. Bárbara se paró del piso y fue a encaminar al amigo.

Ya en la puerta, se detuvieron y se miraron uno al otro. Gabriel le sostuvo ambas manos a Barbie y se las besó. Le agradeció de nuevo por un día grandioso. Recordando su primera experiencia sexual con él, 20 años atrás, ella lo jaló y lo besó en la boca más como amante que como amiga. Él se sorprendió por su acción y trató de resistirse pero empezó a tener otra visión entonces.

Gabriel volvió a sus sentidos y se separó de la boca de Bárbara. Ella buscó su reacción, pero él en cambio le informó acerca de las visiones.

"Tengo buenas y malas noticias, Bárbara. A veces me llegan visiones acerca de cosas diferentes."

Barbie se le quedó viendo, incrédula.

"Deja contarte lo que acabo de ver: Larry, tu administrador, está muerto; se quitó la vida. Estaba enamorado de ti y no podía aguantar tu posición. No sería feliz con solo una parte de ti, pero estaba consciente que no te podría tener. Se dio un tiro y dejó una nota."

"Estás bro... bromeando... ¿Verdad?" tartamudeó ella.

"¿Tenías un empleado de confianza llamado Larry?"

"Sí, ¿pero cómo sabes que se dio, o que se va a dar un tiro?"

"Eso no importa. Vas a ser notificada por la policía en la mañana. Tú vas a ser sospechosa hasta que se verifique que fue él mismo quien se disparó."

"¡No bromeas!" Barbie exclamó, dándose cuenta que hablaba en serio.

Sintió que las piernas le flaqueaban y se sintió muy débil. Gabriel le dio apoyo y le ayudó a caminar a una banca del patio de enfrente, bajo la luz de un farolito, cerca de la entrada de la mansión.

"¡Es mi culpa que Larry se haya matado!" murmuró ella.

"No, Barbie. Él hizo su decisión por lo que tenía en su propia mente. No te eches la culpa por las acciones de alguien más."

El Padre Gabriel se detuvo de aconsejarle en ese momento que ella debería reflexionar sobre sus relaciones con sus empleados, lo cual había creado aquella situación. No era el tiempo apropiado.

"Deja darte las buenas noticias. ¡Tus oraciones han sido escuchadas!"

"¡Yo nunca rezo!" protestó la mujer.

"Quizás fueron las oraciones de tus padres entonces, o de tu hermana o hermano. Pienso que en tu interior tú sí has orado, a tu manera, y que esas oraciones fueron escuchadas. ¡Concebirás un hijo el año que entra!"

Él le sonrió y le puso la mano sobre el abdomen cariñosamente. Ella se mofó de sus palabras.

"¡Amigo mío, has bebido más de lo que debías esta noche!"

"Tu semental blanco, Rocky, se escapó de tu propiedad. Un hombre apuesto, alto, y de piel muy oscura te lo va a regresar. No vayas a dejar escapar a ese hombre porque será el padre de tu hijo y te llenará la vida de la felicidad que no tienes ahora. Tu reino, este Jardín del Edén va a ser vendido y tu vida cambiará por completo."

Bárbara se rió abiertamente, pretendiendo que no le creía ni una palabra de lo que el místico le había dicho, pero en lo más profundo de su ser, una pequeña chispita de esperanza apareció para su alma.

"Quédate aquí afuera por un rato, Hija mía, Dios te está, y te ha estado, esperando a que regreses a Él. Yo solo encontraré la salida."

El ministro desapareció, bajando por el camino empedrado mientras que Barbie se quedaba sentada en la banca y repetía sus palabras proféticas.

"Un hombre apuesto, alto, y de piel muy oscura será el padre de mi hijo. ¡Dios Santo ojalá que fuera cierto!"

Entonces Barb se acordó de que Gabriel necesitaría ser llevado en el bote al otro lado del lago. Se levantó y caminó cuesta abajo para alcanzarlo. Ya había desaparecido de su vista; pensó que la iba a tener que esperar de todos modos en el embarcadero.

"Gabrielín, espérame, Amigo. Yo te llevaré hasta tu auto."

Ella caminó por el empedrado caminito rumbo al embarcadero donde la lancha estaba atada. No lo oyó contestarle, pero se fijó que había agarrado un atajo cruzando el pasto mojado. Vio sus huellas como si se hubiera arrancado corriendo. La última huella de sus zapatos estaba en la orilla del muelle, pero alejada del bote. No se había subido a la lancha a esperarla. Bárbara vio a un lado y otro pero no encontró nada.

Escuchó la máquina del Curimóvil encendiéndose. ¡Ya estaba su amigo en el otro lado del lago! No podía haber nadado para cruzarlo tan rápido, a menos que hubiera... ¡corrido sobre el agua! Miró los faros del Curimóvil iluminando el camino al irse de su propiedad. Descartó el incidente y decidió irse a acostar, pero las predicciones de Gabriel se mantuvieron en su mente toda la noche. Bárbara se tuvo que levantar y, de rodillas, rezarle a Dios, como cuando era niña. Después sí se pudo dormir.

Capítulo XIV

Conclusión

El Padre Gabriel salió a correr después de recitar sus oraciones matinales. Eran las cinco de la mañana del 13 de diciembre. Muy pocas gentes andaban ya levantadas y en acción, algunos distribuidores de periódicos, unos empleados de tiendas preparándose para el día de negocios, o algunas gentes pobres esperando el autobús urbano que los llevaría a sus trabajos.

Siempre estaba pasando algo en la gran ciudad, y el cura parecía tener la suerte de tropezarse con cosas graves aún si solo había salido a dar una corridita. Disfrutaba correr porque era un tiempo a solas para meditar en las oraciones del día y estar en contacto consigo, con Dios, y Su creación.

Algunas veces estaba de regreso en casa sin saber qué tan lejos corrió ni que ruta tomó. Su corrida usualmente le llevaba de treinta minutos a una hora. Su experiencia favorita era cuando en una tibia mañana de verano una lluvia ligera lo mojaba y lo refrescaba al ir corriendo; se sentía como si estuviera en las manos de Dios esas mañanas.

En esta ocasión, iba pensando más en Theresa y menos en las oraciones del día. Era una madrugada fría de diciembre. La temporada de calor finalmente se había terminado, pero el frío no le molestaba.

El rabioso ladrido de un enorme perro suelto persuadió al clérigo a que evitara dar vuelta en una calle y continuara mejor rumbo a la carretera.

Se iba preguntando si fue la decisión apropiada desairar a Theresa en la mansión de Bárbara. Había ya renunciado a sus votos, para entregársele por completo, y él se había negado a aceptar su regalo. Aquello la había lastimado, y él odiaba pensar que podría lastimar a la mujercita a quien amaba tanto. Como siempre, se consoló a sí mismo, pensando que Dios le proveería con el camino apropiado y el alivio a su tormento.

Un rechinar de llantas lo sacó de sus pensamientos. Oyó un terrible ruido de choque de metales mezclado con quebradero de vidrios, gritos de dolor, y el pitar de un vehículo. Un accidente acababa de ocurrir en la carretera, no lejos de donde él andaba. Aceleró su paso rumbo al sitio.

Gabriel vio a un hombre tambaleante, alejándose de la rampa de salida. El hombre aventó una botella y se agarró el brazo, obviamente lastimado. Las luces de una camioneta pasando iluminaron su cara. Era un tipo en sus veintes, sangrando por la boca, y se miraba espantado. La cosa más única del muchacho que el Padre G notó fue un lunar grande sobre su pómulo derecho. El tipo se cubrió la cara y huyó.

Gabriel oyó una mujer gimiendo, pidiendo ayuda desde adentro de uno de los carros envueltos en el choque. Fue hacia allá y vio que sus ocupantes no tenían chanza de sobrevivencia. El pequeño sedan había sido aplastado por el choque de frente contra el enorme vehículo deportivo del fugitivo. Después del impacto, el carrito se había volteado y había acabado con las ruedas para arriba. Había sido culpa del chofer de la camioneta deportiva porque se había tratado de meter a la carretera por la rampa de salida.

El ministro se arrodilló al lado del carro de la mujer. Estaba consciente y sufriendo mucho. Le pidió que la tratara de sacar del auto; no iba a ser posible sin herramientas pues el carro estaba deforme. Los ocupantes del vehículo estaban atrapados. Ella le pidió que viera cómo estaba su esposo.

Gabriel fue alrededor del carrito y miró al chofer. Era un hombre en sus cuarentas, inconsciente y con un color muy pálido en su rostro. El sacerdote le tentó el cuello para sentir si aún tenía pulso. Tenía palpitación muy leve y lenta. El cura le habló al oído; él no respondió. Gabriel oró por él para que fuera perdonado y se le permitiera entrar al cielo.

Se regresó con la mujer quien seguía gimiendo. El Padre Gabriel le dijo que era sacerdote y le preguntó si quería confesarse. La moribunda mujer se le quedó viendo con lágrimas en los ojos; estuvo de acuerdo en confesarse ahí en ese momento.

El clérigo la absolvió de todos su pecados y la bendijo. Ella le pidió un favor. Él le prometió que haría cualquier cosa que le pidiera. La mujer le suplicó que se hiciera cargo de su único hijo quien había nacido ciego.

El pito de la camioneta se hizo más leve y luego se apagó. El silencio envolvió la escena mientras marido y mujer dejaban el mundo de los vivos.

El Padre Gabriel estaba orando sobre los cuerpos atrapados. Sintió la presencia de la muerte; un vientecillo helado le acarició la cara y le puso carne de gallina en la espalda. Le agradeció a Dios por la oportunidad de ayudar aquellas gentes a bien morir.

La patrulla, la ambulancia, y un camión de bomberos llegaron al sitio. El Padre G habló con el oficial de la policía y le pidió la información de los dueños de los vehículos. Las placas del vehículo deportivo reflejaban que había sido robado en otro estado. El policía le dio al presbítero el nombre y la dirección de los dueños del carrito.

Frank y Elizabeth Parker tenían una dirección en la parte noroeste de la ciudad. El Padre Gabriel le pidió al investigador enviado a la escena del accidente si podría ir con él a notificar a la familia de los finados. El Detective Gilbert Powers estuvo de acuerdo en llevarlo con él.

El sacerdote se acordó que el sospechoso había tirado una botella en el pasto, así que llevó al detective allá. Powers la mandó procesar por huellas.

Recogieron muestras de sangre del vehículo deportivo por ADN. Gabriel le dijo también que el hombre del lunar en el pómulo podría tener un brazo quebrado y quizás fuera a buscar ayuda médica, así que la policía se puso alerta para revisar los hospitales del área.

El Padre G corrió a su casa a darse un regaderazo y vestirse. El Detective Powers llegó un poco después a recogerlo.

John Paul Parker había sido nombrado en honor del Papa Juan Pablo I, quien reinó por solo un mes antes de morir. El chico había nacido ciego, como la madre le había dicho al Padre Gabriel, el mismo día en el que el pontífice murió en Roma. Parker creció y se convirtió en un joven guapo, pero su defecto le impedía vivir una vida normal. Había sido protegido por sus padres toda su vida. Ahora quedó solo en el mundo; no tenía ningún pariente conocido cercano que se pudiera hacer cargo del joven ciego.

Los ojos azules de John Paul derramaron abundantes lágrimas cuando se enteró. Parecía inconsolable, desolado, preguntándose qué iba a ser de él sin sus padres.

El Padre G le dijo al Detective Powers que él se quedaría con John para ayudarle con el funeral.

Gabriel platicó con John y escuchó su historia. Había aprendido a leer Braille, y estaba mejor educado que la mayoría de los de su edad. Al no haber tenido vida social, se había dedicado a estudiar una gran variedad de materias. Escuchaba charlas por radio, disfrutaba la música clásica, y tocaba el piano de memoria. Tenía una gran fe en Jesús.

Le aseguró al muchacho que lo iba a acompañar a través de todo el proceso. El cura enfatizó el hecho que Dios le había permitido ayudar a sus padres a bien morir, asegurándose que iban a ser recibidos en el cielo. Estarían ahí, esperando, para cuando fuera el turno de John Paul.

Dentro de su casa, John Paul se podía mover con facilidad porque ya tenía memorizado dónde estaba todo, pero nunca había andado fuera de la casa por sí solo. Nunca fue a la escuela. Solo tenía un amigo a quien le permitían ir a visitarlo cuando eran niños, pero se había cambiado de casa a otra ciudad con su familia.

La Señora Martínez, quien había sido ocupada para que se hiciera cargo mientras los padres estaban fuera de la ciudad, aún se encontraba ahí.

Frank, el papá, había tenido que ir a una conferencia en Nueva Orleáns el sábado y el domingo por su trabajo. Quería llevarse a Liz y a su hijo con él, pero John Paul les sugirió que se fueran solos. Se puso de voluntario a quedarse en casa y dejarlos que fueran solos para que se divirtieran.

La habían pasado bien en Nueva Orleáns hasta el domingo en la noche. Partieron de la ciudad a las 10:00 pm y llegaron a San Antonio justo a tiempo para encontrarse con su muerte.

El Padre G le pidió a John Paul que se concentrara en lo positivo, los mejores momentos, y su amor. El ministro dejó que John llorara y pasara por su luto en lo que él fue y se hizo cargo de hacer los arreglos necesarios para el funeral. La Señora Martínez estuvo de acuerdo en extender su estancia por unos días para ayudar al joven con el quehacer de la casa.

Gabriel entró a su oficina. Había un mensaje del Arzobispo Rosales que quería verlo. Gabriel sabía que era acerca de su relación con Theresa. El reporte escandaloso en uno de los canales locales de televisión le había llamado la atención al arzobispo. Habían exagerado el reporte del incidente en el restaurante; entonces, otras gentes le fueron a dar al prelado reportes sospechosos acerca del cura y la monjita.

Theresa llamó a Gabriel, disculpándose por no estar presente para hacerse cargo de su clase. Él le dijo que ya había hecho arreglos esa mañana para que una sustituta tomara su lugar por ese día.

Informó a las otras hermanas que Theresa no se sentía bien y se había quedado en la casa de Bárbara, lo cual era verdad porque no se sentía bien en absoluto. No solo amaneció con una tremenda cruda por todo el vino que se bebió el día anterior, sino que se sentía también triste que había tratado, sin éxito, de atrapar a Gabriel.

Theresa se declaró ser egoísta y tonta. Empezó a llorar. Para hacer las cosas aún peor, la policía estaba ahí. Le dijeron a Bárbara que su empleado supervisor, Larry Samson, había sido hallado muerto. Bárbara estaba aturdida. Larry le había dejado una carta. Ella se culpaba por su muerte, y le dijo a Theresa que Gabriel ya le había vaticinado aquello.

La profesora del octavo, la Señora Nogarelli, estaba en la oficina de la escuela, recogiendo unos papeles y tomándose un café. Se sabía que a ella le gustaba meterse en chismes. Escuchó por la puerta entreabierta al Padre G hablando por teléfono con Sor Theresa.

Se sentó ahí cerca para oír mejor, mientras fingía leer el periódico.

"No se tú, Tere, pero yo tuve la tardeada más hermosa de mi vida contigo ayer en el Jardín del Edén."

Esther se preguntó a qué clase de tardeada se podría referir el cura.

"Por favor, no te sientas mal acerca de lo que pasó entre nosotros," continuó diciendo el párroco.

Nogarelli levantó las cejas y se echó un traguito de café, imaginándose.

"Estoy seguro que las cosas se van a arreglar de un modo u otro."

La maestra se sonrió con malicia. Sus sospechas acerca de la tórrida relación entre los dos compañeros de trabajo se estaban confirmando.

"Creo que me encuentro en problemas ahora," declaró el Padre Gabriel.

Esther se inclinó hacia la puerta para no perderse ni un detalle.

"El arzobispo ya oyó de lo de nosotros y me quiere ver hoy mismo."

Esther casi se cayó de su lugar en la orilla de la banca por inclinarse junto a la puerta. Echó un vistazo alrededor, pero no había nadie en la oficina que la viera espiando la conversación telefónica privada del director.

"No. No le temo a nada... ¿Qué es lo peor que crees que pueda pasar? ¿Que me corran de la iglesia? Si he aprendido una cosa en esta vida es esto: tengo un destino que cumplir, y lo cumpliré con gusto porque eso es lo que Dios ha planeado para mí, y para ti también. ¡Sí! Siempre te amaré, pase lo que pase... Escúchame. Tómate tu tiempo por allá, y dime si vas a necesitar otro día o dos para lidiar con ese problema. Regrésate cuando ya te hayas recuperado por completo."

Nogarelli se tapó la boca; sospechaba que Theresa ya estaba embarazada y probablemente fue a tener un aborto.

"Tengo un joven ciego que cuidar. Su moribunda madre me pidió esta mañana que me hiciera cargo de él. También me tengo que hacer cargo de un funeral doble para sus padres. Murieron en un accidente."

La Señora White, la secretaria, regresó a la oficina. Nogarelli se levantó de pronto y dobló el periódico. Se empinó el resto de su taza de café, se salpicó su blusa blanca y se escaldó la lengua con el café caliente. White vio lo que le pasó, pero no hizo ningún comentario.

El Padre G fue a ver al arzobispo en sus oficinas de la arquidiócesis.

El arzobispo tuvo una larga charla con el Padre Gabriel. Por un lado, tenía que tomar acción acerca de las acusaciones de conducta inapropiada en contra de su subordinado; por el otro lado, no quería perder al sacerdote más carismático de su arquidiócesis.

Gabriel admitió que tenía una relación amorosa con Theresa y explicó la relación que habían tenido de jóvenes. Las noticias eran verdaderas en cuanto a su relación con la religiosa. Habían salido en una cita el día de su cumpleaños. Bailaban y jugaban. Se amaban intensamente. Los chismes de una relación sexual y que él ya la tenía preñada eran falsos.

Gabriel declaró que él aún era tan efectivo en su ministerio como antes; sin embargo, admitió que estaba pasando más tiempo con Theresa que con ninguna otra persona. El sacerdote le dijo al arzobispo que habían quedado de acuerdo en mantenerse fieles a sus votos pero sin abandonar su amor.

El superior le recordó a Gabriel acerca de la delicada posición pública de un ministro de la iglesia y cómo aquel tipo de escándalo le traía problemas a toda la comunidad de los fieles. Aconsejó al subordinado que se alejara de la hermana y que ocupara su tiempo con su ministerio. Gabriel debería orar por obtener la fuerza para lograrlo, pero era indispensable que se distanciara de toda oportunidad de tentación.

El prelado le ofreció asignarlo a otra parroquia en la arquidiócesis, aunque fuera temporalmente, si aquello le podría ayudar. Gabriel se rehusó vehementemente, pero luego moderó el tono de su voz y predijo que Dios le proveería una solución al tiempo apropiado.

El arzobispo estuvo de acuerdo, pero sin mencionárselo al sacerdote, pensó que él, personalmente, le iba a dar una manita al Señor.

A pesar que salió en una sola pieza de la oficina del arzobispo, Gabriel aún tenía duda en su mente acerca que su decisión de mantenerse como sacerdote célibe había sido mejor que casarse con Theresa.

Cada vez que recordaba su carita, su sonrisa, y su figura, experimentaba un ardiente deseo de seguir su pasión por ella y abandonar su ministerio. No iba a dejar de ser cristiano, podía ser un buen laico católico o un predicador protestante para así, aún servir al Señor y al mismo tiempo hacer muy feliz a la mujer que adoraba.

Alzó los ojos al cielo, abrió los brazos y le pidió a Dios una mente clara para estar seguro de lo que debería de hacer.

Se acordó que tenía varios deberes que cumplir en cuanto al entierro de los papás de John Paul. Además, caviló acerca de lo que iba a hacer con el joven; le había prometido a su madre que se haría cargo de él.

"¡Dios proveerá!" se dijo a sí mismo, y empezó a caminar con energía rumbo a su auto.

Ya en su oficina, el Padre Gabriel recibió una llamada del Detective Powers de Investigaciones de Tráfico. El sospechoso en el caso de doble homicidio involuntario no podía ser localizado. Encontraron el hospital en donde fue atendido bajo un nombre ficticio, pero se les había escurrido. Las huellas que tomaron de la botella eran legibles, pero no existían huellas similares en los archivos policiales.

"¿Cree que podría identificar al hombre si lo volviera a ver?" preguntó el detective.

"Sí, Gilbert. Estoy seguro que podría hacerlo."

"Muy bien. Le haré saber si algo nuevo se presenta. Voy a conseguir unas fotos de posibles sospechosos para que las revise. Mantenga los ojos bien abiertos, en caso que volviera a ver al tipo."

"Seguro. Te haré saber si lo veo de nuevo, o si me entero de algo acerca de él por mi parte, Detective."

El clérigo colgó el teléfono y se preguntó por qué tenía que estar envuelto en ese caso cuando ya tenía bastante de que preocuparse por su cuenta. Se repitió que Dios tiene un plan para todo aún cuando no lo comprendemos, así que continúo su día de actividades con su típica actitud alegre.

El lunes en la noche, Gabriel tuvo un sueño. Un tipo mataba a golpes a una pareja con una botellota. A pesar de ser de vidrio, no se quebraba en lo que el infeliz golpeaba al hombre y la mujer sin misericordia. Gabriel trató de correr a detener al hombre, pero sus pies se sentían pesadísimos. Se iba moviendo en cámara lenta. Aún su grito para que el asesino se detuviera era distorsionado y grueso.

El matón se estaba carcajeando, viendo los cuerpos inertes tendidos en un charco de sangre. Se bebió un trago de la botella que había usado. Luego se volteó a ver a Gabriel cara a cara y habló en un tono diabólico.

"Llegaste tarde, Gabriel... demasiado tarde. ¡Ja-ja-ja-ja-ja-ja!"

La cara del asesino se le quedó muy grabada en la mente a Gabriel. Era la misma cara del hombre del lunar. El tipo tiró la botella con sus huellas digitales impresas en sangre sobre el césped, y corrió. Gabriel volvió sus ojos a los cuerpos. Un niño ciego como de diez años, estaba llorando sobre ellos, sintiendo los cuerpos y con su cara al cielo.

"¡Auxilio, socorro, por amor de Dios! ¡Alguien... por favor, ayúdeme!"

El Padre G lo levantó y lo miró a los azules ojos ciegos; vio la reflexión de su propio rostro en ellos. El sonoro llanto de una sirena de ambulancia acercándose a la escena llenó los oídos del Padre Gabriel.

El sacerdote despertó; era medianoche. Una ambulancia pasó por ahí y siguió corriendo calle abajo.

Gabriel se levantó de la cama y fue a su escritorio. Sacó un cuaderno de dibujo y una pluma para bosquejar la cara que tenía en su memoria y había reaparecido en su sueño, del hombre con el lunar en el pómulo.

Escribió una carta, explicando que aquel era un retrato del sospechoso en el caso que el Detective Powers estaba investigando. Mandó una copia de la carta y el retrato a la Unidad de Investigaciones de Tráfico a través del fax para que el oficial tuviera la información en cuanto llegara a trabajar.

Satisfecho, se fue a acostar de nuevo para continuar durmiendo por unas horas más. Sus sueños cambiaron de dirección.

Se encontró desnudo en el Jardín del Edén. El día era muy agradable. Andaba caminando solo por la orilla del agua, admirando los paisajes y la vida a su alrededor. Un ave multicolor se posó en su hombro. Él se inclinó y recogió un conejito blanco que estaba comiendo alfalfa.

Al otro lado del lago miró a Theresa, también desnuda, agitando su mano. Dejó el conejito en el suelo y el ave voló. Tere corrió sobre las aguas del lago sin sumirse. Se abrazaron y se besaron. Una hermosa música comenzó a sonar. Se pusieron a bailar mientras se miraban a los ojos y se declaraban su amor. Una lluvia tibiecita y ligera los rodeó y los humedeció. Hicieron el amor por largo rato sobre el verde prado a la orilla del lago.

Un relámpago iluminó el cielo, y ellos se sobresaltaron con el trueno. La tibia llovizna se convirtió en lluvia helada. El día soleado se hizo gris, denso con nubes y tormenta. El lago placentero se volvió turbulento río. Los dos resbalaron y la corriente los separó; sus manos se alejaron una de la otra. El río se llevó a Theresa. La lluvia, los relámpagos y truenos continuaron. Gabriel estaba gritando su nombre. Theresa emergió del otro lado del río. Se volteó hacia él, le agitó la mano suavemente, diciéndole adiós y le envió un beso con la palma de su mano. Luego se desapareció.

Gabriel se sentó en la playa, llorando. La música de Bach seguía oyéndose entre los truenos y la lluvia. El sabor del último beso aún permanecía en sus labios. Escuchó una vez más las palabras del libro del Génesis.

"Juro por mí mismo —oráculo del Señor—: porque has obrado de esa manera y no me has negado a tu hijo único, yo te colmaré de bendiciones y multiplicaré tu descendencia como las estrellas del cielo y como la arena que está a la orilla del mar. Tus descendientes conquistarán las ciudades de sus enemigos, y por tu descendencia se bendecirán todas las naciones de la tierra, ya que has obedecido mi voz." (Génesis 22:15-18)

La lluvia se mezclaba con sus lágrimas mientras que él volvía su rostro al cielo y vio la luz regresar al firmamento que se empezó a aclarar. Abrió los ojos y se regresó del sueño a la realidad.

"Levanta tu cruz" de Johan Sebastian Bach sonaba en su radio-reloj-despertador. Llovía afuera, y él había dormido más de la cuenta.

Eran las 7:00 am en vez de las 4:30 cuando usualmente se levantaba. Gabriel se estiró y se tronó las vértebras de la espalda, agarró su librito de La Liturgia de las Horas, y se arrodilló ante su crucifijo a recitar matins.

Se preguntaba si el sueño tendría significado o si fue solo una fantasía sexual, pero se estremeció al recordar lo real que se había sentido. Gabriel se rió, pensando en la canción que lo despertó: "¡Levanta tu cruz!" Se preguntó si Theresa podría haber compartido ese sueño también. Decidió mejor concentrarse en la oración.

El arzobispo hizo una visita sorpresa a Gabriel esa mañana en la escuela. Quería hablar con Sor Theresa. El párroco le explicó a su superior que ella estaba con su amiga, Bárbara Williams, enterrando a su administrador en Fredericksburg. Necesitaba unos días para consolar a su amiga porque Bárbara se sentía responsable por el suicidio. El Arzobispo Rosales le pidió al Padre que mandara a Theresa a verlo en cuanto regresara a la parroquia.

La Señora Nogarelli pidió tener una charla en privado con el arzobispo. La mujer informó al superior eclesiástico lo que sabía acerca del romance. No le había caído bien la nueva religiosa desde que llegó; aún más, había posibilidad que si el director fuera removido de su puesto, Nogarelli podría agarrar el control de la institución como directora. Hablaron los dos por un buen rato y luego el prelado se marchó.

El Padre Gabriel tuvo una junta con su diácono, Andrés García, y con su subdirectora, Sharon Gray. Les preguntó si habían notado que él no estuviera poniendo suficiente atención a sus deberes como pastor de la parroquia y como director de la escuela.

Ambos estuvieron de acuerdo que él había estado más ausente que de costumbre y no tan envuelto en las operaciones cotidianas, lo cual les había dado oportunidad a ellos de ejercitar su poder de hacer decisiones.

También estaban de acuerdo en que ya todos sabían que el cura le estaba dando mucha atención a Sor Theresa, y que chismeaban de ellos. Dijeron que la gente sospechaba que los dos religiosos iban a dejar la iglesia y que Sor Theresa estaba embarazada. Sin embargo, también habían notado que el Padre G había andado deslumbrante y se veía más contento que nunca.

Ni el diácono ni la subdirectora tenían ningún problema con apoyar al sacerdote con cualquier decisión que tomara. De hecho, comentaron que él y Theresa formaban una pareja adorable. El Padre G les dio las gracias por su apoyo y su comprensión. Les dijo que quería tener una junta con todos los empleados para acabar con aquellos rumores el siguiente lunes. Antes de dejarlos ir, les dijo un chistecillo.

"Un cierto Padre Juanito se cansó de la vida de parroquia y decidió irse a un monasterio a buscar la paz y la soledad. Y no me estoy refiriendo a las dos hermanas Aguirre... Bueno, se presentó al superior, el Padre Frank, y fue admitido. El único requerimiento duro con el que tenía que lidiar fue el voto de silencio que todos en la orden debían seguir para permanecer en el monasterio. 'Usted no hablará, ni una palabra, en absoluto, a menos que yo se lo autorice,' le dijo el superior. El Padre Juanito asintió, y no volvió a decir palabra. Al cumplir cinco años ahí, Frank llamó a Juanito y le dijo, 'Padre Juanito, ya que está usted celebrando cinco años con nosotros, le permitiré decir... dos palabras.' Juanito lo pensó por un buen rato y dijo, 'Comida fría.' Frank levantó las cejas y le dijo, "Oh, siento mucho que le hemos estado sirviendo su comida fría. Me haré cargo de que le sirvan sus alimentos calientitos en adelante. Vaya en paz.' Cuando cumplió diez años, Frank mandó llamar a Juanito de nuevo y le permitió decir dos palabras de nuevo. 'Cama dura.' Dijo Juanito esa vez. El Padre Frank pidió disculpas y le prometió que se iba a asegurar que le pusieran un colchón en la cama al Padre Juanito. 'Vaya en paz,' le dijo Frank. Otros cinco años pasaron. Cuando Juanito completó sus quince años en el monasterio del silencio, como ya era su costumbre, el Padre Frank lo mandó llamar de nuevo para permitirle decir dos palabras más. '¡Yo renuncio!' le dijo Juanito esa vez. Frank se le quedó mirando por un momento y luego le dijo, '¿Sabe una cosa, Padre Juanito? Eso es probablemente lo mejor que pudo pasar. ¡Todo lo que he escuchado de sus labios desde que llegó usted al monasterio no han sido más que puras quejas y lloriqueos!'"

Andrés y Sharon se encaminaron hacia la puerta, riéndose.

"Ahora ustedes, ¡vayan en paz!" Gabriel les dijo, palmeando sus espaldas.

El jueves 16 de diciembre, fue el día del funeral doble. Poca gente fue, no había miembros de la familia, solo los compañeros de trabajo de Frank, de la tienda donde trabajaba como gerente del departamento de aparatos electrónicos, y unas cuantas amistades vecinas de Elizabeth. Ella tenía un título para enseñar inglés, pero había escogido quedarse en casa por los últimos veinte años para hacerse cargo de cuidar a su hijo.

Después del entierro, el Padre G se llevó a John Paul a la iglesia. Tenía varios asuntos que tratar antes que terminara el día escolar. El cura le pidió al joven que lo esperara en la iglesia. John Paul estuvo de acuerdo y abrió su Biblia en Braille para leer en lo que esperaba que su nuevo amigo se desocupara de sus deberes. John Paul estaba muy impresionado con el párroco y confió en él desde un principio. Se sentía en paz cuando el presbítero lo guiaba de la mano; ya no sentía ansiedad.

El Detective Powers llamó al pastor para agradecerle por su ayuda. Él publicó el retrato a pluma del sospechoso en las noticias. Gracias a eso, varias pistas fueron recibidas que llevaron al detective a las bodegas de una cadena de supermercados en el noreste de la ciudad. Ahí se encontró a un tipo con la descripción del sospechoso. En cuanto el policía se le acercó, el hombre huyó corriendo velozmente a pie, así que Powers lo persiguió.

El sospechoso, un mexicano llamado Rogelio Ramírez Esparza, corrió a la calle frente al negocio y sacó a una viejita de su automóvil, la derribó sobre el camellón de en medio y después se arrancó a gran velocidad con el vehículo de ella para distanciarse del detective.

Powers pidió que le enviaran ayuda de patrullas, pero tuvo que perseguir al fugitivo en su pequeño carro sin equipo de emergencia. Rogelio perdió el control del sedán donde el periférico da vuelta de norte a oeste. Se salió del camino porque se le quebró la rueda derecha de enfrente. El sospechoso corrió pero el detective de tráfico lo tacleó sobre el pasto de la orilla.

El sospechoso fue remitido al juez, y demandó le asignaran abogado. Sus huellas igualaban las de la botella; su rostro era idéntico al que el artista había dibujado, con el lunar en el pómulo. Iba a tener que encarar varios otros cargos criminales además de los dos de homicidio involuntario por los cuales Powers lo había andado rastreando.

Había un joven esperando ver al Padre Gabriel cuando terminó su charla con el detective. Un tal Marco Antonio Gallegos, quien decía ser amigo de la familia Parker. Había leído los obituarios en el periódico y quería saber a qué horas iban a ser celebrados los ritos funerales de la pareja.

El místico lo encontró en la entrada de la escuela y le informó que el funeral ya había concluido con el entierro, más temprano. El joven se vio muy desilusionado. Le explicó que él había sido amigo de la familia; jugaba con el hijo de ellos, John Paul, cuando los dos eran niños. Marco acababa de regresar a la ciudad a trabajar para un negocio local luego que terminó su carrera en ciencias de computación en otro estado. El Padre G le dijo que John estaba en la iglesia y se pondría muy feliz de verlo.

"¿Quiere decir que ya no está ciego?"

"Lo siento. Se pondrá muy feliz de saber que estás aquí. Me habló mucho de ti cuando nos conocimos."

Se fueron caminando juntos a la iglesia; Gabriel le hizo señas a Marco Antonio que no hablara, para poder sorprender a su amigo común.

"¡John Paul!" El pastor pronunció su nombre muy fuertemente en la casi vacía iglesia.

"Sí, Padre Gabriel. Estoy aquí," replicó el muchacho desde su asiento en la banca del frente.

"Te traigo muy buenas noticias, Hijo."

"Qué bueno, pero primero déjeme leerle a usted mi parte favorita de toda la Biblia: El Santo Evangelio según San Juan, capítulo nueve."

"¡Muy bien! Prosigue, Muchacho."

"Al pasar, vio a un hombre ciego de nacimiento. Sus discípulos le preguntaron: 'Maestro, ¿quién ha pecado, él o sus padres, para que haya nacido ciego?' 'Ni él ni sus padres han pecado, respondió Jesús; nació así para que se manifiesten en él las obras de Dios.'" (Juan 9:1-3)

El místico se conmovió con las palabras de la lectura y sintió al Espíritu Santo descender sobre él en ese mismo instante.

"¡Levántate, John Paul!" el sacerdote le ordenó, agarrándole el brazo.

El Padre G volteó el rostro, haciéndole la seña a Marco Antonio que se quedara quieto y se esperara justo donde estaba.

"¿Cómo curó Jesús al hombre que había nacido ciego?" Gabriel le preguntó a John en lo que caminaban a un patio afuera de la iglesia.

"Bueno, pues, Jesús... Lo hizo de un modo medio asqueroso. Hizo lodo con su saliva y tierra para embarrárselo en los ojos del pobre ciego. Luego lo mandó a que se lavara en las aguas de la piscina de Siloé."

El Padre le puso las manos sobre los hombros al joven.

"¿Tú crees que eso pudo haber ocurrido?"

"Sí, pero ¿dónde está Jesús cuando uno lo necesita? Me hubiera gustado encontrarlo hace dos mil años para que pudiera yo ver."

Gabriel se inclinó y escupió en el suelo donde había coloridas flores adornando la orilla exterior del templo. Se puso a hacer algo de lodo, lo bendijo y elevando una oración al cielo, se lo embarró en los ojos a John.

"¡Ey, órale! ¿Qué me está haciendo?" el sobresaltado joven se quejó al sentir que el ministro le estaba cubriendo los ojos con lodo. "¡Oiga, me está lastimando!" gritó él, perplejo, y le agarró al clérigo la mano.

"Fue el poder de Dios que alivió al ciego del Evangelio según San Juan. A pesar que Jesús nos dejó para ir a su Padre Celestial, nos envió al Espíritu Santo para capacitarnos a hacer lo que Cristo hizo mientras vivió entre nosotros. Dices que crees en Él; lo que hago ahora es en nombre suyo. Vamos a que te laves los ojos. Te voy a dar agua bendita."

Marco Antonio estaba viéndolos, moviendo su cabeza, sin esperanza que pasara algo. John Paul se arrodilló frente al altar con la ayuda de Gabriel y se comenzó a lavar el lodo de los ojos con la bandeja de agua bendita que el sacerdote le dio. El místico se irguió sobre él con sus manos elevadas en una oración de gracias.

Marco Antonio notó que el párroco parecía brillar al estar parado como un Cristo por encima del ciego. El cura le dio una toalla a John Paul.

"¡Aaaaah... Oh, Dios mío! ¡Veo... Puedo ver!"

John se levantó apretando los ojos y se tropezó con el sacerdote. Gabriel lo sostuvo en sus brazos.

"¡Gracias, Dios Padre Todopoderoso! ¡Gracias Jesucristo! ¡Gracias Espíritu Santo!" dijo Gabriel, lleno de alegría.

El joven abrió los ojos muy ampliamente y miró la cara del presbítero; pensó que Jesús debió haberse visto así como él cuando anduvo por la tierra. John besó al cura en las dos mejillas y se arrodilló enfrente del altar para agradecerle a Dios desde el fondo de su corazón.

Gabriel tenía lágrimas de emoción en sus propios ojos cafés. Se volteó a ver a donde Marco Antonio se había quedado esperando. También estaba de rodillas, persignándose después de haber presenciado aquel milagro.

El Padre G le hizo la seña para que se acercara; el muchacho se levantó y se apresuró a acercarse al altar.

"¿John Paul, no quieres oír las buenas noticias todavía?" le dijo al anteriormente ciego amigo, poniéndole una mano sobre el hombro.

"¿Qué cosa podría ser mejor noticia que el poder ver por primera vez en mi vida, Padre?"

"Ser capaz de ver la bondad del Señor es más importante que el poder de ver con nuestros ojos, Hijo mío. Déjame presentarte a tu viejo amigo, Marco Antonio Gallegos," explicó el párroco, jalando al visitante.

"Matony! ¿A poco de veras eres tú?" exclamó John Paul, levantándose a abrazar a su viejo amigo.

"Sí, Jopal! Soy yo."

Se llamaron uno al otro por sus apodos de niño, Matony y Jopal, que eran combinaciones de sus dos nombres. Se dieron un muy apretado abrazo.

"Regresé a la ciudad y me enteré por el periódico lo que les pasó a tus padres, mi Amigo. ¡Lo siento muchísimo, y te acompaño en tu dolor!"

"Gracias, mi Amigo. No te imaginas lo que tu presencia significa para mí hoy. Este es el día más triste de mi vida, cuando tuve que enterrar a mis dos padres... Aún así se ha convertido también en el más feliz. ¡Dios me ha otorgado el regalo de la vista, y tú has regresado!"

El Padre Gabriel los encaminó a la puerta principal.

"Ustedes, muchachos, tienen una vida entera que contarse. ¿Matony, por qué no te llevas a Jopal y le muestras el mundo?"

Marco abrazó al sacerdote y agarró la misión asignada con gran emoción y alegría.

"Ah, otra cosa que quería decirte, John. La policía ya arrestó al chofer que causó el accidente."

Gabriel se le quedó mirando al joven a los nuevos ojos; se le habían cambiado de color de azul claro a un verde oscuro.

"Padre, ya no odio a ese hombre. Lo he perdonado en mi corazón como usted me aconsejó. Ojalá que Dios tenga compasión de él."

El presbítero abrazó al joven y le dio alabanzas a Dios por haberle otorgado la gracia y la paz que se obtiene a través del perdón.

"Vamos entonces a dejar que el sistema judicial se haga cargo de él como lo encuentren justo," dijo el presbítero.

Los dos amigos se fueron con un brazo encima del hombro uno del otro al carro de Marco, un convertible azul de medianoche. John iba volteando a ver para todos lados, queriendo absorber toda la creación con la vista.

El sacerdote los miró alejarse en el auto, eufóricos. Les mandó su bendición desde la puerta principal. Volteó a ver la imagen del Cristo resucitado en el centro del santuario y le guiñó un ojo.

"Ahora veo, Señor, '...*para que se manifiesten en él las obras de Dios.'*"

Gabriel se sintió inspirado por la amistad de aquellos dos jóvenes y al ver su propia amistad con el Señor, así que comenzó a cantar una canción a Dios. Era una canción alegre que se puede cantar a un amigo humano o al mismo Dios. La potente y melodiosa voz del párroco llenó el templo en lo que cantaba desde la puerta. Algunas gentes que iban pasando por la calle le sonrieron y lo saludaron de lejos. Les contestó el saludo, sonriéndoles, pero no dejó de cantar hasta que acabó la canción.

Gabriel sintió que estaba haciendo exactamente lo que Dios quería que hiciera. Debía continuar con su ministerio milagroso y renunciar a sus ardientes deseos de entregar su vida a Theresa.

"¡La fidelidad a Dios debe prevalecer! ¡Eso era lo que el pasaje acerca de Abraham estaba tratando de decirme!"

El viernes fue un día regular de trabajo para el presbítero, misa matutina, citas de la escuela y de la parroquia, y cosas así.

Antes que se acabara el día de clases, los chicos del octavo grado se organizaron para jugar un partido de voleibol contra las chicas del mismo grado. Les faltaba a los muchachos un jugador, así que le fueron a pedir al Padre G que se les uniera en el equipo. Las muchachitas se quejaron de que era injusto que tuvieran a Dios de parte de ellos, si el Padre G jugaba en su equipo. Él se rió y les garantizó que no era así.

Una de las chicas fue y jaló a la Hermana Theresa del pasillo y le pidió que se les uniera para hacer la cosa pareja. Acababa de llegar. Theresa miró a Gabriel desde la puerta; él ya estaba en la cancha con una pelota en sus manos. Gabriel le hizo señas para que fuera a jugar con ellos. Theresa les gritó que regresaría en un minuto.

Tere volvió vistiendo pantaloncillos y camiseta, lista para jugar. Su cabello en una cola de caballo; se veía como estudiante de universidad.

La monjita empezó a servir la bola por su equipo de muchachas. Los chicos no eran tan buenos, así que empezaron a perder un punto tras otro. Un servicio de Sor Theresa le dio en la cabeza a un chico para rebotar fuera de la cancha. Ya iban siete a cero. El siguiente cayó en medio de dos jugadores de los de atrás quienes solo se miraron uno al otro esperando que el otro la levantara. ¡Ocho a cero!

Finalmente los chicos le acomodaron la bola al clérigo para que la clavara. Él se elevó y le pegó muy bonito, pero Sor Theresa la levantó antes que tocara el piso. Las muchachas pusieron la pelota en el otro lado de la red. Los dos jovencitos que fueron chocaron entre ellos y le pegaron mal a la pelota, la cual rebotó en la red para hacerlos perder otro punto más.

Gabriel corría por todos lados de la cancha, tratando de apoyar a sus jugadores, pero aún él estaba mandando la bola fuera. El servicio final se clavó sin que siquiera lo pudieran tocar para un marcador final de 15-0.

La campana sonó, indicando el final del día de clases. Los chicos concedieron su derrota ante las chicas pero prometieron que harían mejor en la revancha la semana siguiente.

Sor Theresa les dijo que probablemente harían mejor papel porque ella ya no iba a estar ahí para ayudarles a las chicas. Sor Kathryn ya había regresado de Irlanda, así que Theresa debía ahora regresarse a Europa.

Gabriel sintió que se le quebraba el corazón al oír aquellas noticias. Ya sabía que eso iba a pasar, como se le había revelado en su sueño, pero aún así era muy doloroso.

Gabriel y Theresa caminaron juntos hasta el interior de su oficina. La Señora White, la secretaria ya se estaba marchando. Theresa se sentó en el sillón. Gabriel se iba a ir a sentar detrás de su escritorio pero cambió de plan y se fue mejor a sentar junto a ella en el sillón doble.

Se miraron a los ojos, sin saber qué decir. Luego, ambos empezaron a hablar al mismo tiempo, y los dos se detuvieron, pidiéndole al otro que prosiguiera. Se rieron. El Padre G la tomó de las manos.

"Tere, tuve un sueño..."

Ella se le quedó viendo, intrigada. Preguntó, "¿Estábamos en el Jardín?"

"¡Sí! ¿Cómo lo supiste?"

"Aparentemente tuvimos el mismo sueño otra vez."

"Yo estaba en un lado del lago..." empezó a decir Gabriel.

"Y yo vine del otro lado del lago a encontrarte. Bailamos con una música que provenía de arriba y de verdad hicimos el amor. Fue la experiencia más grandiosa de mi vida. ¡Se sintió tan real!"

"Empezó a llover, muy recio..." continuó Gabriel.

"Truenos y relámpagos se dejaron venir. Fui arrastrada por la corriente, y acabamos en lados separados del lago," dijo ella, verificando que habían tenido exactamente el mismo sueño.

Se vieron con los ojos muy abiertos.

"¿A dónde te fuiste, Amor?" él le preguntó.

Ella se encogió de hombros diciendo, "No sé. Desperté en eso y eran..."

"¿Las siete de la mañana?" él completó su oración como pregunta.

"¡Sí! Me quedé dormida, pero fue el más dulce y triste de mis sueños."

"Ya sabía que esto se estaba aproximando a su fin, y que ibas a regresar a Europa.'

"¿Tú quieres que me vaya, Cariño?"

"Es la voluntad de Dios, Corazoncito. ¿Quiénes somos nosotros para oponernos? Él nos ha dado este tiempo para que lo disfrutáramos juntos. ¡y también nos concedió la gracia de encontrarnos en sueños!"

"Tienes razón. Debemos ser agradecidos, fieles, y obedientes a la voluntad de nuestro Padre," Theresa dijo, asintiendo. "Me la pasé en grande estos meses que compartí contigo. Fue un tiempo sensacional e inolvidable. Siempre te mantendré en mi corazón, junto a nuestro Señor."

Ella se secó las lágrimas de los ojos y le sonrió. Se abrazaron por un momento; entonces le dijo que tenía que irse a su casa y alistarse para partir. Él le ofreció llevarla al aeropuerto.

El Padre Gabriel fue a la casa de las monjitas a recoger a Sor Theresa esa tarde. Todas las hermanas religiosas estaban muy llorosas diciéndole adiós a la amiga. Llegaron a amar a Theresa con el tiempo que compartieron.

Tere le dio a Sor Magdalene una torta de queso que horneó para ella; sabía cómo le encantaba la comida. A Sor Mary le regaló un libro reciente de las grandes religiones del mundo porque sabía lo curiosa que era la joven en el campo del conocimiento. A Sor Carmen, quien siempre andaba con frío en el salón, pero no se quejaba, Theresa le regaló un suéter largo de lana pura. Aún para la Sor Kathryn a quien acababa de conocer, Theresa le dio un disco con música para meditar. Las abrazó a todas y les dijo adiós, expresando su deseo de mantenerse en contacto.

Las religiosas vieron a la pareja partir hacia el aeropuerto y comentaron que bien se veían juntos. Sor Kathryn descartó sus comentarios como sacrílegos; las otras se la llevaron al interior de la casa para contarle todas las cositas interesantes que habían pasado mientras estuvo ausente.

Theresa iba mirando todo en lo que Gabriel manejaba al aeropuerto. Ella le pidió que no se subiera a la carretera y se la llevara por entre las calles. Quería ver la ciudad por última vez y llenar sus ojos con las imágenes del lugar donde había encontrado el amor romántico, dos veces, en su vida.

"¡Ya estoy extrañando este lugar, Gabriel!"

Él no le respondió; sentía como si trajera una bola de golf en la garganta.

"Dime algo, Gabrielín. Llena mis oídos con tu voz."

"No puedo decir nada en este momento."

"Entonces cántame una canción, por última vez."

"¡Una canción... una canción! ¿Qué canción puedo cantar cuando siento que me estoy muriendo?" Gabriel se preguntó a sí mismo en voz alta.

Gabriel recordó un viejo tango que habla de la tristeza de no tener más a la persona amada cerca. Empezó a cantar cuando ya se acercaban al área del Aeropuerto Internacional de San Antonio. El poeta lamenta el tener que vagar por el mundo solitario mientras que su amada está lejos de su alcance. Le reza a la Milagrosa Virgen por el perdón si es que en su canción él demanda que le regresen a su amada, pero clama que seguramente morirá sin su querido amor. El poeta dice que la encontró cantando y también cantando la perdió, así que se resigna a morir cantando.

Theresa escuchó cada palabra y disfrutó de la dulce amargura de la canción. Atesoró la voz de su amado Gabriel en su corazón, prometiéndose nunca olvidarla. Examinó con gran detalle, sus facciones y su imagen, su cabello, su perfil, y sus poderosas manos.

Tere se le acercó, recostó su cabeza en el hombro de él y aspiró para llevarse su aroma grabado en la mente. Gabriel sintió que el hombro se le estaba mojando con las lágrimas de ella mientras reposaba su carita ahí.

Ella le recorrió tiernamente la cara con sus manos. Estaban ya parados en el estacionamiento del aeropuerto. Él no dijo palabra en lo que ella dejaba sus manos resbalarse de su cara a su cuello, hombros, y pecho. Ella lo jaló y lo besó desesperada. Él le respondió con la misma pasión.

El rugir de las turbinas de un avión aterrizando los hizo abrir los ojos y separarse. Se quedaron sentados, nada más mirándose. Gabriel se salió del auto y fue alrededor a abrirle la puerta. Caminaron en silencio, cargando sus maletas hasta la terminal.

La hora de su salida llegó. El Padre Gabriel traía una camiseta negra de cuello abierto y pantalones grises. Sor Theresa traía un trajecito de dos piezas, falda y saquito, muy recatado, color crema con una blusa de seda café. Por su apariencia, nadie podía decir que se trataba de dos religiosos.

Anunciaron que era hora de abordar la nave. Ellos se saludaron de mano como director y maestra suplente. Él le dio las gracias por el buen trabajo; ella le agradeció por el tiempo extraordinario que pasó a su lado.

No pudieron resistir más, así que se abrazaron apretadamente y se besaron de nuevo, sabiendo que no habría un mañana para ellos.

Una viejecita vestida de rojo se volteó a verlos, enlazados en su largo beso apasionado. Se sonrió con malicia.

Gabriel miró a Theresa con gran ansiedad, tratando de grabarse cada detallito de su cara. Ella volteó a ver que todos los demás pasajeros ya habían entrado al túnel rumbo al avión.

Gabriel le besó las manos; Tere besó las de él. Caminaron al túnel de abordaje. Ella le dio su boleto a la azafata. Él dejó ir su mano despacio. Ella le dijo adiós y comenzó a caminar dentro del túnel. Él se asomó al túnel. Ella se volteó y le sopló un último besito. Él lo capturó con la mano y se lo puso sobre el corazón.

Aquella fue la última imagen que tuvo de ella. Procedió al ventanal a ver el avión despegar. La viejita del vestido rojo lo vio parado ahí y se le acercó.

"¿Era esa tu esposa a la que estabas despidiendo? Es simplemente hermoso apreciar cuánto se aman ustedes dos."

Él no le pudo verle la cara; sus ojos estaban nublados de lágrimas contenidas. Se veía como si la mujer tuviera unos ochenta años y traía unos lentes oscuros negros cubriéndole un par de ardientes ojos rojos.

"¡Sí! Nos amamos muchísimo," murmuró Gabriel.

Gabriel se sacó el pañuelo del bolsillo y se limpió los ojos para ver el avión despegando. Se volvió a verla después que el avión desapareció en la noche. La vieja se había desvanecido como si nunca hubiera estado ahí.

Gabriel sintió una ira incontenible y la necesidad de pegarle a alguien. Apretó los puños y tensó todos los músculos de su cuerpo. Podía ver su reflexión en el vidrio del ventanal que daba a la pista de aterrizaje. Su rostro se estaba distorsionando; sus ojos se estaban poniendo rojos como dos carbones encendidos. Se sintió atrapado dentro de sí mismo.

Todo alrededor suyo había dejado de moverse. Escuchó algo como un grito despavorido y no supo si provenía de su propia garganta, pero el sonido no era humano. Era un desgarrador quejido. El olor del maligno y la náusea que experimentó le advirtieron que Satanás trataba de poseerlo.

"¡Infiel sacerdote! ¡Infiel sacerdote! ¡Infiel sacerdote!" una horrorosa voz le dijo dentro de su mente.

Una profunda oscuridad lo rodeó y sintió su interior lleno de asquerosos gusanos resbalosos. El cura tuvo relampagueantes visiones de los últimos meses de su vida en donde se vio actuando con Theresa de manera indigna para un sacerdote en lo que la voz en su mente lo acusaba.

"¡Infiel! ¡Infiel! ¡Infiel!"

Luchó desde el fondo de su mente y corazón, invocando al salvador.

"¡Señor Jesucristo, Hijo del Dios vivo, ten compasión de mí, un pecador!"

Sintió un poco de alivio de la presión sobre su pecho, así que repitió el divino nombre, "¡Jesús! ¡Jesús! ¡Jesús! ¡Jesús!"

La presión sofocante se levantó, y Gabriel cayó sentado en uno de los asientos de la sala de espera. El bullicio de la multitud de gente regresó a sus oídos y pudo ver claramente lo que lo rodeaba.

"¡Gracias, Dios mío! ¡Gracias, Señor! ¡Gracias, Jesucristo!"

Gabriel se persignó y comenzó a caminar rápidamente hacia fuera del aeropuerto sin querer mirar a nadie. Él solo quería irse a casa.

El Padre Gabriel se sintió adormecido de todo el cuerpo. No supo ni como llegó a casa. Se dirigió a la iglesia a rezar, arrodillado ante el altar.

"Amo al Señor, porque él escucha el clamor de mi súplica, porque inclina su oído hacia mí, cuando yo lo invoco. Los lazos de la muerte me envolvieron, me alcanzaron las redes del abismo, caí en la angustia y la tristeza; entonces invoqué al Señor: '¡Por favor, sálvame la vida!'. El Señor es justo y bondadoso, nuestro Dios es compasivo; el Señor protege a los sencillos: yo estaba en la miseria y me salvó. Alma mía, recobra la calma, porque el Señor ha sido bueno contigo. Él libró mi vida de la muerte, mis ojos de las lágrimas y mis pies de la caída. Yo caminaré en la presencia del Señor, en la tierra de los vivientes. Tenía confianza, incluso cuando dije: '¡Qué grande es mi desgracia!'. Yo, que en mi turbación llegué a decir: '¡Los hombres son todos mentirosos!'. ¿Con qué pagaré al Señor todo el bien que me hizo? Alzaré la copa de la salvación e invocaré el nombre del Señor. Cumpliré mis votos al Señor, en presencia de todo su pueblo. ¡Qué penosa es para el Señor la muerte de sus amigos! Yo, Señor, soy tu servidor, tu servidor, lo mismo que mi madre: por eso rompiste mis cadenas. Te ofreceré un sacrificio de alabanza, e invocaré el nombre del Señor. Cumpliré mis votos al Señor, en presencia de todo su pueblo, en los atrios de la Casa del Señor, en medio de ti, Jerusalén. ¡Aleluya!"
(Salmo 116)

En cuanto se profundizó en su oración y meditación, empezó a brillar. Su cuerpo comenzó a levitar. La paz llenó su interior mientras que le rendía su vida a Dios.

Su mayor tentación había terminado. Gabriel había sido herido y llevaba ahora una cicatriz en su corazón, pero había sobrevivido y se sentía más fuerte en su fe por aquella experiencia. Las palabras del Génesis volvieron a su mente acerca de la recompensa a Abraham por ser obediente a Dios.

Cuando salió de la iglesia, ya estaba amaneciendo un nuevo día. Se la había pasado sumido en profunda oración toda la noche pero había perdido la noción del tiempo.

Fin?

La Tentación del Tejedor de Milagros

ÍNDICE

Diseño de la cubierta – Roberto Rosas

Fotografía del autor - Matthew Rutkowski

Foto del fondo posterior de una escena de la película del mismo nombre

www.ingramcontent.com/pod-product-compliance
Lightning Source LLC
Chambersburg PA
CBHW032207030726
47494CB00020B/656